The Change

TALES OF DOWNFALL AND REBIRTH

EDITED BY

S. M. STIRLING

RoC

A ROC BOOK

ROC
Published by the Penguin Group
Penguin Group (USA) LLC, 375 Hudson Street,
New York, New York 10014

USA I Canada I UK I Ireland I Australia I New Zealand I India I South Africa I China
penguin.com
A Penguin Random House Company

First published by Roc, an imprint of New American Library,
a division of Penguin Group (USA) LLC

First Printing, June 2015

LIBRARY OF CONGRESS CATALOGING-IN-PUBLICATION DATA:

The change: tales of downfall and rebirth / edited by S. M. Stirling.
pages cm.
ISBN 978-0-451-46756-0 (hardback)
1. Regression (Civilization)—Fiction. 2. Science fiction, American. 3. Alternative histories (Fiction), American. I. Stirling, S. M., editor.
PS648.S3C466 2015
813'.0876208—dc23   2014047237

Printed in the United States of America
1   3   5   7   9   10   8   6   4   2

Set in Weiss Std.
Designed by Alissa Theodor

CONTENTS

The Change

HIGH KINGDOM OF MONTIVAL
C.Y. 46

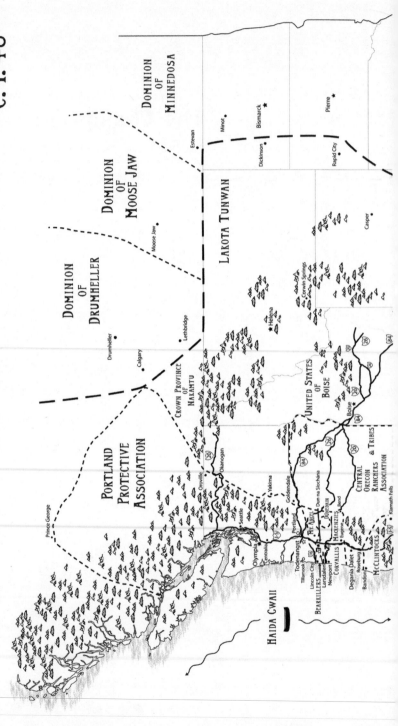

DOMINION OF MINNEDOSA

DOMINION OF MOOSE JAW

DOMINION OF DRUMHELLER

LAKOTA TUNWAN

Estevan

Minot
Bismarck ★

Pierre ★

Dickinson
Rapid City

Moose Jaw

Lethbridge

Drumheller
Calgary

CROWN PROVINCE OF NAKAMTU

Helena ★

Corwin Springs

Casper

PORTLAND PROTECTIVE ASSOCIATION

Okanogan
Oroville

UNITED STATES OF BOISE

Boise ★

Prince George

Yakima
Goldendale

Seattle

Olympia
Centralia

Portland
Pt. Angel

Dun na Sìochàna
Bend

CENTRAL OREGON RANCHERS & TRIBES ASSOCIATION

Tillamook
Lincoln City
Newport

CORVALLIS
MACKENZIES
Eugene

Klamath Falls

Dùthblain

BEARKILLERS
Larsdalen

Degania Dalet
Roseburg
Bandon

McCLINTOCKS

Todenangst

HAIDA GWAII

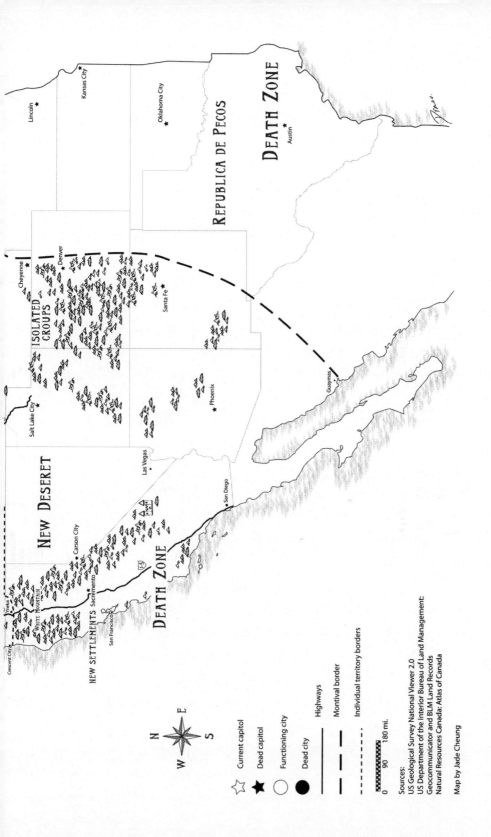

DEATH ZONE

REPUBLICA DE PECOS

Austin ★

Oklahoma City ★

Kansas City ★

Lincoln ★

Cheyenne ★

Denver ★

ISOLATED
CROUPS

Santa Fe ★

Salt Lake City ★

Phoenix ★

Guymas ·

NEW DESERET

Carson City ✛

Las Vegas

San Diego ·

DEATH ZONE

NEW SETTLEMENTS Sacramento ★

San Francisco ·

WHITE MOUNTAIN

Crescent City

N
W · E
S

☆ Current capitol
★ Dead capitol
○ Functioning city
● Dead city

Highways
Montival border
Individual territory borders

0   90   180 mi.

Sources:
US Geological Survey National Viewer 2.0
US Department of the Interior Bureau of Land Management:
Geocommunicator and BLM Land Records
Natural Resources Canada: Atlas of Canada

Map by Jade Cheung

INTRODUCTION

THE CHANGE AS SETTING AND SECONDARY WORLD

There are a number of perils you can encounter when building a fictional world, particularly if you intend to set a number of stories in it. Running out of story you really want to tell, which induces boredom, is one—Arthur Conan Doyle eventually desperately tried to kill off Sherlock Holmes, whose fame was obscuring the historical novels that he felt (with some justification, they're very good) were his best work. Edgar Rice Burroughs' reputation would probably be much higher if he'd written only the first three or four books in his Tarzan and John Carter of Mars series, though more with the former than the latter. Africa was wall-to-wall Lost Races and Lost Cities by the 1940s, and you'd think some would show up from the cabins of the Imperial Airways planes flying over it by then.

Which brings up another potential problem: simply *running out of space*, even if you want to continue and have stories to tell.

Patrick O'Brian ran into this problem with his wonderful Aubrey-Maturin series, set during the Napoleonic Wars; eventually he was reduced to unofficially splitting the year 1813 into, as it were, 1813a and 1813b—sort of alternate history versions of the penultimate year!

The wars against Napoleon spanned more than a decade; if you throw

1

in the beginning of the struggle against Revolutionary France it covers a full generation—around twenty-five years, with one short truce. Men like Stephen Maturin and "Lucky" Jack Aubrey would have spent their entire adult careers in the period between the fall of the Bastille and Napoleon's exile to Saint Helena, and by the end of it most of their subordinates would have been *born* into the wars. That's more than enough for a series of books!

What tripped O'Brian up was simply that he didn't anticipate how many books he *would* be writing with this (quite large) cast of characters, and so passed over a good many years as he skipped between the time periods of the earlier books.

I took this lesson to heart when starting the novels of the Change, what some call the Emberverse. It tied into another desire, that of making a world that felt *ample*. Even if you're worldbuilding for a single novella, it should feel "big," not fading into nothingness beyond the tight frame, not "thin." The characters should be aware of an entire universe around them, full of people and things going about their own business. Look at our own world, even in this age of globalization when there's scarcely a city on the planet where you can't ask directions or order lunch in English. How vast and varied and interesting it is, both in terms of nature and of how human beings live on it and with each other!

Many of the great fantasists—Le Guin, Howard, Tolkien, Martin—have achieved this feeling of having an entire world that exists on its own, with the narrative taking place in only part of it. Howard was one of my early influences; I spent a hot cross-country trip in the late sixties dripping watermelon juice on the Lancer *Conans* as my family drove an un-air-conditioned car from New Jersey to Los Angeles.

He achieved it by using what was supposedly, like Tolkien's Middle Earth, the remote past of our world. Even the maps of the Hyborian Age and Middle Earth are similar, if you look carefully. Both Tolkien and Howard did glorious mashups (the concept is older than the term) of historical cultures in their antediluvian worlds. Tolkien has late-medieval Gondor, Anglo-Saxon riders of Rohan, largely Nordic Dwarves, Regency

English yokel hobbits, vaguely Middle Eastern and Central Asian Easterlings and Corsairs, plus the totalitarian nightmare of Mordor, with its pollution and its population known by their file-numbers. Howard went completely berserk, and had high-camp-medieval Aquilonians, English longbowman Bossonians, ancient Egyptians in Stygia, Afghans in (where else?) Afghulistan, and something close to nineteenth-century Zulus and Sudanese on the "Black Coast." Not to mention Vikings, Cossacks, Bedouin, archaic-Semitic more or less Assyrians and Babylonians in the cities of Shem with their ziggurats and brass idols, seventeenth-century buccaneers, eighteenth-century pirates, Turks, Renaissance Spaniards, and Picts who are pretty much Iroquois as seen by the frontiersmen of the Mohawk valley with the odd demon and giant snake thrown into the slumgullion for flavor.

Conan, of course, was essentially pre-Christian Irish, and cheerfully chopped up an entire multicultural host of opponents without fear or favor.

Taking the planet Earth (geographical amplitude and variety) and historically attested cultures (human, ditto) solves the most basic problem of worldbuilding; it's extremely hard to come up with an entire world and its inhabitants and be convincing, to avoid thinness and sameness as everything takes on the cast of your own mind. Not to mention your own limitations with regard to geography and ecology. Hence the multitudes of one-note planets in science fiction; desert world, ice world, and so forth, often inhabited by races who have only one "hat" or trait. Superlogical, super-emotional, super-aggressive, you name it! As the saying goes, worldbuilding is good occupational therapy for lunatics who think they're God, and a lesson in the almost paralyzing complexity and interconnectedness of reality.

This has become the Stock Fantasy World; an ancient or parallel Earth with historically based cultures. This can be done well (Westeros) or badly (I shall not specify, and let the libel lawyers starve). It has the virtue of giving you an unlimited canvas; after all, our own Earth is the "worldbuilding project" of endless mimetic fiction.

Another possible setting is the post-apocalyptic wasteland, where a "new future past" creates analogues to historical settings; Andre Norton was fond of this and did it very well.

Which brings me to the world of the Change.

When I set out to do the Nantucket trilogy (beginning with *Island in the Sea of Time*) I knew that I'd eventually return to the world Nantucket left behind when it was plunged into 1250 BCE. And that as that ancient world received the technology of the late twentieth century when a community of thousands of Americans from 1998 was dumped into its midst, so the world left behind would be denied the high-energy-density technologies. Electronics and electricity; heat engines of all kinds; and the electrochemical and high-pressure, high-energy chemical processes dependent on them.

That gave me the big world—ours—to work with, rendered even bigger by the sudden removal of fast communications and travel. Naturally, losing the technological basis of the great world-machine in 1998 would cause unimaginable chaos and destruction, comparable to a full-scale global thermonuclear exchange at the peak of the Cold War in immediate devastation and removing the possibility of reconstruction on the same basis.

Old cultures and nations would crash and new would, eventually, be born. *That* basic story has been told many times in science fiction, and generally with more of a time gap is the basis of a fair bit of fantasy as well—*The Dying Earth* by Vance, for instance, or Alyx Dellamonica's new Stormwrack series that begins with *Child of a Hidden Sea*. Even the specific removal of higher technology isn't entirely original to me, of course: Steven Boyett's *Ariel* is a lovely example, though more overtly fantasy. Dragons lairing in the Great Smoky Mountains, anyone?

But what sort of new cultures would arise in the wake of this *particular* apocalypse I'd come up with? Here I got hints from my subconscious, in the way I usually do when contemplating new books—scenes and characters spontaneously appear; one of them was Juniper Mackenzie sitting by a campfire in front of her Romany wagon, and somehow I knew she was a witch (in the strict sense, that is, a Wiccan). Inspiration . . . but inspiration is cheap. It's being able to connect the dots that's important.

The Change is not a random disaster, cataclysmic though it is; it's not an asteroid hitting the earth, and it's not something like nuclear war or ecological collapse that we might do to ourselves. It's precisely tailored to remove certain possibilities. And it involves what is, as far as any human being can tell, a deliberate alteration in the fundamental laws of nature.

A disaster like that wouldn't just have physical consequences; it would have cultural and ideological-religious ones. Modernism, scientistic-materialist naturalism, would be shot through the head for any but the most fanatical of its devotees, most of whom would perish with the great cities anyway. Technology wouldn't necessarily be reduced to a medieval level; there's nothing to prevent people from using McCormick reapers, water-powered machine tools and antiseptic surgery in areas that preserved some cultural continuity. But the structures of belief based on the scientific and industrial revolutions, at least the more overt and conscious ones, would be dead as the dodo because their basic presumptions would be discredited. The invariability of natural law, for instance.

Human beings *need* ideas, though. We don't live in the natural world alone; we live in a world of shared perceptions, assumptions, beliefs. You can't make sense of the raw data of experience without some inner framework of ideas, a theory of how things work. It seemed to me that people in the situation I'd postulated would often fall back on the past, on the ways of their ancestors. To a certain extent that would be inevitable, because the material underpinnings of our high-modernist, post-modernist world had been traumatically removed.

But as a character in an upcoming Change book notes, "History cannot be completely undone, even by the Change, nor can the past be truly brought back even if you wear its clothes."

Groups of survivors—often coalescing around some charismatic obsessive leader and his immediate followers—would think they were returning to the ways of their ancestors. What they would actually be creating would be *new* societies based on *myths, stories and legends* about the past. A group of Wiccans might call themselves a Clan and adopt Gaelic terminology and wear kilts (an eighteenth-century invention by the way), but they wouldn't be much like a group of pre-Christian Celts. A knight of the SCA might contrive to build a kingdom with (ferroconcrete) castles, knights in plate armor made in hydraulic presses and a feudal-monarchical structure, but it wouldn't be much like eleventh-century Normandy. Too much memetic technology has developed in the interim. Isolated ranches in the American West (or estancias in Argentina or stations in Australia) might think they were reverting to a more recent heroic past of bold pioneers, and traumatized English survivors led by Guards officers might think they were reestablishing a myth of Deep England; they'd be just as wrong, though more subtly so, beneath the chaps and the smock-frocks.

This has happened before. The ghost of Rome haunted the Western world for a thousand years and more, with everyone who could trying to appropriate its manna by emulation—it's not an accident that we are governed by a Senate from a marble building with domes and columns. That doesn't mean we're actually Romans, and for that matter the Holy Roman Empire of the German Nation was neither Holy, Roman, nor an Empire, and a lot of its population weren't Germans.

And the *people* who survived the Change would be inescapably modern no matter how disillusioned with the formal ideological superstructure of modernity, often in ways that they weren't conscious of. Though . . . what would their children and grandchildren, raised in a world where a mile was once more a long way, be like? Here insert a glyph of authorial hands being rubbed together in glee.

Throw in the Supernatural (in a Clarkean sense) and you've got what I decided would be a background as big and varied as the real world. It would have an array of cultures as colorful as anything in pulp fiction . . . not least because in some cases they were half-deliberately *based* on pulp fiction and half-remembered historical novels and bad movies. Why not? Charlemagne's Empire was based on equally bogus memories of Rome.

As a bonus, they would usually be more psychologically accessible to modern Western sensibilities than something more genuinely archaic, for the real thing is always alien and often outright repulsive to many.

They would build their castles from our ruins, and conduct their wars and Quests along the crumbling line of our roads. The ancient past that gradually became half-understood myth—was *Jurassic Park* fiction or fact?—would be *our present*. Instead of sending a single individual or small group through a "portal" to another world, I could send the *whole world* to another world.

I had my own Hyborian Age, my own Middle Earth, but accessible through Google Maps! Including a society founded by a mildly insane Tolkien fangirl who thinks that she and her friends are the Dúnedain Rangers amid the Douglas fir and redwoods . . .

The rest, as they say, is histories. The novels of the Change, or Emberverse (what comes after *Dies the Fire* but embers?) have been far and away my most popular work. The setting gives a stage interesting enough and big enough for a large number of stories I've found fun to write, especially when combined with my cunning trick of giving all the protagonists descendants.

Herein are some other authors who've found the world of the Change a fun canvas on which to paint, ranging from seeking fortune and adventure in the ruins of Sydney to Venetian and Greek galleys clashing in the Mediterranean. Enjoy!

Hot Night at the Hopping Toad

⟨∿∿∿⟩

By S. M. Stirling

Órlaith Arminger Mackenzie threw the letter down on the table and buried her hands in her long strawberry-blond hair, squeezing her eyes shut for a moment. That didn't help, since the image she was trying to banish was inside her head.

The Hopping Toad tavern just after the early sundown of November was a good place to have a private conversation, mostly *because* it was so crowded; the noise level was such that you could barely hear someone sitting across from you unless you leaned close and shouted, which the mostly young clientele were doing on every subject under the sun. Often waving their arms and hammering mugs and cups on the battered tables in accompaniment or shaking a finger—or in one case she could see, a half-eaten sausage on the end of a fork—under someone's nose. The Faculty Senate election provided a lot of the material, just as if it were really important.

The gaslights on the walls were turned down for the same thrift's sake that had shunned incandescent mantles, until everything was a sort of wavering umber shadow. Between crowds, noise and dim light even a five-foot-eleven blond princess just turned eighteen could be at least quasi-anonymous as long as she didn't set out to attract attention. Which would have required stripping naked and dancing on the table. Plus a lot of Corvallans were stubbornly republican and went out of their way to be unimpressed by royalty, even though the city-state had been part of Montival since the beginning.

The heir to the High Kingdom felt free to half-shriek at her best friend.

"No, Herry, no! *Tell* me you're not banging my annoying jerk of a little brother!" she moaned.

"I'm not banging Prince John, Orrey," Heuradys d'Ath said agreeably, folding the letter and tucking it back into a pocket in the long sleeves of her houppelande.

The words went with a charming smile. Heuradys was two years older, just a hair shorter and a trifle more full-figured than the Crown Princess; her birth mother was a notable beauty and her father a big ruggedly handsome man, and both showed in face and build. Her dark mahogany hair, amber eyes and pale slightly freckled complexion were unlike either of them.

"You aren't? He's talking about your *tits* in that letter, woman, that he is!"

"I'm not doing it right here and now, am I? And he's using much more elegant terminology than *tits*. Rose-tipped pearls is sort of a sweet, poetic way to say *I'm so horny*, really. Besides, you're my liege-lady and you *told* me to say that I wasn't. So say it I must, regardless."

"You mean you actually did?"

"Yup. And a good time was had by all."

"Euuuw!" Órlaith struggled to find words. "Herry . . . euuuw. He's sixteen! He's a virgin!"

"He's a sixteen-year-old boy, which means he's a penis with feet. I'm only three years older —"

"Four!"

"OK, four. And he *was* a virgin."

"He's Catholic!"

"They do it too, you know, they just feel guilty afterwards. As I remember it—"

She cast her eyes upward in an obviously false searching of memory.

"—you lost yours at that Beltane festival in Dun Juniper when *you* were sixteen. Diarmiud Tennart McClintock, wasn't he? Everyone has to start somewhere, and there's nothing written in the stars saying the boy has to be the older one."

"Beltane . . . that was a sacred rite," Órlaith said a little weakly; it was among her more pleasant memories.

"*All* acts of love and pleasure are sacred rites."

Órlaith had to nod at that, for it was simple truth for her variety of the Old Faith. Heuradys was of a slightly different branch, but the principle held.

Perhaps my repulsion is illogical. Still and all, it's mine.

Heuradys went on: "It's amazing Johnnie made it to sixteen and three months; he *is* a prince, after all. I'd have expected some calculating Court lady or ambitious servant girl to kick his legs out from under him long before this. Probably he knew I wasn't after anything; he's no fool, your little Johnnie. And cute, and charming, and he has a really good singing voice, and he isn't intimidated by me, which is a nice change, and I really like him as a person. But I'll *stop* the banging if you want me to."

"Yes! Yes!"

"All right then, my liege. I hear and obey."

Heuradys half-rose and made a parody of a northern Court bow, doffing her chaperon hat. Its circular roll-edged form and dangling liripipe were markers of *her* new status as a knight, as were the discreet little gold spurs on her half-boots. Then she pushed it to the back of her mahogany curls and leaned back, waving her beer mug to attract a server.

They were drinking the excellent house premium brew, Guaranteed Tenure Ale—whose official slogan was *Three Mugs and Set for Life*—a richly amber-colored beer with taste like toasty caramel to start and a bitter, herbal finish.

"Mind you, I was *going* to stop anyway. That's why I showed you the letter, so that you could help me let him down easily."

"Why didn't you say so!" Órlaith said in relief.

She also made a note to switch to the lighter small-ale called Sophomore after dinner. Being grown-up meant you had to make your own decisions on things like that and stick to them, rather than just taking what was brought to the High King's table with a score of eyes on you.

"Because it's so much fun making you run around in circles waving your hands in the air and screeching in horror," Heuradys said, grinning and wiggling her eyebrows for a moment. "And *now* you're so relieved you're in a cooperative frame of mind. He *is* still a bit callow for anything unbrief. 'Twas one of those impulsive things in a hayloft. Over a stable at Kore Manor."

Technically Heuradys had three manors on Barony Harfang up there in County Campscapell in her own name—in what had once been called the Palouse—as part of her inheritance, but two were still empty range-land, and Kore was only a small village and modest newly built country house. She'd been taking an interest in the land for some years now, and getting to know the people her mother—both her mothers—had working on the new settlement. Also the hunting and hawking were good there.

"Not a hayloft, that's a *cliché*. Stop, for the love of Lady Flidais of the White Deer!" Órlaith begged. "No more details!"

Heuradys smiled in a heavy-lidded way. "Callow, but there's something to be said for frenzied untutored enthusiasm, though, this absolute panting thrashing eagerness to get—"

"Euuuw! I so did not want that image in my *head*, that I did not! John cooties!"

"Well, he's your brother," Heuradys said generously. "It would be odd if *you* thought he was attractive."

"How would you feel if I was sleeping with Lioncel or Diomede?"

"Surprised; they're both extremely married and very Catholic. And I assure you no *sleeping* was involved."

She grinned, continuing the teasing: "Cliché? It was *classic*—prickly alfalfa hay and a smelly horse-blanket, a mad grapple, clothes raining down into the stalls . . . All right, all right, sorry, no more."

Órlaith made a sound of revulsion that was half laughter and drank more of her beer. She was in jeans, canvas-and-leather shoes—what Corvallans called sneakers, for some reason—and a roll-topped sweater, with her academic robe thrown over the back of her chair. That was standard garb for studying at the University, the city-state's ruling institution and pride and joy; she was attending for a few semesters, as much for the experience and of course for politics as anything. Not trying for a degree; only a minority of students did that anyway, and she didn't have anything like enough time. It had been deeply interesting . . . for a while. Especially the course on post-Change ecological trends, and she'd worked doggedly on law and finance though they bored her like augers.

But city living wore on you, she found, even when you could walk to green fields and woods in a half-hour. It helped that she could spend the weekends outside the wall at the Finney steading. They were prominent Corvallan yeomen and old guest-friends of the Mackenzie chieftains, a link that went back generations, even before the Change.

The tavern was a long L-shaped room crowded with tables to the extent that getting to the jakes at the rear required dancing skills. The day's selections were chalked on a board over the flickering fire of the hearth in the middle of the longer wall, and though the tables nearest it must be sweating half the customers howled *close it!* whenever someone went through the outer door and let in a blast of the cold damp. There were even patrons on the dais where musicians sometimes played. That had a small brass plaque on the wall behind it, reading:

Lady Juniper Mackenzie, first Chief of the Clan Mackenzie, was performing here at the time of the Change, 6:15 p.m. March 17th, 1998, beginning the long friendship between the Clan Mackenzie and the People and Faculty Senate of Corvallis.

Which made it a family affair, since Juniper was her grandmother, mother of her father the High King; Corvallans were a little old-fashioned and still used the ancient calendar even after most folk had shifted to the Change Year count for everyday use—currently it was the tag-end of CY 41. Though from what she'd heard from Juniper only the location, name and floor plan remained of the pre-Change hostelry. Half of the other patrons in the taproom were in student garb too, though some of the jeans and robes were patched; the air was thick with the scents of beer, wine, mulled cider, hot chicory drinks and herbal teas, damp wool—it was raining outside, as it did most of the Black Months of winter in this part of Montival—moderately clean humanity and cooking.

The rest of the crowd wore wildly varied garb from all over the High Kingdom and beyond; Corvallis was a center of trade and manufacture as well as education. There were plenty of Mackenzie kilts and plaids since the dùthchas of the Clan was just on the other side of the old Highway 99, and rather fewer of the baggy Great Kilt (and tattoos) worn by their McClintock cousin-rivals whose stamping-ground was in the hill country south of dead Eugene. Benedictine robes marked a warrior-scholar-monk from Mount Angel, a Rancher from the eastern plains flaunted gaudily embroidered and embellished fringed leathers, the picturesquely uncomfortable archaic jacket and tie some Boiseans still favored marked the self-declared heirs of the ancient Americans, and brown Bearkiller quasi-uniforms ostentatiously drew attention by their grim understated modest practicality. Indian garb of several varieties identified various autonomous tribes; some of it was stuff she knew they took out only for festivals and impressing outsiders with their authenticity. Plus plenty of variations on the rough and rather shapeless linsey-woolsey homespun that was what most folk actually wore.

Quite a few were from the north-realm, the Protectorate as the lands of the Portland Protective Association were known. The old border was only about fifty miles north up the navigable Willamette River and the railway, and trade and traffic were lively within Montival under the High King's long peace. Most of those were merchants or artisans or the rougher types who crewed riverboats, though, and unlike them Heuradys d'Ath was in the nobility's full fig.

In her clothes-conscious case that meant skintight claret hose, loose-sleeved white silk shirt closed at the wrists with sapphire-threaded ties, a thigh-length black doeskin jerkin edged with gold thread and a long fawn-colored houppelande coat of superfine merino wool with amber ties and long dagged sleeves revealing a pale gold lining. A jeweled Associate's dagger gleamed on the tooled leather belt looped over the back of her chair that also held a severely plain long sword with sweat-stained rawhide bindings on the hand-and-a-half hilt.

"Did you have to show up in Court dress?" Órlaith asked.

It was attracting a few hostile glances, since not everyone had forgotten the old wars against the Association in the days of the first Lord Protector of the PPA, her maternal grandfather. Who had been, she had to admit, by all accounts an all-around murderous evil tyrant bastard, if also a great man and mighty conqueror. It wasn't everyone who could claim that their grandfathers had killed each other in battle . . .

"Court dress? Nonsense," Heuradys said loftily. "This is *afternoon* dress suitable for informal social activity. For *court* dress I'd be wearing that white-work shirt and the sea-green houppelande my lady-mother just finished. It's trimmed with embroidery three inches deep! And a plume in the hat, and those really dumb shoes with dagged tops and upturned toes and bells that look like a quarter of a jester's hat, not these fetchingly tooled half-boots. And this year parti-colored hose is back. Except when I was going girly in a cote-hardie, of course. My lady-mother and her tirewomen came up with this absolutely heavenly rose-and-azure concoction for me to wear at the Twelve Nights balls this Yule, the two-peak headdress has these tails of woven silk and feathers; I've *got* to show it to you. Stunning, if I say so myself."

"That does sound interesting," Órlaith said.

The Royal household would be keeping this Yule in Portland, and the thought of the round of balls and masques and routs suddenly seemed attractive. It would be the first time she'd done that as more or less an adult.

"Though you are *such* a clothes horse," she added quellingly, while making a mental note to consult Lady Delia about her own dresses.

"Given my parents, I come by it honestly."

Lord Rigobert de Stafford, Count of Campscapell, was noted for dressing elegantly, as well as having been a famous warrior in his day. Lady Delia de Stafford had been a leader of Associate women's fashion for decades and a legendary beauty. Though her other, adoptive mother . . .

"Tiphaine d'Ath giving a damn about clothes? Pigs will fly, lead will float, water will burn . . ." Órlaith said.

"With my lady my mother as her Châtelaine she doesn't have to. Mom sees that it all happens without her noticing."

She was getting some *curious* glances too. Few Portlander aristocrats attended Oregon State University even now; they tended to go to the Protectorate's own college in Forest Grove, or to Mount Angel. And what she was wearing was emphatically male clothing up north, and women knights were rare. Not hen's-teeth rare, but uncommon, more than one in a hundred but much less than one in ten even now.

The waitress bustled up holding two mugs and balancing plates on her arms with an acrobat's ease. She was young and slim and darkly pretty, about their age, and in Corvallis wasn't necessarily poor; there was a tradition here of people from respectable backgrounds working at humble tasks while they were young. Ways of thinking about rank varied even more than local styles of dress in Montival's many lands, from the Clan Mackenzie—which, apart from the Chief didn't *have* much distinction of rank—to the Protectorate, which had a great and intricately detailed deal of it, to Corvallis, where there was a bewildering combination of money and academic status. Understanding such things first-hand was one reason she'd been spending time living in as many communities as possible. Lately Órlaith had been doing some of that living on her own; her parents worried, but they were also determined not to raise her completely enclosed in a bubble of State.

"One bacon cheeseburger done medium-rare with onion and pickled tomato, side of onion rings, one beer-battered fish and chips, two pumpkin pie with whipped cream," the server said.

"Ah, Demeter of the Shining Hair be thanked, I'm *starving*," Heuradys said to her cheerfully, touching a finger to the foam to flick a tiny drop aside as a libation to the face of the Mother she had named. "My gratitude, O servant of the Good Goddess."

She tossed a small silver coin in the air and added: "No change."

The server snapped it up neatly as a trout rising to a fly; it was nearly half again the bill. The lordly unconcern with pennies was typical enough of the northern nobility, but most Associates would have crossed themselves and used the prayer that started *Bless us O Lord through these thy gifts,* they being largely Catholics. The server caught the gesture and phrase, looked at Heuradys sharply, and then turned her eyes to catch the arms embroidered on her jerkin in a small heraldic shield over the heart.

There were a hundred and seventy-odd barons in the Protectorate and several thousand knights with their own blazons, but the d'Ath arms of sable, a Delta Or on a V Argent, were distinctive and well known even outside the lands where heraldry prevailed. Tiphaine d'Ath had been Grand Constable of the Association during the Prophet's War back around the founding of Montival, and Marshall of the High King's Host for the last decade. The latter position had involved a lot of traveling outside the Association lands.

Heuradys went on to Órlaith as she applied mustard:

"I like the way they've done this, with the onion slice in the cheese so it melts in and caramelizes."

She shrugged her coat over the back of the chair, tied back her sleeves and tucked the brown linen napkin into the neck of her jerkin—even the daughter of a Count, a Countess and a Baroness wouldn't risk that much imported silk—and took an enormous but careful bite, mumbling something on the order of *damn that's good* through it.

"I told you it was the best student hangout in the city. But you just like the name of the place," Órlaith said; she'd sent a message up the heliograph line to Forest Grove yesterday.

"I've always liked the word 'toad.' It has a . . . resonance. Toad . . . toad . . . toad."

Órlaith chuckled: "Remember that first winter you were at Court, we were staying at Dun Juniper that Yule, and Grannie Juniper told *The Wind in the Willows* to all the kids in the Hall? You went around muttering *toad, toad, toad* for days and hopping now and then. I liked Badger and Rattie better," she added reminiscently.

"All right, but *toad* is still a noble word," Heuradys said. "And Toad of Toad Hall was a knight-errant."

"I thought he was a self-absorbed idiot with his head in the clouds, that I did."

"What I said. Even if he was from England and not La Mancha. But I meant it about the food. I caught the Portland-Corvallis train at Forest Grove and they stopped for lunch so-called just north of Larsdalen, while they switched the horses. The soup was vile *and* still too hot when they blew the all-aboard whistle. I think they just dump it back into the vat and sell it over again to the next lot of captives."

"It's a scam the West Valley Railway Company runs, that it is, the black disgrace of the world," Órlaith agreed; she had a Mackenzie lilt to her speech, though not as strong as some. "Fell and evil sorcery: they wave a potato over boiling water while chanting *chickenchickenchicken* and call it soup."

Órlaith made the Invoking pentagram over her own plate and recited the Mackenzie blessing:

> *Harvest Lord who dies for the ripened grain—*
> *Corn Mother who births the fertile field—*
> *Blessed be those who share this bounty;*
> *And blessed be the mortals who toiled with You*
> *Their hands helping Earth to bring forth life.*

She dug in. The Willamette River swarmed with sturgeon ten feet long or better and weighing hundreds of pounds each, and the Hopping Toad's cook—she owned the place and ran it with her children and grandchildren—did them a treat. The flesh under the thick crunchy brown batter was moistly firm and almost meaty, much less fragile and flaky than most fish. They ate in companionable silence for a few minutes, if you could call not contributing to the background roar that.

"Good to have you back, Herry," Órlaith said at last.

"Nice to be back, Orrey. I know the last thing you needed while you were winning hearts in Corvallis playing student was an Associate knight hovering in the background."

"Truth. They make a great noise about how cosmopolitan and sophisticated they are here, but they can be as parochial as any dun in the dùthchas or manor up north, that they can. Or Mormon village or backcountry ranch over the mountains, even."

They chatted for a while, Heuradys filling in the latest doings in the north and greetings from her mothers, father, siblings, numerous nieces and nephews, and all their connections. After a while Órlaith chased down the last of the Hopping Toad's own proprietary spicy ketchup with a final fry, took the first forkful of pumpkin pie and held it before her lips in anticipation while she watched her friend thread her way back to the jakes.

I wish there was someone I could bet with, she thought, as the young knight passed a table where they had a platter of thirst-inducing fish tacos and a whole tall gallon pitcher of Dean's Downfall between them, a dark amber brew that was dangerously smooth and fatally easy to drink fast, especially when a jalapeno hit your tongue.

She grinned while she waited, remembering the first time she'd come in here on a crowded night. Nobody with any sense whatsoever tried it with the staff—you did *not* want *La Abuela* Montoya coming out of the kitchen with a frying pan in hand—but with an anonymous out-of-towner there was always some arsehole with one too many in them who thought they could pat or pinch . . .

A confused flurry of movement, a yelp . . .

Yup, she dislocated his thumb when he grabbed, she thought, taking the bite of pie and suppressing a giggle—she was getting too old for those. *Just precisely the same move that I used, so it is. Now is that a* different *arsehole, or the same one showing an inability to learn from experience? To be sure, Herry has an outstanding rump and the hose show it off.*

The similarity wasn't an accident. Heuradys had spent a lot of time over the last eight or nine years at the High King's court, as a page and then a squire; she and Órlaith had had the same unarmed combat instructors. She hadn't even paused in her stride as her left hand did a quick grab-lock-twist-pull on the man's right; the perpetrator yelled loud enough to carry over the background while two of his friends—possibly his friends, they were laughing—held him down and a third popped the thumb back into place, which would reduce the pain from *agonizing* to merely *bad*. Just putting a dislocation back didn't make it all better, of course. The overstretched tendons still had to heal, which could take weeks if you were lucky.

When Heuradys came out again the server who'd waited on their table stopped to talk to her for a moment, smiling and standing with a sort of three-quarter-on hipshot posture. Órlaith couldn't hear what was said—that would have been impossible at five feet, much less thirty. The body language was fairly unmistakable, and more so when the server wound up and tried to deliver a roundhouse slap to the face. The Associate simply pivoted and pulled her head out of the way, then administered a gentle two-fingered nudge to a precisely calculated spot on the back that sent the other woman staggering while she slid past and returned to the table.

"And what was *that* after being about?" Órlaith said innocently, looking at her friend's exasperated expression.

"That insolent churl grabbed my—"

"No, I meant the slap that did not hit, but which was meant with all her heart, so."

"The Three Spinners and their pervy sense of humor. Mostly people get slapped for *making* propositions, not politely declining to meet someone after the tavern closes. Why, why, *why* do people always assume I'm interested in girls that way?"

Órlaith snickered unsympathetically. *Turnabout is fair play.*

"Because of your scandalous choice in clothing? Hose on a woman . . . why, it's unnatural, so it is!"

Heuradys groaned. "Oh, I expect that sort of bullshit up in the Protectorate . . ."

Órlaith nodded. She'd run into the same assumption herself in the north-realm, though it didn't bother her nearly as much.

"But here?" Heuradys went on disconsolately. "The only skirts you see here are on Mackenzies and McClintocks of both sexes."

"Some Corvallan women wear them on formal occasions; forbye they know that people in the Protectorate *don't* regard it that way. And don't be calling the kilt a *skirt*, woman, if you want to get out of here alive," Órlaith said. "And then there's your parents, all three of them, the which is not much of a secret. I think the lass recognized your blazon and her mind sprang into bed, also to a conclusion, so."

"*That's* not hereditary," Heuradys grumbled. "Nor obligatory just because you're entitled to wear the d'Ath arms. And my lady-mother and Auntie Tiph are the most absurdly monogamous people I know, anyway—all One True Love for them; I doubt there was ever any picking up barmaids."

"That we remember. But you can never tell about parents; they start out as folk younger than us, you know. And now we'll have to worry about her spitting in the beer. You should have agreed to meet her."

"Hey! Some sacrifices I'm not going to make even to get my liege-lady guaranteed un-spat-in Guaranteed Tenure. Anyway, isn't that a philosophical puzzle . . . you know, like the tree in the forest with nobody to hear? Is there spit in your beer if you don't see it put there?"

Órlaith waited until her friend was drinking before replying: "I didn't say you actually had to *show up*. We could bolt before your virtue was threatened."

Heuradys choked, sprayed a little beer onto her empty plate, coughed and then wheezed: "No fair!"

"Now you teasing me is funny, but me teasing you . . ."

"Oh, all right," Heuradys said, and laughed as well.

They both stopped when a tall young man in student garb who looked as if he played the local head-butting game forced his way through the crowd to stand by their table, looming over them in a halo of curly dark hair and beard. The man with the injured thumb trailed him, and one or two others—it was difficult to tell in the dense-packed gloom who was with whom. The waitress who'd tried to slap Heuradys was hovering behind them, looking amused but a little frightened as well.

"Yes, goodman?" Heuradys said politely, since his glare was directed at her, laying down her fork and glancing up at him.

Or *reasonably* politely; that was how a noble who was being formal but not ultra-snooty addressed a commoner in the north-realm. The young man was already scowling and clenching his fists. Now he ground his bared teeth in a way that would have been audible in most places. Órlaith carefully laid her hands flat on the table, and brought her right foot forward with the ball pressed firmly to the floor and her knee cocked. It just looked like an interested position, but you could come out of it like a released catapult spring if you had to.

Out of the corner of her eye Órlaith saw two people dressed like Mackenzies who'd been sitting and very slowly sipping one mug of Sophomore each all evening and playing a desultory game of fidhcheall. Now they put the mugs down and packed up the board and pieces on the table between them. They actually *were* Mackenzies, named Dobharchú and Sionnach—Otter and Fox respectively—but they were also members of the High King's Archers, the Crown's premier guard regiment. The Archers provided plainclothes bodyguards for her; they were under orders to be as inconspicuous as possible and do what she told them, but they'd interpret that in light of their first priority, which was keeping her safe. Dobharchú fished in her sporran as Órlaith watched and then kept that hand in her lap, which meant she'd put on her weighted brass knucks.

Their swords were peacebonded, as all bladed weapons over four inches long had to be inside the city wall of Corvallis, which meant a length of lead wire and a crimped seal wrapped around the guard and sheath. You could pull it apart with a quick jerk, but you'd better have a very good reason for doing that.

Sionnach just clenched fists like small kegs and scowled; he was a mountain of a man with a burst-mattress brown beard tied in two plaits dangling down his plaid, and looked as if he could twist horseshoes straight with his bare hands anyway, which in fact she'd seen him do as a joke at a Lugnasadh festival. His nickname was *Sionnach Tréan*, Strong Fox.

"This isn't some goddamned fief full of serfs, northerner," the young man said to Heuradys.

Which was a little unfair, since serfdom had been abolished in the north-realm after the Protector's War, before anyone involved here had been born. On the other hand, the man had probably never *been* to the Protectorate, and had a mental picture of it based on old stereotypes, which had been exaggerated even in her grandfather's day. Most people didn't travel much. Plus he was flushed and weaving a little. Dean's Downfall could sneak up on you unawares. Alcohol removed inhibitions, which turned the passively imbecilic into the all-too-active moronic.

"You can't go around bullying and molesting anyone you please here. Stay away from Shelly . . . from my girlfriend!"

Heuradys ate the forkful of pie, looked at the rest and sighed. When she spoke her tone was as reasonable as you could be when you had to half-bellow. It was difficult not to sound angry when you shouted.

"Goodman, nothing would make me happier than staying away from her. She tried to hit *me*. After I declined to meet her when the Hopping Toad closes to . . . ah . . . *become better acquainted*, she said."

"You lie!" the man blurted.

Then he looked a little apprehensive as well as very angry and slightly drunk. Giving a knight the lie direct was a killing matter in the Protectorate; for that matter, calling someone a liar was pretty serious in most places. You couldn't live like a human being without your reputation, and letting it be put in doubt by unchallenged slander was intolerable. Corvallis was a little different, being a great city with upward of forty thousand people, where a bit less depended on face-to-face dealings and reputation and trust and rather more on formal contracts. But Corvallis was also an urban island in a rural world, and he knew he'd gone too far.

The law of the city-state might forbid dueling, but even here a magistrate probably wouldn't do anything beyond levying a modest fine if Heuradys simply beat the stuffing out of someone who called her a liar to her face. As long as no killing or crippling was involved, of course, since this was a painfully law-abiding and peaceable town on the whole.

Heuradys rose to her feet. She was an inch taller than the young man, whose eyes widened as he realized it. He was probably thirty pounds heavier but she moved like a cougar and suddenly looked as dangerous as one, as the last trace of lazy good humor fled from her face. He had the height and heft and beef for a pikeman, certainly, and if he had any war-training it would be how to march in step while carrying a pike. Not the intensive study of generalized mayhem that a knightly family's resources and tradition gave their children.

"Excuse me, goodman, but what was that you said?" she enquired politely. "It's very noisy in here. I probably misheard you?"

Ah, most excellent, Herry—you've given him a path to retreat. My parents are not going to be happy if there's a sordid drunken brawl over a barmaid . . . regardless of who's in the right or was actually drunk.

"I said I believe Sherry, not you!" the man said, not notably backing down.

Which was gallant, or gallantly inebriated, but stupid. There were times when she suspected that men suffered a brain shutdown when their voices broke and didn't start it up again until they passed thirty, like millwork with a crowbar shoved into the gears. Throw in booze or jealousy, and you had a bonfire on legs.

"Then you're thinking with your dick," Heuradys said crisply.

She reached out with deceptive casualness and gave his nose an emphatic tweak.

"Which isn't what it's for," she added. "Go away and sober up, you silly person, before you get blood on my good shirt."

The Corvallan howled and clapped his hands to his face in reflex as red leaked between his fingers; knight training with long sword and heavy shield made your hands *strong*. Heads were turning as he roared, wound up and swung a wild haymaker—few could have heard what went on, but that was body language loud enough to catch the eye and carry over the white waterfall blur of sound. Most of those who'd noticed just looked, mugs and forks and spoons suspended; others bolted out the door, surged backward or came forward depending on the degree of their curiosity, boldness, sobriety or taste in entertainment.

Some people *liked* brawls. As her mother was fond of saying, whatever happened to the wheat or barley there was never a failure in the annual crop of fools.

She saw two men who looked as if they were members of the northern Guild Merchant glance at each other and then pour the last of their bottles of wine into their glasses and gulp them down . . . before they grasped the bottles by the necks and held them down by their sides, inconspicuously ready to leap up and whack heads. They might or might not dislike the aristocracy at home, and might or might not consider a shindy in a pub fun, but they'd probably pitch in regardless to keep a fellow Portlander from being mobbed. Órlaith felt a stab of dismay, like a splash of cold water in the gut.

Oh, Mom and Da will so not appreciate a sordid brawl that turns into a mass punch-up over who was born where, with me taking sides since I'm certainly not going to leave Herry in the lurch, that they assuredly will not. And someone might get really hurt if that happens. There are enough old quarrels in Montival as it is, sure.

Heuradys swayed aside and ducked slightly, and the punch slid over her head. Órlaith wasn't worried about Heuradys d'Ath *losing* a fight with a single half-drunken tavern bruiser. The duck continued as she sank into a twist and then uncoiled into a blow with doubled knuckles up under the young man's short ribs, putting the strength of gut and legs as much as arm and shoulder behind the pile driver impact. The whole process took about a second and a half, and ended in an audible meaty thud.

Nicely done, Órlaith thought; you had to be an expert yourself to see how elegantly it had been managed.

"Urk!"

He started to double over. That turned into a pitch backward as Heuradys heel-hooked him, combining it with a shoulder-thump that sent him turning and falling facedown into the arms of his friends.

Thus neatly immobilizing them all, and making a brawl less likely, so. Very nice, Herry.

Their shouts turned to cries of disgust as he began to vomit copiously. Órlaith started to smile in relief despite the sharp acidic stink; there was something inherently comic about a man throwing up . . . on someone else. His friends, or acquaintances, dropped him to the sawdust-strewn brick floor with a limp thump. For a fraction of a second she thought the whole thing was about to teeter over into fits of laughter, as folk relaxed and grins spread.

Then the server leapt screeching over the man, throwing herself at Heuradys with clawed hands outstretched like an illustration from a book dedicated to proving men had no monopoly on folly. While she was still in the air the light went out as someone threw a tankard of beer at the nearest gaslamp. In the same instant there was a *c-thuk* sound, exactly what you'd expect from a hard head-butt.

Órlaith surged up, ready to vault over the table and come down beside Heuradys. It wasn't completely dark, the fire still cast a red glow and the more distant lamps were still on, but that was mostly blocked by people who'd also leapt to their feet. There was a confused buffeting and thrashing, and things bumped into her. A bottle crashed somewhere, there was a clang of pewter plates hitting the floor, and the noise rose from its temporary lull to a crescendo. Arms closed around her like winch-drawn cables, and she nearly stamped a heel down to break bones in a foot before she realized it was Strong Fox.

He swung her hundred and fifty pounds around as easily as if she were a moss-stuffed doll, putting his own broad back between her and any danger.

"Let me go, you great ungainly *bachlach!*" she shouted.

She heard Herry calling the war-cry of her House: *"D'Ath! D'Ath!"*

Which sounded exactly like *Death!* when you yelled it, which was pretty much the point.

She struggled frantically. It was futile, as long as she couldn't do anything really harmful to him; Sionnach weighed more than twice what she did, every inch of it muscle when it wasn't massive bones. And his oath was to her father, not her; where her wishes clashed with the High King's orders, there was no contest at all. There was another sound, a panting grunt and a crunch, which was probably Dobharchú slugging someone with her knucks.

Then light flared up, from a Tillman lamp raised high in the hand of one of the Montoyas.

Everyone froze, even the people who were lifting stools or bottles over their heads; one man stood single-footed, with the other drawn back to deliver a really satisfying kick to a set of prostrate ribs. Heuradys was leaning back against the table, her nose dripping blood. The waitress named Shelly was lying at her feet, with a knife protruding from her back just beside her left shoulder blade. As they watched she gave one last twitch and went limp, and nobody who knew practical anatomy doubted for an instant what nine inches of razor-edged steel was going to do when it was put *there*. The young man who'd tried to punch Heuradys crawled forward, vomit still streaking his beard but tears running down into it.

"Shelly!" he said, and began to sob, raw racking open-mouthed sounds. "Oh, Shelly, don't be dead! Please!"

Everyone was looking at the dagger; it was a double-edged weapon, nine inches in the blade. The d'Ath arms were engraved on one side of the bolster, the Lidless Eye of the PPA on the other, and a ring of rubies set into the silver pommel. It was, without question or doubt, the Associate dagger of one Heuradys d'Ath. Broken lead peacebonding wires dangled from the empty sheath on the belt looped over the back of her chair.

"Police!" a harsh voice shouted from the doorway, and a whistle shrilled. "Nobody move!"

One of the first out of the Hopping Toad must have gone straight for the authorities.

*   *   *

Oh, shit, Órlaith thought.

Shelly's self-defined boyfriend—he turned out to be called Tom Dayton—was sitting glaring murder at Heuradys, surrounded by his three former tablemates, tears still trickling down his somewhat cleaner face. Occasionally it would contort with overwhelming grief; she would have felt more sorry for him if he hadn't been trying to pin a murder on her best friend.

Could he have done it himself? she wondered. *That's real sorrow, but it wouldn't be the first time a jealous man went insane. And he may have thought the former Shelly was his girlfriend, but I suspect she had a different view of the matter, so.*

The possibly-friends had tried to sidle out but the constables had at least listened to Órlaith long enough to put a stop to that; two of the blue-uniformed peace officers were standing at the door with their catch-poles making an X across it and more were at the kitchen doors, the rear entrance, and the stairs to the upper story of the tavern.

Heuradys was holding a wet cloth full of ice to her nose. There was a constable right next to her, too, though she hadn't been formally arrested or cuffed yet.

And Police Chief Simon Terwen was stooping over the body, leaning on a chair to avoid stepping in the blood whose raw metallic stink filled the air, dictating technical-sounding details to an assistant who took them down in shorthand on a ring-bound pad. There was a modest pool of it around the dead girl's head, but not the flood there would have been from a slit throat or cut-open belly. A photographer had taken a picture with a flash of magnesium powder as well as a sketch-artist dashing off several more; Corvallis had all the latest and best, including a ceremonial barrier of yellow linen ribbons to keep the curious out of a crime scene. He turned and looked at them, shrewd blue eyes in a lined face, clean-shaven and with short-cut white hair.

Whoever had run for the police had probably mentioned Órlaith's name; there must be a hundred people or even more in the Corvallis city police force, but its commander had shown up only minutes later. Everything was very quiet now, with the crackling of the fire in the hearth the loudest sound. She looked up and saw brightly interested black eyes peering through the balustrade of the staircase beside the hearth, and then a protesting juvenile yelp as the child was pulled away by one ear.

"I don't think we can rule out foul play," the policeman said dryly, examining the angle of the knife.

Heuradys made a gurgling sound. Behind her, Otter and Fox looked at each other. Órlaith turned her head and hissed to them:

"No. I'm not in physical danger, so don't even *think* about just rushing me out. The *Ard Rí* wouldn't thank you for that."

Both bodyguards glanced at each other again; then Otter shrugged and they relaxed. The policeman—he'd been one even *before* the Change, though very junior—acknowledged the byplay with a flick of his eyes.

"It's not the first time I've found members of your families standing over a body scratching their heads," he said. "Your grandfather Mike Havel, for one, Your Highness. That was just before the Protector's War."

The Bear Lord, she thought; the first ruler of the Bearkillers. Her father's father, though on the wrong side of the blanket.

He turned his gaze to Heuradys. "As it happens, that was one your mother killed, Lady d'Ath."

Uh-oh, Órlaith thought.

Tiphaine d'Ath *had* been an assassin for Sandra Arminger in her youth, and a duelist at home, before a military career conventional only by contrast. It wasn't mentioned much these days, but part of that sneaking and throat-slitting had been done here in Corvallis, in the run-up to the Protector's War—or the War of the Eye, as most people called it. As part of a set of intrigues by Sandra Arminger which *nearly* kept the city-state out of the coalition which stopped her dreadful husband from overrunning the whole Willamette.

OK, if I absolutely have to, I could ask Da to issue a pardon . . .

"I honor my lady my mother above all others, save of course my other parents and the Crown," Heuradys said carefully. "However, I am not Baroness d'Ath."

"I'm aware of that," he said. He glanced from her to the corpse. "Including aspects that make this less simple than it appears. Let's get it straight."

Yes, let's, by the Powers! Órlaith thought. Then: *I need to get this settled. I need to get it settled quickly, if I can—before things drag through the Corvallan courts.*

Her parents wouldn't interfere with the judicial process. The Great Charter of Montival forbade—the monarchs could hear an appeal from a death sentence, but they couldn't intervene in ordinary criminal matters in any autonomous realm. Couldn't, and wouldn't try. Corvallis *was* one of the autonomous realms, a founding-member of the High Kingdom, not a Crownland where the High King appointed the judges.

Not that Da would interfere there either.

Terwen ran through the events as the various witnesses had recounted them, referring to his binder for details. Some of those were extremely fanciful.

"Sword?" Heuradys said. "I'm supposed to have used a *sword*? What, and then stuck a knife in the wound?"

"Eyewitness testimony," the police chief said dryly. "I've heard a great deal of it, and it tends to have more to do with what people see in their heads than with their eyes. A hint, my lady: if you're guilty, get an eyewitness. If you're innocent, rely on circumstantial evidence. Now—"

Eventually, after he'd summarized:

"And that's when you got that nose, Lady d'Ath?" he said.

"Exactly," Heuradys said. "Sort of an involuntary flying head-butt."

She pronounced it *eggsacly*, since her nose was swelling shut. Then she went on:

"I saw the hands coming for my face and did a double-knife block."

She mimed it, putting her palms together like the Christian gesture of prayer and then turning both hands up and out, blocking with the bladed edges of her palms.

"She ran her forehead right into my nose. And then I couldn't see anything for a second, because my eyes teared up, and besides it was very dark when that gaslamp went out."

Most of those present nodded automatically. If you got a hard smack on the nose your eyes ran; that was uncontrollable reflex.

"The impact knocked me backward against the table."

The furniture was plain but very sturdy, heavy planks spiked to thick uprights.

"I could feel her falling; she grabbed at me and then gave a sort of jerk and fell away. Then the lamp came on. And she had my dagger in her back."

"You—" Tom Dayton began surging to his feet.

"Shut up," Terwen said without looking around, frowning.

"You can't talk to me that way! My father—"

"Is a tenured member of the Economics Faculty," the police chief said. "Words can't express how much I don't care, sonny. Do you think I mind if they retire me a year early?"

He frowned again, looking at the dagger which was the only hard evidence.

And he as much as said he discounts nearly everything except *hard evidence,* Órlaith thought. *Wait a minute, he said that if you're* innocent *you should rely on the circumstances. Think, woman, think the way you would if you'd just walked in on this and didn't know anybody and hadn't heard the names. Think the way you would if you were out hunting and looking for sign.*

She breathed deeply and cleared her mind; there was a trick to that. Mackenzie priestesses had taught her, and the monks of the Noble Eight-fold Path at Chenrezi Monastery over the mountains when she and her parents stayed there on a State visit. Breathe, imagine a pool of calm water, close your eyes, let the breath out and all emotion with it. No attachment, be pure floating consciousness.

They came open and she looked at the body as it *was*, without the overlay of speculation and her mind talking to itself.

Heuradys took a deep breath of her own. Órlaith *knew* she was about to do something—probably to confess, to get her liege out of the hot water. She thought desperately, and then . . .

"Silent Sentry Removal!" she burst out.

Everyone looked at her. She went on hurriedly: "My aunt Ritva was giving us lessons. We were visiting her down at Stath Ingolf, in the new settlements in Westria."

A stath was what the Dúnedain Rangers called their steadings, and the Rangers did special operations in wartime. Her aunts Ritva and Mary had been legends at it in the Prophet's War; they'd gone with her father on the Quest to Nantucket, too.

"We asked her why she said she'd always used a garrote and not a knife, and she explained how difficult it is to stab someone in the heart from behind, not just the ribs, but the angles reaching across your body because the heart is on the left. And if you just cut their throats, it's loud and messy. The kidney is better—"

About a third of the hearers nodded unconsciously at that, too.

"—but still not quiet unless you can control the mouth or throat too, and if you can do that you might as well strangle them."

Heuradys had been white-faced and focused within herself. Now she looked around at Órlaith, her mind visibly starting to work again.

"Yes?" Terwen said politely.

He's not a warrior, Órlaith thought. *But he's probably seen a lot of dead bodies, sure and he has.*

"You ken . . ." she said, and mimed drawing a dagger.

Then she slowly played out the ways you could stab someone in the heart from behind. The ones who knew what she was talking about looked on with keen interest. All the methods required the point approaching the target from an angle. Perfectly possible, with a long knife and if you were strong and quick, but the knife in the unfortunate Shelly's body stood straight out at ninety degrees, thrust with the flat of the blade parallel to the ground.

The only way an ordinary assailant could do that was with a backhand stab, and even then you'd have to be at exactly the right place.

"And at the right *height*," Órlaith went on. "Look, this girl, Shelly, she's what, five-six? Something like that. Herry . . . Lady d'Ath . . . is my height pretty much, maybe an inch less. And the position isn't right.

Shelly ran right into her, headfirst. And Herry . . . Lady d'Ath . . . is very strong and quick, but to reach back, get the knife, then *turn Shelly around,* stab her without slanting the blade, and then turn her around again so she could fall flat on her face . . ."

"Interesting," Terwen said slowly.

"Her prints will be on the knife!" Dayton blurted.

"Of course they will be!" Heuradys snapped. "It's *my knife.* I clean and wipe my sword and dagger every evening and touch the hilts a dozen times a day even if I don't draw!"

"So you think someone else grabbed the knife and stabbed Shelly Hiver in the back?" Terwen said.

"Someone behind her to begin with. Someone who knows how to use a knife, and who's quick-thinking enough to douse the light with beer . . . I hope nobody thinks Herry . . . Lady d'Ath . . . did *that.*"

Tom Dayton started to go purple. Órlaith extended a hand.

"Not him—he's too tall anyway. There was just time to reach over, grab the knife, stab and let her fall before the lamplight came on. Someone about the same height as the girl. And—"

A thought occurred to her. "Someone left-handed. Or using their left hand."

She looked at the cluster of young men beside Tom Dayton. One of them *was* a little under average height, though broad enough to be a bit squat, with big hands and long arms. His right hand was looking painfully swollen . . .

"That's the one!" Órlaith said. "He's the one who groped Lady d'Ath, and she dislocated his thumb. Look for *his* prints on the knife!"

The young man didn't waste any time on protests of innocence; he just turned and dashed for the front door and the police there poised their catchpoles. His hand came out of his pocket and twitched as he did, and a blade gleamed—flick-knife, prompting a yell of warning from several people. Where he thought he was going at night with the city gates locked shut she didn't know; she was too conscious of the warm flux of relief in her gut.

Sionnach moved very quickly for such a big man; he picked up a globe-bellied wine flask from a table, hefted it and threw fast enough to make it blur through the shadows. It cracked into the man's back, and he staggered with a cry of despair. The hesitation was just long enough. One of the officers at the door darted out her catchpole like a frog's tongue striking, and the open-end of the Y-fork whacked home on his neck. The spring-loaded catch snapped closed, but the man grabbed the pole with his hand and rammed her into the wall beside the door. The other catchpole darted forward in the instant that took, and the constables both twisted to bring the choking pressure to bear.

"Drop it!" the one he'd run into the wall wheezed. "Do it now!"

After an instant the man went to his knees as the intolerable leverage of the long poles made his thick neck creak. His face turned dull purple, mouth moving in silent curses or snarls.

"Drop it or we'll snap your spine!" the constable snarled.

He did a moment later, and several more closed in, nightsticks ready. One smacked him on the side of the head by way of precaution, while another grabbed his wrists and the third put the cuffs on—they were pre-Change and snicked home with reassuring solidity.

"You have the right to remain silent, you backstabbing asshole, not that it'll do you any good," the first constable said as she loosened her catchpole. "You have the right to get your teeth kicked in back at the station if you give us any more trouble. You have the right to be hung by the neck until dead after a fair trial when the jury hears about this."

The man revived enough to start heaving and shouting as the constables dragged him out; the constable hammered the end of her catchpole into his back above the kidneys with evident satisfaction.

"*Told* you," she said. "C'mon, make more trouble, give me an *excuse.*"

The whole thing faded into the rainy night as they pulled him out and four picked him up to throw him headfirst into the Black Maria, which was waiting with its horse standing droop-headed and drowsy and indifferent as the vehicle rocked on its springs. The door swung shut again.

Terwen nodded to his technician, who worked the dagger loose carefully by the ends of the guard and carried it over to a table where his instruments and magnifying glass were ready.

"Nice smooth ivory, sir," the young man said. "I should be able to lift a good set of latents from this."

Tom Dayton was sitting down again, looking stunned. He grimaced and wiped the back of his hand across his eyes as two more of the constables lifted Shelly Hiver's body onto a stretcher and covered her face. Then he turned towards the Associate knight.

"Sorry," he said gruffly. "I, uh, I shouldn't have said that."

Órlaith looked at her friend. Heuradys made a half-leg of acknowledgement, then took the man's hand for a brief shake.

"No offense," she said briskly. "You were honor-bound to take your leman's part. And when you saw my knife, that was a natural assumption to make."

He nodded, started to speak, then blinked and turned away to follow the body. Terwen stood aside, giving unspoken permission for the man to leave, then touched him on the shoulder.

"Dayton, we'll need you to make a statement. I'd think back on how you fell in with that crowd, if I were you. I don't think they had your best interests at heart, and they weren't just hanging around for free drinks, either."

Dayton shambled out. Two of the Montoya family came in and scattered buckets of sawdust on the floor; that would absorb most of the blood overnight. The rest would make a stain . . . but that would probably just be something to make an interesting story. Heuradys sat with a slight thump, exhaling a long breath and rubbing a hand across her forehead before she gave Órlaith a slight significant inclination of the head:

Thanks and *quick thinking!*

Órlaith raised a hand. Then she closed her eyes for a moment and made the sign of the Horns.

Go in peace to the Summerlands, Shelly Hiver, she prayed sadly.

Everyone died, but it was a shame to do it so young, and for such a reason.

Make your peace with the Guardians, and rest in the land where no evil comes and all hurts are healed. Be you reborn through the Cauldron of Her who is Mother-of-All, by whatever name you call on Her.

Terwen sat down facing them, straddling one of the chairs and resting his arms on the back.

"That was quick thinking, Your Highness," he said. "I won't say you saved your friend here from the noose, but you certainly saved a lot of unpleasantness all round. You'll both have to stay in the city until we've taken your statements, but assuming the prints match it'll all be over in a couple of days as far as you're concerned. Josh Burgen has been in trouble before, so we've got his on file. I suspect he's part of a hijacking ring, for that matter, which would account for his cultivating Dayton. Dayton blabs when he's drunk, and, pardon my French, he gets led around by the dick even more than most men his age."

"And it would account for the churl's being able to use a knife like that," Heuradys said thoughtfully.

Terwen nodded. "We may be able to make him rat out his accomplices—maybe he thought your friend was here to investigate him."

"Thank you, Chief Terwen," Órlaith said, trying for her mother's friendly dignity.

He smiled. "Either of you ever think of taking up my line of work? I haven't seen many cases settled so quick and neat. I'm sure your parents would consider a year or two of it valuable experience . . ."

Startled, Órlaith shook her head violently, and Heuradys made a small choked sound of revulsion. "By all the *Powers*, no! Not that I don't . . ."

". . . you don't appreciate the job we do, yeah," Terwen said. "Policemen do hear that occasionally."

"My father says he'd rather be a farmer, too, and I believe him," Órlaith said impulsively.

The man looked even more tired than being in his sixties warranted. And of course that was *old*. Her grandmother Juniper was spry enough in her seventies, but such was rare.

"Yeah, I could see that."

He looked out at the rain streaking the diamond-shaped panes of a window.

"I bought a farm down on the southern border about six years ago, one of my grandsons and his family run it for me. It's got a nice little vineyard and some cherry trees; I call it Uncle Vanya's Place. Next August I'm off there for good, going to sit in the shade and quietly decompose . . ."

"I'm glad you hadn't retired yet, Chief Terwen," Órlaith said sincerely.

Because I might not have been able to do this with someone more hasty or more dense, so.

Then she found herself yawning. "C'mon, Herry. My couch is your couch."

Rate of Exchange

by A. M. Dellamonica

ALYX DELLAMONICA

I am a recent transplant to Toronto, Canada, having moved there in the spring of 2013 after twenty-two years in Vancouver. In addition to writing, I study yoga and take thousands of digital photographs. I am a proud graduate of Clarion West, and teach writing through the UCLA Extension Writers' Program.

My latest novel, *Child of a Hidden Sea*, was released in June of 2014 and is the first in a new trilogy set on a seafaring world called Stormwrack. My first, *Indigo Springs*, won the Sunburst Award for Canadian Literature of the Fantastic. I have several novelettes available online, particularly at Tor.com, where there are two prequels to *Child of a Hidden Sea* and my infamous "baby werewolf has two mommies" urban fantasy, "The Cage." You can find the full details at my Web site, alyxdellamonica.com.

Alternate history is one of my favorite SF subgenres, and I have always been intrigued by Huon Liu, but the real inspiration for "Rate of Exchange" came when I read S. M. Stirling's *The Given Sacrifice*. The story of the Last Eagle Scout and his people intrigued and excited me, and having a chance to peer into their future was nothing short of candy. In terms of the geography of the Emberverse, I had called dibs on setting a story in Northern Alberta, where I grew up. All I had to do was find a way to bring a young Scout and Huon Liu into the familiar, if often implacable, terrain of my childhood.

The totem marking the pass to the Fortress of Solitude was an enormous man with skin the color of cream, clad in blue and red and with a big "S" emblazoned on his chest.

If not for his size, Finch might have believed him real. The blue of his eyes blazed with lively intensity as they bored down into hers, and his cape rippled in the wind in a way that made him seem as a-thrum with life as any cub or grown adult. His jet-black hair was real—horse, perhaps?—braided in long strands, bound with beads and feathers. The illusion was so perfect she thought she saw him tilt a brow . . . but then her pinto danced sideways and she saw the old man on the platform, putting a finishing lick of red paint on one red boot.

"Like him?" he asked, scampering down an old metal ladder and rubbing his paint-smeared hands.

If her liege lord Huon Liu was surprised at the casual, friendly sounding address, he hid it well. The previous year, they had come to this appointed meeting laden with gifts. The bordermen accepted the offerings, then refused to admit them into the Cree Alliance territory north of Drumheller. The year before that, the Baron told Finch, the mission had simply been told: "What, no gifts?" before being sent on their way.

"The workmanship on this totem is extremely fine," he replied now. "Better than I've ever seen. But I wonder . . ."

A canny glance from the craftsman.

He was the oldest spry man Finch had ever seen. She had drawn a portrait of the Last Eagle Scout when he was days from his end, tucked into bed and gasping for every breath. Despite the deep lines on his face and the close-cropped gray bristles on his skull, this elder seemed light-limbed, bursting with the energy of a just-grown boy.

"Yes?"

"I believed the Man of Steel tale was more central to the people south of here," the Baron said.

Delighted guffaw. "Supes was from Kansas, all right. But he keeps his fortress up where the snow flies. So, you bring us anything worth having?"

The Baron gestured, and Finch nudged her pinto forward. She had a wrapped tiger skin bound around the offerings, making an attractive but somewhat awkward bundle. They had paused at the last bend in the trail to arrange it in her arms, so the cat's head rested atop, painted eyes slit, teeth bared.

"The Queen Mother sends greetings and gifts to the Cree Alliance," the Baron said. Inside was a gold necklace, twelve extremely fine arrowheads, a fine wool scarf and a Sawridge Nation beadwork collection, ancient leather goods, intricately decorated, that had been salvaged by Sandra Arminger from a museum in Seattle, decades before. The Drumheller folk had sent word that their return would be appreciated.

Finch raised the striped pelt so the whole party could see it before passing it down to the man. She was conscious that the tiger's eyes were nothing, in terms of craftsmanship, to the lifelike gaze of this Supes looming above her.

Cold air rushed to chill her legs, where the fur had rested.

"Kitty, kitty," the man crooned, bending his ear to its mouth, as if listening. Then he bowed, so deeply he was almost bent double, and intoned the words, "My name is Lester Pica, and I am an alcoholic."

Huon didn't hesitate to reply: "Huon Liu, Third Baron Gervais of the Portland Protective Association, holding from Mathilda, the Lady Protector."

"Charmed." The old man's gaze slid to Finch. "And you?"

"I am Rita, called Finch, a Scout of forty badges, bearer of the Falcon, of the Explorer Patrol of Birdsong troop, Eyes of the Council of Troops of the Morrowland Pack."

Lester straightened, stroking the tiger pelt between its ears: "A gift of cat, then, from a bird?"

"Carried by a bird to a bird," Finch replied, for pica meant magpie, and bird lore was one of her forty.

"May we always outmaneuver our hunters." The old man grinned into the tiger's face. "C'mon, then. You want to go to the Winter Hoedown, Baron, I'll be your sponsor."

Finch's people were those who had fallen from the sky during the Change, into a forest the Baron's folk called Yellowstone. They fought to prove worthy of their territory, learning to survive under the guidance of the Last Eagle Scout. The Morrowland Pack allied with King Artos late in the war with the CUT, and afterward Finch had traveled to Montival to cement the alliance. Her mission: to explore, seek out unknown knowledge, and to learn new skills the Scouts might pass to their cubs in turn.

Sending their Eyes so far from home, even to serve a kind man such as Huon, had been a difficult choice for the Pack. Bright thought she shouldn't go.

"Morrowlanders keep to themselves," he had argued. "A Scout is trustworthy! Is there any need for such a people as we to engage in diplomacy? To learn the art of espionage?"

Finch had, as yet, no answer.

Now she rode north with Baron Gervais and his party, three men-at-arms, and a groomsman.

"We don't run things top down like all you do," Lester was telling him. "Cree Alliance holds Councils for its member tribes: The Night's Watch, Wood Buffalo Insulin Collective, Sawridge Band, Wood Cree, the Twelvesteppers—that's my folk. There's Tar Sandies and Hockey Knights, the Kip Kelly Rodeo, Doubledoubles, Wranglers, Riggers, Zambonis, these Alberta Wheat Pool bastards out of New Kiev—"

He seemed, somehow, to realize Finch was searching for that town—New Kiev—within her remembrance of the northern maps she had studied. "Lloydminster, that is."

He misses nothing. "Thank you."

"You can get acquainted at the Hoedown with some of the Council. Make friends, do some minor horse swapping. You got serious business to discuss—and being as you've come up here and rung our bell all polite three years running, I figure you got serious business—"

"Yes," the Baron said, and his diplomat's mask slipped a little, revealing a glimpse of the concern beneath. "Very serious."

"It's the whole Council decides."

"Is it a majority vote?"

"Hell no. Mother Winter, she demands unflinching unanimity of purpose."

"Consensus, you mean?"

"Yep."

Finch mulled that over. Huon had come, in part, to see if the Cree knew anything about the Haida raids on the western coasts of the expanding Montival territory, and to investigate a trade in the high quality insulin their hosts refined from pig pancreases. Both items that might qualify as minor horse swapping.

The other matter, though, their primary reason for coming . . .

Could any people reach consensus on treason?

As the afternoon wore on, weather smothered even Lester's inclination to talk. Wind played them, driving ice flakes aslant into the faces of horses and riders alike, poking cold fingers into the gaps in their furs. The riders leaned into their mounts, curling inward to hoard body heat. The horses huddled close, plodding along remnants of old highway from the days of the ancients.

The people of the North were said to be aimless nomads, ill-directed, squabbling tribes, but Finch saw signs of forest management here. Along the road, the trail was fifty feet wide, kept free of trees; the clearing provided browsing for deer and caribou. She saw signs of their passage, here and there, among the humps of snow: spoor, cropped grass, even a splash of blood surrounded by wolf tracks. Farther on, a pair of ribs breached the snow, gnawed clean and reaching skyward like fingers.

The road was the quick and easy way up toward the fortress, but there would be others. Whenever the wind broke enough to allow her a look around, Finch scanned the likely ambush sites, finding high points aplenty and, once, a concealed platform, well constructed and maintained, within an especially tall tree. Invaders would do themselves no favors by taking the easy route.

Not so disorganized, then, not this close to the border with Drumheller. For no good reason, this pleased her.

A gust drove her back into her wraps. Tucking her head, Finch imagined how she might draw Lester. How to capture both age and vitality, not to mention that canny expression? Would she render him with the red Supes paint on his hands, or would that simply make him look blood-drenched?

They passed through a checkpoint—the sentries seemed surprised that Lester had sponsored them—and camped, dining on buffalo stew and preserved sugar beets the party had brought up from Drumheller. At dawn they abandoned the highway for the forest, riding for five hours along an ever-narrower forest trail to Gregoire Lake, the Hoedown site.

Lester said: "These oil towns were real shitholes 'fore the Change, but the people who live here now put up a good gathering. You'll stay in the Twelvestepper wigwam."

"We're grateful for your hospitality," said the Baron.

"Lake's got whitefish and walleye and northern pike. Perch, too, though there's a fish I never saw the point of. Use up more life getting 'em than comes back to you in the eating."

"We must take what comes our way," Finch said, perhaps out of turn.

The comment had thrown her back to a memory of an especially harsh winter, elder Scouts dividing a small kill among the cubs, deciding who was most in need of the meat. A mouthful for her, for Bright. Two for a littermate who had not, in the end, survived.

"Sometimes," Lester agreed. "Trick in life's knowing when to throw something back so it can fulfill another purpose."

That, Finch thought, *was aimed at the Baron.*

Gazing ahead, she saw an expanse of wind-burnished ice: Gregoire Lake, presumably. Its far shore was lined with blue spruce, trees dusted silver by recent snowfall. Totems circled its banks: carvings of bears, hawks, fish, and deer. A red-clad soldier on horseback, both of them upside down, stared across the ice with comical, if strangely lifelike, despair. Nearby a stack of white hats, each the height of a girl and all bereft of heads, stood out luminous, bright even against the snow.

Small camps had sprouted along the shore and on the ice itself, clusters of dwellings made of buffalo hide and sapling, the occasional strip of ancient material: fiberglass, aluminum, copper pipe. One wigwam featured, as its roof, a weather-scarred blue canoe.

The Fortress of Solitude loomed up from the center of the water.

It was a spiky bloom of icicles, a circular stockade of enormous proportions, set on a small island a mile from shore. A silvery glint within its radiating spines led Scout to guess that, within, they might find old steel skyscraper beams. It glittered and sparkled, dripped and bristled. In fair weather, you would have to paddle out to it, within plain sight of the grizzly totems who towered above its walls, not to mention the sentries and archers' towers.

In winter's chill, one could walk right to its open gate, over the sturdy ice.

"Council meets here, on the longest night," Lester said. "You've time to chat up people 'fore that. Come on, Huon, I'll take you to meet Chief Jane."

They dismounted, and he showed them where to unsaddle. The groomsmen and the youngest of the warriors stayed behind to brush and stable the horses. Huon spoke to them, quietly, getting them settled.

"All right, Finch?" He was giving her a chance to break from the party, to rest if she wished.

She shook her head, accompanying him and his men-at-arms out onto the lake. The ice muttered as they passed, taking their measure.

They found Chief Jane and a handful of warriors behind a wall of snow blocks, five feet high and curved into the wind. Two of her people were working an old steel screw into the ice, grinding away to make a hole. A third was scooping up the wet, ground ice created by the screw and smearing it on their windbreak, making it thicker and stronger.

Three fur-swathed figures sat around another hole, fishing.

Chief Jane was wide-shouldered, blond, and motherly. Her hair was parted in the middle and divided into snow-dusted braids that hung to her chest.

"Janey," Lester said. "Got some folk to meet you."

"Trifling with *yo ne gi*, Old One?" she asked, neither friendly nor unfriendly, just curious.

"Don't feed me that 'ware the white man crap, honey pie. Your grandma was South African, old Boer through and through."

"Chatter-chatter, Magpie." She put out a hand and said, to Huon. "*Yo ne gi* these days means outsider. No offense."

"We're certainly that," the Baron said, bowing before introducing his followers.

Formality didn't impress her. "You fish?"

"Finch?"

She brightened. "I can net, cast, and angle; I can tie a lure made of feathers and bark. I can spear—"

A bark of laughter, from Lester. "Catch us a perch, little bird?"

Finch borrowed a pole and bait from a stranger whose only visible feature, within his drapes of fur, was a row of stylized coyote tattoos, drawn in arches above a striking pair of smoky gray eyes. She set up with him and two others around the new hole in the ice, happy to listen and learn as Jane made a place for the Baron by their fire, a scavenged metal box set on a tripod above the ice.

For a long time, the conversation circled aimlessly, like hawks on an updraft, casual wanderings as the two became acquainted. Jane asked about Montival and the High King, then told a long story about the annual buffalo hunt, which had gone well, a few weeks earlier.

Conversational warm-up was not the way of the Morrowlanders. A Scout is direct. Finch had been pondering the necessity of it ever since she joined the Baron's service; the nature of diplomacy, how one might frame a badge around what some called small talk.

Bright would have said, *Let the outsiders keep their gabble, their give and take. Morrowland is a small world, with no need for such things.*

But Bright had wanted her to stay. Or wanted her to want to stay.

She had landed a sizeable pickerel and thrown back a young walleye by the time Huon got to business: "A few years ago, when we were at war with the Church Universal and Triumphant, there was an attempt on the life of Órlaith, King Artos' heir. The assassins got into Castle Todenangst. They could never have done it, but one of the kitchen staff left a storage room window open for them, and poisoned a guard."

"Did the girl survive?" Jane asked.

"The assassination was unsuccessful and the baker fled," he said. "Lady d'Ath has learned he is living among your people. His name is Charles Frayne."

"'Spoze you want him back." She scratched the back of her neck, then asked Lester. "This about who I think?"

Lester looked as if he'd dozed off by the fire. "Chuckwagon Charlie."

"You know him?" the Baron said.

"He's engaged to the princess of the Kip Kelly Rodeo."

"He's well liked," Jane added. "Reckoned a nice guy. He makes these crab-apple turnovers, ohmuhgawd—"

"He's—" He paused for a breath, to master his feelings; Finch saw it only because she'd been watching. "We are engaged in tracking down the last of the CUT magi. He might be one."

"So you're here to see if you can rope him from out the Hoedown?"

"The six of us, kidnap him?" The idea that they could take on the entire gathering Cree nation was preposterous. "I'll request he be given up to face justice."

"Allie Sawchuk, the rodeo princess, sits on the Council. She's a fair bet to be the next Grand Chief."

Consensus, Finch thought. *They won't give him up.*

"We can only ask," Huon said. His tone was still light, hiding feelings that, Finch knew, ran deep.

Jane sucked her teeth. "The famed Lady Death—it's her house you mean?"

He nodded. "The one she was in charge of guarding, at least. She had to dash up the stairs and take care of it . . . personally. I was there."

"Kind of an insult, breaching her walls?"

"Indeed."

"Maybe you could never hope to kidnap Charlie, but an arrow might cut him down easy enough. We've heard about your Montival longbows."

Huon shook his head. "We want him, but not enough to risk war. And speaking of our longbows—" They eased gracefully back to minor issues, trade and weapons exchanges.

By now, Finch had landed a third fish, a pickerel as long as her forearm. She cut it open, throwing the guts to an eager, fox-faced dog before bringing the rest to the fire. When Jane gestured—go ahead—she set it out on the grill. One of the others rolled out a cake of flatbread batter beside it.

Lester, she saw, had got into her saddlebag and was leafing through Finch's sketchbook, a gift from the Queen Mother and her most precious possession.

"This your king, then?" he asked.

She had drawn Rudi Mackenzie, Artos the first, standing tall on a hill with the Sword of the Lady drawn and half-raised.

Finch nodded, more interested in the smell of roasting pickerel and the bread dough. Nevertheless she named the portraits as he leafed through them: Lady d'Ath, the Baron's sister, the Queen and the Queen Mother, various people of the court.

"And this?" A Scout, in formal dress, short pants and badges all present and correct.

"Nathan, called Bright."

"Boyfriend?"

"No," she said, forcefully, her tone icing over that inner voice that said her feelings for Bright should run a deeper course.

Lester, who missed nothing, clucked sympathetically.

That night, rather than shelter with the Baron and his men, she dug a sleeping trench in a snowdrift, uphill from the main camp, and lined and covered it with pine branches. A single gap left in the nest allowed her to watch the camps, to see people come and go.

Near midnight a brawl broke out, four agile young-looking shadows from two different camps coming together, seemingly by design, to circle, shout taunts, and then thrash one another. It was a short fight, as fights often were. After, they clasped hands before limping in separate directions.

Newcomers roused her twice, riding in on the southern trail, speaking to the sentries before setting up shelters of their own. Later, Bright came to expel her from a pleasant dream with bitter words: *You care for me, but you do not burn.*

She woke aching and annoyed—with him for demanding, with herself for failing to want him as she should. Lester was slinking across the ice; she watched as he disappeared.

As the moon sank into the trees, the fox-faced dog she'd fed that afternoon nosed its way into her shelter and curled against her chest, a welcome companion and bringer of warmth.

Later, the sky clouded and the cold eased; a warm wind licked down from the west. Snow glistened, melting just enough to form an icy skin over the drifts.

The smell of roasting buffalo teased through Finch's pine screen well before dawn. Drumsong rolled across the ice from the forest as people lit fires: voices singing in languages she didn't understand rose and fell in something that sounded like a lamentation.

One couldn't wait for the sun, not at the ebb of the year, not so far north. Finch walked the edges of the camp in the predawn darkness, the dog at her side. She caught the eye of a lithe young man, familiar only because of the coyote tattoos arching over his eyes. Her fishing companion. He was clad today in a quilted coat and a fur-lined hat.

He had a well-constructed face: smooth red skin, strong nose, straight teeth, and eyes the color of smoke.

He offered her a place at his mother's fire, and a skewer of roasted buffalo. "You came with Lester Pica."

"Does that surprise you?"

He nodded.

"Why?"

"The Old One's partial to the rodeo folk. This thing with your baker; they'll be angry he's helping you."

She ate the meat and then, as the weather was clear and dry, opened her satchel and took out her book. Taking up an ancient charcoal crayon, she began to draw, sketching the lines of the camp, the porcupine shadow of the Fortress, the shadows of totems on the far bank of the water.

"I'm Raki," the young man said.

"Finch."

"Do you sing?"

She nodded; of the five music badges, she had four.

Raki cast an admiring gaze over her picture. Feeling strangely shy, Finch tore it free and rolled it, holding it out. "It's not waterproof."

"I won't get it wet, then." An ember of flirtation within those smoky eyes drew a smile from her—then his mother called, and he darted off with a wave.

Feeling strangely moody—homesick, she supposed—Finch circled back to the Twelvestepper wigwam. The Baron and his men were up, dressed, and armed.

"Did our Scout see anything interesting?" Huon asked.

"They socialized all night, off and on. Chief Jane had more visitors than most."

"People asking our business here."

"Yes," she agreed. "Lester crossed the lake; he went into the Fortress, and later into the woods near the Hat totem."

"And made it back for breakfast." The old man popped out from behind the shelter with a delighted caw at having surprised them. "Lotta folks arrived last night."

"The Kip Kelly Rodeo?" Huon asked.

"Rough riders always run late." Lester shook his head. "C'mon, want you to meet Chief Lundy."

The Lundies were bards, singers of songs from both before the Change and since, keepers of stories and, thus, a useful source of information. They had arrived pulling travois laden with instruments both ancient and modern. Finch recognized a fiddle the Baron had included among last year's gifts.

They brought a drink made of roasted dandelion root, Saskatoon jelly sweetened with beetroot sugar for the morning bannock, and four plump ducks, shot by their archers on the way to the Hoedown. They offered the first serving to Lester and then, while the others were eating, sang a lengthy song about the people of Raven—the Haida, they meant—and that people's first post-Change Chiefs, the ones who had set them on the path of piracy. They said Huon could share this story with his king, by way of thanks for the violin.

Finch wondered if Huon would have to compose an ode if he wanted to ask about Chuckwagon Charlie. But Lester laid the situation out in a few sentences, between helpings of the jam.

Lundy said:

"I know your baker. Was us found him round old Wetaskiwin, like to freezing. He says he was baking that morning, up early. Some fella showed him a badge, covered in rubies. Mean anything to you?"

The Baron nodded. "It happened a great deal: the CUT had put many people under their thrall."

He didn't add that others had gone to them willingly.

"Next thing Charlie knew, Lady Death's guard was kicking him, as a prelude to dropping him in the dungeon. Things were a bit crazy, after the attack. He got a chance to burrow into a wagon fulla horse shit, caught a ride out."

This time the Baron couldn't hide his surprise. "He confessed, to strangers?"

"We Lundies are Winter's historians. We demanded his tale before we saved him."

It was easy to follow the turn of Huon's thoughts: revealing the truth might be the act of an innocent man, or a careful one. The betrayal would be a familiar tale to all who knew Charlie now. There could be no shock or outrage in it, as there would have been if he'd been concealing his history and suddenly exposed.

Lester belched. He was contemplating the Saskatoon jelly, the color of it, Finch suspected. How did he make his totems so lifelike? Carved Scouts, placed carefully at the Morrowland borders and hard to tell from real guards, might deter casual trespassers.

"If Charlie was forced, Baron, would you leave him in peace?"

"If the story is true, certainly." Huon shook his head. "If he's one of the CUT magi we've been tracking, he's a danger to you all."

"We've bagged a couple of the tormented folk. We haven't been worried about Charlie," Chief Lundy said.

"Perhaps you should be," he said. "The damage a magus can do is incalculable."

"Aww, he's fine." But Lundy's gaze flicked to Lester, and he seemed disturbed by the suggestion.

"Our King, Artos, carries the Sword of the Lady. It tells him whether someone is lying."

"Mystic bullshit detector?" Lester said.

"If Charlie is one of them, or if he sought their influence at any time, it would reveal the truth."

"Tell us about it," Lundy said, by which he meant he wanted the whole story of the Quest. Huon told him, in detail, and if the hour it took wore on his patience, it did not show.

"May we tell this tale?" Lundy asked.

"Yes." Huon had apparently had time, as he spoke, to think the present matter through. "If the baker was innocent, why did he run?"

"Little thing called fear, maybe?"

"Maybe. If he returned with us and faced the Sword, I believe the King and Queen would show mercy."

"Mercy? To someone who threatened their infant?" Lester leaned in.

"They have been reasonable, even kind, to those touched by the actions of traitors." The Baron's voice was steady.

"I doubt the Council would agree to send Charlie off on a maybe." Lundy shook his head. "Too easy to lose him on the way, have an accident . . ."

The young knight stiffened, taking offence.

"These things do happen," Huon agreed. "But no harm would come to him by our hand. And . . . I could give my word that if he was exonerated, he would be returned."

"You'd guarantee your King's mercy?"

"Maybe." Huon was considering, and Finch sensed that the prospect pained him.

He could probably tell, himself, if the baker was still under CUT thrall—he'd come close to ending up that way himself. The question, with Huon, would be whether he had truly been surprised by the badge-wielding invaders, or had courted them.

Lester gave him that hunter's look.

"Would you take warriors with you, some of the rodeo clowns? To see to his safety?"

"Certainly."

"Or leave a hostage?" Lester gestured at Finch.

Finch felt herself twitch as all the men's attention focused on her.

Say yes, she thought, though her heart was hammering: the truth about this baker must be exposed, for everyone's sake.

Huon put his large hand over her mittened one.

"Trust isn't grass, Lester, to spring up after a night's rain. It grows slowly, like the trees. Everyone here understands that this friendship between us has only just been seeded."

One of the musicians mouthed the words, clearly liking the phrases, or perhaps memorizing them.

"That is a diplomat's answer," said Chief Lundy.

"You've given me a lot to think about. But the Cree should think, too. Unless King Artos were to see Charlie, he might never believe he was forced, as he says."

"Better make more friends here at the Hoedown, then," said Chief Lundy. "If you want any chance of taking him."

All day they did exactly that, crossing from camp to camp, horse swapping as Lester called it, meeting and greeting and making small deals. They dropped in on the Doubledoubles to see Raki's mother, and her son promptly invited Finch out to something called a track meet.

She looked to the Baron. "Shall I?"

"Yes. Shine those eyes around," he murmured. "And by the way, if you're worried about me leaving you here as a hostage—"

She shook her head, and was surprised to feel a small hum of disappointment, one low chord.

The young people at the Hoedown were engaged in games she knew from her own cubhood in Morrowland, practices that in time led to hunting: ringtoss, a throwing game called chunkey stone. Some of those her age had made foot-powered ice sledges and were racing them: Raki showed her how to drive one, and waited as she drew a plan of its undercarriage and asked its makers exhaustive questions on its construction.

Her gaze kept returning to his smoky eyes, the tattooed arch of his brow. Her thoughts, as she walked with him, became far from businesslike.

He gave her a snow snake, recompense for the picture she had drawn that morning. She tucked the weapon, a short sort of throwing spear whose use she didn't immediately see, into her pack. She would practice with it, take its measure.

After the games, she and he crossed the lake so she could examine the glaze on the totems. The stacked hats rose up fifty feet or more, and had facets beaten into them: a honeycomb pattern, invisible at a distance, that caught the light and reflected it at different angles. Bits of fool's gold on the bands of the hat brims brightened the effect.

"This is Lester's work?"

"The people of Haida Gwai have claimed Raven for their own," he said. "Magpie, Lester says, is that trickster's poor cousin. An illusionist: you should see him do card tricks."

He was saying something important, but before she could puzzle its meaning, he stepped close and kissed her.

She kissed back as a summer storm of feelings gusted up within her. Her arms came round him, barely reaching because of the bulk of their heavy coats.

He tastes like Bright.

She remembered his opposition to the Pack's sending the Eyes of Explorer Troop as far as Montival. What would he think if he knew where she was now, how far away?

She had wanted to go.

She pushed on Raki's chest, lightly, and he stepped back right away. "I shouldn't tangle with—I'm returning to the South."

"I wouldn't hold you," Raki replied, tracing the line of her jaw with his thumb.

She caught his hand, feeling her whole body sing with desire.

What had Lester said? Winter demands unanimity of purpose. A Scout should be certain: mind and body in accord. "May I think about it?"

He nodded, and took her to see another totem, a great metallic riding animal, on a balance, with a big scoop for a head. Liquid black covered it, as though it had just been dipped in thick glossy paint. It had a saddle, and a ladder leading up to it.

"Petroleum pumpjack," Raki said. "The ancients used them to drink the blood of the earth."

Though the thing was more machine than monster, its red eyes had that same lifelike quality; they burned with madness, a need to devour. The whole totem seemed to strain to come to life, to spring to the hunt. She was happy to flee its gaze.

That night, Huon said to Finch. "What do you make of the Cree?"

"The chiefs speak of a Council, but they look to our guide when we talk of the baker."

"Lester pretends to be an itinerant old sculptor, but his voice carries weight here," Huon agreed.

"Are you—" Finch thought better of the question.

"Yes?"

She shook her head.

"It's all right, Finch."

"Your mother betrayed Artos."

He nodded.

"Lady d'Ath wants this man Charlie. To show lenience, even if he was compelled . . ."

"Am I afraid to return home having forgiven a traitor? Given my history?"

"It isn't my place to ask."

"No," he agreed, a little sharply. Then, more softly, "It's a fair question. But the real issue is whether he can harm them."

They let that sit for a moment, before she said: "They seem an honorable people. Worthy of badges."

"The Drumheller folk underestimate them," he agreed.

"That's their design." *Illusions*, she thought.

"We could trade here. They have an eye to all the northern borders. The Night's Watch monitors the west—those troublesome Haida—closely."

"It would be good to have them as allies," she agreed.

"Is Charlie a CUT magus? If not, was he truly victimized by them?" He paced the small wigwam. "To leave him here, if he wasn't an innocent target of opportunity . . . he's placed himself in the heart of their elite squad of warriors."

"I would remain as hostage," Finch said in a rush. "If it would get him away."

"You're in my care," Huon said.

She stood as tall as she could—which wasn't very—and trying not to look all the things she was: young, fine-boned, vulnerable.

"I have duties, too. There are things here for the Eyes to study."

Like Raki. Which was foolish, a thought of the body. There was no guarantee, if she stayed, that she would ride with the Doubledoubles.

"It's a generous offer," he said, and the mask he wore among the Cree was entirely gone: she could see the gratitude, the respect for her and all his vassals that made him such a good leader. "Let's hope it doesn't come to that."

Next day, at dawn, the Kip Kelly Rodeo arrived.

They were a band of fifty, riding light and armed with whips, lassos, and tomahawks. They came over the eastern fringe of the lake, backlit by bloodred sun, yowling like a wolf pack as they galloped out of the brightness. They wore fringed leather pants and jackets, and their hats were wide-brimmed. Their boots had hard pointed toes and were stitched in intricate patterns that rose to midcalf.

The princess rode at their head. Her skin was the gold-tinged red of cedar and her hair was caught in a hundred small braids, each a finger's length and tipped by turquoise beads. She wore a crown of curved ram's horns and the cuffs of her sleeves were wound with vicious spikes of rusted wire, but the show wasn't necessary; merely the look on her face was enough to show she was spoiling for a fight.

Among her wranglers were six warriors with their faces painted white—the clowns Lester had mentioned—capable-looking warriors, dangerous men. The baker was in their midst, under guard. He looked beaten down, unhappy, trapped.

The clowns and the Baron's men-at-arms exchanged glances pregnant with professional implications, weighing one another.

The princess rode to the Twelvestepper wigwam—everyone, from every camp, had found a reason to be out and watching, and when Lester opened his mouth in greeting, she said, "Do not greet me, Uncle."

He spread his arms, shook out his black-and-white cloak, and stood his ground. "I have sponsored these people. They are my guests."

She said, "I'll never give Charlie up, do you understand? Would you waste the Council's time trying to change the length of the day, or the angle of the sun? Return to your easy summer home and forget him."

Huon faced her steadily. "If your baker is a magus of the CUT, he will poison all you love, in time."

She leaped from her mount, giving up the advantage of height, and stepped in close. She was smaller than Huon, and the furs hid her body; she might have been soft as an overfed puppy in there.

Finch doubted she was soft. It took an effort to keep her hand from her own knife. Huon's hand flickered out, reassuring his party: all is well.

The trick of seeming fearless; another skill that was hard to capture in a badge.

Her words carried across the camp. "Charlie has ridden our mean bull, roped a calf, and trained a pony. He's one of us."

"One of you now. What about his past? Guards, loyal to the Queen, died in the attack."

To the rear, surrounded by clowns, the subject of this discussion slumped lower in his saddle.

"Your war dead are nothing to me," Allie said. "I would not let him go if he'd gutted that baby himself."

A hiss and crackling of ice punctuated this, a rattle from the frozen surface of the lake that penetrated the still beating drums. Cawing rose from the trees, then silenced.

What would it be like, Finch wondered, *to love someone that much?*

"Has this Council meeting already started?" Huon said.

Allie's eyes narrowed. "You think twelve hours will change my mind?"

"I will make my petition to your people," Huon said. "It's your law, and Montival respects it."

She hissed before remounting, then galloped west, leading her troop to a bare patch of ground. Throwing down her hat, she marked the place where they would camp. The rodeo dismounted, their show of threat dissolving into the dull work of building shelters from the weather. Few approached them.

Finch went back into the wigwam herself, while the encounter was fresh in her mind, drawing Allie's portrait, the image of her nose to nose with Huon. She drew the traitor, Charles Frayne, attempting to capture his misery.

He feels the wrong he has done, she thought.

Huon put his head inside. "Where's Lester?"

"I didn't see him leave," she said. "What will you do?"

"Ask the Council for Charlie," he said.

"They'll refuse."

"I can hope to get close enough to . . . measure him."

To assess whether he was under CUT influence, Huon meant.

"And if he is?"

"I don't know." A strained edge of a smile. "At worst, send someone next year."

"Allie would ask, I think, if we believed another year would change her mind."

"Yes, she would. What would you say to that?"

She pondered. "That a diplomat is patient?"

"Just so. A lot can change in a year, Finch."

She tried to conceive of the Rodeo Princess' white-hot love for the baker burning down to embers.

I'll never feel that much for Bright, she realized. Was it wrong that failing to feel caused a sort of heartbreak, too?

"In any case," the Baron said, drawing her back to the question at hand, "there's worth in knowing these people."

The day, for all that it was short, passed slowly. She made an attempt to capture Lester on paper, but he was quicksilver: draw his age, and she lost the vitality. She spent an hour working to sketch the sharpness in his eyes, and came away with mere calculation.

The sky clouded to a low gray and ice gritted down, filling the grooves in the lake surface, dulling the colors of the flags and totems, dusting the horses into charcoal shadows.

Near sunset, the drums intensified. There must have been over a hundred of them now, pounding as if to shatter the lake's icy floor. Raki appeared at the wigwam entrance and said to Huon, "My mother asks, Baron, if you will go with her to the Grand Winter Council of Fort Solitude."

Huon looked surprised; Lester hadn't returned.

"Just you," Raki amplified.

Huon gathered his cloak, took a breath, and headed out, leaving the two of them together.

"They'll talk half the night away," Raki said, as she packed away her sketches.

Mind and body in agreement: she smoothed a cowhide that had rucked up on the wigwam floor, running a hand over the place beside her. Raki slipped inside the shelter, bringing one last gust of cold air with him.

He was young and strong, beautiful too, and he wanted only one thing. He would not try to hold her.

"You miss your tribe?"

"My pack," she agreed, kissing his tattooed brow and then sliding her hand into his shirt, where the skin was smooth and warm as the limestone walls of her favorite hot spring.

Well before morning, the drums stopped.

"They're done," Raki said, shifting within the nest they'd made—the dog had come to sleep between them, a belated chaperone. "I've got to go help Ma and the other Doubledoubles—we cater the farewell breakfast."

"Now?"

"No, but soon."

She shoved the dog aside, then kept him so long he had to bolt—vanishing into another gust of cold when his people began shouting for him.

After he went, Finch washed and dressed, listening to the sounds of the camp: purposeful calls, the occasional sound of a hatchet working to break the ice on ropes or other shelters. She packed her belongings. Her touch lingered on the snow snake.

When the Change came, she would tell her people, the world had become smaller. Now, in peace, it was growing again. So, by necessity, must the Morrowland Pack.

They had been children, lost in the forest, but wanting changed nothing. There would be need for diplomacy badges, for espionage, for masks.

She wondered if the Baron, too, had reached a decision.

Just then he appeared, as promptly as if she'd sought him. "Pack up. We haven't quite outstayed our welcome, but we're getting there."

"It didn't go well?"

"There was never much chance, was there?" he said.

"Did you get near him?"

"No." He didn't know if Charlie was safe, then, or a danger to the tribes.

Cries—alarms, from the sentries—brought them outside:

There was a new party at the entrance to the lakeside camp, a great gathering of horses and riders, shrouded against the weather, and heavily armored.

The Cree were moving, suddenly, as one. Some of the braves melted into the wood; others stepped up to defend the camp—spearmen ahead, archers behind. The rodeo clowns rode to form a front line. Teens too young to fight drew the children toward the Fortress.

"My King," Huon said in obvious surprise.

He was right: as the curtain of snow parted she saw it was Artos himself. Standing at the head of the party, cloak whipping, he raised the Sword of the Lady.

Had he followed the Baron? Was that possible? She supposed that, when someone tried to kill your cub . . .

Could it be he didn't trust Huon to bring Charlie back?

A gust threw ice into her eyes. When her vision cleared, she saw the baker.

He had bolted past his guard of rodeo clowns, and was running toward Artos, hands outstretched, feet kicking as he waded through deep snow.

"Charlie," the Rodeo princess, Allie, shouted. She started forward.

Suddenly Lester was there, catching at her horse's reins. She raised an arm, as if to strike the old man.

"You believe in your man or don't you?" he demanded.

Bending, she raised Lester up and tossed him away, on his backside, so he fell harmlessly into the snow.

Finch blinked. Were those feathers, black-and-white ones, falling from the hand that had grabbed him?

By now the baker, Charlie, was almost to Artos. As he ran he was stooping, stumbling, showing his neck. He still had his hands out.

One of the Baron's men had an arrow drawn. "He rushes the King," he murmured. "We'd be justified."

"If the King felt threatened by such as him, we'd have greater worries in Montival than a runaway maker of croissants," Huon replied. "Hold."

Artos and his men waited, untroubled. The cook clearly wanted to touch the Sword.

He wanted the truth known.

Flesh met blade; the flat of Chuckwagon Charlie's bare palms slapped down on the metal with an audible thump, like fish on a grill, as he knelt. He said something, his voice low. Begging forgiveness? The words were shredded by the wind, but they carried the flavor of a sob.

"Come." Huon began striding across the ice to join his King.

Now Charlie was wriggling, strangely, writhing and jerking as if he was caught in a dog's teeth. Guilty after all?

Instead of screaming, or attacking Artos as a magus of the CUT would, he yelled. "Goddammit, Magpie!"

His hands appear to be stuck to the sword.

Jerking, undignified, Charlie put his boot on the tip of the Lady's blade. He gave a mighty yank, and went toppling into the drift, taking half the sword blade and Artos' arm with him.

The party from Montival gasped.

It was a fake, a colored statue. It wasn't the High King at all.

Allie ran to her baker's side, striking the remnant blade with her tomahawk. The King's false arm broke into shards. Beneath the ice, Charlie's hands were frozen to a foot-long length of old steel pole.

She whirled, facing the Baron.

"He reached for your truth-stick!" she said. "He put himself freely to the test."

A false test, Finch thought. "He might have known."

"Did any of us?" She waved a hand, indicating the assembled throngs and their drawn weapons. "Did you doubt this was your precious king?"

Charlie didn't say anything in his own defense. He wrenched himself free of the pole, and dusted snow off his leather pants with the backs of his ice-burned hands.

Up close, the illusion didn't hold. The horses, Finch saw, were mounts borrowed from all around the camp. The host of Montival soldiers was nothing more than snowmen, already slumping and sliding off the saddles.

Charlie said, "I'll go south with them, Allie. Reconcile myself with Artos."

"They might execute you."

"Right or wrong, I let those soldiers into Todenangst."

"It won't be necessary," Baron said.

The hubbub quieted.

"Charles Frayne," Huon said, "as vassal to King Artos and his voice in this matter, I release you from the burden of the crime. You were compelled; you bear no responsibility."

The baker staggered against the horse. "I . . . I should—"

The princess steadied him. Then she reached out, taking the Baron's hand and shaking it. Walking past him, she crossed the drift to lift Lester out of the snow.

"It's like a winter miracle, ain't it?"

"Shut your chatter, Magpie," she said, but there was no heat in it now.

He shook his cloak, and for a moment there was a creak in his movements: he seemed old, achy, and tired, worthy of every line on his ancient face. Then his eyes gleamed, like those of his totems, bright as hungry birds.

"Well! Allie! You oughta take your new pal here to meet those Wheat Pool bastards. They hate my guts, Huon, or I'da done yesterday. And there's a helluva dance at the end of this thing, if you change your mind about going early."

The Baron looked to the princess.

"You shouldn't miss the Doubledouble breakfast," she said, leading him off into the crowd even as it dispersed.

Finch stayed where she was, searching the trampled ground for black-and-white feathers.

Lester interrupted her search. "Guess you know your business," he said, tapping the satchel where the book of sketches was nestled. "Good portrait."

"I'd—" She nudged a piece of ice, the false king's illusory crown, with her toe. "I would like to be worthy of this badge."

"Sculpture, you mean, or trickery?"

"I wish to learn," she said. "I am the Eyes of the Morrowlanders and your skills would benefit my people."

"Come back next winter," he said, "if your boss agrees. In the meantime, our friend Charlie makes an incredible crab-apple turnover. Can you smell it?"

She turned into the wind and it was there: fruit, an unknown spice, fresh flour, and a hint of meat. "Is that real, or is it merely that you suggested it?"

"Should a Scout be so philosophical, little bird?" Lester asked, leaning on her arm for a moment before springing lightly atop a shelf of ice and, from there, to a felled tree trunk. "Seems a little impractical for such hands-on folk."

"I'm beginning to think 'should' is a useless word," she said, hopping up after him, two bird-named people of the forest, balancing on a downed spruce.

"Don't knock 'should.' She's a tyrant, but she's got her uses. Don't ever trump what is, though."

"Says the illusionist," Finch said, and she raised her nose to the freezing air and the cooking crab apple wafting on it, and spread her arms like wings before jumping down to the ice and sliding, twirling like a child, laughing as she cut through the eye-opening bite of the northern wind.

TIGHT SPOT

BY KIER SALMON

KIER SALMON

I'm Kier Salmon, jack of many trades, master at a few. A list of many of the things I've done includes sales clerk, teacher, secretary, executive assistant, programmer, mental health worker, interpreter, copy editor, and first reader.

I have been honing and working on my writing skills in the midst of doing other things like earning a living, being a good witch and community member, and raising my adopted daughter.

My first story, written when I was fifteen, was in Spanish, because I was living in Mexico—I was there between my ninth and twenty-seventh years. I am still fully bilingual.

My first commercial publishing was in *Marion Zimmer Bradley's Sword & Sorceress VI* and under my previous last name of Neustaedter. Then things like real life got in the way and I dropped the idea of writing professionally and focused on earning a living. I'm fairly sure that was the wrong decision. Since 2003 (Beltane) I've been working as S. M. Stirling's first reader, and I've been editing and running his fan-fiction Web site since 2005.

A number of other stories are yammering to be told and between his blunt pointers and the work I do telling people "No, no, no! You can't do that!" I have seen my skill level rise. I'm pleased to present a post-Change story in this anthology.

"**Y**ou're such a fool!"

Colin laughed and juggled the rocks higher and higher, dancing and turning on the narrow path, his great kilt folds swirling around his knobby knees, his dark blond ponytail jouncing on his shoulder blades. One by one he slapped the rocks out of sequence, each one flying over the steep drop-off to the north. He caught the last one neatly and began to toss it, up and up and up, snatching it out of the air as it plummeted down and tossing it again.

". . . And why would I be being a fool?" he asked, catching the stone and turning a bright inquiring gaze to Robin.

She sniffed. Colin reflected that even at twelve she could do a disdainful sniff to rival his stepmother Esther's. As he'd turned sixteen, he'd found himself trying to read female attitudes the more.

He tossed the single stone thoughtfully as they continued to move down the path through the Siskiyous, keeping at a steady dogtrot.

"Well?" she demanded.

"Oh-ho, it's worming the secrets out of the chief's son, is it the now?"

She shrugged and pulled slightly ahead as the trail narrowed, her neatly pleated great kilt flashing stripe, sett, stripe, sett. Colin opened his mouth and shut it. He should really go first, but with two of them alone on the ridge of the world, one position really wasn't safer than another. She was paying attention, eyes, ears, and her sixth sense, and he did the same, still holding the stone.

They'd left Stronghold around midmorning. The aching blue sky of a perfect brisk May day, piled as high with cloud-banks as the earth below was wrinkled into steep ravines and winding valleys, soothed him. Robin was pulling ahead and he pushed himself a bit harder.

"Got it!" she said as he came up to her. "You play the fool every time somebody starts bullying. You did it this morning at practice with that murderer Malcolm!"

Colin clicked his tongue at her. "Well, aren't you the wee bright lassie," he drawled, dodging her sudden fist to the arm. "Di' na, lassie. I'm not truly mocking you the now. But keep that quiet. As I told tha' great brawling bully: when I've the inches and pounds of my sire, I'll smash and bash my way through battle just as he does—I don't think! My faither ain't stupid!

"But Malcolm Robson took two good blows to his kidneys and needed to allow and honor my win. So I made him a laughingstock."

"Robson's got no honor," spluttered the girl. "Murdering bastard . . ."

A cold finger touched Colin's neck. He placed a finger on her lips. "Ah'm thinking we maum go a little milder the now . . ."

She shook off his touch, brown eyes already scanning the forests, barren mountain ridges and arching sky, her ears obviously a-prick and her mind, *the real sixth sense*, thought Colin, working.

They stood quiet for a few minutes before meeting eyes and shrugging slightly. "Something," said Robin, her voice now low. "But I can't pinpoint it."

"Truth," answered Colin, "truth. Keep alert. We have a serious errand to your da and mam, what with young Derek lying on death's threshold. There's no wrong with your anger at the man, for Derek's the second child he's hit too hard. He's not long for our company, not w' two laddies laid out and me but just escaping this morning thanks to Greer Tennart. When m' faither told me to bait him the morn, we di' na expect it to be so effective. Arguing that he nivir meant for to hurt none rings well hollow the now. And Greer did flite him well . . . I reckon the other men will be dishing out yet more scorn today."

Robin's lips had tightened at the mention of her brother's injury. She scanned the rugged land before them again and opened her mouth, and shut it abruptly, freezing. Her eyes met his and they scanned the trail again. Without a word they moved forward at speed, footfalls now as soft as possible and climbed off the trail, up and behind a large rock face overhanging the ravine.

They lay absolutely still, dark green and rust-red plaids thrown over their hair and faces. Slowly the sound that they'd perceived became more pronounced, regular, and Colin felt his gut twist. *Men, damn! Men, for women do not march in syncopation on these trails. And those who do march are not of the Dells of McClintock.*

From the west came a small troop of men, dressed in worn battle camo and laced boots. Billed caps, backpacks, and rattling just the slightest bit from all the hardware they were draped in. Colin kept his eyes in the shade of his plaid, but watched and counted. Swords, daggers, axes, and a few morning stars . . . and where he could see a naked weapon, he could see dried blood. The camo was stained, as well. He could feel Robin stiffen beside him. And slowly force herself to relax again.

They stayed where they were until the sound of the pounding feet faded to the subliminal level that'd first caught their notice. Colin turned his head and looked at Robin. Under the kilt's overdrape, her face was pale. After a long stare into Colin's eyes, she buried her head in her crossed arms, shaking.

"Sherries," she said, fear and loathing in her voice.

Well, Da, that backfired on us . . . Big time. What do I do the now? Colin sat up, pushing his plaid off his head and looked west hoping to see smoke.

Gradually Robin stopped shaking. "Sherries, right?" she asked.

Colin snuck a quick look at her tear-streaked face and nodded shortly, still weighing their options.

"There's no column of smoke," she said, low-voiced, sitting and scanning the western horizon, putting back her own plaid and smoothing down the fluff of hair escaping from her once-neat Dutch braids.

Colin considered. He pointed . . . "Right about there," he said. Robin followed his finger and nodded.

"There, where"—she choked and coughed, rubbing her wet cheeks— "where the eagles fly . . ." They slipped down from their perch back to the trail.

"And the buzzards and war-birds are homing in." Colin chewed his lip. *They got them afore dawn, just like the last time. And nobody left to fire the beacon.*

The midnight planning with his da, the sneaking about, trying to figure out who was the mole in the hold . . . it had been exciting last night as he talked his way past Sean, Stronghold's teacher and accountant, and bluffed him to the kitchen. Now it all felt like a bad spy movie.

We knew RoeDell was fingered as a probable target. But . . . they haven't finished stripping Rachel's Dell. Da didn't expect them to hit another so fast, not before we could warn them; they've niver before. Now what do I do? Or better yet—now what are they going to do nixt?

"It's going to be like Rachel's Dell, isn't it?"

Colin looked down at his companion grimly. "What do you think, lassie?"

"I'm more interested in what you think, Chief's Son!" she snapped back.

Colin shook his head.

"You were there, weren't you?"

"Well," Colin picked up another two stones and began to juggle the three, controlling his emotions by the intense focus needed to move the spinning wheel of stones along several planes. It was like the concentration required to not let his voice break during sword practice.

Robin made an exasperated sound and batted one of the stones out over the ravine. "Stop that, you fool!"

He snatched the other stones out of the air and laid them neatly on the trail, before another betraying rockfall sounded.

"I was," he said shortly, answering the original question. "If RoeDell has fallen, fallen like Rachel's Dell, to the last living creature there, then we don't want to go there . . . at least, I don't want to see it again, and I truly don't want you to see it either."

The serried ranks of heads hanging on poles dug into the ground haunted his sleep. His father had returned to Stronghold and taken down the skulls of his foes from the battles of Eight Dollar Mountain and Redwood Pass, and burned them. He'd made the taking of heads geasa forevermore on the McClintocks.

"Then there's the problem of where the damned Sherries are headed. To their hidey-hole, which we have yet to find, or to hit another dell? Like wasps they are. If I was alone, I'd try to shadow them. As it is, to get back to Stronghold, we'll have to shadow them all the way to Eight Dollar Mountain, and hope they don't set back scouts."

"Bravado," sniffed Robin, trying to recapture her 'tude. "It'd be too dangerous."

Slowly Colin shook his head, looking east, where the column had vanished. "They take no prisoners. If they wiped out RoeDell—that makes"—he thought for a bit—"close on to two—almost three—hundred people in less than a year's time. We can't sustain those kinds of losses.

"Dangerous to follow them, yes, but we've not . . ." he hesitated. *Tell her or not? What she doesn't know she can't tell anyone.* "We're not sure where they are holing up or why they aren't at least stealing the women and children for slaves. Mebee you should go back, alone . . . If only those men . . . If only I could be sure you wouldn't . . ."

"No fear," said Robin flatly. "I'll go, but I'll go careful, very careful."

Colin bent for a stone and then hesitated, looking up at Robin. They made an aborted movement and froze. Around the spur came a man in plain breeks and a shirt. *Can't get off the trail fast enough . . . for sure he's seen us. Two smaller people against one medium-sized man . . . tricky . . .*

"He's not dressed in camo or a kilt. Who is he?"

Colin felt the blood drain out of his face as he recognized the man's gait and short rusty hair and bent hurriedly for the stones he'd put down. He fended off a sudden exasperated push from Robin.

"Let be," he hissed, scowling. "Play along, do!"

He had the rocks up and whirling and began to dance along the narrow trail, sideways, chattering. ". . . So that was Ma's reaction to Da marrying LaTonya . . . but she and LaTonya got to be good friends, 'cause LaTonya's new husband, after she ditched Da, was this guy, Goah, and he came over to work in something called Sirk deh soly. He taught gym at the local school; taught me a lot of things, Goah did. Anyway, he did kid-care for all the kids. We were really a tribe . . . Goah had two plus the other with LaTonya, Mum had two before Da, and three w' Da, and LaTonya had t' one w' Da. He's always liked kids."

Colin felt like he was going to pant and controlled his breath strictly and grabbed another rock and spun around, the pleats of his belted fei-leadh mor flaring and brushing against Sean's pants. Even expecting to find the man close, it was startling and his voice cracked embarrassingly when he let out a gobbled sound and lost his rhythm. Sean startled back, his arms up to shield himself as the egg-sized rocks thudded around them.

"Damn you, fool boy! What the hell are you doing here?"

Colin swallowed and cowered back just a little bit, only enough to convince Sean, without convincing himself. He was remembering an un-expected encounter in the dark passages of Stronghold just hours before. "Taking Robin home!" he said. He shot a quick look over his shoulder and then back to Sean. "I pushed Da to let me do it. I din want her to come alone this way."

"Why are you taking Robin home?"

Colin frowned. *When did Sean leave the morning? Did he not see the kerfuffle at sword practice?*

"Shhh," he said low. "She doesn't know all about Derek, yet." Louder he said, "Me da told me to take her back to talk with her mam and da 'bout Derek being hurt by tha' idjit Malcolm Robson."

What time did Sean leave Stronghold to get here? And what's he doing in the wake of those Sherries?

He turned to Robin and saw a deeply suspicious gleam in her eye. Panic wanted to grab hold of him, but even as he watched, her face went blank and then suddenly, bratty. When she spoke her voice was a perfect whine.

"What're you doing here, Sean? Did you go to warn me mam to go easy on me?" Her voice, petulant and sulky, mimicked an older voice: Sean's. "Ms. RoeDell, sorry ma'am, Ms. MacRoe, Meestair—Maire, An-gus, I've come to warn you Roberta's being sent home . . ."

Sean scowled at her and said, low-voiced, "Sneck it, girl. I needed some missing harvest numbers. I never got to RoeDell—close, but close don't count. I hid up the trail when I heard them climbing up from the Dell."

"How close did you follow?" asked Colin eagerly, patting Robin on the shoulder. It looked like an absent pat—he pinched her good and hard. She grabbed his arm, clinging and whining under her breath. A second "sneck it" from Sean had no effect on her and Colin again patted her shoulder, turning her into his bony chest.

"Let's go back to that place where the overhang makes the trail a bit wider."

He pushed Robin in front and she suddenly ran. "Can't catch me!" she cried, her voice thin in the great open spaces. Colin took off after her, hearing Sean's low-voiced curse behind him. Two quick twists of the trail and she stopped at the wider spot, panting slightly.

"Quick, what am I supposed to do? And why is he coming along behind those Sherries?"

Colin nodded. Sean was coming up, fast. "And he's clean! No blood—dunno what that means, but nothing good. Go figure. We can't ditch him, too dangerous if we don't know where he is or what he's up to. Go home w' him—that'll spike whatever plan he has, having to escort you. I think I know where the Sherries are headed. If I'm right, they plan on wiping out two or three Dells at once and plunder them slowly.

"Da's gotta be warned; tell him the next one is in danger, mebee by dawn tomorrow, mebee the day after. He knows which one that'd be. I can't make the distances work otherwise. Only you can warn him . . . or, I only trust you to do that. When you get to Stronghold, run away from Sean. If he doesn't try to kill you, he'll want to send you up to Selmac and the weavers there. Don't let him touch you, or get in touching distance. Go to Esther or Aisha . . . either'll go right to Da. Keep smart; you missing is a lot less trouble than you sent to Selmac. I trust you, stay alive—get the message to Da."

Colin turned as Sean came up to them.

"You didn't get to RoeDell, you say?"

"Did not. Got within sight of the path, heard something very wrong, went past and hid until they'd gone. Was keeping far enough back they wouldn't see me. I don't think they've got a back scout."

"That was all of them?"

"Aye," said Sean. "Now, you two listen to me . . ."

"No," interrupted Colin. "Did they get to fire the beacon?"

"No, not that I ever saw."

"Did you go down to check?"

"No, I didn't even smell cooking, so I didn't bother."

Colin tried to think how to get the information he needed . . . "What time did you get there? Or, when did you leave, I mean?"

"How'm I to ken? Fine the lot of watches we have now the Change has happened. Now listen, boyo . . ."

Break his train of thought, break it, fast . . . Don't let him give you an order; don't make it a fight . . . Colin began to sway back and forth, bending back at the waist, his back horizontal with the ground. He tried to lift his left leg; just the right holding his whole body and fell in a puff of powdery earth.

"I said," Sean spoke in a low, but very intense voice, bending over him.

"I hierd ye," answered Colin, quietly, flat on his back. "But— Ah'm ordering you in the name o' t' Laird, Hamish McClintock himself, himself, Chief of the Dells and Clans and Stronghold, who sent me on a secret mission to RoeDell, to take Robin back to Stronghold and deliver her richt into the hands o' my aun sire.

"'Tis important, so 'tis, Sean . . . and you the only man I kin trust wit' t' charge of the light o' my life!"

Robin gave an almighty snort. "Like I'd have you to mate any time soon!" she exclaimed, but kept her voice down and quiet.

"I should hope not! We'aun micht too young . . . but it's hope I have for some future date!" Colin rocked, kicked, and forced a jump that landed him on his feet again. He busily patted down his great kilt, sending clouds of the fine dry earth right into Sean's face.

Sean snapped upright, coughing and waving his hands, frustration shouting in every tense muscle.

Wha' e'er yer up to, I hope I've spiked ye. It's hard to come the lordly elder over a boy flat on his back on the ground and joking. And I hope ye have a blessedly bad trip home with Robin. No flies on that girl! Whatever, whatever, I wish I knew what it was yer up to.

And Colin picked up three rocks, started to juggle them and danced down the trail, ignoring Sean's sudden low-voiced order.

He'd have rather let Sean and Robin go ahead. There was danger that Sean might see where he went off trail, but he couldn't trust the man to go fast enough. *When they're no gud choices, son, pick a choice; much better than none or dithering.*

He stopped juggling and started dogtrotting. Eventually he paused where he couldn't be seen from somebody on his back trail and took a sighting. For years he and his many siblings had come up every summer and winter and played tracking games through the entire range of mountains to the west of Cave Junction. After he came to live in Cave Junction a few years before the Change he'd come to know the land even better, winning the games for his gang during their vacations.

Since the Change, his ability to go "off trail" without getting lost and directioneering to any destination he wanted had saved the McClintocks' bacon several times. It wasn't easier or faster, but it did allow for sneak bypasses and spying.

He pulled out the ropes he never left at home, and some carabiner clips, a few pulleys and a pickax and crampons. With a final look down the trail and a heartfelt hope that Robin would arrive back to Stronghold safe, he put her out of mind and began to climb the ridge.

Hours later he rested on another ridge, watching the last wisps of light fade to the west. Overhead stars began to glow; sunset was close to nine.

Mickleson's Dell lay downslope and west.

It was hidden beyond a spur and he couldn't *see* any sign it existed . . . but the scent of the evening meal fires hung in the air. He waited for several hours, but he saw no movement at all along the slopes. All the evidence they'd managed to dig up from Rachel's Dell, which he'd happened upon just two days after the attack, and from the other two smaller hamlets months before led them to believe that the Sherries were arriving and hiding in a wide arc around the settlement the day before the attack and came out, very quietly, several hours before dawn and slaughtered as many as possible before the alarm was given.

Hamish had decided, from the traces left, that no more than ten or fifteen men were involved. But ten or fifteen men, awake and systematic and well led could easily slaughter a hamlet of ten or fifteen households . . . eighty or ninety people, most dead in their beds or at the very threshold of their homes, and from the state of the animals, just before or at dawn. Farmer folk often were up betimes, doing their routine chores, and none of the Dells lost had shown signs of the early chore work.

The moon rose in a blaze of glory, looking as wide as Stronghold, silhouetted against the rough terrain. Colin watched eastward, and was rewarded. There was a fire to the east, possibly several from the smoke trails across the face of the moon. *They would have done better to camp cold,* he thought. *But, unless Sean is one of theirs and they expected him to join them; they've no idea they've been rumbled. Time to warn Mickleson's and trap the trappers.*

He yanked his tousled hair back into a neater ponytail and slung his rope around a rock and began to descend by the tricksy moonlight to the trail down by the river. *At least, when the dogs start barking I don't have to worry that they'll warn the Sherries I'm arriving, and I don't have to sneak through a line of heartless murderers—I hope.* Colin was tired after a full half day of scaling up and down the mountain screes, so he took extra care with the descent. He finally reached the Illinois River Road, the NF-4103. The river brawled and leapt to his left as he set forward at a slow trot.

The moonlight made his path difficult; hard-edged black shadows making him hop and skip over obstacles that weren't there, and stub his toes on hidden ones. The road's pavement was deteriorating from years of neglect. A broken leg, or even a twisted ankle could kill him.

He trotted up to Mickleson's, one of the largest of the Dells, amid a chorus of angry dog barks and shouts and torch lighting.

"Quiet, quiet!" he yelled, feeling ironic.

Mickleson waved a pine knot close to his face, furious. Colin thought that the reflected flame wasn't making the man's face redder and puffier than it really was.

"Put that damned boy in the lockup and Hamish can spring him when we've got the time to send and let him know where his stupid little Loki is!"

Colin grabbed at the torch and doused it on the ground. "Quiet, you dafties!" he said, keeping his voice down. "And less noise and flame!" He dodged a sudden heavy fist, jumping behind the man.

What do I do now? he wondered. *The jokester's all well and good, but it's backfiring the now.*

Two men grabbed him from behind and yanked him back, one covering his spluttering mouth.

"Rory, Rory, be calm!"

Colin started violently. *Aisha? What's she doing here? Oh, damn! Aisha! Here!*

She talked softly to Rory Mickleson. Colin relaxed himself and felt the hold on him loosen. He didn't pull free. After a few more seconds the Dell's commons were moonlit again, just a few horn lanterns, and the dogs under control. At a sign from Rory Mickleson, the men let go.

"Aisha, what are you doing here?" he blurted out.

His father's fourth . . . or second wife—depending on how you counted she could be his first since she was the only one living he'd married in a formal, official ceremony, five months after the Change—was barely visible in the darkness. She came to stand beside him. "I had to bring special supplies for Rory's wife. But she died and he's got some problems, so I stayed."

Colin looked over to the far side of the commons and spotted the llama pack team Aisha generally used when she was wandering about the Westmark, pastured with the Dell's sheep, alpacas, and llamas.

After a minute of trying to put too many pieces of data in order, he settled on the most important. "Rory, 'tis sorry I am to hear that Susan's deid, th' now. Tha's terrible news. But we'll all be deid by the second dawn, do we not work hard tonight and tomorrow. There's a mess o' Sherries camped back a matter of a league or two and they've just wiped out RoeDell. I've sent news to my faither, but it's a question if it'll get through. Problem wi' these narrow mountain trails is how easy 'tis to interdict communications."

Rory Mickleson scowled at him and then waved irritably. "Everybody, back to yer cots. Danuel, Robby, Maire, and Devra, wi' me in t' Hall. You too, Aisha." He grabbed Colin by the arm and hustled him up to the grandiosely named "Hall."

An hour later Colin scowled and gave it up. Mickleson would have his way, and in his Dell he ruled. Loyalty he owed to Hamish McClintock and the clan, but not obedience. Having wrung Colin dry of all the information and speculation he had, he had made his decisions and formulated his strategy.

"You and Aisha make tracks for Stronghold at dawn and tell t' laird," he instructed, reddened eyes glaring, bitten lips cracked and bleeding a tad more. "I'm not having you risk yersel's in my bragle. Yer no loss as warriors, neither, but as couriers . . . mebee you can get Hamish and the affinity out here and catch them, slaughter them, and we'll be done with their threat."

The lanky Dell chief turned away from them and gathered his seconds in a huddle over a relief map in the far corner.

Colin sighed. "But I told you, I already sent a courier . . ." he said to the man's back, and softly.

"Are you hungry, then, Colin?" asked Aisha.

"I'd take it kindly, if you'd feed me," he answered. She took him out to the refectory and found bread, cheese, and jerky, with some nuts and clean cold water. He ate watching Aisha fuss the kitchen back into order.

"Susan's going to be missed," she observed. "Rory's not a bad man, but he was always . . . a man to let women's work rest in women's hands. And Susan would have no second in her own home. And the girls were caring for their mother and not the house, not to mention, they're all young."

Colin nodded, enjoying her voice. *She's the only person who isn't trying to sound like a second-rate BBC historical around here. I wish Da hadn't . . . well, but I don't either.* He sighed and Aisha laughed suddenly.

"Dear Colin, you've been a good boy with the world turning upside down on you twice and three times. And a good friend to me. What's the sigh for?"

And in the gloom of the kitchen, with the friendly low glow from the banked hearth it was suddenly easy for Colin to say, "I wish Da'd nivir left you when Esther came back pregnant that winter. And you with child."

"Esther's Shona is as much your sister as Dhugal is your brother," said Aisha, a measure of reproof in her voice.

He struggled to express himself . . .

"It, it jest warn't right!"

"No, Colin, it wasn't. It wasn't right that Esther had to bear a rape child, or suffer the cruel march south to return, under the slave's yoke. Life isn't right . . . many times. Your father loves Esther. He cared and cares for me, but Esther is the wife of his heart. I'd rather a cold bed than a shared bed. Esther would have said nothing had Hamish honored the vows he spoke to me, believing her dead."

She drummed her fingers on the table, lightly. "But I wouldn't have been happy, either. No, sometimes you get lemons and even lemonade isn't possible, so you sip the sour and accept it." She put her work-roughened dark fingers over his hand for an instant, eyes black in the gloom of the kitchen, skin well nigh invisible.

Colin sighed. He'd fallen in love with Aisha this last year, her dark skin, slender, aristocratic face, patient kindness, and the riot of curly black hair ravaging his adolescent heart. She was—had been—his father's wife; it was icky! And she was abandoned and beautiful and . . . Colin squelched the thought.

"We'll be leaving the morn, then? I'm not too easy in my mind. Moonset is after sunrise, so we'll have no dark hours before dawn to creep past the Sherry camps."

"I don't know, Colin; it doesn't feel right. Are you sure they'll surround the Dell tomorrow? And attack at dawn the next day?"

"No," he said, baldly. "It's what they've done before. But they've not, to our knowledge hit two Dells in two days. So, I don't know."

"Aisha? Colin?"

"Here," called Aisha.

Rory walked into the refectory. "Dennis isn't back," he said. Colin watched him fidget with the ironmongery hanging in the fireplace.

There's a man not as confident as he was showing to his seconds.

"Of course, you've yer aun place here, Aisha, and always welcome. Colin, ye kin bunk with the boys over in t' tower. But . . ."

"Who's Dennis? And where and why is he missing?"

Rory glared at Colin. "Ye'll ha' yer faither's inches soon eno', and probably your faither's brains, though I dun see no sign they's there, just the yet. Any yet—so, Dennis is our shepherd and he an' his dog have been after finding a missing sheep flock. It's but a bellwether and three ewes and their lambs."

"There aren't many places for them to hide," observed Colin.

"It's coming up on midnight, Rory," said Aisha.

Colin shot her a glance; something had changed in her voice. Clearly Rory had heard it, too. He moved behind her and pointed her at the banked fire. "Midnight, the witching hour, black witch. Tell me what you see . . ."

Call her black witch? Colin wasn't sure which noun offended him more and opened his mouth to protest and shut it. Aisha was in a trance and Colin had seen Belle at Selmac Lake go into a trance and prophesy truly; he went very still and shuddered a bit.

I didn't know Aisha tranced.

Rory held Aisha's shoulders gently and pressed; the black woman collapsed to her knees, folding gracefully, arms wrapped around her forehead resting on her thighs. She rocked slowly and Colin heard her words, whispered to the floor.

"They argue; they argue. Their leader is gone. They are splintering, splintering, splintering . . ." Aisha reared up, her eyes wide and blank. "They will destroy my new home, before it is even offered to me . . ."

She fell over and Rory scooped her up.

Colin made a move and then held back. Rory nodded at him.

"Not too useful, the now. But she did that for Susan months ago. And what she said was true. I'll put her to bed with Tracey and Danetta. And you're damn well leaving at dawn! The both of you; clearly they'll attack! Even if they break into splinter groups, splinters kin be deadly."

Colin paced around the refectory for a few minutes more. Aisha's words itched at him, and the missing shepherd and his sheep. Finally he found the outer door and walked into the silent night. Silver moonlight poured down, the small bright disk high in the night sky. There were meadows across the river and both up and down the river where the animals might have wandered, Colin turned and turned.

It was late; he was tired and if there were men hiding in the trees around the commons and by the other cots across the river and up and down the trail, he couldn't see them and finding them would be impossible. A huge yawn cracked his head open, straining his jaw joints. Llama-Dama and Dali-Llama were at pasture at the edge of the trees. He curled up against Llama-Dama and fell asleep. Even for the son of Hamish Mc-Clintock, it had been a long day. His last thought was to wonder if Robin had made it back to Stronghold and Hamish was mustering the rescue.

The night was bright with moonlight, but the corridors of the outer keep, inky black. Late as it was, no light gleamed out of the narrow windows above. Sean felt a faint movement of air on his cheek. He moved his hand abruptly and the hulking shadow paused.

"Where is she?" he asked.

"Bloody if I know! Why the hell didn't you just kill her on the trail?"

"Couldn't get close enough to her, damn it!"

"Things going bollocks-up real fast. Is it worth it to stay?"

"You can't; that boy—Derek—he's dead as a doornail. You just had to kill! We needed you in the muster—and now you'll be hanged at dawn before ever himself leaves with his kilted clowns. I must stay, or give up the whole plan. And I won't! Stronghold is mine!"

The angry swearing of the man hidden in the shadows grew in volume. "Can it, Malc—Quiet! You don't want anybody finding you. I'll try to distract the guard and you sneak out. Get over toward Mickleson's as fast as possible; moon's up. The boys'll be camped out 'bout a league short, where the trail cuts narrow over the Illinois River. I don't know who's in charge. Rick bought it at RoeDell and Andy sent for Dubya and his guys and Warren and his'n were scouting south of the Illinois River."

One soft, heartfelt curse answered him.

Sean walked out into the practice ground, through the forest of pells and targets and on over to the great gate and lounged against the postern, fumbling behind his back.

"What's up, Teach?" asked the on-duty McClintock.

"Nothing much, Sam, nothing much. Been looking for young Robin MacRoe. I was out most of the day, but there's a note on my desk saying she wants to talk with me."

"Haven't seen her since she left with the boy midmorning."

The deadbolt moved smoothly back; the postern door wanted to swing open. Sean stilled it and then walked forward, still talking, talking, talking—distracting the guard, listening for Malc's heavy tread and the sound of the postern door swinging open and shut.

He never saw the fist shoot out of the darkness—only felt the star-spangled pain as it slammed into his temple.

In the brisk chill of the predawn Colin came suddenly awake as Llama-Dama surged to her feet and gave the gargling, squeaky attack scream of her kind. Colin could see the mountain silhouettes to the east; the sky above pale with the approaching dawn. He screamed as hard as he could as the mountainside was suddenly alive with the disciplined movement of camouflaged men.

"Rory! Rory! Turn out the guard!" His voice cracked.

Curses; he could hear curses from the slopes and more from the cots around the commons. Dali-Llama butted him in the chest and he fell over onto the hay they'd been sleeping in. Even as he struggled up, Llama-Dama stepped backward and put one leg and all her weight on his breast-bone.

Doors banged—torches flared—the Dell's adults poured out, armed and ready . . . Colin turned his head and caught a glimpse of the men coming into the Dell. He reached up, trying to shift the llama's foot off his chest. Something was off; if only he could see! Or move!

The clash of weapons, scurrilous yells, a few screams of fear or agony. Colin pounded on the llama's leg. Suddenly Llama-Dama moved forward and let him up. He grabbed her around the neck, hanging on and gasping in deep breaths. The commons were crowded with men and women, weapons waving, ropes being tied . . . Colin counted and then looked again. He'd gotten a fairly close look at the men who'd marched past him on the trail, yesterday.

These weren't them and they'd come from the west, not the east where he'd seen the smoke plumes last night.

Splintered . . . she said they were splintered, he thought. *Only eight of them, and the camo is hunting camo, not the battle camo from yesterday.* He backed up, toward the trees, hoping Rory wouldn't see him and order him down. He was only a few trees in when he heard a chant, "Chop! Chop! Chop!" and on the heels of the chant the meaty whack of an ax landing.

Rory Mickleson wasn't one to waste any time on judging bandits.

Now does that help them or hurt them? he wondered. *It's May; river might be deep enough to toss them in and expect it to take them to sea by Gold Beach. If they keep the bodies and the rest o' them come late today . . .*

He bit his lip, scanning the steep hillside, wondering where he could hide for the day—or should he go back and remind Rory that the danger was to the east? It was all very well to say any decision was better than none, but this time . . . he worked his way east, slowly, hoping to get a better idea of what was waiting for the Dell.

Hours later he'd worked his way several miles east, without ever staying on the road for many steps. He bitterly regretted the lack of a proper breakfast. The jerky and hardtack and cheese in his pack had mostly been eaten the day before, and the leftovers hadn't made a dent in his aching hunger.

He finally found the perch he wanted. If there were more men coming in from the west, they were going to follow the road until they could spread out near the settlement. From here he could see the southwest road for nearly a mile; more than enough warning.

He glanced back toward Mickleson's and froze. Aisha was walking down the road, leading her llamas. He looked forward—saw movement, men marching, and felt *Rock! Hard place!* He waited, the hardest thing he could do, trying to come up with a strategy that would leave Aisha alive.

Me a hero would be a great bonus, but not necessary at all, at all.

The next twenty minutes felt like an hour. He couldn't stop Aisha without the Sherries seeing them. The most he could hope for was that she knew they were there and this was a deliberate strategy to smoke them out.

He looked and judged and looked and judged until he was sure he would be right above the meeting ground. He set about gathering pine mast and broken branches, building a little fire up against one of the trees that had burned halfway and died in the Change year.

He was some yards west of the meeting when it happened a little later. There were almost thirty men, double what he'd seen the previous day. They surrounded the slender black woman and her llamas, shouting and shoving. Aisha stood with a llama on either side and they bobbed their heads, punching two of the men in the chest. Colin grinned fiercely . . . *Go kill a couple for me, Llama-Dama!* he cheered silently.

Two men waved back the rest and walked up to her. Colin strained his ears. "Too bad for you, girlie! Wrong place wrong time, lots of wrong men. And we've a few hours to kill, anyway . . ."

"Andy, just 'cause Rick nivir attacked in the day, dun't mean we can't. We should just take this piece of ass with us and use it there. We're almost there."

"Dubya, we still alive and a gang 'cause Rick knew his business."

"He isn't alive anymore and it was one of these critters killed him . . ."

"Shut it!"

Colin gasped. It wasn't Sean; the hair was too long and redder than the teacher-accountant's, but the resemblance . . . From the distance he could see the shock hit Aisha, too. "We can go on nibbling at the edges, but we need to get into Stronghold if we mean to live much longer. Rick and Sean made the plan and we're following it."

"Alasdair, you're a dummy. Sean's not here and Rick's dead and I want this piece of ass!"

The one called Dubya leered at Aisha. "You are black, but comely, O ye daughter of Jerusalem . . .'"

Colin wasn't aware of thinking . . . of planning, of deciding as he set fire to the grass rope he'd laid to reach the pile of dry tinder; then he was swinging down the scree, recklessly letting the rope run through his hand, the palms of his climbing gloves heating up fast. He landed on the road behind the group of men and dropped the line, stripped off the gloves and ran, full tilt forward.

"Alasdair! Alasdair!" he yelled.

The men spun around, reforming in front of Aisha, swords, cross-bows, clubs out and ready. He skidded to a halt, panting harshly.

"Where's Alasdair? Sean sent me!" He looked up and down the road and complained, "Any road, you aren't supposed to be here. It's not noon yet and you'n's supposed to wait till three to get into position! I been running and running, trying to find you!"

He made his voice petulant and whining. He grabbed a stone up from the ground and tossed it up. Caught it, tossed it, caught it, and waited, waited, waited for the baited hook to catch.

"Alasdair! Sean sent me!"

"How'd he know your name?"

That was the one called Andy, sullen, angry and suspicious. Then Dubya's voice said, "Sean said the brat was fighting his da a lot. He thought maybe he could get the kid to open the doors when the time was right. I heard him telling Rick and Al."

"That's Alasdair to you! Let the boy through, maybe he is going to help us, and if he isn't, more pain to him."

Colin gulped and grabbed another stone and lofted it up and began to juggle as he walked forward. Close up Alasdair didn't look that much like Sean, after all. He was older, a lot older, and a deep knotted scar cut across his left cheek. Colin snatched up two more stones, bending his juggling wheel from horizontal to vertical and back again.

"Sean said you were an idiot with those stones and joking around. Put 'em down."

Colin snatched them out of the air, and carefully piled them up on Llama-Dama's pack and bowed extravagantly, left hand on his homespun linen shirt, right hand waving in a complicated pattern before coming to rest on the short-sword hilt by his side.

Then he laughed, happy, and a little cruelly. "You've got Aisha! Good for you! She is mine, you know."

"I know nothing of the sort," said Alasdair, his ice-blue eyes narrowing.

"That was my price." Colin stepped around Llama-Dama, grabbed Aisha and kissed her soundly, holding on and grabbing her breast. Her first startled stillness gave way to angry shoves and a clout on the head.

He laughed again, meeting her eyes. "Give over. Me da dun want you and I do. You'll be my little slave girl and happy for it, too, if you want Dhugal to survive!"

He bent back fast away from the second blow and snapped up and hopped back, landing on Alasdair's boot with all his weight. "Sorry, sorry!" he gasped, leaping back and jostling Dali-Llama who promptly put his ears back, crouched and spat, spraying indiscriminately as usual. The Sherries yelped and scattered. Colin turned, looking completely aghast. And noted that Aisha had moved the rocks off Llama-Dama's back to the back fold of her kilt.

Alasdair grabbed him, yanking him around, and put a fine-bladed knife right under his eye. "What's this about Sean?" he asked. "He was supposed to go back to the hold and convince the McClintock to ask for help from the Rogue River Valley levees, not come out and attack right away."

Colin looked at the knife, going cross-eyed trying to see nearer and his hands made an aborted movement to toss a stone up.

"Shut it!" ordered Alasdair. "No more jokes."

Colin nodded and let a little whimper escape, leaving his eyes crossed as he looked up.

"Sean got back yesterday and got caught coming in. He had a bloody knife on him and he said it was a dog he'd killed up trail. M' da did'n believe him, but he had to go see to Derek . . . Robson done kilt the boy; he just took a few hours at dyin', and Sean went to let Malc go and the McClintock caught him and . . . kilt him, him and Malc both."

Alasdair frowned. "So why you coming to me now? Just lay low and yer da'll nivir know you'd thought o' taking his place."

Colin grabbed up a stone and tossed it in the air. Alasdair batted it out of his reach.

"Answer!"

"Me da questioned the both of them before he shoved them off the wall with a noose round each neck. He knows, and he knows my price. He's pretty mad. Not to say, rip-shit furious. I got out, just ahead of three crossbow bolts and Greer Tennart's longbow arrow."

He stared into eyes colder and more deadly than Sean's. "Sean—Sean told me he's led the Sherries, has since you guys escaped Sheridan, way back Change Day. Now he's dead, I guess yer the new laird."

Alasdair gave a bark of laughter, and slapped Colin. He stumbled sideways from the force, the flat salt taste of blood all over his tongue. From a crouch, he looked up, cowering away from the angry man.

"I'm the boss of the Sherries if anyone is!" Alasdair was practically snarling. "Not Dubya, not Andy, not Sean. Rick and I, we know how to lead a guerrilla troop. We got the experience in El Salvador. Sean was just my little brother . . . got us all in hot water."

Colin nodded, eager to keep them talking. He could feel Aisha fading back toward the mountain slope, the llamas screening her. He spat redly into his hands and glared up at Alasdair.

"Bastard! Didn't need to hit so hard. I'm only repeating what Sean tol' me. He said you was bank robbers and he kilt a man."

Colin could feel the men around him paying attention, their eyes on Alasdair. He stood cautiously, holding a few pebbles in his hands.

"And if he hadn't kilt the guard and shot the cashier, we wouldn't have landed in federal prison for . . ."

Alasdair shook his head, scowling. "You behave like a good little boy and I'll use you to bribe your paw to open Stronghold to us after we take out this Dell. Been blocking us from Gold Beach for years, he has."

"Dun need to bribe me da. There's a back way in. Only four people know it."

Alasdair drew in a satisfied breath. "Good . . . good . . . An easy way in, and you to kill your father in his bed."

Colin moved as Alasdair looked up, a puzzled frown growing on his face. The click of the stones brought his eyes back and he slapped a stone out of reach. "Fool boy! Why do you do that?"

"Nervous habit . . . but it riles m' faither something awful."

"Well, it riles, me, too. Stop it!"

Colin let the rocks fall. It looked random, but he saw one smack Andy's right elbow. There was a satisfying thunk and he suppressed a grin.

"So what's the plan?" he asked, wishing he could sneak a peek at Aisha or his improvised beacon.

Alasdair slapped at him again and Colin swayed out of the way with a yelp that landed him against the man called Dubya. He danced away, with a sharp belt knife hidden in the folds of his great kilt, leaving a slice through the man's webbing belt. One good tug at the sword and it would all fall apart.

Alasdair clapped his hands once and the seething mass of men quieted.

He pointed at Colin. "Quiet, you!"

"We'll split, soon. As soon as the bank is shallow enough, Dubya and his seven will cross over and hide around the place they call CrossCot. Remember, we don't attack until dawn. It's the best way to make sure we don't get caught.

"Andy, you and me'll go up this slope and I'll lead my six against the Hall while you take your ten to the place they call Table Meadow and . . ." Alasdair looked north and east and they all froze. Colin's dead tree was burning merrily, spewing up a thick column of smoke.

"Where's the woman? She did that! Find her and kill her! Knew that piece of black ass was going to be trouble!"

Colin tensed as one of the men yanked on Llama-Dama's leading rein, lifting a knife. The llama's ears went back, she gave her gobbling screech and rammed the man in the chest, knocking him down. She jumped on him and stomped a few times for good measure and set off down the road at a brisk trot. Dali-Llama followed posthaste, spitting in one man's face. Colin searched the mountain scree, but Aisha's brown and gold and black plaid blended in just as well or better than camouflage and he couldn't spot her.

The men were milling, now, trying to sort themselves into the groups Alasdair had named. Colin faded back, away from the three leaders, hoping to get away and follow the two llamas. He stooped and grabbed some more egg-sized stones for good measure, looking right and left. Climbing the scree was possible, but he was sure Aisha was somewhere on the slope, so having a dozen men struggling up the unstable surface wasn't a good idea. Jumping over the side to the riverbank was another possibility that didn't make him feel very confident. Forward to Mickleson's was out.

He faded down the road, faded again, behind him were five Sherries, two, none. "Grab the boy!"

He turned and ran all out after the llamas' thudding steps. He could hear the men baying behind, like a pack of dogs . . .

That's good! Dogs they are; vicious, unprincipled poorly trained scavengers! Nothing like the well-trained brutes that guard our Dells and Stronghold.

Colin suddenly realized that llamas don't sound like kettledrums . . . or lambegs. They have feet that patter and nails that click. He ran harder and came skidding round a spur to see his father at the head of a mass of men and women.

Behind him he heard Alasdair screaming, "Leave the boy, leave the boy! We've got to hole up at Mickleson's!"

He didn't wait to see if pursuit stopped. Pell-mell he ran for his father's banner: four white and black Tudor roses on a purple background with a silver sword, slanted left-lower corner to right upper. The llamas pulled up and danced uneasily in front of Hamish McClintock. Colin dashed up and grabbed them by the shoulders.

"They're going for the Mickleson's! And Aisha's up on the mountain somewhere."

"Get off the trail and let us pass. We'll take them down once and for all. Sean said there were twenty at RoeDell."

"You did smoke him! The dirty liar! They're forty of them just down the trail."

"Your girl, yon Robin did that. Smart lassie . . . and heir to the Dell. Derek died at Matins, poor lad. So, after Sean opened the postern for Malc, I socked him in the heid . . . and the guard shot Robson like the mad dog he was."

Colin tried to laugh, but the swollen cheek from Alasdair's blow hurt, and all he could do was grimace. He pulled back, happy to let his father and the seventy men from Stronghold go forward.

He followed, leading the llamas. "Aisha is going to kill me anyway, but if I bring you back to her, she might do it fast instead of torturing me," he observed to Dali-Llama, who snorted his disbelief.

AGAINST THE WIND

by Lauren C. Teffeau

LAUREN C. TEFFEAU

Lauren C. Teffeau was born and raised on the East Coast, educated in the South, employed in the Midwest, and now lives and dreams in the Southwest. In the summer of 2012, she attended Taos Toolbox, a master class in writing science fiction and fantasy. When she was younger, she poked around in the back of wardrobes, tried to walk through mirrors, and always kept an eye out for secret passages, fairy rings, and messages from aliens. She was disappointed. Now she writes to cope with her ordinary existence. Her work can be found in a variety of speculative fiction magazines and anthologies. To learn more, please visit laurencteffeau.com.

I t had been a day full of anemic sun and salt breeze. Perfect for sailing. And salvage.

As the *Windfall* crossed the swirling line where the electric blue waters of the Prince William Sound met the slate gray of the gulf, Mitch told the kids to stay alert.

Unlike the storm surges and eddies that ate away the edges of the mainland, the open sea had an energy all its own. Simple mistakes could turn deadly, especially out here. Only a few feet of fiberglass, metal, and wood separated his family from the expanse of the sea. As the snow-draped ridges of the Kenai Mountains faded into the distance, anxiety settled low in his spine. He manned the tiller, keeping the thirty-six-foot sloop pointed eastward.

They were roughly five leagues off the coast, south of Montague Island, when his son Edward let out a cry, pointing starboard. "What do you think, Dad?" Eddie shielded his eyes against the afternoon glare off the choppy water and strained against the railing like an overeager puppy.

Mitch raised his binoculars and inspected the deck of a marooned yacht. Some yuppie's toy left to rot thanks to the diesel engine, the now-shredded sails just for show. The canvas fluttered and snapped in the breeze—a rippling sound like playing cards clipped to the spokes of a bicycle. The anchor had kept the boat in place. That a squall hadn't sent it under was a miracle.

Then again, that's what Mitch was counting on.

"No bodies on the deck," Danielle said from her perch at the bow.

"That doesn't mean anything. We'll anchor here and row over."

"Aww, come on, Dad." Dani had her hand on her hip, the other hand clenching the jack line running bow to stern.

Mitch knew both kids thought him overly paranoid, but it had served them well so far.

"I'll not risk the *Windfall*." He turned back to Eddie. "Prepare to drop anchor."

"Aye, aye, Captain." The twelve-year-old boy clambered across the deck and reeled out the anchor. The heaving waters greedily swallowed the metal links.

"Dani, you—"

"I know, I know. Dad, I got it."

Mitch suffered through the rolled eyes as she helped him adjust the sails so they could set the anchor. She did good work, which made her think she knew it all. Except patience and prudence. Which he didn't have at fifteen either.

Eddie helped him lower the dinghy over the side of the *Windfall*. He had a leg over the railing before Mitch reached out a hand to stop him.

"No. Dani and I'll go over first and scope things out."

"But I always stay behind." His voice cracked on the whine.

"We need you here as lookout. If things go to hell, you'll need to get the *Windfall* ready to sail. That's a huge responsibility. You know that."

Eddie slunk back onto the deck with a pout.

"Tell you what. Next time, I'll have Dani be lookout, okay?"

Eddie brushed his sandy hair out of his eyes and gave him a reluctant nod.

Mitch passed him his binoculars. "Make sure you—"

Eddie looped them over his neck. "I won't drop them, Dad. Even if I did, it's not like we don't have four other pairs belowdecks."

Mitch frowned. "They're for trading. And no excuse not to take care of what we have."

Dani finished securing the mainsail to the boom and joined them at the railing. He helped her down into the dinghy, and followed her in as she settled into the seat at the stern. Eddie passed them wooden oars and then the rope lead.

Winds were maybe five knots at most from the north, but no guarantee they'd stay that way. Mitch scanned the western horizon and saw nothing that gave him pause. Still . . .

"Keep an eye on the weather," he said to Eddie. "If all goes well, we'll pick you up after we drop off the first load."

Mitch pushed the dinghy off the fiberglass hull of the *Windfall* and fought the current with each stroke as he rowed them toward the yacht.

"Easy now," Dani called out when they were maybe a dozen feet out.

He jammed the oars into the water, the drag slowing them down enough the dinghy bounced off, instead of slammed against, the hull of the yacht. Mitch searched the exterior and found a cleat off the rear deck for them to tie off the dinghy.

He handed the oars to Dani. "Once I'm on board—"

"Dad, I know."

He bit back a response as he levered himself onto the yacht. Water sloshed as the dinghy squeaked against the yacht's transom. The metal railings sapped his hands of any warmth. When Dani passed the oars up to him, he barely felt the smooth wood.

"Permission to come aboard, Captain."

So that's how it was going to be.

Dani's voice always took on that grating quality of his ex-wife's when she was pissed, which seemed like always these days. But, he supposed, teens were teens, even when civilization was crashing down around you.

Mitch scanned the deck, his hand hovering over the hunting knife sheath that hung off his belt. After a moment, he relaxed. Still empty. The snapping, lacerated sails the only sound.

"Permission granted."

Dani's brown braids bobbed into view, the rest of her gangly frame followed, emphasized by the way the life jacket over her windbreaker hugged her body. He frowned. Bordering on too thin for a girl her age.

"We'll check below. Cover me."

Dani didn't answer, just kept her oar out in front of her.

The cabin door was shut tight. He tried the handle.

"Locked."

Dani peered around his shoulder. "Do you want me to get the pick kit?"

Mitch jiggled the handle again. There was just enough give to make him think . . . "Stand back."

He brought the butt-end of the oar down on the handle, then once more for good measure. Metal popped, and the cabin door creaked open. The stench of rot—food, folk, and forgotten spaces—smacked them in the face.

"God, I hate this part," Dani muttered behind him.

"Look sharp," Mitch said as he pushed down the short flight of stairs.

Wall-to-wall wood paneling surrounded him. Not cheap veneers. The real stuff. Probably take a couple of days to strip it off the walls, bundle it back onto the *Windfall*. And then? The folks in Homer were rebuilding something fierce. He'd probably get enough foodstuffs and supplies to get the kids through winter.

"What's that?" Dani pointed to the V-berth.

The door was half-closed. An arm was draped across the threshold.

Mitch stepped past the galley right off the stairs. Cupboards hung open. Empty cans, wrappers, used sugar and ketchup packets were strewn across the floor along with an upturned bag of flour. You could live on flour gruel for a while, but without potable water . . .

Vomit stains had soaked into the tightly woven carpet leading to the berth. He pushed the door open with the tip of his boot. The smell intensified, but each subsequent openmouthed breath made it easier to bear.

Mitch stared down at the body, recently dead. Male, middle-aged, wearing better quality outerwear than his own. Real down and lamb's wool, not the synthetic stuff that itched as much as it kept you warm. They looked to be about the same size. Good. He could use a fresh set of clothes.

He eased out of the room. "Stay here." He poked through another berth, then the chart and engine rooms. All empty.

Dani squealed. He wheeled around, clocking his head on the low doorway leading back to the main saloon. He shook off the pain in time to see Dani brandishing her oar against a gaunt young man a few years older and a few inches taller than her. *Where'd he come from?*

Shaggy brown hair shielded his eyes. An inarticulate cry escaped his wind-chapped lips as he lunged toward Dani.

She dodged and darted around the bar. Her eyes widened in relief when she spotted Mitch.

"Dad! He won't listen to me."

"Hey. We're here to help if—"

At Mitch's voice, the guy veered away from the bar and faced him. He seemed too scrawny to do much damage. Mitch revised that assumption when the guy's fist flew out and caught Mitch's shoulder. Agony lanced down his arm, short-circuiting the reasonable part of his brain. He reacted swiftly, smacking the kid in the head with his oar. Hard. He collapsed, knocking against a barstool bolted to the floor. It squeaked as the seat rotated around and around in counterpoint to Dani's harsh breaths.

She came up next to him and leaned into his side. She hadn't done that in years. "He was hiding in one of the lockers, I think." She glanced up at him. "Can we help him?"

Too many times in the months right after things changed, they'd stumbled upon people stranded on their fancy boats that had suddenly stopped working. Most didn't know how to really sail—the pure unadulterated way without radar, GPS, engine backup to get you back to harbor when the winds and the currents weren't cooperating.

In the early days, they'd provided safe passage to the marooned. The law of the sea and all. That didn't keep him from marking each ship's position on his chart and returning to the spot to strip it down of anything remotely useful. Which was usually everything.

He glanced at Dani, then back at the young man. Still out cold. They'd come across folks half-crazed with hunger before, but something had been off about this guy. Mitch didn't like it.

"Keep an eye on him. I'll be right back."

He found the locker Dani mentioned. Inside, bones and gristly joints were scattered across the floor. One bone was too big to be anything other than . . . Jesus. Nausea burned the back of his throat. He lurched back to where Dani hovered over that . . . monster.

He shoved her away and pulled his hunting knife out of its sheath.

"What are you—"

He ripped the blade through the guy's trachea as if he was cleaning a halibut. Blood dribbled down the front of his thermal pullover. Mitch straightened. The barstool slowed to a stop on one last creak.

He faced Dani. "He wasn't worth saving. Ate at least one member of the crew, and was probably saving the other for later. I may not go to church like your mom, but I know what's unholy." He took a deep breath. "You understand?"

Dani nodded. The shock in her eyes slowly shifted to grim resignation. Good girl. On a ship a few months ago, they'd encountered cannibalism, but Mitch had managed to keep it from the kids. No such luck this time. He forced himself to look away from the body. There was enough that needed done it wasn't too hard.

"When we get your brother over here, we'll dispose of the bodies."

Normally they made a point of giving the folks they scavenged from a proper send-off. But Mitch didn't want the taint of whatever transpired here looming over them as they worked.

"We'll load up as much as we can before nightfall. Tomorrow, we'll see how to get this stuff down."

He rapped his knuckles along the paneling, and was rewarded with a beautifully solid sound.

The corners of Dani's mouth drooped. "That'll take forever."

"That'll keep us fed for months," he countered.

That shut her up as they tromped back up and waved to Eddie, duly keeping watch on board the *Windfall*. She had one leg hitched over the gunwale, ready to climb back down to the canoe to bring him over.

He didn't blame her for wanting to get away, but he couldn't afford to coddle her. "Hold up, hold up. Don't want to waste a trip."

He cast about the deck, finding a fishing rod locker set against the wall of the wheelhouse. Gleaming graphite rods and reels with stainless steel bearings. "Jackpot."

HOMER COOPERATIVE, SOUTH CENTRAL ALASKA
OCTOBER 15, CHANGE YEAR 0/1998 AD

Dixon Moore, the elected head of newly formed Homer Cooperative, fingered the wood, satin finished tongue-and-groove oak, turning it over and over again against the table with stubby fingers.

The tap-slide-tap made Mitch's skin crawl, although it could have just been the itchy hemmed-in feeling he got whenever he bundled up the kids with some choice goods to trade and reluctantly rejoined civilization for a few hours. He couldn't stomach it for much longer. Even if the new Homer was more pleasant than most of the communities that had cobbled a life from the ruins.

Dixon, all six and a half feet of him, crowded the end of the mahogany dining room table that must have been scavenged from one of the million-dollar retirement homes that dotted the coast. The room—a converted hangar on the opposite side of the Kachemak Bay from where the original town of Homer sat—served as the Cooperative's chambers. Chairs lined the walls for overflow attendance, Mitch guessed. Metal-folding, factory-assembled, and even one hand-carved wooden throne shaped to look like you were sitting in a grizzly bear's lap—probably taken from some kitschy bed-and-breakfast the tourists used to flock to in the summertime.

Right now, though, it was just the two of them, underscored by the empty woodstoves on either end of the room. At least the chill in the air dulled the smell of old diesel. Mitch regretted taking off his hat when he first arrived and went through the obligatory pleasantries with Dixon and his second, Tom. But Mitch refused to put it back on in the middle of a negotiation. Weakness to a second-generation Alaskan like Dixon. Instead, he kept his hands jammed into the pockets of his down parka.

"You say you have more of this?" Dixon's words created cloudy puffs above their heads.

"Yep. Brought two crates with us. More if you want it."

"Where did you find it?"

Mitch smiled. "Now, you know I can't tell you that."

Dixon knew the rules, knew that too many questions and Mitch would just go to the next buyer on his list. But Dixon was always a touch too suspicious of just how Mitch managed to procure the range of items he had for trade. Mitch billed himself as a go-between for a larger crew, negotiating trades and drop-off points for goods if they were too numerous to carry inland between the three of them.

It kept things simple. But as he met Dixon's gaze across the table, nothing was ever simple.

Dixon snorted. "Trade secrets? Bullshit. We've been working hard to ally ourselves with other communities. Imagine my position if I learn this wood came from one of them. So you tell your boss we need answers."

Mitch forced back a frown. Most communities rolled out the red carpet when he came—desperate enough not to question the origin of the goods he brought with him. But the Homer Cooperative was doing better than most, and could afford to be . . . ethical? No. Careful, cautious.

Some of the folks here thought Dixon was a visionary. Mitch didn't know about all that, but he did know the Cooperative was the first community to request glass, the real stuff, or if not that then Plexiglas, to build greenhouses. For a diet that went beyond fish and elk and wild berries. They were thinking of the future when so many other communities could afford only to take things one day at a time.

Mitch raised his hands. "I can try, but they'll just say if you're being difficult to take it to New Whittier or Soldatna."

He let that sink in, pleased to see the slight panic that crept into the other man's eyes. Dixon was a tough SOB—forest ranger from before— but a terrible poker player. Mitch shrugged.

"I hear they have an influx of refugees from Anchorage and nowhere to house them."

Dixon frowned, suddenly looking tired. "The city's still smoking, if the rumors can be trusted."

In those first few weeks right after, Mitch and the kids sailed up and down the coast, watching everything burn. And while they waited it out, Mitch had to find a way for them to survive.

He'd even considered sailing across the gulf to the mainland, but by then stories of the West Coast going up in flames had reached Alaska. He thought of Kathy in her swanky loft in Seattle—the absolute opposite of their life together in Valdez. She probably never had a chance before the fires found her. Not that he'd tell the kids that.

Dixon finally set the wood sample away from him with a soft snap against the table. For a brief moment Mitch could see the large "H" branded to the inside of his wrist before Dixon's sleeve covered it once more. Every member of the Cooperative had one.

"Winter's not too far off. Folks are wising up, realizing they can't do it all on their own. It's beautiful, really, watching people come together to rebuild."

Mitch raised a brow. "Alaskans working together?"

"This is bigger than you or me. What about your kids?"

"What about them?"

Dixon's eyes widened slightly at Mitch's tone. That was rule number one. No one laid a hand on Danielle or Edward. So far, no one had tested him on that.

"I'm just saying life as traders must be hard on them."

True enough. The kids always brightened when they came to Homer to trade. Mitch tried not to get defensive when they'd dash off without a word to him and tag after the other children their age they'd gotten to know on past trips. Some sort of weird kid radar that must short out when you got older. He might keep them safe and well fed, but in the end he was still Dad.

Mitch shook his head. "Life's hard period. Get to your point."

"Look, we want good people here." Dixon licked his lips and leaned forward. "You've always dealt fairly with us, even if you leave out more details than I'd like. We could use someone like you."

"Sorry, not interested." He slowly got to his feet. "You want the wood or not?"

Dixon nodded without hesitation.

"Then we're done here." He turned to leave, but Dixon stopped him with a hand on his arm.

"Word's getting around, Mitch. People are starting to wonder. One of these days . . ." He shrugged.

"Is that a threat?" Mitch forced out.

"A warning. You'll have to throw in one day. And I hope it'll be with us."

"Geez, Dad. Did we have to get so much?" Eddie struggled with the straps of his bulging pack. Danielle's shoulders bowed under the extra weight, but she hadn't complained since they left the Cooperative and hiked into the forest to the southeast. A cold drizzle trickled down through the trees, liberally soaking them before the moss cushioning their steps absorbed the rest.

"You want to eat for the next four months?"

The words came out sharper than Mitch intended. He'd been on edge as he and the kids packed up the supplies they'd negotiated for and gave Dixon the coordinates for the cache of paneling—in the opposite direction of the route they'd take back to the *Windfall*—that they set up before even approaching the Cooperative.

Eddie sucked in his cheeks. "Does this mean we'll take a break from salvage for a while?"

Mitch frowned. They probably could afford a break, considering all they carried and the cold feeling in the pit of his stomach that Dixon's parting words had created. Maybe they should lie low for a while, let the curiosity die down.

"I guess we could spend a week at camp once we stow everything in the cave."

Eddie beamed at him. "You promise?"

"I don't see why not. But remember, we're like ants. We work hard spring, summer, and fall so we can survive the winter. We can't afford a grasshopper mentality for too long."

Dani rolled her eyes but for once did not make a snide comment.

They pushed through the forest of spruce trees. The fresh evergreen smell had a way of calming the mind, but Mitch fought it, his head on constant swivel. After all, a healthy dose of suspicion had kept them alive. As a bonus, all his precautions kept the kids on their toes.

They had maybe two hours of daylight to find a defensible camp. He made a point never to stay the night in any community they traded in, always camping out of range and keeping watch to ensure they weren't being followed.

Like they were right now. It took a half mile to be sure. Mitch had to swallow his first impulse to tell the kids. But they needed the practice.

It was Kathy's fault they were so far behind. Years lived in Alaska mattered; if you could trace your residency back a generation or more, even better. Mitch had learned that early on when he was subjected to all kinds of questions related to his parents' retirement home on the Prince William Sound, the summers he spent in Alaska growing up, learning her secrets. He liked to think his experiences were enough for most of those born and raised here—the grizzled types at the bar or the marina who were always on the lookout for folks from "back east."

Kathy, on the other hand . . . Too many people took him aside and told him it was only a matter of time before she hightailed it back to the lower forty-eight. He didn't believe them, of course. But she couldn't handle the eternalness of winter, the isolation that forced you to look deep inside yourself, or the way life and death were separated by the sharpest of knife-edges here. A land constantly in negotiation with its extremes.

She took the kids with her. He got them summers and two weeks every March. And since that fateful spring break he had promised them a fishing trip they'd never forget, Dani and Eddie were catching up— learning the land, the sea, growing more confident in the nature around them, and more respectful of it at the same time.

The back of his neck prickled. Mitch just hoped it'd be enough.

Eddie glanced back the way they came, a small frown on his face. He kept walking, holding his pack's straps to rest his arms. Dani faced forward, her steps precise and controlled, despite the fatigue that left smudges under her eyes. Then she cocked her head the same time Eddie shot another look over his shoulder. Mitch held his breath, willing them to make the connection.

"We're being followed, aren't we?" Dani asked.

Mitch nodded, his shoulder relaxing slightly under the weight of his pack. He was nearly at the point where'd he have to cut the experiment short.

"You two keep going. I'll see if I can get behind him, see what we're up against."

He scanned the trees. This was as good a place as any. Shot through with the occasional aspen, spruce surrounded them. But bark beetles had kept the trees from thriving. Resulting in less cover, but more space for a confrontation.

"But—"

"I mean it, Dani."

That they figured it out was enough of a lesson for today. He'd handle the rest. He had to.

"Take your brother, and go on ahead. I'll be right behind you."

A brief flicker of fear passed over her face, then she nodded. Eddie opened his mouth to protest, but Dani pushed him ahead of her.

"Come on."

You can take the man out of the wilderness, but you can't take the wilderness out of the man.

That was something Kathy said to him right before the divorce. She hadn't intended for it to be a compliment, but he thanked God the kids had been with him when everything changed. Otherwise . . .

He wouldn't think of that. A stick snapped somewhere behind him, loud despite the constant drip of water. Then a muffled curse. One person for sure, but Dixon would be a fool to send only one person after them.

Nestling between the brittle evergreen boughs, he hid against the trunk of a sick spruce and peeked out for a count of three before returning to cover. Two men hiked through the undergrowth. Loggers, oil-riggers, fishermen . . . it didn't really matter what they did before. The result was the same: broad shoulders, toned arms and legs well accustomed to work, and the single-mindedness of a job needing done.

Talk and trinkets wouldn't send these two back home. Damn Dixon to hell.

He shrugged out of his pack and partially buried it under moss and needles carpeting the forest floor. His fingers caught on a branch with the diameter of a rolling pin about the length of his forearm. That and his knife would have to do. His breath squeezed his chest as he waited for the men to pass by. One, two . . . Then he snapped his wrist forward, clobbering the first in the head with the tree branch.

Not giving himself a moment to hesitate, he tackled the second to the ground. The man's shoulder dug the air out of his lungs with an agonizing wheeze. Mitch scrambled to his feet, desperately clutching the handle of his knife. Six inches of sharpened steel. He hoped it'd be enough.

The man who got a face full of spruce groaned and careened toward him. Mitch brandished his knife, but the other man was fearless as he launched toward him and knocked him back against a tree trunk. Pain lanced up Mitch's spine and sparked behind his eyes. *Son of a—*

He still had hold of his knife. Right. He slashed out, catching the man across the shoulder. The man screamed, surprisingly high-pitched, and clutched at the red leaking out.

Mitch brought the knife handle down on his head, and the man collapsed in a boneless heap. Still bleeding. He would have to do something about that. But first . . .

He spun around, searching for the second man. He was where Mitch left him, moaning into the spruce needles. He gripped him by the hair and pressed the knife to his throat.

"You tell Dixon: never again."

"Don't know . . ." he gasped out, "what you're talking about."

Unbelievable. Mitch snarled, tightening his grip on the man's hair.

"Dad, he's telling the truth. Just look at him."

Dani. Where'd she come from? Behind him, she held up the wrist of the other attacker. No "H" branding all members of the Cooperative.

"You sure?"

She nodded.

He eased up on the man. Up close, he could see the hollowed cheeks and hungry eyes. Must've been driven into the forest to survive. That explained the stink coming off both of them.

"What do you want from us?"

"Food, supplies . . . anything. We're desperate."

Dani slowly backed away, coming to a stop next to Eddie.

Mitch shook his head. "I can't help you."

And he wouldn't have these two following them back to the *Windfall.*

Or worse. "If you have a skill or don't mind hard labor, I suggest you beg the folks in Homer to take you in."

Mitch knocked the man out and pushed off the ground. Blood plummeted from his head, taking whatever adrenaline he had leftover with it. His knife slipped and thudded to the forest floor. Wiping his hands on his pants, he cast about, mind and heart racing.

"Dad?"

His gaze snapped to Dani and Eddie, whey-faced and wide-eyed a few yards away.

He lurched toward them. "It's . . . okay. Everything's going to be okay."

GULF OF ALASKA, SOUTH CENTRAL ALASKA
NOVEMBER 3, CHANGE YEAR 0/1998 AD

The cruise ship glimmered on the horizon like a mirage. The *Ice King* was picture perfect with the distant Wrangell Mountains in the backdrop, looking as though they'd been recently dusted with powdered sugar. Mitch took one last lingering look, then passed the binoculars to Dani. Her brow furrowed as she scanned the ship, the logo CRUISE ALASKA emblazoned on its side. It was smaller than the vessels used by global cruise lines, but it still eclipsed the *Windfall*.

Since leaving the Cooperative, they'd come across an abandoned motorboat that had already been cleaned out. A new set of charts, a forgotten packet of boat rations, and the glass of the windshield was all they could scavenge. All in all, rather disappointing. Especially for Eddie, since it was his turn to assist.

But an intact cruise ship? The passengers' clothing alone would keep his family fed for months. And the rest? Mitch forced himself to slow down. One thing at a time.

Dani bit her lip. "You think anyone's still alive over there?"

Mitch shrugged. "One way to find out."

As he and Dani rowed over, the *Ice King* stayed silent, still.

"Maybe they all got away on the rescue boats," she whispered.

"Maybe."

They tied off the canoe to a lonely rope ladder hanging over the edge. The last rung was knotted with kelp. Mitch went first. Dani followed him onto the deck.

He raised a finger to his lips and leaned in. "Keep your knife ready."

She nodded and worked the knife out of her leather wrist guard. She'd picked it out herself from their stores. Mitch insisted the kids arm themselves ever since those men nearly got the jump on them. Mitch's mouth twisted. Never again.

She tipped her head toward the bridge, a glassed-in area on the upper deck. Mitch gave her a grim nod. They forced open the door that led to the bridge. Empty.

"Dad, look." Dani pointed to a dark red stain on the metal floor. "You think it's blood?"

"That or rust." He cast about the bridge and found a poster mapping the emergency exit routes for the ship. Besides the common areas, there were two floors of passenger cabins. "We'll start at the top and work our way down."

Amidships, they found a small dining room that showed signs of a scuffle. The tiny galley and attached pantry were empty.

"Think someone beat us to it?" Dani asked.

"That or it was moved to a more secure location on the ship . . . easier to defend that way."

They moved on. Past a bar, massage rooms, dormant exercise equipment. Then a corridor of passenger cabins. He opened the door to the first one with the toe of his shoe. He sucked a breath. Dani followed and looked into the cramped room. Two berths, a couple splayed across the floor, their luggage scattered around them. Throats slashed recently enough decay still lingered on the air.

Mitch moved to the next cabin and the next. "Someone systematically killed all the passengers and secured anything valuable."

"You think they're still here?" Dani asked.

Mitch lifted a shoulder. "We stay together." He waited for her nod before moving on.

Two floors of dead passengers. The main dining room came into view. This time there was no mistaking the old blood that streaked the doors.

Mitch gritted his teeth and slowly pushed the door open. Silence. He poked his head in and gestured to Dani. Her hand went to her mouth. Corpses everywhere. Broken chair legs, canes with screwdrivers duct-taped to them, oars, pipes, and other large heavy objects perfect for bludgeoning.

Mitch sketched the room with his fingers. "What passengers weren't executed in their rooms must have gathered here and fought . . ." He stepped over one body and opened the door to the storage pantry.

"Food. Prepackaged, nonperishable. Though it looks like it's been picked over some."

He toed open a sack on the floor. Jewelry, watches, money. "This must be what they collected from the cabins. Or some of it at least."

Dani's eyes lingered on the treasure before returning to the corpses scattered around the room. A find like this should have been cause for celebration, but like everything, it came with a cost.

Mitch rubbed his face. "Okay. Here's what we're going to do."

They scavenged. Spices and sheets, canned goods and clothing, medical supplies and machine parts. Hours of trips back to the *Windfall*, shoulders and backs aching. When Mitch was trying to figure out a way to cram another load on board, Eddie sighed.

"We can always come back later, you know." He jerked his thumb at the deck. "As it is, we'll have to sleep up here."

Mitch shook his head. Whatever had transpired on board the *Ice King* didn't sit right. Mutiny, infighting . . . the brutality that swept through the mainland in microcosm?

"If we thought to scavenge a ship like this, you can bet someone else will too."

Mitch grimaced and glanced back at the cruise ship. Dani was bringing up another load of suitcases crammed full of hand tools from the engine room.

"I'll help Dani with the last load. Why don't you see if you can catch us some supper in the meantime, all right?"

A reluctant nod was his only answer. Mitch got in the dinghy and rowed back to the *Ice King*. He found Dani collapsed on top of a small Rollaboard.

"How you doing, kiddo?"

She made a face. "I'm not a kid. I brought all this up by myself. See?"

A half dozen suitcases surrounded her on the lower deck.

Mitch grinned. "So you did." He reached out and helped her stand.

She groaned and rubbed her back. "Last trip?" He nodded. "Good. But this time I want to enjoy our treasure before we give it all away."

"We don't give it away—"

She gave him a pointed look. "Or enjoy it either."

"We scavenge because we have to. Nothing more."

"That's just it, Dad. We don't have to. Any of the places we trade with would take us in if we wanted."

"No," Mitch said sharply. "We've worked hard to create a life for ourselves."

"But what have we really achieved?"

Cold fury rooted him to the spot. "If this is about what your mother would have—"

"This isn't about Mom." Dani swung out her arms. "I'm just saying it feels like no matter what we do or how hard we do it, we'll be stuck in this . . . limbo." She sighed. "We just can't keep going like this."

Mitch swallowed an angry reply. "Look, it's been a long day for all of us. Once we get all this stuff stowed, we'll—"

"Whatever, Dad."

That wasn't fair, but he let her go. She pushed past him and started in on the last load. The dinghy sat dangerously low in the water by the time they got all the luggage in. They'd both be straddling a carry-on for the return trip.

Eddie's wolf whistle caught his ear on the breeze. Mitch cast his gaze eastward, along the coast. The details were too shiny to be certain but it looked like a boat . . . He squinted. No. More than one.

He swore and brought the binoculars up. Dani shielded her eyes and turned in the direction Mitch was looking.

A cedar dugout canoe, maybe a bit longer than the *Windfall*, crossed the distance between the cruise ship and a double-masted schooner, complete with a set of sails right out of the age of exploration. Men rowed with deadly precision. Two, fore and aft, brandished bows and quivers full of arrows. War paint covered their faces. What the hell?

Then he saw the skull of a bear mounted to the boat's prow.

Dani's eyes widened when they landed on the dugout.

"Dad?" Her voice held childlike fear, and his chest squeezed.

"Get to the *Windfall*. Now!"

He gave the longboat one last look before scrambling down the ladder rungs after Dani. He dropped into the boat and she handed him the oars. Water sloshed in, the cold grounding him as they pushed off the *Ice King*. Thankfully Eddie had already abandoned his fishing rod and was readying the sails.

Dani said nothing as he rowed. The breeze picked up, and Mitch gripped the oars tighter, frowning into his white-knuckled strokes. The dinghy slammed up against the hull of the *Windfall* with a hollow thud.

Eddie had unfurled the sails and was in the process of tightening the jib.

"Get the anchor up, Dani," Mitch called out as she clambered over the railing. He grabbed the first piece of luggage and chucked it on board.

"Did they see us?" she asked, hunched over the reeling line for the anchor.

Eddie's head popped up and nearly caught the boom. "Who are they?"

Mitch heaved the last piece of luggage and scrambled onto the deck.

"We aren't staying to find out."

His gaze flew to the *Ice King*'s deck where he and Dani had been standing only a few minutes ago. He counted ten men already on deck gesturing at them wildly. Had they come upon the cruise ship first? After eliminating the opposition on board, they were probably coming back with reinforcements to pick the ship clean. Damn it.

Dani returned to his side and helped him hoist the dinghy back on board the *Windfall*. Seawater leaked across the deck, but they got the awkward thing up and lashed it to the side of the cabin.

A sharp tung slammed into the hull. Mitch jumped back and smashed against the mast. An arrow vibrated against the fiberglass, black fletching fluttering.

"High-dah. High-dah."

The strange rhythmic chanting sent a cold wash of fear down Mitch's spine.

Dani was at his side. "Dad! Are you okay?" She gripped his flannel-clad arms as he regained his footing.

He took a hand and gave it a quick squeeze. "Leave it. Get to the—"

A black arrow speared her upper arm. Her eyes widened in shock, then pain, as Mitch clutched her to him.

"Shit. Eddie, get the tiller!"

Mitch helped Dani over to a small bench along the stern. "Dani, I need you to stay here. All right?"

He ripped off his belt and fastened it diagonally across her chest, holding her injured arm in a sling. "Whatever you do, don't pull out the arrow."

She whimpered but nodded.

Mitch glanced back at Eddie. "Just going to be me and you, skipper."

"Aye, aye, Captain." Eddie's face paled as he glanced back at the *Ice King*.

Mitch cursed. Whoever the men were, they had brought one of their dugouts around the cruise ship, angling for the *Windfall*. She'd be able to outrun them eventually, but fully loaded as she was? The telltales streamed out perpendicular to the mast. Good. The wind at least was on their side.

But they needed all the wind power they could get. "Got to trim the mainsail."

With Eddie in the cockpit, Mitch loosened the sail, waited for it to flap, then slowly tightened it so the flapping stopped. Breath gusted out of him as the *Windfall* slowly picked up speed. Maybe they should have held off on the last load.

"High-dah. High-dah."

The chants floated across the water.

"Dad . . ." Dani's pained voice drew his attention to the rear deck.

A stone's throw away, the dugout barreled toward them, the rowers straining to keep pace with the chants that corresponded to the strokes of their oars.

What had they gotten into? He felt for his hunting knife, but it was still attached to his belt holding Dani's arm in place. No help for it.

"Eddie, take cover!"

Mitch crouched below the railing, gripping one of the wooden oars in his hands. In one of the lockers belowdecks blocked by all their treasure, he had four hunting bows and one fiberglass crossbow. But he never thought they'd need them out on the open water. He'd been a fool to think the sea would be theirs alone for so long.

More arrows sailed toward them, but they hit the water or lodged into the hull of the *Windfall*. The cedar dugout edged closer. One of the archers shrugged off his empty quiver. The other shot his last arrow, piercing the mainsail. For a long moment, the arrow stayed put. Then it fell. They couldn't afford a tear now. If they got away, sure, they could limp to shore with just the jib sheet, but Mitch hoped it wouldn't come to that.

The sailcloth started to rip—just a little—but every little bit counted when it came to maximizing the rigging. The dugout pulled alongside the *Windfall*. The archer positioned in the prow of the dugout suddenly leapt toward them. He slapped against the water, a foot shy of the *Windfall*. Were they insane?

Already the dugout was adjusting its heading, closing the distance between the two boats.

"Eddie, grab an oar. Dani, can you take the tiller?"

She gave him a pained nod.

As she stumbled toward the tiller, he tossed the other oar to his son. "Remember your tenth birthday?"

He and Kathy had thrown him a party at the Chuck E. Cheese's in Anchorage. Less than six months later, she'd moved to Seattle. Mitch caught Eddie's eye.

"Think Whac-A-Mole."

One of the rowers stowed his oar and launched himself at the *Windfall*. He slapped against the hull followed by another thud. At least the dugout could no longer keep pace without two of its rowers. They just needed to hold these two off.

Mitch brandished his oar with his left hand as he swiped up hooks from the abandoned tackle box with his right. Then he stalked toward the starboard side where one of the men clung to the *Windfall* like a barnacle.

A head appeared, saltwater dribbling down the strange man's chin as he panted. It was like looking into a mirror—brown hair, brown eyes, pale skin—except for the tanned leather jerkin and the dead bird draped over his head like a macabre cowl. Hell, maybe Mitch would have gone native too if it meant he'd survive. But he'd had the *Windfall*—and it was going to stay his.

Mitch leveled the oar at the man's head. "Leave. Now. And maybe you'll be able to swim back to your ship."

It would still be a long shot—hypothermia would get him if exhaustion didn't.

The man barred his teeth and hefted a leg over the edge. Mitch supposed he'd do the same thing in the man's place. Too bad.

Whack.

Mitch brought the flat edge of the oar down on his hands. The man bellowed as his upper body fell back into the water, his leg still hooked awkwardly around the railing. Mitch smacked the man's knee with his oar for good measure. The man's leg spasmed, lost its hold on the railing, and the rest of him flopped into the water.

"Dad!"

Mitch spun around. Eddie grappled with another man twice his size, his oar out of play and crushed between them.

He reached them in three strides and wound back, jabbing his paddle into the man's side. He stumbled, releasing Eddie, and snarled when his gaze landed on Mitch.

He lunged for Mitch's paddle. Mitch held on but the man was too strong. Time for plan B. Mitch swung out his right fist, the fishhooks between each finger. They latched into skin as Mitch punched the man in the face. His hand bounced off but the hooks stayed. The man howled, an unearthly sound, soon lost in the sea's spray as the *Windfall* surged on.

Eddie hollered and charged, hitting the man square in the solar plexus. Together they fell back. The man's head cracked against the railing. Eddie was still perched on top of him, his small fists punching his torso. Mitch leaned over and tugged him back against his chest. His hand scrabbled against the deck until his hand closed over the grip of his oar.

Mitch held it out in front of both of them as they stared down at the man, deathly still. The oar shook despite his best efforts.

Eddie gulped for air beside him. "They were going to kill us."

Mitch didn't say anything, just watched the dark stain that spilled out along the planks.

Mitch gave Dani some whiskey pilfered from the cruise ship to help her sleep in a makeshift berth belowdecks, cradled by their hard-won treasure. He and Eddie kept the *Windfall* pointed east despite their exhaustion. But there'd be no rest for him until they reached land.

The wind had gentled and the sailcloth had held up enough that they needed to make only a few adjustments to keep them on course. Eddie hunkered down next to him in the cockpit.

"She going to be okay?"

He'd gotten the arrow out and dressed the wound, but he didn't want to leave anything to chance.

"Once we get a doc to finish patching her up."

"We're going back to Homer?"

Mitch frowned. He didn't know what irritated him more—that Eddie assumed they were going back to the Homer Cooperative in the first place or the hopeful throb in his voice as he said it.

They'd been doing okay, hadn't they? He'd kept them fed, clothed, safe . . . well, as best he could. Didn't that count? But heading back to Homer felt like they were giving up. Going backward, after all they'd done to survive and thrive.

He took a deep breath. "Yeah, that's the plan."

He didn't see any other options. The Cooperative had a few medical professionals in their ranks, and was big enough to protect them against whoever those crazy bastards were. Besides, he was fairly certain Dixon would treat them right. If not, the booty below would do the trick.

Eddie nodded to the body lashed to the railing. "Who do you think they are?"

Mitch forced back the revulsion that lurked in the back of his throat. "I don't know." Their war cry lodged in his brain. "Wait. High-dah . . ."

He snapped his fingers. "Haida are a native people that live off the coast of mainland Canada near the Alaskan panhandle, if I remember correctly."

He thought back to the faces in the dugout. Had they really been Haida? Or just a group of men mimicking their traditions to survive?

Eddie frowned. "That's all the way across the gulf."

They were either very brave or very desperate. He felt Eddie watching him and shrugged.

"Maybe the folks in Homer will know more."

HOMER COOPERATIVE, SOUTH CENTRAL ALASKA
NOVEMBER 4, CHANGE YEAR 0/1998 AD

Gray-tinged dawn heralded their approach to the Kachemak Bay. The ruins of Homer were to the north. Dixon had told him fires, fighting, and the need for more resources had pushed survivors to the southern, less-populated side of the bay. Before things changed, supplies had to be airlifted in for the tiny cluster of homes there. The now useless airstrip and hangar had been a community center for the surrounding areas for years and made a natural starting point for the Homer Cooperative.

Until now, Mitch had never risked going near their new harbor. People would kill for the *Windfall*. But as he laid eyes on the folks from the Cooperative who gathered along the shoreline, he hoped it wouldn't be today.

They dropped anchor a ways off, and after the initial alarm, a small rowboat with three men slowly crawled out toward them.

"Declare yourself," a man's harsh voice rang out, while another kept a crossbow leveled at Mitch's chest.

"Mitch Davis. We have news, and, if you wish it, a proposition."

The faces in the boat flickered in relief before suspicion clamped down once more.

"But I'll only talk with Dixon." Mitch's chest squeezed tight as the men on the boat conferred, then slowly rowed back to the docks.

Minutes ticked past, then a half hour. When the boat returned, Dixon was in it.

"Permission to come aboard?"

He couldn't quite keep the eagerness out of his voice, but at least Dixon's face betrayed no emotion.

Mitch waved him on. Dixon came with Tom, his second, who scanned the deck with undisguised hunger. Mitch positioned himself so he was blocking their view of the dead Haida warrior.

Dixon smiled. "It's a fine ship, Mitch."

"That it is."

"You bring news?"

Mitch nodded, his throat suddenly dry. "I do, but before we get to that, you meant what you said last time?"

Dixon's face broke into a smile. "The Homer Cooperative would be honored to have you. That's still true."

"The *Windfall* is mine."

Tom's mouth dropped open. "Now, wait a second—"

Dixon slapped Tom's shoulder, silencing the younger man.

"The *Windfall* is yours, but if she harbors here, we'll occasionally require use of her."

"Understood. But only so long as I train the folks who take her out, and have final say on when she sails. I want no risks to her."

Dixon held out his hand. Mitch slowly relaxed his hold on his oar, and shook. Then he stepped aside.

The crackling woodstove made Dixon's cabin quite cozy. Or maybe Mitch was so worn out it didn't matter where he was so long as he didn't have to do anything for a while. Sitting beside him at the table, Eddie could barely keep his eyes open, his chin propped up by his hand. Dani slept soundly on a pallet, snuggled under a handful of furs and a home-made blanket. Once Dixon heard their story, he had wasted no time getting someone to see to her injury.

Mitch supposed he should feel grateful, but he was too weary, all momentum gone. That nearly all their goods from the cruise ship had been taken from the *Windfall* didn't help.

Across the table, Dixon cleared his throat.

"Folks along the coast from Yakutat to Cordova have spotted the Haida warriors. Pillaging like goddamn pirates. That you three got away with just one arrow-shot shoulder is amazing."

"So you knew about them?"

Dixon frowned. "I heard stories, but it wasn't enough to trouble us much."

The unspoken pride that Homer was bigger and doing better than the other settlements filled the silence. "But what you've described is more disturbing. If they're doing such large-scale salvage . . ."

"They'll target Homer eventually."

Dixon nodded. "And thanks to you, we'll be ready."

Mitch swallowed his whiskey—just one of the prizes he hadn't turned over when he showed Dixon and his men their plunder from the cruise ship. Eddie dozed in his chair. Something popped and settled within the stove.

"I always wondered how you did it."

Mitch raised his brow. "Did what?"

"Get all those goodies you'd trade." He thumped the table with his hand. "I knew you didn't have a bigger crew."

Should he deny it? He was just so damn tired. Of everything. Mitch bit the inside of his cheek. "Really?"

"You don't get to be a leader of a group like this without knowing a thing or two about people."

He stabbed a finger at Mitch. "You're a loner. That you've survived this long means you're lucky or crafty or both. And frankly we need more of those people here. I'd hoped you'd come around eventually."

Mitch took another swig of his drink. Dixon didn't have to rub it in.

Dixon leaned in. "How'd you keep the *Windfall* hidden?"

It might have been the exhaustion or the whiskey, but Mitch didn't see any point in lying.

"We kept her moored a ways off the coast and rowed in, taking all the sails with us."

Dixon whistled. "Jesus. I'm surprised your kids didn't mutiny."

Mitch flicked a glanced at Eddie, then Dani, both sound asleep. He shrugged. "They're good kids."

"What about their mom?"

"She lived in Seattle. Anyway, they were visiting me when things . . . Well, you know the rest."

Dixon winced and nodded. "You've done well, for them and yourself."

Mitch grimaced. "We'll see."

"I won't lie and say I'm not thrilled you're here, however it came about. And with the *Windfall*, we're going to be able to do so much." Dixon caught himself. "With your permission of course."

"It's all right. Get it out of your system. The sooner you and your engineers figure out how she works and get to shipbuilding, the better."

Dixon chuckled. "The hell of it is, I never liked the open water."

"Too bad. With my contacts and your boats, this could become a big trading center."

"That's quite a proposition. You and your kids going to stick around long enough to make it happen?"

"I don't know. At least through the winter. Then we'll see."

Dixon gave him a hearty slap on his shoulder. "At least you're honest. We'll see what we can do to change your mind."

HOMER COOPERATIVE, SOUTH CENTRAL ALASKA
MARCH 14, CHANGE YEAR 1/1999 AD

The trebuchet launched a pile of stones to sea, the momentum rocketing the whole apparatus back on greased rails.

"See that?" Harrison grinned ear to ear, practically dancing. "The rails'll distribute the force and make sure the boats don't tip or get knocked off course."

Mitch quirked a brow. "Or split open the deck?"

The ex-high school physics teacher looked sheepish. "That too."

It was Harrison's idea. Dixon's chief engineer. He'd burst into a council session, clutching a book to his chest.

"Look at this: the Battle of Caishi in China. Trebuchets mounted to riverboats."

Since then, they had eagerly set about to put the plan in place with the Cooperative's slowly growing fleet of sailboats—only to find out the torque generated by the war machines could rip them from their mount on the ship deck. The damage to the *Windfall*, since fixed, had been almost a physical wound when Mitch first heard the whomping crack and then saw the deck planks torn apart. And no way to treat a loyal friend.

"Well, what do you think?" Harrison asked.

Mitch walked around the floating arm trebuchet. Rather than swing the counterweight around the axle like a traditional catapult, the axle rolled out of the way on rails so the counterweight could fall straight down. As it did, it pushed the arm away, then jerked it back with the full force of the weights dropping. The compact machine also packed quite a punch with a hundred-plus meter range.

For the last six months, the Homer Cooperative had prepared. A good percentage of folks already had hunting experience. Alaska was rife with elk, bear, moose. Everyone had mandatory bow practice twice a week, on top of some hand-to-hand basics taught by two black belts who used to run a karate studio downtown.

According to survivors' accounts, the Haida not only stole goods, tools, and weapons, but people too—primarily skilled workers and young children. Someone had a book on the First Nation peoples of British Columbia. With how Vancouver went up in flames like so many other major cities, the Haida, living on the islands to the west, must have dealt with refugees fleeing the more populated areas. Resource-strapped and desperate like everyone else, it seemed they'd fallen back on the teaching of their ancestors to survive.

That explained their impressive dugout canoes and weapons. But not their targets or the savageness of their attacks. Who was he to judge, though, wearing clothes he stripped off of a dead man? Anyone who'd lasted this long had done things they weren't proud of, himself included. But at a certain point, you had to let that go. You had to do better than just survive.

After much discussion with Dixon and his advisors, they settled on the need to protect what they'd already built in Homer, and to demonstrate to the Haida they were not to be trifled with.

Hence the war machines and the calluses on everyone's draw fingers.

"Mitch?" Dixon prompted.

What Dixon was really asking was whether he and the kids would stay long enough to see this through. Mitch had held off getting his wrist branded with an "H." Dixon hadn't pressed him, but Mitch knew some of those in the Cooperative were getting impatient with them hanging around if they weren't ready to commit.

He gave the trebuchet one last look and nodded. He didn't like it, but was it really any crazier than the salvage operation he and the kids had run? Mitch glanced at Dixon and Harrison who still jittered beside him.

"The wind gods will have to be smiling down on us."

Dixon waved his hand impatiently. "Of course, but . . . ?"

Mitch nodded. "What do we have to lose?"

HOMER COOPERATIVE, SOUTH CENTRAL ALASKA
APRIL 3, CHANGE YEAR 1/1999 AD

Mitch kept his hands buried in the pockets of his jacket as he headed back from the harbor. Despite his foul mood, he registered the few curt nods he received from members of the Cooperative he passed on his way to the cabin Dixon had granted him use of until they came to a more "formal arrangement." Dixon's words, not his.

He slowed his approach at the sight of Dani speaking to a young man outside the cabin, a soft blush on her cheeks. Mitch came up behind them.

"Danielle, who's this?"

She jumped and turned, fluster intensifying her blush. "Dad, this is Charlie from school."

Once they got settled, Dani and Eddie started taking classes with the other Homer children, using books and textbooks that had been saved or salvaged. It had kept the kids busy during the winter months, but now it was just one more thing tying them here.

"I see."

In a few years, Charlie wouldn't have to look up to meet Mitch's gaze. Today, however, Mitch used his height to remind the young man just who he was talking to, and he was rewarded when Charlie swallowed.

The young man gave Mitch a deferential nod, mumbled something to Dani, then scurried off. Mitch watched him go, partly bemused, partly annoyed.

"Remember what we said about making connections here?"

Dani huffed. "He's just a friend, Dad. Anyway." She gestured vaguely toward the harbor. "How did it go?"

Mitch couldn't hold back his groan. "Bunch of landlubbers. Don't know how they're going to be ready in time."

One of the men he was training to crew the *Windfall* ended up in the water before they'd even gotten out of the harbor—and it had just gotten worse from there.

"There's an answer to that."

"No."

She placed a hand on his arm. "Dad, I mean it."

"We've been over this, Dani. I won't put you and your brother in any more danger if I can help it."

"Even if it gets you killed in the process?"

Mitch didn't answer, just entered the cabin. Eddie glanced up from where he was sitting cross-legged on a wide-plank floor in front of the woodstove, book in his lap.

"You two fighting again?"

Mitch shook his head. "No."

"Yes, we are."

"Dani, the matter is closed."

"The hell it is."

Mitch looked at her in surprise. "What—"

"You're always saying we need to think for ourselves, but as soon as we do, you say the matter's closed."

"Honey, that's not—"

"Dad, please. Listen for once."

Mitch glanced at Eddie. No help there. Mitch faced Dani and crossed his arms.

"We've done everything you've asked of us and more. Now, it's time you do something for us. Let me and Eddie crew for you when the time comes."

"Absolutely not."

"Name one person here who's better than us."

"That's not the point."

Dani arched her brow. A slightly smaller but scarier version of Kathy. "Do you even want the Cooperative to succeed?"

Mitch held up his hands. "Where'd that come from?"

They'd put off their departure a couple of months to see this through, hadn't they? Originally, he told the kids it was just for the winter. As soon as the snow melted, they'd take the *Windfall* and—

"Because it seems like you'd rather fail than take us along."

"At least you two would be safe."

"But without you, where would we be?" Eddie piped in. He slowly got to his feet. "You're our dad. You're all we have."

His ears turned bright red, but he held Mitch's gaze.

Dani stepped toward him. "We're a family. Our place is with you."

"You don't know what you're saying."

Dani glanced at Eddie and nodded. "We do. We want to help."

"You don't owe these people anything."

"What do you mean? We have a chance to start over. A place to call home. Do you really want to go back to salvaging? What's going to happen when we run out of boats to loot? When we run out of luck?"

Mitch shrugged. "We'll figure it out like we always have. We're a team."

The corner of Dani's mouth lifted. He saw his mistake too late. She went in for the kill.

"That's right. And that's why you're going to let us crew for you."

Outmaneuvered by his own daughter. He didn't know if he should be proud or ashamed.

ENTRANCE TO THE COOK INLET, SOUTH CENTRAL ALASKA
MAY 18, CHANGE YEAR 1/1999 AD

The deep groan of the alarm call seemed to reach into Mitch's rib cage and give it a sharp tug. It was time, but until that moment, he didn't realize how much he had been dreading what they had to do. Armed with mirrors and a month's worth of rations, Dixon sent his hardiest men east along the coast to camp and keep watch for the Haida. And now they were finally here.

Dani and Eddie joined him on the deck, blinking back sleep. The *Windfall,* and the four other sailboats they'd managed to build or cobble from cannibalized remains of other ships, all waited at the entrance to the Cook Inlet, barring the way to the Homer Cooperative and the settlements beyond.

"Get the anchor up. Let's see what we got."

Eddie started reeling it in while Dani unfurled the sails, both working in near silence. Mitch closed his eyes and listened for the wind. He rotated until it ruffled his hair and slid into his ears with a persistent sigh.

When he opened his eyes, he swore to himself. The Haida schooner was running downwind straight toward them. Double-masted, just like before.

The plan was to approach the ship, launch the trebuchet, then circle back around. Meanwhile one of the other sailboats would take their shot, giving them a chance to reload. But the *Windfall* couldn't sail directly into the wind. They'd have to tack like crazy and take their shots when they could. As it was they had limited mobility because of the weight of the trebuchet mounted to the rear deck. So much for strategy.

"We'll keep her close-hauled as long as we can." It was the best they could do given the conditions. He just hoped the captains of the other boats could keep up.

Dani and Eddie made the adjustments to the sails. The *Windfall* crept closer to the schooner at a slight forty-five degree angle. Mitch glanced back. The rest of the "fleet" followed. Good.

"Dani, take over."

She took hold of the tiller while Mitch and Eddie manned the trebuchet. The basket was already filled with petroleum-laced bombs. Rocks and cement blocks wrapped with foul-smelling fabric. *Light, let it go, and make sure the sailboat doesn't catch fire.*

It sounded simple enough on land. But with the sea heaving under his feet, his two children, ever trusting, even in this, he wished far away from the concerns of men.

"On my mark," Mitch called.

Eddie had the torch lit, his body shielding it from the breeze. Mitch could make out cries of alarm from the Haida, carried on the wind. The *Windfall* edged closer, and something told him they wouldn't get a better shot.

"Now!"

Eddie plunged the torch into the basket. The flame gutted, then a soft glow crept over the contents, growing in intensity.

"Get back!"

Eddie flinched away, nearly knocking over a bucket of sand they had on hand in case of fire. Once he was clear, Mitch loosed the lever. With a deep-seated groan, the trebuchet released its flaming contents. Like fireworks, the bombs separated in a glowing display before they smacked into the schooner.

The Haida loosed arrows in response, but they pelted only the water around them.

"Away, away!" Mitch cried.

The *Windfall* kicked up spray as she hit the first wake wave from the schooner. Dani turned the ship around, and the sails started to flap. They couldn't lose speed now. Mitch and Eddie worked to get them rigged properly so they'd be out of the way when the rest of the fleet made their approach.

"Another hit!" Eddie cried out.

A few more adjustments to the sails, and Dani had them pointed back at the schooner, which had slowed its approach. The wind had shifted so they didn't have to tack so hard to get back into position. Once the *Windfall* was lined up, he and Eddie lit the basket and let it fly.

By now, flames licked up the hull and had caught the sails. Haida warriors lowered a dugout canoe onto the water, the men recklessly following after it.

Time to go. "Dani?"

She got the *Windfall* turned about, taking advantage of a strong crosswind, only to find one of their sister ships on fire. Arrows had fouled up the trebuchet's launching mechanism, and its basket of flames had spilled out across the deck.

Dani steered the *Windfall* as close as she dared, and two of the crew dove into the water and swam toward them. When the first one got close, Mitch leaned out and helped him on board. Tom, sputtering and coughing.

"Dad, hurry!" Eddie pointed at the Haida dugout speeding toward them.

Shit.

The other man was still a ways out. Mitch slung the life preserver toward him, and he hooked an arm through it. That would have to be good enough.

"Dani, get us out of here."

She'd maneuvered the *Windfall* into the wind so they'd slow down enough to help the other crew, but she'd sacrificed their momentum in the process. Now they were in irons. Dead in the water. But not for long.

The scariest thing about being in irons was that you had to go backward in order to get moving again. It felt unnatural, like you weren't in control and losing ground, but really it was the boat and the wind setting everything back to rights again.

"Dani, you need to—"

"Back wind to port!" she cried out.

Eddie was already moving, swinging the boom to port before Mitch could do anything. Then they waited. The silence on board the *Windfall* was interrupted by chants as the dugout closed in on them.

A few boat lengths away and gaining. "High-dah. High-dah."

Mitch tried to ignore their cries as the sails slowly filled, pushing the Windfall backward, but ultimately around.

Eddie brought the boom back over the centerline, tightening up the mainsail and adjusting the jib so they could take full advantage of the wind and outpace the bastards. Dani, hunkered down in the cockpit, already had them back on course and picking up speed. All without his help.

"Dad, watch out!" Eddie cried.

Mitch spun about. He caught a Haida war club in the chest, knocking him back over the jack line.

Eddie helped him up. "You okay?"

He'd have a wicked bruise but . . . "I'll live."

Mitch glanced back. Thankfully, they'd finally outstripped the dugout and were out of range of their weapons. In the distance, the Haida's schooner blazed higher, wood creaking and popping, backlighting the warriors' canoe, still tailing them. At least there was that.

Working together, Mitch, Eddie, and Tom managed to haul in the life preserver. Thankfully Harrison had managed to hold on as the *Windfall* surged forward. He clung to the railing as he cleared his lungs of seawater, then straightened. He whooped for joy at the sight of the flaming schooner and kissed the inside of his wrist, where his "H" brand lay.

Mitch's own wrist itched. The kids would have gotten theirs months ago if it weren't for him and his refusal to take what was offered. Maybe they'd been going against the wind for too long. Dani kept them pointed toward land. As the Kachemak Bay came into view, it didn't feel like they were going backward.

It felt a little like they were finally coming home.

With the schooner lost, only a dozen Haida warriors survived. They refused to speak, but the anger buried in their eyes told them they understood Dixon's pronouncements that they'd be allowed to live so long as they pledged never again to plunder the Alaskan coast.

"You would let them go without a verbal agreement?" Tom hissed.

"Better to let them slink home with tales of this battle than to silence them forever." Dixon lifted a shoulder. "That way they'll know what it'll cost them to return here."

Mitch rubbed his chin. "If this didn't cripple them, then we must hope it'll force them south to other targets. Make them someone else's problem."

"You think it'll be enough?" Tom asked.

Dixon gave him a grim nod. "If not, we'll be ready."

THE DEMONS OF WITMER HALL

BY M. T. REITEN

M. T. REITEN

M. T. Reiten lives and writes in Los Alamos, New Mexico, where he also works as a research scientist at the lab bearing the same name. Before grad school, he served in the U.S. Army and had tours in Bosnia and Afghanistan. M.T.'s stories have appeared in *Writers of the Future XXI*, *All the Rage this Year* (Phobos Books), and *Jim Baen's Universe*. He and his wife have welcomed a beautiful baby girl to their home and are trying to achieve a new equilibrium. Although M.T. spent an inordinate amount of time in Witmer Hall at the University of North Dakota as an undergraduate, he doesn't wish the apocalypse on the building or any of its former occupants and must emphasize this is a work of fiction. Thus the characters are neither real nor purely imaginary, which means they're complex (math joke).

"This has to be a mistake," I said, flipping the light switch.

Nothing happened. The tiny flame from a single candle barely cut the darkness in the large office space.

"Mistakes that don't go away become facts." Kirk Vandermeer turned the thick Acer laptop on his desk, revealing the black display. He stabbed the power button several times for my benefit. "It's not just a blown transformer in a substation, Jason."

His office was on the third floor of Witmer Hall, the physics and math building at UND. Minutes earlier I had experienced a blinding flash of light and an intense pain. I had thought it was a migraine, but as quickly as it hit, it was gone. I had groped through the dark stairwells from my lab in the basement. My flashlight had stopped working—I assumed just old batteries—so I couldn't check the breakers in the complete blackness of the mechanical room.

No one was around on the first or second floors. Not too surprising for after-hours during spring break. When he went home at six, the physics department head, Dr. Murali Rao, kicked out the few faculty and students who hadn't taken vacation. He had forgotten about me in the Radon Monitoring Facility, trying to catch up on the backlog of test kits. Candlelight shone from Kirk's office when I reached the third floor. Kirk would have deliberately hidden from Dr. Rao, so he could keep working undisturbed.

Now Kirk pointed out the window toward Columbia Road. I bent to peer through the half-closed blinds. The traffic signals and streetlamps were off and the vehicles were motionless dark lumps. Stopped on the railroad overpass behind the industrial tech building. Stopped on University Avenue. Stopped in the parking lot outside the Memorial Union.

"Nothing is working." Kirk, again at his desk, held out the phone handset. Silence.

"Sweet. Just what we need," I said.

Grand Forks had just survived the flood of 'ninety-seven, billed the flood of the century during a slow national news period. The town had been evacuated as the Red River overflowed. The whole Valley region was flat as a pool table. The highest point between Grand Forks and Fargo was the Buxton overpass on I-29. So the north flowing river ran into impassable ice in Canada and had consumed the town with nowhere else to go. A year later and we were still recovering.

"Wonder how long this will take to fix?"

Kirk shrugged. Kirk Vandermeer was a wiry, short guy. At five-four, he stood about a head below me, but he was always hunched over something—his desk, lab equipment, or his coffeepot—making him seem shorter. His ever-present narrow leather tie constantly dangled into things. I would have thought a Texan would wear a bolo and cowboy boots, not secondhand eighties fashion.

But what did I know about fashion? I still wore sweats, though my main exercise had been physical therapy since I blew out my knee early freshman year. No NFL contracts in my future. But as grad students in the physics department, no one cared how we looked, and my sweats were comfortable.

"EMP?" I asked.

Electromagnetic pulses could knock out the power grid and electronics, just like in Moore's *Dark Knight* graphic novel.

"Something hitting the Air Base?"

Grand Forks had always been ground zero, due to the SAC base and Minuteman missile silos scattered throughout the farmland.

"That could do it." Kirk smoothed his thin moustache with a finger as he thought.

"For computers, certainly, but . . ."

"My dissertation!" I had made backups to the point of paranoia, 3.5 inch floppies at my apartment, in my car, multiples in the drawers of my desk, labeled with dates and revision numbers.

"Wait." Kirk stopped me before I could run toward my dark office in a panic. "If it's zapped, you can't fix it. If it's safe, you can't work without a computer."

I took a deep breath and ran my hands across my smooth scalp. I shaved my head since I started balding during my junior year in high school. Passing for thirty when I was seventeen made me popular with friends who wanted me to buy them beer, but it had been hard on my nonexistent love life. Acing my ACTs didn't help either even though I made the all-state defensive line.

"Whoa. This is crazy. What do we do?"

"I want to check my car to test your EMP theory," Kirk said.

We grabbed our coats and took the north stairway to the loading dock entrance. The weather had warmed from the previous week when it had dropped into the negative teens. Still it was crisp enough outside to wear my hood up.

Kirk had "borrowed" a staff parking tag from his advisor who had gone on sabbatical, so he had snagged primo parking nearby. His car, backed into the spot, was a 'seventy-two Plymouth Duster, baby blue and rust speckled with balding tires. Kirk opened the hood for me and climbed behind the wheel.

"Let me know what happens," he called after cranking down the window. He turned the ignition.

Exactly nothing happened. No turn over. No clicking. No faint flicker of dome light inside.

"Didn't think this old heap had computers," I said.

"It doesn't. The battery is dead, too. Strange." Kirk climbed out and stared with me into the oily blackness of the engine compartment.

He shivered. "Let's try a push start."

I looked around the mostly empty parking area. My eyes had adjusted to the faint moonlight. The worst we could hit was the Dumpster or the half-melted snow mound at the far end.

"I guess. You want me to push?"

"Well, I could push you, but all that will accomplish is give me a hernia." He hopped into the car with a derisive snort.

"I wouldn't want you to strain your milk," I grumbled as I leaned onto the trunk and heaved against the cold metal.

The Duster rolled forward, refrozen ice crunching beneath the tires. Kirk popped the clutch, but the car didn't even buck. It just slowed to a squeaky stop.

"What? You have it in fifth?" I asked.

"Only have three gears. It's like the pistons fell out of the engine." Kirk rubbed his moustache with a knuckle.

As he thought, I pulled back my hood and listened. As dead as campus normally was in the evenings during breaks, an eerie silence permeated the night. No distant rush of traffic heading to Columbia Mall. No crash of freight trains from the nearby tracks. No blasting music from the frats along University Avenue.

"We might as well stay put," Kirk said, warming his hands in his armpits.

Three years up north and he still hadn't acclimated to the cold.

"Let the confusion die down."

"What confusion?"

"You'll see."

Kirk got out of the Duster and opened the trunk after fiddling with the lock. He retrieved a large black case that looked like a soft-sided golf bag and slung it over his shoulder.

"Blackouts do strange things to normal folks."

"An excuse to play some D&D on a work night, huh?"

"Don't have enough candles for that," Kirk said as we abandoned his car to return to the warmth of Witmer Hall.

We stopped at the double glass doors at the west entrance and searched for the right keys.

"Hold it right there!" came a command from behind us.

The campus officer's uniform looked bulky with his jacket and a bulletproof vest beneath and his voice was hoarse from heavy breathing. He wore a white bicycle helmet perched on his large round head. He dumped the mountain bike he was straddling into the dirt-laden snow next to the sidewalk. Probably hadn't exercised this much since he joined the university police force.

"This is my lab," Kirk said, pointing to the third floor.

"Me, too," I added.

"No one is allowed into evacuated buildings until physical plant gives the go ahead," the campus officer said. He sounded young to be a cop and had an odd, clipped accent. "Too many hazards. Can't allow looting."

"Looting?" I asked.

Kirk pointed at the black bag slung over his shoulder. "I'm bringing things inside. That's the opposite of looting, so it should be okay."

"No, not okay."

The officer reached for the walkie-talkie microphone on his shoulder and pressed the button, but nothing happened aside from a plastic click. Must have been reflex.

"I can't check if you're authorized with dispatch, so you can't proceed. It's a public safety issue. You'll have to leave the area immediately."

"I've got keys to prove we're allowed."

I held out my wad of brass-colored do-not-duplicate keys that would make any custodian proud and jingled them as if I was trying to entertain a baby. Perhaps that wasn't the smartest move. Short police officers didn't like big guys like me.

The officer's hand dropped to rest on the butt of his sidearm.

"I am delivering a final warning. Depart the premises."

"Don't you have better things to do?"

Kirk must have thought he was being reasonable and fair. But he really sounded pissed and condescending, which was why he got low teaching evals from his students. It had taken me a few months to get used to him.

"I have to get my stuff. It's in there."

"Show me what's in the rifle case."

Kirk sighed and set the black bag down. He blew on his hands. "It's not a rifle case. It's just my exercise equipment—"

"Open the goddamn case!" The frustrated officer drew his pistol.

I stepped backward with my hands in the air. I thought that was what you were supposed to do. I'd never had a cop point a gun at me. Which was exactly what happened when I suddenly moved. The automatic was leveled at my chest.

Kirk unzipped his case, exposing a handful of smooth sticks.

"See?"

"Dump it on the ground!" the officer ordered.

The gun was trained on Kirk now.

"I'm not dumping anything." Kirk crouched and carefully shook the bag.

The sticks slipped out, but then one of them separated with a gentle click of metal on wood. A shiny length of blade awash in moonlight appeared on the pavement. It was a real Japanese katana—the first time I had seen it—with wooden practice swords sprawled around it. Kirk reached for it. I believe he meant to keep it from getting scratched on the sidewalk.

The recognizable metallic clack of a pistol hammer slamming home made me wince. But there was no bang. We all stared at the gun pointed at Kirk.

"You were going to shoot me!" Kirk sounded offended.

The officer worked the slide as he backed away. The unfired round flipped out. The slide snicked forward. Click. Click. Click. The officer repeatedly squeezed the trigger.

Kirk growled and the katana was in his hand, free of its scabbard like a magic trick, as he rose from his knees. In a single fluid motion, the tip of the blade stopped at the officer's throat.

"You wanted to kill me!"

The officer whimpered with the three-foot length of steel, presumably razor sharp, threatening his neck. His left hand had begun to reach to his belt, but now he seemed frozen. What did he have to counter a sword? A telescoping baton or pepper spray?

"Kirk?" I asked, trying to appear calm. "What are you doing?"

Kirk stood in a deep stance. A martial arts movie pose with arms extended. His back was perfectly military straight. Breath steamed from flared nostrils.

"Self-defense."

"I don't think that works against cops." I eased forward. "Let's not make another mistake tonight. Okay?"

"Drop the gun," Kirk snarled. "Then the belt."

The officer thought about being a hero. I'd seen the same wild animal look countless nights around two in the morning outside bars. However, never with a really, really big knife involved in the decision-making process. The officer dropped the gun and the equipment belt at his ankles.

Kirk withdrew the blade and held it high, ready to strike. "Leave."

The campus officer snatched the bike and pedaled away.

"You're in deep shit," I said. "He'll be back."

Indignant, Kirk said, "He was going to shoot me." He scooped up the pistol and belt.

"And we're both in deep shit, my friend."

The cop didn't come back, but we barricaded the doors with scrounged chains and padlocks and piled classroom desks anyway. We hoped we could explain to the authorities when the lights came on.

DAY 1
WITMER HALL, UND, GRAND FORKS ND

The lights didn't come back on, but the sun did rise in the east. The steam radiator beneath the window had lost pressure during the night, the popping and creaks faded, and the building had grown chilly.

I had retrieved my sleeping bag, kept for overnight data collection, from my lab. I sat with my back against the wall in Kirk's office facing the door. My stomach had been in knots all night and I jerked awake at every imagined sound. Kirk sat nearby with his sword across his lap and the cop's gun on the desk.

"I saw you wearing those black skirts in the gym a while ago. I thought you did aikido, like Steven Seagal. What are you doing with that sword? On campus?"

"I practice iaido," Kirk said.

He didn't sound worried at all, explaining as if it was a lecture question I had almost understood, but not quite.

"Same black *hakama* as aikidoka, but deeper roots. Basically fast draw with a katana."

"Still shouldn't have pulled that on the cop," I said.

"He was an incompetent ass." Kirk gently tossed a large caliber shell at me.

I caught the heavy round and peered at it. The brass casing had a dented primer. "You're lucky it was a dud."

"The second one, too?" Kirk pulled the pistol off the desk.

He racked the slide and tossed the other shell to me.

Dented primer again.

"Bad lot?" I guessed.

"Mistakes that don't go away become facts."

Kirk pointed the pistol toward the wall and pulled the trigger. He worked the slide and repeated. Eleven more shells fell on the floor with dented primers.

"The world has changed, or at least this part of the world."

"Oh."

The power going out was understandable. Computers, too, if there was an EMP. Those events had explanations, although unlikely. But gunpowder? Batteries?

"We need to test the limits," Kirk said. "Find out what still works."

Then Kirk jumped up and went to the door in the back of his office. He carried the sword in his left hand. "Breakfast?"

I followed him to what I had assumed was a storage closet the hundred times I'd been in his office. Kirk opened the door into another slightly smaller, windowless room. Must have been left over from when this was lab space. Shelves were lined with cans of food with faded labels or no labels at all. Water-stained cardboard boxes were piled on pallets. Some bore MARK DOWN and DENTED stickers like a cheap warehouse store. A camp stove sat in the corner next to a cot and a full laundry bag.

"How long have you been living here and does Dr. Rao know?" I asked.

DAY 2
WITMER HALL, UND, GRAND FORKS

Kirk Vandermeer was a connoisseur of aged food. At first I thought he might be a nut-job survivalist preparing for the next flood. He explained that an ex-girlfriend who worked at the Human Nutrition Lab had turned him on to food that was past its sell-by date. The girlfriend had dumped him, which was why he lived out of his office, and he decided to conduct his own culinary experiments.

"The flavor evolves," he said. "Like very slow cooking. Just avoid botulism."

Most of his stock was relatively fresh, bought from Hugo's or the Walmart discount aisles. Some of the older tins had gone quite pungent, becoming an acquired taste or perhaps a test of courage. My dad had talked fondly of *surströmming*, fermented herring, from his trip back to Sweden. I miss the tuna and sardines though.

We ate, slept, and sat holed up in Witmer Hall for the second day. Kirk had opened his undergrad physics text on the desk. I remember the bright yellow USED sticker on the red binding. I reread Leiber's *Swords Against Wizardry* since it was lying around. But no one came for us.

"I think I should get my stuff," I said later that day, feeling antsy.

Kirk didn't look up from the textbook. "They probably won't be after you."

"Yeah. Must have better things to do," I said. "Like looking for a lunatic with a sword . . ."

Kirk slammed the book closed. "Stay away from the supermarkets. Those will be getting ugly."

So I hiked from the loading dock into the crazy changed world toward the graduate apartments. Hand-printed signs warned people to stay home and not enter main campus grounds by order of the provost. The university cops were taking their duties to heart. So I skirted into the residential neighborhood to trek west. For all the strangeness, it was quiet as dusk settled. Most folks hunkered inside, staying warm. The lucky houses had wood smoke drifting from chimneys or old fuel oil furnaces that didn't need electricity. The frats and sororities all had fireplaces. I crossed the English Coulee near the deserted dorms. Some pedestrians, wrapped more tightly than the previous days, waved at me in anonymity provided by scarves and knit caps. I kept my hood low. Overall there was a stoic sense of wait and see. Hadn't we just survived a major catastrophe? At least the water wasn't rising and nothing had burned down. The government or someone else would be here soon to sort things out. Sure. You betcha.

DAY 3
GRADUATE HOUSING AND WITMER HALL, UND

I returned the next morning with a duffel bag and large rucksack full of everything I could scrounge that might be useful. That meant my stereo system, television, and computer were left behind in the furnished apartment. I retrieved camping gear, my kitchen cutlery, blankets and towels, a bottle of vodka, and the other contents of my freezer. I also grabbed my Redwing work boots, my articulated knee brace, and my pouch of gaming dice. Even a valid excuse to not write on the dissertation made me feel guilty.

I had cut across campus, but everyone else seemed to obey the warning signs. We were a law-abiding people, mostly. I didn't see anyone else among the redbrick buildings, but carried a camp hatchet just in case. I banged on the steel loading dock door to have Kirk let me in. I dumped my load in his office.

"I'm working through Halliday and Resnick."

At his desk, Kirk flipped the aging beige pages. He looked haggard, dark shadows under his eyes and dark stubble on his chin.

"So far dynamics seems to be unchanged. Gravitation, too."

"Did you do the ball drop?"

I hated that lab exercise as a TA for Physics I. The spring-loaded apparatus that launched a ball bearing horizontally and dropped another one straight down must have been sixty years old. If I never had to do that experiment again, I'd be perfectly happy.

"Raided the teaching lab and did pendulum measurements. The timing works out."

Kirk held up a self-winding Seiko dive watch, fat against his slender wrist. "Also looked at the orbits of Mars and Venus. Took the telescope to the roof while you were gone last night. Good viewing without sodium streetlights. But it might be a while before anything changes at that scale."

"Very systematic." I blinked at the morning sunlight that was warming the cold room. "I wonder if the sun is still working."

"Fusion? That's beyond the scope of this course." Kirk smiled and his bloodshot eyes glittered with a strange enthusiasm. "But I'll check the spectral lines if I can locate the correct filters."

"It'll be years before we see dimming." I remember solving the stat-mech problems to determine how long a photon took to escape from the core to the chromosphere. Eight years or something. Then it would really get cold for everyone. No more North Dakota bragging rights.

Kirk nodded. "Now's our chance to make a real impact. To understand what's happened."

I found a cheap solar-powered calculator on the desk and picked it up on the off chance it might work. It didn't. I tossed the useless calculator onto the desk.

"Calculators on the fritz . . . what did they use before? Slide rules and log tables? Isn't that what Dr. Soonpa uses?"

"We chose this path," Kirk admonished. "We chose understanding the universe over an easy life. If we hadn't, we'd be down on South Padre Island right now with the rest of the spring break partiers, getting drunk."

"And meeting women."

"Drunken women," he said with disdain.

"Your point?" I leered down at him and he finally laughed.

DAY 4
WITMER HALL

"First we should check Boyle's Law."

Kirk led me to the roof through the service stairway. He had his katana tucked into his belt.

"Which one is that again?" I asked, a bit sheepish. "An ideal gas?"

"The product of pressure and volume of a gas remain constant," Kirk said. "Remember pushing the Duster? There was no compression from the engine. Strange, don't you think?"

We stepped onto the flat asphalt and tar-lined roof. It was a sunny day and well into the mid-forties, so the remaining snow created puddles. I noticed a dusty Weber grill with a broken wheel and beat-up lawn furniture in an empty patch of roof next to the air handling enclosure. The department's eight-inch Schmidt-Cassegrain telescope was on a tripod next to the chaise longue. The piston and cylinder experiment for demonstrating hydraulics to the education majors sat by the grill.

"What do you need me for?" I asked.

"You need to confirm my methods and results, so I know I'm not going schizoid."

Kirk set his sword on the chair and knelt by the hydraulic experiment: two clear Plexiglas cylinders, one half the diameter of the other. Fancy plungers with gaskets and handle grips were inserted in the cylinders and tubing ran between them. Two dial pressure gauges poked out the side of both. He pressed gently on the fat plunger and the skinny plunger rose up slowly as air transferred through the connecting tube. The needles on the gauges barely registered.

"Now you try. Give it a real shove."

"I'll probably break it." I leaned over and gripped the plunger. Then I shoved it down with all my strength. A momentary resistance vanished and the volume in the fat cylinder decreased without corresponding movement from the skinny plunger.

"There must be a leak."

We repeated the experiment several times. I couldn't find the leak. The rubber gaskets were sealed. But sudden pressure change much above one atmosphere seemed to bleed off. For the first time in a long time, I felt scared, because I really didn't understand.

"How did this happen?"

"It's not the overall pressure. It's the delta, the rate of change of pressure. I wonder if there would be any sonic booms?"

"No, not just the experiment. Everything. How did this happen? Why doesn't anything work? What changed?"

"One question at a time." Kirk, seeing my face, switched topic.

He glanced up at the large water tower to the south, past the geology building. "We should collect fresh water while there's still pressure in the pipes. We might be here a while."

"How long? I'm worried about my folks," I said.

That was mostly true. My dad would be fine, except come deer season if guns really weren't working. My mom would have a harder time if she didn't get her soaps.

"Are you going to walk forty miles with that knee?" Kirk asked, mockingly.

His mother was in Houston, fourteen hundred miles away.

I shut up.

DAY 5
WITMER HALL

The next day on the roof, we got a metal piston in a fitted barrel, once used to compress ceramic powder samples for Dr. Soonpa, and a propane torch for brazing pipe fittings. The small green propane cylinder still held gas, supporting the change in pressure hypothesis. The piston didn't have a gauge, so we piled graduated weights on the top. We heated the piston with a few millimeters of water trapped inside. Kirk removed mass after mass, waiting for the piston to move. The temperature was high, above boiling, but no expansion.

Kirk took the last ten-gram weight off the piston top. "A tea kettle might whistle, but not much else. Good-bye Industrial Revolution."

"Is mass no longer conserved?"

I quenched the small torch. PV = nRT was a law. Had Avogadro's number changed with temperature? How could it? It was just a number and supposed to be constant.

As the cylinder cooled, the piston slowly sucked down. Kirk pulled the piston out with a vacuum pop as it released.

"It's as if all the hot molecules just escaped."

We repeated the same experiment several times, varying the added water, the heating time, everything we could think of. The same results, a dramatically irreversible process.

"Maybe it's a bubble universe, a brane, that's enveloped our region of space," I proposed.

Branes were the big thing in theoretical physics. A separation between universes had slipped somehow.

Kirk scoffed.

"A brane wouldn't be permeable to physical matter. Otherwise there would be mass diffusion and no separation of universes."

"Okay, maybe another fundamental force has frozen out of a cooling universe? Like the electro-weak did."

"Doesn't match with observables and it's not testable." Kirk rubbed his moustache with a finger. "It's like Maxwell's demon has taken control."

"And Maxwell's demon is testable?" I asked.

Maxwell's demon was a thought experiment. In the 1800s, James Clerk Maxwell proposed an imp gatekeeper between two containers that would allow only hot molecules from one container to the next. Eventually all the hot molecules would be in the same side, circumventing the randomizing chaos of entropy. I forget what Maxwell's point was, but there was no real demon.

Kirk just rubbed his moustache and gave a sly smile. "You'll see."

I wanted to smack the smug right off Kirk's face.

DAY 6
WITMER AND STARCHER HALLS

The Simplot plant sent its reek of rotting potatoes as the early thaw settled in. I could barely stand to be on the roof with the wind coming from the north, but the warm sunshine was too enticing. I scratched my itchy stubble and then the ruff of hair on the back of my head. I had stopped shaving. The last thing I needed was a nick to go septic and then die from the infection.

The fires in town started the previous nights. Smoke and flames from various neighborhoods near the river on the Minnesota side. There was no one to put them out. One week without power or gasoline or guns and civilization was starting to crumble. But when people started to feel hungry and frightened and abandoned, what could be expected? I guess I was lucky, having fallen in with Kirk. We had begun rationing the food.

"We can't stay up here forever." I leaned over the Weber grill. The last of my frozen hamburger patties stored in the disappearing snow sizzled on the grate. I flipped them with Kirk's long Williams-Sonoma grilling spatula with serrated edges and solid steel handle. I liked the heft of the spatula, but Kirk complained about it being too heavy. So I cooked. I put the lid on the grill to dampen the smoke.

"That depends on how you define forever." Kirk had taken it upon himself to outfit the roof of Witmer for survival. He was intent on the staple gun attaching wire mesh to the plywood supported by a Unistrut frame, the green metal beams we used for experiments like an erector set.

"What are you building?"

"Chicken coop. We'll have eggs," Kirk answered.

"Raising chickens here? What about salmonella?"

Kirk ignored me and squeezed another staple into the wood with a thunk.

"More important, where are we getting the chicks?" I asked.

"Biology department."

I was glad to have a break from the pistons and cylinders and scribbling down rows of measurements on an engineering pad and clipboard. We had tried different liquids, alcohol, acetone, etc., and even tried igniting the gunpowder from the handgun shells in the piston. Nothing except fizzle.

After lunch, I followed him to the basement and through a metal floor grate into the steam tunnels. We crossed under the campus in candlelight, following insulated pipes in musty concrete passages. It was strange, maybe a bit liberating, when we broke into the basement of the biology building. We snuck to the second floor and found the incubators in a dark lab. I smashed down the locked door. Most of the chicks were dead. I felt sorry for the damp little fluffs of feathers, abandoned like this, but Kirk rescued the surviving ones. I carried the bags of birdfeed back through the tunnels.

MARCH 28
WITMER BANDIT LAIR AND CAMPUS

Our criminal looting spree couldn't be stopped after that. We roamed through the tunnels, Kirk with his sword and me hefting the "universal key," bolt cutters liberated from the machine shop in mechanical engineering. We grabbed drugs and antiseptics from the medical building. The diseased organs and fetuses in formaldehyde on display were creepy in the half darkness. The stench of something decomposing filled the basement and we left quickly. We hit Leonard Hall and scavenged the precious metals and gemstones from the geology displays. I don't know why that seemed like a good idea at the time, living out a role-playing fantasy, or maybe planning ahead. Kirk seemed fascinated with a gritty, twisted rock like a branching piece of sandy gingerroot. He said it was fulgurite, as if I should know, but I couldn't find it on the list of semiprecious gems in the DM guide.

When we broke into the Student Union, we ran into trouble. The first hint was that the potato chip rack outside the Subway had been ransacked. The roll-down metal gates had already been jimmied open. The second was the trio of young cops picking through the bookstore. None had stripes on their sleeves. The shortest one—I recognized his clipped voice from our previous encounter—threw aside a crumpled Doritos packet and shouted, "There! The one with the sword!"

The cops turned as a unit and hefted nightsticks with the funny handle on the side. They rushed toward us, yelling "Drop it!" and "Halt!"

Kirk and I ran without exchanging a word. We instinctively knew we were in the wrong, although the cops had been doing the exact same thing we had planned. A thrown nightstick, meant to trip one of us, clattered to the tiles behind me. We crashed into a dim stairwell as the heavy boot steps from our pursuit echoed in the deserted corridors. As we descended, I kicked open an emergency-exit-only door that led to the street. We continued into the service basement as doors slammed in the stairwell above.

"Just like high school!" Kirk laughed as we dropped into the pitch-black steam tunnel.

He had obviously gone through a different kind of school system. We hurried to our bandit lair by feel. Once inside Witmer, we tipped a heavy desk onto the steam tunnel cover in the basement. I stayed to reinforce our barricades while Kirk went upstairs to check on another of his pressure experiments. This time we rigged a gradual increase in compressive force using a massive hourglass fabricated from a water cooler jug that trickled sand onto the piston.

Still hopped up on adrenaline, I went to the main entrance, passing through the astronomy and Einstein displays in the sterile foyer. Previously, I had arranged desks into interlocking mounds like a Roman shield wall and bolted lengths of two inch Unistrut to reinforce the structures. Under cover of night, we had hauled in sandbags left over from the flood and then filled metal bookcases with them against the glass doors. I had been working on bracing everything in place by chipping into the cement floor and wedging the Unistrut to entirely overengineer the barricade.

The faint sound of smashing glass came from the second floor. I lifted the six-foot length of Unistrut that I had been fitting and dropped the hacksaw.

"Kirk?"

I knew better. He would be all the way upstairs tending the chicks or his experiment. I rushed up the single stairwell we—meaning me—had not heaped with obstacle furniture and bookcases. On the second floor landing I heard them in the department office. They must have come in from the south side of the building above the big lecture bowl, hidden from view. I eased past the secretary's station and peered into the short hallway lined with closed doors. We had left the faculty offices alone, mostly, half from respect and half from habit, but no professors had returned to campus from the fateful spring break.

The three cops from the Union stumbled out of Dr. Lykken's office, heaps of papers avalanched from overloaded shelves and desks. They wore black Kevlar helmets and struggled with clear riot shields in the tight quarters. They also reeked of alcohol. I had wondered what the police did with the booze confiscated from underage students.

"Kirk!" I shouted.

"He is big," one officer said and lifted a long baton. They pushed forward. "Goddamn squatter."

I lowered the strut and thrust it like a spear. The sharp edge I had just cut gouged into a shield and the impact rocked the cop backward. The other shields tried to bat my metal strut aside. I dipped the end under a swinging shield and thrust again at an exposed chest. The blunt end thumped into the soft torso of a cop. He collapsed, gasping. A baton struck downward on the strut and made a dull ringing. The bone-tingling vibration nearly made me drop my only weapon. The other cop lunged forward as I maneuvered out of the cramped office area. I caught a glancing blow on the side of my head and the hard plastic bouncing off my skull hurt like hell.

They covered their fallen comrade as he struggled to his feet. I repeatedly slammed the strut into the raised shields like a battering ram. The metal strut transferred a lot of momentum. They grunted in pain with each shock. The barrage of strikes kept them on defense and me outside the reach of their batons as I shuffle-stepped backward. One drew a machete. I was pretty sure that cops weren't allowed machetes.

"Kirk!" I yelled again.

I swiped the strut across the useless florescent light fixture overhead, knocking the plastic cover away. Two white tubes fell free and shattered over the cops in a faint dust of phosphors and glass shards. While they hesitated, I retreated to the department entrance and stood my ground. They'd be squeezed into a single doorway, while I now had room to swing.

One cop came through the door as I finished a wide swing with all my weight and muscle behind it. He lifted his riot shield, but I kneeled at the last instant. The whistling metal strut whacked him on his unguarded leg. The meaty pop of his dislocating joint made my own knee twinge in sympathy. He toppled and cried out. The other two, including the one with the machete, moved around him, muttering curses at me with murder in their eyes.

Kirk seemed to leap out of nowhere. He was beside me in the hallway with his katana tucked into his belt and shoulder tilted forward.

The machete cop lifted his blade with a yell. Before he could slice down, Kirk's sword was free of the scabbard with a hiss and in a single graceful sweep, sliced across the cop's forearm. Before the machete hit the floor, the last cop charged. I lifted the tip of the strut to catch the bottom of his riot shield, prying it up, and Kirk's blade slipped beneath. The police body armor couldn't stop the chisel tip of the katana and the blade parted Kevlar and sank four inches into his belly.

Blood welled out as Kirk withdrew the katana in a flourish. The cop made a retching sound as he doubled over and covered his stomach with his hand, hiding behind the clear shield. The cop with the busted knee had crawled into the office, shield and baton forgotten.

"Witmer is our territory. Don't mess with us and we won't mess with you." Kirk glared through narrowed eyes and bared his teeth like a snarling cat. "*Comprende?*"

"There's nothing here we'd want," said the cop with the slashed arm.

His hand was curled against his side as he clamped on to his wound. He looked for a quick escape despite his bravado. "Just trash."

Kirk whipped the sword up to his throat. The steel tip rested on the soft skin below his jaw leaving a smear of red. "See yourselves out the way you came."

We followed as they dripped blood onto the carpet and hobbled into Lykken's demolished office. They crawled out the busted window.

"Asshole cops always pick on Mexicans," Kirk said.

"Isn't Vandermeer Dutch?" I asked as we pulled up their ladder.

"Mom's side." Kirk rubbed his moustache as he watched the rogue cops slowly cross the spotted brown lawn. "We probably should have killed them."

That was the last time Kirk willingly left the building.

APRIL 5
WITMER FORTRESS

I fitted bars over the windows with the last disassembled Unistrut, scrounged pipe fittings, and broken apart furniture. I made do with hand-powered drills and screws and clamps until my wrists and forearms ached. My sweat and labor had transformed Witmer into a fortress.

Kirk had found a gold leaf electroscope in an old box in one of the professors' offices. The electroscope was an old demonstration apparatus where two strips of very thin gold foil dangled inside a glass bottle attached to a protruding plate electrode. Rub a plastic rod with fabric and touch the electrode. Static charge would transfer to the gold foils and they'd repel each other. Honestly, not a very exciting demonstration, but when Kirk discovered the static charge still caused the gold foils to dance apart, he stole it away.

When I went to the pantry to find lunch, Kirk called me over to his desk. He was hunched over the electroscope and a small circuit board attached to a nine-volt battery. He consulted a Mouser Electronics catalog.

"The chicken room is getting rank," I said. "When do we move the hens to the roof?"

"Do you mind clearing it out?" he asked, distracted. "Oh, you need to see this."

I sighed. Kirk had sworn he would take care of the chickens, but that duty had fallen to me as he got obsessive about his discoveries.

"What? Batteries don't work, right?"

"Apparently batteries do work."

"Okay . . . ?" I combed my fingers through my beard. It had come in orange-red and finally stopped itching.

Kirk had removed the plate electrode from the glass bottle, so the enclosed foils weren't connected to anything. He stacked three heavy lead bricks from the X-ray lab between the electroscope and the circuit. Then he connected the battery and stood back.

"So what is supposed to happen?" I asked.

"The light should glow."

Kirk pointed at the circuit board where a small bulb poked out. It didn't glow. Then he pointed at the two foils on the other side of the bricks. They spread apart like golden butterfly wings.

"Whoa!"

"The electrons in the current tunneled out of the circuit. Then reappeared someplace else. Here."

Kirk discharged the electroscope, the foils flopped limp, and then they slowly spread apart again. He disconnected the battery, discharged, and the foils remained inert.

I bent to peer at the experiment from a tabletop level.

"How could they go through the lead?"

"Because they didn't. Maxwell's demon picks out the fast moving electrons, dephases them, steals their energy, and dumps them back nearby."

"Steals their energy?"

"The momentum is gone, the battery drains without doing observable work, and that energy is going someplace else to do something else."

"Like feed Maxwell's demon?" I asked.

"Mmm." Kirk rubbed his carefully trimmed moustache. "Preliminary results, but your guess about mass not being conserved may be right. Although nonlinear interparticle forces require energy too."

JUNE 17
WITMER FORTRESS

"I need to send a letter to NDSU with details. Have them reproduce my"—Kirk corrected himself—"our results."

Kirk had mapped the diffusion region for hot electrons escaping circuits. He said that it matched the radial expansion for suddenly freed electrons in vacuum, down to his measurement uncertainty. We revisited the piston experiments and detected reappearing alcohol and the faint sulfurous taint of gunpowder with our noses. But the heated molecules weren't subject to the same space charge expansion as electrons, so they remained localized, rephasing back into the test chamber, mostly, according to Kirk's theory.

"There aren't many folks left here," I said. I had watched the exodus of people moving through town from the roof with the telescope. "I'd bet everyone else has migrated into the farmland or to the lakes in Minnesota."

"We'll take that chance. Find someone to go south."

"Like a postman?" I asked, but he ignored me.

We recovered the ancient mimeograph from the department office and cranked out copies of Kirk's handwritten and illustrated letter, "Evidence of Maxwell's demon after the Change." Now it was up to me to find an honest courier headed elsewhere.

Armed with my hatchet and the cop's machete, I emerged from the steam tunnels like a gopher on north campus. I passed the old St. Michael's Hospital and went parallel to Columbia Road. I discovered the expansive community garden plots beyond were teeming with people. Maybe not everyone had left. Chunks of old concrete and stacked sandbags formed walls. Barbed wire was strung between pickets and a few plastic sheets and tents were set up behind. The houses along the nearby frontage road had been ransacked for building material. But I saw rows of sprouting crops on the protected acreage within.

I ducked into deserted neighborhoods to keep out of view. I came across signs of torn apart houses consolidated into sturdier ones in cul-de-sacs with barking dogs and NO TRESPASSING signs, or other dwellings simply abandoned and gutted. I moved quickly and quietly down alleys fenced off from yards and beneath the shade of leafy cottonwoods. Single family homes once filled with people who prided themselves on knowing who lived next door and the state of their lawns, were empty and overgrown. Now with the "Great Equalizer" of the handgun gone, people had banded together for protection whether needed or not.

I went through the downtown that had been underwater a year ago and passed the *Herald* newspaper building that had burned during the flood. Hell and high water. The mall and commercial developments on the south side had destroyed downtown long before the water. The looters had finished the job, giving the coup de grâce. Glass shards from storefronts scattered the streets amid abandoned vehicles. Delivery trucks were peeled open like sardine cans spewing torn plastic and discarded packing peanuts.

I crossed through the partly constructed flood wall near the DeMers Bridge and the proposed "river walk." It had worked for San Antonio, so it must work here, according to civic leaders. I scrambled down the gentle bank, cautious of my braced knee and wary of the shadows under the bridge. I found a cottonwood and sat beneath it to rest.

In the shade near the river, I admitted that I wasn't likely to ever finish my dissertation at this point. Who cared about the impact of radon on health now? Lung cancer versus Alzheimer's? You would have to live long enough for it to matter anyway. Did radon even decay anymore?

I returned at dusk with the unopened packet of letters stuffed in my shirt.

JUNE 19

BANKS OF THE RED RIVER

The next two days I followed the same routine. I snuck out of Witmer, spied on the growing community gardens, and took a route through the backstreets to my place by the river. As I sat beneath my tree wondering how long it would be before I could abandon this fool's errand, but enjoying the solitude, I heard the splash of oars. Two canoes came plodding along the muddy waters from the south. They saw me on the bank and one canoe turned toward me with paddles dipping strongly into the river.

The strangers were dressed in leather and furs like French voyageurs or Lewis and Clark scouts. Probably members of a black powder reenactment club. Tomahawks were tucked into beaded belts, but they had aluminum Coleman canoes and hunting crossbows with razor tips on their gear. The canoe crunched into the dirt on the shore and the lead voyageur, a bearded man with a paunch under his fringed buckskins, stood cautiously and pulled off his sunglasses.

"I'm Tapio Hakula," the bearded man said with a big smile. "We represent the Fargo community. We're contacting folks to join with us. Working together is better than being left on your own, wouldn't you agree? So who is left in charge up here?"

"Anything from Bismarck?" I asked, standing. I wiped damp dirt from my behind and kept my hands away from my weapons. "Minneapolis?"

Tapio looked to the south and then at the other canoe, which had turned to hold position in the slow river. "Those're overland, so that'll be a few days before we hear from the cyclists."

"I'm from the university," I said. "We need an important message delivered to someone at NDSU."

"Who?"

"Anyone in physics, engineering, or chemistry, I suppose. We've got a theory about the Change and observations to support it."

I held out the manila envelope stuffed with a dozen letters. "We need to spread the information."

"You don't look like a professor," he said.

"You don't look like a politician," I said. "Why are you dressed like that?"

Tapio looked at his leather outfit and spread his arms in a welcoming manner. He laughed.

"It gets people talking before fighting."

"Will you take the letters?" I asked.

"Fair enough. We won't be headed back for a while. We're going up to Pembina before turning around."

He gripped the envelope as I let go.

"Your responsibility now." I just hoped they wouldn't use all the copies to wipe their ass along the way.

AUGUST 3
WITMER FORTRESS

"Everything we worked for can't just go away. Science can't turn into something called magic for our grandchildren."

Kirk's fingers were blue from the mimeograph ink.

"We'll never have grandchildren or even regular children at the rate we're going."

I flipped through a *Penthouse* magazine and then tossed it onto the couch we had pulled up the stairs.

"I need some air." Kirk didn't like having the windows open in the bandit lair, because the breeze would blow his papers all over the place. "Could you check the chickens?"

I climbed to the roof. I caught Kirk with a stethoscope checking the heartbeat and breathing rates of the chickens once, but only for estimating the pressure flow and how it matched his demon theory. Other than collecting eggs, he left it to me to play Igor to his scientist. I approached the fine metal mesh, meant for a high frequency Faraday cage, and the enclosed birds.

The flock stared with evil beady eyes to see if I had brought food. Oatmeal, to my surprise, was their favorite. They scattered when I had empty hands, except for one dark brown hen. The dark brown hen had peck marks on her neck and broken feathers. She still wasn't laying while the other chickens were. The rest of the brood would eventually kill her if I left her in there. I did feel hungry, and not for more eggs or aging potted meat product. Hatching a plan, I opened the coop and grabbed the pathetic hen. Kirk wouldn't approve, but I did it anyway.

AUGUST 3
COMMUNITY GARDENS

I began to doubt the wisdom of my gut as I drew near the guarded entrance to the community gardens. I had seen outsiders approach the gate when I spied on them before, so I assumed it wasn't by invitation only. There were two guards on either side of the makeshift entrance, just like you'd expect for a castle from the movies. When I saw the corpse with an arrow with green plastic fins protruding from its chest on a concrete slab, I nearly turned away with my cardboard box. A burlap sack covered the dead man's head and sprinkles of white powder had been thrown over the body. Lye or carpet deodorant?

A cardboard sign hung from the corpse's neck. PETER RABBIT.

"Hey, Gunderson, what are you doing here?" one of the guards called out to me.

The big black guy was named Pennington and had been a trainer in the sports department. He held a baseball bat and wore the green and white Fighting Sioux tracksuit.

"Hardly recognized you with the beard."

I tore my attention away from the corpse. "I need a salad."

"I hear ya," Pennington said. He waved me through. "I could kill for a real, honest-to-god cheeseburger."

"I heard some whacko let the beefalo out of the pens west of town."

The other guard, a shorter, squatter white guy, leaned on a long pole tipped with a pruning hook. Must have been a hockey player judging from the missing teeth and mullet, but I couldn't recognize him without a jersey.

"To establish great herds on the prairie again."

I stepped into their compound. A dozen people tended the fields beyond, once gridded into family plots, now a single large farm in the nearly abandoned city. A mountain ash shaded a small lean-to of plastic tarp, sandbags, and two-by-fours.

"If any buffalo get in my gardens, they'll get an arrow through their heart," came an older woman's voice from the shelter.

Patsy Helmsrud, one of the administrative staff responsible for students with athletic scholarships, ducked out of the lean-to. I remembered her because she presented a bag of zucchinis to me when I'd first in-processed nine years ago this autumn.

She wore a Harley-Davidson leather motorcycle jacket, tight on her barrel frame, and carried a red compound bow with confident ease. Stickers for Forx Archery and Red River Bow League were plastered on the flat steel limbs holding the cams and four arrows with florescent green fletching hung from the mounted quiver. Patsy had a square, no-nonsense look about her, dark hair chopped short that would be butch on anyone

younger and touched with gray. A judgmental middle-aged aunt or opin-
ionated shirttail in-law.

"Then we'll eat good again, eh?" the hockey player said.

Patsy gauged me slowly. "I know you. You came through my Twamley
office a few years ago. Football scholarship?"

"Yes, ma'am."

"Did you drop from university?" Patsy tilted her head in disapproval,
which tucked her chin into the folds of her neck.

"Messed up my knee. Got my engineering degree instead of playing.
Now I'm in grad school. Well, I was."

"Well, good for you. You seem to be keeping well." She assessed me
like I was a show animal at the state fair.

"Doing okay, I guess."

"Now, what do you want from our growers' cooperative and do you
have money?"

"Dollars?" I asked.

"Gold or silver," Patsy said with a sneer. Pennington and the hockey
player snickered.

"Better," I said, and opened the cardboard box. The brown hen poked
her head up and tried to flutter out. I snatched her legs and held her
splayed upside down for Patsy.

"This should be good for a sack of fresh produce."

Patsy's lips pursed in a sour expression. "She laying?"

A nearby garden worker, a bottle blond sorority type, had stood when
she heard the hen's alarmed clucking. The blonde had a pleasantly round
face with high cheekbones that had taken a nice tan over the summer.
She wore shorts and a loose T-shirt that exposed straps from an athletic
bra over her broad volleyball player shoulders. Her nails were crusted
with dirt. When she made eye contact with me, I sucked in my gut out
of habit, though I'd slimmed since the Change.

To Patsy, I said, "No, but I'd bet she'd taste better than scrawny red
squirrels from the park."

The blonde smiled and distracted me.

AUGUST 25, 1998
WITMER FORTRESS

The memory of the blonde's gray eyes troubled me, as if she had asked a question I wasn't prepared for. I could only guess what she had seen, a hermit trading a chicken for a rucksack of vegetables. All I knew was that I felt dissatisfied and angry. Back at our lair, I told Kirk, "We have archaic knowledge. What use are we now?"

"Archaic? It's been six months, Jason. Some rules may have changed, but we're capable of discovering the new rules."

Kirk dropped effortlessly into lecture mode. "How often have you imagined going back in time with the knowledge that you have now? We're opening a new field, a new era. Discovering the workings of the universe after this change. It's the new edition of science. Version 2.0."

"Why bother? We're running low on food." I desperately groped for any excuse. "There's no reason for me to stay here."

"I've been reading." Kirk's challenging tone changed to something closer to mollification. He patted the stack of old theory journals on his desk. "Maxwell's demon may violate entropy locally, but if you expand the box to include this demon, eventually he will add disorder to the system. It can't go on indefinitely."

"So this Change will go away?" I asked.

"Yes. Eventually."

"We'll find a fix? We're after a solution?"

"Yes, of course."

So I believed him and continued to help. He needed me.

SEPTEMBER 13
WITMER FORTRESS AND SIGMA CHI HOUSE

"We'll need to fill the balloon before the last of the helium leaks out."

"So late in the day?"

I'd have to hoist the heavy metal cylinders to the roof from the lab in the basement. I had already changed into jeans and a clean T-shirt.

"Yes. Launch at dusk so the balloon catches the light from the setting sun over the horizon against a dark sky. That way I can track it."

Kirk touched the binoculars dangling from his neck. Then, as if he remembered I was standing behind him, he asked, "What else do we have to do?"

"I thought we'd go to the harvest dance that Patsy Helmsrud is throwing."

I'd been invited by Pennington the last time I visited, trading extra eggs for chicken feed and fresh veggies.

"Free food and music. Haven't heard music in a while."

"You go. I have to protect our lab."

"Kirk, this is getting old."

"Old?" Kirk asked. "The easy stuff had already been done in physics. Didn't you ever notice? What was the last big scientific breakthrough?"

"High temperature superconductors," I said glumly.

"That's nearly ten years ago, but no paradigm shift. Now the universe changed. We can be the first to use old techniques to discover the new paradigm."

Kirk dropped his left hand to the sword at his belt as he paced in front of the dusty chalkboard. "Since stellar behavior seems unaffected, I believe Maxwell's demon, while pervasive, must be confined to an envelope close to the Earth's surface. The balloon payload will contain a strobe light connected to a battery that I've saved that will start blinking when it goes above the demon's limit."

I was sweating by the time I got the steel cylinder to the roof. Compressed gas cylinders had been dangerous, called "Sleeping Giants" by Dr. Rao in his lab safety course. But since the Change, I had lost my caution, dropping the cylinder with a clang. Kirk waited with a limp weather balloon attached to a Styrofoam payload box. The last of the helium hissed into the expanding sack of white rubber. Those high altitude balloons always seemed so pathetic and droopy when released. It rose rapidly in the last golden light of evening. The harvest moon rose fat and pumpkin orange in the east.

"I'm heading out then."

"If you want to miss this," he said as if only a dimwit would pass on the opportunity.

I left Kirk tracking the balloon with his binoculars. He craned his neck back and had the telescope nearby for when it got too high for the low power optics.

I took a quick birdbath using our collected rainwater to remove my sweat. I left through the loading dock; the steel door slammed and locked behind me. I walked across the overgrown campus.

I heard music as I reached University Avenue and fraternity row and, except for the dusty and smashed cars on the street, it made me think of previous autumns when school had just started and all the freshmen were being rushed. I crossed near the burned husk of the Sigma Chi fraternity and arrived at the old Sigma Nu house next door, a formidable brick and tile-roofed structure. Patsy Helmsrud and her crew had taken it over, expanding their control from the gardens to the north into campus. A handful of haggard-looking people milled around on the weed-choked lawn and backed off nervously as I walked through them.

Pennington, acting the bouncer in his green tracksuit, waved me up the steps and shook my hand. He smiled and clapped me on the back.

"Heard a story about you messing up the provost's gang."

"Just a misunderstanding," I said. A momentary flash of guilt nearly drove me back to Witmer.

"We had some misunderstandings with them too." Pennington nodded in casual agreement. "Hey, we're starting a five-man football league, to pass the time, if you're interested?"

"I'll think about it," I said. I forced myself through the massive wooden door, banded with metal and studs like it was stolen off a castle.

"Don't start any trouble, okay!" Pennington called after me and laughed.

Inside, a three piece acoustic band covered Nirvana, Sheryl Crow, and some other popular songs in the large, first-floor party lounge. The band might not have been particularly good compared to what once played on the radio, but they compensated with enthusiasm. Their music quenched a thirst in me that I hadn't noticed I had until now. Too many silent, sleepless nights had passed in hiding, hypervigilant for any sounds beyond Kirk's faint breathing.

I ate grilled squash and onions and boiled beans with bits of ham served from pots in the corner. The cook had splurged on the black pepper. A pleasant contentment flowed from my belly while I scraped my plate clean.

I surveyed the room, but I didn't recognize the guests, a mixture of older neighborhood couples and college-age kids. They all had forced grins and a vast desperation that came with being lost. I wondered what they had gone through outside that I had escaped by hiding in Witmer. The wood floors creaked as people huddled in small groups and the faint odor of stale beer permeated the building. The bottle-blonde from the gardens—Mandy as I had learned—leaned against the stone fireplace and listened to Patsy Helmsrud voicing her opinions on the Fargo emissaries and the lack of common decency among those who stayed behind within the town limits.

Patsy was no fool, nor was she generous by throwing a party or raising civic morale. Everyone who remained nearby attended and saw her wealth and power over the local food supply. Even if someone grew their own, they'd eventually come to Patsy for help in some way. Rabbits, both two-legged and four-legged varieties, had a way of ransacking unguarded gardens. Everyone gushed their thanks and well wishes as they shuffled past her.

After wiping my beard on a sleeve, I approached Mandy. She had cleaned up nicely in a simple skirt and gray cardigan. She looked at me with a strange desire, as if I had a sports car and a massive stock portfolio. We chatted. She had been an elementary ed major from Williston and had been Patsy's work-study before the Change.

"Dance?" I asked with a newfound bravery.

Patsy nodded at Mandy and she accepted. The band played "Candle in the Wind" as we moved close. Mandy curled against me and rested her head on my chest with her hands tucked beneath her chin in a surprisingly vulnerable gesture. She seemed to melt as I caressed her well-toned back. Her hair smelled of dandelions.

Mandy brought a mug of watery beer to me and suggested we should sneak off into the bushes for alone time. I downed the brew and laughed, picking her up by the waist. She giggled and kicked playfully. Then I noticed that Pennington and the other jocks weren't there anymore. I set Mandy down gently and rushed out the unattended door as she called after me to wait.

At the loading dock, with my knee aching from the run, I banged my hatchet against the steel door. I could hear the hollow echoes inside. No Kirk. I considered the tunnels, but we'd left lead bricks on the grating. I circled around the building, but my fortifications held, even against me, their creator. On the south side, I saw silhouettes in the light of the full moon scaling the thick ivy covered wall. I gripped the tough vines and scrambled after them as if I were on a cargo net at an obstacle course.

The climbers had partially torn the vines from the brick above me, so I had to be careful with each hand and foothold. As I crushed the soft leaves in my fists, the tendrils popped free and I could taste the bone-dry mortar dust. The climbers crested the lip of the roof. The damn rooster started crowing as they disappeared from my view. I found a dangling rope, the explanation of how the climbers had reached the top so quickly, and latched on to pull myself up before they destroyed our refuge.

A grapnel fashioned from a fishing boat anchor was attached to the end of the rope holding it at the top. I heaved myself over the short wall onto the roof. I swung my bad leg over the edge and my hatchet slipped from my belt, tumbling to the dirt three stories below. I wiped sweat from my forehead with my hand and realized I had smeared sticky leaf pulp smelling of peppery lawn trimmings on my face.

The five men were near the coop holding pillowcases and a fishing net. The chickens clucked in uncertainty as the men whispered and lifted the coop entrance. I then recognized the white stripes of a tracksuit on Pennington holding the net.

"Those are our goddamn chickens!" I bellowed.

They turned toward me, standing taller and angrier, no longer attempting to sneak. Pennington lowered the net he carried and the four jocks who were with him spread into a semicircular formation. The short white guy was the hockey player from the gardens. The others I didn't know.

"You're not supposed to be here, buddy," said the squat hockey player.

He drew a machete that had been strapped to his back. The other four also pulled machetes and came at me.

How did everyone in North Dakota get machetes? We didn't have jungle vines, bamboo, or even kudzu to chop through. As they circled, I lunged for the Weber grill. I snatched the domed lid and the heavy steel Williams-Sonoma spatula, a greasy match for any of the battered military surplus Vietnam-era machetes these jocks wielded. I kicked the grill over to spray a cloud of ashes at the ones on the right and slashed with my spatula at Pennington, their leader.

Pennington raised his arm and the edge of the serrated spatula bit into his muscle like a cleaver. The hockey player lunged at me, but I caught his machete in the impromptu shield. The tip pierced the thin metal. I twisted my wrist and pulled the machete out of the short guy's grip. I roared in fury as I smacked the spatula with a backhand swipe across his face. The utensil bent slightly, hitting with the flat. I continued to slash after that. I bashed them with the now dented Weber lid and hacked at limbs and necks. The pent-up rage from not understanding and always wondering what the hell was really going on flared out. The cathartic sense of bone-crunching tackles flooded back in to my deepest sinews, except there were no pads, no refs, and no rules.

I must have gone berserk. I didn't care about the sharp weapons, but only destroying the enemies who held them. I didn't feel nicks or gashes. White ash clung to my sweaty skin coated with coagulated blood, mine and theirs. I felt where they were, where they moved, my detached mind viewing the battlefield from above and the beast inside me clawing across the pebbled asphalt lunging for throats and seeing red and smelling raw meat.

A disemboweling attack rose from below. I lifted my knee to protect my groin. The machete blade scraped against the metal support joint of my brace. I punched him with the spatula's solid handle. I felt a bone compress and give way in his cheek. The jock dropped with a bulging eyeball, unconscious or dead.

Then the silver arc of Kirk's katana appeared out of the night. A dancing tip of deadly accuracy to my brutal, primitive assault. A handful of dismembered fingers bounced off my face. I sank the spatula edge an inch deep into Pennington's skull and then stomped on his neck after he fell on his back. Bloody black innards dropped from the belly of the hockey player as the katana slashed him open. Kirk was the blade's shadow, a servant rather than master.

Then there was silence and I could only tremble. I had crossed the threshold and there was no going back.

"You were awesome!" Kirk exclaimed. "You fought just like a Bubba of the Apocalypse."

"What's a bubba?" I asked with someone else's hoarse voice. My ears felt hot.

Kirk feigned surprised as he wiped his sword clean. "No bubbas up here? Well, like a redneck, but without the bigotry and more barbecue."

I dropped the mangled grill lid and the gore covered spatula. Patsy had to be behind this.

"Oh, Jason," Kirk said morosely. "This is bad news."

"Yeah?"

I looked at the mess of dead bodies strewn across our roof. What do we do with these? And, I wondered, who would come next?

Kirk sighed.

"Negative results with my balloon. The envelope extends at least ten miles in altitude."

DECEMBER 21, 1998
SIGMA NU HOUSE

I had snuck away to see Mandy often throughout the darkest months. She had holed up for winter with the rest of Patsy's crew in the Sigma Nu house. She had been shy at first, pleading that she didn't know about the raid, but I knew she wasn't involved and told her to shush. I threw a snowball against her plywood covered window and waited by the back door as usual.

Patsy opened it and confronted me like an offended sorority housemother.

"What do you want?"

I put my hand on my hatchet and loomed over her. She had avoided me since the harvest dance and I didn't like her sudden courage.

I announced, "I'm here to see Mandy."

"She works for me."

"And I don't. Let me see her."

"Everyone works for someone. You might as well come over, too. I can always use a smart, big guy like you," Patsy said. "You can't eat principles."

"We're doing okay."

But that's when I fully realized my size had become important again, and not just for football. No one cared about my dismal score on the physics GRE or that I failed my prelims twice.

"I am sorry about my former colleagues' behavior," Patsy said with an empty smile tinged with nasty. "They must have misunderstood my observation that you'd be competition since we didn't have chickens. I never meant for them to attack you. That's not how you get on my good side."

"They learned the hard way," I said.

"I guess they did. Come in." Patsy led me into the warmth of the kitchen. "Mandy, you have a caller!"

MAY 30, 1999
WITMER FORTRESS

Winter had passed, thankfully a mild one, and we'd survived on the dwindling supply of canned goods, eggs, and the most troublesome chickens. I had collected grasses and fallen ornamental plums from the quad to help feed the chickens. I ground the eggshells to feed to the hens to keep them healthy and laying. I also was glad they were back on the roof and not inside where it was hotter. The previous day had been a scorcher, nearly ninety degrees, and it had brought storms. Kirk had sent me to fetch a sandbag from downstairs.

The wind always blew in the Valley, so I wasn't surprised when I caught Kirk sending up his kite on that blustery afternoon with lightning flashing in the distance. I hefted the sandbag and set it down next to Kirk and a tall plastic bucket.

Kirk had made the box kite with aluminized Mylar and wood in our lair when we could barely feel our fingers from the cold. I had helped scrounge the reels of fishing line from deserted basements and garages. The coppery filament coiling the length of nylon line did catch me by surprise. He had tied the end of the line and copper filament to a protruding rooftop pipe and trailed it through a hole in the bottom of the bucket.

"Dump it in there," he said as he kept tension on the string.

The clouds looked suspiciously green and roiling. Almost close enough to touch, it seemed. The sand came out in clumps as I squeezed the fraying burlap. I juggled the sack as it emptied.

"We shouldn't be up here."

"Nonsense."

Kirk fought against the tugging kite with one hand and fussed with the slack end of the string. He kept the filament centered like he was setting a candlewick.

"Break up the sand and spread it evenly."

"What are you doing?"

"I'm making my own fulgurite!"

I recalled the ugly chunk of useless rock stolen from the geology building that Kirk kept on his desk. "Why do you want more?"

"Because it's petrified lightning."

Another drawn-out jagged lightning flash rolled over us. Fat raindrops spattered across the roof, but I felt the hairs on my arms lift. A bad time to be the taller of two. I dumped the remaining sand and retreated to the stairs. Kirk followed walking backward. The filament tugged the sand-filled bucket, but didn't tip it over as the kite danced in the clouds above.

I looked up in time to see faint white nimbus form near the bucket and leap along the gentle hyperbolic arc of the copper filament to destroy the box kite. The crack of superheated air sounded hollow and distorted as the nimbus coalesced into a writhing rope of light. The white actinic flash turned a Crayola canary yellow to my eyes. That was not an afterimage, the blue of bleached photoreceptors that I had experienced for over twenty years of watching storms, but the glow of a dying lightbulb. Mother nature had changed her palette.

"Holy shit!" I cried out involuntarily. We'd been standing there mere seconds ago.

Kirk rushed to the intact bucket. He knelt and thrust his hands into the sand. It should have been molten. However, sand streamed from his fingers when he pulled them out. Kirk laughed as the growing rain pelted him.

"Nothing happened! No fusing, no melting!"

"Get back here!" I yelled.

Kirk trotted back to where I sheltered in the stairwell. "I've figured a way to test quantum theory. We'll build a solar-powered laser. Atomic iodine has the right absorption bands and favorable state lifetimes. I'll need you to find a big parabolic reflector."

"No one cares anymore, Kirk," I said. "It's time to grow up and stop playing around."

"Everyone should care. When it all changes back, we'll have to be prepared. We can't forget."

"If it changes back. Even then, why rely on technology that could switch off again at any moment?"

"I thought more of you, Jason," Kirk said with pain. "What if something else switches off? Slow combustion? No more fires. Photosynthesis? No more plants. The sun?"

"And what could we do about it? Huh? If that happens, we die."

His single-minded obsession with what-ifs and his toys blinded him to the world around us. We had imprisoned ourselves in this squat tower for what purpose?

"What have we really learned in the past year?" I burst out in frustration and anger. "The world has changed and we need to change with it."

Kirk shook his head in defiance. "The society is only as strong as its pinnacle members, the artists and scientists."

"You think we're the pinnacle members? The farmers and ranchers and militia leaders are the pinnacle members now. They're special. We're crazy. No. You're crazy!"

Kirk closed his eyes and rubbed his temples as if he was tired of arguing with a moron. "You can check my math. It all works out."

"So how long will the Change last?" I demanded. "So what's the answer?"

"With my estimates, between ten thousand and two hundred thousand years. That's assuming no energy is supplied from the outside. But I'm still refining my estimates."

Rain flowed down his face and he recognized the betrayal I felt. To Kirk those were just results, values scratched on paper. 1×10^4 to 2×10^5. Arbitrary and unit dependent. To me those were unobtainable lifetimes outside Witmer Hall, impossible to bridge except by imagination and faith in math. We were stuck with this world where a couple of guys with machetes got to be in charge.

Kirk drew his sword with slow deliberation as he faced me. "I'll show you why this is important."

"You're making a mistake, Vandermeer."

"Mistakes that don't go away become facts."

Kirk stepped to the edge of the roof. His tie fluttered in the wind as he raised the steel of the sword. Lightning struck him. His muscles twitched and he grimaced from the shock as the nimbus surrounded him. I could smell the tang of ozone and burnt hair through the rain. But he stood apparently unharmed in the pose of a hero anointed by Zeus or Thor himself.

I hoped to God no one saw him from below.

10 YEARS POST-CHANGE
REPUBLIC OF FARGO, VALLEY CITY ENCAMPMENT

"So I killed him with my bare hands. I had always been bigger and he stood in the way of progress. And that's how I got this sword."

The big NCO slapped the hilt of the Japanese katana. His squad of young soldiers huddled around the campfire, listening to his stories, groaned.

They were all kids, maybe in kindergarten when the Change came. Now they marched to war in the service of the Republic of Fargo against the Neo-Sioux Nation in the far-flung badlands. Hand selected as engineers—sappers—they carried shovels and axes with their kit. Similar campfires dotted the rolling hills above the Sheyenne River where their northern contingent had bivouacked.

The sergeant didn't mention how Kirk Vandermeer had been struck by a second bolt of lightning. The onetime physicist suffered no burns as he'd predicted, but he had fallen into a seizure and lay in a coma for six days, wasting away. It doesn't take much rephasing electrical current to disrupt the intricate circuitry of the brain. The sergeant patted his chest pocket, beneath his padded leather jerkin, where he carried copies of his friend's scientific letters.

One of the new recruits, who had the tilted grin of a smart-alecky troublemaker, said, "My dad told me the magic smoke was let out of the computer chips. Like a genie from a bottle. That's why nothing works like old times."

"Nothing was let out."

Sergeant Jason "Girder" Gunderson shook his shaggy head. He'd have to keep an eye on that private. Maybe too smart for his own good. Perhaps even ready for calculus.

"No. A new demon came in."

BERNIE,
LORD OF THE APES

೧౪౪౪౦

BY JOHN JOS. MILLER

JOHN JOS. MILLER

I've been with the Change/Emberverse from the beginning because Steve and I have both been in the same writing group since he first conceived of it. It's been a real pleasure watching the series develop and grow to its well-deserved level of popularity. It was an even bigger pleasure when Steve asked me to become part of it.

Of course I accepted immediately and also almost immediately assured him I had an idea for a story. And I did. But having an "idea for a story" and an actual "story" are two separate and distinct things. In this case, as often happens with me, I had a title, a beginning, and an ending. Writing a story, whether a short-short or a novel, is always a journey for me. I view outlines as restrictive and a waste of time. I have to live the story as it happens, be the ultimate first reader, if you will.

The title "Bernie, Lord of the Apes" made me think of safari parks abandoned after the Change. I needed a tropical climate, so there you are: Florida.

I had planned to introduce Bernie in the first scene, though it was pushed back to second place, as Doc had to be introduced while it was still night. And so it went. The closing scene remained pretty much as I'd initially envisioned it, though more detailed, of course.

I'm not going to say more about the story because I don't want to ruin surprises and/or belabor the obvious, but I do want to mention that Edgar Rice Burroughs was one of my gateway authors into the field and in my own poor way this is a tribute to his work, which has stayed with me over the many years since I first read it.

I've had about ten novels and more than twice as many short stories published, as well as comic book scripts, gaming books for the Wild Card series, film commentary for the Jean Cocteau Theatre of Santa Fe newsletter, and pop culture articles/reviews for the blog cheese-magnet.com. I've also written extensively on baseball history, especially nineteenth-century baseball and the Negro Leagues.

I'm one of the original members of the New Mexico writing group that created the Wild Cards franchise, which is the longest-running shared-world universe (twenty-three volumes and counting in America, as well as having British, Italian, Russian, German, Spanish, Mexican, Brazilian, and Japanese editions) in existence. Besides having stories in four of the books currently available from Tor, I have also authored two role-playing-game volumes about the series for Green Ronin Publishing. My adaptation of George R. R. Martin's "In the House of the Worm," a Gothic-style horror story that takes place in the far future on a dying Earth, has recently been published by Avatar Press. My columns in Cheese Magnet deal mainly with fantastic cinema and pulp fiction, but sometimes include musings on whatever pops into my head on any given day.

Doc Potter lay on her bedroll in the middle of the biker pack, pretending to be asleep. It wasn't easy. The stench was unbelievable. An incredibly ripe odor emanated in almost palpable waves from the mass of unwashed bodies pressed close around her. It'd been a long, hot, and bloody day and the bikers' body odor, the stench of their filthy, blood-stained denim and leather clothing melded with their farts, belches—Doc had never before realized that you could belch in your sleep—and a continual cacophony of atonal snoring made her breathe shallowly through her mouth and want to stick fingers in her ears.

Today had been the last straw. She'd been an unwilling witness when Los Guerreros del Diablo had come upon a small, struggling farming community, looted every morsel of value and burned the rest. The slaughter had been minimal because only a few of their victims had dared to stand up to the hundred or so bikers. Also, the bikers needed slaves to replace spent workers back home on the outskirts of a devastated Miami. But in the end, the brutality lavished on the captive men, women, and children had been awful and sickened Doc to her core.

Things had been bad enough when Chito Diaz, the late—and by Doc anyway, lamented—leader of Los Guerreros had been running things. He'd had a modicum of brains, which was more than you could say for his idiot son, Manuelito, who'd taken over after Chito had combined one too many bottles of rotgut tequila with a handful of pills of dubious manufacture, fallen into a coma, and never woken up. Chito had appreciated her. He'd hung Doc with her nickname because of the three years she'd put in as an engineering student at the University of Miami before the Change had ruined that particular life path. Delighted with the crossbows she'd built for the gang, he'd conferred the name "Doc" upon her with the dignity of a dean handing out a diploma. She'd accepted it with grace, though making weapons for gangbangers in a post-apocalyptic Miami wasn't the type of thing she'd wanted to do with her life.

Dawn was approaching quietly, except for the bikers' various bodily noises and the sobbing from the prisoners chained to the supply carts.

I can't take this anymore, Doc thought.

She resisted the urge to check the old watch ticking in the front pocket of her heavily worn jeans. It was a big old silver-cased twenty-one jeweled marvel of an earlier age. Her railroad man grandfather had given it to her dad, who'd passed it down to her when she'd gone off to college. It was a minor miracle that one of the shit-heads hadn't taken it from her, but she kept it out of sight and therefore out of mind. Besides, now watches were mostly useless. No one needed them. Except her. Somehow that remnant of the old technology reassured her that some laws of nature still held. Anyway, it was too dark to read the face.

Dawn must be approaching, Doc thought, and she wanted to mask her break under the cover of darkness.

She opened her eyes a crack and furtively glanced around. Everyone was dead asleep, thanks no doubt to the exertions of the day and the following celebration where many bottles of tequila had been consumed. She'd built the still that produced the rotgut and she purposefully made the liquor raw and harsh. It was the best she was willing to do for the jerks who held her captive. Especially Manuelito.

She raised herself up on one elbow and looked at him lying asleep an arm's length or two away, blubbering like a beached whale. He kept her close these days and he wanted to get closer. Doc knew what he wanted and she was nauseated by the idea.

Manuelito had inherited his father's size, more than his share of mean-ness, and a low degree of animal cunning. That was about it. He was about six three and packed three-sixty on his admittedly large-boned, big-muscled frame. He wasn't built for bicycles, which the Change had forced on the Guerreros as their major means of transport. Doc had whipped up an extra-large three-wheeled sidecar pulled by two bikes attached by a universal joint.

This chariot, as he liked to call it, was pedaled by a rotating cadre of gang members. No one thought it was an honor to pedal Manuelito ex-cept for Manuelito, but also no one ever said no to Manuelito. Chito had stomped down many hard men when he'd led the gang to the top of the heap in what was left of south Florida, but he'd been smart enough to rule with a judicious hand. That word had about three too many syllables in it for Manuelito to know what it meant.

She could see his bloated, unlovely face in the moonlight, his mouth gaping open, drool running into his scraggly beard. Doc sighed softly. *No sense prolonging this shit,* she thought.

As a child Manuelito had watched *Star Wars* too many times and had a special favorite part. He certainly resembled Jabba the Hutt and during the looting spree had made Doc play the Princess Leia role, chaining her at night to the rear of his chariot by an iron neck collar that she herself had made. He especially liked that. It appealed to his sense of humor. The collar fit tightly around her neck and had rubbed her skin raw, but that just added to Manuelito's fun.

Doc looked around carefully, then reached into the front pocket of her worn jeans and removed a crudely wrought-iron key. *Dumbass,* she thought, as she slipped the key quietly into the lock and turned it slowly. She carefully opened the collar and set it and the chain silently on the ground. She got to her feet and gathered up her bedroll.

She slipped through the campsite like a ghost. Everyone was sleeping after a grueling day of travel and fighting and an equally grueling night of drinking and raping. Even the guards Manuelito had posted.

Thank God, Doc thought, *for their sense of duty. Or lack thereof.*

She plucked a crossbow from the side of a snoring gangbanger to arm herself, and then extricated her bike from among the others. Silent in her worn red low-top Keds, Doc jogged along the grassy verge of the asphalted county road. After a couple of hundred yards she shifted to the road itself, mounted her bike, and pedaled off silently into the night and, she hoped, another life.

The sun's rays slanted through his bedroom window and smacked Bernardo Diaz right in the face and woke him up. He'd always been an early riser, so he was fine with nature's wake-up call. He threw back the rumpled sheet and swung his feet over the side of the bed. The polished wooden floor was warm against his soles. It was midspring in central Florida and a quick glance out the open window told Bernie that it was already shaping up to be yet another beautiful day.

He yawned hugely and rubbed his face. He didn't know the exact time, though he kept an old alarm clock on the nightstand by his bed for nostalgia's sake. He hadn't wound it in two years. It didn't matter anymore if it was six oh nine or six nineteen. The world now ran on a less specific schedule. Nature was Bernie's timepiece, and he was happier for it.

He stretched to get the night-kinks out of his muscles. When he'd come to Jungleland ten years before he'd been a tall, scrawny kid. Now he was even taller and not scrawny at all. Ten years of hard work and good food had filled him out. It was yet another thing he owed to Don Carlos, another debt he could never repay. He missed the old man every day. His death was Bernie's biggest regret.

Bernie strapped on the loincloth that was on the bedside nightstand and stepped into his handmade moccasins, padded over to the small but comfortably appointed bathroom and washed up. He decided to skip breakfast, figuring there'd be plenty of chow at the business meeting later in the morning. He whistled for the chimp, who was probably in the kitchen stuffing his face, and in a few moments the ape waddled into the bathroom with Bernie's morning glass of fresh-squeezed orange juice.

"Morning, Cheetah."

The chimp chittered at him, exposing his strong white teeth in a wide grin. Bernie drained the glass and Cheetah took it back into the kitchen and set it on the counter by the sink. They met at the bungalow's side door. It was twenty-six feet to the ground from the branch of the baobab tree that cradled Bernie's tree house. Cheetah clambered down the rope. Bernie followed.

As usual, Bagheera was waiting for them at the base of the tree, stretched out in the early morning sun. The panther chirped as Bernie approached. The big cat stood and leaned against Bernie to have his black-tipped ears scratched, emitting a contented purr. Bagheera was a Florida panther with a tan pelt, a creamy white underbelly, and black tips to his tail and ears. He was oversize for his species, about a hundred and eighty pounds, seven feet long and three feet high at the shoulder. Orphaned as a kitten, Bernie had hand-raised Bagheera. It was the first important task that Don Carlos had given him when he'd run away from home and come to Jungleland, no more than a cub himself.

"We're going down to the *chikit*," Bernie told him. "Want to come?"

The big cat seemed amenable. He fell in next to Cheetah as they padded toward the canal. They stopped by the grave site at the edge of the baobab's overhanging branches, fifty feet from the rope that gave access to the tree house. The baobab was an ancient tree, having been planted several centuries before by one of Don Carlos' seafaring ancestors who'd brought a sapling back from Africa. It was only one of the many exotic species of plants and animals that contributed to Jungleland's fantasy-like atmosphere.

The animals waited patiently in the shade while Bernie fussed about Don Carlos' grave, cleaning up a bit of litter and trimming and watering the plants. The grave mound was covered by a blanket of flowers. Bernie judiciously applied the watering can. It had been a warm and dry spring so far.

"I'm meeting with Johnny Tiger at the *chikit*."

Bernie liked to keep Don Carlos informed of current happenings.

"Things are going well, though I'd like to get a metal shop going." He sighed. "Not enough people, not near enough knowledge when it comes to technical stuff. I've been studying the books hard, but . . . Anyway— we're keeping it together. The center will hold."

He put the can down and turned to the animals. "Let's head out, guys."

Jungleland was awakening all around them. The staff was up and about. Bernie didn't have to tell them what to do. They knew the schedule, who had to be fed and watered, what needed to be cleaned, what fences had to be checked and mended.

Of course, things had changed since the Change. Most of the predators had been released. The apes, also.

The gorillas were doing well in the nearby forests. The chimps as a whole tended to stay closer to the humans. Various monkeys had spread all over the place and for all Bernie knew were colonizing the ruins as far away as Miami. The rhinos had wandered off, the hippos had taken to the nearby swamp as if it was home. The elephants roamed where they pleased, though some were kept close as working animals.

A couple, in fact, were approaching now, heading down to the canal for a morning washup. They were led by Tantor, the old bull who ran the herd. He'd led them in a charge that'd broken the siege during the Parking Lot War when a horde of starving looters had come up from Miami soon after the Change. But not before Don Carlos had fallen in the hand-to-hand fighting. Fallen saving Bernie's life, as Bernie could never forget.

Tantor stopped and offered Bernie a leg up. He hoisted himself up on the elephant's thigh so that he was eye to eye with the old beast. Bernie always felt that Tantor's eyes contained an ancient wisdom that humanity in general was too dumb to understand. Certainly, Bernie felt he was, though he never stopped trying.

Bernie scratched energetically at the deeply lined wrinkles around Tantor's eyes.

"Sorry old fellow," he told the beast as he snuffled at Bernie's hands with his trunk, "but I left the peanuts in my other loincloth."

The elephant let Bernie down gently, saluted him with a blatt from his raised trunk, and led the procession on toward the canal at a stately pace.

Accompanied by his accustomed shadows, Bernie followed them to what he liked to think of as the mooring where Jungleland's navy docked and chose a wooden canoe from among the vessels. The aluminum ones tended to get a tad hot to the touch on a sunny day. Bernie got in first and held it steady as Bagheera leaped in lightly, hardly rocking it. The big cat settled down in the middle as Cheetah climbed in cautiously at the bow—he was leery of the water. Bernie climbed into his place aft, untied the mooring rope, and pushed away from the bank with the paddle. They floated out into the middle of the canal and were caught by the gentle current.

Bernie hummed as he paddled, cleaving the water with deep, powerful strokes. He really missed music you could take with you and listen to as, for example, you paddled your canoe down a peaceful canal on a beautiful spring morning. That, and Dr. Pepper.

They had gotten maybe twenty feet away from the bank when a galloping horseman spotted them, wheeled about frantically, and shouted, "Riders on the road! Armed riders on the road!"

Doc pushed on for as long as she could. It'd been an almost pleasant ride, but the temperature was rising with the sun and she needed a rest and something to eat and drink. The raiding party had been on the road for several days so they'd consumed almost all their fresh food, but there was also the stock of preserved items that the Guerreros had stolen or bullied from the original owners whenever and wherever they could. Two-year-old Slim Jims weren't Doc's favorite, but she'd become less finicky when it came to eats than she'd been before the Change.

She coasted onto the sward on the left-hand side of the road, a strip of grass paralleling the canal and road that ran along the flat and virtually featureless landscape. What had once been the bustling city of Miami lay to the east and sprawling Lake Okeechobee was to the north. Doc, always prepared, had studied maps of this sparsely inhabited region. In fact, she'd stashed some in her saddlebags along with the water and food she'd filched over the last couple of days in preparation for her escape.

"Son of a bitch," she said quietly as she opened the saddlebags and saw they were empty.

Someone had stolen her stolen food and water. The thought outraged her. She didn't even want to contemplate the fate of her maps in this toilet-paper-less world. She stared back down the long and unwinding road and shook her fist in the general direction of the biker horde.

"Crap," she said as she saw two figures traveling in her direction. "The Dalton brothers."

The only gringos in the gang, they were lean as whippets and twice as fast on their custom-built racing bikes. No doubt Manuelito had sent them after her, either to drag her back or immediately dispense the Guerreros brand of brutal retaliation against those who'd broken the brotherhood's rules.

They were a couple of miles away and clearly moving fast, though it was hard to judge speed and distance. One of them was waving at her, damn it. She climbed back on her bike and began to pedal as fast as she could, trying to think of something.

As the chase began her sense of time vanished. She forced down an irrational urge to pull out her pocket watch and try to time how quickly they were catching up to her. Her leanly muscled thighs soon began to burn. She doggedly pushed on. It wasn't too long before her throat, already dry, had turned to parchment and she could feel her precious bodily fluids leaking out of every pore. *Damn,* she thought, *it's hot.* She glanced over her shoulder and saw that the gap between her and the Daltons had already narrowed by a disappointingly large margin. She could see where this was heading, and she didn't like it.

Suddenly it became clear what she had to do.

She slowed down. The last thing she needed now was to cramp up. Another glance over her shoulder showed that her pursuers had put on more speed and were catching up even more quickly, probably thinking they'd broken her.

"Manuelito is real pissed!" she heard one of them yell.

"We're gonna be real pissed too if you don't slow down right quick," the other added.

She admired his lung capacity. He wasn't even panting.

Doc's mind was surprisingly calm and clear. *Dad loved those old cowboy movies,* she thought, and she'd loved sitting on the sofa watching them with him. *He's maybe gone now. Those movies certainly are. What the hell was the name of that one with John Wayne?*

"I'm talking to you, bitch," the cry came from not very far behind her. "Slow the fuck down right now or we'll take it out on your ass before we hand you back to Manuelito."

True Grit? Doc thought.

She yanked the bike's handlebars, scattering gravel over the steaming road, popping the tar bubbles that were rising to meet the afternoon heat. She stood on the pedals for six or seven strokes of her long, lean legs, then plopped down on the seat. She was maybe thirty yards from the brothers and riding straight toward them in the deadliest game of chicken she'd ever played.

One was still laughing at what the other had said. She probably imagined it, but she thought she could see expressions of eager anticipation on their faces quickly turn to looks of shocked surprise.

Anticipate this, assholes, she thought.

She let go of the handlebar and flipped up the crossbow dangling from its cord around her shoulder. She slammed a bolt into place, shifted one hand to the bar as the bike threatened to veer off course and held up the bow with the other. Her arm shook but she was almost at point-blank range. The crossbow was just window dressing anyway, intended to scare the crap out of them. She popped the trigger, dropped the bow, gripped the handlebar with both hands, and pulled with all her strength sending her bike swooping across their path, and unconsciously ducked at the anticipated collision.

Doc felt her heartbeat clang loud as a gong in her chest, almost drowning out the noises of rubber raking asphalt and a surprised scream cut short. Her heart gonged again and there came the sound of metal scraping road and metal clashing with metal, and at the third gong some great, invisible hand grabbed her and yanked her off her bike. She felt herself flying through the air. She tried to relax, but she didn't have the time and she hit hard, skimming across the macadam like a stone skipping on water.

Pain shot through her knee and thigh and hip and she bounced a couple of times, shredding denim and skin, then rolled some and finally came to a rest lying faceup, half on the asphalt, half on the road's pebbly verge.

Ow, she thought, closing her eyes as the rays of sun speared down on her. She lay there thinking, *That's it. I've had enough. I'm going home now.*

When nothing happened for a long enough time, she sat up dazedly, wincing as she put a scraped palm on the ground to lever herself up. It took her three tries, but she finally made it. She stood shakily, then turned to face the other way as she realized that someone was cursing up a storm behind her.

Her eyes widened as she observed the wreckage. It was worse than anything they'd ever seen in Driver's Ed in high school. There was, literally, blood on the highway. She dragged herself closer. One of the Daltons, the mouthy one, she thought, was entangled in the combined wreckage of his and her bikes, draped like some insane parody of the *Pietà* among bent wheels with broken spokes and twisted frames. His left leg was as twisted as their bikes.

"You crazy stupid *puta!*" He tried to work up enough energy to shout, but couldn't quite make it. "You broke my leg, you fucking bitch! Eric! Eric, help me! Get this bitch!"

Doc shuffled slowly around the whining Dalton and approached the other. "Son of a . . ."

Her lips clenched simultaneously with her stomach and she would have thrown up if there had been anything in it. As it was, she swallowed bile. She'd seen a lot of death after the Change, but had never killed anyone herself.

Before.

Not that he was dead yet, but the bolt had drilled him right through the throat and had obviously hit something important. There was blood all over him, a lot of blood, and it was slowly pulsing out of his mouth and out of the wound the barbed shaft of the head had torn in his neck. He looked at her, but couldn't speak. She knew that he knew that he was dying. She fought down an irrational urge to apologize. The least she could do, she thought, was maintain eye contact while he still had something left, so she did. It didn't take long.

She turned to the other. "Eric's not here anymore," she said.

The remaining Dalton blinked. "You . . . you killed him?"

Doc licked her lips. "Seemingly so." She could hardly believe it herself.

"You bitch—"

"Come up with a different insult already," she said tiredly, stretching cautiously.

She didn't think any of her own bones were broken, which was a minor miracle, but her ass was sore as hell, her right thigh and knee were scraped, raw meat, bleeding more than she'd like, and her hip wasn't doing too great, either. She'd landed on her right side, and she kept her pocket watch in her left front pocket, so it was probably all right. That was something, at least. She put her hand to her face, but it came away bloodless.

All right then, she thought.

In the meantime, the remaining Dalton was spewing an obscenity-laden invective in great and, Doc felt, somewhat repetitious detail as to what he would do to her when he got his hands on her.

To be fair, she thought, *he is in great pain and I just did kill his brother and he's also making a difficult decision easier for me.*

She glanced at Eric's bike, which was the only one that held out a shred of hope, but it too had been damaged beyond her limited possibility of repair. It did have saddlebags, though.

"Hey—" Her tormentor interrupted his rant. "What are you doing?"

"Looting the dead," Doc said. "Now shut up."

The pickings were slim, but he did have a canteen. She raised it to her lips and chugged half of it. The water was hot and metallic tasting, but it went down great.

"You! You—"

"Yeah, I know. Bitch."

She went halfway across the road, bent down and picked up the cross-bow she'd dropped. She pointed it at the remaining Dalton, who flinched. It wasn't loaded, but he was too shaken to realize it.

"Shut. The. Fuck. Up."

He complied. She turned her back on him and started to walk up the road.

"Hey! You can't just leave me." His voice shook with agonized fear. "You can't!"

She turned and looked at him. "Why not?"

"That'd be cruel, just cruel, man."

Doc bit back a laugh. "What are you, stupid?"

He stared at her silently. She looked back at him a long time, finally sighed, and walked back toward him. He watched her, beseechingly.

"I can't do a thing for you," she finally said. "And even if I could . . ."

She paused, cutting herself off. *I'm not like him,* she thought. *Not like the rest of them.* She tossed him the canteen. Surprised, he caught it.

"Say hi to Manuelito for me when you see him."

She turned away and headed back up the road, thinking to herself, *I should have my head examined.* It was a hot day and only going to get hotter.

Bernie paddled back to the mooring, disembarked, and coaxed the story out of the messenger. He was young, frightened, and excited, a combination that didn't allow for a coherent recitation of events. By the time Bernie learned that the sparsely settled area to the southeast had awoken to the smell of smoke on the air with wispy tendrils still reaching out to the sky, almost all the Jungleland staff had been attracted by the ruckus and were gathered around listening with intent concern.

Scouts, the messenger continued, had stumbled upon what the kid called a horde of well-armed bikers camped out on the road—hundreds of them, with shackled prisoners. They were breaking camp and preparing to go on.

Bernie looked around at his people. He could see the fear in their eyes, hear it on their voices. Panic was threatening to rise. He wet his lips. Don Carlos wasn't here to stop it. Someone had to.

"All right," he heard his voice say, though he thought it didn't really sound like him. "Stay calm. No need to get too excited."

He stopped to think for a moment, surprised to see that all eyes had turned to him. "I'm going to go check things out. We have plenty of time before they can get here. I'll probably be gone all afternoon, so don't worry if I'm not back right away. Jose—give me your clipboard and pen."

Wordlessly, he handed them over. Bernie scribbled quickly on a blank piece of paper, folded it, gave it to the man. "Take this to Johnny Tiger down at the *chikit*—we're having a Coalition meeting today, so the word can get out quickly from there."

Jose threw up a hand in a quick salute and hurried away, grabbed a canoe, and headed off down the canal.

"Emily—you're in charge until I get back. Get the place on lockdown, just in case."

"You got it, boss."

Bernie nodded. "Look—we've been through this before. This won't be our first rodeo and if we stick together, watch out for each, it won't be our last, either."

To Bernie his words seemed inadequate, but it was the best he could do on the spur of the moment and there were murmurs of agreement from his troops. What, he wondered, would Don Carlos have said? What would he do? Bernie kept up a stoic front, but he wondered if his people could see through the facade.

Doc was pissed, hot, hungry, thirsty, and worried. She'd loved her bike and now it was gone. It had been a fine piece of machinery and its loss diminished the world. When she'd left it behind she felt as if she'd had to shoot her broken-legged horse. Her concern for the remaining Dalton brother was somewhat less and she'd tried for the last several hours not to think about the other one with her crossbow bolt in his throat, but had failed miserably.

The afternoon had progressed considerably and with only a floppy hat, half-shredded long-sleeved shirt, and a bloody, torn to hell pair of jeans to shield her, it was baking the hell out of her. The road was no picturesque avenue. The heat had liquefied the tar in the asphalt and it was bubbling up like bizarre mushrooms. The bubbles popped when she stepped on them, stinking and sticking to the soles of her beat-up Keds. Now that her bike was gone, she wasn't limited to the road, but naked and ugly as it was, Doc felt no inclination to wander off into the countryside. The road was the only trace of civilization in this entire godforsaken area. She had to stick to it. She'd seen the maps and she knew that it led somewhere. Undoubtedly somewhere backward and insignificant, but maybe with people willing to help her. That, or willing to club her over the head and add her to their collection of slaves. She sighed deeply, grimly limping on.

Her stomach rumbled and she had dreams of a nice club sandwich and—

She paused, blinking. Up ahead a couple of hundred yards on her left was a clump of actual by-God shade trees, nodding leafily over the canal that still paralleled the road. The grass on the bank was tall, thick, lush, and comfortable-looking. She was also thirsty as hell. The sun hit like a hammer and sweat soaked her ripped jeans, wife-beater tee, and her long-sleeved cotton work shirt. She could feel it trickle down her face, neck, and arms, and runnel down her legs. At least, she hoped it was sweat and not blood. She was quite suspicious about the quality of water in the canal. It was full of slimy things and dangerous microbes and fish fucked in it. But what choice did she have?

She limped toward the blotch of welcoming shade, when to her sur-prise she realized that a canoe was tied by a rope to a stick protruding from the canal's bank. She smiled, momentarily not believing her incredible good fortune.

"Maybe this day won't turn out to be so bad after all," she said aloud.

She limped as quickly as she could toward the canoe. Not only was it the first sign of civilization she'd stumbled across, it was her ticket to freedom. No way Manuelito could catch her if she took to the water—

A great wild beast, a huge cat of some kind, suddenly reared out of the tall grass from where it'd been lurking not twenty yards away and glared at her, fanged jaws slavering and evil intent in its baleful eyes.

"Holy c-c-crap!" Doc stuttered.

It padded forward a step or two, growling dangerously, eyes boring into her, and Doc went into action. She unslung her crossbow with lightning speed, cocked it, popped an iron bolt into place, raised it to her shoulder . . .

. . . and literally out of the sky a whirling lasso fell over her head, slid past her shoulders, and jerked tight, pinning both her arms to her side, causing her to drop the crossbow. A powerful tug yanked her upward and left her dangling and kicking two feet off the ground. The big cat approached relentlessly as she twisted helplessly like a side of beef strung up in a butcher's shop.

It didn't make her feel any better as she revolved around to see a tall, hard-muscled naked guy with flowing black hair and the greenest eyes she'd ever seen glaring at her. She had no idea where he'd come from. Veins stood out in his neck, beating time in accord with another in his forehead. His face was clenched in an expression of fury and murder was in his eyes.

"You were going to shoot my cat!" Bernie shouted, glaring up at the woman twisting in the loop of his lasso.

And then, he realized that he was looking at a woman and she had an expression of utter terror on her face. But that expression was gone in a moment, as if a shutter had slid down over her features.

"I'm sorry," she said in an utterly controlled voice. "I didn't know that it was your cat."

"He," Bernie automatically corrected.

"He," she agreed.

Bagheera reached his side and sat down next to him. He automatically put his hand on the cat's head, scratching behind his ears. Bagheera purred like a distant motorboat. Bernie watched the woman's eyes flicker with something. He wasn't sure what. They were blue.

The rest of her was tall and slim. Her hat had fallen off, exposing tousled blond hair cut much shorter than his own. Her features were finely chiseled with a snub nose, high cheekbones, and expressive mouth. It twitched, Bernie saw, and he realized that she was probably hurting. All the anger drained out of him. He reached out and grabbed her around the waist. She flinched, but remained steady in his arms.

"Sorry," he said, trying not to sound contrite.

Something else moved in her eyes and across her face. Bernie looked away from her, back over his shoulder.

"Let go of the rope!" he yelled, and her entire weight suddenly pressed against him.

He relaxed his grip a bit and she slid down his body. She felt like a feather rippling across his chest. He set her down on the ground and saw that he was only a couple of inches taller than her, and he was six two. She moved her eyes from him to Bagheera, who was already looking bored.

"Is he really your cat?" she asked.

"Oh, sure," Bernie said. "I raised him from a cub. His name's Bagheera."

She looked like she might say any number of things, but finally settled on, "Who were you talking to?"

"Oh"—he gestured over his shoulder, pointing briefly to the tree—"just Cheetah."

She looked at him blankly.

"My ape," he explained.

Cheetah stuck his head out from the tree's leafy branches and chittered. She looked blank for a few more moments and then it was like a light dawned. Her expression turned guarded.

"You know—" Bernie said, beginning to explain, then noticed the stains on her jeans and the flesh beneath. "Hey, you're bleeding."

He turned back to Cheetah. "Get the first aid kit from the canoe!" he shouted and Cheetah went down the tree quick as a monkey.

"Oh." She seemed to rouse herself from a daze. "I'm all right. I just scraped my leg when I fell from my bike—"

"We should take a look at it," Bernie said. "Wounds turn septic out here, fast."

She nodded. "Yes, of course."

"I'm Bernie, by the way."

"Bernie?" She seemed surprised. "I thought it'd be—"

He frowned, slightly. "I'm not delusional," he said.

She nodded. "No, of course not." She thought it over for a moment. "I'm Doc."

Bernie nodded stiffly. He didn't want to give the game away immediately.

"Well," he said. "Fine. I'll get you bandaged up and then you can just go on your way. Doc."

He said the name doubtfully and looked around, almost suspiciously. No one else was on the road. She was probably one of their scouts.

"Wherever that may be."

Doc grinned weakly. "I'm sorry," she said. "You're being . . . most kind. I'm afraid that we've gotten off on the wrong foot. It was my fault. About the cat and all."

She looked at Bagheera lying at Bernie's feet, his big black-tipped tail flipping about impatiently. He yawned hugely and the girl flinched again at the size and nearness of his teeth.

Bernie sighed inwardly. "No, I understand. My lifestyle is not . . . usual. Most people don't get it."

Cheetah arrived, brandishing the first aid kit, a white, medium-sized plastic box adorned with a red cross. Don Carlos had been something of a survivalist. He'd stockpiled all sorts of useful equipment and supplies. Ironically, the space he'd dedicated to guns and ammo had turned out to be totally wasted.

Cheetah handed the kit to Bernie, and then grinned hugely at Doc.

"This is Doc, Cheetah. Doc." The chimp nodded energetically.

"You may feel more comfortable doing this yourself," Bernie added, and gave her the kit.

"Thanks," she took it and sank to the ground, wincing.

She tore the jeans away from the thigh wound, the worn denim parting easily, and frowned at the sight of it. Suddenly she looked up, glancing at Bagheera.

"The smell of blood won't, um, affect him, will it?"

Bernie sighed, again. "No. He's really not used to eating people," Bernie explained.

Doc nodded. "Yes, of course not."

The skin of her leanly muscled thigh was pale, Bernie noticed. Apparently she didn't get out in the sun much. The sight of it might not be affecting Bagheera, Bernie thought, but he wasn't too sure about himself.

"So, uh, what," he asked, "are you doing out here, anyway?"

She didn't look up as she swabbed her scraped thigh with antiseptic and flicked away bits of gravel and dirt.

"Running away from a biker gang," she said.

He wasn't, Doc thought as she glanced at him out of the corner of her eye, naked after all. Quite. He wore a pair of really nice moccasins with some great beadwork and fringe and a plain loincloth with front and back flaps. Nothing else was left to her imagination.

In her three years in Florida she'd seen a lot of near-naked male bodies and even a few naked ones in her day—

Though that day seems like quite a while ago, she mused—

And she had to admit that Bernie's was pretty much near the top of the list. His skin had been turned a deep bronze by the Floridian sun and his face was rather pleasant, too, as he studiously looked anywhere and everywhere except right at her, except when he was looking right at her. Not like when she'd first seen him, burning with raw emotion, veins standing out in his neck like cords, visible even in his forehead, throbbing in time with his pounding heart, pressing her against his hard body . . .

She lost track for a second, then caught herself, finished bandaging her thigh and repacked the supplies. She held the box out to Bernie, but the monkey snatched it away with a curiously human-looking expression of suspicion on his face.

"That's all right, Cheetah," Bernie said smoothly. "Doc is a friend."

Bernie, standing behind the animal, gestured discreetly at her with his chin.

"Oh," Doc said, smiling rather more widely than normal. "Yes. Me—I mean, I, I'm your friend, Cheetah."

Bernie nodded encouragingly and made an encircling gesture with his arms.

Her smile faltered, but she caught it before it could entirely slip away and she opened her arms. The monkey waddled forward and put his rather long and ungainly arms around her and pulled her to him. Doc could feel the ungodly strength in those limbs and had the sudden uncomfortable realization that Cheetah could tear off her arms and beat her to death with them without really exerting himself. His big, white, strong-looking teeth were damn close to her throat. The hair on his thickly furred body was coarse against her skin. He smelled a little less terrible than she thought he would.

"See, he likes you," Bernie said. Cheetah pulled back and grinned widely, too close to her face. Doc looked up to see him smiling smugly down at her. "Okay, Cheetah, let's go."

Cheetah released her and waddled over and put an arm around Bagheera's neck. The big cat came lithely to his feet and they walked off together. Bernie extended his hand toward her and automatically she took it. He lifted her, utterly, she was sure, unconscious of his strength. It felt almost as if she were being pulled toward him by some completely previously unknown variety of gravitic force. They stood closer together than she normally liked to be, especially to a stranger, and then Bagheera made a strange huffing sound. Bernie looked away at him.

"Right," he said to the cat. He looked back at Doc. "We have to get going. Lots to do today."

"Of course," Doc said.

Neither made a move. Bernie frowned at her. Not at her, actually, but clearly something was bothering him.

"You'll be all right?" Bernie asked.

"Sure," Doc said, and cursed silently.

What's wrong with me? she wondered. *I'm certainly not all right, stuck out in nowhere with no food no supplies no transportation nowhere to go with nothing to do, but I'll be damned to admit it to this big ape—*

"I don't want to pry," Bernie said thoughtfully, "but a moment ago you said something about escaping from a biker gang? What was that all about? Because I don't like the idea of those hombres roaming around here on the loose."

"Oh." Doc felt vaguely disappointed. "Them. They'll get tired of the country quickly enough and head back to Miami soon. Just . . . just keep out their way and you'll be fine."

She hoped. Bernie himself seemed to have doubts about her explanation, but she didn't feel like going into detail because it was a long story and none of his business. But his eyes had narrowed and she didn't like the look in them.

"Okay. Here's the story. Short version. Soon after things had Changed, I was with my boyfriend in Miami, and you know how bad it was—"

Bernie shrugged. "No, not really. I was up here at Jungleland—"

"Jungleland? You mean, the safari park?"

"Sure. Me and Cheetah and Bagheera and the rest. Yeah, it was tough, but—"

"You want to hear my story?" Doc was getting a little angry.

She wasn't sure why, but here was something she rarely—well, never—spoke about and at his request she was trying to tell him—

"Sure," he said, calm as a pond on a windless day. "Go ahead."

"All right."

He nodded, made a gesture to continue.

"All right." Doc gathered herself. "Anyway, in Miami it was bad, really bad." She looked at him as if expecting him to dispute her statement, but he just gestured again. "So, after a while, Chad, my boyfriend, traded me to this biker gang for a case of canned chili—"

"Wait—Chad? Canned chili?" Bernie seemed somewhere between bemused and outraged. "What for, I mean, why did—"

"I'm getting to it." The memories threatened to derail her narrative.

At the time the humiliation and the terror had nearly broken her, so she'd put it all behind a wall she'd built in her mind and never looked at it, ever again.

"I told you, it was awful. There wasn't enough food, so Chad sold me to them." She frowned grimly. "Sometimes I wonder whatever happened to that bastard. His trust fund has surely gone the way of my engineering degree, so I suppose that he's out there somewhere peddling his latest line of horseshit. Unless someone killed and maybe ate him. Sometimes that thought cheers me up when things are looking gloomy."

Doc looked up to see Bernie staring at her. *Have I overshared?* she wondered. She hurried on.

"Anyway—I had almost gotten my engineering degree and the gang figured that they could use me. Like I said, everything in Miami had fallen apart. The center could not hold. Nothing worked anymore. Chaos, crazy shit you can't even imagine. These bikers were big in the drug trade. Cooked most of the meth in southern Florida. But their stuff started breaking down and it just got worse. They knew how to cook meth, sure, but the theory, the science, crap, it might as well have been nuclear physics to them. I found work-arounds, held things together for a while. But eventually even that all went to hell. They started looking for something else to exploit to keep their little empire together, because almost by default they'd become The Man. When the jefe died and his moron son took over, I knew I had to split, so I came up with this scheme."

Bernie was listening intently. "Scheme?"

"Yeah. I had an idea." Doc was proud of this part. "Sugar, man. Sugar."

Bernie's frowned. "Sugar?"

Doc nodded eagerly. "Of course. Everyone likes sugar. I sold the gang on the idea. I knew that there was a cane-growing area near Okeechobee with a refinery and everything. I thought we could head out into this wilderness, check out the setup, see if we could salvage anything from the refinery, whatever—but I actually planned to run off. But Manuelito, the old jefe's son, gummed up the works. He has a brain like cement. Once it congeals around an idea it becomes hard as rock and impossible to change. He insisted on coming along, with a looting party. The boys were getting bored and to tell the truth supplies were running out. He also, well, he had a liking for me. He kept his hands off when Chito was alive, but when the old jefe died, well . . . I finally managed to slip . . . away . . . early . . . this . . . morning . . ."

Her voice ran down as she saw the expression on Bernie's face. It was as if he'd lost all the color under his tan. He'd taken on a unhealthy-looking grayish pallor and his eyes were as expressionless as stones in a statue's head.

"So . . ." He didn't look at her as he spoke. "Chito's dead?"

"Yeah," Doc asked. "Did you know him or something?"

When he looked up she was caught between a shudder and a gasp.

"He was my father."

"Your . . ." Doc's voice trailed off. "Then, Manuelito—"

"Yes, of course." His voice was dead calm. "My brother." He continued on musingly. "You came up with a good plan," he said, "but you weren't the first to think of it. There were farmers, a refinery and the people who worked it. Indians in the swamp. Jungleland employees and the animals. It was hard here, too. At first we fought over the scraps, but Don Carlos pulled us together. The center held here. We're just starting to build again. It's finally coming together. And you sicced the beasts on us."

Doc felt the truth of his words hit her like a fist. "They may just go home," she said in a small voice.

"You know Manuelito," Bernie said grimly.

"I know Manuelito," she agreed.

He would grab this land with his fat fingers and squeeze until all the blood had run out.

"Does he have maps?"

"Yes."

Doc had never heard a man growl before. The hair on the nape of her neck rose at the sound of it. She felt the flesh on her arms prickle. The noise coming from his throat brought an answering snarl from Bagheera with angry swishings of his tail and put a horrifying expression on Cheetah's face. The ape bared his fangs and hooted like a maniac, hopping around madly and looking for an enemy to sink them into. The vein throbbed in Bernie's forehead, his powerful hands clenched and the muscles stood out like stone on his arms.

"Come," he muttered through clenched teeth.

"I—"

He looked at her.

"All right," she said quietly.

He strode to the canoe and she and the animals followed. He leaped in with an animal-like grace himself and held it steady.

"Can you paddle a canoe?" he asked. There was no real emotion in his voice. Doc didn't know whether to be frightened or grateful.

"I did when I was a kid, on the Finger Lakes."

"Get in the bow."

She managed to climb in without tipping it. Bagheera and Cheetah followed. They both sensed Bernie's urgency and made whining noises that made Doc feel uneasy.

"Cast away," Bernie ordered, "and paddle your ass off."

Bernie's anger started to fade after a couple of minutes of furious paddling as he came to the conclusion that it really wasn't Doc's fault. She had every right to take reasonable steps to ensure her survival. She wasn't responsible for the actions of others. He wouldn't have liked it if she'd been a willing participant in a ring that barbecued babies or something, but her scheme to mislead his brother had been clever. Admirable, even. He sat back and held his dripping paddle, watching as she matched him stroke for stroke. It took a moment, but she realized that she was the only one paddling. She stopped and looked over her shoulder.

"What now?" she asked, aggrieved. "I thought you were in a hurry."

"We are," he said.

"Well?"

"I just wanted to ask you something."

"What?" she asked sharply, then glanced quickly down at Cheetah, who was staring at her and frowning.

"I mean . . . what?" she repeated in a more modulated voice.

"How'd you get that ring around your throat?"

"What?" Her hand flew up to her neck.

"I've been wondering about it since I first saw you."

"Oh." She looked at him steadily. "Manuelito chained me up each night so I couldn't run away from him."

Bernie nodded judiciously. "Sounds like Manuelito. Listen, I'm sorry I was angry at you. I was out of line."

"Oh."

Her expression softened into a relaxed uncertainty that almost made Bernie laugh, but he was good at projecting a stoic front.

"Whatever happens," he said, "it's not your fault."

"What's going to happen?"

Bernie shrugged. He didn't want to get into details. It might destroy the mood he sensed developing. "Who knows?" He dipped his paddle into the water, propelled the canoe forward with a powerful stroke. "Let's go."

She watched him, seemingly studying him, Bernie thought, as if he were a particularly interesting bug. Finally she nodded and turned back to the task herself. Cheetah gripped the sides of the canoe and held his face up to the breeze as they slipped smoothly through the water. The chimp grinned widely, making little sounds of delight. Bernie wished he could emulate his friends and faithful companions, but the days of living in the present had slipped away from him without him even realizing it.

The towering presence of Don Carlos had shielded him from responsibility even as the old man had deftly passed it down to him. With him gone, Bernie realized that he'd stepped into the role he'd been unsuspectingly groomed for. The old devil had done it slyly, starting him off by giving him a tiny, sharp-clawed kitten to care for and ending with, well, as he'd said to Doc, who knows? Perhaps Don Carlos had already shown him the best path forward.

Take in those who come to your doorstep and make a place for them.

He watched Doc as she paddled steadily. He didn't have to bear this burden alone. He had Cheetah and Bagheera and their kind who were trusting as children and loyal as saints. They would follow him to Hell if he had to take them there and be parted from his side only by death. He had human allies, too, fractious and uncertain at times. Some, like Don Carlos and Johnny Tiger were as dependable as Cheetah and Bagheera ever were.

He found himself staring at Doc's tall, slim form, wondering what she looked like without the dust, blood, and sweat-stained old clothes. She was so close that he could smell her over all other things and he wanted to be closer, much closer, but they were already at the junction with the creek. They'd been traveling pretty fast.

"We turn here," he said.

She glanced back without missing a stroke. "Do you mind telling me where we're going?"

"Of course not."

He steered into the creek. It was wider than the canal with irregular banks, twists and turns, and rock outcrops and silt bars to be wary of. The character of the surrounding land also started to change, becoming forested.

"We're heading for the *chikit*."

"What's a chicklet?"

Doc was concentrating on the more uncertain waters they suddenly found themselves in. Cheetah hooted excitedly. He knew where they were going. There was food there. Bagheera was majestically unconcerned, insouciantly licking his paw.

"*Chikit*," Bernie corrected tolerantly. "It's the Mikisuki word for their native dwelling—also what they call a group of them, like we'd say village or hamlet. It's not a place name, but we use it as shorthand for the indios territory in the Coalition."

"And that's?" Doc asked.

"What we call our community—the alliance between the Native Americans, Jungleland, local farmers, and plantation and refinery workers."

"That's—impressive." He could tell she actually was impressed by the tone of her voice.

"All due to Don Carlos," Bernie said.

"I'd like to meet him," Doc said.

"He died," Bernie said briefly, "in the Parking Lot War. He died saving my life from a hammer-wielding maniac before the gates of Jungleland."

"Oh. I'm sorry."

Bernie shrugged, though she couldn't see him. "Me too. But what can you do?"

"Remember him?" Doc asked, and they moved farther up the creek and into the reaching fingers of the swamp, which seemed to draw them in.

Doc welcomed the shade, but not so much the swarms of gnats that threatened to carry her off. She batted fruitlessly at them, and Bernie called a halt.

"There's some insect repellant in the first aid kit. Give it a try."

She took a deep breath, regretting it immediately as she spit out half a dozen of the annoyingly tiny insects she'd inadvertently sucked into her mouth.

"Cheetah," she said, "hand me the first aid kit."

She was kind of surprised when the monkey passed it over with a big smile.

"Thanks," she found herself saying without half realizing it. She slathered some gooey gray paste on her face and hands. It smelled surprisingly sweet, like lilacs.

"We still have some of the commercial stuff," Bernie said. "But this is better. Tiger's people make it."

"Tiger's people?"

"Johnny Tiger's the indio chief." Bernie paused for a moment. "He's . . . kind of hard to describe, but he's my best friend. You'll meet him soon enough."

Doc nodded and offered the bottle to Bernie. The gnats were swarming him as badly as they'd bothered her pre-lotion. And, she observed, there was a heck of a lot more of him to swarm.

"Want some?"

At the last moment she bit back an offer to slather his back that had popped unbidden into her mind.

Bernie shook his head. "I'm used to them," he said.

"You get surprised at what you become used to after a while," she said.

"Yeah," Bernie agreed, "but I gave up using stuff like this before the Change. It just—I don't know. I kind of accepted it all, even these petty annoyances. It's part of my world. It's natural."

He smiled briefly. "I draw the line at mosquitoes, though. I hate those vampires."

"Bugs belong in the woods," Doc muttered.

"And you don't?" Bernie asked with a raised eyebrow.

"It's not my natural environment," Doc said.

"What is?"

"Somewhere where I can figure out how to build stuff."

Bernie brightened. "Plenty of things need building around here."

Doc's lips quirked. If it was a pitch, it was clumsy, if sincere. She looked around as they worked their way up the creek. The swamp was gloomy and stinky. It could do with a lot of improvement, but she doubted that that was what Bernie had meant.

She thought of ribbing him a little about it, but she wasn't sure how he'd take it. So far he didn't seem to have much of a sense of humor. But it had been a trying day all around. She was really running low on energy. For a while she'd been caught up in the excitement and she'd forgotten that she was hungry, but now it had come back to bite her in the stomach like a pack of ravening weasels. Her arms had stopped aching a while back. Now they felt like wooden blocks. The numbness was spreading into her shoulders, but she wasn't going to let Bernie know that as long as she could grip the paddle. The big stiff.

Still, she pondered over his last words. What was it she'd heard in his voice? A note of relief? Gladness? She peeked back over her shoulder. For a moment she simply enjoyed the sight of his muscles rippling in coordination under perfect control like a well-oiled machine.

His face was fixed in a goofy grin, somewhat unfocused, totally carefree.

What a strange dude, she thought. *Quick to anger, quick to, what, joy? Contentment, maybe?*

Another thought struck her, not for the first time. *Is he simple?*

He hung out with animals, treated them like friends. Yet, except for the obvious flashes of anger, he seemed kind.

He's certainly been kind to me, Doc realized, even when, to put it frankly, she'd been alone and, face it, pretty much at his mercy in a world that had forgotten the niceties of civilization. She appreciated his restraint. She had a sudden thought. *Maybe he is gay?*

He shifted his gaze fractionally and for a moment their eyes met. She literally caught her breath. Incoherent thoughts flashed through her brain and then he blinked and broke eye contact, breaching the current that had passed between them.

She turned and looked straight ahead. *Jesus Christ,* she thought, *not gay. Not fucking gay at all.*

She couldn't catalog everything she'd seen. Hunger. Uncertainty. Need. Worry. Burning lust and quiet tenderness.

Simple? she thought. More like multiple personalities clamoring to escape. Her gaze narrowed. Or maybe like someone with a complete array of feelings. Not emotionally stunted. Not solely fixated on his own needs—*I'm looking at you, Chad*—but fully aware of the world around him and the part he could play in it, for good or bad, depending on the path he chose to walk.

Doc started when he quietly said, "We're here," and guided the canoe to the shoreline.

The *chikit* seemed deserted, but Bernie knew that it wasn't. He waited at the stern as Doc disembarked, his eyes glued on her tight, round buttocks clad in torn, fragile jeans that he could rip off her with a single finger, swallowed, and shut his eyes to break the spell. Once on land she turned back to the canoe, holding the prow as Cheetah clambered out and Bagheera, graceful as ever, levitated himself onto the bank.

Their eyes met for a brief second and Bernie grinned goofily. No wonder she thinks I'm an idiot, he thought, and erased the smile from his face. He replaced the grin with a stolid expression of frank noncommittal. She frowned and turned to tie the canoe to the mooring bar sunk into the creek bank. She looked around, briskly.

"So, this is a *chikit* . . . Where is everybody?"

The communal area with *chikits* scattered about it like toys abandoned by giant children was bereft of noise and activity. The romping children, their barking dogs, the women gossiping by the ever-present cook pots, which were in fact not present, the men working leather and making arrows as they told lies about their hunting skills and prowess in bed, all were gone. The empty stillness made Bernie feel queasy. There was always life here. It had all vanished in the face of the approaching threat, leaving a vacant landscape alone and waiting. Only a single parrot, a red and blue feathered behemoth sitting on the branch of an oak draped with Spanish moss—one of the multitude that helped define the living-space—watched them, mute and stony-eyed, looking down from his perch like a judge.

Doc followed Bernie's eyes, looking up into the tree. "Nice bird," she said.

"Yes."

She looked around. "He's not the only one who lives here, is he?"

"No." Bernie glanced around the forest margin whose sketchy circle was broken only by a gravel lane that crossed an arched bridge over the creek. "You can come out now."

For a moment there was silence, then the branches of a large shrub parted soundlessly. Doc started at the unexpected newcomer. He was a big, genial-looking, moonfaced man in his middle years, muscular but now running to fat. He had long, straight black hair and dark eyes. He was carrying a long spear with a wooden haft and a sharp-looking metal tip.

"Forgive my eavesdropping, but—"

"He enjoys his dramatic entrances," Bernie told Doc.

"Well, I was in show business when I was younger."

"You wrestled alligators."

"True enough."

"Doc," Bernie said, "this is my friend, Johnny Tiger. Johnny, this is my, uh, this is Doc."

"Doc?" Johnny asked. "Nice to meet you, but what kind of name is that for such a pretty girl?"

"Well," Bernie said, "to tell you the truth, we've been so, uh, involved in things . . ."

Tiger shook his head. "No wonder you never get anywhere with the *chiquitas.* When you meet a pretty girl, the first thing you do is ask her her name. Anyone will tell you that."

Bagheera interrupted them with a low growl that raised hackles all around. Bernie and Johnny locked eyes.

"We'll have to discuss the deficiencies of your love life later," Johnny said.

"What?" Doc said.

"Right." Muscles rippled across Bernie's chest as he unconsciously flexed his hands. Tiger offered him his spear. Bernie took it, gripped it. "Thanks. Everything ready?"

Tiger nodded. "As you outlined in your message. You sure this is all you want?"

"Hey—" Doc said.

Bernie looked at her. "They're coming."

"Oh. You mean—"

Bernie nodded. "Listen, we have no time. Whatever happens, I want you to stay."

Doc's eyes widened.

"We need you here. Your knowledge—"

"My knowledge?"

"Yes." Bernie paused.

He couldn't say it yet, that he needed her, too, more than anything. Her eyes were all he saw, all the world. "And, other things."

"You silver-tongued devil, you," Tiger said.

Bernie looked at him.

"Hold this," he said, and handed back the spear.

He turned to Doc. He had always lived his life through action, not words. He reached out and put his hands on her shoulders and felt her shiver at his touch. He leaned forward, put his lips on hers. He didn't know how it happened, who made the first move or if they made it together, but suddenly she was against his chest, against his body from his shoulders to his knees. She was stronger than he'd thought and as hungry as he.

After a moment a voice said, "Hurry up!" and both started. They broke away and took a step apart. For the first time Bernie became aware of certain limitations in wearing a loincloth. Everyone pretended not to see, but he did notice Doc taking a second glance.

"Whatever happens," he said again, "stay."

Doc opened her mouth but for a moment no words would come. She gulped, then was able to say, "We'll talk about it."

Johnny Tiger got Bernie's attention by tapping him on the shoulder. He held out the spear and Bernie automatically took it.

"She means 'yes,'" Tiger explained. He cocked his head as Doc opened her mouth, and wagged a finger. "We have to go now."

Bernie nodded. "Please, Doc, go with Johnny."

He looked down at Bagheera, who had been padding around staring alertly at the path leading from the county road over the bridge, his ears quivering.

"Bagheera. Tree."

The cat slunk off among the surrounding oaks and vanished without a sound. Bernie turned to Cheetah, who was looking up at him with a humanlike expression of concern.

"Go with Johnny, Cheetah."

The ape shook his head silently. Bernie went down to one knee before him.

"Cheetah, my friend. Go with Johnny. Protect Doc."

The ape made a strange keening sound. Bernie pulled him in close and hugged him. Cheetah hugged him back and Bernie felt his ribs creak.

"For me, Cheetah. Protect Doc for me, because I must stay here."

The ape chittered, finally nodding, and Bernie stood up. He and Tiger looked at each other and nodded. He looked at Doc. She raised her hand and touched his chest in a gesture Bernie couldn't quite grasp, but he knew that she wasn't pushing him away. Cheetah went to her and took her other hand and they walked away, Tiger with them.

Bernie hefted his spear and turned to stand before the end of the bridge, the weight of the world—his world—on his shoulders.

"All right," Doc said to Tiger as they went into the forest and settled behind cover so that they could see out into the clearing but were unlikely to be seen themselves. She was confused and definitely unhappy. "Mind telling me what the hell is going on? I mean, I get that it's some masculine bullshit for sure, but why is Bernie waiting there all by himself?"

"He's not alone." Tiger gestured around the forest. "There's more than a hundred people out there, but you can't see them. Fighters from all factions of the Coalition."

Doc nodded, a light dawning. "I get it," she said. "You're testing him."

"Partly," Johnny admitted. "Everyone wants to see how he'll react. He's just a boy to them. Sure, he fought well in the Parking Lot War but, Bernie has to show everyone that he can face the demons from Outside who encroach on our land—"

"You sound like a professor," Doc said suspiciously.

"Why shouldn't I?" Tiger asked. "I have a Ph.D. in anthropology."

"Oh." She nodded. "I get it. Native American culture from the inside."

Tiger drew himself up. "I should say not. I did my dissertation on the social and economic mores of Young Urban Professionals."

"Yuppies?"

"A most fascinating culture with an extremely interesting social system. Now stop interrupting. Bernie must replace a legend in these parts, whose family has been here since the beginning of the European encroachment."

He paused. "Who in fact has a Spanish land grant over a swath of central Florida larger than many of the smaller states that once made up our sadly devastated nation."

Doc was about to say something, but restrained herself.

"Yes, of course. It's complicated. Don Carlos was a wise and great man. He understood. He never pressed the claim. He knew that you don't own the land. The land owns you. You are its steward. You guard and protect it, use it wisely to nourish the people and animals upon it, then pass it down the line."

He paused, looked, Doc thought, searchingly at her. "For a while Don Carlos was in despair, for he had no suitable heir. And then Bernie came to Jungleland, eleven years old, seeking sanctuary from his terrible life."

"Bernie told me Chito Diaz was his father, but I couldn't believe him."

Tiger nodded. "Bernie felt the call of the land so greatly that it brought him here from Miami."

From where they watched they could see bikers come over the crest of the bridge, Manuelito's chariot in the lead.

"And now," Tiger said thoughtfully, "he must not only face the de-

mons of the outer lands, but the personal demon who abused him phys-
ically and emotionally when he was a helpless child—"

"Manuelito?" Doc said. *Of course,* she thought.

Tiger nodded. "His father Chito was merely indifferent to him. His
mother had died of a drug overdose before he could know her. But Manuelito, ah, he was the one who really tortured Bernie. That's why Bernie
stole his car when he left Miami to seek sanctuary in Jungleland. He took
the man's ride, a most grave insult."

Tiger gazed at Bernie who stood his ground as the chariot came to an
uncertain stop before him. "Truly demons and giants again walk the
Earth. This is the time of legend and Bernie must begin to build his today."

Doc felt a fierceness grip her heart. She didn't know if it was mostly
fear or pride. Both, certainly. It was all she could do not to fly to his side.

Bernie watched them approach. He held the spear horizontally, hands
gripping the shaft three feet apart, a barrier to those who would despoil
his land and harm his people. It was weird, but he felt calm and collected,
as if he'd totally expected this sudden turn of his life for years and had
not had it suddenly thrust upon him in the course of a very pleasant
spring day when he'd finally met the woman he loved.

In the long run, he thought, *it is better this way.* He'd had a lot less time to
worry about it.

The chariot coasted down from the bridge's crest and skidded to a
halt twenty feet from where Bernie stood on level land. Behind Manuelito's bizarre vehicle the bridge was crowded by at least two-score Guerreros on their bikes pushing forward to see what was going down. Bernie
looked at them looking at him and wondering, and he smiled.

"Hello, Manuelito," he said.

The gross man in the sidecar leading the clown parade stood ponder-
ously. Placing one hand on the shoulder of one of his drivers, he heaved
himself out of it onto the ground. He took a step forward peering at
Bernie uncertainly.

"What," Bernie said, "you don't recognize your own brother?"

"Bernardo?" Manuelito said incredulously.

Bernie nodded. "It is I, in the flesh."

Manuelito laughed. "You have grown," he finally said.

Bernie shook his head sadly. "So have you, Manuelito. And not in a good way."

His laughter ceased and he scowled. "You crazy motherfucker," he said. "You always was loco. I thought you crawled into an alley somewhere and died. No one missed you," he added maliciously.

"I know," Bernie said. "That's why I stole your car and found a new home."

"You stole my car, you crazy *puto*. For that alone you'll die. I was just going to squash you like a bug, crazy man, but now I will make you beg to die."

"I stole more than a car from you," Bernie said.

"What the fuck you talking about?"

"I also stole your woman."

Bernie watched the thought tracking slowly through Manuelito's brain and when the train finally pulled into the station, he roared.

"Doc! Where is she, motherfucker? Where's that worthless bitch?"

Bernie shrugged. "Somewhere where you'll never touch her again."

As Manuelito seethed, Bernie looked up past him at all the *Guerreros* who were watching with mixed expressions of bafflement, wonder, and uncaring boredom.

"I have no argument with any of your men. You may all turn and go back to Miami, or if you want and if you are willing to do your share you may stay with us in peace and plenty and find a happy life."

His gaze narrowed as he looked back at Manuelito.

"But you, brother"—he spat the word—"I cannot permit you to leave. I know you too well. You would go back to Miami and nurse your hatred and no matter what it took you would come back with a thousand men and you would burn this land black."

"A thousand men! I will bring five thousand and you will all die screaming, every man, woman, child, and dog. All because of you, Bernardo, because this is how you treat family."

Bernie felt the flush run up his neck, over his face and to the beating vein in his forehead. He growled and it gave all pause. Even Manuelito was taken aback. Bernie gripped his spear to keep from shaking.

Through a red veil washing over his vision he spat back, "My father was a bull ape and I never knew my mother. I have no family, Manuelito, no family at all."

He took a step forward, his spear pointed at Manuelito. The big man moved fast. He unslung the crossbow and his trembling hands managed to slap a bolt into the slot and he threw the weapon up to his shoulder. He couldn't miss at this distance. He fired. Bernie shifted, his spear flashing, and the bolt made a dull clang as it ricocheted harmlessly aside.

Manuelito screamed, "Kill him!" and his drivers reached for their crossbows and in the tree above them came an explosion of sound and color.

All eyes but Bernie's flew upward as a great squawking parrot, brilliantly red and blue, erupted from a branch, cackling like a madman, and a bolt of tawny brown and white fell from an adjacent tree, landing on one of Manuelito's drivers. Bagheera swiped once across the man's face with his great taloned paw and the biker screamed, his hands clutching his ruined eyes. Bagheera leaped, his claws digging in and pushing off the man's chest. The second driver held his crossbow dangling in nerveless hands and his scream was cut off as Bagheera closed his jaws around his throat. The man went down, Bagheera atop him. The panther shook his head once and then spat out man blood and flesh. He did not like the taste of it. He crouched and growled.

Bernie approached slowly and raised his head to the sky and called out in a weird, ululating cry that brought shivers to Manuelito and the other listeners. He paused and his smile made them shiver even more.

"Hear that?" Bernie asked conversationally. From afar, but not too far, came the sound of distant thunder, but it did not come from the sky. "That's the sound of your approaching doom. You'd better run."

Some listened to him and turned their bikes on the crowded bridge. Wheels locked, men cursed, panicked, and began to fight. Some just jumped into the creek over the bridge's waist-high walls, but those in the middle were stuck by the press of flesh and machinery. The ones at the rear succumbed to the panic and tried to pedal away as if Hell had opened up behind them and Satan himself was reaching out his gigantic clawed hand to pull them screaming into the Pit, but their way was blocked. The few, the smart, the brave, paused a moment until they could see the herd of twenty stampeding elephants and the chimp sitting astride the big male leading them. They were moving fast.

That convinced them, too.

Only Manuelito stood his ground. He stared fixedly at Bernie as he approached with a leveled spear. His mouth moved, but no words came.

Again, as it always did, the sudden anger left Bernie as it had come and he lifted his spear as he came within reach of his brother. Manuelito still tried to talk but could not.

Bernie was genuinely puzzled.

"What is it?" he asked.

Manuelito's face was that of a worried child. The hate had gone out of it, the anger, and the lurking fear that Bernie had always seen in his eyes.

"My arm hurts, Bernardo."

"Your arm?" Bernie asked.

His brother's left arm was dangling uselessly at his side. The biker reached out with his right hand and tried to touch it, but he was weak and shaky. The big man sagged forward and Bernie caught him before he could hit the ground. The weight of him almost bore Bernie down, but somehow he managed to hold him up as the elephants went by, dust clouds following in their trail, trumpeting their triumph. They swerved to miss the two men, as well as Bagheera, now sensibly crouched under Manuelito's chariot. The elephants stomped up the bridge. There were screams and the tortured sounds of rending machinery and bodies. The great beasts slowed somewhat as they went over the bridge and on down the road, chasing the bikers. Now that the rush of the moment was over they moved halfheartedly, but they still managed to catch a few.

Doc and Johnny Tiger were close at the elephants' heels. Other people were coming out of cover more slowly, not exactly sure yet what the hell had happened.

Tiger went down on one knee before Manuelito's body as Bernie let him down gently and stood over it, staring. He automatically put his arm around Doc's waist as she ran up to him, and he held her closely.

"What happened, Bernie?"

He shook his head. "I think—" He looked down at Tiger.

"Yep. Heart attack. Dead as a doornail." He stood, blew out his breath gustily. "Well, I guess that'll do as well as anything for the start of the legend."

"What?" Bernie asked, puzzled.

"Bernie, Lord of the Apes," Tiger said. "The man who doesn't even have to lift a finger against his enemies. He just scares them to death."

Tiger walked off, shaking his head and chuckling.

Bernie looked at Doc and she smiled back.

"I guess," she said, "I better stick around just to see what happens in the second act."

"I think you'll like it," Bernie said.

"I bet I will."

He bent in to kiss her again, but stopped when their lips were less than an inch apart.

"By the way," he said softly, "Tiger was right. I should have asked you your name."

"I forgive you," she said, her lips brushing his as she spoke. "It's Jane."

"Jane Potter," Bernie mused. He shrugged. "Close enough."

Don't Miss Their Next Amazing Adventure:

"Bernie and the Jewels of Okeechobee"

THE SEEKER: A POISON IN THE BLOOD

⚬〜〰〰〜⚬

Victor Milán

VICTOR MILÁN

I've written and seen published more than one hundred books. My next is *The Dinosaur Lords*, volume one of an epic fantasy trilogy, due out from Tor in July 2015. I came to the Change world by reading and enjoying Steve's stuff in writers group. When he invited me into the anthology, I asked what he was looking for.

He said the world was his own "personal Hyboria"—I could do whatever I wanted, so long as I played by the rules. So, cool. (It also gave me considerable insight into the books themselves.) I was intrigued by the notion of a protagonist who wondered so hard just what the hell happened to the world that he devoted his life to seeking answers. I'd also felt like writing a Western for a spell, and having a hero sling knives instead of guns suited me fine. So I combined the themes and plopped my pulp tale of revenge in a setting remote from the glittering courts of Montival—the Chihuahuan Desert, where a battered, wandering badass finds himself caught in the oldest game in the book: bad god . . . worse god. And learns that, not only do all knights not wear shining armor, they don't always volunteer for the job . . .

"**B**rodie? Brodie? *Ay, ¡hijo de puta!*"
His best friend wasn't just dead.
He was dead bad. Real bad.

Zamora had been seeking Brodie since the man missed a rendezvous in Silver City ten days back. At a general store outside the *ciudad de* Chihuahua ruins he'd got a tip that his friend had been seen traveling south with a strange woman.

It led him here, to this derelict hacienda. Even in the shadows of the roofless, half-melted adobe toolshed, Zamora could tell his friend's pallid Anglo features were mottled dark, and their somewhat ratlike skinniness bloated into near unrecognizability. He looked as if he'd been dead for days. But from the smell . . . not long at all.

"Don't touch that body!" Recuerdo called from the doorway.

Zamora froze in midcrouch, with the tails of the black frock coat he always wore, hot or cold, just brushing the bare dirt floor. "What?"

"Something's wrong."

"No shit, Recuerdo. *Mi hermano's* dead."

"Besides that. With the body."

"You better be right. It's your fault if I get stuck like this. I am way too old for this shit."

He backed away from the contorted corpse and cast around for something to prod it with. He wasn't concerned about proprieties. The friend he'd known since they were kids wasn't there anymore.

Where he might be now, if anywhere, was the kind of question Zamora was obsessed with finding an answer for. It was one reason he'd earned his nickname in the two decades and more since the Change.

This part of the Chihuahuan Desert ran mostly to yellowed grama grass and scrubby-ass creosote bushes. Which meant plenty of fuel available for heating and cooking, especially here in the dry belly of the springtime. And the nearby Sierra Madre Occidental provided good pine and oak timber. The weather-grayed and cracked hardwood staff Zamora found had been the handle of a tool whose head had long since been scavenged for the metal. Maybe a rake.

He hefted it in his left hand and drew one of his fighting knives, his big twin bowies, with his right. His stomach roiled: with grief, and with misgivings that had nothing to do with the warning. Childhood superstitions, he'd have called the sensations that raised the hairs at the nape of his neck. If not for one teeny-tiny piece of evidence he liked to call the whole last quarter-century.

Holding the stick by one end he gingerly prodded the corpse.

Something writhed from beneath it. Several somethings.

Quicker than thought, one of the sinuous forms coiled itself and lunged. Zamora thrust upward with the knife. He felt an impact and found himself staring down both barrels of the business end of a striking rattlesnake. He had stabbed the creature through the throat, right behind its head.

The tail of the now thrashing body was black to the rattles. Its body was shades of gray with crisp black diamonds.

"Fuck," he breathed.

He threw down the rake handle, drew his other bowie, and with a quick motion severed the neck behind the gaping head. Flinging the still dangerous head at the body, and the half-dozen or more rattlers that had crawled out from under it, he backed out of the shed. Once clear he sheathed his thirty-centimeter blades.

"What now?" Recuerdo asked.

He stooped down, feeling his age and even more, and picked up his dusty black wide-brimmed hat from the ground where he'd laid it to one side of the door.

"Follow who did this," he said, "and pay him back for what he did to Brodie. That's no way to die."

"What about your friend?"

Though he'd been mostly raised in *el norte*, he'd been born in an onion field here in Chihuahua. He'd been a grad student in psych in Albuquerque, with a degree in physics, no less. But the views of his father's people, the Ndé'indaaí band of the Chiricahua, made more sense in the world where he'd spent the latter half of his life.

He'd devoted that life to trying to reconcile those two worlds. And how to make the one everyone was stuck in now a better place.

"Brodie wasn't carrying anything worth dying for," he said. "And he's gone now, so I'll let his bones go back to the Earth."

That was the Apache world talking, with its distaste for dead bodies.

"Three sets of tracks, boss," Pensamiento, his second scout, reported. "Heading north. Not in much of a hurry."

"Thanks, *ese*."

He squinted up at the springtime sun. It was barely half up the cloudless sky, and already stung his forehead.

"Maybe we can catch up with 'em while it's still daylight," he said, and clamped the hat firmly on his head.

Inside the cantina was dark and cool as a well. Or seemed that way after the hot and dusty afternoon. It smelled of fresh pine sawdust and not so fresh cerveza, sweat, and vomit. The usual for a place like this in a place like this. Maybe a little better.

Zamora walked inside. He immediately took a step to his left to stop being a target conveniently silhouetted by the light of the lowering sun outside. The tracks had led him here. And the sizes of two sets would conveniently fit the two tough customers jacking up some kind of itinerant peddler in a corner of the bar.

The doors swung shut with a creak of hinges that hadn't been oiled in recent history. They were the double-leaf kind, proving that cowboy movies had made their mark south of the border as well as north. Which was only fair, Zamora reckoned, because the whole "cowboy" thing was largely a ripoff of the Mexican vaquero and his culture in the first place.

As his eyes became accustomed to the dimness he saw a blade glint in the smaller mugger's hand. Didn't look like steel, but that made little difference. A blade was a blade.

He started forward. The barkeep barely glanced up from wiping the long hardwood bar—premium scavenge, Zamora guessed—beneath a neon sign, long dead like all the rest of artificially powered civilization, which read, idiosyncratically, THE CLIENT IS ALWAYS WRONG. In English.

The bartender seemed no more concerned by having a big, scar-faced Mexican lumber through his door than he seemed to be by the violence in progress in the corner.

The handful of other patrons drinking standing up at the long bar, or sitting in ones and two at the ratty ramshackle tables, paid no more obvious attention. This close to the border with Trans-Pecos, it paid to mind your own business, especially when that business was selling drinks. Plus the usual things that went along with them: weed, girls, gambling, information.

"This a private game?" Zamora asked, deliberately harshening a voice already made gravelly by years of bad tobacco, worse booze, and the occasional throat punch. "Or can anybody play?"

The mismatched pair reacted faster than Zamora expected. The bigger, lighter-skinned guy spun right around. Just enough light bled in from the late afternoon outside that Zamora could make out his Mohawk and beard were rust-colored and his nose had been broken more than once. He was taller and wider even than Zamora.

"Back the fuck off!" he shouted in badly *norteamericano*-accented Spanish. He raised a beefy fist and started forward, not waiting for Zamora's reaction.

Zamora saw his partner put his blade away and make a quick move toward his waist. That changed everything fast as an electron jumping shells around a nucleus. If they even did that anymore.

Zamora had walked in bare-handed. Even a *norteño* cantina would regard it as an unfriendly act to walk in the door holding a naked blade. But his left hand dipped fast under the long black coat he wore despite the day's heat, and then whipped out again, quick as that black-tailed rattler had gone for his face.

The Anglo bruiser was quick for his weight class. He got a hand up. And howled and staggered back as he consequently took the throwing-knife meant for his bull throat through the palm of his left hand.

The little leaf-shaped blades Zamora carried in pockets sewn on the front of his vest were intended more as distractions than lethal threats. Not so the big bowie he whipped free of the sharkskin sheath he wore, Hollywood gunslinger-style, tied down his right thigh. It was of a size and weight that kids born since the Change would flat call a short sword, not any kind of knife at all.

A wise man had told Zamora once that the problem with throwing a knife at an enemy was that the enemy wound up with your knife. With his little specialized throwers, inexpensively stamped out and ground down from scrap steel, that didn't matter much. But the big fighting knife was a serious thing to put in ill-intentioned hands.

Zamora threw it anyway, underhand. Hard. As the smaller, darker-skinned assailant spun it hit him right in the notch of the rib cage, angled up. The man jerked, squealed like a frightened horse, and sagged back into the wall beside his erstwhile victim. The crossbow he'd been raising shot its bolt into the pine floorboards with a thunk that rang out before the twang of the spring-steel bow had finished.

It was a better shot than Zamora had even hoped for. Maybe it even cut into the bastard's heart, though Zamora knew from knifer's experience even that wouldn't always take a man down at once: he could still keep blood flowing through frantic, big-muscle activity, even if his heart was stopped. Of course, in this day and age, that just put death off for however long it took your legs to get tired . . .

That didn't concern him now. That dude was no threat for the moment, which was all he needed. The huge Anglo was still very much in the fight. And somewhat better motivated than he'd even started out.

Howling, he plucked the throwing-knife from his blood-streaming hand and flung it at Zamora. Zamora ducked his head aside and drew his left-hand bowie from the sister of the rig on his right. The thrown blade rang off the indifferently whitewashed adobe wall behind him, which he suspected was pretty well pockmarked from similar impacts already.

The Anglo roared and rushed him. Thinking fast—the way he always did when the shit came down—Zamora calculated that his opponent didn't get quite that ugly, at least that kind of ugly, by doing things like running straight onto a foot-long knife blade. Especially not with just his bare fists, giant clubs of scar tissue and gristle though they happened to be.

Sure enough, even as he charged he reached over his shoulders to draw a pair of hatchets. By the glint of backscatter sunlight Zamora could tell they were drop-forged, head and haft alike of a single piece of steel: primo salvage. So the Anglo was smart enough not to rely purely on size, strength, and a bull-rush to beat a foe. Especially one who was even less pretty than he was.

The right-hand ax flashed down, aiming to lock up Zamora's knife, or even knock it from his hand. Zamora took it, rolling his thick wrist slightly to make sure he met steel haft with flat of blade. At the same time he launched a straight right punch into the bearded pale face.

It landed hard—a boxing punch, with the last three knuckles of his fist hitting flat, lined up with the sturdy radius bone of his arm. As a general thing Zamora followed the rule of not hitting hard things with your fist, but in the current case he felt a powerful need to make a fast impression.

It made an impression on him. He felt a tooth gash a knuckle. As he pulled his hand back fast the flight of a dingy sharp shard told him the beard-fringed gape was lacking another tooth. At least.

The punch, delivered with skill, will, and two bull-sized masses rushing together, didn't concuss the Anglo enough to put him out. But it did rock his world enough that the ax cocked over his left shoulder failed to carry through to split Zamora's skull. And that was all Zamora needed. He grabbed the triceps of the upraised arm with his right hand, slipped his blade free of the hatchet, and swiped it hard across the thick gullet.

Blood splashed hot over Zamora's chin and down his chest. The bearded bravo fell gurgling and clutching his neck with both hands, as if that could seal up two severed jugular veins.

Zamora whipped attention to the smaller man, the one with the crossbow and the knife through his brisket.

The man was still slouched against the wall beside his erstwhile victim, holding the bowie's hilt in both hands. His features had gone bloodless and saggy. But he still seemed to be breathing.

Zamora had a few too many scars, and not just on his mug, to take for granted that either man was completely out of the fight. Just like the rattler he'd decapitated in the shed, they could still avenge themselves. Even on their way out.

And speaking of which . . . , he thought.

"Why'd you do my friend Brodie?" he demanded in Spanish.

The man croaked something in a language he didn't recognize. Not Spanish, English, Apache, or any tongue he knew. He suspected it might be Nahuatl.

There'd always been plenty of people in Mexico who spoke their own traditional tongue and no Spanish. But he doubted the white guy bleeding out into the sawdust understood enough of the old Aztec lingo for the two to communicate. To say nothing of their still undiscovered third partner.

"*En Español*, asshole," he snarled.

"Fuck . . . you," the man said in English.

His left hand had slipped from the knife hilt. Zamora had not failed to note that. He wasn't surprised when it flashed up, with astonishing speed from a dying man, and a hard glint in it.

He slapped it aside. It did surprise him that the knife that spun away from the not-very-strong grasp had a rudely triangular blade of black stone. Obsidian.

The trader, who was short but sturdier-looking than Zamora had first taken him for, reached over and twisted the bowie's hilt, hard. The killer's eyes rolled up in his head and he went limp.

"Why didn't you show that kinda enterprise earlier?" Zamora demanded.

The man shrugged and grinned. "Maybe I was looking for a hero."

"Will you be my hero?"

The voice was low, husky, and feminine. Zamora wheeled to face its source. She was short, dark, and deeply curved. She had a curious sort of stone-bead tiara around her head and a large jade medallion around her neck. The cotton shirt she wore had fallen open far enough to show that was all she had on under it.

Her eyes met his. And held them like magnets.

She reached a slim hand up to trail her fingers down his chest. "I could use a big, strong man like you."

Zamora's reason was screaming, *Get away! It's wrong! She's obviously not a whore. If she needs a big strong man so badly, why is she running all over the Mexican Plateau with her big old titties flopping out?*

But it had been a long time—uncomfortably long—since he'd had a woman. And with his looks and age the prospect of another had been looking none too bright. His brain, in other words, had had its throne usurped by other parts.

And those eyes. They were pools. Black pools. Like gazing into an abyss . . .

"Watch her other hand, *coño!*" a voice screamed from the doorway.

Not the voice of reason, maybe. But the voice of Thought.

It was as if he'd dunked his head in a Sierra Madre snowmelt stream. He swung the bloody knife in his left hand hard up and around. He barely had a chance to notice what the hand she'd had hidden behind her hips was holding before the massive blade chopped through its delicate wrist.

The small rock rattlesnake struck futilely at air as the hand that held it bounced against the mud-stuccoed wall.

Hard as he could, Zamora smashed the pommel of his bowie into the side of the woman's face. He had no idea what other tricks she might have in store for him. He wasn't minded to find out the hard way.

The way Brodie did, he realized. Before they tossed a bunch more rattlers on him to make good and sure.

The sound of her right cheekbone imploding was immediately drowned by the noise of her neck snapping. It put Zamora in mind of a handgun going off. A sound no human on Earth had heard for over twenty-five years, so far as he knew.

She fell straight down. The smells of various bowels emptying in death suddenly made the cantina feel very crowded.

The serpent squirmed free of the fingers of the severed hand, which were spasming open and closed, and tried to burrow into the sawdust. The trader's right foot stamped on it with a surprisingly solid sound, as if there was stone inside the simple moccasin, instead of flesh. It crushed its arrowhead-shaped skull against a floor of clay set with fresh blood and trampled hard by countless feet.

But the eyes of the woman whose neck Zamora had just broken were open and aware. They drew his as if by some even stronger version of the magic that had held them before. This time he was sure his pecker wasn't involved.

But where before the eyes had seemed like black pools they were really that now: all black, even where the whites should be. They glared at him with cold and infinite fury.

"*I . . . See . . . you,*" the lips said, in a voice that no more belonged to the woman who had tried to seduce him into accepting venomous fangs than it did to him.

Then the eyes returned to what they had been before: brown irises around dilated pupils, in slightly yellow whites. They were unseeing as marbles. The woman was well and truly dead.

"Get the fuck out of my bar, *cabrones!*" the proprietor shrieked. Zamora looked over to see him half crouched behind the counter, brandishing a woodsman's ax. "I run a respectable place, here."

"Yeah," Zamora murmured. "Respectable enough for murder, but not self-defense."

The trader had shouldered his well-stuffed pack. The trader had a shaved head, an eagle beak, and maybe a few years on Zamora. He wore an ancient T-shirt that read I'M WITH STUPID. He touched Zamora lightly on the arm as he brushed by.

"He's right," he said in well-educated Mexico City Spanish.

It sounded quaint even to Zamora. You didn't hear it much these days.

"Best we find someplace else to be, pronto. Before more of them come along."

Zamora was reaching down to recover his bowie from the first man's chest. He froze as he saw the heavily stylized eagle tattooed on the corpse's right biceps.

Then he grasped the hilt, braced his boot sole against the man's ribs, and pulled the big blade free.

"You said 'them,'" he said, straightening. "You don't mean the white guy too?"

The trader grinned with yellow but surprisingly straight teeth. "Check him out, *chico*."

A glance showed a second eagle tat on the pallid thigh-thick arm.

"*¡Hijo de la chingada!*" he said fervently. "An Anglo Eagle Knight?"

"Huitzilopochtli has an equal-opportunity blood cult, these days."

In passing—purely by accident—Zamora's glance strayed across the woman's upturned breasts, which were now entirely bare and lay sprawled off by gravity toward either armpit. They didn't count, anyway; they were dead-chick breasts.

But what did catch his glance was the equally stylized, and far more hideous, figure carved into the jade medallion lying on her sternum between them.

"What's one of Her priestesses doing hanging out with a pair of Eagle Knights?"

The trader just smiled at him and pushed out into the now visibly waning sunlight. He limped heavily, favoring his right foot—the one he'd used to crush the rattler. The crow that stood right beneath the swinging doors hopped peevishly to one side to let him pass, but did not take wing.

"Hey, mister!" One of the drinkers at last stirred himself to speak. "It was like that bird warned you. Does he talk to you?"

"Just random cawing," Zamora said. "What do you expect? It's just a crow."

"Well, that was a new twist," said Memory—Recuerdo—fluttering down off the parapet of the flat cantina roof to light on Zamora's shoulder. "Killing off all your potential informants before they could give you any information. You think you learned enough mystic human bullshit to follow 'em into the afterlife?"

"They forced my hand."

"They wouldn't have told you anything, anyway," the trader said. "So, the crows do talk to you."

Zamora shrugged. "They talk to anybody, man. I just listen."

As a grad student in Psych, he'd been studying communication among birds—crows in particular, since they were clearly smart and also common as assholes in Albuquerque—when the Change hit. Funny, but it was only since then that he'd really begun to understand them.

He reckoned it was because he started paying more attention. He had incentive. Like survival.

"I say you should make them let us in," said Pensamiento—Thought—fluttering up to Zamora's other shoulder. "Discrimination."

"I hate being indoors," Memory said. "No place to stretch your wings. Nothing in there for a crow, anyway."

"¡Yo quiero tequila!"

"You can't handle that shit. You're even stupider drunk. And you fly into things."

"TEQUILAAAAA!"

"Enough," Zamora said. Then, to his human companion: "So how come you understood what he said?"

The trader just shrugged back and smiled. Again. He had dark Indian skin and dancing eyes. He limped south along the track that passed by the cantina. Zamora found he had naturally fallen into step beside him. Even though it was back the way he'd just come.

It wasn't as if he had any better direction to go, just now.

"I'm Zamora," he said after a moment.

"The one they call the Seeker, right? Born in an onion field near Nuevo Casas Grandes, son of a Chicana law student from Albuquerque with a social conscience, and a Mexican-Apache day laborer without much evidence of a conscience at all."

"My father was a good man," Zamora mumbled. "In his own way. How do you know all this about me, anyway?"

The trader shrugged.

"You're quite the legend, in some circles. Also distinctive, with that hat and the two crows. Plus your proficiency with knives."

"Eh. People gossip. Without TV, what else they got to do?"

"I don't have much memory of television."

"I do. Plenty. And I had you sized up as maybe older than me."

"Oh, I am, I am . . . but I forget my manners. Thank you for rescuing me, Señor Buscador. I am Nocheviento."

Zamora grunted. It was something he was finding himself doing even more than usual. The name didn't really make sense. It was the Spanish words for "night" and "wind," but crammed together into one. Which was more the English way of doing things than the *castellano*.

Then again, the Mexican and U.S. cultures had gotten pretty well crammed together themselves, before the Change. And the recent reversal of the military fortunes of Trans-Pecos' ally, Boise, had caused an upheaval in the Republic that had resulted in a fresh influx of refugees south. Most of whom were Anglo, which was ironic, since for the last few years Trans-Pecos had been trying to block immigration.

"So why were Eagle Warriors beating on you, anyway?"

"They thought I had something they wanted. Even cultists of Left-Hand Hummingbird and the Rattlesnake Mother have their reasons to stoop to highway robbery, I suppose. Why did you want to question them?"

Zamora frowned. But he couldn't think of any reason, paranoid though he was, not to tell Nightwind the truth.

"My buddy was murdered," he said. "By rattlesnakes, looked like."

"An ugly way to die."

"Yeah. So I followed the tracks that led away from the scene. They matched the three I found jacking you up in that cantina. And the fact that strange woman tried the same trick on me tends to back up that they were the guilty ones."

"Why would they want to kill your friend?"

"No clue. Brodie was a con man, sure. But totally nonviolent. He even disapproved of me being violent, even when I had to beat some ass to save his. Why would he get mixed up with a bunch of hard-core bloodletters like Eagle Knights—or that priestess with the crazy eyes?" He shook his head. "But I reckon that doesn't matter anymore. I've avenged him."

"Maybe. And maybe not."

Zamora gave his companion a narrow look.

"I believe he may have been caught up in a larger scheme," Nightwind said. "Much larger."

"How do you mean?"

"You asked why a priestess of Coatlicue would be keeping company with a pair of Eagle Knights—dedicated warriors of Huitzilopochtli, at least since his cult re-arose after the Change. Well, in the course of my travels, I have run across evidence that they're up to something together. My brother—"

He stopped.

"Your brother what?" Zamora prodded.

"He's . . . caught up with the Eagle Knights. And he won't listen to me. Even though the Rattlesnake Mother has always had an agenda of her own—and definitely doesn't have Huitzilopochtli's best interests at heart."

"You talk about 'em as if they were real people."

"Who's to say they aren't?"

I am, the rationalist part of Zamora's mind wanted to say.

But he kept his peace. Arguing with people didn't do much good, he found. And until he found out the whys and the wherefores of the Change, he didn't feel as if he was standing on ground firm enough to go throwing many stones . . .

"Okay. I know a lot of people have gone back to believing in old ways. Even phony old ways, like that *Lord of the Rings* was an actual history book."

"So you've encountered the self-proclaimed Dúnedain, have you? You've been northwest, to Montival?"

"I've been everywhere, man."

"Like the Johnny Cash song?"

"Yeah. You know about Johnny Cash?"

"Know about him? I knew him. We were like that."

"Huh."

But you don't remember much about television, Zamora thought. *Funny.*

The two crows, getting bored, took off again and winged south.

"So they spy for you?"

"Good to have eyes in the sky."

"Did they track your friend's killers, then?"

"I'm a better tracker than they are, actually," Zamora said. "But they're good at spotting tracks in the open fast. Aerial reconnaissance and all."

"A mysterious wanderer with a broad-brimmed hat and two corvid servants? So you're basically a Mexican Odin."

Zamora laughed. "Not hardly. Still got two eyes, you'll notice. And no plans to go dropping either of 'em in any wells. So where we headed now?"

"You and I are parting company. Here, in fact. You will want to follow this road south."

"Where does it lead?"

"To the reason your friend was murdered. That's the first part of my reward to you for saving my humble life. And it may be your eventual reward would become greater still, if you got to the bottom of what our cultist friends are planning. And survived, of course."

"You'd pay me?" Zamora asked skeptically. "How would you get in touch with me? Not like we got telephones anymore."

"I have my own ways of knowing. Some almost as cool as having a pair of crow spies. And now: farewell, my child. Good luck. Even you will need an abundance of it."

And with that he set off toward the hills to the west, with a swinging gait that belied his years and gimpy foot.

Frowning, Zamora watched him go for a moment. Then he turned his head, put two fingers in his mouth, and whistled.

Another moment, and Pensamiento and Recuerdo were circling three meters over his head.

"What is it, boss?" Recuerdo asked.

"How about you keep an eye on that dude, find out where he's going."

They spiraled higher. Almost at once they swooped back down to orbit Zamora's hat once more.

"Funny," Recuerdo said. "No sign of him. But there's a jaguar, loping down the far side of that hill he went up. Big one."

"I hate those bastards," Pensamiento said.

Zamora didn't care about any damn *tigres*. They didn't fuck with humans. Usually. And none had been known to fuck with him twice.

A lot like humans, come to think of it.

"How'd he vanish into thin air?"

"You're the naked monkey with the big brain," Recuerdo said. "We're just birds."

"Sarcastic asshole birds."

"What do you expect? We're crows."

"Have you seen this man?"

The old lady's face was wrinkled like a raisin. She had a blue-green bandanna wound around her head and was puffing on a fat joint as she hung steaming clothes on a line to dry. From inside the little adobe hut came the sound of an infant crying.

She paused in her work to study the object he held out in his hand. It was a hand-formed slab of red clay, into which he'd engraved a sketch of Brodie's face with his not-inconsiderable drawing skills. He had fired it overnight in the banked embers of his campfire, and then rubbed a slurry of charcoal and water into the engraving to add contrast.

She frowned and shook her head.

"No, I haven't. Kind of a fish-faced gringo, ¿qué no?"

She offered her joint. He took a deep, grateful hit.

"He's a friend of mine who's dead, ma'am," he said, exhaling. He handed back the joint.

She crossed herself. Then she frowned.

"If he's dead, why are you looking for him?"

The ground got higher as he followed the road south. He asked about his dead friend at every settlement, outpost, and random hut he came to.

People reacted with a certain amount of suspicion. They were poor, but not so poor that they might not attract the attention of bandits. Especially if those bandidos were the local baron's men. Nor was it unheard of for a lone hombre to scout for a gang of whatever sort.

But the mysterious—and improbably named—Nightwind was right. Zamora was the Seeker. Even if he had seen little evidence his fame had spread quite so far and wide as the trader made it out to have. And after all, he could be forgiven for laying it on a bit thick with a man who had rescued him and asked for no reward. Zamora had a well-practiced way of seeming harmless.

Which, unless you tried to do ill to him or his, was perfectly legitimate.

It was at least no particular disadvantage that his scarred, craggy features, which had never been mistaken for a movie star's even when he was young, now looked like a hundred hectares of malpaís: lava rock and heartbreak. North of the Río Grande he was a scary Mexican, even to

Latinos who were U.S. born and raised, like his mom, bless her memory. And with the Republic of Trans-Pecos trying to strengthen its hold by stirring up old racial feuds and divisions, he would've run shit out of luck in short order there.

Here, he was just another campesino scuffling to get by.

It was as such that he hailed a couple of farmers hoeing weeds out of an acequia: "¡Escuchenme, hombres! Give a brother a little help, here?"

He walked up to the irrigation ditch where they stood waiting with their hats pushed back on their heads. After all these years he still wasn't used to seeing Mexicans wearing conical constructions he thought of as "coolie hats." But Asian influence was stronger in Mexico before the Change than most norteamericanos realized, and woven straw hats cost way less than a proper hat like his, with felting and such.

In their patch the bean plants were already beginning to twine their way up stalks of spring corn. Beyond them a huddle of adobe houses stood on the far side of a stream running down from the foothills. Let the gringos in the Northwest cling to their odd, parochial notions that native peoples around the world had mostly died out; they sure hadn't down here in Mexico. The people adapted to the fall of technology just as they had to its rise. A village like this looked little different than it would've a hundred years ago. When the lights went out, there were plenty of abuelos who remembered what things were like before electricity and running water.

Hell, there were plenty of people who never had 'em to miss.

As usual, people working in the hot sun weren't any too averse to taking a break. "What you got for us?" asked the gap-toothed older one. The pair were small, dark, and sturdy even by Mexican standards, suggesting they were mostly indio.

"Was wondering if you'd seen this dude," he said, holding out his clay tablet. "He's my friend, man. I'm looking all over for him."

"Your friend?" the older man asked. The grooves the sun had dug in his face got deeper. His eyes almost vanished into them as he squinted at the image.

"He's one of them!" the younger guy shouted. And he took a swipe at Zamora with his hoe so hard he overbalanced and splashed into the ditch.

The older dude jumped back. He crouched, menacing Zamora with his out-stretched hoe.

Over his shoulder he yelled to the other workers, "It's a child stealer! ¡Matenlo!"

"I think you lost 'em now," Recuerdo said, fluttering down to perch on a rock near Zamora's temporary hideout on top of a ridge. "They're stumbling all around with their hoes and machetes a good half kilometer off."

"Good thing they weren't very good shots with those bows and arrows, huh?" Pensamiento said.

Zamora took a last swallow of water from his gourd, stoppered it, and let it hang from its sling across his shoulder. He wasn't too worried yet that it was nigh empty. Even if his father's people hadn't taught him the skill of finding water in the desert, he had the crows to scout for it. Though the rainy season was a month or two off, this close to the mountains it wasn't hard to find springs or even streams.

The rocks that hid him were black, part of an ancient lava flow. Which also meant they had fangs. They smelled, unsurprisingly, of sun-heated stone and the sage that sprouted plentifully from them. He had to be careful or they'd tear the soles of his keban, Apache-style moccasin-boots, to shreds.

He frowned. Something in his coat pocket felt hot. And was . . . buzzing.

He wasn't sure how a cold-blooded rattlesnake could make his pocket warm. But he wasn't taking any chances. Especially where crazy Magic Snake Priestesses were involved. He turned its contents out without even grasping the pocket directly. Much less sticking his hand inside.

What plopped out on the wind-drifted pale sand beside him wasn't an animal at all. At least not obviously. It was a rock. Its rounded back had sunk halfway into the dirt, exposing a face of glasslike black stone as flat as water in a jug.

Something like steam wisped from it. Something like condensation clouded the face of it.

"Shiny," Pensamiento said, flaring his wings to land on a rock.

"Don't touch it," said Recuerdo, landing beside him.

The pair had been kiting on updrafts from the lava ridge, to keep eyes on the outraged villagers.

Fog began to clear from the obsidian face. "I'm starting to have a bad feeling about this," Zamora said.

"Don't be a wimp," Pensamiento said. "Go for it."

Zamora picked it up.

"Monkey curiosity," sniffed Recuerdo.

"Hasn't killed me yet," Zamora said.

"Yet."

The obsidian lump was just bigger than his hand. It now felt only modestly warm, though it still vibrated. The rounded part he held it by was almost smooth, with a slight knobbly texture. After the fashion of the other obsidian chunks of Zamora's experience, that hadn't vibrated, got hot, or given off . . . smoke.

"You have got to be shitting me," he said, staring at his own reflection in the black volcanic glass.

"I get that a lot," said Nightwind's face, replacing his, as if the mirrored face was a tiny TV screen.

Zamora recoiled. "Cool beans!" squawked Pensamiento.

"Nocheviento," Zamora said. "I thought that was a bogus-sounding name."

"I admit that I was a bit surprised you didn't twig right away that was a kenning for Tezcatlipoca," said the face in the smoking mirror. "But you'd had a tough day."

"You mean I finally have direct interaction with an actual supernatural entity," he said, "and I don't even find out about it until after? In a phone call?"

He surprised himself how cool he sounded. Tezcatlipoca—Smoking Mirror—had been one of the chief Aztec deities. And one of the bloodiest. A god of sorcery, as well as war. Although lots of the Aztec gods were war gods, most notably his brother and rival, Huitzilopochtli.

The trader laughed. "What kind of god would I be if I couldn't outsmart a mortal? And don't call it a phone, Seeker. Technology's over. It's magic."

"I don't believe in magic."

"While you're talking to a god? Okay. But how do you account for the fact that one day—one minute—technology stopped working? Poof— no more gunpowder, electricity, cars. Even steam engines. But the sun still burns, and lightning still strikes."

"I don't account for it. Yet. I'm looking for the physics behind it."

"You think physics still works? Even as a concept?"

"'Course it does. The rules have changed, that's all. And if there is 'magic'—well, that's just a different kind of physics. One we don't know the rules of yet."

"Circular arguments are the best arguments," Tezcatlipoca said. "Because they're impossible to answer. Still, it may be that what you say isn't that far from the truth. Or maybe I'm trying to tantalize you, keep you in the game, draw you deeper?"

"I'm thinking"—Zamora drew a deep breath—"both. So what now?"

"You're on the right track," Tezcatlipoca said. "You keep on the way you have been, you'll find the key to your friend's death."

"That's it? You called to offer encouragement?"

"It's better than not getting any. You are getting close to your goals. You have the word of a god on that. Doesn't that make you feel better?"

"From the god of deception? No. But I do want to know what the fuck is going on. *Mi amigo* Brodie was a lot of things, and a 'good' man in the way most people meant was seldom one of them. He was all kinds of fucked up, even when we were kids growing up in Albuquerque. He used his slick talk to cover my ass when I was small. Then when I started to get my growth, I used my size and strength to cover his.

"He was a con man, a *ladrón*. But never violent. And he'd never ever get mixed up with anything involving hurting children. He loved kids."

He was eyeing the sky as he spoke, lying on his back in the little pool of sun-warmed sand between the rocks. The day was fleeing. Its departure should make it a bit easier for him to make clean his escape from the vengeful townsfolk.

He remembered that night was Tezcatlipoca's special domain. He doubted, somehow, that was actually going to turn out to be any use for him.

"And he was my bro. So what's your stake in this? And why me?"

"I told you. I need a hero."

Zamora chuckled. "And I'm the best you could find at short notice."

"Bingo."

"But why? You're the god, man."

"Well, don't gods traditionally act through heroes? Or proxies, anyway? And there are severe limits to what I can do in your plane. It stretches my resources just to talk to you, and as you might imagine, I have a special affinity for the object I'm using to communicate."

With a racket of wings Pensamiento took off from the black rock he'd been perched interestedly on. "Uh-oh, boss. Trouble!"

"What kind of trouble?"

"Angry peasant trouble," Recuerdo said.

"Fuck," Zamora said. Then to the smoking mirror, "Gotta go."

Before Tezcatlipoca—fucking Tezcatlipoca!—could say anything more he stuck the rock back in his pocket, rolled over, and wiggled through the sand so he could peep out and down the slope he'd come up.

"They got a dog to track you," Pensamiento said before Zamora could start digging his binoculars out of his light pack. "Looks like he got a lot of Shar Pei in him. Got a face like an old *vago's* ass, all saggy and wrinkly."

Zamora thought about asking how the hell a crow knew what a Shar Pei was. Or what a bum's ass looked like, for fuck's sake. He decided that, even as a Seeker after truth, he didn't really want to know.

He himself couldn't make out near that much detail through the gloom that had gathered at the base of the frozen flow. His eyes weren't what they'd been. But he could see the dog raising his big head and gazing up the slope vaguely in what he took for confusion.

"He can't follow us, anyway," Zamora said in satisfaction. "Slope's too rocky for him to haul his big ass up."

A couple of women trotted up to where the big black dog stood. They reached back for the baby carriers slung over their shoulders, then stooped down to release what they'd been carrying in them.

"Fuck! Chihuahuas!" Pensamiento yelped. "I hate those yappy little bastards!"

The little big-eared dogs came racing up the hill, weaving easily among the man-sized stones, or springing like little hyperkinetic cats to the top of them, barking furiously if shrilly the while.

Zamora sat up and clapped his hat on his head. "*¡Vámonos!*" he said. "Let's blow this joint."

"Have you seen this man?"

The townsman squinted from the tablet up at Zamora's face. He had a stonemason's blocky build and big, callused hands. Though he stood a head shorter than the Seeker, he could do some serious hurt if he teed off on him, Zamora reckoned.

Also this was a bigger, meaning more prosperous, settlement than the one he'd managed to turn into a lynch mob raving to see the color of his insides. The road here was broad and in good repair, as it wound its way among low, grassy hills and the houses scattered over them. Some of which were pre-Change cement or cinderblock. Like the one he'd braced the laborer by, obviously an old Pemex gas station, though what scavenging might have left of the pumps and any sort of signage, a couple of decades of weather eradicated. Now only memory remained to suggest what the structure with the formerly wide windows largely filled in by adobe blocks, and the mother outside teaching her preteen daughter to grind corn on a metate, had once been.

"Why do you want to know?" the mason asked suspiciously.

Judging from the white dust on the front of his leather apron, and that flew from his hands when he dusted them together, he worked in limestone.

"I'm a bounty hunter," Zamora said in his best guttural growl. Which given his breadth of chest and normal voice, was mighty good indeed. "He's a child stealer. Got a good price on his head."

He had wised up some since his last debacle. Started thinking with the head that held up his hat, instead of the other one. Though that one hadn't been getting much of a workout lately, either, if you lay aside the incident with the rattlesnake-priestess in the cantina. And Zamora was inclined to let Señor Feliz off the hook for that one, since magic had no-shit been involved.

"Yeah, we know him. Took away two of Widow Susana's *niñas*, and Old Lady Martinez's grandson Rico, whom she took care of after Feder-ales killed his parents. Not a one of 'em over nine years old."

Zamora's gut clenched as if in preparation to take a blow. *What was Brodie doing mixed up in scaly shit like this?* he wondered for closer to the thousandth time than the hundredth. Why would he even be dealing with bloodthirsty freaks like Huitzilopochtli cultists and a Coatlicue priestess at all, much less for something like stealing kids? He wouldn't even run a scam on somebody if it might make a child go hungry . . .

The key to finding the truth, as Tezcatlipoca said, was to track down the kids Brodie had, apparently, helped snatch. If any of them were even still alive . . .

"How do you know it was him?" he asked.

It may not have been strictly in character for a bounty hunter—who, logically, wouldn't care about such niceties, so long as he got paid for the head. But he really wanted to know.

Maybe he was hoping it would all turn out to be a mistake after all.

"He told us he was looking for a few orphan kids to take to an *instituto* where they'd be raised up right," the workman said. "They'd get edu-cated, even fed better. Even though Susana's kids aren't really orphans, she don't have much family left to help her raise four of 'em, after Hum-berto got eaten by wild hogs and all. They liked the gringo's line about how much better life would be at this fancy school. Got pretty excited. They were her youngest, Ramona and Isabel."

"Did he say what kind of *escuela* this was?"

"Naw. Just that it was good. And run by priests."

Zamora grunted.

I bet it was, he thought. *Just maybe not the sort the people here thought.* Catholicism had never been far from the main vein of Mexican life. But it had become a more powerful influence than ever, after the Change.

"They vanished in the night. The gringo paid good steel washers for a bed at the inn, but come the morning, he and the kids were gone."

"Did you go after them?"

The mason shook his head. "Not far," he said. "They got a good head start. And we're a poor village. We all got to work sunup to sundown to pay our taxes, or Barón Alonzo sends men with crossbows and armor to make an example or two. To encourage the survivors to work harder."

"Looks like the gringo everybody's talking about," the trader said, nodding. "Weedy little bug-eyed motherfucker. Bad teeth."

The lead caravanner was a woman whose face had been sunburned into a mass of leathery wrinkles despite the straw hat she wore—Panama style, rather than the currently more-common Asian variety—over a gaudy red-orange-blue floral bandanna wrapped around her head. She had a stub of Cubano cigar sticking out a corner of her mouth as she looked up at Zamora.

"Everybody says he's one bad dude," she said, and laughed. "Wouldn't think it to look at him. Like a puff of wind would blow him away."

"Stealing children," a black drover said. "Don't need to be strong for that."

The half-dozen traders led three times that many burros, each with big, sloshing clay jugs hung on framework carriers strapped to their backs. The jugs, they told him, contained tequila from the blue earth country. Zamora wanted to ask about how they did business: did they mean to trade for the nails and needles *norteños* stamped and filed out of scrap metal? Fine swords from New Wazoo? Did they follow the common practice of buying carriage-beasts at the same place where they bought their goods, and then selling off the creatures as their loads were delivered and became surplus?

Because that was what he did, ask questions. About anything and everything.

But today he was Seeking other information.

"Any idea where he's taking them?" he asked.

The traders seemed glad enough to break and chat, as folk usually did hereabouts. Even in the old days Mexico had moved to its own pace. Zamora had been raised enough of a *norteamericano* still to feel pangs of impatience with their deeply ingrained cultural lack of urgency, sometimes.

The exception was a silent indio—Zamora sized him up for a Rarámuri, or Tarahumara—who never stopped scanning the surrounding hills, and especially their back trail.

Traders carried lever-action repeating crossbows, with relatively light springs, and wore crossed bandoleers of quarrels.

The Rarámuri, though, carried a full-on sniper model, with a heavy bow cut from car springs and a pre-Change four-power scope. All sported a variety of cutlery, most prominently machetes and steel-headed hatchets.

They were bandit-wary he reckoned, naturally enough. But they were also probably watchful for predatory local barons, whether or not nominally associated with the Federated Kingdom. The fact was, Cuauhtémoc II couldn't even claim to control more than a day's travel from his own capital. But that didn't stop him and his vassals from sending patrols far and wide to loot in the name of tariff and taxation.

Zamora expected scorn in reply to his question, though he had to ask. The easy answer was, If anybody knew, they'd go get their kids back. And burro-drivers had a reputation for especially caustic speech and manners at the best of times.

But to his surprise the woman nodded.

"People say they go off toward there," she said, taking the stogie from her mouth to hold it between the first two fingers of the hand she pointed southwest with. He saw a plume of gray smoke rising into the cloudless afternoon sky.

"Why don't people go after them?" he asked in surprise.

"Locals are afraid to go there," said another trader, with long, drooping moustaches, a none-too-sanitary looking eye patch, and a nasal Veracruzano accent.

"Because they think the smoking mountain is an evil spirit?" Zamora asked.

The traders all laughed. Even the indio grunted amusement.

"No, ¡norteño estúpido!" the lead trader said. "That's just a volcano, like a hundred others in Mexico. They fear the evil spirit who lives there. They say it kills men and eats children."

Zamora nodded. Inside him exultation warred with a deep sense of, *Oh, fuck me.*

"Thanks," he said.

"You're not going there," the black guy said.

Zamora shrugged. "Dude's got a good price on his head."

The traders looked impressed at his balls. Or something.

"Lucky for you," the chief trader said, "you're too ugly even for a *demonio* to eat."

Zamora rubbed his chin. "We'll see about that," he said.

"Yeah," Zamora grunted softly. "Fuck me was right."

The good news was he'd found the place where Brodie—or, more likely, Brodie's customers—had brought the stolen children.

The bad news was—well, that.

"So this thing does work both ways," he said to the face that resolved out of the mist on the obsidian mirror.

"It wouldn't be much use to me, otherwise," Tezcatlipoca said. "Though like any god, I reserve the right to ignore prayers and other calls upon my divine attention if I damned well feel like it."

"But you picked up this time."

"Of course. What have you got for me, Buscador?"

"Found the camp. It's near an active volcano—vent, anyway. Sends up clouds of ash and makes a nasty sulfur stink. Haven't seen sign it's been doing much else lately, but all the rocks are old lava and igneous shit."

"And the camp?"

He lifted his head over the jagged boulder he'd found shelter behind, on a handy lava-flow ridge, and peered through his binoculars. At least the laws of optics hadn't gone *chingado* with everything else.

"They got the kids, two dozen or so, in a wooden pen built against a big old rock. It just has a crappy ramada, with latillas and brush for shade, a few water jugs, and that's pretty much it."

"And the cultists?"

"That's the problem, now. They got a bunch of adobe-hut barracks. Some of 'em look to've been here a while; dunno if they took them over, or have just been here that long themselves. I see maybe a dozen hefty dudes with those obsidian-edged sword-club things, and various Eagle Society regalia."

Whether formally trained or just combat-seasoned, the way the Eagle Knights carried themselves told Zamora they were pretty serious bad-asses. As a largely self-taught pretty serious badass himself, Zamora knew the signs.

"Macuahuitl," Tezcatlipoca said.

"Gesundheit."

"The swords. That's what they're called."

"I knew that."

"Go on."

"They also got some women I make for Rattlesnake Mother priest-esses. At least six or seven. They all have the ugly stone medallions. Plus there's a shitload of random cultist dudes. I've seen at least thirty-forty, and got no clue how many others may be inside. They got housing for twice that many, if everybody's real friendly-like."

The cultists were not by and large a prepossessing bunch. To Zamo-ra's surprise most of them looked to be middle-aged—men who could remember what the world had been like before the Change. Some of them looked to be almost as old as he was, if not near as old as he felt right now.

But to be doing something as bad as mass child sacrifice, they had to be stone fanatics. That and sheer numbers made them dangerous. Plus the Knights probably acted as cadre, training and leading them.

"Excellent," Tezcatlipoca said. "You've found what we both were seeking. Now you can disrupt the rites, and avenge your friend."

"Not so fast," Zamora said. "There's way too many of them for me to take on by myself."

"Ah, but you have no choice."

"Sure I do. And I choose 'hasta la vista, baby.'"

"You misunderstand. The sacrifice is due to happen tonight. As soon as the sun dies—or goes down, as you moderns would put it—the children's lives will be offered to Coatlicue."

"And I feel terrible about that. But I told you: I got no chance. They're way too active, and there's way too little cover, for me to sneak in. And much as I hate the idea of them murdering those poor kids, it's not gonna help them one little bit if I die trying to rescue them. Which is what'll happen."

"And what of Brodie?"

"Órale. I reckon revenge isn't just a dish best served cold, but in individual helpings. Over time. And unless I get to come back as history's most kick-ass ghost, I won't be doing any avenging after I'm fucking dead. So, sorry. But the deal's off. Not that we even had a deal."

"As I say, you misunderstand me. The Rattlesnake Mother wants—needs—this sacrifice to let her enter more fully into this world. And act in it."

"Why do I have a bad feeling about that?"

"Because sacrificing the stolen children will be like opening a door. Once Coatlicue comes through, she's going to need a whole lot more sacrifices to keep her here. And she's pissed. She was never that sweetly reasonable to begin with, I assure you."

"And that would be a bad thing?"

"The worst," Tezcatlipoca said. "That's when the real *matanza* begins. You dig?"

Zamora sighed. "I dig."

"But I will sweeten the pot for you, Seeker. If—when—you stop the ceremony from happening—"

"And free the kids."

"—that, too. Then you will learn why and how your friend was really tied up with this scheme."

"If I survive."

"That, too."

"Bastard."

"Tezcatlipoca." The god chuckled. "You know what you must do, my friend. Unless you want the world—and your own life—to end in blood and fire and screaming and all that Lovecraft jazz. So I'll leave you to it."

"Yeah," Zamora said glumly.

He looked up at the sky. The sun was close to the mountains, which were themselves much closer than they had been when he started this latest crazy quest of his.

"My dad's people always told me my curiosity would be the death of me," he said. "Well, I got a couple hours to kill . . ."

The altar stone was uncomfortably hot on Zamora's naked back and ass. But surprisingly smooth. The woven-yucca ropes were uncomfortably tight on his wrists and ankles, though.

Okay, he told himself, looking at the sun.

Which was big and red as a ripe tomato, and just about to burst like one on the peaks of the Sierra Madre Occidental.

I did plan on causing a diversion. Except this sure as fuck isn't what I had in mind.

The second part of his plan—freeing the kids and escaping in the ensuing confusion, hopefully into quickly gathering darkness—seemed to have run right off, and be receding farther and farther from view.

He heard chanting from many voices, male and female. The language might have been Nahuatl, or another of Mexico's myriad native tongues. Or it may be just some made-up bullshit.

He sensed, somehow, it didn't really matter. So long as they believed.

Even less encouragingly, he smelled tangy mesquite charcoal smoldering in a brazier not far away. Aztec gods, he remembered, liked their hearts grilled. They got nourishment by huffing barbecue fumes like glue.

He rolled his head back farther. Two figures stood a few meters away, silhouetted by the sun they were both looking at and discussing in muted but professional-sounding voices. The male wore a cotton loincloth elaborately embroidered in gold and red. The female wore a skirt of rattlesnakes. Live fucking rattlesnakes. All writhing slowly.

Both appeared to be nude beneath. In the case of the man that was flat unfortunate, in Zamora's eyes. The female, though as middle-aged as her companion and likewise on the . . . compressed side, had kind of a nice ass, though, he had to admit.

They turned back to him. Both of them wore elaborate headdresses that looked as if they had been designed by Carmen Miranda's hatmaker on a bad acid trip, with feathers and shiny bits of metal and rock in place of fruit. The man's had an eagle beak, the woman's a stylized rattlesnake head.

They were naked from the waist up except for bulky stone medallions. Hanging over the dude's hard biker paunch was a standard image of Huitzilopochtli, showing the War God in a beaked and plumed helmet, carrying a shield and a curved macuahuitl. Like his boss, the Eagle Knight had an obsidian-bladed sword and a shield slung by either hip.

An idol sporting a wide rattlesnake head with doubled sets of fangs, four hands, beast feet, and, of course, a skirt made of rattlesnakes nestled between the priestess' sagging breasts. Her face and her companion's were painted with what looked, given the light and the nearly setting sun dazzle forming halos about them, like simple broad swatches of color.

"So," Zamora said. "You gonna do me with rattlesnakes, the way you did my pal, Brodie?"

She smiled. "Oh, no. We prefer to reserve that means of sacrifice for the innocent."

Zamora laughed. It wasn't even faked, to cover the rapid spinning of his mind as it sought a way out of this mess.

"Brodie was a lot of things, sister," he said, "but 'innocent' wasn't one of them."

She laughed. She had a surprisingly nice laugh. She looked like a handsome, unusually well-preserved peasant woman of mature years. But people like that didn't always have the best kind of life even before things Changed. So he could at least see why she might enjoy a power trip like this.

He could also see, with some sense other than his eyes, that she had no real idea of the nature of the Power she was fucking with.

Well, I was Seeking for reasons why the world turned out this way, he thought. *And at least now I'm getting some pretty strong hints. If only it looked like I was gonna have more of a chance to integrate them . . .*

"He was, you know," the priestess said. "Innocent. At least, he was remarkably credulous, for a man of his . . . background. He so eagerly embraced what we told him, about a mythical orphanage where children could be raised right and taught the means to a better life. And his abilities served us very well, until he began asking the wrong sorts of questions."

"He always did say it was easiest to scam a scammer," Zamora said ruefully.

"He just didn't like the answers he was getting," the priest grunted.

He looked as if he might once have been among the goofy dentists and accountants who'd fancied themselves as restoring the proud heritage of the Meshika people, whom Zamora had run into when he visited the Federal District—Mexico City—as a boy. Just another silly-ass reenactor.

But now he bore the badges of an Eagle Knight, including the tattoos. His fat was hard, and his biceps were big. Whatever he had been, he was no soft upper-middle-class poser now.

And after all, reenactors had inherited the Earth.

The Knight waved what he was holding in his right hand at the pen. With a heart that managed to sink farther from its present position, Zamora saw younger rattlesnake-priestesses already dragging out the first quartet of children, while Eagle Warriors poked the rest back into place with long poles. The big, brave bastards.

"We told him the truth: they are being groomed to serve, in a far finer way than grubbing in the dirt. They are to become food of the Goddess!"

He was using one of Zamora's own pet bowie knives as a pointer.

"That's right," the priestess said. "We shall sacrifice the innocent to Our Rattlesnake Mother, in the purest way: using Her children!"

As if on cue, the dozen or two snakes tied by the tails around her waist stirred and stuck out their tongues. They seemed to be moving in slow-motion, as if under the influence of drugs. Or—something else. And not just that the sun was going down and their exotherm batteries were running low.

"You, however," she continued, "are called a mighty warrior, Seeker."

Sure, he thought glumly. *Because I gave right up when your people started popping up from the brush all around me pointing crossbows at me?*

Not that he'd had a whole bunch of choice. He hadn't even had a knife drawn while sneaking down toward their camp in the slanting, buttery light of late afternoon. And they had a lot of crossbows. It wasn't like with the one dude back at the cantina. He'd have been lucky to nail one before they quilled him like a porcupine.

It wasn't as if his Pensamiento and Recuerdo, had been much help. They'd been preoccupied by the Mexican eagle, the snake-eating one from the flag—and the old Aztec legend—circling overhead. Really a big type of falcon, the caracara preyed on crows, when it couldn't get anything better. More often, it bullied them off carcasses they were scavenging.

Turned out that while the crows were being Zamora's eyes in the sky, the fucking caracara had been doing the same for the cultists. As the crows themselves called to Zamora in passing, as they fled the suddenly stooping raptor, and every bush sprouted an Eagle Warrior or a cultist with a cocked arbalest.

Now the caracara sat, appropriately, on a prickly pear not thirty paces away, eating what looked like a baby green rattlesnake. Maybe it hadn't been up to Coatlicue's standards . . .

"As such, you shall be given as thanks to our Mother's son Huitzilopochtli," the priestess said, "in thanks for his assistance to his Mother, at the moment the sun goes down."

Which'll be any minute now, thought Zamora. *Much as I hate to think this—Tezcatlipoca, if ever there was a time for a little divine intervention—*

"Only using your own blade," the Eagle Warrior said, "rather than the customary obsidian one."

He turned the weapon over in his hand.

"Nice knife. Not as sharp as volcanic glass, but keen enough. Less likely to turn in my hand and cut me like a *pinche güey cabrón,* too."

"And in case you were hoping your jaguar-loving friend would help you—" the priestess said with a knowing smile. She held up the Smoking Mirror. A wisp of vapor coiled from its flat surface, stained as if with blood by the dropping sun.

"Do you hear me, Tezcatlipoca? Night and Wind, Lord of the Near and the Nigh? Or are you in your Aspect of Tepeyollotl, and can't answer because you're skulking around on little cat feet?"

She tensed, then hunched in interest over the stone. Her compatriot joined her, jostling bare shoulder to shoulder in his eagerness to see too.

With a rustle a black shape landed by Zamora's left wrist. Another lit by his right.

Zamora kept his face turned resolutely upward, to a mauve sky already turning indigo in the east, lest the slightest hint of motion—or twist of his attention—betray the birds. But from the corner of his right eye he saw Recuerdo whip him a quick wink as the brothers began pecking the woven yucca fibers that bound his wrists to the sun-heated granite.

For some reason none of the other assembled cultists spotted the birds. Even in the twilight, that was strange. But Zamora figured they were all engrossed either watching the two senior sectaries trying to get a rival god on the phone, or watching the reluctant captives being led to four priestesses who waited with rattlesnakes semiquiescent in their hands.

Or maybe they were just eyeing the snake priestesses' bouncing bare titties. Some of them were young and not bad looking.

The High Priestess yipped. She threw the stone/Mirror to the sand by her feet. Smoke seemed to fairly billow from it now.

"¡Mierda!" she exclaimed. "The *puta* got hot as a coal!"

As one she and the Eagle Knight looked back at the altar. The priestess screeched in fury at seeing the crows working on Zamora's bonds.

"Get them!" she cried.

The caracara snapped its head toward the altar. Zamora looked at him.

Even in twilight, even though the bird's eyes were already dark to the point of near blackness, he saw them go blacker. As if they'd suddenly turned into obsidian themselves. Or portholes into Void.

With a booming of wings it launched itself from the cactus. Recuerdo immediately took off and flew away at an angle.

"I'll draw the bastard off!" he cried.

Pensamiento continued stabbing at the rope around Zamora's right wrist with his beak. "Go on," Zamora grunted at him. "Get out of here. It was a nice try, but—"

For just a moment, the raptor dithered, five meters off the ground, treading air with its wings like its much smaller cousin the kestrel. Then it arrowed in possessed fury for Pensamiento. With a squawk of terror the crow fled.

But the bigger-winged caracara was faster and had a head start. He caught the crow with an audible thump of his claws thirty meters beyond the camp's bare-beaten earth. Pensamiento gave a despairing cry and fell into the bunchgrass.

Its wings never missing a beat, the eagle continued in pursuit of Recuerdo. They vanished in the gloom.

"Hurry!" the High Priestess hissed to the Knight. "The sun, he dies!"

Belly jiggling, the man scuttled toward Zamora on his skinny bowed legs. He held the bowie poised over his right shoulder, point downward.

As he loomed over Zamora the knife came down. Hard and fast.

With a grunt of effort Zamora snapped his left wrist free. Too late to try to stay his knife on its traitor course.

Instead he shot his freed-up hand under the Eagle Knight's loincloth, grabbed him by the balls, and squeezed for all his mighty grip was worth.

The Eagle Knight howled like a gut-shot wolf.

With a thunk! clearly audible over the scream the bowie planted itself four fingers deep in the cultist's thigh.

Violent femoral-artery spray painted Zamora's arm instantly red. Hot drops stung his face. He let go the man's well-violated parts. Batting now nerveless fingers from the hilt, he grabbed his bowie and wrenched it out of the Warrior's leg. With a swipe that flung blood in a darkly glistening arc into the black velvet painting sky, he slashed through the rope that held his right arm to the altar. He nicked his own skin in the process— painful and unhygienic, but also the least of his worries.

Slightly higher on the list was the fact that he was butt naked. But he had to play the hand he'd been dealt. Even if a couple of jokers had turned up at an opportune moment to help him, the other side had plenty of high cards left to draw.

The priest was doubled over, shrieking and clutching at his blood-hosing leg. Sitting up fast, Zamora gave him an overhand right to the side of his head. He sat down. As he did Zamora yanked the macuahuitl from his belt with his right hand.

With icy deliberation the High Priestess walked toward him. She held a huge rattlesnake in her hand, fully roused, jaws opened almost flat, fangs protruding for Zamora's face like curved spears. He had no time to defend himself with steel or obsidian, and was off balance to do so.

Her eyes had turned dead black. "I . . . See . . . you," she said.

"Yeah? Well I raise you!"

And he kicked her hard and straight in the crotch.

That blow wasn't quite as virulent to a woman as a man. But from experience Zamora knew it could still take one out. But that wasn't the purpose.

It wasn't really a crotch shot. It was a snake shot.

It succeeded beyond Zamora's wildest expectations. The whole skirt full of rattlers seemed to wake up at once. And they woke up *pissed*. The High Priestess stopped in midstride and screamed as they buried fangs in her bare flesh.

The snake she was holding twisted around and bit her in the cheek.

She reeled back as the megadose of hemolytic toxins started popping her blood cells like bubble wrap in her veins. They turned into a black network, spreading rapidly beneath her skin. Neurotoxins started her convulsing.

Zamora rolled the other way. He didn't want to be near a passel of enraged rattlesnakes. As he did he felt something brush air across his bare back. His ears picked up the hum of a crossbow quarrel turning to the angle of its vanes as it whipped by.

Fresh screams broke out all around him like fires set in dry grass by a shower of sparks. Apparently the other sacrificial snakes had all snapped out of whatever spell held them docile to the priestesses' will. And they were expressing their ire in the only way they had, to the agonized dismay of the Rattlesnake Mother's servants.

But other, burlier figures were converging on Zamora fast from all directions: male cultists, led by several Eagle Warriors armed with spears and macuahuitl.

Zamora decided his best bet was to take the offensive. He put his head down and charged straight at the nearest knot of attackers.

An Eagle Knight shorter than he but wider across chest and shoulders swung a club edged with razor-sharp rock at him.

He guided it by with the flat of his own stolen macuahuitl. A couple of decades' experience fighting with big knives had taught him that movie sword-fighting was a load of horseshit. At least where it came to parrying with your edge. You never, never did that, unless you wanted to wind up smart quick holding a dull club. Or an even more useless stub.

As he dashed past the Knight he hit him with a powerful backhand. And found out something surprising about the macuahuitl: while the volcanic-glass flakes set into it were indeed sharper than the finest steel, their square edges acted like saw teeth. His stroke didn't just send a dozen teeth flying, but ripped half the skin off the man's lower face.

Which gave him something to do other than press the attack on Zamora, such as falling down while trying to scream and not choke to death on teeth and blood.

Zamora kept running. He had no clear destination. Just away from the point on which several score angry enemies were converging. A cultist appeared in front of him, jabbing with a spear. Zamora jinked as far to the right as he could. The spear tip gashed his left hip just below the bone. He slashed the man across both forearms in passing.

Another Eagle Knight came in from the right. Zamora blocked his horizontal macuahuitl swipe with the bowie in his left hand. The tip of his own macuahuitl was flat and wide; its wooden "blade" narrowed straight to the grip on both edges. It still worked for poking his opponent hard in the Adam's apple and dropping him choking to his knees.

A Knight loomed in front of him. He blocked a cut from Zamora's sword-club with a clack of his wooden shield. Worse, he forced Zamora to slow down.

Strong arms gripped Zamora from behind. He thought for a heartbeat he was lucky it hadn't been a spear through his kidneys. Then he realized his enemies were still trying to capture him alive to sacrifice him. Just the way their ancestors—or anyway the people they were imitating—had.

The dude was going for a full nelson hold. But he wasn't good enough or quick enough—quite. Zamora jackknifed forward with all the power of his ample core. He flung the attacker right over his head. And literally into the surprised, painted face of the Eagle Knight with the shield.

But that well and truly fucked Zamora's forward momentum. His foes were all around him, a wall of sweaty, grunting, grimacing meat.

And then it was all wild twisting: hacking, stabbing, slashing, with steel and laboriously flaked black stone; elbows and knees and punches and head-butts. Blades gashed Zamora in a dozen places, so that his blood—and others'—covered him like a net, diffusing quickly into a slippery coat. No wounds large enough to be serious, yet. He would weaken in time. But time wasn't something he was worried about.

Even though the cultists had put themselves in the classic mob dilemma of getting in one anothers' way a lot more than they were stomping their would-be victim, it was only a matter of hammering heartbeats before they beat Zamora down. Even though he tagged at least a dozen of them, and dropped five or six more dead or hurt bad enough that it made no never mind, given the antibiotic-lacking standards of today's medicine.

Most mobs, it would've been more than enough to send them all packing off in search of easier prey. But this one had fanatic zeal driving them on. Backed by a head of plain old vengeful anger.

A blow from a club or macuahuitl-side on the temple sent sparks shooting through his skull. His vision got even darker than the sun's fall behind the mountains would have made it. His stomach sloshed like a stormy sea and his knees got weak. He continued to swing his arms feebly, tried to keep moving. Moving at all costs—to stop was to die—

Something big and dark flapped overhead. It came close enough to make the dark blurs of faces surrounding him turn upward. His vision began settling back into focus as he looked too.

In time to see the caracara fly by, low and fast. Whatever evil spirit had gotten into it was gone—Zamora could feel it. Now it winged in clear terror beyond the cultist summer camp and around the brush-dotted hip of the smoking mountain.

And behind him came Recuerdo, at the head of a vast flock of crows, a few burly Chihuahua ravens, and a mess of various kinds of jays, all squalling in joyous rage. Corvids hated birds of prey like poison. And a fraction of that number could fatally mob a much larger bird than the caracara.

"Get 'em, boys!" Recuerdo cried.

While a dozen or so of the crows and cousins kept pursuing the cara-cara, the others suddenly descended. Onto the upturned faces of the cultists and Eagle Knights. They clutched with cruel claws, jabbed with their beaks, and battered with their powerful wings.

They provided, needless to say, a powerful distraction.

Using which, Zamora dropped to hands and knees and, still clutching his weapons, still clad only in a coat of blood rapidly drying to stickiness and salty itching, crawled out of the midst of the yelling, flailing mob.

As soon as he was clear he stood up fast. Somebody blundered into his right side. He turned and lashed out by reflex, laying open the bare back of a male Coatlicue cultist who was trying to punch it out with a pair of punk-Mohawked Steller's jays. The man screamed and fell down. The birds flew off in search of more victims.

Most of the cultists seemed to be struggling with their feathered as-sailants. At first by blind impulse, Zamora headed toward the cage where the children were kept. Then by iron purpose.

A pair of the less-prepossessing cultists, one fat, one skinny, el gordo y el flaco, each a head shorter than he, tried to bar Zamora's way with spears. He knocked the weapons aside with his bowie and hacked them both down. With the macuahuitl, without remorse.

A trio of topless Coatlicue priestesses barred his way with machetes and a regular woodsman's ax. Fortunately for them, only the High Priest-ess got to wear the full snaky skirt. And apparently they hadn't been snake-handling when the subdual spell was broken.

"Scoot," he told them. "Get outta here."

But they stood their ground before the rush of the burly, angry man who'd been their impending sacrificial victim until moments before. He had to give them credit for their courage. Or their crazy.

The middle one, a tall, lean, light-skinned woman, uttered a piercing scream and began swinging at him in figure-eights with her machete. He only just managed to avoid getting gutted like a trout by stopping flat and sucking his big belly back away from the blade.

She still might've got him had she advanced. Instead she stood where she was, screeching and slashing air, until he timed her and decapitated her with a single backhand stroke.

As her head, elaborate headdress and fierce expression both firmly in place, fell away to be displaced by a pulsing jet of blood, her associates threw down their weapons and scattered into the twilight.

He ran to the pen. Small, frightened faces stared at him through the peeled-sapling bars. "Better stand back, kids," he said gruffly.

Then he realized that was a pretty silly thing to say. They were all pressed as far back toward the granite outcrop that formed the enclosure's rear wall as they could fit, staying back away from the naked, bloody, crazy dude who had just hacked a lady to death in front of them. Even if it was a lady who was about to kill them.

The enclosure was fastened with an old-fashioned padlock. He hacked it partway free of the wood, breaking his macuahuitl in the process. Dropping the weapon, he started pulling on the door with both hands, even the one that still held his own knife.

A couple of small shapes appeared beside him, to help tug on the bars. He looked down to see two of the first four kids who'd been led out to sacrifice. The other two squatted nearby, too small to help and smart enough to notice.

In a moment they—okay, mostly he—got the pen open.

"Okay," he declared. "We gotta get going. The birds won't keep those *cabrones* busy for long."

They stared at him. He looked down at himself.

"Don't mind me," he said. "I'm the good guy."

He got them all out of the pen. The ones who'd survived to this point, anyway: twenty-odd kids from just barely walking to just-shy-of-marriageable. Which, granted, wasn't all that much older these days. It hit him hard to reflect that the reason they all were fit to flee was that only the near perfect had been kept alive for sacrifice to power Coatli-cue's return. But he still thanked the Virgin that they were.

They hadn't made it more than a couple hundred meters from the camp before he heard the angry sounds of pursuit firing up behind them. And barely half a klick beyond that when he heard the crashing of enemy scouts in the brush off to their left.

They were caught. No way to hide that many fugitives, even small, well-motivated ones, from people who knew the area. Even though it was full dark now, with the light of a million stars offering little more illumination than they did heat.

He held a brief debate with himself. The outcome was never in much doubt. Between not being able to live, and not being able to live with yourself, was no real choice at all.

He shook his head.

"You kids keep going that way," he rumbled, pointing southeast, at an angle to their course but basically away from the pursuer blundering around to the north of them, with one of his bowies.

He'd recovered the second from the corpse of the High Priestess. Who was in shape to make Brodie look ready for an open-casket funeral when he found him. He had also snagged a cultist's cotton shirt that wasn't too bloody, and bound up his loins. Because even with everything else on his mind he just didn't feel right, running around with his business swinging freely right next to a bunch of kids.

"Keep together, help each other, and keep quiet."

"Mister," said one of the bolder ones, an indio-looking boy of maybe nine or ten. "There's lights coming from the east."

Zamora looked. He shook himself like a wet dog.

"All right," he said, "change of plan. You all hide out in the scrub here and keep out of sight. And remember—you never saw me!"

They nodded solemnly.

"When can we come out?" a girl asked.

"You'll know."

And just like that, they vanished as if they'd teleported out of there.

And right about then several dozen cultists, led by a handful of Eagle

Knights, ran headlong into several hundred pissed-off peasants with pitchforks and torches, led by the young local priest. Who was waving an arming-sword, of all the gods-damned things.

"Careful!" squawked Pensamiento from the inner pocket of Zamora's coat, as the man squatted to reach for the Smoking Mirror, beside the horribly contorted and bloated High Priestess. "You'll squash me!"

"Yeah," Zamora told him. "Sure. After I went to all the trouble of setting your broken wing after your *hermano* found you in that bush, I'm gonna forget and fucking sit on you."

Off to the east of the now deserted camp it sounded as if some cultists were still busy dying. That sort of sound carried a long way, especially at night up here on the Chihuahua Plateau.

Zamora didn't hold with torture, even a little. But he figured what was going on was strictly between the local peasants and the fanatics who wanted to murder children to unleash untold horror into the world. None of his business.

"Neat trick with the locals," Tezcatlipoca said, as soon as Zamora turned over the obsidian node. "Why'd you play it that way, though?"

"You mean, why'd I pretend to be the Devil, taunting farmers as they made their way to the local church?"

It was a stroke of luck today was a Sunday, with Mass celebrated twice.

"And why'd I tell 'em my worshippers had their missing *hijos*, and were fixing to feed them to me? Here I thought that was a nice, theatrical choice. With my best growly voice and everything."

"But why not rally them and lead them yourself?" Tezcatlipoca asked. "And given what your normal voice is like, I'm not sure I want to hear your 'growly' one."

"Hey, man. That stings. Anyway, you're a Mexican deity, right? You know how things work around here. If I tried to gather me up an army and bring them back, we'd be setting out about noon Tuesday."

He shrugged. "Guess that's better than it would've been back North in the old days. Anglos'd take twice that long, just to set up a committee to study the issue.

"Anyway, nothing gets these folks riled up like a threat to their children. Or any other folks. And belief in Luzbel is mighty powerful in these parts, which up until a few days ago I would've said was rank superstition. So I figured I'd scare 'em and piss 'em off to the max."

"But why not try the direct approach? You still might have been able to frighten and anger them sufficiently to act at once, persuasive chap that you are."

"And from a standing start, the cultists would eat their lunch. Those Eagle Knight assholes are pretty heavy dudes, and between them and fanaticism, the locals would lose. Also I worried about the bulk of the cultists holding off the rescuers until a few of their buddies could complete the sacrifices. Or just kill the kids out of pure meanness. So I decided to give the anthill an almighty kick, then sneak back in and see what kind of diversion I could cause here."

"You weren't expecting divine assistance, then?"

"Not from you."

"Point taken. So it all went according to plan?"

"So it all went nothing like the *chingado* plan," Zamora said. "Yet here I am. And the kids are safe."

"So they are. And so is my Mother, in the other world. I wonder how she and Buddy are taking it."

"Buddy?"

"Huitzilopochtli. My brother."

"Oh. Not so well, I think. Now: I reckon you owe me, *vato*. You said if I did this you'd tell me what Brodie was doing mixed up in all this evil shit."

"But you know," Tezcatlipoca said. "Don't you?"

Reluctantly, Zamora nodded. "Yeah. The damn weird-ass High Priestess told me, right before her eyes started going all black and shit. The eagle did that too. What was all that about, anyway? Demonic possession?"

"Close enough."

"Anyway, I reckon the Priestess was old enough to have watched too many movies before the Change. The ones where the bad guy explains everything to the captive hero, for some damn reason, instead of just offing him."

He drew a deep breath.

"But that wasn't all you promised."

"You expected some other reward? I thought knowledge was what you were Seeking."

"And it's all I want now. I don't got much need for money. Also, I already tossed the camp and the stiffs. How you think I got my own stuff back? But you promised to tell me just what the hell broke the universe."

"Not the universe, my boy. The sun still burns, doesn't it? The Change is a pocket phenomenon, clearly. So—remember the notion that consciousness was a quantum phenomenon? And that sufficiently intense and particular observation could lead to an ability to resculpt Reality itself?"

"Yeah. But that was all a bunch of bullshit pseudoscience."

Tezcatlipoca chuckled. "Ah, you mortals. You're so amusing in your presumptive arrogance. When you behold a truth that clashes with your prejudices, you have to turn away. For a generation or two. And in this case—"

From his head movement, Zamora could tell he shrugged.

"You didn't have that much time. You see, you mortals—therefore we gods—had a problem."

"Which was?"

"Remember the creatures we protected your ancestors from?"

"The monsters below the horizon? We had to feed you guys hearts and blood because you were all that kept them out—and they were even worse than you?"

"Precisely."

"They fucked up the world?"

"They brought the Change about, let us say."

"Wait. You said, 'we gods.' That implies those Montival crazies are right, and all kinds of gods are real."

"Of course they are."

"¡Hijo de la chingada! The world is even more fucked-up than I thought. So what about human sacrifice? You used to be a big fan of that yourself, back in the day. Are you really any better than Huitzilopochtli and the Rattlesnake Mother?"

"Yes," Tezcatlipoca said. "I don't want to drown the world in blood and fire. I like the world."

"But don't you need blood and souls too?"

"That's Arioch, from the Michael Moorcock stories. He wrote about a character—"

"Elric of Melniboné. Yeah, I know. So, blood, anyway. And the smoke of hearts."

"Our particular type of deity—our *familia*, if you want to call it that— do obtain sustenance from human sacrifice, yes. But all that ended with the conquest of the Spanish, who burnt offerings to different gods."

"So that really is what made you go away?"

"Not exactly," Tezcatlipoca said. "There is another kind of sustenance you mortals can provide."

"Which is?"

"The one thing more powerful than any god. Or rather, the lack of it is: attention."

Zamora laughed. "So when we forgot about you, you went away?"

"Not all the way. Faded into the background, more."

"What brought you back?"

"We were forced to act, by what you might consider pooling our wills. Otherwise, your kind would simply have been destroyed. And the Change—well, human sacrifice is a potent energy source for my kind. The attendant loss of life refueled all of us, willy-nilly."

Zamora was frowning. The gears were turning in his mind. Slowly; he'd had a rough day. But turning.

"So after the Change people started thinking about the old gods again," he said, "since the technology that supplanted them had failed. And that brought you all the way back?"

"As near as may be, yes."

"So—I'm feeding you right now."

"Of course."

Zamora shuddered.

"So why'd you drag me in on this in the first place? You used to have your own Jaguar Knights. Why not use them?"

"You were already in it up to your shaggy eyebrows," Tezcatlipoca reminded him. "These days I employ Knights more on a . . . contract basis. What you might call a different enterprise model."

Zamora's eyes went to slits.

"You don't mean—"

"Of course you're serving as a Jaguar Knight. What did you think you were doing?"

"Acting on my own damn hook."

"You can show surprising naïveté, for one so crusty, Buscador."

"Don't you have to go through all kinds of training and rituals and stuff first?"

"I waived all that. I am Tezcatlipoca, after all. And you are a highly useful servant—and so entertaining. Now, are you ready to hear your next assignment?"

"Count me out, ese. Just 'cause I'm forced to believe you exist doesn't mean I gotta worship you."

"Who said anything about worship? I want your strong back and occasionally strong mind, not your good opinion."

"No way."

"But you're the Seeker," Tezcatlipoca said, almost imploringly. "Think of the knowledge I can impart—in dribs and drabs, of course."

"Because my puny mortal mind can't handle the truth."

"That, too. Mostly to keep the game going on. It's so much fun for both of us! So be a good little mortal and serve me."

"Fuck that," Zamora said. He cocked his arm back and threw the Smoking Mirror out of the camp, as far away into the night as he could.

"You think that's gonna do any good?" asked Recuerdo, who was perched on top of his hat.

"Not a chance in Hell. But it makes me feel better."

With a startled squawk, the crow leapt into the air. "Whoa! Did you see that? A jaguar just slipped from behind those rocks right outside of camp! Big bastard. Looks like the one we saw by the cantina where you messed those *pendejos* up big-time."

Zamora heard a sound that might have been a big cat coughing.

Or a god's laughter . . .

Grandpa's Gift

by Terry D. England

TERRY ENGLAND

Terry D. England is a former journalist who's covered topics from types of hay to the development of the atomic bomb. He has also reviewed books and movies and did stints as a copy editor. Recently he edited combat narratives as part of the Afghan Study Team for the U.S. Army. One traditionally published novel, *Rewind,* is available as an e-book, and an e-novel; *The Tyranny of Heroes,* is available from online booksellers. Recent projects include writing a descriptive scenario for a top-down video game.

The huge ax-head made a mean sound as it sliced down. Petra screamed as it hit right next to her left ear. She tried to pull away but her hair was snagged. With a grunt, the wild man yanked the blade free. Petra rolled over, tried to claw her way over the books and boxes. The wild man shouted and raised his ax, glittering eyes fixed on her.

"Bastard!" came a scream as someone hurled in from Petra's left and smashed into the wild man, momentum carrying both over the side railing of the wagon. Petra heard their bodies hit the ground, followed by a shout, then a grunt, then nothing. She scrabbled her way to the railing, peeked over carefully. A slim woman in brown and green yanked a sword out of the wild man, wiped it on the man's dirty tunic and sheathed it. She stepped up on the wagon's wheel, locking eyes with Petra.

"You hurt?"

"No, Momma," Petra said. "He missed."

"But you didn't. I saw."

Petra looked down and saw a blue, rectangular object on the ground not far from the body. "I hit him with that dictionary. Daddy will be angry."

A brief smile formed through the green and brown face paint. Momma leaned over and kissed Petra's forehead. "No, he won't. Now get down and stay alert." She leaped down.

"You too, Momma," Petra called.

"Liam!" Momma's voice cut through the sounds of fighting and yelling. A slimmer, shorter figure wearing a helmet ran to her side. He carried a short, curved blade in his right hand.

"You're supposed to stay in the wagon with your sister—"

"Momma, I—"

She grabbed his shoulder, turned him around. "Look. That bone-cracker nearly gutted your sister. And where were you? Not where you were supposed to be. Now get in that wagon!" She shoved him forward.

Liam stiffened, but then his shoulders slumped. "Yes, Mother."

"And pick that up." She kicked the book, then dashed off.

As he climbed into the wagon, he tossed the book at Petra, but she dodged.

"Always causing trouble!" he said.

"Not this time, stupid!"

He muttered something and stepped up on a stack of boxes behind the driver's bench. He stood with one foot resting on a box, the sword Black-smith Gunnarson helped him forge at the ready. In his helmet and long, plated jacket, he looked like a small version of the Wingate Rangers, the irregular coalition militia hired to provide security for the convoy. She climbed to the front of the wagon, keeping her distance from Liam. The wagon shook as the two oxen in harness stamped and huffed, disturbed at the noise and the smell of blood. Most of the fighting had moved beyond a tangle of bushes. Two other bodies sprawled on the ground.

The wild men who had jumped them hadn't figured on a detail of the Rangers shadowing the convoy.

"Sounds like it's over," Liam eventually said, sheathing his blade. He pulled his helmet off, set it on the seat. He wiped a hand over his long, light hair, but that just made it more tousled. Sweat dripped down his face but he didn't wipe his brow until he'd pulled off his gauntlets and could pull a cloth from a pocket under the coat. From his tone, Petra knew he was angry because once again he'd been shunted off to the side.

The combat master said he had great potential, but he was only four-teen, a fact that irritated Liam. He wanted to be like Momma, a warrior of courage, sharp fighting skills and steely resolve, but her protectiveness of her only son caused him to chafe. Petra could see this in her brother even now, and Momma once said she suspected even the Rangers were going to wonder what hit them when Liam came of age.

A tall man with dark hair tied behind his neck strode rapidly toward the wagon from the direction of the battle. His plated jacket was long and dark brown and he wore a long sword in its scabbard at his side. He climbed into the wagon and looked at his son.

"John and Gary said you jumped into the fray without permission."

"Poppa, I—"

"Leaving your sister vulnerable."

"I wasn't going to let anyone near." The boy stood straight, glaring at his father.

"Then what's that?" Poppa pointed to the wild man's body, the hand-ax lying nearby.

Liam's face and neck turned deep red, but a wave from Father cut him off. "We have no time for this now."

Petra tried to shrink into a small creature, out of sight and mind. She hated being the source of conflict between Liam and Poppa. Eight years old, not a little baby, certainly, but that's how she was treated. Poppa turned to her.

"Momma said you bopped him one."

She picked up the dictionary. "I hit his ugly face with this," she said. "He almost fell off the wagon, but jumped back and tried to hit me with that ax. Mud got on it—"

Father tossed the book onto the pile. "That's all right, it's old, printed well before the Reckoning. Any others?"

"He chopped that one with the green cover."

Poppa climbed over and picked it up, but it nearly fell apart. "My God! It's been nearly sliced through—what . . . Petra, come here!"

He touched her chin and turned her head to the right. She felt his fingers along her left neck and ear. "Didn't cut skin, but look."

He held up the book in one hand, lifted a tangle of dark hair with the other. He turned, held the items up for Liam. "See? That's how close—Liam!"

The boy leaped down and ran off. Father took a deep breath, turned back to Petra. "Did you get a good look at his eyes? Were they just, like, black, no whites?"

"I don't think so, Poppa. I—I couldn't tell—"

He placed a hand on her head. "Never mind, *petite fleur*, it's OK." He began pulling off his gloves. "Almost not worth this trip."

"But we found Grandpa a gift."

Poppa looked at her. "Is it still here?"

Petra clambered back forward, reached under the seat, pulled out a cloth bag. She opened it, pulled out a package wrapped in bright purple paper tied with white string.

"Well, that's a plus, I guess," he said.

One teamster and two Rangers suffered light injuries, but four wild men were dead and the others had fled. As the injured were being tended to, Momma came by the wagon leading two horses.

"Yates is going to be furious," Poppa said as he opened a clear bottle, took a drink of water. "To him, this side trip is a waste of time and effort."

"All books are a waste of time to him," Momma said. "Is he right, Mycroft?"

"I . . . Marian, that old plantation was exactly as described. A half-buried concrete bunker in back, one of the most elaborate I've ever seen. They had moved the whole family's library down there, where it all stayed nice and dry for decades. And this was before the Reckoning hit. And the books, Jesus, honey, some real valuable stuff. The librarians are going to be knocked on their butts. So"—he pointed to the stacks in the wagon—"no, Yates is wrong."

"What about the black books?"

Poppa shook his head. "They're in the other wagon, untouched. I don't think these guys knew about them." He gave Petra a hug, picked up the sliced book, left the wagon and mounted one of the horses.

"What I should've done, though, was send the kids with Yates. I didn't expect cultists this far south."

"Neither did we, but it looks like it was just a small group. Ready, Pettibone?"

"All set, ma'am," said a stocky, barrel-chested man as he climbed into the wagon, setting his sword and club under the seat. "Where do we meet Yates?"

"On Old 90, or if he's already passed, in Welsh on eye-ten," Poppa said. "Petra, stay safe."

"Where's Liam?" She settled at the end of the driver's bench.

"In the other wagon," Momma said. "I will deal with him later."

"All right," Poppa said as he rode away.

"*Allez!*" Pettibone shouted as he flicked the reins. The two oxen huffed their displeasure but they started moving. "I know, I know, my pretty ones, you almost ended up in a bone-cracker pot, but you're all OK now, so let's concentrate on our job, eh?"

Petra could see Liam in the lead wagon. He had to be sweltering in his armored gear; she felt the heat and humidity in just a cotton pullover shirt, denim shorts and leather sandals. Shortly after they got under way, though, Momma rode up leading another horse. Liam leaped out of the wagon, climbed on the horse and both rode into the bushes off the trail.

"He gets to go horseback riding again," she muttered.

"I don't think this is a pleasure ride," Pettibone said.

They reached Old 90 quickly. Yates had left a message at a way station just south of the intersection saying the convoy had gone on to Welsh. Because of the late hour, Poppa called a halt. The two wagons pulled off the road into a fenced area where two families with horse-drawn wagons had already set up camp. Fresh-killed rabbit and steamed vegetables were prepared over a fire. Momma and Liam soon returned, but Liam just stomped by, looking neither right nor left. His eyes were red and face set in anger. Petra gasped when Mother tossed the cut book into the campfire. Petra looked at Poppa.

"What kind of book was it?" she said as the flames began to devour pages.

"Just some old political tract," he said.

But "political tracts" were important, weren't they? And here was one burning in a fire. Because of her. And Liam was in trouble. Because of her.

After dinner, Momma sat Petra on a log and began to untangle, then cut her hair. "We can't have you looking off-kilter."

"And erase Liam's mistake."

The snipping stopped. "Yes." The cutting continued.

"But, Momma, he might've been killed—"

"Doing his duty." Petra looked around at her. "Honey, let's just say he'd been given orders to follow and he didn't. Let it go."

Momma was combing out her now-short hair when Poppa walked up.

"A new 'do,' eh?" He squinted at her, hand on chin. "It's gonna take some getting used to not seeing that tangle on your head."

"It'll grow back," Petra said.

"I have no doubt."

"'Croft, we've got to get these kids to Athena. Please, no more side trips."

"No, no more delays. We join the rest of the convoy tomorrow, then it's a straight shot to Lafayette. Getting to Ezra Hawks' place should be quick 'n easy."

Just the sound of "getting to eye-ten" excited Petra.

"Why? Is just a big ol' road," said Pettibone the next day as the wagon rumbled along.

"Because of the eyes."

"The what?"

"Eye-ten, doesn't that mean there are eyes watching or something?"

"Eyes?" Pettibone whooped. "Yah, that would make it interestin' all right. Whooee!" He laughed again, but worse, Liam joined in.

"Eyeballs all over the road, that'd be a sight all right. Ha, Ha! Squish, squish, squish as we run 'em over. Hah! No, no, missy, no eyes, too bad, eh? The 'eye' means the letter 'I.' Just a letter and a number, yes."

Petra felt heat flush her face. "Well, what does 'I ten' mean, then?" she said.

Pettibone's laughter stopped and he turned thoughtful, though Liam snickered and jabbed her side.

"I do not know," Pettibone said. "Just a letter and a number. A road, that's all, one of those huge Before-Reckoning mothers."

Yates had the main convoy lined up and ready when they arrived in Welsh. Poppa placed the two book wagons as third and fourth, which Yates had anticipated.

Poppa didn't wait; with a "Move out!" the convoy began its ponderous progress. They had to cross the "big road" first, going over it on a bridge.

"Two roads," Petra said.

"Nope, same road," Pettibone said. "See? On this side, traffic goes thataway"—he pointed to the right as they passed over it—"an' on the other side, the one we want, it goes thataway." He pointed left. "Keeps everyone from bumpin' into each other, see?"

The convoy had to travel over the bridge and turn left on a narrow road that angled up until it disappeared into a long ribbon of gray. As they merged into the flat road, which was mostly gray, except where patches of white or red stone had been used for repairs, convoy masters trotted back and forth making sure all the wagons stayed in line.

The convoy stayed to the right, while smaller wagons—some with brightly colored cloth tops—a four-wheeled buggy with covered openings pulled by two dark horses driven by a man in a tall hat, and two men dressed in green riding horses with one leading a pack mule passed on the left. Otherwise, traffic was sparse.

The land changed from hills and forests of their home village on the Calcasieu River to flat fields, some with crops rippling in the light breeze. Sometimes she'd see human figures in these fields bent over in their labors. Other sections were bare where dust devils played. The gray and green flatness was broken up occasionally by passage under bridges, except for a crossing where one had fallen, forcing the traffic on the other lane to go around at surface level.

Progress was rapid despite the rest stops, mostly for the oxen as the teamsters fed and watered them. The final stop was just a field next to the highway. The convoy broke up into four groups of six, except for two that had one extra wagon each, each forming circles, oxen in the middle. The Rangers patrolled along all four groups while the convoy masters and teamsters took up defensive positions along the wagons. It was a no-fire night, so dinner was dried meat, dried vegetables and fruit, crusty bread and a little cheese. The trip the next day was more of the same, so Petra thumbed through a heavy paper book called the *Sears, Roebuck &*

Company General Merchandise Catalog, Spring/Summer 1956. She wondered what it'd be like to wear a frilly dress, little pink socks, petticoats and hard shoes.

"What's RV?" Liam asked as the convoy pulled into the Frog City RV Park that night.

"Dunno," Pettibone said. "Something the Before People had, I reckon."

Dinner was a delicious beef stew made from meat a convoy master had traded hooch for. They slept under the stars to the sounds of peeping frogs.

"The frogs in the RV city," Petra said.

"A frog city and eyes on the highway," Liam said. "You're just weird, Pest-a."

Petra stuck out her tongue and turned her back on him.

Rain fell from a gray sky the next morning, causing a scramble to cover the book wagons. Travel was wet and miserable despite the rain gear. By early afternoon, the rain had let up, but as the convoy began passing tall buildings, several horse-mounted soldiers crossed the green strip between the lanes and headed right for them. Pettibone and the other teamsters started to grab bows, spears and clubs, but Poppa rode forward and raised a hand. After short discussion with the lead horseman, Poppa rode back.

"That's the Lafayette Escadrille, the local militia," he said. "The Acadia Parish governor sent them to accompany us through Lafayette."

Petra watched as the horsemen took up escort positions along the convoy. They wore green and silver under their chain-mail and plate-armor coats. Their domed helmets had nose and cheek guards, which served to hide most of their faces, but Petra saw an occasional beard or strong chin and broad nose. Their shields were emblazoned with a man's head wearing a bonnet of long, flowing feathers. A flag carried by a man galloping by carried the same image.

"They say they used to fly, the Escadrille," Pettibone said. "Long time ago, across the ocean. Their forebears flew and fought in the air."

"But people don't fly," Liam said.

Pettibone shrugged. "They say they did. I'm not arguing wit' these guys."

After about two hours, the convoy left I-10 and traveled down a narrow road until they came to another large road that went underneath the big double-road. The wagons gathered around one another on the flat concrete surface. Someone had painted a giant fleur-de-lis and the words University of Louisiana on an angled concrete wall below I-10. Soon the road was crammed with wagons, protesting oxen, horses and convoy workers grumbling as they ran around with brooms and bags collecting what the animals left behind. Petra and Liam jumped out of the wagon and dodged oxen, wagons, horses and people to where their father stood next to his horse.

"This is where we split," he was saying. "The Lafayette wagons will take this road to the town's commercial center accompanied by most of the Escadrille. Dillon, we'll only need a few Rangers for that group, leave the rest with the main convoy. A detachment of Escadrille will go with you to help navigate through the town. Yates, you're in charge of the main group because I'm going into the town. All right? Then let's move."

Petra ran up to Poppa as he pulled out his water bottle. "Do you have to go, Poppa?"

"Yes, honey, I do. It's business. Your mother's going with you, though. I won't be long." He kneeled, gave her a hug. "Be good for me, eh?" He eyed her for a moment, then stood. "Liam—"

"I know my duty, sir."

"I was going to say, take care, son."

Liam nodded. "Come on, Pest-a."

As they reached the wagon, the sun appeared. Pettibone shed his rain cloak as they climbed aboard.

"On the road again," Pettibone said as he snapped the reins. "I heard that somewhere, but I don' remember where."

Petra checked the bundle under the seat, then sat between the two. The convoy again climbed a narrow, angled road, then joined I-10 again. When Yates started to pass on his tall horse, Pettibone waved.

"Goin' the long way round, ha?" Pettibone said as the taciturn Convoy Second pulled up alongside. "I don' think this is much faster than Old 90."

"Safer," Yates said. "This convoy is too tempting for bandits and other sleazebags. Plus, on Old 90, we'd be stopped every five miles to pay 'hood tolls.'"

"That'll happen on the Evangeline."

"Not so bad now, they say."

"Hah. We'll see."

"Indeed." Yates spurred his horse and headed to the front of the convoy.

"What's the Evangeline?" Petra said.

"A road named for the town it ends in, I think. It's still Old 90, where it takes a bend south, actually. See, there? The old signs are tellin' us where to go."

The signs were mounted on a framework that stretched across their side of the road. EXIT SOUTH, U.S. 90, read the one that pointed to the narrow road the convoy was taking. It curved around in a long loop, then merged into another big road, this one with three lanes instead of two. Almost immediately, they ran into the first checkpoint, but the convoy didn't even stop.

As they passed through the gate in the wall that stretched across the road, a fat man in an ill-fitting brown shirt waved. Wagons made up most of the traffic, but the inside lane was reserved for single-horseback riders, many of whom were youths, even girls her own age. Petra envied their high spirits as they passed laughing and shouting in their bright clothing, but they were also accompanied by dour-faced men carrying swords and wearing armor.

Buildings tall and low crowded the roadsides. Most of the taller ones had blank fronts with empty window openings, but one or two sported signs proclaiming themselves as hotels. Several of the smaller buildings were covered in symbols and odd words. Petra could read French, but many didn't make sense and some of the drawings looked scary. This wild artistry was often accompanied by snatches of music when the traffic noise abated, a mix of what she'd heard back at the old settlement but others that scraped her nerves.

They passed a huge sign way up on a pole that proclaimed JESUS IS LORD!

Crosses, fish, birds and flowers were painted on the pole and a large metal cross stuck out from the side. A church with stained-glass windows and a cross at the top of a tall steeple stood behind the sign.

Farther down the road, another sign rose out of the tangle of buildings, but this one said SATAN IS TRUE LORD!

Snakes, skulls and faces with horns adorned the pole. It stood behind a long, high fence, with the words BELIEVE IN BAAL and LET LUCIFER LIGHT YOUR WAY painted in large letters surrounded by deformed animals, odd-shaped moons and planets. Naked men and women cavorted through the scenes.

Pettibone crossed himself, mumbled a prayer. "You childs don't look, that's blasphemous! Turn your heads away! Damn, I wish the gummint would get rid of this place!"

Once past the wall and signs, though, the roadside buildings, while still garishly painted, took on a more normal look. Things didn't go so well at the next checkpoint. As Yates and the Escadrille haggled with the 'hood's militia, a general rest was declared to water—and clean up behind—the oxen. Momma rode up and she, Petra and Liam bought some water and fruit at a roadside stand. By the time the convoy was finally allowed to pass, the sun was low in the sky and the long twilight of summer in full swing as they arrived at the Beaver Field campgrounds.

A shallow lake filled the center of the field, and a river of brown water curved three-quarters of the way around. The layout prevented formation of complete defensive circles, so the book wagons were parked along the riverbank. Yates told Pettibone he wasn't real happy with that, and Pettibone said he didn't like to see the Escadrille departing.

Fires were lit in the pits, but dinner was dried food again because of the late hour. Petra and Liam bedded down with several Raiders in a shelter tent, but Momma was on first watch. It took a while before Petra fell asleep, and her dreams were plagued by crawling and oozing things, like those she'd seen on the walls.

A shout in one of those dreams jolted her awake where she found the shouting was real. "Alarm, Rangers!" She crawled over next to Liam. Shadowy figures ran back and forth in the dim dawn light. Petra ducked as unseen arrows whistled through the air. Oxen bellowed, horses galloped by and men shouted and waved swords and spears. Petra gasped as someone grabbed her shoulder.

"Easy, it's me, Annie. Marian sent me to check on you guys."

"What's happening?" Liam said.

"A raid we were told wasn't going to happen."

Annie wasn't as tall as Momma but she packed power in her broad shoulders and compact frame. "Good thing we not believe that, right? Stay put, this is a defensive position." She hurried off in that odd lumbering gate of hers.

"Stay here."

"Liam—"

"I'm just going up there. You're safe here."

"Stay here, stay here, that's all everyone says." The noise and the occasional arrow dampened any desire to follow. It was like back home when raiders attacked; she would crouch somewhere and wait. Then she heard what sounded like a sick ox bellowing. Someone cursed, but someone else cheered.

"It's the horn of Ezra's guard! This'll clear those bastards out!"

The bellow sounded again much louder. Petra pushed herself up in time to see three horses gallop by with riders waving swords. She scooted along the canvas until she saw Liam, and crawled to his side.

"Good guys or bad guys?" she said.

"Good, lots," Liam said, once again sheathing his sword.

More horse riders appeared but slowed their mounts to a walk. Petra could make out more of the details in the morning light, mostly three wagons across the way from them. She looked toward her left and saw what looked like wheels sticking up. She stood up, trying to see better.

"Oh, no!" Petra dashed away.

"Petra!" Liam shouted, but she ignored him. She jumped over the tongue and ran around the wagon's front but froze when she saw someone tossing books aside.

"Well, what's this, a little pig to gut, eh?" The face that turned toward her was covered in a white mask with dark eyes and a rictus grin. His dark clothing made it hard to tell what he was wearing. He dashed forward and grabbed Petra, who screamed and kicked.

"Shut up y'little b—uh!"

Someone plowed into the man, making him stumble and drop her. The attacker whirled around, stopped with sword point forward. Liam looked very slender and small against the masked man's bulk.

"Ha! Another little worm, this one with a toothpick." The man whipped a shield around from his back and grabbed a heavy club. "You first, then."

He swung hard with the club; Liam tried to parry it but his sword was knocked aside and he barely held on to it. The man swung back in an awkward backstroke, but Liam ducked, then managed to return to a proper stance. His gaze didn't waver but his sword shook slightly.

"Hot shit, you think, eh, worm?" The man feinted, then hit Liam squarely with his shield. Liam staggered. "Little boys shouldn't—"

Liam screamed and lunged, putting all his momentum behind his sword. The point hit the man's groin just inside the right leg. It must have penetrated because the man grunted and jerked to a stop. He reared back with the club, but Liam twisted the sword, then turned his body and pulled so the blade sliced across and ripped out with a gout of blood. The man screamed, dropped both club and shield, and clutched the wound. The blood flowed down his leg. He staggered back, tripped and fell backward and rolled down into the sluggish river. He splashed at the edge as red spread into the brown of the water. His struggles gradually lessened until they stopped. Only his legs showed on the shore.

Liam stood breathing hard, sword shaking in his hand.

He crouched, wiped the blade in the grass. "Come on, Petra."

Petra turned back and climbed into the wagon.

"Now, damn it!"

"Wait!" She grabbed the bundle just as Liam yanked her away. She barely managed to hang on to it.

His grip was hard as he hauled her back to the Rangers' tent. "Stay here."

"Where are you going?"

"To check—find—never mind."

"Liam!" Petra yelled but he turned and left in rapid strides. She clutched the bundle to her chest, stood frozen, suddenly fearful and alone, until a familiar shout pierced through.

"Petra Marigold Landreaux! What do you mean running off? Practically in the middle of a battle, Annie tells me."

Momma, eyes ablaze, stood above Petra, hand on hips. "What were you thinking?"

"I had to save Grandpa's gift!" she shouted. "There was a guy—"

"You could've been killed, child! That was irresponsible—"

"I had to save Grandpa's gift! It's special!" She tried to glare back at Momma but tears made it all go fuzzy. "Poppa helped me find it. I had to save it, Momma, I had to. Liam got to give Grandpa a birthday gift! I want to give him one, too, Momma, I had to save it!" Petra's words dissolved into a long series of sobs.

"Oh, child, child, child," Momma said in a gentle tone as she kneeled and wrapped her arms around her. "My *petite fleur*, no book on this planet, not one, is worth your life. Grandpa would be devastated if he knew—if he lost you. There are more books, many more, we could find another just as nice. But there is only one of you."

She wiped the tears from Petra's face. "You have to be careful out here, *petite fleur*. There is so much danger—" She stopped, looked at Petra a moment. "You definitely are your father's daughter. Now. You got your bundle?"

She picked it up from where she'd dropped it. "Y-yes."

"Good." Mother gave her another hug, stood, took Petra's hand.

"Momma, Liam killed a man."

Her mother's steps faltered. "I will find him."

They walked a bit farther, then Momma yelled, "Mycroft!"

A horse came to a sudden halt and the rider leaped off and ran toward them. Petra quailed, expecting another lecture, but the tall figure scooped her up.

"Oh, baby. Are you all right?"

"I'm fine, Poppa, I'm fine." She fought more tears as he pressed her to his hard jacket.

"I have to find Liam," Momma said.

"Annie said she saw him at the water station, white as a ghost. Take my horse."

"Right. You two behave yourselves." She mounted and rode off.

"I think the mess tent is in operation." There they got plates of scrambled eggs and sausage; Petra was hungry enough to clean hers. A messenger came by and he and Poppa had a quiet conversation.

"Just a local band of bandits, looks like," Poppa said after the man left. "We'd gotten word of the plans and came as quickly as we could. Fortunately Ezra sent help." They left the tent and walked to the overturned book wagons.

"Th-that guy in a mask was going through the books," Petra said.

"I don't think he was after dictionaries and atlases."

Petra walked over to the riverbank, pointed. The red had disappeared, but a pair of legs still stuck out of the water.

"Come away, honey," Poppa said.

"What will we do now?"

"Once everything is secure and the wounded are taken care of, Ezra's having a party. And, by God, we need one."

Petra put on her one dress. Not like the frilly ones from the catalog, but one that fell below her knees and with long sleeves. Mother despaired because it came out of the luggage wrinkled, but Petra didn't care.

Musicians played on a stage and when she danced with Poppa, she loved the way the dress swirled around her legs. There were barbecued pork ribs, chops and chicken; jambalaya, potatoes—both white and sweet—fresh collard greens, beans and corn bread. After dark, Petra joined Poppa, Momma, Liam, Ezra and his petite wife, Adele, sitting in a circle near the fire. Everyone was relaxed, even if there were weapons on belts and bows and quivers within quick reach.

"When the Reckoning came, some folks thought they could enslave the blacks again." Ezra was a huge man, tall and deep-chested, with a high forehead and wide shoulders. His voice was deep and rumbled in his chest. "But the blacks had tasted freedom for too long. And they had learned history, and they had learned to fight, so it wasn't so easy. So here I am, a black man, descendant of slaves, owning a huge plantation where there once was a country club and an airport. I named it Justice Oaks because it's just that I should be in this position. But I don't own slaves. Everyone who works for me, I pay them well with what is valuable."

"Must've taken a lot of hard work," Poppa said.

"Three generations, going on four. All carefully recorded. My great-grandpappy was a kid when the Reckoning came, and he wrote it all down. Wasn't much of a warrior by all accounts, but he was a good . . . what d'you call it?"

"Scholar," said Adele.

"Scholar. Wrote it all down, then my great-uncle took over, then my pappy, now my son. Complete family history of the After times with a bit of Before."

"The library at Athena would love to have that history in its files—"

Ezra shook his head. "Those journals do not leave this land."

"No, no, they'll send scribes here to copy them, word for word, just as they're written."

"Well, I don't—"

"We would be honored to have our story in the library," Adele said.

"We would?"

"Ezra, people will read about the Hawks family, our struggles, our deeds, our triumphs, all in our own words. Our family history will inspire future folk."

"Well, then," Ezra said, gazing at his wife, "I guess you'd better tell your librarians to send their scribes, Mycroft."

The next morning Poppa, Petra and Pettibone were removing books from the book wagon with the broken axles when Yates and four convoy masters rode up. Poppa barely glanced at them.

"Yates, bring wagon fourteen, please, there's room around the bottle gourds and clay vessels, we should be able to cram most of these around—"

"Sir, delay could mean we'll miss the salt train at New Iberia."

Poppa looked at his Second. "We're slightly ahead of schedule, Yates, plus I think McIlhenny will be willing to wait a day or two."

"Sir, I—this stuff just isn't worth the trouble."

"I see." Poppa looked down at the book he was holding. *A Brief History of Time* by Stephen Hawking." He held it up. "You think this is junk, right, Yates?"

"Sir, I—"

"Fine." Poppa flipped through the pages. "You're in charge, then, go on, take the convoy, I trust you. We got some nice goods in Lafayette and Ezra's six cotton wagons are valuable, but reserve at least two for Athena. I'm going to salvage what I can because I'm just damn fucking dumb enough to believe there is value here, value beyond the paper and the ink, value even beyond the old metal parts and the cotton and the timber and the crops and the chickens and whatever the God else we carry for short-term gain."

He waved the book. "This is most definitely pre-Reckoning and I don't have a fucking clue what it's about but that doesn't matter because somebody else will come along and understand it and what it means to us and our future. Odd things are going on in our world right now, Yates, a rise of fear and dark things we once thought we'd put behind us. The Before people valued this book, all of these books, because they realized knowledge was a way of fighting the dark and the terror. All damned worthless now, right, because where are the Before people now? All gone, the Reckoning having swept them all away along with their useless knowledge. Still, the Before people did amazing things whether you believe it or not, and one day perhaps we can do those things again. But even if we don't, we need to know what they once did, what they once thought, how they dealt with darkness and fear, what they once dreamed, because we need to dream, too.

"There's poetry here, Yates, tales of hope and beauty, and knowledge, information to guide and inspire us. The Before people built huge palaces to store these things in and keep them safe. We're trying to do that again at the library at Athena. So I'm going to stay here and save as many of these as I can because by God I think they're important and I will get them to the library if it takes me the rest of this goddamned fucking year!"

He wiped his brow with his sleeve, carefully set the book on one of the stacks. "Be on your way then, Yates."

Nobody moved as Poppa and Yates stared at each other. Finally Yates straightened, ran a hand over his face and muttered something Petra was sure was a bad word.

"Armandriz, get wagon fourteen, please." He dismounted, stepped over and grabbed a handful of books. After a moment, the other convoy masters followed.

"Raphael, Manuel, Arlen, let's see if we can right the unbroken wagon."

Once the work started, more hands arrived and soon all the wagons were ready. Book wagon two was crammed to capacity, wagon fourteen's merchandise was buried under books with a few stuffed into empty vessels. The oxen from the broken wagon were turned over to a couple of Ezra's wranglers.

"Ezra will have the wagon repaired for us," Poppa said.

After Yates mounted his horse, Poppa called to him.

"Thanks," he said.

"Sir." Yates touched the brim of his hat, rode off.

Before giving the go-ahead, Poppa turned to Petra. "Any, uh, funny words you might've heard today are not to be repeated to your mother. Got that?"

She put on her innocent face. "Which words, Poppa?"

He wagged a finger at her. "You little devil."

She shrugged. "Where's Liam?"

"Riding with your mother."

"Oh. He gets to ride with the big folk."

"Because he is one now, *petite fleur.*"

"Yeah." She shook the memory of the incident that made him one from her mind, then checked to make sure Grandpa's gift was secure under the seat.

"Ready to roll?" said Pettibone as he climbed aboard.

At Petra's nod, Poppa yelled, "Move out!" and the convoy resumed its journey down Old 90.

McIlhenny had to wait only half a day. New Iberia station was a huge yard crammed with ox-pulled merchandise wagons, salt wagons behind their six-horse teams and even a couple of fancy beer wagons pulled by teams of large, beautiful horses. Poppa was a happy man as they left the chaos behind.

"Six salt wagons, three barrels of pickled peppers and nine barrels of beer. With the stuff from Lafayette and Ezra combined with what we brought from Oakton station, this is going to be a very profitable trip."

"And the books," Petra said.

"The icing on the cake," he said. "But, before that, a little bonus." He opened a small box stuffed with wood shavings, pulled out a small bottle filled with red fluid. "This'll spice up your breakfast tomorrow."

After New Iberia, the land changed again from fields to swamps and bayous with their strange sounds and odors. Each town seemed pretty much like the last, the days were hot and oppressive and the nights were barely less so as they slept under the stars and a waxing moon. Liam was allowed to break the boredom by riding with the Rangers, aiming a smirk at Petra each time until she was ready to smack him with the Sears book.

Just outside of Berwick, a line of horsemen passed in formation. The riders rode with backs straight and faces stern. The metal in their armor gleamed in the sunlight, and round shields were slung on their backs. Red plumes curved down behind their helmets; their white tunics were short, leaving their legs bare. Spear shafts protruded from sheaths attached to their black and silver saddles. Their white flag was emblazoned with a golden shield crossed by a red lightning bolt above two green branches.

"The Athena Legion in fancy dress," Pettibone said. "Show-offs."

The convoy stopped in the center of Berwick while, as Pettibone said, "they figure out what it'll cost us to cross Miss Atchafalaya." He and Petra bought roasted chicken pieces stuck on a stick from a nearby stand. Just as they finished, the word came to move out.

Once again the teamsters yelled their peculiar calls and once again the convoy creaked forward. The road went straight through the town, then began a slow, angled climb up a huge embankment. Petra climbed onto the driver's bench.

"Long climb up the giant levee," Pettibone said. "These towns'll wash away without 'em. When Ol' Man River came, he took no prisoners. In the Before time, it was different. The Before people, see, they wanted the Ol' Man to keep going on down to the Old City where they and their machines lived. The Before people did that a lot, making Ol' Man River go *here* but not *there*, not where *he* wanted to go, but to go where *they* wanted him to go, to make him toe the line until he got to the Big Water. Miss Atchafalaya, now, she knew the Ol' Man be gettin' tired of the old ways. Oh, she worked her wiles on him, sayin' sweet things, flatterin' the old coot, telling him she knew a shorter way to get to the Big Water. But the Before people didn't like this, not at all. So they built levees and dams and ditches to keep them apart. Miss Atcha, though, she was patient. She knew the truth about the Ol' Man, and all she had to do was wait."

Petra had learned about the Atchafalaya and the Mississippi in her schooling, but Pettibone's singsong version was a lot more interesting.

"Then the Reckoning came. The Before people had other things to worry about 'cause they were becoming the After people and that wasn't an easy thing. So Miss Atchafalaya pushed, she dug, she scoured, trying to get to the Ol' Man. Then she got unexpected help: the Big Devil Wind came roaring up from the south after drownin' the Old City. And finally

Miss Atcha could speak to the Ol' Man, and she asked, just as politely as could be, if he'd like to go with her to the Big Water, and he said 'Ma'am, I'd be obliged. It's been a long time I've been runnin' the long road, and I'd be happy to join you on the Short Road.' So, Ol' Man River and Miss Atcha carved a new route, drowning towns and sweeping away many of the After people. The Old City in the Delta died and the new city on the banks of the new river rose. 'Course, these big levees had to be built first to contain the power of the new Miss Atchafalaya."

Pettibone timed his tale to end just as the wagon topped the levee. Stretching before them was a high, wide bridge with a stone road four lanes wide. But it was the river that made Petra gasp. The landscape itself was moving, sliding under the bridge in a massive and constant flow. The shores were reduced to irrelevance the farther out on the bridge they rolled. Petra saw a path where people were walking right along the edge of the bridge, so she leaped down, stopped, looked both ways for horses, then ran to the path. She raced along the sidewalk, dodging the other strollers, until she came to an overlook. She could see just enough of the bridge's shadow in the water directly below to make out the shapes of the tops of the arches. A log rolled and bumped between the massive piers.

She raced down to the next lookout next to a tower. The river was the only thing in her view now. She began to feel like *she* was moving, not the river, she and the bridge receding backward toward an unknown destination.

The illusion was dispelled when horses rode up behind her.

"She acts like she's never seen a river before," Liam said.

"Cut her some slack, son," Poppa said. "She's never seen *this* one before."

"It is an awesome sight," Momma said as she stepped up to the railing on Petra's right, Liam and Poppa on the left.

"It's smarter than us, too," Petra said. "In school they say we aren't sure what's in the places north of us, the interior, as teacher calls it. But this river has flowed past all those places, so it knows what's there and we don't."

"Well, that's interesting," Poppa said slowly. "Nice to have the bridge in any case. Up until last March you had to cross on a ferry. Took forever to get a convoy across. Yep, the Consolidated St. Mary–St. Martin Parish people say their shiny bridge matches anything the Before People built. Might be true, 'cause all the B.R. metal bridges that used to be here were swept away."

Poppa attached their horse's reins to the wagon when it reached them and everyone climbed aboard, Petra and Liam on the bench, Momma and Poppa sitting behind.

"What's that down there?" Liam said, pointing to a latticed tower downriver.

"That's Mr. Charlie," Pettibone said. "Used to be right next to the shore, but the new river left it stranded. One of them things the Before People used to dig out that magic black stuff."

"Petroleum," Poppa said.

"My old grenma use to say people could travel from Oakton to Old Morgan City in less than a day using that magical stuff in their machines. I never believe her 'cause they'd have to be almost flyin'."

"That sounds silly," Liam said. "People don't fly."

"A lot of B.R. things sound silly," Momma said. "Hard to know which is myth and which is truth."

"Aye that," Pettibone said.

"Where's Morgan City?" Petra asked.

"Athena was carved out of Morgan City. The idea was to repeat Alexandria, in ancient Egypt, the library, the harbor, and the lighthouse that you can see way down the river."

Petra had to stand up in order to see the tall, white tower.

"At night, you can see the bonfire at the top. Ships that anchor here are asked to send any books they have to the library so they can be copied. Just like they did at the library at old Alexandria. The founders here were planning to call this place Alexandria, too, but there's already an Alexandria in the Louisiana Federation. So they named it for the Greek goddess Athena."

"It's better they named it after a woman, anyway," Petra said.

"Well put, my daughter," Momma said as Liam made gagging sounds.

Once across the river, Poppa cut the book wagons from the main convoy and sent it to the central market with Yates in charge. As usual, Momma would go to the library, but for the first time, Liam was given a choice: the library or the Ranger barracks. Liam dithered less than a second and rode off with Annie, leading Momma's horse.

The library was a large structure, rising skyward in white stone. An even larger building was rising behind it, still incomplete inside its cocoon of scaffolding. Pettibone guided the wagon to a sheltered area and pulled up next to a low dock. Poppa went inside as Pettibone, Momma and Raphael, the teamster from the other wagon, lowered the railings. Poppa returned with a short, curly-haired woman, a taller dark-haired woman and three men pushing wheeled carts.

"My daughter, Petra," Momma said after they all greeted one another. "Petra, this is Kathy and that's Elaine. The guys are Don, Dennis and Mark."

The wagon teamsters began handing out the books as Poppa handed a notebook to Kathy, the short woman.

"OK, complete set of *Foxfire* books," she said. "Can't have too many of those. *The Complete Book of Tanning Skins and Furs*, good. The *SAS Survival Handbook*. *When Technology Fails*. *Seed to Seed*. *Tom Brown's Field Guide*. Books on Chinese and herbal medicine. My goodness, sounds like your bibliophiles were preparing for the Reckoning."

"Except they didn't know it was coming," Poppa said. "They must've thought some kind of catastrophe was, though."

"Are these black books?" said Don as he and Mark lifted a large trunk wrapped in chains.

"Yes," Poppa said. "The Satanic Bible, along with books of spells and curses and other black arts."

"Don, Mike, that goes straight to the vault," Kathy said.

"Yes, ma'am," Don said.

"We think at least one raider in Lafayette was after them," Poppa said.

"He threatened Petra, but Liam took care of him. Later, we took a look at him. He had the CUT sun-sign on a metal disk, but he had a lot of icons attached to his armor. We didn't think he was one."

"Did his eyes go black?" Kathy asked.

"Liam says no, but the guy was wearing a mask. That mask also precludes him from being a Cutter because they've never been known to wear any."

"A wanna-be, likely," Kathy said.

"Here's a 1956 Sears catalog," Petra said. "Is it any good?"

"Doesn't matter," Elaine said, leafing through it. "We can't buy these things anymore, but we might get ideas on how to make items we can use."

"Like those frilly dresses? And those petcoats—"

Elaine leaned down and whispered. "Petticoats, right? And girdles? God, I wouldn't be caught wearing that stuff in a pigsty."

Petra giggled.

"This goes on the wagon with the encyclopedias," Elaine said. "What's in these boxes?"

"Mystery novels an old lady in Lafayette insisted we take," Poppa said.

"OK, they go on that other wagon."

"What's the difference?" Petra said.

"Fiction and nonfiction. What's real and what's made up." She shrugged. "Most of the time."

Petra didn't understand that last remark, but she felt a pang of regret as the last of the books came off her father's wagons. She felt sad she would never see them again.

"That's it, then, Pettibone, Raphael," Poppa said. "You guys rejoin the convoy." He unhitched his horse from the wagon, hitched it to a nearby post. "I'll probably catch up before you reach Center."

"Right, sir," Pettibone said as he climbed into the driver's seat.

"Wait!" Petra shouted.

"Yes, yes, missy, here it is." Pettibone pulled the bundle from under the seat, handed it down.

"Thank you for everything, Mr. Pettibone," she said, clutching it to her chest.

"You're quite welcome, missy. We'll see you soon." He touched his brow with his fingers as the wagon pulled away.

The library people wheeled the carts inside and pushed them against a wall. Poppa followed Kathy into an office and Momma led Petra through a double door into a huge room with long tables arranged in straight lines. Books were stacked on carts and the floor. People sitting on stools at the tables were bent over, until one would place a book on a cart behind, then take another from a stack.

"Are our books coming in here?" Petra said.

"Yes," Elaine said as she joined them. "These folks are classifying the books, nonfiction by topic and fiction by type, for instance. Some we'll copy using the printing presses next door, duplicates we'll send out for trade in other cities. The ones we keep will be available for anyone to come and borrow."

"Any new contact outside the Gulf Coast Coalition?" Momma said.

"Yes, we've heard solid reports of a stable government up in Oregon. It'll be tricky getting there, but it'll be worth it. We've also heard some strange tales about some sort of magic sword."

She shrugged. "I hope it's more myth than reality, but you can't tell these days."

"All done," Poppa called from the door. "We got good prices and credit this time," he said as they walked back to the dock. "As I expected, this will be a profitable trip."

"Good," Momma said. "I'd hate to go through all this for nothing."

They embraced, kissed, then Poppa got on his horse. "Say hello to Grandpa for me, *petite fleur*, but don't give him that present until I get there."

"All right, Poppa." She waved as he left, turned to Momma. "What are we going to do now?"

"We are going to Grandma and Grandpa's in style, that's what."

Momma hired a fancy one-horse, four-wheeled black carriage with red interior and brass fittings. Once settled on the thick velour seat, Petra took the book out of the bag and found to her dismay that the wrapping had wrinkled and torn.

"It's been through a lot," Momma said as she untied the white string and smoothed and readjusted the paper. She rewound the string, tied it with a bow. "Small wonder it's a little ragged and worn. Just like the rest of us."

After a while, the carriage turned into a curved street. Momma pointed out the window. "Look, that's the house we're going to live in."

They passed a structure with only one floor and no roof. "See, it connects to Grandma and Grandpa's house right next door. You'll have your own room and there's a lake in back so you can still go swimming and a small woods to go exploring in."

"In between chores," Petra muttered, but Momma laughed. "Why did we come?"

Momma slipped an arm around her. "It's safer here, little flower. When I'm on duty and your Poppa is on another trip, you'll be safe with Grandma and Grandpa Landreaux. The old village area was getting too dangerous with those cultists and dark-arts people in the forests. Plus, we're a lot closer to Grandmére and Grandpére Gautreau in the Houma Nation. We'll go for a visit soon."

The carriage stopped and as Petra got out, a screen door opened and a tall, lanky white-haired man came down the steps.

"Grandpa!" Petra shouted.

"Is this my *petite fleur*?" Grandpa said as Petra ran into his arms. "Not so *petit* anymore is she? Soon she'll be too big for old Grandpa."

She wrapped her arms around his neck and giggled as his beard tickled her. He set her down and she ran over to Grandma, who smelled of baked bread. Momma, after paying the driver, came up and more hugs and hellos were exchanged.

"Where's Liam?" Grandpa said.

"He'll be along later with Mycroft," Momma said. "He rode in with the Rangers."

Grandpa arched an eyebrow. "Oh, really?"

"So young," Grandma said, a look of concern wrinkling her brow.

"He saved me, Grandpa," Petra blurted.

He look down at her. "Did he!"

"Yes, I—"

Grandpa knelt, placed a hand on her shoulder. "Wait until he arrives, honey, so he can tell us in his own words."

"All right."

"Right now, my stinky *fleur*," Grandma said, "it's bath time for you."

Petra protested, but once immersed in the hot water, she found she enjoyed it. There were bubbles, there was Grandma scrubbing her back with a brush and washing her hair with sweet-smelling soap. She put on a clean-smelling shift that was soft against her skin. Momma then took a bath, and meanwhile neighbors came in whose names she quickly forgot. Grandpa showed her the communal gardens, the house and the stables, then took her to the greenhouse where she picked several big, ripe tomatoes and carried them into the kitchen.

Liam and Poppa arrived to another round of loud talking and hugs, and when Poppa gave her a hug, he said, "Someone smells sweet. Did'ja save any bathwater for me?"

"Was I supposed to?"

The neighbors stayed for a dinner of glazed ham, hominy grits, mustard greens, and a corn and red pepper dish along with fresh cucumbers, carrots and the tomatoes. Spiced apples and little nut cakes served as the dessert and the adults offered toasts with goblets of wine while Petra drank grape juice. She suspected Liam had wine in his glass, but he was on the other side of the table so she couldn't be sure.

Finally, Momma said, "Petra, the bundle."

Petra raced upstairs. She carried the gift carefully into the dining room, noticing that Momma stopped talking when she did.

"I'm sorry this is so late, Grandpa," she said. "But I wasn't here for your real birthday—"

"It is no never mind," he said, putting his free arm around her. "I am truly touched by your devotion and determination to bring me this. Your Momma told us about the troubles you had."

Petra felt her face flame. Grandpa didn't seem to notice as he untied the string and removed the wrapper.

"Ooo, pretty gold color," Grandma said.

"This book still has a slipcase," Grandpa said, turning it over in his hands. He tilted it and slid the book out, set the slipcase on the table and opened the cover. *"The Hobbit, Or There and Back Again."* He gazed at the gold cover a moment. "I remember this."

Petra's heart sank. "You read this already?"

He smiled. "Long time ago. Now it's your turn." He slipped the book back into the slipcase. "But now—Jacob did you bring your accordion?"

"But of course."

"Then we shall dance first."

Once cleared and the dishes done, the tables were moved, leaving a large open floor. The music started and the dancing took over. Before long, though, Momma took Petra by the hand and led her upstairs, had her change into a long nightgown, say her prayers, then crawl into a soft bed.

"Don't fall asleep yet," Momma said after kissing her good night. "Wait for Grandpa."

Petra sat up in the bed when she heard the slow tread coming up the stairs. Light flickered on the walls as he made his way to her room. He set the lantern on the chest next to the bed, then pulled a chair over. He sat down, took the book out of the crook of his arm and slid it out of the slipcase, which he set aside.

"Are you going to read that whole book to me?"

"I am. Unless you have an objection."

"I brought that for you."

"And we'll read it together. This is something that should be shared. Besides, it's my duty."

"Duty?"

"It's a grandpa's duty to read stories to his grandchildren. It's a tradition that reaches way, way back, before the Reckoning, back before they could print books, back before folks could even write, back to the ancient times when everyone lived in caves and listened to the old stories. So settle back and we'll get started."

Petra plumped her pillow, adjusted the covers, put her hands together, rested them on her lap, looked at her grandfather with her best polite face.

He laughed lightly. "You are a pill, no doubt about that. Well, anyway." He opened the book. "*The Hobbit, or There and Back Again.*" He cleared his throat. "In a hole in the ground, there lived a hobbit—"

"A hole? Who wants to live in a hole?" She remembered hiding in holes back home that most times had water in them, and sometimes big bugs or other icky, crawly things, or even snakes. And the holes always stank.

"Well, now, I'm sure"—Grandpa flipped the pages back—"Mr. Tolkien will explain why this particular character likes to live in a hole. That is, of course, if certain of us can set aside our impetuousness for a moment to hear what he has to say."

Petra shifted, frowned. "All right, Grandpa, I'll be patient."

"Good." He shifted the book in his lap, then resumed.

The hole, the story went, was snug and comfortable because the individual who lived there wouldn't have it any other way, and as Grandpa's voice rumbled into Petra's thoughts, she discovered that there were also dwarves who danced and sang and ate a prodigious amount of food, a wizard who made secret plans, and possibly a dragon, a creature she'd only heard about but she knew to be dangerous and powerful, who had stolen a vast treasure. At some point, all those things became part of a dream, though if asked she couldn't say exactly when that had happened, just as she was unaware exactly when Grandpa had stopped reading, tucked her in, kissed her on her forehead and said, "Sweet dreams" softly into her ear. And if she had stopped to think about it, she would recognize that these new dreams contained things she'd never seen before, places she'd never been before, with adventures she never could have imagined otherwise, because there, in the safety and warmth of Grandpa's house, it was possible to have such dreams.

FORTUNE AND GLORY

BY JOHN BIRMINGHAM

JOHN BIRMINGHAM

John Birmingham is the author of the Axis of Time series, *Weapons of Choice, Designated Targets, Final Impact,* and the *Stalin's Hammer* e-book spin-offs. Because you always wanted to see a time-traveling rainbow alliance kick Hitler's ass.

In "Fortune and Glory," he revisits some of his favorite characters from *Without Warning* and the Disappearance series. Cap'n Pete Holder, Fifi Lamont, and Lady Julianne Balwyn of the good ship *Diamantina*. In this alternate-alternative history they take on a direct commission from the King of Darwin to track down a vital document lost somewhere within the great crypt city of Sydney. But being ambitious, self-starting pirates they also find time for a little side project and a running battle with the city's ferocious cannibal horde, the Biters.

The old sailboat was a twin-masted forty-footer carved out of thousand-year-old Huon pine from the Tasmanian Highlands, a beautifully preserved museum piece. She placed third on corrected time in a Sydney–Hobart race way back in 1953, and in the decades since had logged enough miles to make it to the moon and back. In that time she had been the plaything of a builder, a manufacturing tycoon, one dot-com millionaire, and a pirate by the name of Pete Holder.

He was a nice pirate, though, if you asked him. Quite handsome in a derelict-surfer-bum sort of way, in spite of, or maybe because of, the scars. Damsels dig scars, after all. And he only ever stole from the other pirates, and when he wasn't doing that, he was busy rescuing said damsels and hunting hidden treasures, as the better sort of pirate is wont to do. Commendable pursuits that had furnished him fortune and glory and Jules and Fifi: a dark-haired, deadly English rose and her messy blond bestie, redneck princess to Lady Julianne's bona fide if distant claim to the blood royal.

The fortune he'd salted about here and there. A little in the Royal Vault at Darwin. A little more on his account at the Townsville Arsenal. At least half in the First Republican Bank of Tasmania. And a few little trinkets and baubles buried in watertight capsules on lonely, unpeopled islands up and down the Great Barrier Reef.

The glory, of course, he carried with him everywhere. Sometimes it even got a little ahead of him and it wasn't unknown to hear tales of Cap'n Pete that had escaped and run wild and were enjoying themselves hugely at the dockside taverns of Hobart or Fort Lyttelton well before the man himself turned up to help them along with a few more drinks and a little adventurer's license with the literal truth of things.

Jules and Fifi meanwhile were crouched below the armored gunwales fore and aft as Pete steered the *Diamantina* up the harbor through the dark hour before dawn. Water as black as oil hissed by as he spun the wheel a quarter turn starboard to take them around the rusted hulk of an old guided-missile destroyer. The warship had sunk close to shore and her bow knifed into the night sky, silhouetted by fading stars and a quarter moon. The dead city of Sydney held itself closely around them. No campfires burned where he could see them, which might be a good sign, or very bad news indeed.

On the final approach they had slipped past three large encampments on the northern beaches, spaced at least ten miles apart, and before they'd weighed anchor in Townsville, Shoeless Dan had warned him of a large tribe of Biters living in the cliffs around Bondi.

"Took down a whole salvage company out of Hobart, was what I heard, Pete," he warned over mugs of Old Scrumpy.

"Yeah, but we're not softcocks out of Hobart," Fifi had scoffed.

She wasn't scoffing now. As the first birdsong reached them from the overgrown slopes of the inner harbor, Fifi swept the shoreline and the waters behind them with the *Diamantina*'s swivel-mounted harpoon launcher. The antique whale killer took all three of them more than a minute to load and prime and they couldn't leave it primed to fire for too long, lest the thick rubber slings that would send the heavy javelin shrieking away, became stretched and lost some of their snap. He'd intended to fit a spring-loaded launch mechanism at the Arsenal.

Only half a minute to load, and by just two crew members at that, and another two hundred meters effective killing range, but it was a new technology and the price was too steep, even for the legendarily fat purse of Cap'n Pete Holder. Indeed, the legend of his fat purse may have worked against him there. Sometimes, it turned out, having a reputation as a very well-to-do pirate wasn't altogether helpful. For instance, when negotiating terms with the Colonel's First Armorer.

Fifi crouched over the harpoon gun. At the bow, Jules used a standard pair of old binoculars to sweep the ridgelines of the north shore, home of the three Biter Clans whose fires they'd seen as they ghosted past, a few miles out. She scoped up and down the shoreline, lowered the glasses, and took in the landscape as a whole. Nothing. The northern side of the harbor had gone back to brute nature harder and faster than the south. All those garden suburbs. And the Zoo of course. The Zoo had been over there too.

Jules crab-walked over to the port side gunwale and recommenced her surveillance. The haunted towers of Potts Point were visible as negative space where they blocked out the still bright constellations of the southern sky. The greater density of cement and steel and glass on the southern shore held back the wild with more success, but Pete's shoulder blades twitched anyway as he followed her sweep of the wasteland. He knew from long, hard-earned experience how many more hiding places, and hazards and unpleasant surprises were to be had in a concrete jungle than any other kind.

Ah, but more rewards too. More fortune and glory.

The gentle nor'easter carried them past the listing hulk of a passenger liner that had run aground on Cremorne Point. The breeze moaned a little through the bones of the rusting ghost ship, which was still festooned here and there with rat lines that hung like a few, drab strands of dead man's hair. Pete heard a deep, arrhythmic thumping that set his heart to beating faster until he realized it was just a lifeboat, still hanging from a steel cable halfway down the side of the liner, swaying in the wind, bumping up against the flanks of the ship.

"Clear south, clear north," came Julianne's voice from the prow.

Years from a home now lost forever, she still spoke in the sort of cultured English accent that would announce the discovery of a cannibal horde rowing madly toward them in the same tone as she might declare morning tea ready to be served. Pete smiled at the thought of similar voices echoing across these waters for the first time some two centuries earlier, as Cook nosed the *Endeavour* up the harbor to drop anchor at the very edge of the dark unknown. Although, he had to admit, there probably weren't many genuine aristocrats among Cap'n James Cook's crew. Not like Lady Julianne Balwyn. They were all hardworking mariners.

"Clear on the six," Fifi reported quietly, her voice an heirloom of the vanished American South.

To the casual observer, the waters appeared to be free of obstruction, with nine years of tide and storm having cleared away much of the free-floating wrack and debris and the hulls of derelict ferries and powered pleasure craft, some of which they'd passed washed up on harbor beaches. Others had foundered on rocky points or been carried out to sea, probably with all those passengers unable or unwilling to abandon the presumed safety of the vessels when the Blackout hit them. But they were in more danger astern than ahead. This was not the *Diamantina*'s first visit to the vast tomb of Sydney, and Pete Holder threaded them through the hazards he knew of, and those he could guess at. The unknown and uncharted they would just trust to the famous luck of Cap'n Pete.

As they passed Garden Island Point and the junkyard of giant, gray naval ships at Woolloomooloo Bay, the first sails of the Opera House loomed skyward, framed by the great arch of the Harbour Bridge. He forced himself to concentrate on their passage, steering around the sunken wreck of a submarine he had missed on his previous trip, but which Shoeless Dan had been kind enough to mark on his maps—in return for one percent of any salvage taken in the voyage.

"Aye, Pete, don't quibble about pennies," Dan had cackled. "Conning tower of that bitch'd rip the keel right off your pretty wooden fancy. Try your luck if you doubt me."

But he didn't doubt Shoeless Dan, not when Dan had a payday in the offing, and he didn't try his luck.

Luck was a finite commodity, in Pete Holder's experience. Finite and scarce. It ran out quickly.

The sandstone stronghold of Fort Denison loomed off the starboard bow and both girls swung their weapons around to take it under fire if needed. Avoiding Dan's unseen sub took them a little ways closer to the fortress than Pete would have liked, but he spent a few coins from the purse of his good fortune and it paid off. Denison was a Martello Tower, an old nineteenth-century redoubt built to secure the colonial township from the predations of the Spanish, or French, or even the American navies, but they were all gone now, like the millions of souls who once lived here. Only bones and crumbling brick remained.

And Biters of course. Plenty of them.

But the Biters weren't much for the study of naval tactics in the age of sail and it had obviously never occurred to any of them to occupy the fort and thus take control of all the harbor and back up river.

Jules didn't realize she was holding her breath until she let it go with a gasp. She didn't take her aim off the squat, crenellated battlements of the fort, however. Not until they were well past and out of bowshot.

The Biters weren't much of a threat at a distance. Such ranged weapons as they had tended to be of the crudest design and limited effect. Sticks and stones, quite literally, for the most part. They were also, it was generally agreed, barking mad. The perils of down-breeding and a diet heavy in man-meat. But you couldn't deny them a suggestion of animal cunning. They were, after all, fast devolving into animals.

With the threat of a surprise attack from Denison receding she lowered the bow and turned her attention back to the course Pete was steering. Fifi would scan the waters behind them for trouble until they had tied up and disembarked. Gooseflesh came up on her arms as the shrieks of some large animal drifted across from the forests of the north shore. She did her best to ignore it, concentrating on the more immediate threat of the green chaos off to port. They had no reports of any Biters in the dense, overgrown tangle of mismatched scrub, forest, and jungle that grew wild in the old Botanical Gardens. Shoeless Dan, who would surely have shaken them down for another point on the back end if he had more information, was adamant the Gardens remained empty.

"Biters aren't for growing and tending much, missy," he'd cackled when she pressed him on it. "Less'n it's their unrivaled collection of shrunken heads."

Shoeless Dan's shrunken head had fairly tipped back and near fell off as he roared at his own wit, at least until Fifi had kicked his chair over and sent him tumbling to the floor of the tavern amid the appreciative uproar of a hundred plus drinkers.

Still, who was the stupid one now, eh? Dan was safely abed in Townsville, protected by the massed pikes and swords of the Colonel's First Regiment, while she was inching her way into a city of the dead and undead. Pete steered them carefully through the sunken and half-sunken vessels that still lay about Farm Cove. The largest was a paddle steamer, a floating restaurant she supposed, that had gone down in front of the old governor's residence. Tiny waves lapped at the paddles halfway up the giant wooden wheel and slowly poured through the broken windows on the second deck. Only the third was completely free of inundation and she watched it closely for signs of movement. As they wove around the abandoned hulls of smaller power craft, their course took them close enough to the flat bottomed steamer to make of them a perfect target, even for rock throwers. The old hulks clinked and creaked in the nor'easter. Magpies and crows cawed and cackled at one another, and somewhere nearby a kookaburra began to laugh. She startled at an enormous black bat that flapped close overhead, its leathery wings sounding just like the whuffling snap of sails in a moderate breeze.

"Bugger me," she breathed. "This is less fun than the brochure promised."

"Too late for a refund," came Pete's voice softly. "See to the sails, Julesy."

She reduced the canvas bellying in the breeze and they bled off speed as Pete brought them up on their mooring point, an old floating dock at the Man o' War Steps. Moving quickly now, wanting to be done with her work so she could get back to keeping an eye out for Biters or scavengers or any of the myriad types of ne'er-do-well you tended to meet in a necropolis, Jules shimmied up the mainmast carrying a length of torn and wretched looking sail. The sun was just peeking over the hills of the eastern suburbs then, revealing the *Diamantina* to be a wreck every bit as dilapidated and woebegone as any she had passed on her passage up the harbor.

Or at least that's how it would appear to an observer. The rust streaks were lovingly painted on, as were the gaping holes on both port and starboard flanks, just above the waterline. The torn rags she fixed to the mast were held in place with industrial strength Velcro, but ready to be ripped down with one strong tug. The decks did not gleam, hiding under a fresh coat of coal dust, applied thinly to create a patina of age and neglect.

Pete maneuvered them around to point the bow back out toward their escape route, at which moment Fifi at last gave up her vigil on the whale gun and relaxed the firing bands with a mechanical crank. The skipper dropped anchor and tied them up while Jules went below and hurried back with their equipment. Each of them carried a mix of essentials: rope, ChemLights, copies of the maps they would use, a little food and water, some very basic emergency medical supplies. These went into small backpacks, which in turn were stowed in slightly larger ones. Each crew member carried their own weapons load out, and one piece of unique equipment: lightweight binoculars for Julianne, a small grappling hook for Pete, a couple of smoke bombs in Fifi's kit.

They were dressed lightly, for fast movement. No chain mail, no steel plate, nothing that would weigh them down, sap their energy, or drag them to the bottom of the harbor if they ended up in the drink. Knee and elbow pads, sunglasses, and bandannas seemed to be their only common items. Pete clipped on his boiled leather breast-and-back plate, the heaviest armor any of them would wear. Jules snapped the fasteners of her old SWAT team tac-vest. Fifi wore Ray-Bans and attitude.

"We cool?" she asked.

"We're cool," Pete said.

"ERPs?" asked Jules, giving Fifi reason to roll her eyes before she recited the list of emergency rendezvous points like a bored schoolchild.

"Gatehouse of the governor's mansion. The old library. The Mint. That restaurant you used to like."

"Which is where?" said Jules.

More eye rolling.

"Corner of Martin and Phillip," Pete said, to wrap it up. "But we won't need it, will we, ladies? Because this payday will run smooth as poo through a duck with runny poo problems."

"Touch wood?"

Jules passed him his secondary weapon. A wooden tonfa, which looked like a riot baton, but with both ends of the long striking-and-blocking arm filed down to wickedly sharp points.

"Thank you, m'lady," he said, slipping his arms through the straps of his pack and taking up the tonfa and his primary weapon, a cruel-looking club with four steel blades embedded in the knobbly head.

Fifi settled into her pack and took up the short-bladed ninjaken sword and Okinawan sai trident she routinely favored for close-in work. Julianne was already wearing her sword belt, from which hung a pair of khukuri blades. She passed out pistol grip slingshots and forty rounds of steel shot in two pouches of twenty, half-inch rounds each. Fifi and Pete stowed theirs in the leather holsters at their hips, while Jules, who was by far the best shot, carried her larger and more powerful model with three balls loaded and the wrist brace extended.

Jules obsessed about the kit as she had once obsessed about properly accessorizing her wardrobe. She'd been on a flying boat to Cairns when the Blackout hit. The pilot got them down alive, mostly, but she'd crawled out of the surf in the rags of a once beautiful silken shift by Akira Isogawa with nothing but a plastic bottle of spring water in her handbag for a three-hundred-mile trek to Townsville where the army kept things together at bayonet point.

"You ever wonder what we'd be doing if it weren't for the Blackout?" Fifi asked as they geared up.

"Shopping," said Jules.

"Let's be about it then," said Pete. "The shops await."

And he swept his hand toward the city.

"Yeah, let's fuck this cat," Fifi agreed.

The sun had climbed high enough to dapple the harbor with a net of golden sparkles. Each of the three took a moment to look around. It was always hard to leave the relative safety of the boat. A line from an old movie surfaced from Julianne's memory:

Never get out of the boat. Never get out of the boat.

But they did.

Fifi took point, preferring it to the role of tail gunner she'd made her own on the *Diamantina*. They cut a path through the vines and tanglebush spilling down the headland and onto the forecourt of the Opera House. Funny. That place always reminded her of big ass turtles humping each other. Woulda been a helluva lot easier to just walk up Macquarie Street, even with all the piled-up traffic wreckage, but it woulda been kind of an epic dumb-ass move too. The first couple of hundred yards of Macquarie were sunk between the towering sandstone retaining wall that marked the western edge of the Gardens, and on the far side of the road a long terrace of once luxurious apartments that dominated the waterfront facing Circular Quay. A shooting gallery, in other words, where even the most retarded Biter could rain down fire, or pointy rocks, on her pretty head, without having to think much about it.

So Fifi took them along the high road, a walking path, still easily navigable for most of its length. It skirted the edge of the Gardens, and afforded them a decent lookout over lower Macquarie Street and into the abandoned catacombs of the apartments on the far side. She mostly kept her attention forward, stopping at random intervals to listen for sign of pursuit or ambush. When the way forward proved impossible because the jungle had sent so much thorny creeper, or lantana or wait-a-while vines out to climb the old iron fencing, she would call Jules up to chop a way through with those wicked fucking Gurkha knives of hers.

"Reckon we might bring some garden shears next time," Pete offered after the second delay.

"And a weed whacker," Fifi grinned as Jules cursed up a storm at an especially thick knot of creeper.

"I thought Jules was our weed whacker."

The obstruction was thick enough that when she'd hacked her way through, Julianne took a sharpening stone out of her tac-vest and spent a minute or so putting the edge back on her babies. While she did, Pete doubled back a ways and checked their six. Fifi used the break to scope out the roadway below, using Julesy's binoculars to trace their intended path uptown.

The Blackout hit Sydney smack in the middle of lunchtime, at least according to Pete. Reckoned he'd been halfway to Tasmania at the time, running a charter for a bunch of merchant bankers as some sort of "team building" exercise. As best he knew, the team was building outdoor latrines in a potato field somewhere north of Hobart now. Still, better than starving to death, or being eaten alive in a place like this.

You could see where the traffic had been flowing freely the day it happened. As drivers lost control of their vehicles, long lines of cars and trucks and buses and taxis had been crunched together like God was a big old accordion player who'd decided at that moment to just mash everything up for no good reason. Some of those pileups had burned, of course, and they burned all the way down to the ground because no fire trucks had come to put out the flames.

At other places she could see where the drivers had been lucky enough to be stopped at red lights, or caught up in the grind of the slow-moving traffic jams that were once endemic to big cities everywhere. At those intersections, and along those stretches of road you could still see daylight between the front fender of one vehicle and the ass end of the next one. Many of the doors stood open, and here and there she could see where windows and windshields had been smashed, perhaps to let the occupants escape, perhaps to break into the cabins days later as order broke down and the looting and riots began.

Jules grunted and swore, and hacked away as the morning sun climbed higher in the sky. They were all sweating by now, but their English rose was drenched with it. The heat didn't bother Fifi much. She liked to tan. On the day of the Blackout she'd been the sous chef for a yachting party cruising around San Francisco Bay. Woulda been a total death sentence except that the geekboy millionaire who owned the big ass yacht was also a sci-fi super nerd who had about a dozen different plans worked out for all his favorite flavors of the Apocalypse. Mostly they involved sailing away to Tasmania. They'd all been very hungry by the time they made the South Pacific and she was sick of cooking fish and seabirds. But she had a great tan.

Summer was two or three weeks gone here, but the heat lingered and in the last couple of days it had been warm enough to brew up a decent storm by midafternoon. Fifi didn't envy Julianne the job of cutting path, but Jules wouldn't let anyone else use her choppers, and nobody wanted to carry the extra weight of a machete they wouldn't need for more than a couple of minutes at most. She heard footsteps coming back up the path behind them, and saw Pete returning from his backtrack. He signed "All Clear" and she took a moment with the binoculars to sweep the buildings across the street. The mirrored sun blazed off panes of glass where windows and sliding doors were still intact, but she concentrated on those darkened caves that threw off no reflection.

No movement. No sign. Nothing.

Awesome.

The scrape of steel on whetstone told her Jules was done with the gardening. They paused to allow her to tend to her blades, which went back into their twin scabbards when she was done. The small, wiry noblewoman took a drink from her water flask and retrieved her slingshot from its holster.

"Next time, we'll just take a taxi, I think," she said.

They covered the rest of the way up past the charred ruins of Government House in good time, slowing only to negotiate a snarl of traffic that reached neutron star densities at the eastern end of the Cahill Expressway. A bus had tipped over on the ramp that swept down from the elevated roadway, blocking dozens of vehicles behind it. Fire had raced through the pileup that was now an impassable hazard of rusted, jagged metal.

"High road or low?" asked Jules.

They could use the grappling hook to climb up the off ramp, or detour deep into the wilderness of the Gardens gone wild.

"Why don't we just fast rope down to Macquarie?" asked Fifi.

"Because Captain Sensible doesn't like taking shortcuts," Jules answered, waving the blade of her short inward-curved sword at Pete.

"Shortcuts are the road to Hell," he confirmed, but he didn't look like he loved the idea of a walk in the park either.

"Anyone hear that big cat earlier?" he asked.

Both women raised their hands, although Fifi was sure the nor'easter had carried the noise to them all the way from the north shore. As dangerous as it was navigating the streets, the only things likely to bite you down there were crazy people. The scrub, on the other hand, was crawling with snakes. Blacks and browns and king browns with venom enough to kill a man, painfully, with one lightning quick bite.

She hated snakes. They were the reason she missed shotguns so much.

"I'm cool to play Spider-Man," she said. "Worst of the bad ground's back yonder anyway," she added, gesturing over her shoulder with the three-pronged sai.

"Pete, how far up is this place we're headed?" asked Jules.

He didn't need to consult his map. He well knew the city from before the Blackout and had been studying the maps all the way down the coast. Nor was it their first salvage run on old Sydney town.

"Three blocks."

"Biters don't like to wait for their breakfast," Jules pointed out. "If they were going to have at us they'd already have put on a cauldron of tea and buttered up a couple of muffins."

"Man, I'd love a breakfast McMuffin," said Fifi.

"OK," said Pete. "The low road it is."

"I miss McDonald's."

"OK. We'll get you a Happy Meal later," said Pete.

"And curly fries."

"Of course."

"Man, I loved curly fries," Fifi recalled wistfully.

"Didn't you used to be a proper chef?" said Jules.

"A deputy," said Fifi. "Sous chef. And I just cooked that snooty shit. I didn't eat it, Judgy McJudgerson."

The fence line had collapsed a little farther on, allowing them to rope down to Macquarie where the drop wasn't too far. Fifi went first, doubling the rope around an anchor point at the base of the iron railing where it still held strong. She rappelled down the sheer sandstone retaining wall, kicking off with her boots, zipping downline, and landing with a soft thump on the roof of an old Volvo that had mounted the curb when the driver lost power and steering. Jules followed and they formed a basic perimeter as Pete descended. He pulled the rope through and stowed it in his pack.

As soon as they were all down in the canyon between the Gardens and the apartment blocks, Fifi regretted it. Her skin crawled with the sensation of being watched and her heart beat faster than the meager exertion of a fast rope descent really warranted. She took point again, leading them forward, sword and sai in guard position, bent low to drop beneath the roofline of the cars. Behind her, Julianne's boots crunched on the accumulated grit of nearly ten years that lay on the road surface. She would be sweeping their flanks and the high ground with her slingshot, the ammo pouch loaded with four or five balls for area suppression. Fifi didn't need to look back over her shoulder to confirm the detail. This wasn't their first rodeo. Pete, she knew, would hang back just a little, occasionally stopping and dropping out of sight to cover their back trail.

In this way they moved quickly up the gentle gradient toward the intersection where the Cahill Expressway looped back into the city grid. It was a junkyard of rusting cars, all snarled together, but easily skirted on foot. They cleared the canyon and jogged the length of the next block, which was almost free of traffic. Weeds and razor grass had sprung up in the cracks of the tarmac and curb, but not so thickly that she had to worry about snakebite. Not that she really had to worry at all. Her boots laced halfway up her calves and the camouflage pants she wore were reinforced below the knees with a thin titanium mesh, carefully removed from a "shark-proof" old wet suit. She knew there was no such thing as shark-proof, unless it was staying out of the goddamned water in the first place. But it made her feel better. She'd been snake-bit once.

Never again.

They halted and spread out at the next intersection, taking a minute to scan their surrounds. They were on open ground now, or as open as it got in a city, a wide apron of tarmac and granite in front of an old colonial building. Real big sucker too, like a Roman ruin, or would be in a hundred years or so.

"Library," Pete informed her when he saw her looking.

"A real one, with Danielle Steele?" she asked, almost hopefully.

"Probably not," said Jules. "Looks a bit grown up for that."

"Hey, I'm a grown-up and I like Danielle Steele," Fifi protested.

"No time for browsing, sweetheart," Pete warned. "Not this trip. We can get you some new stories in Hobart."

"Yeah, for about a million bucks," she scoffed.

"We make this score, that won't be a problem," he promised. "Come on. Not far now."

And it wasn't. The building marked on all of their maps, committed to all of their memories, was only another half block past the big mall that dropped downhill into the city. It took them less than a minute to hurry along on past the stupid library without any Danielle Steele stories. They crouched behind a taxi, sunken down to its wheel rims right in front of the target building. It looked old, but not like the library. The Art Deco features, the green tiles and faded silver banding, advertised its origins in the 1920s or thirties.

Pete had told them on the boat that it was mostly doctor's consulting rooms. All of Macquarie Street, or at least this end of it, was full of doctors, probably because the first hospital in the colony had been built right behind them, on a high ridge overlooking the original sweep of Gardens. Then, being Pete, he'd spent the next hour pulling a cork and telling them a lot of boring stories about how some assholes had paid for the hospital with rum running, or some shit, and there'd been a rebellion, again because of rum, or something and . . . well, Fifi tuned out and tried to remember what listening to the Spice Girls sounded like.

There wasn't a thimble small enough to hold her lack of interest in Pete's history lessons, and she sorta wished that he'd just drink his god-damned rum rather than think up a lot of super-tedious stories that he used to explain why drinking rum was such an interesting goddamned pastime.

"Third floor," he said now. All business. No lectures or cork pulling.

"It's a jeweler, not a doctor. A. A. Finkle and Sons. Place should be secured. But not so's we can't break in. Now, Finkle's sister who lives in Darwin . . ."

"Pete," sighed Fifi, "why are you telling us this? You already told this on the boat. About a hundred times."

He smiled. "Because you forget things, Fifi."

"No," she retorted. "I just choose not to remember them, unless they're interesting. I'm not interested in Double-A Finkle's sister, or what she told you. I just want to get the salvage, finish our commission, and fuck off back to Darwin."

"That does sound a worthy plan, Pete," said Jules, who was not nearly as rude as Fifi, except when she was very angry, and then she was a very rude and very scary lady indeed.

She wasn't angry now. She just looked like she wanted to get on with it. Luck seemed to be with them this morning. A whole city to them-selves, nobody bitten or tossed into a cooking pot, not even freebooters or scavenging shitheads to rassle with.

"All right," sighed Pete. "But you know, the journey is the destination."

"Shut the fuck up, Obi Wan," said Fifi. "And let's go get our loot."

Another scan up and down the street revealed no sign of lurkers or stalkers. The birdsong, which had started up as they moored, was loud and continuous now. No mysterious breaks in the chorus heralding an untoward change in their circumstances. Jules put her slingshot away and tooled up with the Gurkha blades. As much as Fifi liked the idea of the cover provided by her friend's skill with the ranged weapon, she felt much safer when she saw those bad boys glinting in the sun. They spent a lot of time at sea, and when it wasn't terrifying, which was only rarely, it was mostly dull. Endless hours to fill as they made the long run between the top end of Australia and the ass end of New Zealand, via the bizarro theme park of modern Republican Hobart. Endless hours that they filled with weapons practice.

Kata, in Pete's case, a series of basic forms adapted to the modified tonfa he carried—he didn't see much point training with his big ol' club.

And blade training for the women. As good as Jules was with a slingshot, thousands of hours of training on the unstable, heaving deck of a sailboat had made her even deadlier with a pair of choppers. The way those things whirled in a blur around Julesy reminded Fi' of an old cartoon from primary school about atoms and the littler atoms that flew around them in a solid cloud. When Jules got going she was like the little atom inside a cloud of razor-edged steel.

They crossed the street quickly. First Pete, then Jules, then Fifi, all of them threading through the dead traffic, covering one another. The door to the building stood open, held in place by a house brick wrapped in fraying, faded cloth. A decade of dust and leaf litter had blown in and covered the old marble floor to a depth of inches in some places. The mulch squished rather than crackled under Fifi's bootheels as she took point again, leading them deeper into the shadows. A café stood trashed and looted on the immediate left, the furniture all turned over and smashed to kindling. Old-fashioned mirrors, frosted with DRINK COCA-COLA had once added an illusion of depth to the dark, leather booths, but they were all cracked and shattered. One had been splashed with a thick dark liquid, dried to a brown smear. There was nothing to be had in there.

Sword and sai at the ready she glided forward to the end of the hallway, where an elevator door stood half open, the floor of the car at least three feet above the level of the corridor. A stairwell wrapped around the service core of the building and she took them up that.

The natural litter blown in through the front door gave way to the familiar chaos of a looted building on the first floor. Doors smashed open, furniture dragged out of waiting rooms, an abandoned hospital gurney, empty boxes she was sure would once have contained drugs. They climbed to the next floor, then waited while Pete backtracked and lay in wait for a tail.

Nothing.

The second floor was a repeat of the first. Doctors' rooms, all of them plundered long ago. They repeated the procedure of sweeping past and waiting as Pete doubled back to ambush any stealthy pursuers. Again, nada.

Awesome sauce.

The third floor was different. The corridor was narrower, darker. The rich marble flooring gave way to worn wooden boards and a thin carpet runner. There were more offices on this level, tinier and meaner-looking. Fifi checked with Pete and he nodded, pointing with his chin to an office secured with steel grillwork halfway down. Fifi took a deep breath and stilled her pulse, settled her nerves, before stepping out of the stairwell.

It was good fieldcraft to pause before you leapt onto the pot of gold at the end of the rainbow. Excitement, greed, impatience—they were all calculated to bring you undone. You got carried away with the prospect of all those gold doubloons and next thing you knew some cannibal fucking leprechaun had caved your skull in and you woke up in his dinner bowl.

She stood, as still as an old tree in an ancient forest, letting her senses flow out into the world. Listening for the snap of a hard and dirty bare foot stepping on a twig, or a discarded syringe two floors below. Eyes scanning and scoping, not looking for any one particular detail but letting it all flow in over her, as alive to unusual absences as the presence of some giveaway tell. She sniffed the air, tasting it.

Nothing. No rank sour stink of unwashed humanity. Just dust and decay.

Neither of the others pressed her forward. They would wait until she was ready.

A full minute later Fifi stepped off.

*   *   *

It was all as Miss Finkle had said it would be. Her brother's workshop, tucked in between a once infamous private detective and a less notable astrologer-by-appointment. The door to the detective agency stood open. There was only one room, no space for a receptionist. The shattered remains of a whiskey bottle littered the desk, which was also strewn with papers and something Pete hadn't seen in a long time. A handgun. He pieced the story together. The private eye putting away one shot after another as everything fell apart around him. Draining the bottle. Putting the muzzle of the revolver to his forehead for that last, white-hot shot that would carry away the troubles of the world, forgetting . . .

Forgetting . . .

Forgetting the gun didn't work anymore. Nothing worked anymore. The trigger clicking impotently. The hammer falling uselessly. And the drunken, bewildered man lashing out with the cold lump of steel, smashing the bottle, glass shards flying everywhere. He'd probably find a few dried, brown bloodspots in there if he bothered to look.

He didn't.

"So, what now?" asked Jules as they pulled up in front of the frosted glass door stenciled with A. A. FINKLE—WATCHMAKER. The concertina security grill looked as old as the building, a relic of the 1930s, but that simply meant it had done the job of securing the Finkle family business for eight decades. There would be no breaking in by brute force. Not without raising an unholy racket that'd bring every hungry Biter on both sides of the harbor looking for them.

"Yeah, Obi Wan. Nice work. The journey is the destination but the fucking destination is locked up tighter than a gnat's ass."

Pete just grinned.

"Such a lack of faith in your celebrated captain would speak poorly of him, if he didn't know what a feckless pair of bitches you are."

He reached into his breast plate and fetched out a brass key on a long chain.

"If you'd listened to my improving instruction on the voyage down, instead of murdering the Spice Girls' back catalog, you'd have learned that Miss Finkle, sister of the dear departed Double-A, has provided us with a key to her brother's place of business for the very reasonable consideration of ten percent off the back end of any salvage."

"Fuck me!" said FiFi. "Ten percent? For a cut like that the old bitch should've dragged her wrinkled ass down here and helped us haul out."

Pete smiled and shrugged as he fitted the key into the lock. It turned easily.

"Well, she is, as you say, a rather wrinkly old bitch. Perhaps you'll get lucky and she'll die before we return with her share."

"Fifi," sighed Jules. "You know we have to pay her. Good information always pays off. That's how it works. It's how we work. Otherwise we're just picking over the scraps like the rest of the bottom-feeders."

Fifi rolled her eyes. "I know it, but I don't have to like it."

"Come on," said Pete as he pulled the grill aside. It squeaked in protest. "Lets see what Double-A has for us."

A. A. Finkle had treasures indeed. The watchmaker had specialized in old, super premium timepieces. Most of his business had been in repairs and maintenance, but every year he took a handful of commissions from high-paying customers, crafting exquisite watches and clocks for the city's elite. Increasingly, according to his sister, he'd been also taking work from Asia, mostly China and Hong Kong.

The safe was locked of course, but Pete had the combination from Miss Finkle committed to memory and written down in his notebook. His memory was fine. The dial turned, the tumblers fell, and the heavy steel door swung open.

"Holy shit," said Fifi as Pete carefully removed fifteen finished pieces, each one stored in a small velvet-covered box with the owner's name embroidered in gold stitching on the lid.

Nine of them were men's watches—big, chunky chronometers that would need winding every day or two. Once upon a time that would have made them hopelessly old-fashioned. Nowadays it made them priceless.

Two were slightly more modern in their design—newer models that relied on the kinetic energy of a swinging wrist to power their workings. Pete knew they'd be worth slightly less because the suspicion most people had these days, quite reasonably, of any technology that seemed to run off "invisible" sources of power. He might even keep one for himself, as a backup for his old windup Breitling Navitimer.

Jules and Fifi cooed over the remaining pieces, four bejeweled ladies' watches of quite breathtaking beauty. Julianne held one up into the weak gray light that struggled through the dusty office window. It still sparkled like a newly revealed secret.

"Girard-Perregaux," she whistled. "Sweet."

"Into the bag," said Pete, holding up a large black velvet sack.

Julianne gave the watch one last rueful look before replacing it carefully in its little box and passing it to Pete.

There were another twenty-two watches under repair, and he took them too, careful to keep each wrapped separately.

"We taking the cuckoo clock?" Fifi asked, admiring the giant polished walnut unit that stood in one corner.

"If you can carry it," said Pete.

"Guess not then. So? We done?"

"No, we need to grab up all the tools as well. Pack them properly."

"Seriously?" Fifi asked, holding up an instrument that looked like it belonged in a dentist's surgery.

"Yep. They're worth more than the watches, according to old Miss Finkle."

"Then who the fuck could afford them?" asked Fifi. "Only a watchmaker could use them, and no way those guys are loaded."

"I don't even know how many of those guys are left," Jules added. "Wouldn't have been a high demand skill set when everyone was starving to death and killing one another. So what are you thinking, Pete?"

Pete Holder moved over to the window and took a moment to survey the street. Old and cautious habits made for old and cautious captains.

"I'm thinking you're both very perceptive young ladies, easy on the eye too, and not at all stuck up, except for Lady Julianne on occasion, but you're not thinking of the long game."

He held up the black velvet bag, now stuffed and lumpy with priceless chronometers.

"When these things hit the market in Darwin or Christchurch or even fucking Portland someone in some royal household is going to want their very own Mickey Mouse watch too. Maybe they don't have in-house watchmakers, although I'll bet that mad fucker in Portland does. The tools are worth more than the watches because with the tools you can make more and repair what you have."

"You got a price in mind?" asked Fifi, suddenly interested.

Pete grinned. "Oh these old things?" he said, picking up another inexplicable utensil. "Free to those who can afford it, very expensive to those who cannot."

"What?" Fifi frowned.

"Favors," said Jules, in a flat voice. "He's going to trade them for royal favors."

"You'll make a fine pirate captain one day, Julesy," said Pete.

They gathered up the rest of the watchmaker's tools, finding a handy carryall that seemed purpose built to, well, carry them all. It went into Pete's backpack, the watches into Jules'. Fifi would carry the treasure they'd actually been warranted to salvage from the city.

Another prudent check of the streets below, and they effected a careful exit from the office and workshop of one Double-A Finkle, watchmaker, deceased. Pete slid the security grill shut and locked it behind them. When he saw the looks both girls were giving him, he shrugged.

"I promised old Miss Finkle. And Cap'n Pete always keeps a promise."

They removed themselves from the building with just as much watchfulness as they'd entered, moving no less easily with the small, but immeasurably valuable load they'd picked up. Back out on the street Jules swapped over her weapons again, sheathing the kukri daggers and taking up her military slingshot. She extended the arm brace, squeezed, and shook out her fingers a couple of times before loading three ball-bearings into the soft leather ammo cup. She checked her position against a mental map of the city and the actual map they'd just reviewed in the foyer of the building. They weren't far from the second objective, just a couple of blocks this way and that, the sort of distance she would once have walked in high heels simply to get a better cup of coffee. But in a city of the hungry dead those extra minutes could make all the difference.

Fifi took point. Pete covered their six. And Lady Julianne Balwyn watched the high places, ever alert for the telltale movement that would warn of an attack from the higher floors of the haunted skyscrapers that towered over them. Their path took them down through the legal district, away from the overgrown wasteland of Hyde Park and into the shadowy canyon of Castlereagh Street. Apart from the low moan of the morning breeze passing between the high-rises and through thousands of broken windows and the soaring steel cable lacework of Centerpoint Tower, their footsteps were still the loudest noise she could hear.

She never got used to that. She had grown up in London, studied in New York, partied in São Paulo, Bangkok, and Sydney. Or at least she partied until her father had utterly dissipated the family fortune. Quite an achievement that, pissing away all the wealth extorted from the peasantry over the better part of the millennium, and all in less than half a lifetime.

Still, she knew cities. Old and new, alive and dead, they each had their own particular . . . feeling. And this one felt wrong to her. She grew more anxious about it the deeper they pushed into the old abandoned central business district. It wasn't anything as simple as a sudden cessation of all background noise that would warn of predators moving through an area. It wasn't the way that their boots, crunching on years of grit and litter and broken glass, were the loudest noise she could hear. It was the uncomfortable pressure of silence. The way the creeping stillness and quiet of a great necropolis like this seemed to push down on your chest. As though the absence of life was a physical presence in and of itself.

She shuddered and shook it off, turning around to make light of it to

Pete, and gasping in fright when she realized he wasn't there anymore. Her heart lurched, but he had simply backtracked to cover their path again. He reappeared just as she was getting her panic reaction under control, stepping back onto Castlereagh Street from some alleyway he'd used as a shortcut. He waved to her with his heavy club, signaling "All Clear."

"Hey Jules, check it out."

She almost ran into Fifi, who had pulled up just short of the entrance to another alleyway and was speaking in a low whisper.

The blond woman hung her three-pronged sai through a loop on her belt and used her free hand to pass Julianne a compact mirror. Fifi slid away from the corner, making room for Jules to take her position. She sensed her companion signaling to Pete to quiet down and approach them with caution. Julianne used the mirror to peer around the corner without exposing too much of her own body. It took her a moment to find whatever Fifi had been looking at, but she swallowed hard and took a slow, deep breath when she saw a thin tendril of smoke and followed it down to its source, a small campfire, the ashes smoldering within a rough circle of broken bricks, which were in turn surrounded by upturned boxes and plastic crates. That was enough for Jules. She handed the mirror to Pete and took up a firing position from where she could cover them with her slingshot, next to a burned-out people-mover.

Holder did as she had just done, surveilling the alley without stepping into it, but he took a few moments longer.

"Looks like it's been tamped down for an hour or so," he said quietly as he joined her in cover. Fifi stowed the mirror and recovered her short, fighting trident.

"Y'all wanna deep six this?" she asked.

"Hell no," said Pete. "Little campfire that size? Looks like a three or four man outfit. Probably freebooters. Maybe scavengers, not real salvagers. Jules?"

Julianne frowned as she swept up and down the street with the high-powered slingshot. Nothing. No movement, no sign of occupation beyond the cold campfire.

"Well, we know they're not here looking for what we're after," she said. "Although I'm sure they'd be more than happy to relieve us of those watches."

"Well that's not gonna happen," hissed Fifi. "But they're welcome to get themselves killed trying."

"I vote we press on," said Pete.

He was not the sort of captain who just ordered people to do stupidly dangerous things. He rather expected them to agree with him that there was a balance to be struck between the stupid and dangerous choice, and the profits to be had from occasionally paying them less regard than they might otherwise deserve.

"Fuckin' scavengers," spat Fifi, again. "Ass-feedin' cocksuckers don't bother me none. I'm for going on, getting our salvage, and if we find these assholes I say we kill 'em on principle. They ain't got no warrant to be working this city. Ain't right they're even here."

"Jules?"

Julianne let the strain off the slingshot, taking it back to a half pull.

"Another block? Right?"

"Yep," Pete confirmed.

She shrugged. "Well, it's the reason we came. Can't rightly show ourselves in Darwin without it."

"Nope."

"I suppose we best kick on."

"And we should totally kill the scavengers too," said Fifi.

"Totally," agreed Pete, but in a tone that betrayed his lack of enthusiasm for the idea.

Fifi led off again. She'd been careful before, of course. The King of Darwin did not issue Royal Warrants of Salvage to any old asshole. The King of Darwin was a righteous dude who paid his bills and suffered no fools. Especially not the sort of fools who went into unlicensed scavenging, picking over the loot and plunder of the dead cities that rightfully, legally, belonged to righteous dudes like the King of Darwin and his official retainers or agents or Royal fucking appointees or whatever you called them.

Which was what she and Jules and Pete were, goddamn it, because they had a Royal Warrant and she would bet beans to bullshit chips that the worthless, scavenging cocksuckers who'd built that campfire back there did not. That meant they were not just stealing from the King of Darwin. They were stealing from her.

And nobody stole from Fifi Lamont. Nobody took anything from her she didn't feel one hundred percent like giving up.

So as careful as she'd been when leading them to the watchmaker's place, she was doubly vigilant now. Not because she was frightened of running into these worthless thieves, but because she was frightened she might miss the chance of running into them if she didn't pay attention. Pete and Jules, she understood, were a little more laid-back on this topic, a little more inclined to live and let live. They would be just as happy to avoid any encounter with the scavengers, to execute their Commission, and get the hell back to the boat. She respected that. But she had to be true to herself and if there was one truth you could say of Fifi Brianna Lamont, it was that she had never met a scavenger she had not taken the time to put down like a diseased dog.

Well, almost.

There was one. The one Pete had rescued her from. But that made it important she never let a chance slip by to settle up with every other scavenger asshole she happened across. So she crept through the wreckage and over the bones of Sydney, her sharpened steels before her, her senses alive and raw. She stepped ever more carefully, placing each foot where it would make the least noise. She breathed through her nose, sniffing them out, detecting the faint smell of burned flesh as they passed the open alley, almost certainly the remains of some rodent or possum they'd cooked up over the fire for breakfast or even supper last night.

She suppressed a smile at the thought of them being so stupid, gathered around a campfire, staring at the flames, ruining their night vision, probably passing a bottle, roaring and shouting at one another in the dark. If these clowns hadn't brought the Biter clans down on them, then the Biters probably weren't within miles of the CBD. It made sense. They tended to be nomadic, the tribes orbiting around one another in a slow dance that might take years to cover the whole city. That left Fifi free to deal with as many lowlifes as she could get to with her blades before Jules and Pete dragged her back to the *Diamantina*. She was cool with that.

But first they had the Warrant to execute.

She led them past the rear of some once grand hotel, around a small snarl of fire-blackened cars, and across the street to the address Pete had made her repeat to him a dozen times before they'd stepped off the boat. She could find it on a street map at a glance, and had known exactly the path she would take to lead them here before they'd even set foot on dry land.

"Nicely done," said Julianne behind her. "Will you be okay, sweetheart? You know, with the scavengers and all?"

"Obi-Wan has taught me well, Jules. I am the path of least resistance girl now. Sure, if I see them, I will kill every motherfucking one of them. But if I don't, that's cool too."

She smiled as innocently as she could with all of the old rage welling up inside her.

"Okay," said Julianne uncertainly. "Just so we don't get distracted by all the killing and oaths of blood vengeance and everything. Again. We still have paying work to do here."

She nodded toward another old building, this one of 1940s or fifties vintage. The facade and the ground floor were in much worse shape than the old Art Deco high-rise where Double-A had his crib. Probably because there was a cluster of sandwich shops and coffeehouses in this part of the street, and they had all been attacked by starving hordes a couple of days after the Blackout.

"Let's stick to doing the simple things well," said Pete as he joined them after yet another backtracking exercise.

Since discovering the scavengers' campfire he had increased the frequency and length of his efforts to uncover any tail they may have picked up.

"Any sign?" Jules asked.

"Just the campfire," said Pete. "You cool, Fifi?"

"Fuck! Why does everyone keep asking me that?"

"Because," said Pete, "the last time we ran across scavengers, you rode a horse right at them screaming and firing crossbows and throwing ninja stars into their faces."

"So?"

"Fifi," said Jules. "You don't know how to ride a horse."

"And the time before that . . ." Pete started, but she cut him off.

"Omifuckinggod just back the fuck off would you. I ain't like that no more. I done chilled out and cured myself of all that anger. And I've only got two ninja throwing stars with me this time."

She held them up. "And no horse."

Jules looked like she wanted to go on with the argument but Pete put a hand on her arm.

"Come on. We're here now. We can get the papers and be back on the boat before lunch. Be out the Heads and making sail for Darwin before cocktail hour. Let's focus. The King's Commission. Escape the city. Cocktails."

That seemed to mollify Julianne, and Fifi let go of her temper.

"OK. I'm chill. Let's get 'er done."

But as they stepped into the darkened vestibule she threw a look back onto the street. Just in case they were being followed by scavengers. Because if they were, those motherfuckers were totally getting a face full of ninja star.

Jules folded the brace of her slingshot away, and stowed the weapon in its holster. Her twin blades came out of their scabbards with a whisper as Fifi and Pete picked a path through piles of upturned furniture, long shards of broken window glass, and three shopping trolleys that had been loaded up with crap and then abandoned in the middle of the building's entryway. The dark space smelled of rot and old piss. One of the coffee shops had burned at some point, but the fire hadn't spread. She had no idea why. Perhaps there'd been a storm. The piles of debris and abandoned pillage made their passage difficult, but spoke of a building that had not been touched by human hands in many years, possibly not since the city died.

"Look," said Fifi, gesturing at a small, scattered pile of bones and rags in one corner of the fire-scorched café. They looked human, but only just. Animals had gnawed at them and carried off most of the protein. Jules recognized a hip bone and maybe half a femur.

"I can see why the King of bloody Darwin was disinclined to pop down and run his own errands," she said.

"But he's paying us handsomely to run them for him," Pete pointed out as he put his shoulder to a piano that had somehow made its way onto the stairs at the back of the entry hall. It was blocking access to the upper floors, but threatening to topple down on anybody foolish enough to try to move it.

"Gimme a hand, Fifi," he grunted.

The American was the stronger of the two women and put her own broad shoulders to the job while Julianne kept watch over them and the street outside. Her skin crawled at the jangling racket they set up, grunting and heaving the thing aside, but as before, they attracted no attention, not even when the enormous weight did suddenly shift and drop with a loud crash and the sudden discordant music of untuned strings. Jules was instantly thrown back to her teenage years, watching shitty horror movies that were all about the sudden noises and flashes of movement.

She breathed deeply and waited for the hordes of enemies to break upon them.

Nothing happened.

First Pete, then Fifi slipped past the obstruction, while she waited a little while as a hedge against any stalkers who might have been drawn by the noise.

Nothing.

She wanted to relax and believe this was going to be a milk run, but the absence of any trouble so far just made her more anxious. When she was sure they were indeed alone and unsought by scavengers or Biters or ne'er-do-wells of any kind, she followed her crewmates up the steps. They were headed for the sixth floor this time and she calculated it would take them at least another ten minutes before they were done if they moved as cautiously as they had back at the watchmaker's. She tarried behind Fifi and Pete, watching their rear, pausing on each landing, waiting a full minute, moving slowly to the next floor and . . .

"Got it."

"What?" She almost jumped out of her skin.

"We're good," said Pete, tucking a sheaf of documents into Fifi's backpack. "Easy as a drunken nun. Lets go."

"Bugger me," said Jules, struggling to still her rapidly beating heart. "You sure you got the right one?"

"Checked it against the Warrant. Come on. This place is giving me the creeps."

"There was dead people upstairs," said Fifi. "Heaps of them."

"How? When?" asked Jules, suppressing the note of panic in her voice.

"Don't sweat it," Pete said. "Looked like a suicide pact back in the day. Whole bunch of them got together in some meeting hall one floor up and necked enough pills to do the job."

"Nasty," said Fifi. "Little kids and everything."

"Ugh, I hate these places," said Jules. "Let's just go."

They hurried through the detritus, pausing for a moment to surveil the street and, finding it clear, plunged back out into the surprising chill of a morning that had turned gray and overcast in front of a southerly change. That would mean tacking down the harbor against a prevailing wind, but still, they were on the home run now. Only needing to retrace their steps, return to the boat, haul anchor, and haul arse. All for fortune and glory.

Everything turned to shit one minute later.

Fifi took point, as always. Pete brought up the rear. Jules had swapped kukri blades for her slingshot again. They moved a little faster now they had secured the salvage. They shouldn't have. Each of them knew enough to take the business of getting out without being seen or heard as seriously as they had taken sneaking into the city. But it was hard. It was always hard when you felt yourself this close to getting away with it. This close to stepping back on the boat, and laying on sail for the open waves. Out there, they knew they could outrun pretty much anybody. The heart always beat a little faster when you knew you were getting clean away. Your breath came a little shallow, and your steps quickened. You . . .

"That'll be far enough, Pete. The redneck and the fuckin' Thloane Ranger can hold up there too."

The voice was rough and loud and vaguely familiar, and as soon as she heard it Julianne didn't think or pause or hunt around for the source. She dived for cover, and while she was diving she swept the crossroads of the intersection they had been moving through, looking for any sign of movement.

She saw it as she flew horizontally through the air. Two figures darting between an overturned postal van and the charred metal skeleton of a taxi. Already airborne, diving for her own spot sheltered in the lee of a sun-faded station wagon, she still had time to draw her sling back a little farther and loose three heavy steel balls in the direction of the attackers. She heard glass shatter, and steel punch through steel with a dull clang. Two shots had missed then.

But the third struck home with a satisfying, meaty thud that was lost in the gargling scream that followed. It was enough to take some of the sting out of landing heavily on the concrete.

"Smoke!" yelled Fifi, somewhere ahead of her, lighting and throwing both of her smoke pots from somewhere within the traffic pile up.

The crude grenades wouldn't explode, of course. But they did an admirable job of filling the intersection with thick, gray chemical clouds. Julianne pulled the bandanna around her neck up to cover her mouth and throat. Fifi's smoke bombs always tasted like shit.

"OH PETE! COME ON, NOW, MATE! THITH ITH UN-

NETHETHARY! DAN THAID YOU'D BE REATHONABLE ABOUT THINGTH!"

Jules cursed to herself.

Fucking.

Shoeless.

Dan.

That treacherous cunt. Was there a world somewhere in which he didn't fuck them every fucking time?

She recognized the voice now, too. The harsh, rasping lisp of Dan's one-time first mate, Jake "The Cobra" McTiernan. The Cobra liked to put it about that he got his nickname by virtue of his being so fast and deadly in a fight, but everyone knew it was because Dan had slit his tongue in two during a drunken disagreement over a salvage rights split six or seven years ago. Jake the Snake, as Jules preferred to think of him, had drifted from salvage into scavenging, but it seemed the rumors he'd patched it up with Shoeless Dan, at least in private, were no longer rumors.

"Fucking Shoeless Dan," hissed Pete, warning her of his approach as he slid out of the acrid smoke to crouch beside her. "Treacherous motherfucker."

Jules had already swapped out her slingshot for the twinned daggers. They'd be of much more use in this fight now. Pete's club and sharpened tonfa, she saw, were already slicked with blood.

"Where's Fifi?" she asked.

"Fucked if I know. She was moving fast when she popped smoke, should be headed for the rendezvous point by now, but . . ."

They heard a scream.

A scream with a noticeable lisp.

Then, "I am not a redneck, you ignorant cocksucker."

"Bugger," said Jules, at almost exactly the same moment as Pete, causing an odd, echo effect.

There were at least nine of them.

At least. Maybe ten. That was the rough number Fifi thought she counted in the sight-picture she took in the mad chaotic second after she sprang the ambush and Snake McTiernan's little worms had all come wriggling out to play. That could mean there were only nine of them, but more likely meant they were facing a dozen or more.

Pete and Jules would head for the first rendezvous point as soon as the smoke gave them a chance to get gone. And she would too. She would totally do as she was supposed to do.

But by her best reckoning, that forked-tongue spudfucker McTiernan was standing between her and the quickest path to the first ERP, and that meant she was totally entitled to a reckoning with him for getting in her goddamned way.

She didn't pause for sake of caution, or falter out of timidity. Sword and sai raised she moved into the thickest of the smoke, toward the voice that was now yelling in fury and exasperation to "Kill them, kill them all and get their thtuff."

Fucking scavengers.

She hated these guys.

A face came at her out of the gray chemical soup, a leering fright mask of facial tattoos, nose bones, lip rings, and long, oiled hair. The eyes went wide as he saw her, first in triumph, then in horror as her hand licked out, driving the trident sword deep into his throat. The thrust destroyed his voice box, opened up the trachea, and he died trying to scream, but failing as Fifi ripped the sai out of his neck and spun on her heel, cleaving a trail through the smoky air with the razor-edged metal blade of her ninjaken sword. The sweeping blade failed to connect with the other scavenger who'd come up behind her, but the flash of lethal steel unmanned him completely. He stumbled over his own feet, trying to back up even as his earlier momentum and intent served to carry him forward.

She lashed out with a front kick, missing his groin but connecting with the inside of his upper thigh. Her heavy, steel-capped boot dug into the soft flesh around the femoral artery and he collapsed with a howl that she cut short by opening his throat with the chisel point of her longer weapon.

"Kill them all!" cried McTiernan, and he was very close now. Fifi homed in on his cries.

"Hey! Thnakey," she called out as his rotund profile emerged from the smoke. "Behind you."

The leader of the scavenger band whipped around, raising his machete to guard against the flurry of blows he expected to face. But Fifi had already stowed her sai, replacing it with a seven-pointed shuriken that she flicked into his face with practiced speed. Over the years since the Blackout, she had made tens of thousands of practice throws into a series of scarred wooden tree stumps on the deck of the *Diamantina*, gradually reducing the fat, hardwood logs, one after the other, into kindling and wood chips.

Over the same period of years, the Snake had enriched himself, in a meager fashion, by sneaking up on travelers in their bedrolls and bashing out their brains, by raiding isolated farmsteads in low and vicious company, and by ambushing small parties of legitimate salvagers with genuine Royal Warrants to be about their business. None of this prepared him for close combat with an experienced and committed foe and one who, in the person of Fifi Lamont, was authentically bugshit on the topic of scavengers.

McTiernan made a ham-fisted attempt to knock the throwing star off its course, but badly mistimed the fend and screamed in pain and violation as the missile bit deeply into one of his eyes and the hairy curve of his cheek. His hands flew up involuntarily, pawing at the wound, and Fifi leapt forward in a fluid blur, slicing down across the front of his poorly protected belly, hacking through the ties of his boiled leather-scale vest with her first strike, then biting deep into his unprotected flank with a return technique that caused her sword to describe a glistening figure eight in the smoke, before gutting Jake "The Thnake" McTiernan at the intersection of Castlereagh and Market Streets.

For his dying declaration he chose "Thupid redneck thlut," which gave Fifi reason to cry out in protest.

"I am not a redneck, you ignorant bigot," just before she kicked him in the face, driving the shuriken in so deeply there was no sense in trying to retrieve it.

"That's her," said Pete. "Come on."

"Behind you!" Jules cried out, and Pete spun as he came up, already raising and sweeping the tonfa in a defensive arc.

A scavenger was leaping at him from the bonnet of a car. Pete poured even more torque into his turn, whipping his hip and shoulders around in a tight circle that perfectly recalled the old graphical representation of yin and yang. The real-world effects were not so pretty. The move took him off the line of attack and the long arm of the tonfa smashed into the man's unprotected elbow, doing little structural damage but probably stunning the arm. He was already too close for Pete to get a good swing in with his club, so he lashed out with an elbow, connecting lightly with some part of the guy's head as he flew past. Graceful technique fell apart in a tangle of arms and legs as ballet gave way to messy kinetics. The city blocks swirled around him in a sick miasma of washed-out colors and he drew in a deep breath ready to raise the club and bring it down on the neck or spine or anywhere soft. The attacker flew past and crashed into the car against which they had been sheltering. Pete readied himself for the kill, but then . . .

No point.

Julianne was already there, Gurkha blades flashing out in short, efficient strokes that neatly removed his head. Blood jetted from the body in extravagant fountains of hot, red horror.

"How many of them?" he asked, feeling stupid and numb.

"Same as before," answered Jules, flicking gore from her blades. "Fucked if I know."

With McTiernan no longer shouting orders, there was no sense of a coordinated assault, but that hardly made their position any less perilous.

"This way," said Pete, leading Jules in the direction from which they'd heard Fifi shouting at the scavenger chief.

Club in one hand, tonfa in the other, ready to block or stab, he felt his way through the smoke and chaos, expecting at every moment to fall into a desperate close quarter fight for his life. He could sense Julianne just a few steps behind him, her long, bloodied daggers ready to spin up like an old-fashioned threshing machine at the first provocation.

A gust of wind thinned out the smoke for half a second, revealing two bodies just ahead of him, one of them was the sprawled out corpse of the so-called Cobra, one hand clutching at a sharp and decidedly foreign object lodged in his face, while the other had tried to hold in a butcher's bag of gizzards that had come spilling out of his once generous paunch. He was dead, but there was no sign of Fifi.

No sign of the Cobra's crew either though, and that shouldn't be. As cowardly and vicious as they were, by Pete's best guess the scavengers still had them outnumbered two or three to one. He hefted the club, and gave the tonfa an experimental twirl, burning off nervous energy.

"Where are they? Where'd they go?"

"What part of fucked-if-I-know are you having trouble understanding, Pete?" said Jules in her clipped, pissed-off voice.

The wind freshened as they found the edge of the smoke and stared up the gentle slope of Market Street toward Hyde Park.

"Bugger," said Julianne in a flat voice.

It took a heartbeat, maybe two, for Pete to understand. At first he thought the southerly front was simply whipping through the dense forest and undergrowth that had taken dominion over the park lands. His body seemed to understand before his brain kicked in. He felt his balls trying to crawl up inside him before he had processed what he was seeing.

What looked like hundreds of Biters emerging from the foliage. They were camouflaged not so much by design and cunning, as by caked-on filth and long reversion to brute nature. They had one of McTiernan's men, who'd foolishly run toward them, or rather away from the sudden danger presented by the small salvage crew he'd meant to murder and rob.

He wasn't screaming, so he was already dead. Pete was paralyzed by the sight of crude cutting implements rising and falling as the cannibals chopped him up on the spot.

"Bloody savages," marveled Julianne. "I don't think they're even going to cook him."

A few drops of rain spattered on Pete's sweating face, surprising him with their sudden chill. He saw lightning flash in the distance. More and more cannibals emerged from the undergrowth of Hyde Park, clustering around their fresh kill, but some of them had already attended to the smoke and carnage at the intersection. They raised crude spears and clubs, and a couple of them, stupidly true to form, tried to lob stones all the way down the hill, hoping to hit Pete and Julianne and, he supposed, any of McTiernan's men who were still hanging around.

They were well out of range.

Pete felt a tug on his elbow and turned expecting to find Jules. Instead, he looked dumbly at Fifi.

"The journey is the destination," she said quietly. "And our destination is the fuck out of Dodge. Let's haul ass for there, now, Cap'."

It broke the spell. He took one step away from the Biters, and then another, and then he started to run.

They ran through the city of the dead, pursued by the open mouths and insane howls of the inhuman. They ran without turning or looking back, because to do so was to lose all hope. They did not stand and fight, they ran and prayed or ran and cursed each according to his or her own disposition. They ran through long empty streets that soon thronged with hundreds of savages. They ran through the first fat, heavy drops of rain. They ran through the first moments of the cloudburst that broke over them with a blue-white flash of lightning bright enough to end the very world. They ran through hard, stinging sheets of rain that lashed at them and soon caused the gutters to fill and overflow, puddles to spread and deepen, great fantails of filthy gray water to fly up at their heels.

They ran for one brief mad moment alongside a scavenger, a survivor of McTiernan's band, his weapons and equipment discarded, his eyes bulging with terror, beseeching them to carry him along with them, to deliver him from evil, for surely whatever differences they might have had, they were all united now in flight from this most horrible of fates.

Fifi flicked a shuriken into his leg and he went down in a screaming tangle of limbs. Half a block later they heard his desperate pleas for mercy turn into shrieks of horror as the fastest of the Biters fell upon him.

That's cold, Julianne thought, but didn't say so, because she was not foolish enough to waste her breath. Cold, but totally reasonable.

She still clutched both kukri daggers in her hands and wished for time enough to sheath them, to unfold and load her slingshot, time to put a couple of heavy balls through the foreheads of their lead pursuers. Splashing their brains over the second rank would surely slow them down, if only because they stopped to snack.

But she knew there was no time to even break stride.

The three veterans and friends hammered down the footpath, racing past burned-out cafés, the ruined facades of luxury boutiques, and looted and "salvaged" jewelry stores—the only difference between one and the other being the imprimatur of a Royal Warrant.

They took Martin Place at the diagonal, stretching legs that were already hot and trembling with fatigue, pushing themselves up the incline, past the polished brown marble pile of the old Commonwealth Bank headquarters, its heavy iron doors still sealed, broken windows protected by iron grates. On Elizabeth they took a barricade of heavy wooden desks in a bounding series of steeple jumps. As she sailed over a great, leather-topped bench she saw it had been scarred and gouged at sometime in the past by the blows of edged metal and heavy bludgeons.

Lungs burning, knees aching, backpack full of useless treasure grinding and slapping painfully into the base of her spine, she followed Fifi around the corner that led into a broad, almost semicircular line of road in front of an old 1960s era building, topped with a fading, broken sign that read QANT S.

The traffic wreckage here was horrible, but somehow Fifi threaded them through the worst of it, jumping and sliding across the bonnet of a convertible that was half filled with water. Pete rolled across the hood, cursing as he jabbed himself in the hip with one of the sharpened ends of his baton.

"I'm good," he gasped. "Keep going."

The temptation to hunker down behind the metal barricades, to make a stand somewhere that felt secure, even if it wasn't, almost robbed her of her strength and speed. But Pete pulled her on, dragging her through the last of the wreckage by the strap of her backpack. She struggled to control her breathing, drawing in deep drafts of air, squinting against the stinging rain, tilting her head forward so she didn't suck in too much water. Strobe lightning reducing their progress to a series of eerie still images; lightning that cracked with a physical force that she felt deep inside her burning eyes. And still they ran.

Don't be stupid, don't stop, don't fight, she told herself. *Just run.*

They charged up the hill toward Macquarie Street, taking the shortest route rather than the safest one, throwing aside all their previous caution about being trapped in the long canyon between the sandstone cliffs of the Botanic Gardens and the haunted apartment blocks on Circular Quay. Water squelched in her boots and she felt the weight of it soaking into all her clothes, slowing her down.

But she knew without looking, because to look behind was to lose hope, and to lose hope was to die, she knew without looking that the Biters were gaining and she had to keep running. Lightning flickered and flashed again, strange contrary winds trapped and channeled through the tunnels of the city pressed at them, further slowing any forward momentum. She could hear the shrieks and bellows and cries of the Biters closing in from behind, imagining, because it helped, that they were screaming in fear at the storm and the anger of the great Skylords who did not want them to catch this fleeing trio and eat their livers with a nice Chianti. Hysteria bubbled up from the roiling brew of terror and madness and Julianne Balwyn found herself giggling and then laughing without sense or purpose as she ran for her life.

The roughhewn sandstone walls to her right passed in a blur. Fifi was pulling ahead of her and Pete, her greater strength and speed telling in the final moments of the race. Perhaps she could get away at least. Then Pete put on a burst of speed, despite the blood that was running freely down his leg, dripping into the shallow stream through which they now splashed, pursued by monsters. Julianne's daggers had grown heavy in her grasp, slippery in the rain, and for a moment, just a moment, she thought about dropping them, or even tossing them over her shoulder, hoping to catch a pursuer in the face with a million-to-one throw.

But then they were around the end of the point and bursting into the wide open spaces of the Opera House forecourt, and she seemed to find new life in her legs, fresh air in her lungs, and an inexplicable, impossible, utterly magical second life as Fifi leapt onto the deck of the *Diamantina* and prepped the boat for an emergency departure.

She seemed to fly about the deck and masts, reefing down the Velcroed tatters of the camouflage sails, hauling up as much good canvas in their place as she could, hauling anchor and cutting ties as Pete put on his own quite unbelievable surge of speed and took the last few strides toward deliverance like a champion triple jumper.

Something long and dark flashed past Julianne. A spear.

Sharpened stones and rocks began to crash around her. She felt a dull impact in the middle of her tactical vest, but it served only to add impetus to her flight. The storm reached its height as Jules skipped across the rotting, nonslip decking of the little wharf at the Man o' War Steps before launching herself into clear air and landing amid the coiled ropes and crumpled canvas of the tattered sails Fifi had ripped down.

Now at last she turned and looked behind her, horrified to see how close the Biters were. Dozens of them were already around the point of the Gardens and most of the way across the forecourt. A barrage of crude missiles landed in the water and crashed into the Huon pine boards as Julianne whipped out her mil-grade slingshot and bent her knees against the violent inertia of the moving yacht as it pulled away from shore.

She let fly with the first ball, which put out the eye of the nearest cannibal.

He screamed and fell, taking down a couple of pursuers who were right on his heels. Two more shots and two more bodies hit the concrete. She gulped in horror, her face a mask of revulsion as the Biters fell on their fallen kin with teeth and claws and old kitchen knives. They were like sharks in a feeding frenzy.

All except one.

The largest and fiercest of them, armored in a sort of bone-mail cuirass that rattled as he leapt from the dock into the sky, landing neatly on the balls of his feet right in front her. She threw the useless slingshot into his face but he didn't so much as flinch, coming on at her with hands outstretched, his long filthy nails grown into slashing claws. He smiled and she saw his teeth had been filed to points.

"Get down," cried Fifi from behind her, and even though years of training and experience meant she almost unconsciously disobeyed the direction, instinctively reaching for her daggers, years of trust won out and Julianne dropped to the deck.

She heard the huge metallic chunnng as the harpoon mount fired. It sounded different, duller or thicker, and she realized Fifi would have had time to load only a quarter crank into the firing mechanism. It didn't matter. She wasn't firing on a ship. Just a man. Jules buried her face against the wave of offal that exploded from the spot where the cannibal had been standing when Fifi loosed the artillery at him.

Two smaller, briefer reports, sounded as Pete fired a couple of crossbow bolts into the pack that had pulled up at the Man o' War Steps, ready to make the leap across the water until they saw their strongest warrior turned into pink mist by the terrible magics of the Mighty Salvagers.

Julianne hurried to her station, where bow and arrow waited, but she didn't need them.

The Biters cursed and shook their fists but the fight had gone out of them. A few broke off to return to the feeding circle that boiled around the remains of the cannibals she'd put down. Within a few moments, they were far enough removed from land that there was no prospect of anyone leaping after them. Fifi appeared at her side with a crossbow that she casually raised and fired into the group that still stood watching them. It took a young male in the throat. He screamed and went down.

His tribesmen fell on him in the rain.

"Now that's a Happy Meal," said Fifi.

DARWIN
THREE MONTHS LATER

They had suites at the Royal Darwin Inn, which they could easily afford with the profits they had from the Sydney run. Hell, the one percent they weren't going to be paying Shoeless Dan anymore would have covered the room and service charges with plenty to spare. But there was no charge.

The King of Darwin was well pleased with the crew of the *Diamantina* and their execution of the Warrant of Salvage. He was even more pleased with the gift of watchmaker's tools Pete had presented to him. Thus the rooms at the Inn were comped, the bars stocked with the finest spirits and liquors and jugs of Saltie Bites Lager. There was even ice to keep the beer chilled.

Ice!

Jules had no idea where that had come from. Some mad bastard adventurers probably got themselves killed going after it. But as she sipped at a frosty gin and tonic she found she did not much care.

They even had tickets to the Royal Command Performance at Princess Anna Stadium.

"You couldn't get us better seats than this?" she asked, gazing out over the heaving crowds, but the quirk of her lips gave away the teasing intent of the question.

"Doesn't take you long to revert to type, does it, M'lady Mucky Muck?" said Pete as he tipped the neck of the oversize beer jug to his lips. Saltie Bites Lager came in two jug sizes: Epic, and Fuckin' Epic.

They weren't ensconced within the Royal Enclosure of the Stadium, but then none of them, not even Lady Julianne Balwyn, were of a mind to endure the tedium of Court when they could kick back and enjoy themselves in a gentry box with its own pukka-wallah laid on and another insulated cooler of more mystery ice. There were thousands of people in the stadium. It shook with the roar of cheers for the performers and for the monarch who insisted on introducing each of them.

Darwin is not like other Kingdoms, thought Jules.

"Ooh! Here's our bit," said Fifi who, like Pete, was drinking strong cold lager from brown jugs beaded with condensation. There was an impressive collection of empty jugs behind her and she almost tipped out of her chair as she tried to better look at the stage.

The king stepped up to the enormous speaker horns that would amplify his voice, at least for those who were sitting in the Enclosure and adjacent private boxes. Town criers, reading from scrolls, relayed His Majesty's words to the rest of the crowd.

King John, Jules noted, was wearing shorts. And a blue wife beater.

No, Darwin was not like other Kingdoms.

"Hey!" His Majesty roared out in a voice that would have been strong even without the magic of passive audio engineering. A loud voice was a must for a leader on the modern battlefield.

"How fucking sweet is this, Daaaaaarwin?"

The crowd noise indicated that the fortified city thought the Royal Command Performance very sweet indeed so far. The king stood back from the shouting tube and waited for the tumult to die down. It took a while, because of the echo effect of a half dozen town criers repeating his every word to the stadium.

When the roar had backed off, King John stood up again.

"We've got a treat for you tonight Daaaaarwin. A treat from the Olden Days."

He tried to damp down the reaction, but the crowd needed a full minute to quiet themselves. Treats from the Olden Days were a King John specialty.

"But first," roared the monarch to his adoring, if rowdy, subjects, "you gotta put your paws together for the mad bastards who made it all possible."

Jules reared back as flash pots went up in front of their box and long royal banners unfurled to draw the crowd's attention to them. Pete was already on his feet, waving his jug of Saltie Bites at the crowd. Fifi stumbled drunkenly when she tried to join him and Jules was forced to help her up.

"Thanksh, Juleshy," she slurred. "Will you hold me hair back if I vomit later?"

"Oh for fuck's sake," muttered the Englishwoman.

They all waved, but Jules was sure the loudest cheers were for Pete with his jugs. Until Fifi flashed hers. Her ears actually hurt, the crowd noise was so loud.

Darwin, she sighed.

The king was back at the giant speaking horns.

"Give it up for Cap'n Peeeete," he bellowed. "The Lady Jules and Fifi Lamont."

He drew out the last syllable of Fifi's name until the entire stadium was cheering and roaring it along with him.

Julianne dragged her shipmates, who were a lot deeper into the drink than her, back down to their chairs.

"The crew of the *Diamantina* have voyaged long and far . . ." shouted the king.

"Long and far?" said Jules skeptically.

"He's a fucking king," said Pete. "Cut him some slack."

"Yeah, bitch," Fifi agreed. "Nobody died and made you the sheriff of Nott . . . what . . . to doingham."

They both collapsed into giggles as the King of Darwin recounted the details of their adventures in Sydney, which were already more exaggerated than Julianne recalled. And that was truly saying something.

"And they did it all for you, Darwin," the king informed the crowd.

No, we didn't, she thought.

More cheering.

"And for me, because I fucking dig this album."

And with that, the showman monarch gestured to more flash pots that popped and flared in front of the Royal Symphony Orchestra.

A giant bell rang out. The horns and drums fired up. And the strings did the best they could to re-create the crunching whine of long-dead electric guitars.

"To fortune and fucking glory," said Jules, tipping her gin and tonic gently against Pete's lager jug.

"To fortune and fucking glory," Pete and Fifi returned, raising their drinks as the orchestra launched into "Hells Bells," the first track on AC/DC's *Back in Black,* and a ghostly echo of the Olden Days rolled out into the night.

They played from long-lost sheet music, recovered from a shop in the dead city of Sydney, by the fearless and legendary crew of the *Diamantina,* for fortune and fucking glory.

THE VENETIAN DIALECTIC

BY WALTER JON WILLIAMS

WALTER JON WILLIAMS

Walter Jon Williams is a bestselling, award-winning author of twenty-seven novels and three collections of short fiction. Among his works are *Hardwired, Metropolitan, The Praxis*, and a series of alternative histories about writers: Edgar Allan Poe ("No Spot of Ground"), Mary Shelley ("Wall, Stone, Craft"), and Mark Twain ("The Boolean Gate").

"The Venetian Dialectic" was inspired by a trip to the Arsenale, the world's first industrial complex. Says Williams, "I realized that the Arsenale could be retrofitted to resume its original role as a factory for ships and other objects necessary for survival in the late Middle Ages, and that this could give Venice a crucial edge in surviving a catastrophe such as the Change."

The fleet swept round the northernmost point of the island, and there the harbor of Rhodes lay plain before them, jetties of brilliant white embracing the bay like the loving arms of a mother. Giustinian Foscari had raised flags and banners as soon as the island had come into sight, so that the lookouts on the watchtowers, powerful binoculars pressed to their eyes, would recognize his squadron as Venetian, and allied to the Rhodian citizens who now swarmed the great ramparts.

For the sheer style of the thing he paraded his line of eight ships and two fast dispatch boats past the headland, lateen sails cutting fine arcs in the brisk southeasterly wind, and then he had the helm of the *Agostino Barbarigo* put up, and the galley crossed the wind's eye with the luffing sails booming thunder. As the galley hesitated in the face of the wind, the sail handlers ran the big bowed yards across the ship, the sails filled with a pair of cracks, one after the other, and the *Barbarigo* surged ahead, water singing under its counter. Foscari's heart sang at the sheer perfection of it.

Each galley in the fleet followed, tacking in succession across the wind's eye, each maneuver performed flawlessly under the critical eye of the Rhodians watching from the city's walls.

"Hoist the signal for a pilot," Foscari said. "And blow the trumpet to tell the fleet to furl sail and proceed under oars."

Foscari was a few centimeters below average height, with a compact body, a small mustache, and the sun-browned face of a sailor. He wore a cap with the lion badge of Unione Venezia, and prowled his quarterdeck like a young, restless lion, seeing everything, making sure there wasn't a line out of place.

The sails were brailed up to the yards, and the oarsmen were sent to their work. *Barbarigo* had twenty-four sweeps per side, though one was unused at present to leave room for the cook's station. Each sweep had a crew of three—an arrangement known as *di scaloccio*—who stood at their stations and pushed the sweep ahead of them rather than sitting at benches and pulling. The benches themselves—actually low platforms with hinged lids that turned them into storage chests—were used to brace each oarsman's foot when he shoved himself forward. The system was easier for untrained oarsmen, which had been a problem a generation before, when the Arsenale began building galleys for the first time in four hundred years.

In addition to the hundred forty-four oarsmen—each of whom could fight at need—*Barbarigo* carried sixty marines, which along with the bowman, steersman, bosun, quartermaster, cook, carpenter, surgeon, their assistants, ten sail handlers, the eight *sifoni* who worked the mechanism for the Greek fire, and the *ammiraglio* himself, raised the complement to two hundred and forty. All on a hull only twenty-four meters long. The deck was packed, a sea of rhythmic motion as the oarsmen chopped at the water with their long sweeps.

The pilot boat, moored to the outside of the southern mole, came dashing out under its six oars, and the Venetian ships hovered in the water while the pilot came aboard. The pilot was a weathered woman in her forties named Soteria, and Foscari had met her before.

"Good thing you're here, Admiral," she said. "It's bad news we've been hearing from Cyprus."

"Tell me." Foscari turned to the percussionist who called time for the rowers. "Slow ahead."

The percussionist rapped out three fast bangs on his sounding boards—with a pair of simple tuned boards and a pair of mallets, there was no need to bring anything so bulky as a drum on board—and the rowers responded by readying their sweeps over the water. Then both mallets came down together, one on the bass, the other on the treble, and the great sweeps dipped, then rose.

Soteria stationed herself right forward, on the forecastle where she had a clear view ahead, and while she guided the steersman by flipping her hands left or right, gave Foscari the news as she'd heard it.

"King Spiridon sent another ultimatum," she said. "He's sent one every year for four years, and nothing's happened, but one of these days, maybe after we've let our guard down, he'll come. And this year he's gathering an army and navy at Episkopi, so it's pretty clear he's going somewhere."

"What does the Afentiko think?"

"The Afentiko doesn't confide his thoughts to the likes of me, Admiral. Though everyone else does, as they come in and out of the port."

"What does everyone else say?"

"That Spiridon deflowers a virgin every day before strangling her with a silken cord, and that he worships Satan, and sacrifices children down at the old temple in Paphos. They say he got djinn from the Turks, and that the djinn fight for him, and that they can't be killed."

"I thought Spiridon killed all the Turks. Why would they give him djinn?"

"The djinn don't share their secrets with me either, Admiral. But fortunately some boy down in Archangelikos had a vision of the Virgin saying we'd all be safe, so nobody's afraid anymore."

"Ah," said Foscari. "We've been getting Virgins, too. And every saint in the catalog."

Since the Change, the number of people experiencing religious visions had grown—or maybe they hadn't, but instead the credulity of the population had increased.

Some of these people, Foscari thought, *it's as if the Mother of Christ stopped by every afternoon for tea.*

Foscari was a skeptic where the spiritual claims of the Holy Roman and Apostolic Church were concerned, particularly under the new Pope, who as head of the Umbrian League was a rival of Venice for supremacy in North Italy.

Still, Foscari supposed that religion helped to maintain public order, which was to the benefit of the State. Visions of the Virgin could have their uses, if they were the right visions.

Over the sound of the percussionist, Foscari heard the clack-clack-clack of the enormous capstan at Fort St. Nicholas as it lowered the great chain that blocked the harbor entrance. Had the chain been made recently, with hand-forged iron links, it would have been a vast enterprise consuming much time and capital, but instead the Afentiko had secured his harbor with the anchor chain of a cruise ship stranded in the commercial harbor during the Change. The ship itself was still there, looming over the old Custom House, where it served as a giant, and nearly unscalable, fort.

As the galley passed by Fort St. Nicholas, Soteria with a flip of her fingers directed the galley to the left, and *Agostino Barbarigo* swept in slow grandeur between the two jetties that marked the harbor entrance. The wondrous bronze Colossus had stood there in ages past, but now the entrance was marked by two ancient pillars topped by statues, one of a hind, the other of a stag.

Mandraki Harbor opened up on either side, supernaturally blue water and quays lined with shipping, fishermen, and merchants. At the south end of the harbor were the sheds where the Afentiko's four war galleys rested, drawn up on the shore. They weren't like the Venetian ships, built to a single pattern, but were all experiments, with different hull designs and arrangements of oars. One was surrounded by scaffolding, undergoing a refit. Behind them loomed the decayed superstructure of the old cruise ship.

A band on the shore began to play with a flourish of trumpets and snares. The odors of the land floated on the breeze: fish and lamb being grilled over hardwood or charcoal, bubbling stews and baking bread, all mixed in the breeze with the outpourings of the sewers.

Soteria took the Venetian squadron to a series of buoys laid on in a line near the southern end of the harbor. The bowman lassoed the buoy with a mooring line, the sweeps dipped one final time and rose dripping from the water, and *Barbarigo* checked and swung at its mooring.

As soon as the other ships moored, Foscari ordered the trumpeter to blow "captains report aboard," and sent the crew to lower the ship's boat, which hung from the stern. In the heyday of the Venetian Republic, deck space—and rowers—would have had to be sacrificed to give the boat a place, but in the intervening centuries someone had invented davits, and now boats could be carried outboard.

The boats were lowered briskly, but still the Afentiko beat Foscari into the water. As his barge swept up to the *Barbarigo*, Foscari heard the foghornlike voice of the Rhodian asking permission to come aboard.

"Of course, my friend!" Foscari answered.

The trumpeter knew to blow a flourish as the Afentiko's shaggy gray head appeared in the entry port just forward of the poop, and the percussionist embellished the music by banging a quick taradiddle on his sounding boards. Foscari stepped forward to grasp his friend's hand, and instead found himself wrapped in a great bearlike embrace.

"Blessed is your arrival!" the Rhodian cried. "For war comes soon!"

Foscari was skeptical—war had been on the brink of arriving for years now and had not yet turned up—but perhaps the Afentiko knew something he didn't.

Loukas Kanellis had been a young lawyer in the City of Rhodes when the world was struck by the Change, and in the years since he had been a lot of things: a judge, a military leader, a mayor, and a prime minister. At the moment his official title was nothing more than the Vice Chairman of the Peace and Liberty Party, but all the threads of power on Rhodes ran to his fingers, and those with grander titles, the Council and the Ministers and the President and the Prime Minister, were all his creatures.

Unlike King Spiridon the First of Cyprus, who gave himself royal airs and wore a crown and purple robe, Loukas Kanellis sought no grand titles, but was known simply as the Afentiko, which meant nothing more or less than "boss." He was so completely the man in charge that a throne and a purple robe would have been redundant, if not ridiculous.

He was the reason Rhodes had survived and prospered after the Change.

But by now, Foscari thought, *Loukas Kanellis had probably served his purpose. Perhaps there would have to be a change of power.*

*   *   *

After the Change, Foscari knew, Venice and Rhodes had each been re-founded on a great crime. In Venice it was called the Black Annunciation, when the visitors who thronged the city were driven across the bridge, through Mestre, and out into the countryside, where almost all had died of starvation, exposure, or murder. There had been nearly fifteen thousand tourists in Venice at the Change, and it had been impossible for the city of sixty thousand to support them. There had been attempts to sort out visitors with useful skills and occupations, but there hadn't been time to do it properly, and in the end the Feast of the Annunciation, 1998, was a feast of death, desperation, and despair.

Foscari had been a boy at the time, and he remembered watching from his father's fishing boat as the long line of visitors trudged across the railroad bridge—white-haired tourists out of the luxury hotels, students with backpacks, families with children and babes in arms. Foscari had been more puzzled than frightened.

"Did they do something wrong?" he asked his father.

The older Foscari's answer was simple. "They wanted to take our food."

The answer satisfied the boy, and he watched with complacency at the long line of people being marched to their deaths, all told that they must follow the railroad tracks until they found someone to feed them.

The cynical remarked that Venice had given up tourists for Lent. The devout had made the anniversary a day of repentance and expiation, with homemade altars and belated offerings of food to the restless spirits of the dead.

A few weeks later there was another exodus, as citizens of Venice and Mestre were marched out into the countryside to help the farmers plant and bring in the year's harvest. The city survived, just barely, on the harvest of its lagoon and the agricultural area surrounding Mestre. Foscari's father had died a few years later, of a case of diabetes that had been minor on the day of the Change, but had subsequently run out of control. His mother survived her husband by only a few months, and died of one of the infections that had become so common after the city had consumed its stock of antibiotics.

Foscari had become a ward of the Republic, and it was the Republic that raised him to be a sailor like his father. The State had fed him, housed him, trained him, and trusted him with offices, with commissions, with command of a squadron of warships.

Foscari hadn't forgotten that long, sorrowful trudging line of doomed visitors, but neither had he forgotten that from the day of the savage Annunciation the city had begun its revival, and subsequently its reconquest of the Veneto and its overseas empire. The Republic had required the sacrifice for its own survival, and events had proved the city council right.

The new, independent Rhodes, like Venice, was likewise reared on the bones of strangers. On the day of the Change, Rhodes had fewer tourists, the season not having started, but there was more disorder. The cruise ship alone held nearly three thousand souls, all of whom were blockaded aboard to starve. Others were put in boats and pushed out to sea, penned in buildings without food and water, or simply hacked down by citizens given sanction to kill strangers. And though he preferred not to speak of those bloody days, the young lawyer Loukas Kanellis had done his part to rid his island of foreigners, and begun his rise to power.

Now the Afentiko, leader of a prosperous, independent state, walked in procession alongside Foscari on the road leading past the New Market and through the colossal Gate of St. Paul, marked with the arms of the crusading Grand Master who had built it. Walking with the party were President and Prime Minister of the island, both loyal lieutenants of Kanellis, and Foscari's counterpart, Homer Georgallis, the commander of Rhodes' navy, who had been awarded the rather grand-sounding rank of Archiploiarchos. Following was the Autocephalous Archbishop of the Orthodox Church of Rhodes, a small, bespectacled, smiling man who sweated in his heavy black robes. The Afentiko towered over them all, a huge man with a shaggy gray head and the full beard that had become popular after the last of the safety razor blades had run out.

The band continued to blare out from the walls as the Afentiko led the group to his own residence, the former palace of the Grand Master of the Knights of St. John, the crusading order that had ruled Rhodes for over two centuries. The palace was less a palace than a broad-shouldered Gallic fort that hulked just below the highest point of the city, covered with the blazons of the conquerors. The building seemed a foreign imposition—built in the heart of a Byzantine city, the palace was a military structure that could have been dropped into the city straight from France, a fact that reflected the hierarchy of the Hospitallers themselves, who came from many nations but were usually led by a Frenchman.

Yet the gate, with its towers, was magnificent, and as Foscari passed through it he noted not only the blazon of some half-forgotten Grand Master, but also the name of Benito Mussolini, who during his own heyday had rebuilt the palace—though not, Foscari assumed, personally.

Beyond the gate was a large courtyard, or drill field, surrounded by buildings that looked very much like barracks. Foscari's heart gladdened at the small party awaiting him, their finery glittering in the sun of the courtyard.

Smiling, he doffed his cap to the Afentiko's family and approached. He took the hands of Serafina Kanellis and smiled into her deep blue eyes, and kissed her on both cheeks.

"Contessa, I myself perceive you remain as lovely as the day of your marriage," he said, employing the redundant subject pronouns of their native *Venexiàn*.

"You yourself are kind," Serafina said, in the same language.

Foscari looked at the two girls, fourteen and twelve, who curtsied.

"The young ladies they grow in beauty," Foscari said. And it was true, Efimia and Anastasia had both inherited their mother's chiseled patrician looks—though Efimia, the eldest, seemed also to have got a dose of her father's burly build.

She might well grow to have the face of a goddess on the body of a middleweight boxer, Foscari thought, *in which case any man in her life would have to beware.*

He turned to look at the seven-year-old boy who stood, hands braced defiantly on hips, and grinned up at him.

"And the *puteleto* he thrives, clear enough," Foscari said.

"Go *arancioneroverdi!*" the boy shouted, raising a fist. "Go winged lions! Goooooooooal!"

"Goooooal!" Foscari echoed.

Thanks to his Venetian mother, young Nikolaos had been raised a ferocious partisan of Unione Venezia, the greatest and most glorious football team in all the world.

It further struck Foscari that Nikolaos was wearing a tunic and trunks that strongly resembled the orange-black-green colors worn by his favorite team.

"We will ourselves kick the ball soon," he promised the boy.

Serafina smiled and touched his arm. "You yourself bring news from the Rialto?" she asked.

"I myself have, madonna. And I also myself bring letters."

"We shall ourselves speak at dinner," Serafina said.

When the Afentiko's first wife had died fifteen years ago, it had been Foscari who suggested that Kanellis enhance the then new Venetian alliance by choosing a second wife from the Republic. When the Afentiko seemed interested in the idea, Foscari had then promoted the fortunes of the lovely, well-educated, twenty-two-year-old Serafina Zentil.

She was the child of an old Venetian noble family, one of those who had social prestige but no political power, and who still clung to their pretensions and their decayed ancestral palazzos. As a class they'd expected to step into their old roles after the Change, and fully intended to run everything again; but they'd reckoned without the city's mayor and administration, who back in 1998 had been Communists. Thanks to the Communists' firm refusal to stand aside for the old families, the nobles had been kept from power, and an orphan from the working-class island of Giudecca had a chance to rise to the rank of Ammiraglio.

Foscari considered himself a good Communist. Not that he believed in Marx—with no industrial base there were no industrial workers, there was no bourgeoisie to rise against because everyone was poor and near starvation. Foscari's brand of Communism consisted of making sure that the poor kids got a fair shake, that all adult citizens were allowed to vote, that state offices were filled on the basis of merit, and that power wasn't handed to a bunch of inbred nitwits.

Nevertheless the old nobility had its uses. The Afentiko was flattered by the idea of marriage to a woman who could call herself "contessa," especially a contessa who was beautiful and nearly thirty years younger than himself. Serafina, for her own part, had quickly seen the advantages of marrying the master of an island republic, particularly when the alternative was to spend the rest of her life in a damp, dark, crumbling structure slowly sinking into the lagoon.

The marriage seemed happy, and that happiness had promoted Giustinian Foscari's career and given him the command in the Eastern Mediterranean, where managing Serafina, her husband, and the alliance had become his principal responsibility.

After the meeting with Serafina came a feast in the refectory of the palace. The fires had been lit as soon as the lookouts in the city had seen Venetian sails floating up over the horizon, and the cooking had been going on all day. Foscari shared a long trestle table with his officers, with the Afentiko and his family, the Archbishop, Archiploiarchos Georgallis, and members of the Rhodian government and military.

The meal had started with formal toasts made with glasses of ouzo, each of which had to be drained on the spot. With the ouzo came mezedes, appetizers of olives, tzatziki, goat ribs, sardines, sausage, fish roe, anchovies, brains, skewered meats, and pitaroudia, the chickpea fritter that was a local specialty. After this came main courses—the special moussaka of the island, sea bream and red mullet grilled with oregano and cumin, lamb chops grilled with oregano, garlic, and lemon, cheeses, octopus, baked Cretan potatoes, salads, rabbit stewed in red wine with pearl onions, Smyrna meatballs, red cabbage slaw, lamb marinated in honey and baked underground in the style of the Klepht guerrillas, and hilopites, a local pasta served two ways, with tomato sauce and in a hearty chicken soup.

Clearly, nearly thirty-two years after the Change, the island was no longer in danger of starvation.

With the main dishes came wines—red, white, and pink—and along with the wine more toasts. Fortunately it was not customary to drain the cup of wine at each toast.

The Knights Hospitallers, who had eaten in this hall for centuries, had probably never seen such a glorious meal.

Foscari's crews were being feasted as well, on the lovely beaches on the north end of the island.

Conversation in the refectory was polyglot. Foscari and Serafina could speak their native *Venexiàn*, and also converse in Italian, which was a separate though closely related language. The Afentiko was a native Greek speaker and knew some Italian, and though Foscari knew a fair amount of Greek, most of his conversation with Kanellis and his staff took place in English, even though there was no native English speaker in the room, or possibly on the island. English remained the international language because no other nation had achieved sufficient political dominance to force its tongue on anyone else.

Though if Foscari had anything to say about it, *Venexiàn* would be the language of the Eastern Mediterranean for centuries to come.

Foscari gave Serafina news of home and of her family, and to the Afentiko he spoke of the possibility of opening a pilgrimage route to the Holy Land. The pilgrim trade had provided vast profits to Venice throughout the Middle Ages, and now Italy and other nations had recovered to the point where they might have enough surplus wealth to take up pilgrimage again.

"Where would these pilgrims go, exactly?" asked the Afentiko. "Jerusalem is abandoned—no water."

The Middle East had seen one of the greatest tragedies of the Change. Outside distant and backward Yemen, the cities and towns of the arid region lived almost entirely on fossil water, and once the electricity was gone, the water could no longer be pumped. People had died very, very quickly, and in appalling numbers.

"You survived here with your cisterns," Foscari said. "The Holy Land is not without rainfall. And there is the river Jordan, of course, and other watercourses."

The Afentiko tugged his beard. "There is Cyprus," he said. "There is Spiridon. Between here and the Holy Land."

"Do you think Spiridon is foolish enough to fight Venice? Our forty-third galley is being built in the Arsenale even now."

"Ah," said the Afentiko. "Your miraculous Arsenale." There was a touch of envy in his words.

The Black Annunciation was the reason that Venice had survived the Change, but the Arsenale was the reason it had reclaimed its empire.

The Arsenale had been founded at the beginning of the twelfth century, and had been the world's first industrial plant, all for making ships and boats. Purpose-built structures were erected to make rope, cut timber, cast cannon, fashion oars, weave sails, boil pitch, bend timber frames. All forty-five hectares of the Arsenale were enclosed by a strong ten-meter wall, the only part of Venice that had been fortified. At its height in the late Middle Ages it could launch one fully equipped warship per day, built assembly-line style out of prefabricated parts.

The Arsenale had been converted to other uses in the late twentieth century, being used as an army base, a museum, an exhibition hall—but it had never ceased to make boats, and on the day of the Annunciation, all the old buildings were still standing, safe within their powerful walls, and still under military guard.

After the Change, the Arsenale was put to use converting every motor vessel in the area to sail or oar power. The sea and the lagoon would provide the protein necessary to keep the population alive, and anyone with access to a boat became a fisherman.

But supplies of cordage and sailcloth were limited, and when they ran out they needed to be manufactured. So a traveling exhibit of modern art was chucked out of the old ropewalk, the museum emptied, and the Arsenale's ancient manufacturing centers were brought again to life.

Sailcloth remained a problem, because the output of an entire village, for an entire year, would create but a single sail—as long as the looms were hand or foot powered. So barges were anchored in the flow of the Brenta and Bacchiglione rivers, each flanked by paddle wheels that powered large, industrial-sized looms, all components of which had been ripped from industrial museums or crafted in the Arsenale.

Inexpensive cloth led to increased demands for raw materials: wool, cotton, flax, hemp. These had to be traded for, or the areas where they were grown brought into Venetian influence. So the first expeditionary forces were sent from Venice onto the mainland, to secure the food and resource-producing areas of the Veneto. The Veneto, like all Italy, was dominated by medieval walled towns and hilltop castles; but many of the surviving inhabitants were eager to rejoin civilization, and the rest were too few, or too disorganized, to use their defenses wisely. Venetian forces triumphed everywhere they marched.

Venice had been a city filled with ancient arms and armor, all sitting in museums or displayed in the old palazzos of the nobility. The sheer amount of arcane weaponry helped first to maintain order, then to expand the influence of the city. Only the Pope, with his Swiss Guard who actually knew how to use their halberds and great swords, could field a comparable force.

For the first decade or so Venice depended on its fleets of converted motor craft to carry its trade and transport its armies. But in time the Arsenale produced its first purpose-built warship, built on the pattern perfected in the Middle Ages with flourishes added by modern engineers.

At present the Arsenale was far from producing the warship-a-day that had marked its prime. Such a schedule required a greater surplus of raw materials than was currently available, and a nation that was less precariously placed than at present.

But trade had followed in the wake of its warships. There had been no piracy after the Change for the simple reason that there was no seaborne trade to plunder; but when hulls began plying the seas again, other ships dashed out to acquire the contents of those hulls. Those who had survived through cannibalism were hardly going to stop at piracy.

The fleet was sent after the pirates, but there were logistical problems. A twenty-four-meter-long galley with a crew of two hundred and forty couldn't carry much food or water, and there was no room aboard to sleep the entire crew at once: normally the galleys were drawn up on the beach at night, and the hull rested alongside its slumbering oarsmen. A safe harbor every thirty or forty kilometers was a necessity, and so Venice found itself establishing settlements and forts along the Adriatic, mostly on islands like Hvar and Korčula where there were safe harbors.

Split was on a defensible peninsula, and Dubrovnik's old town already possessed splendid walls. All these places had once been a part of the Empire of Venice, and now they rejoined, usually with the consent of the inhabitants.

Pirates in the Adriatic were exterminated with admirable efficiency and ruthlessness. Farther south the Republic absorbed Corfu and the other Ionian islands. Foscari and his mentors and allies had always pushed a forward policy: the more area controlled by Venice now, the firmer footing the empire would stand on later. And so far the forward policy had prevailed. Crete was too large, and would have to come later, as would the Morea—or, as the locals called it, the Peloponnese.

And Foscari had another dream—to advance up the Dardanelles to Constantinople, the greatest city of the ancient world, the glittering prize that would unlock the wealth of the Black Sea . . .

Yet all that was later. Venice was well organized but overstretched, and though its hand was felt in many places, its touch was light. No one was more aware than Foscari of the Republic's fragility.

"You may have forty-three galleys," the Afentiko said, "but will they all come if Spiridon attacks?"

"They'll have to," Foscari said.

No challenge to the Republic's supremacy could be tolerated, not if it might reveal the city's weakness.

"Spiridon's own fleet is substantial. Fourteen galleys according to our latest information."

"He is far from matching us on the sea."

"And on the land? His army is said to be twenty-five thousand."

"Of which he can transport only a fraction."

"You didn't see the ambassador he sent. A man with burning eyes. The most terrifying thing I've ever seen."

Foscari paused for a moment. "A djinn?" he said.

The Afentiko barked an uneasy laugh. "You've heard that rumor? It's absurd, and yet"—he shivered—"for a moment I wondered. There was something uncanny about that man."

"There must have been," Foscari said, "if you were so impressed by him."

He turned as Serafina touched his arm. "I do not believe in djinn," she said, "but having seen Spiridon's man, I am more than ever convinced that demons can walk the earth."

Foscari considered this. "Demons or not, perhaps I should sail to Episkopi and see what His Cypriot Majesty is up to."

Serafina's voice was low as she spoke in *Venexiàn*. "If you yourself make that voyage, you should yourself be careful."

"Venice itself is not at war with King Spiridon."

"Spiridon himself makes war on whomever he likes."

It was difficult to separate the truth of King Spiridon's life from the stories he had spread about himself, but the most common story was that he was a Russian gangster named Zubov who, with many of his colleagues, had moved to Limmasol a few years before the Change. He and the other Russians had formed a hard core of survivors during the massive population crash that followed, and subsequently Zubov, under the Greek nom de guerre of Spiridon, emerged as a general leading armies of Greek Cypriots in the massacre of the Turkish Cypriots, who lived in their own enclave on the northern part of the island.

Having accomplished this holy and most Christian slaughter, Spiridon had graciously acceded to the request of his army that he become King. Since then he'd busied himself with settling his followers on the rubble of the old Turkish republic, eliminating his remaining enemies among the Greeks, and making threats against his neighbors.

And, if Serafina was to be believed, recruiting demons.

"And you've prepared against this threat?"

"Our towns are fortified," said the Afentiko. "The militia drills regularly. But none of them have ever fought a war, and we have no professional soldiers."

"Would you accept Venetian soldiers in Rhodes?"

The Afentiko considered this. "Yes," he said. "It would hearten the people."

Foscari concealed the elation that burned in his veins.

"I will send a message to Venice," he said, "and see what the Council and the President have to say."

One of Foscari's fast dispatch boats was sent to Venice. Proceeding under sail, with its sixteen oars providing power when the wind was not favorable, and swapping in a fresh set of oarsmen at each stop, Foscari reckoned the journey would take ten to fourteen days. Since he knew what the Council's decision would be once the message arrived, he was reasonably easy about the outcome.

Venice would take any steps necessary to secure Rhodes and prevent Spiridon, or anyone else, from threatening Venetian hegemony. More ships, plus Croatian and Albanian mercenaries, would soon arrive to buttress the island's defense.

Foscari settled into a routine of pleasant activity. He dined with the Archbishop, the President, the Prime Minister, prominent citizens, and the island's small Venetian community. He toured the island, and inspected the local militia and the fortifications. He drilled his ships every other day, and integrated the Afentiko's small fleet into his maneuvers. He played football with young Nikolaos in the courtyard of the Grand Master's Palace, and told the boy of Unione Venezia's great victories over the wretched, stumbling teams of the Umbrian League.

He didn't take his ships to Episkopi to look into the port for Spiridon's ships. The Afentiko had agreed to the arrival of Venetian soldiers, and Foscari wanted to be on hand to prevent Kanellis from changing his mind.

Two weeks after his arrival, Foscari invited the Afentiko to dine aboard his flagship. He spread Venetian and Rhodian banners and flags, and brought aboard cold mezedes, plus stews and ragouts that could be kept warm at the cook's station till needed. Two-thirds of the rowers were given leave ashore, along with the marines, and once out of the harbor the *Barbarigo* traveled under sail alone while the oarsmen gathered forward, by the cook's station, for their own meal.

Foscari saw the barometer was falling. This might be the last fine day for a while, his last opportunity to offer hospitality to the Afentiko.

Foscari shared a table with the Afentiko right aft, shaded by the poop awning. The table itself, and the pair of carved high-backed chairs, had been borrowed from a local Venetian merchant.

Long silver clouds scudded on the western horizon. The sea was so bright and alive with reflections that it looked as if the sun had scattered gold dust on the waters. Water splashed under the counter, and the lateen sails formed brilliant crescents overhead. The scent of the pure sea breeze made Foscari's nerves tingle.

Foscari sipped wine from his Murano goblet, nibbled mezedes, talked with the Afentiko about their business: about the island's preparedness, about where the Venetian soldiers would be garrisoned.

And he thought about poison.

It was unfortunate, he reflected, that Rhodes was simply too small to survive on its own. It had to be incorporated into something larger, either the Venetian empire or the kingdom of Spiridon.

Consider the choice: Spiridon in his purple robes, a crazy butcher, a genocide, and an unpredictable, vindictive, murderous master.

Or Venice, which wanted only money and power.

Given all that, Foscari knew how he would choose, were he the people of Rhodes.

Not that he was prepared to offer Rhodes the choice. The Council had provided Foscari with a poison, made from the castor bean, that would kill the victim in three to five days, and would appear at first to be a bad case of influenza, maybe one that degenerated into pneumonia.

There was no way to diagnose the poison, no way to connect Foscari to the death, taking place as it would several days after the administration of the toxin.

After which Venice would act to protect the Afentiko's Venetian wife and children.

Serafina might rule the island in place of her husband—with a staff of Venetian advisors, of course—or it might be necessary to take the whole family under Venetian protection, to be sent back to Venice for their own safety. Another husband might eventually be found for Serafina, but her children would be sent to convents, where they would remain for the rest of their days.

There could be no question of their being given a chance to have children of their own. The Republic would not countenance a Greek dynasty taking root in Rhodes. The Afentiko's line would die with his children.

The main question was the matter of timing. It might be better for the Afentiko to die after the Venetian troops had already landed and were in a position to intervene. But then again, such a death might be seen as too convenient for the Venetians.

Whereas now the death would create confusion and fear, a situation that would be resolved by the arrival of Venetian reinforcements. And Foscari judged that his own sailors and marines could secure the city if necessary.

It was sad, of course, that the Afentiko had to die. Foscari liked him. He was a remarkable man, and he'd been a loyal ally of Venice during a period when the Republic was weak and needed a bulwark on its eastern flank. But now Venice was ready for another round of expansion, and a sovereign Rhodes would just get in the way.

The Venetian State, the same State that had decreed the Black Annunciation, required a death, and Giustinian Foscari was a servant of the State. The State had saved him, raised him, trained him, and given him purpose. He would put his personal feelings aside and act as the State required.

Foscari turned to the Afentiko. "Loukas," he said. "I have a special bottle of wine I've been saving, a Bardolino blended with a very fine Rondinella. It would be splendid on such a lovely afternoon, don't you think?"

The Afentiko smiled. "I will take the *ammiraglio's* recommendation."

Foscari went to his cabin for the bottle, returned, opened it, and poured equal measures into the Murano goblets from which they'd been drinking all afternoon. The poison fell easily into the Afentiko's glass from the ring on Foscari's second finger—poison rings carried with them an absurd air of melodrama, but they worked.

Foscari felt his heart beating fast as he raised his glass in a toast. But the Afentiko wasn't returning his gaze, but instead was looking aft, over the taffrail.

"Is that my barge?" he asked.

Foscari spun and pulled the old Fujinon 10x50 binoculars from their waterproof case.

Yes, the Afentiko's barge was flying toward them, its lugsail set and its oars thrashing the water white.

A few strides brought Foscari to the break of the poop, where he began shouting orders to the crew. Oarsmen ran to their stations. The helm went up, the lateen sails rolled around their masts as the galley wore around, and the *Barbarigo* pitched as the bow bit into the waves from a new angle. The oilskin seals were removed from the row ports and the sweeps deployed.

Once the sweeps bit the water, *Barbarigo* was within hailing distance of the barge within minutes.

"War!" came the cry. "Spiridon's landed at Lindos!"

Foscari clenched his teeth and turned to see the Afentiko looming over the stern rail, a fierce look on his bearded face. He held the Murano glass in his big, clenched fist.

Alarm clattered in Foscari at the sight. He took a step toward Kanellis, snatched the glass from him, and hurled it along with his own glass into the sea.

"This isn't the time for wine!" he shouted. "This is the time for fighting!"

The Afentiko looked at him in surprise, and then amusement crossed his face.

"You Latins!" he said in his broken English. "You're such drama queens!"

It was too late in the afternoon to send the fleet south to Lindos, a port town about sixty kilometers south of Rhodes City. The town itself was assumed to be holding out: there would have been plenty of warning as the Cypriot fleet rolled over the horizon, and the town featured a massive thick-walled acropolis built, like the Grand Master's Palace, by the Knights of St. John. Foscari had inspected the fortifications only the previous week, and the militia and the stored provisions seemed perfectly adequate to hold such a strong place.

Foscari sent his fast dispatch boat west at nightfall, with instructions to head straight for the Corinth Canal to warn the Venetian relief force. Plans were made to row to the aid of the town next morning. The allied galleys were made ready, their masts and sails taken down and stowed ashore, and a full complement of catapults and other large weapons set up on board.

The Venetian galleys also set up galleries amidships, a kind of raised bridge running athwart the vessel at its midpoint. These were stations for the marines, who could fire crossbows and ballistas down into enemy ships.

But there was one Rhodian ship still under repair. "I've accelerated the work on the *Leo Gabalas*," the Afentiko told Foscari. "But the earliest the ship can touch water is two days from now."

"We'll fight without it," Foscari shrugged. He had confidence in his squadron, in his men.

If he could defeat the enemy ships, he thought, he'd strand a large part of Spiridon's army onshore where they could be trapped and killed, and probably capture a large number of his transports as well.

But as it turned out the allies were unable to go to the relief of Lindos the next day. As the barometer had predicted, the weather turned: a storm blew up overnight, a northerly gale battering the mole and sending spurts of white water shooting over the jetty and up the walls of Fort St. Nicholas.

Because they were designed to be propelled by human muscle, and to be wrestled by their crew onto a beach at night, galleys were light, fragile craft, and did not fare well in storms. Foscari would not risk the island's defense by defying the weather, and he worried that his small dispatch vessel, set out into the teeth of the gale, would be overwhelmed.

Over the next three days the wind shifted easterly, then south. Rain darkened the walls of the city. Foscari could only hope the Cypriot fleet was being hammered on an iron shore.

No such luck: on the fourth morning, the rising sun broke through storm clouds to spread a bloodred stain on the water and to illuminate enemy ships approaching. King Spiridon's navy came on in a long line: sixteen galleys, two more than the Afentiko's information had suggested.

Foscari, using his binoculars from the battlements of Fort St. Nicholas, saw that they were a heterogeneous group, built—like the Afentiko's fleet—from a variety of designs. Some had a single bank of oars, some double, some triple. Some, like the Venetian ships, carried their rowers inboard the hull; others, like the ships of ancient Athens, had a very narrow hull with outriggers staged out from the bulwarks to house the oarsmen. Some, like the Venetians, carried a spur jutting out from the prow, just at the right height to smash through the bulwarks and tear a red swath through enemy rowers. Others, judging from the curl of white water at the bow, deployed an underwater ram.

Whatever their design, the ships were extravagantly painted: greens, blues, crimson, and gold leaf. It was as if the circus had come to town. The dyes alone must have cost a fortune, let alone the gold.

Platforms had been built above the bow of all the Cypriot ships, and Foscari could see smoke drifting downwind from each enemy forecastle.

That meant each of Spiridon's ships carried Greek fire, jellied gasoline from the fuel tanks of cars and boats stranded by the Change. Jellied gasoline worked well enough in firebombs lobbed by catapults or hurled like grenades, but if you were going to squirt the stuff from a siphon, you had to warm it up first and turn it liquid, and so each gasoline tank rested over a carefully controlled fire.

"Are they themselves attacking?" Foscari turned at the sound of Serafina's voice—she'd dashed down from the citadel on word of the enemy approach.

"I myself don't think so," Foscari replied in *Venexiàn*. "They themselves can't get in, and I'm not myself going out."

"They'd pick off your ships as they cleared the breakwater."

"If they themselves had any sense," Foscari said, "that's what they'd do. But I myself don't know how sensible their admiral is, since he blew himself all the way up here in a gale, half his men at least are going to be seasick, and he's going to have a hell of a time getting home rowing straight into the wind."

Serafina raised binoculars to her eyes. "They themselves are keeping formation well enough."

"Well enough," Foscari admitted. "Can you yourself tell if they're roped together?"

She seemed surprised. "They themselves are too far apart, aren't they?"

"They could themselves use long hawsers."

Serafina peered through his glasses. "But why?"

"To keep us from getting in between them."

It's what he would have done if he were the Cypriot admiral, lashed every vessel together and turned any action into a land battle, where superiority of numbers would give him an advantage.

The Afentiko, called away from a meeting inland, arrived a few minutes later, out of breath from his run along the mole. The enemy fleet paraded past the walls, turned neatly in succession, and paraded back the way it had come. Then one ship—the largest, with three banks of oars—turned and made across the gray swells toward the harbor entrance. White flags blossomed from its forecastle.

"A parley," the Afentiko said, in mild surprise.

There was another surprise when the galley came to a halt just short of Fort St. Nicholas, and a man with a big voice called out from the bow.

"We want a parley with the Venetian commander!"

Foscari looked at the Afentiko and shrugged. "With your permission? We might learn something."

The Afentiko returned his shrug. "If you like."

King Spiridon's envoy was a woman, a rangy, green-eyed creature in her thirties who stalked like a leopard onto the quay, dressed in olive-green suede pantaloons, a chain-mail byrnie so brilliantly polished that she seemed clad in silver, and a steel cap. She carried a curved saber at her waist, and identified herself as Colonel Chadova.

No one wanted to take Chadova through the walled city to inspect the defenses, so she and her two aides were escorted by a double line of Venetian marines to the old town hall, a gray, bunkerlike Brutalist building on the waterfront now used mainly for storage. Foscari had a word with the marine lieutenant beforehand about what was expected, and so the envoy and his two aides were made to surrender their weapons, then thoroughly searched, before being allowed into the presence of Foscari and the Afentiko.

The Afentiko said the room had been used for "press conferences," whatever those were, but in any case it was well lit by the tall windows overlooking the water, and once stored furniture had been shifted to the side, and a pair of thronelike chairs set up for the allies, there was a clear space for both the marines and the envoys. Serafina stood quietly in the corner, watching with cautious eyes. Behind her was an old carving of an ancient coin, a godlike face crowned with the proud motto Demos Rodion, the People of Rhodes.

Colonel Chadova padded into the room with a dancer's glide, lithe and purposeful, a performance directed at her audience of two. Her silver chain mail rippled. Her green eyes looked out from beneath dark hair accented by a white streak. She looked first at the Afentiko—Foscari sensed Kanellis' muscles tense, as if he was under threat—and then the eyes slowly turned to Foscari, and he felt the almost physical impact of that stare, a sense that his entire being was being read, as if he were the text of an inferior recipe and Chadova a masterful and scornful cook. His heart gave a sudden lurch, and he felt the hairs on his nape rise. He tried to force his body to relax, not to give himself away as had Kanellis.

"You are the Venetian?" she asked in Greek.

With effort, Foscari held her gaze. "I am Ammiraglio Foscari," he said.

The green gaze shifted again to the Afentiko. "I did not ask Loukas Kanellis to this conference," she said.

"Anything you can say to me, you can say in front of him." Foscari ground his teeth at the hash his inexpert Greek made of this complicated idea, but Colonel Chadova seemed to understand him well enough. The emerald eyes turned again to Foscari.

"Perhaps it is news to you that Lindos has fallen," she said, and Foscari felt the Afentiko stir on his chair.

"The acropolis was taken the morning after our landing," Chadova continued. "I myself led one of the storming parties." Satisfaction curled the corners of her mouth. "The defenders were killed to the last, for the crime of defying His Majesty King Spiridon."

The Afentiko took a moment to recover from the surprise, and when he spoke, his voice had deepened with anger.

"Your king will pay for this atrocity."

Colonel Chadova didn't even bother to look at Kanellis. "When His Majesty Spiridon is crowned King of Rhodes in your Grand Master's Palace," she said, "you may then repeat that threat."

Now her green eyes finally turned to the Afentiko, and they glittered with menace. "I can promise that you will still be alive at that point, though perhaps you may not be . . . entirely intact."

Foscari sensed that Kanellis was about to unleash an angry retort, and saw no point in letting the conference degenerate into a pointless exchange of threats.

"Colonel Chadova," he said quickly. "I believe you carry a message for me?"

Chadova's amusement was almost palpable. She turned back to Foscari.

"I beg your pardon, Ammiraglio," she said. "I intend merely to point out your situation. Lindos has fallen, and as the army of Spiridon is superior to the local militia, the City of Rhodes will fall. Our fleet outnumbers yours, and you have no hope of a victory at sea. If you continue in a futile effort to support the Kanellis regime, you will inevitably fail, and your life will be forfeit."

She paused for a moment to gauge Foscari's reaction. He hoped he managed to keep his face immobile under her unsettling gaze.

"It is your misfortune to be matched against an invincible leader," she said, "one given dominion by the Powers of Land, of Sea, and of Air."

Foscari smiled thinly. The only Power of the Sea that he recognized was the Republic of Venice.

"Powers of Air?" he said. "Does your king intend to fly here?"

Her eyes flashed. "Were you to confront the Powers directly—were you to be so unlucky as to meet Them—you would not mock."

Foscari allowed skepticism to drift across his face. Chadova watched for a long, intense moment, then returned to her subject.

"We offer you an honorable alternative to a pointless death," she said. "If you agree to sail your ships through the Corinth Canal to Corfu, we will permit you to leave peacefully."

Foscari had expected something of this sort. "You wish me to abandon the alliance formally contracted between Rhodes and the Venetian Republic?"

"I offer an alternative to your own extinction," Chadova said. "Why not take it?"

"Because the choice is not mine. I am a soldier and a servant of the Republic. I can neither create nor abandon policy. That is the function of the Council and its President."

He touched a finger to the corner of his mustache and caught a surprised look on the face of his marine lieutenant. "My duty requires that I decline your kind offer, Colonel."

Chadova lifted an eyebrow. "This is your decision? You will die for your ridiculous republic, and sacrifice all those who depend on you?"

"Perhaps I won't be the one who's sacrificed," Foscari said. "Venice has many more ships than those you see here."

"When we capture your squadron, we will nearly double the size of our fleet."

Which tells me something of your plans, Foscari thought. Again he touched his mustache, a signal to the marine lieutenant.

"Unless you have a more sensible proposal, Colonel," he said, "I believe our parley is at an end."

"You will die," Chadova said.

"So will you, madame," he said. "So will everyone."

The important thing, Foscari thought, was not death, but the life that preceded it, ideally a life in service to an ideal. An ideal such as the Maritime Republic, which guaranteed peace and order and prosperity wherever its ships rode the water, and which provided poor children like young Giustinian Foscari a chance to rise in service to the State, rise at a time when so many others were dying of starvation, of banditry, of war . . .

Colonel Chadova's last words were for the Afentiko. "The Powers will burn your sad little kingdom to ashes," she said, and turned to go.

Foscari looked at the marine lieutenant and gave a nod, this time a more explicit instruction. The lieutenant stepped behind Chadova, put his hand on his short saber, half drew it, and hesitated.

He had probably never attacked treacherously before. Very likely he had never had to kill a woman. Possibly he had never killed anyone at all.

The hesitation was the lieutenant's undoing. Chadova sensed his intention and acted instantly—she took a step rearward, her leg between his, and as she turned banged him with a hip to unbalance him . . . She reached for the lieutenant's short saber, and snatched it from his hand and drew from the scabbard all in the same motion.

Foscari shoved his chair back and reached for his cutlass as the lieutenant reeled back from a pair of cuts to his head. Everyone else in the

room was frozen in surprise—the Afentiko was partly turned away, looking by his chair for a briefcase full of papers and reports, and probably
had only the vaguest idea what had just happened.

Chadova's burning green eyes swung to the Afentiko, and the reddened sword swept upward, poised for another cut as she charged.

"For God's sake kill them!" Foscari shouted into the surprised room.

Chadova was already arrowing for the Afentiko, who only now turned
and realized his danger. Foscari's heart thundered in his ears. He lunged
forward with his cutlass and knocked Chadova's sword up, but she kept
going, ducking under both blades and lashing out with a boot to kick the
Afentiko in the face, knocking him back into his chair just as he was
trying to stand. The chair swayed, threatened to tip . . .

Foscari kept moving forward and knocked Chadova bodily back, out
of range of the Afentiko . . . and then she seemed to turn into a whirlwind
of steel, the sword appearing to come at Foscari from everywhere at
once. Her emerald eyes were ablaze, seeing straight through Foscari to
the Afentiko he protected, and her face appeared to become almost
translucent, as if she wore a mask and now her true self was revealed, a
feral, unholy being of burning energy that radiated through her translucent skin.

Foscari gave way under Chadova's attack, barely able to parry the
blade that seemed to whip at him from every angle. Chadova's attacks
were strong beyond reason, and Foscari felt every impact all the way to
his shoulder. With each strike Foscari's hand grew more numb from the
repeated impacts. Terror tangled in his nerves as he feared that soon his
sword would fall from nerveless fingers.

One of the marines saved him, lunging at Chadova from behind
with a boarding pike and piercing the polished chain-mail coat. She
barely registered the thrust, her snarling expression unchanged, but
there was a slight hesitation in her next attack, and Foscari was able to
parry it and make a cut on her arm. The cut seemed to do nothing: her
riposte was so fast that Foscari had to make a leap backward to avoid
being skewered.

His back heel came up against the Afentiko's chair. He could retreat no farther.

The marine made another thrust with his pike, and this time put more weight behind it, so that Chadova was forced to take a staggering step away from her prey—she might possess unnatural strength and speed, but the marine was heavier than she, and physics still worked. Foscari slashed again with his cutlass, and this time he felt the right ulna crack under the weight of his blade.

Chadova's sword dropped from her useless right hand, but in a move so fast that Foscari saw only a blur, she snatched the hilt from the air with her left and turned away from Foscari to sweep it in a long arc behind her, catching the marine in the knee. He gave a yelp and fell heavily, and Chadova whirled again to bat Foscari's next thrust aside.

Foscari tasted blood and fear. More marines charged into the fight, armed with boarding pikes or with cutlasses and target shields. Chadova gave a shriek as she fought them, not a cry of fear but a scream of rage that left the Venetians half stunned. A far-from-human light burned in her eyes.

There was a wild chaos of slashing blades. Foscari's own attacks flailed empty air. One of the marines staggered back with a wound to the throat that spurted red, another jerked back a hand missing two fingers. But two more pikes drove through the polished chain mail, and Foscari hacked into the melee and felt an impact as he slashed through Chadova's wrist.

A third pike struck home, and three strong young men put their weight onto the shafts and bore the wildly flailing woman to the floor. A swarm of Venetians surrounded the body and pierced and hacked in a frenzy of inept and desperate butchery. Blood sprayed and filled the air with its coppery scent.

And eventually Chadova's bloody head turned, and Foscari saw a promise in those green, inhuman eyes—a promise that this was not by any means over—and then the light in her eyes went out.

Foscari leaned on the chair and tried to catch his breath. His marines were standing around the room still half-stunned, still trying to understand what had just happened. Chadova's two companions, unarmed and apparently without supernatural aid, had died quickly. And he'd lost two marines, one of them an officer, with a number of others wounded.

He turned to see the Afentiko in Serafina's arms—during the fight he had got out of his chair somehow, and Serafina had pulled him off into a corner. She was trying to staunch the flow of blood from the nose that had been broken by Chadova's kick.

Foscari straightened, took a breath, and limped over to the Afentiko. "Are you all right, Contessa?" he asked.

Serafina was still tidying her husband's face. She looked over her shoulder at Foscari, a ghost of fear still haunting her face.

"Demons," she said. "I told you."

"Was this the one you met earlier?"

"No. He was a man with"—she gestured toward her face—"with a red beard. Forked."

"How many more of them are there?"

She turned back to her work. "God knows."

The Afentiko took Serafina's handkerchief and held it to his nose. "You attacked an emissary," he said.

"Yes," Foscari said. "And treacherously, at that."

The Afentiko gestured with his free hand. "Why? Spiridon will find it very hard to forgive."

Foscari looked at Chadova's corpse. "Chadova tried, a bit crudely, to drive a wedge between us. I wanted to show everyone in this room— everyone in Rhodes—that I and the Republic are committed to your defense."

And he wanted as well to force commitment from the Venetian Council. There were those at home who opposed Foscari's policy of expansion, who regretted the expense of the fleet that took ten thousand fit young men from the city for years at a time, and who might have tried to compromise with Spiridon, or even hand Rhodes to him in return for a non-aggression pact. Now an enraged Spiridon would prosecute a war with Venice and give the Republic no chance to back out, even if it wanted to.

Foscari turned back to the Afentiko. "At least she told us the enemy's plans."

Kanellis was surprised. "Yes? How so?"

"She said they plan to capture the fleet and add it to their own. That means they intend to take the city quickly, by storm, and take our ships at the same time. Their blockade is here to keep us from escaping to sea." He shook his head. "It won't be a siege, my friend. Spiridon plans to come right over your walls, just as he did at Lindos, with creatures like that"— he pointed to Chadova—"in the lead. Do you think your militia can face them?"

The Afentiko turned pale beneath the blood that stained his face. Foscari turned away from the blood on the floor and looked at the medallion, Demos Rodion, on the wall of the chamber.

"If not for the storm," he said, "they could be here already."

He turned to the Afentiko. "Thousands of refugees will be coming into the city and to the other old Crusader forts like Kritinia and Monolithos. You should take care that the enemy isn't among them—I wouldn't put it past Spiridon to send infiltrators into the city."

The Afentiko nodded. "I'll take care. And I'll warn the militia captains about the . . ." Words failed him, and he nodded at Chadova. "Those."

"Call them 'champions,'" Foscari advised. "Words like 'demon' or 'djinn' might be too unsettling."

The Afentiko nodded, then winced at sudden pain from his broken nose.

"And the official story," Foscari said, "should be that Chadova attacked treacherously, not anyone else."

Again the Afentiko nodded.

"I'll ready the fleet to sally tomorrow, before dawn," Foscari said. "If we can hand them a severe enough defeat at sea, Spiridon's army may try to withdraw before they're stranded." He shrugged. "And in any case, we can keep them from landing reinforcements."

Serafina looked up from her ministrations.

"Go with God," she said simply.

The other side seems to have the gods, Foscari thought. Little ones, anyway.

But he bowed, and thanked her for her concern, and then turned to see that the bloody mess was cleaned up.

The heads of Colonel Chadova and her two aides were delivered to the boat that awaited them off the mole. The sailors aboard the boat were horrified, but there was no immediate reaction from the enemy warships, which rowed off just before sunset, presumably so they could find some safe beach somewhere to run the galleys ashore and let the crews get some sleep.

Foscari was aboard *Agostino Barbarigo* by three in the morning to ready the fleet for war. Slow fires were lit below the tanks of Greek fire to make sure the jellied gasoline liquefied, and turns were taken at the pumps that filled the hydraulic reservoirs that would shoot the flaming gasoline at the enemy. The bows and forecastles of the ships were covered in hides, and the hides drenched in sea water to protect against Greek fire, their own as well as that of the enemy.

Stores and fresh water were carried aboard, and then the pilot Soteria was brought aboard to lead the fleet past the breakwater and into the open sea. The eastern sky was beginning to turn pale as *Barbarigo* first took the deep-sea rollers, and turned its prow toward the enemy. The other eleven galleys, each following the stern lantern of the ship ahead, trailed in an obedient line. The galley rowed east to clear the land, the lights of the city twinkling off its starboard quarter, and then the squadron arrowed southeast. The sewage-smell of the city was washed away by the rich scent of the sea.

Soteria remained aboard. Her thorough knowledge of the coastline might be useful, and for the occasion she'd equipped herself with a spear, shield, and an old Italian helmet dating from the Second World War.

At dawn Foscari raised three flags onto his poop to mark his ship as that of the *ammiraglio*. The central flag was that of Venice itself, with the winged Lion of St. Mark. The flag to port was Foscari's personal ensign, the silhouette of a black galley sailing on an indigo sea. And the flag to starboard was the banner of Unione Venezia, with a slightly different version of the winged lion.

The Cypriot fleet was not visible, no silhouettes on the pale eastern horizon, and no shadows skulking against the shoreline. Foscari could only hope they were sleeping late, and that he could trap them drawn up on the shore in some little cove.

Spray crashed over the bows as the *Barbarigo* knifed into a wave, and Foscari felt moisture on his face as far back as the poop. The sea had moderated since the previous day, but there was still a storm to the southeast that was pushing long lines of rollers straight into the galleys' teeth. The wind itself had veered southerly, bringing a faint scent of land, and was raising smaller waves that ran across the rollers like swarms of fish darting just below the surface.

That southerly wind could prove crucial, Foscari knew. You could spit Greek fire only downwind, and the enemy fleet would be coming with the wind behind them. If the Venetians used Greek fire against their enemies, it might get blown back in their faces.

The sun rose out of low clouds, and scarlet winked on the foam that flew from the sweeps. Spray crashed along the length of the hull as the squadron took a more southerly course.

And then the lookouts at the bow gave a cry, and Foscari grabbed his binoculars and hurried forward along the gangway to the forecastle. From a position between the two catapults, he leaned forward, binoculars pressed to his eyes, and got a face full of foam for his troubles. He snarled, wiped the lenses of the binoculars, and took a few steps back, out of the spray.

His heart shifted to a faster rhythm as he recognized the Cypriot fleet, not in the single disciplined line they'd adopted when parading past Rhodes Town the previous day, but in a gaggle with their sails set, billowing in every color of the rainbow, their admiral taking advantage of the southerly wind to spare the oarsmen's labors. They were due south, still ten or twelve kilometers distant.

They might not yet see Foscari's ships, which lay close to the water and had left their masts and sails at home. Foscari decided to set his course more easterly, to keep the enemy between his ships and the land and give himself more room to maneuver.

He returned to the quarterdeck and ordered the course change, then told the trumpeter to signal the ships into battle formation. The call sang out in the still morning, and was reinforced by a wigwag signal from the ship's signals officer, standing in plain sight on the poop with his flags flashing in the sun. The signal was passed up the line, and the other galleys, drummers rapping out a faster pattern, began to surge forward to take position on either side of the flag, until they formed a line abreast.

The eight Venetian ships were on the left, with the flagship seventh in line. The four Rhodian ships were on the right, in the place of honor, because the engagement would be fought in their home waters.

Foscari went forward again, with his binoculars, to view the enemy fleet. They continued to sail on for some time, oblivious to the approaching allies until the distance between the ships had been halved—and then there was a sudden change, the colorful sails blooming like great bladders as they spilled wind, the yards dropping on the run, the masts toppling like falling timber into their cradles . . . Surprise was complete.

Foscari ordered the allied fleet to turn directly toward the enemy and increase speed. He'd engage as soon as possible, and hope to keep them on their heels. As the Cypriots straggled into line abreast, Foscari kept his binoculars pressed to eyes, looking for sign that hawsers were being passed between the ships to rope them together.

Apparently not. The enemy response was too frantic to suggest any kind of plan at all.

And the enemy ships, once they straggled into formation, demonstrated poor station-keeping. Which was unsurprising, considering they were all built to different designs.

Foscari returned to the poop. Below him the hundred and forty-four oarsmen surged back and forth in one great mass, like the tide advancing and retreating into a narrow chasm, each surge in answer to the drummer, below Foscari's feet under the break of the poop, as he beat the sounding boards. The sea-rollers were coming in from right abeam now, throwing spray over the ship, and *Barbarigo* rolled heavily as the oarsmen hurled her forward. That would make it difficult to aim the catapults properly on the approach, but it would affect the two sides equally, so Foscari decided not to worry about it.

Instead he watched the approaching line of ships and considered matters of timing. If his maneuver was too early, the enemy would have time to respond—and if too late, he could expose his fleet to a ramming attack by the enemy.

Salt spray doused his face. He took off his Unione Venezia cap and wiped his face, then looked at the cap in surprise.

He'd forgot to put on his helmet. *Well*, he thought, *too late now.*

The enemy galleys, their sides brilliant with red and gold and green, scuttled closer across the ocean, like angry, purposeful centipedes with scores of flashing, thrashing legs.

Foscari's heart thundered in his chest. He looked from one enemy ship to the next, and then snatched his speaking trumpet from the rack.

Then, eyes darting among the enemy ships, he waited three . . . long . . . seconds.

"Splitting speed!" he shouted. He pointed at the trumpeter and his signaler. "Signal the *spaccato!*"

The drummer rapped out the knock-knock-knock that signaled a change in tempo, and then brought both mallets crashing down onto the sounding boards. The trumpet rippled out a series of high, brilliant notes that danced in the air. *Barbarigo* lurched as the sweeps hurled it forward at a greater pace.

Foscari looked over his shoulder to see the galleys on either side pick up speed, then turn to follow in *Barbarigo*'s wake.

"Starboard your helm." Foscari stood atop the break in the poop and shouted down at the helmsmen, who were sheltered from enemy fire by the deck above. "Good. Hold her. Now amidships."

He'd chosen his target, or rather his lack of one. He wasn't heading for an enemy ship, but rather the space between enemy ships. He, and the two galleys following, were going to arrow right between enemy ships, then spin and attack them from the rear, where they couldn't defend themselves.

The other Venetians were engaged in the same maneuver, forming themselves into another pair of arrows, one of three ships and one of two, aiming to cut through the enemy line.

The ancient Greeks called the maneuver *diekplous*, "the splitting," and it required a high level of training and discipline both among the captains and the oarsmen. Foscari's crews had been training for years to perform just this maneuver, and he was confident that the Cypriot crews weren't up to this standard.

And this was why Foscari had been so worried that the Cypriots might have strung hawsers between the ships, a tactic developed in the Renaissance to prevent just this maneuver. A hawser not only would have stopped his ship dead in the water, it would have pulled the enemy ships down onto his flanks and rear.

His allies, the Rhodians, were unpracticed at the *diekplous*. Archiploiarchos Georgallis would have to engage the enemy head-to-head, and hope for the best.

There was a percussive thrum in the air as one of the forecastle catapults tried a shot. Foscari followed the smoking track of the projectile in the air—it was a glass bottle filled with jellied gasoline, wrapped in a burning fuse of tarred rope—but the *Barbarigo* was rolling too much for proper aim, and the missile fell short and plowed a white furrow in the sea.

As the galley raced between the enemy vessels, catapults from both sides sang out . . . a giant steel arrow whistled over Foscari's head . . . but so far as he could tell, nothing struck home.

"Port your helm!" Foscari shouted. "Starboard oars drag water!"

Barbarigo shuddered as the rudder bit the water, not only turning the galley but acting as a brake. The oarsmen on the right side allowed their oars to drag in the water, slewing the galley around on a new heading.

"Rudder amidships! All oars flank speed!"

Foscari had chosen his target, not the galley he'd passed on his right but the one just beyond—the nearest craft he could leave for the ships behind him. The ship he'd chosen was vivid with gold and vermilion paint, and featured a single rank of oars. Officers on the poop were running in consternation as they stared at the Venetian ship that had just swung around onto their quarter and was bearing down on them. They had only an instant to respond, and that instant had passed.

"Port your helm!" Foscari cried. "Hard over! Now!"

The helm went over and *Barbarigo* slewed to the right just before impact. The galley's prow crashed through the rank of oars—Foscari could see shrieking oarsmen hurled through the air by the looms snapping back with the weight of an entire Venetian galley behind them—and then the great spur over *Barbarigo*'s bow buried itself in the enemy gunwale right amidships, punching a bloody path through ranked oarsmen. Foscari staggered as the *Barbarigo* came to a lurching, rending halt.

Catapults on both sides fired, unable to miss at this range, and adding to the barrage were marines firing crossbows and crewmen heaving firebombs and hurling spears. Crossbow bolts whistled past Foscari's head. The air rang with screams and curses and the sound of crossbow bolts striking wood, armor, and flesh. Gazing across the short span of water at the enemy quarterdeck, Foscari saw half the Cypriot officers go down before a volley of crossbow bolts fired from *Barbarigo*'s overhead bridge structure.

A firebomb landed on the poop, and flaming gasoline leaped over the planks. A marine, his legs afire, made a frantic dance away.

Foscari glanced at the fire, pointed, commanded, "Sand!"

Marines picked up the sand buckets that stood ready and doused the flames that water could not quench. The burning marine was thrown to the deck and his flaming legs smothered in a cloak.

Foscari raised his speaking trumpet. *"Sifone uno*—shoot!"

A dragon's roar filled the air as flame arced from *Barbarigo*'s bows, fired under pressure from one of the two siphons beneath the break in the forecastle. Getting behind the enemy meant they were now firing from upwind, and the *sifoni* had full use of their weapon. The entire enemy crew seemed to shriek as one, and there was a crazed stampede away from the flames, the enemy deck all astir with panicked men.

Foscari clenched his teeth at the screams of the men wreathed in flame. He would rather have just set the enemy galley on fire and left the crew to survive as best they could, but the decks were so packed with oarsmen that there was literally no other target.

"Helm amidships! Back oars!"

The siphon sputtered as it ran dry. The drummer beat three times for attention, than began a slow beat that drew *Barbarigo*'s prow from the enemy vessel in a long groan of tortured timber. The Cypriot was truly alight now, liquid flame spilling over the rolling deck, racing along the sail that, hastily secured, still bagged out from the fallen yard.

Foscari snatched off his Unione Venezia cap and waved it. "Goaaaaal!" he screamed. "Go *arancioneroverdi*!" He heard nervous answering laughter from the marines on the poop.

As he heard the clanking of the pump that would refill the siphon's reservoir, Foscari looked for his next target. To starboard, a Cypriot galley had lost its rudder after having been rammed astern by the *Doge Dandolo*, one of the Venetians in his squadron. Greek fire was now beginning to play on the enemy poop, and Foscari decided the *Dandolo* wouldn't need his help.

To port, an enemy trireme was spinning in the water, one set of sweeps backing, in order to set itself for an attack on one of the Afentiko's galleys, which itself was lashed head-to-head to a Cypriot galley and fighting a boarding action.

"Ahead half speed! Starboard your helm!"

Barbarigo slowed, then began to gain way as it curved slowly across the stern of the flaming Cypriot. Foscari's victim was now completely unmanageable, the panicked crew hurling overboard their oars, gratings, anything that could help them float once they leaped from the flames into the sea.

"Flank speed!" The oarsmen surged back and forth as the sweeps lashed the sea. Someone on the trireme saw them coming, and suddenly the enemy ship spun again in the water, trying to dodge away.

Too late. The trireme's oarsmen were not quite up to the maneuver they were attempting, and the trained Venetian oarsmen outsped them.

Barbarigo's spur drove into the packed oarsmen on the enemy's port side. They weren't inside the hull but sitting in an outrigger lightly attached to the bulwarks, and *Barbarigo* peeled the outrigger away from the hull, spilling men and dropping part of the outrigger into the water. Suddenly Foscari was shouting and waving his cap.

"No Greek fire! No *sifone!* Don't shoot, you bastards of *squillatoria*, you squirters!"

The Cypriot galley was unmaneuverable and helpless, and could be finished off later. There was no point in wasting Greek fire on them.

The *sifoni* heard him, miraculously, and held their fire. Foscari backed the *Barbarigo* away and looked for another target.

The ocean streamed with smoke from ships burning on the water. The reek of gasoline and burning flesh clung to the back of Foscari's throat. He couldn't see a likely target, so he swung *Barbarigo* to starboard and began to pace along the battle's edges, looking for an enemy.

Whatever ships he could see were locked together in combat. The nearest was the *Carlo Zen*, lying alongside a green-and-white striped Cypriot galley, the crews battling over the decks with pikes and swords. Oars drooped uselessly in the water as their oarsmen battled across the locked decks.

"Starboard your helm! Quarter speed!"

The drummer slowed the beat. *Barbarigo* turned lazily to port, aiming for the Cypriots' unengaged side.

"Helm amidships! Grapnels ready! Sweeps in! Sweeps in!"

The sweeps rose dripping from the water, and then the oarsmen pulled them inboard, getting them out of the way of the collision that was about to come.

"No *sifone!*" Foscari called. A fire on the enemy galley could all too easily spread to the *Carlo Zen*.

The clash of weapons from the engaged galleys rang clear in the absence of the crashing drumbeat and the rhythmic sound of the oars. Foscari could hear the sound of water chuckling under *Barbarigo's* counter, the snap of the flags on their staffs.

"Stand by to board! Ready for collision!"

Foscari braced himself against the poop rail, and the galley began in an almost leisurely way to crash through the sweeps hanging unmanned over the side of the Cypriot galley. Since the enemy oarsmen for the most part weren't at their stations, the destruction wasn't as horrific as it might have been, but still Foscari heard sweeps snapping, saw sweep-looms scything across the deck to break knees or hurl crewmen to the ground, saw white splinters flying.

The ship lurched as *Barbarigo's* spur crashed into the enemy side abaft the beam, chopping the bulwarks into kindling, ruining the white stripe atop the sea-green hull. *Barbarigo* came to rest head-to-tail with the other galley, its forecastle laid alongside the enemy poop. Foscari could see the ship's name picked out in Greek characters on the forecastle: *Iason*, *Jason*.

"Grapnels! Grapnels!" Foscari turned to his trumpeter. "Call for boarders!"

He looked in dumb surprise at the trumpeter's body stretched on the planks, the man's eyes starting, his fist curled around the crossbow bolt that had punched through his chest.

No more trumpet calls. Damn.

Foscari snatched off his cap and waved it. "Boarders! Boarders! For God and San Marco! Boaaaarders!"

A massed shout rose from over two hundred throats, a vast sound with an almost physical impact. The marines on the forecastle were already leaping to the enemy poop, and the oarsmen raised the hinged lids of their rowing benches to grab the weapons stored inside. Shields were snatched from the bulwarks where they had protected the rowers from enemy fire.

A raging tide of adrenaline urged Foscari to charge up the gangway to the forecastle and join the boarding party, and he went so far as to put his hand on his sword and take a step toward the poop companion; but then he realized he would have to fight his way through a mob of nearly two hundred of his own crewmen to reach the fight, which might well be over by the time he arrived.

No, he was the *ammiraglio*, his job was to stay above the mundane details of the fight, command his ship, and try to stay in touch with the rest of his fleet.

If he could work out a way to do that.

A crossbow bolt whirred past his nose, fired from *Iason's* forecastle only ten paces away, and Foscari began to pace the poop deck to make a more challenging target. His own crossbowmen on the poop were returning fire, he had to hope they'd keep the enemy suppressed.

The boarding fight was going well. The enemy had already been engaged along their port side, and his men had roared over the starboard poop and hit them in the rear. The poop had been cleared, and the Venetians were now trying to fight their way onto the main deck, but that involved battling along the narrow gangway and over the rowing benches, a challenging task. Fortunately there was steady fire from the bridges built over the waists of the two Venetian galleys, aimed at clearing the enemy decks, and sooner or later that would tell.

Another crossbow bolt whistled past, and Foscari accelerated his pacing. He scanned across the sea, seeing fire, smoke, wreckage in the water. Wreckage dotted the waves, and some of the wreckage had figures clinging to it.

Then, off the port side, the smoke parted to reveal an enemy galley with two banks of oars. The hull was white, striped in gold and green, the colors of the Cypriot flag, and it had clearly been in a fight. Some oars were missing, and the wet hides that covered its bow were scorched, either from its own Greek fire or someone else's. But the forecastle bristled with armor and weapons, and white water curled from the bronze ram just on the waterline. Even over the sounds of fighting, Foscari could hear orders being shouted from the bireme's poop, and the two rows of oars picked up the pace, white water churning on the bireme's flanks . . .

"Sound recall!" The words were on Foscari's before he remembered that the trumpeter had fallen. He ran to the break in the poop and shouted down into the packed mass of crew.

"Enemy to port! Enemy to port! Brace, brace, brace!"

Few heard him. The ram struck *Barbarigo* right amidships, and the entire galley was thrown sideways with such force that half the crew was hurled off their feet and crashed to the deck in a tangle of bodies and clashing weapons. The sideways movement pushed up a steep wall of water that fountained up between *Barbarigoi* and *Iason* and rained down over the decks.

The lightly built midships bridge, full of crossbowmen and catapult crews firing down into the *Iason,* was knocked off its foundations, and it listed heavily to port and then fell, spilling crew onto the decks.

And then—Foscari was struck dumb with astonishment—the enemy bireme bounced off the Venetian galley like a rubber ball hurled at a stone wall.

Barbarigo had withstood the attack. There was a reason galleys in the middle ages had stopped carrying rams, and that had everything to do with modern shipbuilding techniques invented in the Arsenale of Venice. A modern ship, with the planking stretched around a sturdy frame, was much stronger than a ship built by the older method, where the hull was built first and the frame inserted later. Strong enough, anyway, to repel a strike by an enemy ship powered only by human muscle.

And then a barrage of steel-tipped missiles leaped from the bireme, falling into the tangled mess of the broken midships bridge and the sprawled crewmen, wreaking scarlet havoc.

"Port watch to your stations!" Foscari bellowed down into the chaos, and the port-side oarsmen scrambled to their feet to run to defend their ship.

Foscari clenched his teeth, expecting at any second for Greek fire to spurt from the enemy forecastle, firing straight into the teeth of his crewmen. But the fiery blast never came. Apparently the bireme had exhausted its reservoirs of gasoline.

More shouted orders came from the Cypriots' poop. The two banks of oars thrashed the water, and the helm was put over to bring the enemy ship alongside *Barbarigo*. Grapnels flew through the air.

"Cut those lines!" Foscari drew his sword and slashed at a grapnel that had lodged on the taffrail. A crossbow bolt whistled overhead and he ducked. He rose, hacked at the line again, and it parted.

But slashing at the lines proved useless. The bireme ran alongside *Barbarigo*—not as neatly as Foscari had run alongside *Iason*, but well enough, a little too far forward, the poop overlooking *Barbarigo*'s waist, the bireme's waist beneath *Barbarigo*'s forecastle. And, beneath the enormous flag and streaming pennants on the enemy's poop, Foscari could see the bireme's name glittering in raised gold leaf on the flat poop, SPIRIDON RIGAS, King Spiridon.

The enemy flagship, he realized, and then the bireme's flank ground against *Barbarigo*, and a storm of missiles rained down from the enemy poop onto the Venetian's waist. A wave of defenders went down, and then there was the resonant thud of a catapult firing, followed in a split second by another.

Foscari growled in frustration as he saw two glass vessels plunge down into *Barbarigo*'s main deck and shatter amid the crew. He expected a wave of flame to sheet over the defenders, but instead a ferocious white mist boiled up from the deck, and the crewmen screamed as if they'd been plunged into fire. The lines of crew recoiled from the bulwark.

Acid! Foscari thought, and he shouted for sand to quench the flesh-eating liquid.

Too late. Even as he gave the order, he saw enemy crew leap down into *Barbarigo*'s waist from the poop, led by a figure in golden armor. The attackers all wore thick-soled boots that gleamed with some shiny substance that was presumably intended to repel the acid that had given them a footing on the enemy deck.

Other than the boots, the leader seemed entirely encased in plate, from his greaves to the helmet plumed in the Cypriot colors of gold and green. He glared out at the world through a T-shaped slot in his helmet, and even though Foscari couldn't see his face he felt a sudden shock of recognition.

Yes. Another of Spiridon's champions. Or djinn. Or demons. Whatever they were.

And already he was attacking, charging straight into the disorganized mass of defenders, the point of a wedge of boarders.

Spiridon's champion carried a sword in each hand, a straight sword in the right, a curved scimitar in the left. His group of boarders was also heavily armored, big brawny men who wore plate and mail and plumed helmets, and who carried heavy kite-shaped shields in addition to broad-bladed falchions.

Not expected, Foscari thought. Not in naval warfare, where heavy armor would restrict the agility necessary to maneuver on a crowded, complicated vessel. Shove any one of those titans overboard, and he'd plummet like an anvil to the bottom before he could get the armor off.

But that didn't alter the fact that these armored giants were on his deck, now, at this very moment, doing a very good job of killing his men.

Foscari ran across the poop and began pulling crossbowmen off the rail facing *Iason* and sending them to the break in the poop. Once he'd got half a dozen, he joined them and pointed at the enemy champion.

"Kill that man," he ordered.

At the moment that he spoke, the enemy champion turned his head and looked straight at him, as if somehow, in the midst of the shouts and screams and the clang of weapons, he'd heard the order. Foscari's nerves sang a warning as he gazed into the invisible eyes shadowed by the golden helmet, and then the golden figure turned and began slicing his way toward the poop.

There were two ways to climb *Barbarigo's* poop, a steep companion-way on either side. So as not to interfere with the rowers, the companionways made a ninety-degree turn to descend to the gangway that ran between the towing benches.

"Shoot him! Shoot him!" Foscari urged.

A crossbowman fired and hit the champion right on his armored chest. The bolt shattered on the armor, and the champion came on, his two swords slashing through Venetian crewmen. Another bolt was intercepted by the kite shield of the champion's supporters, and a third bounced off the golden helmet and struck a Venetian sailor.

Foscari was willing to give his right foot for a large enough rock to crush that golden helmet, but unfortunately his ship didn't carry any rocks. He grabbed marines armed with pikes and shoved them to the poop companionway.

"Just fend that bastard off," he said.

The armored champion had killed his way to the base of the poop, and he began the steep climb up the port companionway with the marines jabbing down at him with their three-meter spears. He slashed and parried the spear points, took a step upward, paused and slashed again. His butcher's work had stained the golden armor with scarlet.

Foscari looked desperately for help and saw one of the leather buckets of sand that stood by ready to douse an attack by Greek fire. He seized it by its rope handle, ran to the companionway, and hurled it overhand straight for the champion's golden helmet.

He'd hoped for a rock, but this would have to do.

The strike rocked the champion back, and he lost his balance and took a step back before one of his party caught him. A gauntleted hand wiped sand from the T-shaped slot in the helmet. The boarding pikes jabbed down again, and one caught the champion on the left shoulder and punched through the armor. The golden fighter dropped his sword, grabbed the pike's haft, wrenched the point free, reeled, and then came up the companionway again.

Foscari looked wildly for another sand bucket, saw it, and ran for it. Crossbow bolts whirred near his head. He snatched the bucket, ran back to the companion, and hurled it. If he could just knock the man down, he thought, the fighter might never be able to rise again, not against the weight of his armor and the trampling of fighters surging back and forth over his body.

But this time Spiridon's champion was ready. He saw the bucket coming and fended it off with an upraised arm. It spilled its sand and fell harmlessly into the crowd on the main deck. And the man in golden armor came on.

"Porco dio!" Foscari swore. He was going to have to take care of this himself—that or die like a good Communist.

He drew his cutlass, and felt distinctly at a disadvantage in facing the armored colossus. He wore only a cuirass of boiled leather, reinforced with steel plates over the shoulders, and he'd forgotten his helmet in his cabin.

Spiridon's champion rose to the poop like a golden god rising from the sea. The two tails of his braided red beard hung from beneath his helmet, and that marked him as the man—demon—who had frightened Serafina when they met. The pike wound had made his left arm nearly useless, and he was fighting only with the right hand, but he still fought well enough to cut down two of the marines who were trying to stop him.

Foscari stepped toward the golden fighter and casually flipped his Unione Venezia cap in the man's face, blocking the limited vision of the helmet. The champion slashed blindly. Foscari ducked under the strike and his lunge went neatly between the helmet and gorget, with all Foscari's weight behind it. He distinctly felt the release of the cutlass point as it parted the champion's spine.

Goal! he thought.

The champion fell in a spastic crash of metal, so uncoordinated that the armor seemed to have no bones in it at all. Foscari stepped over the body to slash at the very surprised Cypriot standing just behind his fallen champion. The cutlass caught him in the neck before he could raise his heavy shield, sliced through his chain-mail coif, and sent him reeling back down the companionway, right into his heavily armored companions, who all went down like skittles in a game of *cinque birilli*. Foscari was about to throw himself down the companionway and stab them all before they could rise, but the remaining marines began thrusting down with their long pikes, the steel points driving down in a perfect frenzy, and Foscari decided it was too dangerous to dive into that, and he'd leave the job to the crew.

He bent to retrieve his cap, then looked up as he heard a massed shout. His heart gave a leap as he saw *Doge Dandolo*, which must have finished off the Cypriot galley it had rammed, come crashing alongside *Spiridon*, and a torrent of boarders pour over the side as crossbows and catapults hurled missiles into the defenders.

Spiridon had lost its champion and was now being boarded from its unengaged side while most of its marines were aboard *Barbarigo*. The result was a massacre. *Spiridon*'s crew was so packed together in the waist that they could scarcely wave a sword to defend themselves. Foscari rallied *Barbarigo*'s crew to press them from the other side, and the Cypriots died in heaps.

Iason's crew had by this time succumbed, and the five locked galleys rolled on a sea that grew red with the blood that rained from the scuppers.

The three Venetians recalled their crews to the oars, and cruised as a squadron across the battlefield, looking for enemies to fight and finding none. The allied fleet had won a complete victory.

Six Cypriot galleys had been burned, and three made a successful escape when the battle had decisively turned against them. The remaining seven had either been captured, or they'd been crippled in such a way as to make escape impossible. These last surrendered when offered the chance.

One Venetian and one Rhodian galley had been burned, and one from each allied fleet had been successfully boarded by the enemy—both by crews led by *Spiridon*'s parahuman champions—but each of the captures had been abandoned when the battle had turned against the Cypriots. Foscari had killed one of the champions, and another had been burned when his ship had been set on fire.

The allied fleet returned to Rhodes City with their captures under tow, and the enemy crew were taken off the surrendered ships and into captivity. While the city erupted in mad joy, and icons of the Virgin were paraded along the ramparts of the old town, Foscari stayed aboard his flagship and made plans for the next day's sortie.

The Afentiko and Serafina both came out to *Barbarigo*, bearing hampers of food and drink, and loud in their acclamation for the victory. Foscari accepted their embraces and asked for food and wine to be sent to his crew. The Afentiko complied, and also sent drafts of his militia on board to act as marines.

Once the dead and wounded were carried to shore, Foscari had enough crew to fully man five ships, and the Rhodians could send another two under Archiploiarchos Giorgallis, whose flagship had been overrun, but who had miraculously survived despite numerous wounds. Giorgallis refused to leave his ship despite his injuries, and was carried up to his poop and slung in a kind of hammock, so that he could remain in personal command. Foscari sent him a bottle of brandy as a token of his admiration.

The allied fleet cleared the harbor before dawn, and this time Foscari gave his oarsmen a rest by raising masts and sails. The exhausted crew slept on the deck in neat windrows, and covered every square meter of the planking.

The allied fleet located the enemy by midmorning, and found them in the midst of an evacuation. Cypriot ships had taken their army off the shore near Cape Vayla and were heading home. Their sails straggled out nearly to the eastern horizon. The three surviving galleys stood guard, hanging between the fleet and Foscari's advancing ships.

Foscari exulted at the sight. He'd been worried that Spiridon's army would stay on Rhodes and storm the city with or without naval support, but apparently the loss of their fleet and their three champions had convinced them to give up the campaign.

The allied fleet swooped close, lowered masts and sails, and under oars they charged the three enemy galleys. These manned their oars and fled, scattering through the transports.

Foscari let them go. The transports, with Spiridon's army, were by now his real target.

The Cypriot fleet had ships of every size, from pre-Change converted yachts and fishing boats to large, tubby cargo ships. All were crammed with well-armed soldiers—veterans, presumably, of Spiridon's victorious campaigns. The smaller boats would cause few problems, but the big merchant ships towered like castles above the Venetian galleys, and their bulwarks swarmed with soldiers ready to volley arrows, spears, and other missiles down on any galley that threatened to board them.

Barbarigo approached within hailing distance of one ship, and Foscari's call for surrender was answered with jeers and catcalls. So the Venetian galley swept in under the merchant's counter, and a full tank of burning gasoline was hosed over the decks. The ship was burned to the waterline, and hundreds of soldiers died horribly.

After that convincing demonstration, there was no more resistance. Only a handful of small boats with the greatest head start escaped: the rest were herded together in one bunch, and told to sail for Rhodes Town. Foscari ordered all weapons and armor heaved overside. Foscari watched the steel rain as it splashed into the water alongside the ships, and regretted the waste of good material; but he was determined not to allow the prisoners any chance of regaining the initiative.

The captive ships were ordered to drop anchor off the commercial harbor. The larger ships were told to send down their yards, topmasts, and topgallants, to make it impossible for them to set any amount of sail. While the warships patrolled a short distance away, the prisoners would be taken ashore in small groups by boat, and introduced to captivity.

"There are thousands of them!" said the Afentiko, as he received Foscari in his office. "What am I to do with so many prisoners?"

"I'd execute the officers," Foscari said. "They'll be the most loyal to Spiridon, and the ones who organized the massacre at Lindos. The rest should be sent to hard labor, repairing fortifications, sowing crops, digging new wells . . . Whatever is needed. Offer freedom to those who earn it."

"It's slavery," Kanellis said. "So many things have come back since the Change, but I never thought I'd be the one to bring back slavery."

"We've seen worse," Foscari shrugged. "And it's better than killing them all. If Spiridon wants them back, he can ransom them."

And if there's trouble you may have to kill them all, anyway, he thought. *Another Black Annunciation.* But that, fortunately, was not Foscari's problem.

Three days later, the Venetian squadron from Corfu arrived off the port, nine galleys. Foscari's dispatch boat had survived the gale, and passed through Corfu on its way to Venice. The commander at Corfu had decided to reinforce Rhodes on his own initiative, and bring one large merchant ship full of Epirote mercenaries.

And less than twenty-four hours later, a dispatch boat arrived from Venice after a miraculously swift journey, and informed Foscari that more troops and ships were on their way.

And so, one night after sunset, Foscari played host once more to the Afentiko. There was no wind and *Barbarigo* swung aimlessly at its buoy. The night was still, with the warmth of spring hovering around them; and the sea was quiet, just a distant flowing hiss as waves loped along the mole.

"I'm not going to wait for reinforcements," Foscari said. "I'm going to take the ships and troops I've got and—with your permission—your ships and some of your militia as well. I'm going to Cyprus, and I'm going to show Spiridon what naval superiority means."

A smile formed beneath the Afentiko's bushy mustache. The bruise around his broken nose had poured down his face, turning him into a near abstract composition in blue and yellow.

"What do you mean to do?" he asked.

"I'll take a city, if I can. Kouklia, Limassol, Famagusta . . . Not because I want a city particularly, but because it can be a base for the fleet to raid anywhere we like on the island. I'll destroy those three remaining galleys, and I'll burn or take every ship I can. And it's more than possible that I can come to an understanding with one of Spiridon's commanders—

money will be involved, most likely—and then"—he smiled—"that will be the end of Spiridon."

"You seem confident."

"We've seen a lot of these little warlords in the Balkans. None of them have founded a dynasty, and precious few die in their beds. Despotism is simply . . . not sound. At best, it's a stopgap. And despots who rule through terror . . . well, all it takes is one person not to be terrorized, and to be in the right place."

"And Spiridon's . . . supernatural assistants?"

Foscari considered the two he'd met and suppressed a shudder. He tried to sound confident as he replied, "We've killed three of them. It wasn't easy, but it will get easier."

"I hope you are right."

"May I have the loan of your ships and men, then?"

The Afentiko made an expansive gesture. "Of course, my friend."

"Let's drink on it." He reached for the bottle on the table, then feigned hesitation. "I promised you a drink from a special bottle," he said, "on the day the Cypriots arrived."

The Afentiko inclined his shaggy head. "I remember. You said it wasn't time for drinking."

"I've changed my mind."

He had the bottle brought from his private spirit locker, along with another pair of Murano glasses. Regret sang softly through his veins as he poured, as he employed the poison ring with its castor-bean cargo.

"To the alliance," he said, and raised his glass.

The alliance was solid now, with the memory of Spiridon's bloody invasion firm on every mind. Better that the Afentiko fall ill when Foscari was leading the allied fleet to strike the enemy, and thus free from any suspicion. Then Serafina would take charge—or would be put in charge by Venetian reinforcements—and Rhodes set on its way to becoming another obedient island in a Venetian sea.

"To our friendship," said the Afentiko, and Foscari felt a sharp spear-point of remorse enter his heart.

Necessity, Foscari reminded himself.

Karl Marx might have thought that certain political developments were inevitable, but in Foscari's experience the inevitable usually required a little help.

He clinked glasses with his friend, and then drank deep of the waters of Fate.

THE SOUL REMEMBERS
UNCOUTH NOISES

BY JOHN BARNES

JOHN BARNES

I write a lot of things besides novels, and I've also written a lot of novels—thirty-one commercially published, two self-pub, so far. Latest is *The Last President*, top sellers ever were *Mother of Storms* and *A Million Open Doors*, nearest to my heart are *Tales of the Madman Underground* and *One for the Morning Glory*. I was a bit surprised to calculate, a couple of years ago, that I had written about five million (lowest estimate) paid-for words across the last three decades or so. So I have taken to calling myself a widely published obscure writer.

This story had its origins in the experience of teaching for one term in a high school program oriented toward the "difficult" (i.e., behavioral-issue) gifted and talented. I found some of my students to be fascinating, not so much for how different they were as for how well they were able to adapt to their own differences and create a life that worked for them. And that led me to contemplating how many of the commonly accommodated, treated, and sometimes medicated behavior problems would be actual advantages, or at least not disadvantages, in a different world. Furthermore, many things we consider "pathological" would probably be common enough to be "the new normal." At other times in my life that might have led me to thinking about Foucault and epistemes, or the Turing Test for neurotypicality, or whether generational psychodemographics drive long-wave economic cycles. But as it happened, in autumn of 2013, it led me to think about three very odd kids facing a very big problem, and . . . here you are. Hope you like it.

The survival of the least unfit will ultimately give the world to the fittest.
When music rises in a city street, every man who hears
it with his soul forgets the uncouth noises.

—REV. JOSEPH COOK, *SCEPTICISM AND RATIONALISM: ELECTIVE AFFINITIES*
AND HEREDITARY DESCENT (1881)

MONDAY, 8 JUNE 2015, ABOUT 10 A.M.
RAFTER XOX RANCH, WESTERN NEBRASKA

Glory Cardenas, who is fifteen and excitable, barrels into the little room where I like to sit over tea while I do the books for the Rafter XOX, yelling "Miz Claire!"

"Right here, Glory." I'm already standing up and reaching for the belt that holds my hatchet and knives. "What—"

"It's Mister Matt! Raiders outside the gate, they got him tied up—"

"Tell James to keep talking and stalling, and I'm on my way." Good thing it's James; he's steady like frozen stone, for-defs the guy I'd have picked to have on duty for something like this.

When I go out into the compound, it's dead quiet and motionless everywhere within the palisade. I look around. "A lot of people who should be working are staring at me, and that's not gonna help. Now go on my 'go.' Set up to defend the palisade. All snipers to the loopholes around the front gate. Squad Four, arm up for a dash, set up to sortie behind the front gate. Medical right behind them. Squad Three, guard

403

the medical. Troop A, mount up for pursuit behind the rest. All other forces to ready positions. Wake the day sleepers with my apologies. Hold your hand up if you know where you're going and what you're doing."

They've been drilled. Hands snap up, no hesitation.

Glory is back at my side, whispering in my ear, "James says tell you it's bad and come quick."

I nod, then look back at my people. "Chaplain, join me on the bridge, prepped for EF. Everyone in place pronto, on my 'go.' Hands up if you understand."

Hands are up again. Chaplain Marjorie looks sick. She was one of Mattie's first recruits when we started Rafter XOX; she doesn't want to give him an emergency funeral.

"Go."

They swarm to it.

"Come with me to the bridge, Glory. I need a messenger right with me. Stay in close so you can hear anything I mutter." I walk to the gate as quickly as I can maintain a pretense of calm, Glory trotting beside me. I hear a few clanks and thuds from dropped buckets or spears, and some of the fool chickens start clucking. The dogs are good; we don't keep them if they can't shut up. A guy with good ears outside the gate would learn that lots of stuff is moving around, but he'd expect that, and that's all he'd learn.

The gate bridge is another of Mattie's ideas: a plank bridge on steel trusses that runs above the sliding main gates, with ports in its deck so enemies can't hide under it.

Old car hoods spaced a couple of feet apart are mounted on the waist-high front wall, so our people on the bridge are always one step from cover.

James is standing at the center gap with his crossbow cradled ready in his arm, and the two gate guards are standing to his sides. About twenty feet below us, maybe forty yards away, maybe fifteen grubby-looking assholes are decked out in scraps of the old world; I think the earmuff hat with all the CDs glued shiny side out is kind of striking. The skull on a stick is probably supposed to look scary, but in a country still littered with unburied bodies, really it's more pathetic.

Among the assholes, a half-starved-looking elderly donkey stands patiently, facing away from us. He's harnessed to a travois with a bicycle wheel at the point.

Mattie looks up at us from the travois. He's tied with hands and feet under the frame, splashed with blood and dirt, and gagged tightly enough to pull his cheeks back.

I bet that hurts. At least I can see he's breathing.

"Chaplain's on the way," I mutter, looking down.

Without expression, James says, "They're staying on message."

A raider stands on each side of Mattie, one with a machete, the other with a hatchet.

The leader, standing back by the donkey's head, seems to recognize me. Not that it's all that hard to identify the only six-foot, two hundred ten–pound Asian woman on this range. "We got something of yours you gonna want back."

"Let's skip the villain-talk. There's no movies anymore. We don't bargain for hostages here. James, if they move to harm Mister Matt in any way, or to take him away from the gate, shoot Mister Matt."

James raises his crossbow and sights it; Mattie looks back, quietly, nodding his agreement. It's how we've always handled these, and it was his idea in the first place.

Their leader looks contemptuously up at me. "You won't do any—"

I let him gabble and speak to the guard next to James: one of my best shots, another stroke of luck. "Diego, can you kill me that donkey, for sure, on one bolt?"

"Hard shot, ma'am."

"But can you?"

"Think so."

"Do it."

On the "t" of *it*, the bolt lashes out of his crossbow and plants between the donkey's ears, just back of his poll, up to its steel fins. "Perfect shot," I say.

The donkey falls sideways. The wheeled travois twists and cracks; the bicycle wheel bends under it. Mattie hangs down half off the travois, held by his tied hands and feet behind the frame. That *really* looks like it hurts.

The leader jumps back. "Fuckin' mother fucker—"

"Now you can't take him away," I say. "You can kill him but if you do you're all dead. Or if you force us, we'll kill him ourselves, and *then* you're all dead. Since Mister Matt rode out this morning with five guards, we already have five good reasons for revenge. So you're probably already dead, but if you throw down your weapons and put your hands up—"

"You won't kill your husband," the leader says. "I can't believe that you don't feel—"

"I'm not responsible for what you can't believe."

TUESDAY, MARCH 17, 1998, 7:15 P.M.
WESTMINSTER, COLORADO

For one second I thought that stupid shrink-o-doctor had been right and I was having the first bad migraine of the rest of my life. More light than I had ever seen pierced through my eye sockets, and my head hurt like it was being squeezed to pieces. But when I opened my eyes, half thinking I'd see swirling colors and tumble from my chair like Mom did whenever it was convenient, instead it was just real dark. The living-room computer in front of me had gone black-dead and so had the lamp. I couldn't even see either of them, within arm's reach. All the curtains and blinds were closed, and it was dark outside.

In the kitchen, the little lights on all the gadgets were out, too. Dad had been making a pot of coffee like he always did when he was going to work till dawn. The splut-splut-bloosh of the coffeemaker faded into two dwindling little splorches and a brief trickle.

Dad said, "Aw, fuck, power failure." He felt around in a drawer for the kitchen flashlight. It didn't work either.

Mom yelled from the bedroom that her laptop was dead, ". . . and it had a full charge too, I had it plugged in all day."

Dad ran down the hall into his office and yelled, "Aw fuck," again 'cause his UPS was out.

Stepping carefully—you never knew what would be underfoot—I went to the hall closet where Mom kept her spiritual healing candles, grabbed the first box on top of the pile, found the matches in the kitchen drawer, lit a candle, and stuck it to the table. It couldn't be any worse for the finish than the crusted-on Coco Puffs blobs from last month.

I'd grabbed a box of pale blue ones, scented with a mix of lavender, vanilla, and "natural floral" to bring peace and tranquility, a good idea given Dad's yelling and kicking things in his office, and the whining and raging from Mom in the bedroom.

I lit four more candles, clustering them together on the table.

My folks were irresponsible and flaky but we went camping a lot; it seemed real unlikely that the flashlight batteries would've been dead. *And* the laptop that Mom always left plugged in? *And* the UPS?

Weird.

By candlelight, my digital watch was silvery-blank.

I stepped out on our porch; the chinook that had been blowing all day was still on, wet, warm, and gusty. It would turn to a blizzard, but not right away. That was at least one thing I'd learned from all that stupid X-C skiing we all had to go do every fucking weekend all stupid fucking winter, and pretend was fun, because they were trying to run the fat off their roly-poly giant of a daughter.

Behind me in the house, Dad and Mom were yelling at each other about using good expensive candles and ruining the kitchen table and who broke the electricity. Dad picked up one of the candles with *Not the good potholder!* and went down to look at the circuit breaker box, Mom trailing after, yelling because he wasn't holding the candle where she could see where she was walking.

The street was its same old identical-beige-boxes Denver burb, but way darker: no electric lights, no moon, way past sunset, and about half the sky was socked in with low dense clouds. Pale red-yellow light flickered in a handful of windows—I guess they'd found the candles too. Black rectangles of doors opened up and down the street.

Normally at night in the Front Range, the city below lights up any clouds in the sky brighter than the moon, and the reflected light is plenty to see by. Tonight, the irregular, lumpy black clouds overhead reflected nothing.

My friend Mattie could probably have figured out how far away that meant the lights must be out—he was already taking trig in ninth grade—but the short answer had to be a buttload of a long way away.

The thought of Mattie completed the brain-circuit: *Shit, it's started.*

Mr. Burke next door came out carrying a lighted candle, unlocked his BMW, and popped the hood.

I went over there. "Nothing with electricity is working. Battery or plug."

"Looks that way," he agreed. He scraped a big screwdriver across the battery terminals. "Not even a spark, and I drove two hundred miles yesterday. There should be a full charge. I wonder if this is going on everywhere."

"I think at least everywhere on the Northern Front Range," I said. "Look how dark the clouds are."

He looked up and realized that I meant they weren't reflecting any ground light. "Hey, if I get in, and you give it a good push, we can try to roll-start the car and see if the alternator can still make current."

"Worth a try."

We checked everything over several times, since the driveway slope was gentle and this was going to be our one try.

"Okay, push, Claire!" he said, through the open window. I leaned into his front bumper, getting the car rolling down the driveway in neutral.

Whump-bump-bump. It stopped.

Burke got out. "I didn't hear anything that sounded like a cylinder firing, did you?"

"No."

"So no city current, no battery, and the alternator doesn't work," Burke said. "Well, shitburgers."

"Hey, I know a disaster prepper who's got a shelter—I'm going over to his place. You want to come along?"

He sighed. "Karen's flight from Miami is supposed to be coming in at ten thirty. I better stay here. Good luck, Claire."

"Thanks."

I hurried into the house, trying to get away before Burke realized that Mrs. Burke's flight would have been in the air when everything stopped working.

Mom and Dad were screaming at each other down in the basement, their usual flapping around uselessly, like they did about who forgot to pay the cable bill or register the car, or whose fault it was that I had shitty grades and had gone up another pants size. Mom was ranting that Dad was being patronizing, interrupted by his yipping about her being childish.

Food, shoes, pack, go.

I poured the remaining half box of Cinnamon Toast Crunch into a big mixing bowl, added the last milk from the fridge, and started gulping.

I was almost done when Mom came running up the stairs, crying, with Dad following and desperately apologizing. Then they saw me.

"Claire," Mom said, in that bitchy tone of exasperation she put on to impress her friends with how tough she had it, "we are going out for Mexican just as soon as this crap with the electricity gets straightened out, and that cereal is supposed to be half a cup a day because it is loaded with carbs—"

I kept shoveling it in, and said, with my mouth full because she hated that, "It's started."

"*What* has started?" Dad demanded. "You got something to work?"

"Duh." I gulped a big bite because no one could say the next name intelligibly through a mouth of cereal. "Morton Orczegowski was right. Something's happened, something big. No light on the clouds, the whole Front Range is down, and the batteries and Mr. Burke's alternator and digital watches and *nothing* works. So I'm going over to Mattie's and then him and me and his family will go over to Orry's and then to the shelter. You should come along and see if he'll still take you."

I picked up the bowl and chugged the rest, letting a little of it run down my face.

"Claire, that is so vulgar—" Mom began.

Dad said, "I am not going to go beg a crazy survivalist libertarian gun nut to save me from what's probably just a big solar flare."

I opened the refrigerator, took out a bottle of water, and used a handful of it to wash my face.

"Claire, that's Evian, it's expensive—"

"There won't be any water in the sink," I said. "The pumps are electric."

Dad angrily yanked at the faucet to show me I was wrong; it guttered and burped as the very last of the city water ran backward down the pipe.

I was already heading out of the kitchen to go change my shoes. Dad grabbed my arm. "You are not going off into some fallout shelter with some gun nut libertardian—"

I shoved him in the chest; no time for this bullshit, I'd been taller than he was since I was twelve, and he was scrawny anyway. To make sure they stayed out of my way, I dropped the bomb: "I bet Richard would have gone, and he'd have taken Mom along so he'd have something to fuck."

See, a couple of years before, Mom and Dad tried this thing called being poly, and Mom had a big romantic thing with a big muscular construction dude named Richard. Meanwhile Dad couldn't get a date. They ended up spending twice as long in counseling as they did being poly, just to get back to being their same old whiny miserable selves.

It worked like always. Mom ran into the bedroom wailing and slammed the door; Dad followed her, pathetically mewling, "Abby, she just said that to—"

I dashed to my room, ditched my little strappy silver sandals, and pulled on heavy socks and the butt-ugly hiking boots they'd given me for Christmas. From their bedroom, her sobbing and his apologizing blended into familiar meaninglessness.

My big thick knee-length down coat had pockets all over it; it had been my favorite coat for shoplifting last year. (I gave that up; if you're good there's no excitement and if you're not there's too much.) I put the coat on, dumped everything out of my school backpack onto the floor, and loaded the pack and coat pockets with everything from the cabinet where Mom kept all her bags and boxes of cookies and candy, plus all the bottled water I could fit in.

I could hear Mom subsiding into talking mean shit about how disappointed she was in Dad, punctuated with wracking angry sobs, and Dad pleading in between.

I tied the top of my pack loosely over a bag of tortilla chips and fit a jar of Cheez Whiz into my last pocket. Time to go.

Dad ran out of the bedroom and down the stairs, realized he couldn't see, came back, and got a candle, shielding it with his hand, before going down.

I sighed. One more time, I'd try.

Down in the basement, by the light of the candle, Dad was taking the front panel off the washing machine. "Your mother was just thinking she'd feel better if she could get caught up on laundry, and we didn't always have to take it out, so—"

"Dad, the washing machine hasn't worked since before Christmas. You will never need to fix it now. There is no electricity. Not from main power, not from a battery, not from nothing. Cars don't run either. *Nothing's* working."

"Your mom just gets so frustrated, Claire—"

"I'm going now," I said.

"Over to Mattie's house, you said? Tell Ravikumar I could sure use help on this washing machine."

"'Kay, Dad. Gotta run."

Back upstairs, Mom was on their bed, eyes closed, blanket wrapped against her face. "I just want . . . I just want . . . I just want . . ." Classic Mom. Her breakdowns seemed real enough but her timing was always suspect.

"Mom, I hope you feel better soon."

"Be careful, baby." All of a sudden, she lunged out of the covers and hugged me.

I pushed her arms apart. I didn't like either of them touching me. It always felt like they wanted something.

Mattie was either my best friend or the closest thing I had ever had to a friend. His real name was Mahtab Kaushik and he was one of those scrawny all-feet-and-head kids, with a beaky nose and huge horn-rim glasses, dark enough to be mistaken for black or Mexican; his folks had a little Indian lilt in their accents but Mattie was Colorado born and raised, and sounded like it.

He constantly fact-spouted. That was what the counselors and special ed people at the alternate school called pouring out all the random trivia that a guy who reads too much and remembers all of it accumulates. He also couldn't seem to shut the fuck up even when he wanted to.

Much of his fact-spouting was about games and computers and sci-fi TV shows, but he also spouted a lot about school stuff, which helped me get by with less reading.

We fit together real good at crazy-weird school. His fact-spouting was fine with me; I liked to hear Mattie talk, and so did he. Mattie drew bullies like shit draws flies, so he was safer standing next to that scary giant psycho Korean bitch. And teachers always put us together in groups and committees; they categorized us both as All Other Non-White. Probably they thought Busan and Jaipur were both in All Other Non-White Land.

Anyway, Mattie was for sure my friend, probably my best friend, maybe my only real friend.

When I pushed the doorbell button (out of habit) it didn't ring, probably the first time, ever. Normally if anything had malfunctioned at Mattie's house, Ravikumar, being a repair contractor, would've died of shame.

I knocked, loud.

Ravikumar yanked the door open. "Claire! Good to see you! Are your parents coming?"

"Couldn't get them to."

Mattie had way better folks than mine; all Ravikumar's comment was one little wince, and then a change of subject. "We are trying to sort things out here; it is so dark without power I don't see how we can get to the shelter safely in the dark. We may be better off if we stay put till it is light."

I nodded. "If you think so—"

"Also, can you help us understand something? Mattie tried an experiment—"

Mattie was holding up a plastic yogurt container that reeked of vinegar.

"Mattie," I said, "if it's science stuff, you'd be better off talking to Orry—"

"Just look," he said. "Alligator clips to Mom's wedding ring and an aluminum can pull tab. Both in straight white vinegar. Okay? Should be a simple battery. But none of Dad's multimeters budge. And a multimeter is basically a magnetic needle inside a coil, so I also wrapped my Boy Scout compass in bell wire and hooked that up, and the needle never budged from north."

Feeling stupid and helpless, I reached for the phrase I'd heard from him and Orry many times. "Electromagnetic pulse?"

"See, I told you you'd get it!"

"Get what?"

"That that's what it can't be! I mean what it isn't! I mean . . . look, an electromagnetic pulse might destroy electrical things, maybe even fry the multimeters, destroy car wiring and even wreck batteries if it was big enough, but I put the compass and wire together after the whatever. So it's not that all the electrical stuff got destroyed. It's that electricity doesn't work anymore. See?"

I didn't really, then, but I nodded.

Kanti said, "You see? She's smart like Mahtab. And she says so too. Electricity does not work anymore. We have to get away before people realize you can't fix things."

Ravikumar looked miserable. "What if electricity starts working again in five minutes? Or a year? So many years into this business—"

A window broke upstairs and someone yelled "Ragheads!" out front. Then another window broke. I charged out and found Danny and Zach Davis, ten-year-old twin spawn of Tammy Davis, the neighborhood trash-drama queen, winding up with more stones.

"Hey!"

They ran. With my heavy pack, coat, and hiking boots, no way I could catch them right now. Next time I did, though, they were going to hurt real bad.

Mattie trotted down from upstairs. "Some broken glass on the floor. My bass tipped over, but it's a block of wood, and electric anyway."

"There will be more of this," Kanti said, quietly.

"Right," Ravikumar said. "As always." He closed the door. "All right, we'll finish packing and go."

Five minutes later, Kanti's pack held a couple of photo albums, some jewelry, and mostly clothes. Mattie had clothes, a big bag of rice, and the Boy Scout *Fieldbook*. Ravikumar had less clothing and as many hand tools as he could manage. They all had water bottles in the side pockets and sleeping bags tied on. "That was fast," I observed.

"One of those things Morton insisted on," Ravikumar said, smiling. "We had to have packs handy with lists in them. Let's go." He opened the door and we walked through.

As we hurried up the street, Ravikumar said, "During Partition, one day my grandfather had walked over to the next village for some work, and when he was coming back, he saw the smoke rising and decided to go to his aunt's house instead of home. So he lived. Three sisters, his eldest brother, their mother, all of his nephews and nieces, and his fiancée, they all were killed, every one, after they had spent three days talking about whether they had to go. Grandfather didn't even stay to bury them; he started for Jaipur with just the money in his pocket. Mattie, I hope you will always remember you are descended from people who knew when to run away."

"It's sad, though," Kanti added. "We've been happy here."

"We can be happy again. Somewhere else. But we have to be alive for that."

We headed for Orry's house. I guess Orry was the logical name for a kid whose real name was Marcus Aurelius Orczegowski, especially because he hated "Mark." Only teachers called him that.

About a block from the Orczegowski house, we heard the crowd shouting.

"Morton's place?" Kanti asked, quietly.

"Could be," Ravikumar said.

"I know a back way in." I told the truth because it was simpler. "Morton lets Orry smoke weed, but not at his house because he's paranoid about cops. Sometimes I smoke with Orry, out and around the neighborhood. Sometimes we have to run. There's a way into the house through the back."

Ravikumar didn't waste time judging. "Mattie, go with Claire. We will take a discreet look from the front. If everything's okay, we all meet up at Morton's, if not, we meet back here. Go!"

Those burbs were a maze of fences and dogs, but the house behind Orry's place had three big distinctive evergreen bushes trimmed into cube shapes. Strangely, the car in the driveway had a glow coming from under its upraised hood. As we ran past, I caught a glimpse of candles all around the engine, an open manual on top of the air cleaner, and a man with white hair and a lined face bent over it reading, hands resting in prayer position, so that it looked as if he were trying to follow the Sacred Book of Chilton's invocation to the Mighty God Horsepower. Even having forgotten so much, that momentary picture has stayed with me all these years.

We heard him shout behind us but I was already yanking open the emergency gate in the high back privacy fence.

Flickering orange light glared over the top of Orry's garage. I heard shouts interrupting shouts, and Morton's voice cutting through, sounding like calm reason. *A little late for him to start now,* I thought.

The long-dead electric meter on the garage wall swung on its hinge. Morton had realized Orry might not want to turn a light on while evading cops, so the release was concealed but easy to work in the dark. I grabbed the house key and opened the garage and kitchen door.

Orry's voice from upstairs was soft. "Who's there?"

"Claire and Mattie." I tried to speak as soft as Orry.

"I'm in my room. Crawl when you come through the door."

We rushed up the stairs and down the hall, bending forward awkwardly in our heavy coats with our backpacks, crawling across the dark floor, sliding on books, papers, CDs and DVDs and games. Orry crouched by the corner of the curtain, sighting a rifle whose muzzle rested on the sill. A pale redhead, he looked like Mattie's pigmentless twin.

"No one's noticed me," Orry breathed.

The flickering light in the front yard was from candles, burning sticks and boards, and a couple of Coleman lanterns held aloft. Morton stood in the driveway, in front of a row of five wheelbarrows loaded with stuff. He faced a crowd of about thirty neighbors, who stood along the concrete gutter that separated the street from the narrow sidewalk, held for the moment by suburban property rights habits.

The argument was about whether the supplies in Morton's wheelbarrows meant that he had been hoarding, and whether everybody should be allowed to share it.

"Dad knew you and your family would come, Mattie," Orry whispered. "So we loaded five wheelbarrows. If we'd been sure that you'd make it, Claire, we'd have one for—"

The shout from up the street froze *my* blood. I can't imagine what it must have done to Mattie.

You know the kind of asshole guys that always have three cars out front of their house, and stand out there pretending to fix them so they can drink beer and yell things at girls? Four of those, and of course Ms. Tammy "Speak English, Don't Wear Cloth On Your Head, and Don't Be Brown" Davis, were pushing Ravikumar and Kanti by the arms up to the crowd. "They'as sneakin' up to join their Jew buddy," Tammy shouted. "Jews and ragheads!"

Morton Orczegowski lowered his rifle to point at the ground, walked forward quietly, and stood at arm's-length from the front rank of the silenced crowd. "I *invited* Mr. and Mrs. Kaushik to come with me to my shelter. We bought and paid for everything, including the wheelbarrows, and they are ours. Just let us go with our families and the property we need, and we will leave the whole house, and everything in it, unlocked for you to take what you want from there."

Ravikumar said, "My house is also unlocked, and we have only what is in our packs and what my friend Morton is sharing with us. Please go take what you want, but leave us alone."

The crowd was quiet, looking at one another. Morton said, "Just let Mr. and Mrs. Kaushik walk over to me. Don't hold them that way, you're hurting them. We can't get away from you, anyway, any of us."

A big guy in a Confederate strap-cap released Kanti's arm, and the scrawny, scruffy, probably meth-head holding her other arm did the same. She walked quietly out of the crowd to stand next to Morton; a moment later, so did Ravikumar.

"Now," Morton said, "We will be gone in five minutes, and you can have—"

A woman with a loud voice, the kind my mom called "brassy" I guess because it cut through all the other sound like a trumpet, announced, "This is so fucking silly. I just need that box of powdered milk that I can see right there in that one wheelbarrow, for my kids." She walked up the driveway.

Morton said, "Ma'am, I can't let—"

"It's just milk for my kids." She kept walking. "You are not going to shoot a mother who just needs milk for her kids. That's just silly."

Watching him from behind, I didn't see Morton's face, but there was a weird twitch in his back muscles, around the shoulder blades, like he was fighting himself for just an instant, before he raised his gun.

A loud click. Nothing more.

He tried the trigger again. Click.

"See?" she said, triumphantly, holding aloft the box of powdered milk and another whole canvas bag. "I'm taking this other stuff too so I don't have to make extra trips."

The crowd wavered for a second. Morton pulled a pistol from his shoulder holster.

A man in sweatpants and a Homer Simpson T-shirt stepped out of the crowd with a shotgun and pointed it at Morton. Startling, loud clicks beside me: Orry pulling the trigger over and over. "It isn't firing at all," he whispered.

Morton turned at the clicking of the gun behind him, took one step forward, and pushed the muzzle down. "Looks like guns don't work either." He was looking right into the man's eyes. "So we'll have to—"

The lady stealing the bag of food, trying to walk out through the crowd, wailed, "No!"

People were grabbing and pulling at the bag. Someone pushed her forward onto her knees, and the powdered milk burst. Morton took one step forward, his arm outstretched—maybe to help her, or to calm the crowd—and that ratty little meth-head slammed him in the head with a shovel. Morton fell; Ravikumar jabbed the meth-head in the face with the gun butt, and bent to look at Morton.

Orry, beside me, was screaming, "Dad! Dad! Daddy!"

Ravikumar Kaushik looked up at us. For an instant, even the people tearing the bag of supplies apart froze. Mattie and I, later, both agreed we remembered the same thing: Ravikumar saw his son, looked into his eyes, and said something we couldn't hear.

Then a man whipped a garden rake over his head, down onto Ravikumar's shoulder, dragging him to the pavement, and some people closed in, kicking and stomping, shoving Kanti away, while the rest rushed up the driveway to the wheelbarrows.

I grabbed my friends' arms and stepped back hard, twisting them around to break the spell. "Orry, your coat and pack! Out the back! Before we're cut off! Downstairs! Now, now, *now!*"

The boys leaped down the stairs after me, through the kitchen. The first shoulders were already crashing against the front door.

We raced through the garage, across the backyard, and through the open gate. The man I had seen seeming to pray to his engine was standing there with a shotgun, but he let us by and kicked the gate shut behind us. Orry jammed a screwdriver through the hasp and said, "Guns don't work either, run!"

I never saw whether he did; we just fled across his yard and down the empty street, ducking behind the first big hedge and creeping over to an alley.

Wild yelling and cheering behind us, but they didn't seem to be coming our way. Mattie started to run back, but Orry and I grabbed his arms and dragged him along that alley. "I heard my mom call me!"

So had I, but I hissed, "It wasn't her, it's a trick!" I knew Kanti wasn't calling *for* him, she was calling *to* him; it wasn't *help me*, it was *good-bye*.

We ran along that alley in the dark until we were all stumbling. Orry said, "This way!" and we followed him back onto a wider street, heading west to judge by the dark shape of the mountains against the stars.

In the street, little clusters of people wandered aimlessly. There were some fires starting to burn in every direction. Behind us, there was a sudden high flame; Orry looked back and said, "I'm guessing that's Dad's spare fuel tank."

At the edge of the big park-with-a-pond west of our subdivision, Orry stopped and held up a hand. Between gasps he said, "Always imagined it would look like this when Dad talked about it. Sounds so different though. Never imagined no motorcycle or chain saw motors, no sirens, no car horns, no guns."

I looked up from where I'd been bent over, coughing hard; I was in shitty shape in those days and the air was already thick with smoke. "I never imagined it at all." We all gasped for air for a minute or so; at least with the wind from the west, it was only a little smoky so far.

Orry said, "Okay, no way we can go much farther in the dark. One of us would turn an ankle or somebody'd ambush us or we'd fall into something we never saw. We have to hide till we have light to move by."

"Where are we going?" I asked. I realized Mattie wasn't talking, which was a first, and not a good one.

"Trails Park, for tonight. Up to the shelter tomorrow. I'll explain more once we're safe for the night. Meanwhile I have a bolt cutter and crowbar in my pack, and the pump building for West Lake is close."

It took less than a minute to break in; inside, Orry produced a candle from his pack and lit it. There was a little workbench with tools, a big, now silent, pump and motor, and a little room on the concrete floor. "No windows," Orry whispered, "so we can have a light."

He dragged on the door to make sure it was shut all the way. "I didn't pack much food," he said, apologetically.

"I did." I started pulling things out of my pack. We all gulped a bottle of water, wolfed things from the bags, and then swallowed more water. Mattie still wasn't talking.

Orry investigated the small refrigerator under the table. "Ha, lucky day. Some naughty maintenance guy was keeping beer here."

"Not really time for a party," I said.

Orry shook his head. "It'll help us sleep. We need to do that."

Mattie spoke. "My mom and dad say . . . they say . . . I promised them I'd never drink till . . . till . . ." He began to cry.

"You don't have to," I told him, "but it might help."

Orry and I had three beers each; Mattie reluctantly had one. I'd been thinking about how cold that floor would be, sleeping in my coat, but Mattie said, "My sleeping bag is a big double and . . . and I want to have somebody hold me. My mom used to hold me when I couldn't get to sleep."

He looked pretty pathetic. I said, "Okay, but don't even think about trying to get a feel."

He was warm, almost like the big dog I'd always wanted. Even though he was still sobbing and whispering "thank you for holding me," between the beer, the warmth, and too much exercise I fell asleep right away.

I had no idea that this sharing a bed thing was going to be the rule for the next seventeen years.

WEDNESDAY, MARCH 18, 1998, 5:50 A.M.
TRAILS PARK, WESTMINSTER, COLORADO

Who was this person hanging on to me? Why wasn't I in my bed? Why was it so hard and cold under me?

I remembered, poked my head out into the pitch-black chill, and tried to crawl out without disturbing Mattie, feeling to find my boots and coat. Mattie wriggled out beside me.

Three feet away, Orry was crying, very softly, choking it down and plainly trying to pretend to be asleep.

I wondered about both boys, and if they'd be okay. I knew I wasn't like other people—my folks had spent almost as big a pile of money trying to find out what was defective with their big fat ungrateful daughter as they'd spent buying me out of the Busan orphanage in the first place. I guess it was worth it for Mom to have something to say when the other moms were bitching about their kids, and Dad maybe 'cause I was somebody to talk to that wasn't as crazy as Mom, and only got in his way a little bit when he happened to think of it.

I tried to imagine seeing my father killed, like Orry and Mattie had seen last night.

No idea, no clue, no feeling. Dad was okay and I kind of liked him, so maybe I'd be pissed off.

I figured I'd better stay real quiet on the whole subject. I needed Orry and Mattie to live through whatever this was, and who could tell what they'd do if they found out how weird I was, or how weird they looked to me?

Orry was crying harder now, still inside his sleeping bag. Mattie touched my arm, took my hand, guided me to my feet, and led me to the door. We carefully opened it, finding the beginning of gray daylight, and a huge moon halfway down the clearing western sky.

The chinook was on its way out, but the bad weather still wasn't here. Mattie dragged the door shut behind us. He was holding Orry's crowbar. "I think we can probably get into the bathrooms," he whispered, "and it might be our only chance today for a comfortable place to go."

We pried the women's side door open on the little building; it seemed like a good idea to take turns keeping watch while the other one went in peace. It was freeze-ass cold to drop my pants in there, but at least there was toilet paper. By the time I'd finished, Orry was walking down the slope toward us, and if his face was kind of red and smeary, he seemed to at least be done crying for the moment.

We let him have his turn; he emerged with a wry smile. "Good thing there's only three of us. That's all the toilets there were and we'll have to bring up buckets of water from the lake to flush," he said.

"Why would we bother?"

"For the next guy. That way he doesn't get sick from our crap and spread disease, which will find its way to us." He held up an REI folding bucket. "There's a cook pot in my pack too, so we can boil water once we make a fire, and I've got water purifying tabs."

"If we boil it do we need the tabs?" Mattie asked.

"Oh, yeah. Pretty much all surface water in Colorado has cryptosporidium. You want to shit your guts out for two weeks?"

"There's a soft drink machine in the rec building," I pointed out.

"There's no electricity—" Orry began.

"There's no cops and we have a crowbar," I said.

"I'm still going to grab water to flush the toilets," Orry said, and headed down to the lake. Meanwhile, we broke in and found the machine was mostly full. We started stacking bottled water and Mountain Dew.

"Can't believe I didn't think of that," Orry said, joining us. "That private property libertarian thing, I guess." He seemed on the brink of tearing up, probably thinking of his father again.

Afraid he would set Mattie off, I asked, "So where's the shelter?"

"Up by Lyons. Dad equipped it with pretty much everything we're likely to need."

"How far?" Mattie asked.

"Thirty-two miles. We might even get most of the way there by dark. Going west from here, there's a whole chain of public parks, school campuses, and software company campuses. Dad said to go this way 'in case of civil disorder,' which we sure got. So . . . you guys have any better plan?"

We didn't, so we all sat down and ate more chips, cookies, and candy for breakfast. My pack was getting emptier, so we reshuffled to even out the load of water and soda.

"I'd like to get a look at the city before we go," Mattie said. "Just to see what's happening down there. I mean, what if the power came back on overnight?"

"The Coke machine would've been working," I pointed out.

"And I'd rather not go up the slope and maybe show on a skyline," Orry said.

I looked at Mattie's face and shrugged. "Maybe if we're quick?" I was guessing Mattie was hoping to see cars moving and traffic lights working and then go back and find his parents still alive. I'll never get those parent and kid things but I knew Mattie needed that last look to be sure.

From where we lay prone on the ridgeline, we had big, long views to the south and east.

Eastward, the sun was just above the horizon, a huge ball of red, dark as a fresh wound, slashed by black lines of retreating clouds. I-25 was a horizon-to-horizon smear of abandoned cars. In the nearby housing developments, some fires burned, and some swaths of burned buildings were still smoldering. The big refinery in Commerce City was pouring out black smoke, as were the tall buildings downtown and in the Tech Center. And it was *quiet*, quiet like when you're backpacking.

"Let's go," Mattie said. "Let's get away before more people are out."

MONDAY, 8 JUNE 2015, ABOUT 10:20 A.M.
RAFTER XOX RANCH, WESTERN NEBRASKA

Marjorie comes up the ladder with her minister's robe bunched around her waist, tucked into her belt. The bread-and-wine kids scramble up after her. I step to the side with James, to make room for the emergency funeral party in the center space.

Glory is at my side; she knows there will be a message. But *what* message?

I can tell Glory to take one of three words to the fighters getting ready below:

Straight, meaning as Marjorie finishes the funeral service, James will shoot Mattie. Then our fighters will swarm out and slaughter the assholes.

Bent, meaning on that last Amen, James will shoot the leader of the assholes, the snipers will try for everyone close to Mattie, and the rescue party will try to reach Mattie before the surviving assholes can kill him.

Broken, which means that on some cue that Marjorie won't know, we go all out to take them by surprise before any of them can kill Mattie.

Mattie was the one who explained the three plans to me, back when he came up with them:

"We're a ranch. We don't have fences and fortifications everywhere and some of our hands have to work out on the range, miles from home, completely out of touch with base, for months at a time. And we have to raise cattle and drive cattle to stay in business. We *can't* spend all our time rescuing our people, or avenging them. So to keep our people safe, at a price we can afford to pay, the crazy evil men out there on the range have to know in their bones that harming one little girl carrying water up from a creek to the chuck wagon is tantamount to dancing on a greased branch with a noose around your neck. The reason to pick any of the alternatives is supposed to be, always, to make sure no one ever, ever, ever gets anything out of taking a hostage from Rafter XOX.

"So," Mattie said, "no matter what, and this applies to us too, Claire, these are the rules. If a rescue looks likely to fail, if there's any chance they could get away still holding the hostage, even if it looks like they can kill the hostage before we get there, we play Straight. We never, ever let them have any power or success; better to kill our own people than let them do it. So we play Bent only if we're damned close to certain that they can't take the hostage back. Broken is when the odds are bad but we're being stupid and trying anyway. I'd rather we never used it."

Since we built the Rafter XOX compound, Mattie and I have stood on this gate through nine hostage situations. We have never yet played Broken. We've played Bent three times, Straight six. We rescued the hostages in every Bent, though one died of wounds later.

I know Mattie would call this situation the "classic case" for Straight. The rescue party will have to cut him out of that travois and there's a good chance he's injured badly enough that they'll kill him trying to move him, and there are three armed enemies a step away. He might even have been killed already, if he had a broken neck or internal bleeding, when the travois turned over. He may be my husband and the other owner of the Rafter XOX, but no one is indispensible.

So I turn to Glory to tell her we're playing Straight, steel myself, and lean down to her ear. "Tell them Broken. On the Cup."

I only realize what I've said when I see her cover her mouth to hide her grin, and she has plunged down the ladder before I collect myself enough to call her back.

Well, the die is cast. I mutter, "Broken on the Cup" to James.

The asshole below is prating on about how he wants a third of our cattle now and a quarter of every drive through "his" territory forever.

"We'll talk after the funeral," I say, loudly. He looks up, blinking; he has only been performing for his followers. I feel a flash of sympathy, knowing how that is.

WEDNESDAY, MARCH 18, 1998, 1:15 P.M.
NORTH OF LAFAYETTE, COLORADO

We were eating the last of the chips and cookies from my pack and coat on the porch on the southwest side of a boarded-up farmhouse. The chinook was holding but the sky was clear deep blue, the distant mountains were sharp as a laser print, and the wind was freshening. The blizzard would be here before sunset.

Mattie was going on about how all those boarded-up farmhouses were the result of corporate agriculture. Years later, on cattle drives along the Deseret Trail, he would go on about how once farms got small again, those very old houses came back into use.

The one pleasant constant was that Mattie would go on; it was the most comforting, dependable sound I knew.

"We've made just over sixteen miles," Orry said. "And it's way past noon. We can't get there in daylight; we should find somewhere to hole up pretty soon."

"Okay by me," I said. "You skinny little boys can keep going forever but hauling my fat ass all this way is *work*. And we need to make sure that hole is warm—there's a blizzard coming."

Mattie asked, "How do you know that?"

"Years of cross-country skiing," I said, "which is skiing for people so stupid they try to ski uphill."

Orry laughed. "That's exactly what my mom always told Dad when he'd make us practice because—because—" And just like that he folded up into tears and sobs. "Daddy."

Mattie looked at me like I would know what to do, then fell into tears himself, reaching out to hang on to Orry.

Dad had explained, during Mom's many breakdowns, that people who have those feelings need some time before they can be of any use.

So I just took Orry's map from his limp fingers, turned it around to put the mountains on my left, US 287 on my right, and eventually found the stretch between Ruth Roberts Park and Mineral Road. I put my finger against the scale, then kind of crooked it around on the map and figured things out. By then the guys had gone quiet, just sitting and holding each other. I asked, "Is there anything in Niwot?"

"Where?" Orry asked. It came out real shaky.

"Niwot. We lost all that time swinging wide around Lafayette to avoid the fighting, and the fighting seemed to be about looting, and looting happens around stores. Are there stores in Niwot?"

"Not many," Orry said. "It's mostly office buildings and some houses."

"Then there's at least a fair chance we can find a place to hole up there, and we can go through, not around. We should keep moving while it's light." I stood up and put on my pack, and so did they. The blue-black clouds of the oncoming blizzard were pouring upward from the mountains in front of us.

WEDNESDAY, MARCH 18, 1998, 4:45 P.M.
NIWOT, COLORADO

The last three miles west along Mineral Road, a freeze-ass-cold wind blew into our faces and right through my big bulky coat. Grit and dirt sanded our faces. Orry forged ahead like he was trying to finish a marathon. Behind him, I plodded along with one hand between Mattie's shoulder blades to keep him moving.

I don't know what the others were thinking; in Mattie's case probably nothing, or he'd have been fact-spouting. I thought about Mom and the way she'd always wanted me to say I had feelings that I didn't. She'd probably just lain in the bed crying till someone killed her, or set the house on fire, and Dad had probably died trying to protect her.

I tried to feel bad that she wouldn't bother me for a hug again, or tell me what to feel. I wondered—

"That's Diagonal Highway," Orry said, "that traffic light up ahead."

"Hope we don't have to wait too long at it." Yeah, it was a stupid joke; sometimes that's just what you do.

Orry explained, "It's the southeast corner of Niwot. I'm hoping we can beg our way into somewhere with heat. Lots of woodstoves up here."

Close to the intersection, we walked past cars sprawled across the road in a jumble; a few were smashed or down in the ditch, but mostly they had just stopped at strange angles.

Mattie coughed and gasped, "All their engines must've gone out right at the same moment, and power brakes and power steering too. It's a lot tidier on Diagonal than on Mineral because Mineral Road had the light at the time."

I was just glad he could notice anything besides how cold and sore he was. I wrapped an arm around Mattie, dragging him along with me, and Orry took Mattie's other side.

At Diagonal Highway itself, a sign pointed to the right with a hand-lettered message:

Refugee Shelter in IBM Building→

Orry said, "Let's see if they'll feed us. At least it'll be out of the wind."

When we were about three yards from the main door, a gray-haired lady in a pebbly-gray skirt-suit pushed the door open. "Come on in. I'm Jennifer Shaw. Let's get you in here so I can close this door and open the inner one. We don't have heat so we're trying to keep everyone's body heat in."

A big man, heavyset with a thick beard and bald head, pushed the door shut behind us. "Sorry about this but we've had a couple people who tried to get violent, so I gotta pat you down while Ms. Shaw talks to you for a minute. I'm Harry Uhlman."

"Okay, but I'll need my knife when we leave," Orry said.

"No prob. But we need to keep it at the front desk. Already had one stabbing, don't need more." He was respectful and polite about frisking the guys; Ms. Shaw frisked me.

"You'll have to forgive Dr. Uhlman for not patting you down properly," she said. "He's normally a chemist, not a cop," she said.

"If there's even such a thing as chemistry anymore. I spent all afternoon trying to get gunpowder to do something besides fizz, and gasoline to burn fast enough to power anything."

Mattie, reviving now that we were out of that freezing wind, told about his homemade battery experiment, and glowed when Uhlman said, "Excellent thinking!" and scribbled a note about it.

They asked us about where we'd come from, and what we'd seen. That started Orry and Mattie crying again. Shaw and Uhlman looked at me really weird when I said, "My mother has mental problems, my dad wouldn't leave her . . . I just, you know, I couldn't stay, not with what was happening down there."

I was careful to say it kind of flat and dead, so that they assumed I was just in shock.

"Well," Shaw said, "we've already kept you standing here too long. Let's feed you and bed you down for the night. At least it's out of the weather—sorry it's not more." As we followed her through the second set of doors, into the main lobby, she said, "Mr. Andrews, your turn," and a guy in a suit went out to join Uhlman.

We followed her through the lobby and down the hall in the dim, failing light from the skylights.

Everywhere people leaned against walls, sat or lay on the floor, some chatting, most just staring.

"Most of these people were stranded in the big traffic jam last night, but all day we've had people walking in from Longmont and Boulder, even one family from Lyons," Shaw said. "You've got the record for longest walk to get here, though, I think."

In a glass-roofed atrium, they had set up tables with plastic baskets like cheap restaurants used to serve sandwiches in. The basket she handed me contained an orange, a bag of SunChips, a bag of pretzels, three slices of bread, two slices of Velveeta, a Slim Jim, and a can of Sprite. "One basket to a person, take the one we give you. You can trade among yourselves if you want. We were all here last night setting up for a big conference that, obviously, didn't happen, plus the King Soopers up the road donated a lot. Please do plan to move on soon; with as many people as we have, we won't have enough to last beyond noon tomorrow, and we have no idea where to get more."

We gobbled our food baskets. Then Shaw guided us, by candlelight, to a small windowless conference room, where the tables and chairs had been cleared out. Two families already sprawled asleep on the floor along the back wall, and didn't even stir when we came in.

We took the remaining corner that wasn't at the door, with our packs for pillows and our coats for bedding under the sleeping bags. With so many people in a small sealed room, it wasn't terribly cold.

"Good night," Shaw said, and took the candle with her.

I was almost asleep when Mattie breathed, "Claire?" in my ear.

"Yeah?"

"Did you hear what my dad said, just before they hit him? I thought he was looking right at me and I didn't, I couldn't, I want to know—"

I lied, slightly. "I thought he said, 'I love you.'"

"I thought so too. But I can't get it out of my mind that maybe it was the Hindi for 'Run away!'"

"Which he would have said because he loved you," I said, taking a wild guess at what Mattie wanted to hear.

"Yeah." His arms went around me and he buried his face in my shoulder. Oh, well, if he really needed the comfort, he could sleep holding me for another night, anyway.

MONDAY, 8 JUNE 2015, ABOUT 11 A.M.
RAFTER XOX RANCH, WESTERN NEBRASKA

Marjorie makes the funeral very impressive. Of course, she might really be commending Mattie's soul to her god. As she raises the chalice aloft, two dozen crossbows *slap-buzz!* in unison. Asshole Leader falls dead, and so does the hatchet man, nearest Mattie.

Machete Guy is only hit in the calf, and falls forward, closer to Mattie. He heaves himself forward with his hands as James stomps on the pedal of his crossbow, and has a head and a hand under the travois before James' next bolt strikes him square between the shoulder blades.

Soon enough?

When the sortie party reaches the travois, seconds later, they slash it loose from the harness and lift it up. Horsemen ride past them, lances held high, pursuing the three assholes still on their feet; a moment later, the fleeing enemy are all staked to the plains.

Mattie stands up, supported between two of Squad Four, waving madly with his left hand; his right arm hangs funny.

I have not heard so much cheering in many years, maybe ever.

All of a sudden, I can't breathe and my face is all wet, and I barely squeak out to James that I'd like everyone to just carry on their duties. I almost fall going down the ladder.

As I walk, wanting to run, to my quarters, Glory circles me like I'm a herd she's outriding, and everyone trying to approach me is a wolf.

Safe in our rooms at last, I just wash my face in the basin and sit down to breathe. Things will be taken care of, and Mattie will have to see the medics before he can come to me.

Now that we know that Broken can work, he'll be so interested.

I curl up, hugging myself, sobbing and more afraid than I've ever been.

THURSDAY, MARCH 19, 1998, 6:45 A.M.
NIWOT, COLORADO

We all sat up instantly. Outside our room, somewhere else in the building, glass broke with a crash, and a woman's shout of "What are you—" ended in a shriek and moan.

Orry said, "Pull on your boots. Don't wait for a light."

I did, and I could feel Mattie doing it too. "Now coats on," Orry ordered. "Make sure you have hats and gloves. Then feel around, stuff anything else into your pack, and shoulder up. There's no time to roll sleeping bags, we'll have to leave them."

I'd taken nothing out but I felt around in case there was anything of theirs, finding one of Mattie's gloves and handing it to him.

Nearby, in the dark, a man asked, "What's happening?"

"If I'm guessing right, the building is being overrun by a mob," Orry said. "They're already inside. We're going to hope they were not organized enough to surround the building, and try to run out on the side away from them. If that doesn't work, we'll try something else. Come with us."

"Maybe we should stay and help—" the voice quavered.

"Suit yourself." Orry grabbed my hand. "Claire, take Mattie's hand. We're all going to stand up. Can you guys see the light under the door?"

"Yeah," I said.

Mattie moved beside me. "Now I can."

"All right, any of you that aren't coming with us, pull your legs and stuff in so we don't trip. Is the pathway clear?"

"Yeah," "Unh-hunh," and "Yes," came at us from the dark.

"Here we go." Orry dragged us to the door in about three big steps and threw it open.

He lunged into the sudden light, crossing the hall and putting his back to the wall. That dragged me halfway out the door. I half fell across the hallway and backed up against the wall next to Orry.

That pulled Mattie through. He looked kind of strange; it took me a moment to realize he had his socks in his mouth. Probably hadn't wanted to take the time to put them on, but didn't want to lose them either.

Right then I was too scared to laugh or even smile at this skinny boy, glasses slightly askew, in two sweaters and a heavy coat with bare ankles sticking out of snow-sneakers, and these two brown-and-red argyles hanging down from his mouth like he was a dog playing fetch. But I've smiled every time I've thought about it since. I took his socks and rammed them into one of my now empty pockets. "For safe keeping," I said.

The conference room door opened and a young couple came creeping out, holding hands.

Tossing his head, Orry indicated we should go down the hall, away from the reception area where we'd come in. The couple came with us.

At the end of the corridor, there was a glass door, marked EMERGENCY EXIT ONLY and DOOR IS ALARMED.

Alarmed? In that door's position I'd be terrified. It didn't seem like a time to share that joke.

Snow was piled against the glass at least two feet deep. It took all five of us shouldering against it to break the door from its hinges and knock it down across the drift.

Orry and the man heaved it out of the way, and we were out into the snow, running west across the old parking lot, the thick snow sliding under our soles and grabbing at our pant legs. Behind us, the yelling was louder. When I looked back, a handful of people were fighting in the parking lot. The couple was headed north, toward the smoke plumes of the town.

"I feel kind of bad about running out on everyone else," Mattie said.

I never felt bad about things like that, so I distracted him. "Let's get around to the back side of that building over there, so I can give you your socks, and maybe there's someplace dry to put them on."

There was a dry, though cold, concrete bench in a northeast lee corner of the cross-shaped office building. Mattie sat down with a sigh of relief and pulled his shoes off, and I handed him his socks. While he put them on, Orry crept back and peeked around the edge. He said it looked like the mob was mostly still inside the IBM building, and the few people running out were heading north to Niwot.

"Okay, I'm ensocked and be-shoed," Mattie said. "How far do we have to go?"

"Eleven miles from here," Orry said.

"What if we get lost in this blizzard?" Mattie asked.

"Around here," I explained, "blizzards blow in from the northwest. So if we keep the wind and snow in our faces, till we hit Colorado 7, we'll be good enough."

"How do you know all that?"

"She read it in *Journal of Blizzardology,* the special Niwot edition," Orry said.

"Don't be mean, Orry. I know it from cross-country skiing up here. We had to know how to not get lost. In fact, I kind of wish we had skis."

"There's a full set of different sizes at the shelter," Orry said. "Not that it does us any good here. What I'm really wishing for is a good knife. Uhlman took mine for safekeeping and I don't think he'll be giving it back."

THURSDAY, MARCH 19, 1998, 12:00 P.M.
NEAR LEFT HAND VALLEY RESERVOIR, COLORADO

Around noon, we saw a house by itself with a big flapping note on the door:

> *Honey, electricity/phone don't work, going to ride Shadowfax into town for milk &*
> *coleman. Will keep trying to get you on phone. Call(when phone comes back)no*
> *matter how late.*

The barn in back was closed, with a dead frozen Labrador lying where he'd tried to push his way through the locked door.

"Figure they're not coming back?" Orry asked.

"If they do, we'll apologize our asses off," I said.

With a short split log from the woodpile, I broke the porch window, and climbed into the living room. A little yappy dust mop of a dog came running out. I yelled, waved my arms, chased the little bastard into a bedroom, and shut the door. He went all crazy in there, howling and yipping and jumping at the door.

Orry and Mattie laid a fire in the woodstove. I took a mattress off a bed in the spare room and used firewood and the couch to brace it up against the broken window. Orry's search of the cupboards turned up a bong and an empty lighter; we splashed rubbing alcohol on an electric bill, sprayed the sparks from the lighter onto it, and used that to light the fire.

The bag of meat scraps labeled ELK4STEW and the big bag of frozen mixed vegetables in the freezer were still cold, so I started them thawing in a big stockpot on the quickly warming woodstove. I brought in shovelfuls of snow from the porch and added them to the pot till eventually we had enough water to cover all the food. The room was getting pleasantly warm by the time the pot began to boil, and we took turns napping and watching.

When I woke from my turn napping, the blizzard was dying down, the boys had taken off their coats, and the food smelled overwhelmingly good. We found bowls and silverware, served out the improvised soup, and ate as much as we could.

The house seemed too dangerous and exposed to stay in, and Orry thought we had enough daylight left to reach the shelter. So we set all the pots we could fill with snow on the woodstove to thaw, and refilled our bottles; treated ourselves to sharing a real live toilet that still had one flush left in its tank; and armed ourselves with kitchen knives and shop knives. When we left, Mattie put the soup pot down on the floor, and opened the back bedroom door. The little yapper fled under the bed, but Mattie said, "He'll come out when we're gone, and at least the house will be warm and there's something for him to eat for a while, and if the weather turns nicer he can get out. Better than what happened to the poor guy outside."

We left the fire burning when we left, and for at least an hour afterward we could see the smoke streaking black against the deep blue sky, through the cold, still air.

THURSDAY, MARCH 19, 1998, 5:15 P.M.
ABOUT FOUR MILES SOUTH OF LYONS, COLORADO

The dead woman was still wearing a good pair of jeans, but she'd been stripped to the waist; she still had one boot on, and the other had been flung down the hill.

"Must not have fit," Orry said. I laughed because that was funny, and he stared at me like I was weird.

I knelt to look. Blood matted the hair on the back of her head, and her skull felt squashy and cracked where I pushed with my finger. Up ahead, Mattie said, "Aw! Aw shit!"

He'd found a dead little boy, who couldn't have been more than four. His neck was at a funny angle; someone had broken it. He was in socks and underwear.

"That's the one whose clothes fit," I said. "Somebody wanted that kid's clothes for their own kid, so first they killed his mom, and then they chased him down—"

Mattie blubbered and hung on to my arm for the next couple of miles. Once all the footprints turned off toward Hygiene, I felt a lot safer, but Mattie was silent and moody for another hour.

MONDAY, 8 JUNE 2015, ABOUT NOON
RAFTER XOX RANCH, WESTERN NEBRASKA

"Ma'am, did you want lunch?"

"Thank you, Glory, if they send over some bean soup and a barbecue sandwich, that'll be fine."

"Right away!" She's gone before I can say "thank you" and "no hurry."

The crowd noise outside tells me that everyone is going by the infirmary to reassure themselves that Mister Matt is just fine, because for the Rafter XOX community that's somewhere between knowing that God is in his heaven and that the sun will come up in the morning. Not that I blame them.

I don't know what I'm going to say.

Mattie's such a reasonable person that the fact that it all worked out will be fine with him, and when I admit that I don't know, really, why I said Broken when I meant Straight, he'll probably just shrug and say he's glad to be here. He has never, never, never second-guessed me.

It's just . . . I feel so afraid, now that it's over. And I'm afraid to tell anyone, even him, especially him, what I'm afraid of.

Ages ago, Mattie looked up reactive attachment disorder and spectrum disorders and all the other weird-kid things in the old books, and figured out how in the new, post-Change world, they might be more advantages than drawbacks. He was the one who picked my brains about how to make people like myself comfortable enough to stay with us and give us their hearts and loyalty, and along the way taught me how valuable I was.

Of course there are some regular people at the Rafter XOX too, refugees who just wandered in and found it congenial, but basically we've got a population that could have filled a special-needs school or even an outpatient mental health clinic before the Change, and it was Mattie who understood how, nowadays, that made us stronger and better.

Mattie makes all our weird, not-good-with-people, but talented and capable, people feel valuable and needed, and they stay, and they're loyal as dogs or angels. Me, I couldn't win anyone's loyalty in a million years. After all, reactive attachment disorder means you don't ever really like people, or hardly any people, or care about them really. They can tell, and they hold that against you. At best, you're a useful jerk.

I run Rafter XOX and fight for it and protect it. I'm its decision-maker and its strong arm, but Mattie, he's the memory, and most of all the heart. If I had given the order to kill him, or if the rescue had failed, everyone here could have been left with mean, cold, practical old Miz Claire, who never knew when a touch on the shoulder or an extra plate of chili might save a soul.

Miz Claire who never cared about anyone except herself, and who is sitting here so scared I want to crap my pants, realizing that I came within inches and seconds of finally being able to taste love and trust, and then having it go away.

Through our early years in the refugee camps, and then scrounging work as cowboys, and grubstaking the Rafter XOX and building it up, it was Mattie who taught me to see the way I was as a gift. My RAD meant I could lose people and just say, well, they're not here anymore, they're not useful anymore, that's that. I could keep going, without hesitation, calmly and precisely, taking care of our people, no matter what the loss.

And today I almost lost *him*.

Today I found out I no longer have my gift. Not where he's concerned.

THURSDAY, MARCH 19, 1998, 6:20 P.M.
JUST SOUTH OF LYONS, COLORADO

Daylight was fading and the sun was already down when we turned in at Twilight Drive, a cluster of houses around a short stretch of road just off 7. Orry led us to the north end of the road and undid the combination lock on one backyard gate. "Is there a dog?" Mattie asked nervously.

"Little Yorkie, probably inside if anyone's home," Orry said. He pulled the gate open. "Fuck."

"What's the matter?"

"Tracks—all those tracks from the house to the back gate. That's the way up to the shelter. Nothing else up there."

"Well, so—"

"So Dad offered to let them share if they'd let him use their property for free. But they didn't want that. Dad paid them three hundred a month to have the shelter on their property, and they took all that money, because they said they'd never need the shelter and—"

"Maybe they'll give you a refund," Mattie said.

Orry nearly exploded before I said, "Mattie."

"Guess that was stupid," he admitted. "Sorry, Orry."

"We're all tired," Orry said. "Okay, so there'll be Dave Buchanan and his wife, Angie. Her brother Kevin usually lives at their house too, and they have two real little kids. So at worst I guess it's three against three."

That last trudge up the snow-covered hillside was hard work. Near the top, we crouched and crawled up to the ridgeline, and looked over.

"Fuck," Orry said. A bright campfire was burning in front of what looked like an open bank vault door in the hillside. From the open doorway, brilliant light poured into the gathering darkness. "They tore off most of the camouflage, broke the door open, they built a fire outside;

shit, shit, shit, who knows how many other people have seen that by now? I can understand stealing it but they ruined—"

A man came out. "Dave Buchanan," Orry said. Buchanan set up lawn chairs around the fire. "What the fuck, are they going to hold a fucking sing-along?"

A woman and two little kids in snowsuits came out to hold long sticks over the fire.

"Oh, Jesus God, they're holding a weenie roast," Orry groaned. "Okay, now—"

"What are you kids doing?" a voice said behind us.

I rolled over. There was a man there with a shotgun.

"Kevin, you're wearing one of the spare coats from the shelter," Orry said to him. "That belongs to me. The whole shelter belongs to me. You assholes need to get your shitty asshole looter selves out of my shelter."

"Oh, shut up, boy—"

I stood up. Kevin swung the gun to point it at me, and I walked straight toward him. "You're a pussy," I told him, "and you don't have the guts to pull the trigger, so put the gun down and—"

"I'll shoot. You put your hands up."

I walked toward him. "Pussy, pussy, pussy. Pussy won't use his gun. Pussy's too much of a pussy."

He raised the shotgun to his shoulder and I was looking down the barrels.

"The safety is still on, dumbshit," I said.

He looked down. With both hands, I grabbed and yanked the barrel toward me, then wrenched it around like a big steering wheel. He let go with a cry of pain—his finger had been trapped in the guard. I swung the gun out and back to bring the butt into his crotch.

He gasped and bent over. I brought the gun back around, then over my head, then swung it down like John Fucking Henry being a Steel Drivin' Man on Dad's old CDs. The stock smashed into the back of his head hard enough to face-plant him. Then I just pounded up and down like a crazy bitch churning butter with a shotgun, whamming the stock on his head till he stopped moving. I kicked his shoulder to turn him on his back; blood had gushed from his nose and mouth.

I knelt and pulled out the big chef's knife from my coat pocket, felt for a pulse in the man's neck, and didn't find one. "Where are the carotids?" I asked Mattie.

"Uh, they run straight down from the ear, there's one on each side and um—"

Mattie gabbled about blood veins till Orry said, "Shut up. They might hear you down there."

Since I'd already heard what I needed, I ignored them. I grabbed Kevin's bloody chin by his stupid neck beard, swung his head to one side, and cut as deep as I could along his jaw and into his neck; I felt bone scrape. Then I flipped his head the other way and did it again.

Blood just oozed out, though there was a lot of it.

"No spurting," Mattie said. "So he's dead."

"That was the idea," I said. "Did the happy-happy family down there hear us?"

They were still all gathered around the fire; it sounded like one of the kids was crying and Angie was trying to soothe it.

"I guess he didn't realize guns don't work anymore," Orry said.

"He should have tried one out," Mattie said. "If it *had* been working, at least he'd have known whether the safety was on."

Orry giggled. "That shotgun doesn't have one. Did you know that, Claire?"

"Nope, but I guessed *he* wouldn't know."

"If I could guess what people know," Mattie said, "the world would make more sense."

"No shit," Orry said. "Let's follow Kevin's tracks in the snow toward the shelter. If we go that way maybe we'll meet them coming the other way, and we can ambush them."

Kevin's tracks led us down around the ridge to a big backpack. Orry opened it and said, "Yeah, canned goods and frozen food. Couple jugs of milk. We should remember to pick this stuff up after we settle with Buchanan; we don't need it right now."

"What was he doing with it?" Mattie asked.

Orry shrugged. "Probably he was coming back from looting the neighbors, saw us on the ridge, and just walked right up. We're not exactly woods scouts, are we?"

The weird thing was, those were his last words, ever. Like one minute later, as we followed the tracks toward the shelter, Buchanan stepped out of the shadow of a pine tree and jabbed a bat under Orry's chin, full force, then brought it up and back down savagely across Orry's forehead.

I pulled the linoleum knife from my pocket and lunged forward, raking Buchanan's face from cheek to cheek across the eyes. Buchanan dropped the bat and screamed.

I jabbed forward with the steak knife in my other hand, but it just bent on his leather coat. Meanwhile I backhanded with the linoleum knife across the hands covering his face, slashing through flesh and tendons. By then Mattie was behind him, swinging with a hard sidearm to jam a wood-drill bit deep into the man's back.

Buchanan fell to his hands and knees. I stepped over him, jerked his head back by his mullet, and cut my second throat of the day. This one spurted, so I guess his heart was still going, but not for long.

We turned Orry over; he was breathing but unconscious. "We need to get him into the shelter," Mattie said.

"Turn him on his side so he won't choke," I said. "We need to get those assholes out of our way."

At the fire, the wife was huddled with the two kids, trying to quiet them with, "Daddy will be right back."

"Your husband and your brother are both dead," I said. "This is our shelter now. Get out. Run and keep running."

She screamed.

I remembered Orry lying back there in the snow, and how bad we needed to get him in, and the mess these redneck dipshits had made of the shelter, and just snapped. I grabbed the end of a stick in the fire and threw it at the bitch's head. She jumped back, still shrieking.

Mattie threw another one that hit her on the chest, maybe singed her coat, and she burned her hands keeping it from landing on the kids. She grabbed her little brats by the hands and started running up the hill, slipping and stumbling on the snowy slope. Mattie and I threw some more burning sticks after her. I yelled, "Don't come back, bitch!"

"Should we tell her she's heading straight for her dead brother?" Mattie asked.

"Does it matter?" I shrugged. "Think she's gone for good?"

"Probably. But let's make sure we stay alert while we carry Orry in."

A minute or two later, as we were scooping Orry up, with me taking the shoulders, we heard a screaming wail. "See, she found out about her brother anyway," I told Mattie.

We both laughed too long and too hard. It sounded all sick and weird. Maybe she heard us. By the time we stopped, she'd quit wailing.

We carried Orry inside into the brightly lighted bedroom, undressed him, and put him under the covers. "Never would have thought I was going to see his dick or care so little when I did."

Mattie snorted. He felt Orry's head very gently. "No soft spots on his skull. Big bump high on the back." We peeled back his eyelids and held the kerosene lantern close. His pupils were different sizes, and there was some blood on the whites. "All I remember about that is that it's bad," Mattie said, "but we'll have to look that up in the survival library that Orry said they have here."

The shelter was like Bilbo Baggins' summerhouse: three bedrooms, kitchen, toilet, common living area, workroom. A whole wall of useful books contained a bunch of medical and first aid manuals. We confirmed that Orry probably had a bad concussion, from which he could recover, but might have worse brain damage and could die from it any time. All we could do was to keep him warm and clean and gently put water into his mouth till he woke up. "Speaking of warm," I said, "why is it so freaking cold in here? And I could really use some food."

"I have an idea," Mattie said. "Smell all that smoke? Bet you for sure they didn't know to open the damper on the woodstove." He turned the damper. "Yep. Orry said the smoke goes up to some kind of condenser system that prevents a big plume going up into the air, so it's safe to have a fire here. And you can see they laid this one and couldn't get it going. Thank God they didn't think of taking kerosene from that lantern."

"Yeah. Hey, does it have to be so bright?"

He twisted the little valve at the base. "Nope. All right, well, the damper's open, I'll re-lay this fire—it's way more than we need—and see about some cleanup." The kitchen was a mess; apparently the family had just been breaking into things and dumping them on the floor. "We should probably put that fire out, outside, and see if the door can be blocked, will you please?"

Outside, I kicked the fire apart and dumped dirt and snow on it with a shovel. The thin crescent moon showed tracks on the snowfield, plainly and clearly. If this didn't melt tomorrow, good luck staying hidden. For sure there'd be more crowds on the roads soon. But for tonight, the dark and cold would probably shelter us.

When I went back inside, Mattie had the fire going. I dragged the door closed on its remaining hinge, then lashed it by its handle to a board I propped diagonally across the frame, and stuffed some spare towels into the remaining crack. I hung a string of bear bells on that diagonal brace; if anyone tried to break in, we'd know.

That night Mattie and me shared the double bed that was probably built when Orry's mother was still living with his dad.

Mattie curled up against me with his face in my neck. I could feel his tears running down.

"You okay?"

"Just thinking about how scared I am not to have Mom and Dad anymore. And about how hard I cried for that poor murdered little boy on the road, and taking care of the dog . . . and then I thought, I just chased a mother and her kids out in the snow to die. After I killed her husband."

"We don't *know* that they're gonna die."

"*Claire.*"

"Okay, *you* don't know. And I don't *care.*"

He cried harder, and hung on to me. It was easier to put an arm around him than anything else.

What the hell, he was warm.

FRIDAY, MARCH 19–SUNDAY, MARCH 22, 1998
JUST SOUTH OF LYONS, COLORADO

The snow melted early the next morning as another chinook came in. We moved Buchanan and Kevin into a dry creek nearby. Mattie said that bears or coyotes or dogs gone feral would mess them up enough so that no one would be able to tell we'd killed them, and anyway probably no one cared.

We rested, ate, and made sure that condenser chimney was really working.

Two days later, we got up to find another blizzard blowing, and Orry, who had never awakened even when we'd dripped water into his mouth, was dead.

We gave it some time in case it was just a coma, but after we'd had breakfast and cleaned up, he was cold and stiff.

"I was thinking," Mattie said. "We've been seeing billows of black smoke south toward Boulder, north toward Lyons, and southeast toward Denver, right? And the cities will run out of food soon, but right now everyone's locked down by the snow, right?"

"Right."

"Well, before whatever it was hit us, where would you have thought to go if you had to get out of Denver or Boulder to survive?"

"Into the hills," I said. "Not just the survivalists, everyone thinks that way. I get what you're saying. They'll come this way."

"Yeah, and now we don't have Orry to take care of. All these supplies are great but we could get killed trying to keep them, and anyway they won't last forever. So, if everyone else is going to head for the hills, let's not sit here and wait for them to dig us out and take this place away."

"And instead we should—"

"Go where they grow the food—east onto the plains."

I nodded; he was making sense.

He asked, "How long would it take me to learn to use cross-country skis?"

"If we spend the rest of today packing, and eat a big breakfast tomorrow before we go, you could be sort of decent by tomorrow night at dinnertime," I said, "and we could be a long way away. Maybe where people are still opening the door to refugees. The snow won't last this time of year but we can at least get out of the way of trouble, and maybe better than that." I spread out the map and we looked at it. "If we head due east, eventually we'll pick up 76 and we can follow it into Nebraska; that goes up into farm country and there's no big towns on it for a long way."

"I guess we just leave Orry here, eh?"

I could hear the tears in Mattie's voice, and I knew what answer he was looking for, so we wasted time putting our friend in as much of a grave as we could dig and piling stones on top of it.

That night in the bed, Mattie started crying. For a moment I thought of moving to another bed. But then I thought about trying to do all this alone, and how much smarter he was and how much more stuff he knew.

So I wrapped my arms around him. Considering how valuable he was, if I had to hug him now and then, I could get used to it.

Next morning, we slept late, ate huge, and skied away. Mattie caught on faster than I'd promised, and we spent the day laughing and zooming along the snowy roadsides, almost unaware of the burned-out cars and frozen bodies. It was the first good day since the Change, the first of many.

MONDAY, 8 JUNE 2015, 1 P.M.–11 P.M.
RAFTER XOX RANCH

After a while, I dry my eyes, and tell myself to cowgirl up. I go out to walk around with Mattie while he visits everyone and shows off his splinted right arm and stitches and makes them all laugh that Mister Matt is too tough to die, and Miz Claire is too mean to let him.

Mattie insists on holding kind of a party from dinner till bedtime, and we have to put in an appearance at Marjorie's Service of Delivery and Thanksgiving. So it's a little late before we finally get into bed next to each other, and he snuggles up to me in a weird, gingerly awkward fashion because he's in more pain than he has been letting anyone see.

"I didn't mean to say Broken," I confess, as soon as we've blown the candles out. "It just popped out. For no reason."

"*No* reason?"

I admit, "Well, not for *no* reason. I, uh, I'm used to you. I'm really used to you."

His lips brush my cheek, and he awkwardly strokes my hair with his left hand. "Thanks, honey. I'm used to you too."

TOPANGA AND THE CHATSWORTH LANCERS

~~~

BY HARRY TURTLEDOVE

HARRY TURTLEDOVE

Harry Turtledove is an escaped Byzantine historian. He found that telling lies for a living was more fun than putting in the footnotes. His books include *The Guns of the South, In the Presence of Mine Enemies, Ruled Britannia,* and *Every Inch a King.* He has lived in the west end of the San Fernando Valley for the past thirty years, and quite enjoyed imagining it ruined for the purposes of this story.

J ared Tillman sat in his front room, carefully winding up the phonograph. You had to feel how tight the spring was. It wasn't the original, but it wasn't new, either. One of these days, it would break. He
just didn't want that day to be today. He felt like listening to music, not
messing around inside the mechanism to install the most nearly matching
spring he could pull out of his junk drawer.

As things went, the phonograph was modern. It probably dated from
the early 1950s, made to be taken to picnics and parties where there was
no power. That meant it could play 33⅓ RPM records, instead of speeding them up to a shrill gabble the way an older player with settings only
for 45s and 78s would have.

Where there was no power . . . Jared's mouth twisted. No power anywhere now, not these past thirty years. He scratched at his mustache and
plucked out a hair. It was white. He let it fall to the ever more threadbare
wall-to-wall carpeting. He'd been in his mid-twenties when the Change
came. He remembered how things had been, and how he'd grown up in
a different world.

Carefully, he set the needle on the record's outer grooves. The needle
wasn't sharp. The record wasn't new, which was putting things mildly.
The speaker was a cheap piece of junk. But Steely Dan—tinny, scratchy
Steely Dan, but Steely Dan even so—filled the room in the house off
Topanga Canyon Boulevard. Like the ruins that remained from before
the Great Southern California Dieoff, it reminded him things hadn't always been this way.

"Shit, I didn't even like Steely Dan back then," he muttered. But you
took what you could get. Bands he had liked, bands like Nirvana and
Green Day, put their music out on CDs. These days, CDs were good for
nothing but scaling through the air and for seeing rainbows.

Eucalyptus leaves dappled the sunlight that poured in through the west-facing windows. Eucalyptuses sent roots to the center of the earth to pull up what water they could. Along with olives and scrub oaks and pepper trees and a few hard pines, they were what could grow in arid Topanga Canyon.

He'd grown up in the canyon. He was a second-generation hippie; his folks had moved here to join a commune, and never left. They'd sold candles and pots from a little shop, and sometimes pot on the side. There'd never been a lot of money, but there'd always been some. Enough, or close enough. They'd always said that, if you didn't sweat it, close to enough was enough.

And maybe they were right, and maybe they were wrong, and certainly they were dead. Old Doc Leibowitz gave Jared's mother statins and blood-pressure meds as long as he had them. She had a coronary a couple of years after he ran out, and that was that. A Topangan scavenged more from a Valley house not long afterwards. Someone else got help for a while, but not Mom. Dad . . . Dad had smoked tobacco as well as weed. Lung cancer would have been a bad way to go even with twentieth-century medicine. Without it . . . He smoked lots of weed, and as much opium as he could get, and died in less pain than he would have without them. And Jared's wife had hemorrhaged when Connor was born, and the doc and the midwife couldn't stop it.

Muttering, Jared pulled a paperback off the shelf. *The Pocket Book of Ogden Nash* had been old even before the Change. Before too long, the cheap paper would crumble, but it hadn't yet. Paper made these days lasted longer, but there wasn't much of it. Ben Franklin would have understood post-Change printing just fine. Books sold across a continent for pocket change were as dead as everything else from the old days.

He found the poem he was looking for, not that he needed to: he'd long since memorized it. No great trick—"The Middle" was only four lines long. But seeing the words made him see the world the words came from. He remembered that world, ached for that world, with a terrible longing that would never go away and that would never do him any good.

Nine and a half million people lived in Los Angeles County when the Change came. They took water and food and electricity for granted—till all of a sudden the power and the internal-combustion engine disappeared. Most of the water came from hundreds of miles away, so it disappeared, too. The food arrived in trucks and ships with engines . . . till it didn't any more.

Some people tried to get to less crowded, wetter parts of the world on foot—or by bikes if they had bikes. Some hunkered down, trying to ride out what they hoped would be a temporary disaster.

Before the Change, Jared had read that the natural carrying capacity of the area was about a quarter of a million. About ninety-eight percent of the people had died either trying to escape or waiting for help that never came. His nose wrinkled as he remembered the stench that had filled the air for months.

Topanga was lucky, as places around here went when the Change hit. It was isolated and not too crowded. People were more used to doing for themselves than most Angelenos. Streams ran year-round, in good years anyhow. The canyon gave the Topangans an outlet on the sea, and another on the San Fernando Valley: a prime scrounging resource. And, being a canyon, it was defensible.

He read the poem again. It talked about remembering bygone days. The last two lines had the meat. *So many I loved were not yet dead,* Nash wrote. *So many I love were not yet born.* Yes, that was the truth, sure as hell. Any middle-aged person through all the history of mankind had been there. But, for his generation, the Change was The Middle. Reworking the poem, you could say *So much I loved was not yet dead.*

You could, but how much would it help? Steely Dan was singing about the Royal Scam. The song should have had a proper stereo system. Yeah, and I should have a Mac and a modem, Jared thought. People in hell were sure they should have mint juleps to drink.

They wouldn't get them. Jared wouldn't get his computer. No one under forty had any idea what the Internet was, or had been. The record would play as well as it played on this windup piece of junk. This was the way the world went on, not with a bang—explosives didn't work any more, either—but a whimper. *Tough shit, Eliot.*

Shoes scrunched on dead leaves and dry grass outside. Jared's mouth twisted again. Here was Connor, nineteen now and home from patrol. This brave new world was the only one he knew. He had all the answers— he was sure of it. At nineteen, who didn't? Fathers and sons had butted heads since the beginning of time. The Change, the chasm between Before and After, between who remembered and who didn't, only made things worse. And they said it couldn't be done . . .

Oh, for Christ's sake!

Connor Tillman shaped the words without saying them. His old man was listening to music again. That was always a bad sign. Whenever Dad started playing records, he fell as far back into what his generation called the Good Old Days as you could now.

Get over it, Pop. Connor didn't say that, either.

He'd yelled it often enough when he and his father brawled. It was an easy rock to grab and hit with. The world was what it was. You had to roll with it. The Good Old Days were over. Finished. Done with. Done for. Kaput.

Connor was tempted to believe things couldn't have been all that great. He was tempted, yeah, but he couldn't. Too much remained behind that nobody now could or would match: everything from dead cars to the crumbling paved roads they'd run on to the incredible warren of empty houses and shops and who knew what that filled the Valley.

Even Connor's pants were pre-Change Levi's, patched at the knees and butt with leather. His boots and sleeveless leather vest and his broad-brimmed straw hat all belonged to here-and-now. But the zipper and copper rivets on the pants spoke of other times. And no one now made binoculars like the ones on the strap around his neck.

He turned the doorknob. The lock had failed; a bar secured the door at night. The locksmith might have fixed it, but putting in the bar had been easier and cheaper. Dad did it himself. He could deal with the real world when he decided he wanted to.

"Hey," Connor said. Electric guitars sounded funny to him. No instrument that still worked was anything like them.

"Hey," Dad answered, nodding. His eyes were a million miles and a million years away. They always got like that when he started listening to records. With an obvious effort, he came back to the present. "How'd it go?"

Connor shrugged. "I climbed up to the high ground. Saw some rabbits and some quail and a coyote. Nothing got close enough for the blowgun." He had a green-painted aluminum tube on his back and a pouch of darts by the short sword on his belt. "Oh, and there were a couple of deer way off in the distance. Nothing much going on on Old Topanga Road."

"Surprise!" Dad said. "There never was." Old Topanga Road ran into Topanga Canyon Boulevard from the west right here, where Topanga village lay. Even back before the Change, Old Topanga Canyon had been sparsely settled compared to Topanga Canyon proper.

"I know, I know," Connor said impatiently. "Gotta keep an eye on it, though. It's our back door, like. The Lancers have come that way before. Don't want 'em doing it again."

"Nope." Dad nodded again. "The Chatsworth goddamn Lancers! Is that funny, or what?"

"Not funny when you've fought them." Connor had a puckered scar on his left arm from a skirmish with the Lancers a couple of years before. That had been his first fight, and came too close to being his last.

"I've done it." Dad had a scar, too, an old pale white one, in almost the same spot as Connor's. "But still . . . When I was your age—"

"Spare me," Connor said. He'd heard Dad's rap too often. Back before the Change, when everything was wonderful and it was all one country, Chatsworth had been far enough out in the boonies that a lot of people there kept horses. Because they did, now they ruled the west end of the Valley. Petty lords in places as far away as Pacoima and Studio City had a healthy respect for their fighters. So did the Topangans. Chatsworth dreamt of conquering the canyon and reaching the Pacific. For Topanga, that dream was a nightmare.

"Right," Dad said tightly.

"What's to eat?" Connor asked. "I'm starved."

"Still some of the dried, salted grunion left," Dad answered. "Olives. Cheese. Oranges. The porridge is cold, but it still smells okay."

"Cool," Connor said. The porridge was beans and peas from the garden in what Dad still called the backyard, with garlic and onions and wild mushrooms thrown in for flavor. Boil it into mush, and it was . . . food. Connor'd been eating the same kinds of things his whole life. He took them for granted.

Dad had been eating this stuff even longer—ever since the Change. He let out a sigh, the way he did every once in a while. "What I wouldn't give for a Double Whopper with cheese, onion rings on the side, and a big old chocolate shake," he said, and sighed.

"Yeah, Pop," Connor said patiently.

Chocolate was good, but he could count the times he'd tasted it on the fingers of one hand. Onion rings were fried. Who had oil to waste on such luxuries? Nobody in these parts, that was for sure. Olive oil and a little butter—that was about it. What didn't get eaten went into lamps . . . when there was any that didn't get eaten.

Connor fed his face. He was still a little hungry when he finished. Most people, at least in these parts, were a little hungry most of the time. His father stood just under six feet. His mom had been five-nine. He was barely that himself. Food had been something you took for granted when his folks were kids. There'd been times when the only meat in his stew came from the big green caterpillars that chewed up tomato vines. The scary thing was, they hadn't been too bad. Hunger made you not worry about such things.

The sun set not long after they finished. He and his father went to bed. No need for a blaze in the fireplace. It wouldn't get cold. It hardly ever got really cold, even in the winter. A blanket, maybe two on a bad night, and you were okay. You could easily starve or die of thirst. Millions of people around here had in the years before Connor was born. As far as he knew, though, not a single one of them froze.

Sherman's hooves clopped dully on the faded, potholed asphalt as Bruce Delgado rode south down Topanga Canyon Boulevard toward the Ventura Freeway. Just past the freeway lay Ventura Boulevard. A couple of miles south of the Boulevard—a Valley phrase that had connoted money back in the day—his Chatsworth Lancers no longer ran things. The hippie freaks from Topanga took over.

Bruce scowled behind his catcher's mask. His armor wouldn't have made the SCA cream its jeans. Covering the rest of his head wasn't some blacksmith's finest creation. He wore a German helmet his grandfather'd brought back from Europe after World War II. Good luck making manganese steel like that these days! He'd sanded off the swastika decals. They would've given too many people the wrong idea of what the Lancers were all about.

Thick leather gauntlets covered his hands. His pre-Change work boots had steel toes. Greaves and armguards had started life as sheet metal on one dead car or another. His Kevlar flak jacket had steel under it, front and back. The shit had been bulletproof, but that didn't mean it would keep out arrows or sword points. Quite a few people had made their last dumb mistake trusting it too far.

Once upon a time, the aluminum tubing that formed the shaft of his lance would've had a broom on the end so some guy home from work could sweep the bottom of his pool. A blacksmith had forged the point topping the lance, and put a little lead in the other end to improve the balance. For now, the lance sat in a boss on the right side of his saddle. He was still well within Chatsworth territory; he didn't expect trouble.

He especially didn't expect trouble with four other Lancers along. Their armor, and that which covered their horses, was of the same catch-as-catch-can style as his own. *Something old, something new, something borrowed, something blue* ran through his mind. The rhyme fit, every bit of it: the nylon fabric covering his Kevlar was cop-uniform blue, somewhat faded now from years of sun.

They ambled past a long-dead 76 station. "You ever gas up here before the Change, Eddie?" he asked one of his comrades.

"Couple times, maybe," Eddie Epstein said. "I hadn't had my license long. How about you?"

"Same deal," Bruce said. He leaned forward and laid a hand on Sherman's neck. The gelding was named for the old tank. These days, a mounted lancer was the nearest equivalent. "Who woulda figured cars would crap out and horses'd be the real thing?"

"Not me, that's for goddamn sure," Eddie said. "I didn't give a rat's ass about 'em till the Change, I'll tell you that. We lived in Chatsworth 'cause my mom and my sis were horse people."

"My dad bred 'em—but he got the dough to buy 'em from his used-car lot," Bruce said. "Just goes to show you, don't it?"

The other three Lancers rolled their eyes. They were young bucks, born since the Change. Listening to old farts yatter on about bygone days bored the crap out of them. But they had the sense not to show it too much when one of the old farts was the ruler of the west end of the Valley and the second was his right-hand man.

West of the defunct gas station, some fig trees had been planted on ground cleared after the power died. They looked peaked. There wasn't enough water to keep them happy. There was barely enough water to keep the people who took care of them happy. Cisterns, catch basins in the concrete-bottomed L.A. River, using pipes and lining canals with old plastic sheeting wherever possible . . .

In dry years, none of it was quite enough. You got through as best you could. The Lancers and their kin and the warhorses had first call on what there was. The rest of the people took their chances and prayed for rain.

The freeway sat above the usual street level. A watchtower built atop it gave the Lancers a long look to the south. Semaphores—fire signals at night—could relay news north the half-dozen miles to Chatsworth proper in a matter of minutes. As modern as last week, Bruce thought sourly. But with radios and phones and even telegraphs dead as Stalin, it was the best system he'd been able to dream up.

He muttered to himself when he rode under the 101. He'd been starting high school when the Northridge quake rocked the Valley in 'ninety-four. One of these years, a new one would bring down the overpass. If you happened to be below it just then . . . well, at least everything would be over in a hurry, anyhow.

A wagon pulled by a two-horse team came along Ventura Boulevard. Front and rear axles had been taken from a car. The wheels were wooden, with iron tires, and bigger than the old rubber tires would have been. The teamster on the wagon doffed his straw hat—not quite a sombrero, but close—to the Lancers.

Gravely, Bruce returned the salute. He demanded respect from his subjects. But you had to show you deserved it. He'd learned that playing Pop Warner football a million years ago. A coach who was an asshole might get the outward trappings of respect, but people would tell jokes about him behind his back. Bruce didn't want that happening to him. So when he got, he gave, too.

A couple of blocks south of Ventura lay what had been a shop that sold cameras and telescopes and binoculars. Some of its products extended the range of the signal towers. What had been the parking lot next to it was a field now. Opium poppies, redder and darker than their native cousins—which had been the state flower when California was a state—nodded in the breeze. Pre-Change painkillers were hard to come by these days, and of uncertain worth. You fought pain any way you could; it was everybody's enemy.

The land to either side of the road rose as you got deeper into the canyon. The Valley's street grid disappeared; the little streets that branched off from Topanga Canyon Boulevard wandered every which way. The land got greener as the Valley floor gave way to the Santa Monica Mountains—not green, but greener.

Then the ground dropped away from the west of the main road, down a slope that had made many a drunk driver in the old days go *Oops!* or

Shit! just before he hit bottom. Even on horseback—hell, even on foot—getting down there or back up again was a bastard and a half. No wonder the Topangans chose that Glenview stretch to hold as their frontier.

Well before he got there, Bruce held up a hand and reined in. The Lancers with him also stopped. The Topangans had a watchtower there. Somebody with binoculars or a spotting scope would be keeping an eye on them right now. The road was open—trade mattered to Chatsworth as well as to the hippies down the canyon. But the Topangans could close it in a matter of minutes, and have the closed stretch as strong as the rest of their works inside of an hour.

"So what you got in mind, boss?" Eddie asked. He figured Bruce had to have something on the fire.

"We can't go through 'em. It'd cost us too much. We've got to find some way to slide around 'em."

Bruce had less in the way of a scheme than he wished he did. But he knew he was right about that. He had more people to draw on than the Topangans, but they would enjoy the defenders' advantage. They had catapults by their walls, too. They wouldn't just throw man-squashing boulders. They'd throw big pots full of pre-Change oil and gasoline: homemade napalm. If that stuff clung to you, you begged somebody to cut your throat. And you thanked him with your dying breath when he did it for you.

"Go down Old Topanga?" one of the younger Lancers suggested.

"We've tried it before, Garth," Bruce said. "It wouldn't be a surprise even if we hadn't. They're ready for it—and they hold the high ground."

"You wouldn't have come all this way if you were just gonna do the peaceful coexistence thing," Garth Hoskins said.

All this way. They'd ridden maybe eight miles, and they'd ride back before the end of the day. With the horses walking, an hour and a half or so in each direction. Probably two hours on the way home—take it easy on the beasts in the heat of the afternoon. By modern standards, it was a long way. No hopping in the car now. Too bad.

But Garth wasn't wrong. He was only about five-seven, but he was built like a brick. When he wasn't practicing with sword and lance and ax and mace, he was pumping iron. He got off on exercise the way stoners got off on pot. He wasn't stupid, either. Not subtle, maybe, but not stupid.

He sure did have the post-Change view of distance, though. In Bruce, it still warred with what he'd known as a kid. He'd flown in an airliner. He'd seen the ground from six miles up. Garth never had. He never would.

"We've got to have the right approach," Bruce said. He might have been channeling his old man. Nacho Delgado had got rich unloading clunkers on suckers with bad credit. His son cared little about money. Power was a much headier drug as far as Bruce was concerned. He wanted that outlet on the Pacific so bad he could taste it. It would put the Valley back into direct touch with the rest of the world, make it a force to be reckoned with.

It would . . . if only the Topangans weren't in the way. They didn't want to follow his orders. They didn't want to follow anybody's orders. Rotten hippies! What were you supposed to do with people like that?

"We'll smash 'em for you, boss," Garth said confidently. "Just tell us what to do, and we'll take care of it."

Listening to him made Bruce feel good. Garth was a human pit bull. Point him at something and he'd bite chunks out of it for you. With enough guys like him at your back, you could really accomplish something. And if the hippies stood in your way, hey, that was just their bad luck.

Jared and Connor trudged north up Topanga Canyon Boulevard toward the Theatricum Botanicum, where the Topangans' assemblies had met since not long after the Change. The little outdoor theater held maybe three hundred people. Most of the time, that was plenty.

A redtail lazily circled overhead, peering down at the grassy hillsides in hopes of spotting a rabbit or a ground squirrel. A neighbor rode by on a bicycle. He lifted a hand from the handlebars to wave. "Hey, guys!" he called.

"Hey, Stu," Jared answered. Connor nodded. Stu pedaled on.

"Lucky bastard," Connor muttered once Stu was out of earshot. Jared nodded. Bicycle tires were something for which the Topangans had found no good replacement. Time and bad roads had done in most of the ones from before the Change. Jared and Connor had bikes that sat under tarps from lack of rubber. Connor went on, "Ought to go into the Valley and scavenge."

"The Happy Hunting Ground—if you're lucky," Jared said. The Valley was square mile upon square mile of houses and shops, almost all abandoned, almost all crumbling. Even this long after the Change, you could find almost anything there. Fancy booze, medicine, clothes from fabrics bugs wouldn't touch, bicycle tires, tools, books, spectacle lenses . . . You could, yeah. But— "The Lancers don't exactly love foreigners on their turf."

"Fuck 'em. In the neck," Connor said.

"That's what they want to do to us," Jared said. "That's what the assembly's about. Bruce is cooking something up."

"We ought to have spies up there so we'd know what's going on," Connor said.

"My guess is, we do," Jared answered. The Valley was a big place. You could be inconspicuous there. In Topanga, strangers stood out more.

"Yeah, but they'd have to do, like, what Bruce's stooges told 'em to most of the time, wouldn't they?" Connor might have been describing the ultimate perversion. Chances were, he thought he was.

"If we aren't careful, we'll all have to do what Bruce's stooges tell us all the time," Jared said dryly.

"In his dreams!" Connor exclaimed. He didn't really grok that some people did dream that way, and that some of the dreamers made others dream along with them. Bruce Delgado was one of those. He wasn't a monster like that guy up in the Northwest sailors had talked about in the early post-Change years. He was only—only!—a hard-nosed, power-hungry SOB. Whether that made him less dangerous or more was an interesting question, but not one today's assembly would debate.

At the grounds to the Theatricum Botanicum juncos hopped under the shade of small-leaved pepper trees, pecking for seeds and bugs. They were winter birds in most of Southern California, but lived here year-round. Jays screeched in the branches above them. More trees gave some shade to the theater itself. The bench space under the shadows went first; Jared and Connor had to sit in the sun. Jared had long since quit worrying about melanoma. His son may never have heard of it. They were both tan as leather. Something else—quite possibly, one of Bruce's stooges—would kill them before skin cancer mattered.

The five men in folding chairs on the stage were called the Brains when they were called anything at all. Topangans distrusted every kind of authority. That was a big part of what made them Topangans. They sometimes saw the need for it, though. Somebody had to keep a handle on dealing with the Chatsworth Lancers.

Pete Reilly looked at his watch. It was, of course, a rude mechanical, adjusted every so often by gauging noon from the shortest shadow. "Well, let's get this show on the road," he said. He was the Brainiest Brain of all. He'd landed an engineering slot at UCLA the year before the Change came. That he could think in numbers made him unusual, and unusually useful, in what had been one of the touchy-feely capitals of the world till the Change forced a certain pragmatism on everyone who managed to live through it.

He nodded to Kwame Curtis, who sat to his right. As a very young Marine lieutenant, Curtis had lost three fingers from his left hand in Iraq. He wasn't young any more. He was the Brain who worried about military matters.

"They're going to try something," he said flatly. "We've got to find out what. We don't know yet. But something. Our boys at the wall spotted Bruce looking us over. He doesn't do that shit for the fun of it."

His deep voice held an odd mix of scorn and worry. Once upon a time, he'd been a professional soldier. Bruce Delgado was very much an amateur. But Bruce was a shrewd amateur, and he had a lot more men and resources at his disposal than Curtis did.

"What would you do if you were trying to get rid of us?" Reilly asked.

Curtis' medium-brown face twisted into a scowl. "Drop a match in the woods when the wind was right and hope he could come by three days later and stick apples in our mouths after we roasted."

"Christ!" Jared muttered. Beside him, his son nodded. Jared had feared fires long before the Change. No more chemical-dropping airplanes. No more fire engines. Hell, no more fire departments. No more water mains. Nothing but hand pumps and picks and shovels and prayer.

Reilly nodded as if the answer was no surprise. No doubt it wasn't. The Brains would have worked this out ahead of time. "How are the fire-breaks?" he asked Connie Wong.

The only female Brain brushed graying bangs back from her eyes. "Bad," she answered. "We have so many things to do just to stay alive from day to day, we don't put enough work into the stuff we need maybe once every twenty years."

People were supposed to spend a couple of hours a week in the woods, cutting brush and knocking down saplings to keep fire from getting a running start. Jared knew he and Connor hadn't gone out there anywhere near so often as they should have.

"We'll have to start taking better care of that," Reilly said. Heads in the Theatricum Botanicum bobbed up and down. Whether that would translate into work . . . They were Topangans. Organization and discipline didn't come naturally to them.

"We have to do something else, too," Kwame Curtis said.

"What's that?" Reilly asked, as he was no doubt meant to do.

"We have to let him know that we understand about mutually assured destruction. If he plays with fire, we'll play with fire, too," Curtis said savagely. "The Santa Anas blow things down onto Chatsworth, same as they do with us. If he wants to fight a war, we'll fight a war. If he wants to burn us out, does he think we can't get around him and light up the Santa Susana foothills? He better not!"

Pete Reilly nodded. "I could say I don't want to give him ideas, but that one's too obvious. He's bound to have it already. He needs to know he's not the only one who can play that game. If the Lancers lose their horses, they won't be able to boss the Valley around any more, and all the ranches are up at the north end, near the Santa Susanas." He looked out at the assembly. "Any volunteers to go bell the cat?"

Jared's hand rose, almost of its own accord. "I'll do it," he said. "The message is pretty simple. And it'll be interesting to see what the Valley looks like these days. I haven't been up there for a long, long time."

"This is better," Reilly said.

"Sure it is." Jared nodded without even thinking. He'd grown up an American. He was a Topangan patriot now, though. "But I'll see what they're selling, too. They've got a lot more stuff to scrounge through than we do."

"Have any money?" Reilly asked, his voice dry. Topanga was small enough that it mostly ran on barter. The Valley wasn't.

But Jared nodded. "Yeah, some." Gold and silver were always good. So were pre-Change metal-sandwich coins. No one now could make anything like them. The metal might not be precious, but the package was.

"Okay, go for it," the big Brain told him. "And check out how things are. If we can stir up trouble for Bruce from his own people, he'll stay too busy to give us grief."

"I'll do it," Jared said.

That seemed to settle the meeting. As the crowd filed out of the Theatricum Botanicum, Connor said, "I want to come, too." He sounded like a small-town kid who longed to see the big city. The way things were these days, that was about what he was.

"Let's see what Pete says," Jared answered. The idea of having his headstrong son along didn't thrill him. Neither did the idea of quarreling with Connor. If he could say no and blame it on someone else, he had the best of both worlds.

Because they were ambassadors, Jared and Connor rode horses out of Topanga and into the lands the Chatsworth Lancers called their own. Pete Reilly, blast him, hadn't minded Connor coming along. Jared hadn't learned to ride till he was an adult. He could do it, but feared his clumsiness showed. Connor took horses for granted. He wasn't betwixt and between in the post-Change world the way his old man was.

They hadn't gone far north of the fortified frontier before a couple of men with strung bows came out of what had been a State Farm office back in the days when there were such things as State Farm offices. They had quivers on their backs, but didn't bother nocking arrows. "What's happening, dudes?" one of them called.

"We've got a message for your boss from Topanga," Jared answered.

"Oh, yeah? What kind of message?"

"One for your boss," Jared repeated—pointedly enough, he hoped, to get the point across but not to piss off the archer.

He must have gauged it about right. The man frowned, but said, "Well, go on up to Chatsworth Boulevard and turn right for a couple blocks. He's, like, at home, far as I know. You know where Chatsworth Boulevard's at?"

"Past Devonshire. Yeah." Jared had studied a Thomas Brothers road atlas before setting out. His memory of Valley streets was old, old, old.

"You got it. Awright, go ahead."

Ahead they went. Men with picks broke up the asphalt on what had been a parking lot in front of a Ralph's supermarket. Men with wheelbarrows hauled away the rubble. No one moved very fast, not on a hot day like this. Deadlines were, well, dead. Sooner or later, the work would get done. If not today, tomorrow. If not tomorrow, the day after. *Mañana.*

The farther up Topanga Canyon Boulevard they rode, the wider Connor's eyes got. "Buildings fucking everywhere," he said in a low voice. He stared east, toward the mountains. "Do they go all the way there?" He pointed to show what he meant.

"They sure do," Jared said. "More than a million people used to live in the Valley. Most of them are just bones now, but still . . ."

"People throw those big numbers around. They don't mean squat. Then you see—this." Connor shook his head in wonder. "Where do the ones who are left get their food?"

"Here and there, around the edges and in what used to be parks and torn-up parking lots like the one we've seen," Jared answered. "Not a million people now. Say, twenty or thirty thousand. That's a lot next to Topanga, but it would've been a small town before the Change."

"So what are we?" Connor asked. "Ghosts rattling around inside all that stuff they built?"

Now that you mention it, Jared thought, *yes*. Topanga didn't prompt such gloomy reflections. Topanga had always been way the hell out in the boonies. Being out in the boonies and built to human scale was the whole point to Topanga. Long before the Change, someone had written of Los Angeles, The future is here—and it's coming to get you. That future might be past now, but it sure left a big corpse.

As Jared and Connor came to the north end of the Valley, things began opening out again. There were empty lots that looked as if they'd been empty since before the Change. The vineyards and half-grown olive trees came from after the Change. Wine from these parts would probably be crappy, but even the nastiest plonk, as Jared had reason to know, beat hell out of no wine at all.

A little naked blond boy with a stick watched chickens pecking under the olives. Jared smiled; he could have seen the same kind of thing in Topanga. "This looks more like home," he remarked.

"It's too wide," Connor answered. The Valley was a valley, yeah, but a big valley. Topanga Canyon was, and looked like, a canyon. Jared's son went on, "I feel like a bug on a plate."

Jared had the same feeling. There were mountains on the horizon, but you could tell that horizon lay a long way away. He wondered how he would do somewhere like Kansas or Nebraska, where all you could see was miles and miles of miles and miles. Not too well, was his best guess. But, while he was more likely to end up in the Midwest than in, say, Tibet, he wasn't much more likely, so he didn't waste time worrying about it.

"This has to be Chatsworth Boulevard," he said after a while. They swung the horses down the narrower road. Calling it a boulevard didn't make it one. Houses sat on big lots. Horses grazed. Knights—Chatsworth

Lancers—practiced with spear and sword. Archers sent arrows whistling toward far-off bales of straw. Men wrestled under the shade of trees. When war was personal again, training was like paying life insurance premiums.

Just past the first street east of Topanga Canyon Boulevard, they rode up to a house set well back from the road. A tough-looking fellow opened a gate in the rusty chain-link fence fronting Chatsworth Boulevard. "You the Topangans?" he asked. When Jared and Connor nodded, the man went on, "Semaphore said you were on your way. Well, c'mon in. The boss wants to hear what you got to say."

Bruce Delgado scowled at the men from Topanga. One was older than he was, the other plainly a chip off the old guy's block. "You're telling me how I can fight a war?" Bruce growled—Eddie and Garth were listening, so he had to sound tough. "You got your nerve."

The older Topangan—Jared Tillman—shook his head. "That's not what I said," he answered. "I'm telling you what we'll do if you set fires. If you don't, we won't. We think fires are a nasty way for anybody to fight."

As a matter of fact, Bruce thought the same thing. That didn't necessarily mean he wouldn't do it. Plenty of weapons were nasty but effective. The military history books filling the shelves of his study showed that all too well.

He spread his hands now, and sipped from a glass of brandy. His henchmen had their own, and he'd given the Topangans some, too. The kid had drunk most of his. The older man had sense enough to go easy. Oh, well. It had been worth a try.

Leaning forward, he said, "You think you can sneak firebugs past my patrols? Good luck!"

"You think you can stop us if we try?" Jared Tillman returned. "Good luck to you."

There was a bluff called. Eddie clucked sadly. People in the Valley— in all of Southern California—were too thin on the ground for patrols to do much good. Moving at night, holing up in empty buildings (and how many zillion were there to hole up in?) by day, the Topangans almost surely could get up into the hills north of what had been the 118 Freeway. Wait till the winds started blowing, pour the oil, drop the matches . . . It could work.

"We're not even fighting," Bruce protested, again hoping he could sound as sincere as his father getting a lemon off the lot.

"I hope we don't," Jared Tillman said. "But you people have been scoping us out for a while now. Maybe you think that even though it didn't work the last couple of times, it will now. We're ready—that's the biggest part of what I've got to say, aside from talking about fire."

He made more sense than Bruce wished he did. But the Chatsworth Lancers had to use their army every now and then. Just having it wasn't good enough. An army that sat around or rode herd on peasants all the time started crumbling. It was like a football team that practiced endlessly without ever playing a game.

The other thing, of course, was that when you had an army and didn't use it, somebody else would stab you in the back and take it for a spin himself. Somebody like Garth, say. Bruce didn't think Garth was disloyal— the pup would have had an accident by now if he did. But somebody like him. Somebody who hadn't fought in several wars and didn't know there was no such thing as an ironclad guarantee, double your money back, for victory.

Bruce wondered if Tillman was delivering his warning not least to stir up that kind of trouble among the Lancers. He wouldn't be the only one who kept an eye on the past to guide him through the present. The Topangans were dopers, yeah, but not dopes. They knew what kind of position they held, and they knew how to defend it.

He had to answer the hippie, and in a way that wouldn't turn his own men against him or make them think he'd gone soft. "We'll do what we do," he said, his voice as harsh as he could make it. "You do what you do, and we'll see who comes out on top in the end."

"It doesn't have to be an I-win-you-lose kind of game, you know,"

Jared Tillman said sadly. "Can't we do better than that? How many million died, just in this county, when the Change came? Do we still have to
do all the same stupid shit they did in the old days?"

"Are we not men?" It wasn't philosophy—it was a Devo song you still
heard on the radio when Bruce was a kid. Or maybe it was a Devo song
and philosophy both. "You think human nature's changed? That would
take more than what we went through more than thirty years ago."

"You know what? I'm afraid you're right," the Topangan said. "You
know what else? It's a goddamn shame. Okay. Do your worst, and we'll
do our best—"

"Your worst, you mean." Bruce knew stolen Churchill when he heard
it, and he wouldn't let Jared Tillman get away with that. "Like you
wouldn't jump us, start inching into the Valley, if you saw the chance.
Yeah, right. Tell me another one."

He didn't look at Jared's face. He looked at Connor's. Sure as shit, the
kid dreamt of empty houses and offices and shops to plunder. The Valley
wasn't Egypt, dry enough to preserve things for thousands of years. But
it hadn't been thousands of years. It had been only thirty. Plenty of stuff
from the old days, the great days, was still good, still undiscovered, just
waiting for tomb raiders smart enough or lucky enough to grab it.

Like me. Bruce jerked a thumb at the door. "Go on. Beat it. You said
what you had to say. Now the time for talking's done. Now it's time for
doing."

They left. He sat in his fancy office chair, thinking hard. He wondered if you could find enough people to cut a big firebreak through the
brush on the other side of the freeway. Not without regret, he decided
he probably couldn't, not if he wanted to eat through the winter. Subsis-
tence sucked, when you got right down to it.

He remembered the days when poor people had been fat. If you were
fat now, you were either rich, rich, rich or you had something wrong with
you. People worked a lot harder than they had when machines did the
tough jobs for them. They had less to show for it, too. No wonder they
weren't fat. The wonder was that they were here at all.

Too damn bad the Topangans were here. With a little luck, before too long they wouldn't be any more.

Jared and Connor rode south down De Soto, a mile or two east of Topanga Canyon Boulevard. Jared wanted to see more of the Chatsworth Lancers' domain than the chief thoroughfare. A dead McDonald's sat at the corner of De Soto and Devonshire. Actually, it wasn't quite dead: kids played on the slides and crawled through the translucent plastic tubes, squealing the way they had before the Change. Jared had scorned the Golden Arches then. To him, they'd been a big part of what was wrong with America at the end of the twentieth century.

What was wrong with America a good way into the twenty-first century was a lot more obvious. It had nothing to do with French fries and burgers the consistency of hockey pucks. The grease, the salt, the yum . . .

The salt . . . "You know," Jared said thoughtfully, "if the Lancers attack us and we win, we ought to stop selling them sea salt for a while, see how they like that."

"What's so special about sea salt?" Connor asked.

"It's got iodine in it," his father answered. Just because electricity and internal combustion and explosives were gone, that didn't mean knowledge was. People couldn't use it all any more—but they still could use some. "Without iodine, people get goiters." He put a hand to the base of his neck to show what he meant. "They get stupid, too—not real, real stupid, but stupid. It used to be a big deal. Then they put iodine in everybody's salt, and it wasn't. Since the Change, it is again, unless you live near the ocean."

"They could probably get it from one of those far-off places—Santa Monica, or even Long Beach," Connor said. "They'd have to pay through the nose, though." He smiled, liking the idea.

Jared also liked it. He wasn't sure Pete Reilly would; he didn't know how much Topanga made from selling its larger neighbor sea salt. Well, if the Lancers attacked—and if they lost—he could bring it up.

One of the street signs at the corner of De Soto and Vanowen still stood. Seeing it made Jared guide his horse north, which he hadn't intended to do till he got to Ventura Boulevard. Just on the off chance . . . Connor came with him. He could see they were heading back toward Topanga Canyon Boulevard.

Shouting kids played soccer on a vacant lot that likely hadn't been vacant when the Change came. The way the grass grew suggested the shape of a vanished building. Chances were some long-ago fire took it down. It must have been a calm day, or more would have burnt. Soccer was finally conquering the remains of America. All it needed was a ball and a couple of goals, and you could mark those off with rocks if you didn't even have posts and a crossbar. This wasn't the kind of soccer that would take anyone to the World Cup, but there was no World Cup any more, so who cared?

The next good-sized street north of De Soto was Canoga. As the Topangans neared the corner of Vanowen and Canoga, a slow grin spread across Jared's face. "I'll be damned," he said. "It is still here! C'mon—we'll stop and get some food."

"Okay by me," Connor said.

SIERRA'S, the sign announced in script, and, under that and in smaller letters, SINCE 1959. The red-brown paint and the white background were just the way Jared remembered, and just as neat—it had obviously been touched up several times since he last ate here. One or two lightbulbs remained in their sockets after all these years, useless these days except maybe for swank.

Most of the old parking lot was a vegetable garden now. The people who ran the place had put big windows in the east-, south-, and west-facing walls. Sierra's had been a dark place before, even in the daytime. That didn't work so well now. The hitching rail and trough in front of the door were new. Jared and Connor let their horses drink a little, tied them up, and gave them feedbags before going inside.

"Welcome, strangers," said a gray-haired Hispanic man in a leather apron.

"I'm no stranger," Jared said, "even if I haven't been here since 1997 or so."

"Welcome anyway," the gray-haired man said. "I was here then, too, working for my father. What brings you back after so long?"

"I'm up from Topanga with my son here," Jared answered. "I thought I'd see if the place was still around—and here you are."

"Here we are," his host agreed. "Well, come in, sit down, and get something to eat. First drink is on the house."

The beer wasn't Dos Equis, the way it would have been. It was home-brew, like all beer these days—good homebrew, though. Choice of meat in the tacos and enchiladas was pork or chicken. Jared wasn't sure it all tasted the way he remembered, but it tasted like Mexican food from a place you'd want to come back to. Both meals came to two dollars. Prices weren't what they had been before the Change. Jared set a dozen sandwich quarters on the table.

"You're too kind," the gray-haired man murmured as he scooped up the money.

"Worth it," Jared said. "Eating here makes me feel like I'm my son's age." He clicked his tongue between his teeth. "Been a few changes since then, though."

"Sí, señor, just a few," his host agreed gravely. "In the kitchen, for instance. No gas stove now. No running water, either. But we keep going on. What else can we do?"

"We're lucky if we can do that much." Jared got to his feet. So did Connor, a beat later. "Way too many people didn't."

"Sí, señor," the other survivor repeated. "Where do you go now?"

"Back to Topanga," Jared said. "But you can bet I'll come again the next time I head north—say, after your country and mine fight another war."

"It will be a shame if they do." The gray-haired man clicked his tongue between his teeth. "Topanga. Another country. Who would have imagined that when we were young and one flag flew from sea to shining sea?"

"Not me. Not you, either. We've got it anyway. Stay well, friend."

With a nod, Jared walked out. His son followed. They swung up onto their horses and headed for their home in that other country.

There were trails through the Santa Monica Mountains. Back before the Change, this had been the Santa Monica Mountains Recreational Area. The way Connor's father and the other old farts told it, people who worked in offices in the Valley and the rest of L.A. drove in cars to the edge of the mountains and then hiked for the fun of it.

Those trails were mostly overgrown now. That they were there at all, though, argued that the old farts weren't just blowing smoke. Connor didn't grok it. Why would you hike for the fun of it? Hiking was work, often hot, sweaty work. Few things you had to do seemed like fun. Most of the time, he had to get from hither to yon on foot.

He was patrolling north and east of the village of Topanga, near Eagle Spring. He wanted to fill his canteen at the spring. Most years, water flowed even through the dry season. Here at the end of summer, it wouldn't be a lot, but he didn't need a lot. He didn't have to have any—the canteen wasn't empty—but he wanted to top up when he got the chance.

Faint in the distance, horns bleated. He cocked his head to one side, gauging the direction. Sure as hell, that racket came from Glenview, where Topanga kept its border with the Valley. "Shit," Connor muttered. The Chatsworth Lancers were attacking after all. They wouldn't blow the alarm for anything less important.

Or was it a fire? He scanned the horizon, or the limited part of it he could see. No plumes of smoke jumping into the sky. The Riders, then. He wanted to run back to the village and join up with his father to fight off the invaders. He wanted to, but he didn't. His orders were to stay on patrol even if the fighting started. Compared to the Topangans, Bruce Delgado had men falling out of his ass. He might use some to distract with a big, showy fight while others cornholed the canyon from behind.

Connor got to the spring. After he filled the aluminum bottle, he splashed water on his face and arms. It wasn't savagely hot, the way the weather could get this time of year, but it was warm. The water felt good. He took a few steps down the trail to the east, then froze. Somebody was coming the other way.

Quite a few somebodys were coming, as a matter of fact. They weren't making a lot of noise, not any one of them, but they weren't tiptoeing along, either. You couldn't very well tiptoe in country like this. And they were talking among themselves, the way people will just because they're people.

Connor flopped down behind some bushes near the trail. He put a dart in his blowgun and set several more on the ground beside him so he could reload in a hurry with minimum motion. He wanted to make as much trouble as he could, then bug out. The blowgun was the right weapon for that. It was silent and next to invisible. If only it had more range!

When you're nineteen, though, you don't really believe anything bad can happen to you. Not by accident do very young men fill out armies. Here came the soldiers from the Valley. They were on foot and not especially looking for trouble. The guy at the front had what looked like a page torn from a pre-Change road atlas. Peering down at it, he said, "Looks like we're coming to a spring."

"Good deal," said someone right behind him. "I'm dry."

They were within twenty-five yards. Connor took a deep breath, aimed, and blew. The business end of his dart was a tenpenny nail. It caught the guy in the lead right between the eyes. He went down on his face.

"The fuck?" said the Valley man behind him. Then he fell over, too. Connor got him square in the right eye. That was fool luck, and he knew it.

"What's wrong with those assholes?" another soldier asked, and bent down to see. He had his helmet slung on his belt so his brains wouldn't bake as he tramped along. They got punctured instead. Connor put the dart an inch or two behind his ear. Down he went, grabbing at his head.

Which was pressing things as far as they'd be pressed. Connor did his best snake impression to slither away. He left his blowgun and the other darts he'd set out. He'd already done more damage than he'd expected. As soon as he got in back of a reasonably thick tree, he scrambled to his feet and ran like hell. The Valley soldiers were still milling around by their fallen buddies. Every second they gave him was like a lifeline.

Then one of them yelled, "There goes the hippie freak!" That wasn't how Connor thought of himself, but the Valley guys wouldn't be in any mood to discuss semantics. They'd want to kill him, fast or maybe slowly.

Wheet! That was an arrow whistling by. Arrows could kill you from a lot farther away than darts could, and Connor didn't even have the blowgun any more. He didn't feel so brave any more, either. All of a sudden, this wasn't a game or an adventure. They were playing for keeps. He had to play the same way. If he won, he'd get to keep his life.

Thunk! That was another arrow, this one slamming into a tree. He ran harder than ever. He knew the trail better than they did, and some parts of it took a good deal of knowing. But some of the bastards behind him would be faster than he was, damn them. And if he tripped over a root and landed on his face, it was all over but the shrieking.

Whatever fickle gods there were doled out a little more luck for him. The one who tripped and did a faceplant was the fastest Valley soldier. The two men on his heels fell over him, too. By the way they yelled, they'd busted ankles or dislocated shoulders or maybe even both. Hope it's nothing trivial, Connor thought, stealing a phrase from his father.

It was a little more than a mile back to the village. Connor somehow kept ahead of the cursing Valley soldiers chasing him. Because he was literally running for his life, he had an incentive they didn't.

And he got one more break when he got to Topanga village. The men from the Valley could have torn it up in spite of his arriving ahead of them, only a detachment from Fernwood farther down the canyon was on its way north to the fight at Glenview, the only one it knew about.

"The Lancers are coming! The Lancers are coming!" Connor wheezed, making like Patrick Henry or Paul Revere or whoever that guy back in the old days had been.

"Say what?" demanded the man in charge of the little contingent from Fernwood.

Connor pointed in the direction from which he'd come. The sun glinted off the helmets and shields of the Valley men. If that didn't get the message across, he had no idea what would.

"Holy shit!" said the Fernwood commander, so evidently it did. He pointed in the general direction of Eagle Spring, too. "Come on, boys!" he yelled. "We've got this to take care of before we go on to the other. Fred, you head on up to the mouth of the canyon and let 'em know we'll be late."

"I'll do it," Fred said, and took off up Topanga Canyon Boulevard. The rest of the Fernwood men drew swords and slung bows and ran toward the houses on the east side of the road. If you were going to fight, fighting from cover beat the hell out of doing it any other way.

Connor trotted back to the east, too. Now he drew his short sword—he hadn't had time to worry about it before. He wondered if he was too tired to fight. Then he realized he had to be fresher than the Valley men.

Arrows whistled by, going in both directions. One of them pierced a fighter from the Valley about halfway between the pit of his stomach and his belly button. He folded up like a concertina, clutching at himself. The screams that burst from his throat had nothing to do with language. They were animal sounds of agony. They made Connor's stomach want to turn over. Anywhere on the trail back from Eagle Spring, he might have made noises like that. Oh, the arrow that got him would have gone in from back to front, but that wouldn't have changed the kind of shrieks he let out.

Brandishing his short sword, he rushed at a Valley man. The other fellow, similarly armed, traded a few strokes with him. Neither of them got home on the other, though Connor had to leap back at the last instant to keep a thrust from shish-kebabing him.

The Valley man didn't press his advantage. His comrade's anguished howls seemed to unsettle him worse than Connor. He must have decided that fighting somebody, anybody, even a little bit satisfied his honor. Now that he'd done it—and now that he'd discovered he and his friends weren't taking the village by surprise, the way they must have hoped—he seemed content to fall back into the brush and woods again.

Connor wasn't all that thrilled about chasing him. The Valley men could stage some kind of ambush, and they might come out on top with it. The Fernwood detachment didn't go charging into the undergrowth, either. They'd made sure the village was okay and would stay that way, which was plenty for them.

"Look at the gutless wonders skedaddle!" a Topangan whooped. "They won't stop till they get back up to the Valley!" Connor hoped the man was right. He thought he was. This prong of Bruce Delgado's attack hadn't worked. Maybe the men would be able to get to Glenview and help the Lancers. But weren't they more likely just to give it up as a bad job?

Up on the crest above the village to the west, a semaphore tower's arms began to wigwag. With luck, the towers would take news of the attack and its failure to the defenders at Glenview. Maybe somebody up there would be paying attention. Or maybe everybody would be too goddamn busy trying to keep the Lancers from breaking through.

A Topangan came up to the gutshot Valley fighter. He knelt and asked him something, probably *Do you want us to try to patch you up or just to get it over with?* When he drew his belt knife and slit the other man's throat, Connor knew what kind of answer he'd got.

Suddenly, Connor realized he'd killed three men himself. He swallowed bile again, even though the screams were gone. That blowgun was good for something besides bagging rabbits and doves for the pot. He wouldn't have wanted a big old nail driven hard into his head.

There was something in the Bible about that, but he couldn't remember what. Maybe he'd look it up when he got the chance. He was glad his father'd taught him to read. It was a good way to kill time when nothing else was going on. It was even useful every now and then, though it wasn't such a big deal as it would have been before the Change.

He hoped Pop was okay. Right this minute, all he could do was hope.

*   *   *

"Let 'er go!" the boss of the trebuchet crew shouted.

Jared sprang away from the windlass, along with all the others who'd been raising the heavy counterweight. Down it thumped. Up flew the long throwing arm. Away went the hundred-pound boulder from the leather pouch at the end of the arm. It flew through the air with the greatest of ease. The Chatsworth Lancers and their friends on foot all did their best not to be under it when it came down a quarter of a mile away.

A quarter of a mile . . . That was about the best you could do without explosives to help. "Crank it up, boys!" the crew boss yelled. "Shoulder to shoulder, we'll fling another boulder, and fight for the town we adore!"

"Stick a sock in it, Ronnie!" That wasn't Jared, but only because somebody else came out with it first. Ronnie, predictably, went on singing. If he couldn't inspire his men into action, he'd annoy them into it.

Jared didn't know how much the counterweight weighed. A ton or two, anyhow. The men wrestling it up again with the windlass sweated and strained and swore. This was the kind of hard physical labor that would give you a coronary if you sat around on your middle-aged duff all day.

But, post-Change, who sat around on his middle-aged duff all day? There was always gardening and chopping wood and hunting rabbits and simply walking anywhere you needed to go. No hopping in the car to visit the store two blocks away. Cars were metal mines, nothing more. There wasn't so much food these days, either, and what there was had less fat. Doc Leibowitz said he saw far fewer heart attacks and strokes than he had just after he got his M.D.

A good thing, because he couldn't do much for the ones he did see. Yes, knowledge survived. Drugs mostly didn't. And no gauging pulses past a stethoscope and a watch and a trained index finger. No EKGs. No X-rays. He had ether, sometimes, and brandy for a disinfectant. You were better off if you didn't get sick or badly hurt. Doc Leibowitz was the first to admit it.

Which meant you were smarter not going to war. Unfortunately, that wasn't an option. Jared's sword banged on his hip as he heaved at the windlass. His helmet and shield lay close by, along with his comrades' gear. If the Chatsworth Lancers broke through, they'd do what artillery-men always did when things went south: fight as hard as they could till they bought a plot.

"Boy, this is fun," Jared grunted, straining to raise the weight a little more with every yank.

"As a matter of fact," said one of the other sweaty, smelly men doing the same thing, "no. How many men do the fucking Lancers have, any-way?"

"Too many," Jared said, which was always the right answer. The Valley would always have a big lead in manpower. Topanga's advantage lay in geography. Fortify the narrow place and hang on tight—that was Topan-ga's strategy. "Where are the clowns from Fernwood? Shouldn't they be here by now?"

"Didn't you hear?" the other man said in surprise. "They'll be late if they show at all. There's some kind of dustup back at Topanga village."

"Shit," Jared said. "No, I didn't hear that." Connor was out patrolling down there. Jared had to hope his son was okay.

A couple of shoving, swearing men loaded another boulder into the leather sling. "We ready?" Ronnie asked. When nobody denied it, he shouted, "Let 'er go!" Away flew the stone.

It smashed a man to pieces coming down. Crimson sprayed in all di-rections. There were worse ways to go—he would never have known what hit him. Even so . . . A lifetime of hope and love and rage, all done before the poor sap knew the bell tolled for him this time.

But armored men on foot were banging away at the wall with a batter-ing ram. Others protected them with heavy shields. It wasn't quite a Ro-man testudo, but it came close. If they broke through . . . *Houston, we have a problem.* Jared scowled. He hadn't been born the last time men went to the moon. All he'd done was see *Apollo 13* with a cute girl named Gail. They wouldn't fly to the moon again, not unless the laws of nature changed once more. They wouldn't make any more movies, either, dammit.

The Lancers hung back, waiting to see if they could push through a breach. They couldn't force one themselves. But they could exploit one if it came.

Two Topangans ran down the wall toward the men on the ram with a big kettle of hot oil or hot water or something else unfriendly. An arrow from the Chatsworth side hit one of them in the neck. The Topangan let out a bubbling shriek. Blood poured from the wound, and from his mouth and nose. He staggered and clutched at himself, forgetting what he carried. The kettle tilted and spilled. The other guy who was hauling it also shrieked, on a high, pure, thin note. So did fighters on both sides who got splattered by the horrible stuff.

Jared felt like shrieking himself. Burns were the worst thing that could happen to you these days. About the best treatment Doc Leibowitz had for them was tannic acid—tea, in other words. It had been horribly outmoded at the end of the twentieth century. There'd been a state-of-the-art burn center in the Valley then. But the Change set the state of the art back most of a hundred years. The guy who'd got shot was the lucky one. He'd peg out pretty fast. The other burned warriors would hurt and hurt for a long time.

And the hot stuff in the kettle didn't come down on the bastards serving the ram. They kept pounding away at the wall. Each thud of their iron-tipped telephone pole—which was what the ram had been born as—sounded like the crack of doom.

Which, for the wall, was about what it was. The bricks and chunks of asphalt and cement and rubble that made up the works could take only so much. The wall fell down with a tired groan, as if it had been sick of standing there for so long anyhow. Topangans on the wall shouted in fear. Some of the Chatsworth men from the ram crew shouted along with them, because the garbage coming down from the wall didn't care who got in its way.

Valley foot soldiers scrambled into the breach with spears and swords and axes and anything else they could get their hands on. The Topangans did their best to hold them back, but more Valley fighters kept coming.

Bruce Delgado's kingdom might have been little by any standard this side of Greek city-states, but it dwarfed its western neighbors.

"Well, fuck me," Ronnie said, which was just what Jared was thinking. The boss man stepped away from the trebuchet, stuck his helmet on his head, and slid the straps of his shield over his arm. "Looks like we're gonna have to work for a living." He drew his sword and held it for a moment, as if wondering what to do with such an archaic killing tool. Then he trotted up toward the fighting at the breach with a shout of "Topannnnnga!"

Brawling at close quarters wasn't anywhere near so much fun as serving the catapult. The other guys couldn't reach you then. Now . . . "I'm getting too old for this shit," Jared announced to nobody in particular. But he was putting on his helmet and picking up his shield, too. You always forgot how heavy the damn thing was till you had to use it.

When he drew the sword, the sun glinted off the sharp edges. He made a pretty fair martial display. All the same, he would sooner have been back in Topanga village smoking dope or drinking bad wine.

Along with the other men from the trebuchet, he trotted after Ronnie. You did what you had to do, not what you would sooner do. If they could keep the Valley soldiers from widening the breach and letting the Lancers get through . . .

If they could do that, they'd be goddamn lucky. He saw as much right away. The Valley had too many men, and too many of those men carried pikes. With a pike, you could skewer a swordsman before he got close to you. You could, and they were. Troops from a Swiss hedgehog or a Greek phalanx would have gone through them like a dose of salts, but they weren't up against pros like that. The Topangans were odds-and-sods, too.

You did the best you could for as long as you could, that was all. Jared scooped up a handful of dirt and grit as he ran forward. Flipping it in a foe's face might not be sporting, but this was no sport. This was the real thing.

He got the chance sooner than he'd thought he would. The Valley fighters had no quit in them, and they could see they might make a lot of progress if they pushed the Topangans back from the wall. One of them drew back his spear to finish off a downed Topangan already bleeding from a leg wound. Jared flung the stuff in his left fist with a backhand scaling motion, as if he were flipping a Frisbee. Kids still played with the plastic disks. Every so often, new ones—well, new old ones—turned up.

The Valley pikeman couldn't fight with his eyes suddenly full of dirt. No one possibly could. He threw up one hand to claw at his face. Jared stabbed him in his unarmored belly, and twisted his wrist to make sure the blade cut guts. Without antibiotics, peritonitis and blood poisoning would kill even if the wound didn't. The Valley man squealed like a shoat and doubled over. Just in case he was still feeling frisky, Jared kicked him in the face. He grabbed the pike, too. The guy from the Valley sure wouldn't need it any more.

Then he hauled the wounded Topangan upright. "Here." He pressed the pike into the fellow's hands. "Can you get away with some help from a stick, Greg?"

"I better try, huh?" his countryman said.

"Well, unless you want the Valley guys to catch you," Jared answered. Murdering POWs wasn't a favorite local sport, which didn't mean it never happened. What held people back was more a fear of revenge than respect for the Geneva Convention. That was just one more relic from a bygone age. You did what you could get away with.

Using the pike as a staff, Greg stumped away. Jared went in the other direction, toward the center of the fighting. The trouble was, the center was coming his way, too. The Chatsworth men were pushing the Topangans back from the breach and widening it.

"We won't be able to hold on," panted a man fighting next to Jared. He had a cut under the brim of his helmet and above his eyebrow. His face was all over blood—head wounds always bled like mad sons of bitches—but he hardly seemed to know he'd been hurt. If he didn't catch anything worse, the gash would probably heal without much of a scar. No need to worry about lockjaw, not with that gore everywhere.

"'Fraid you're right." Jared turned a spear thrust with his shield. He chopped at the staff. He nicked it, but that was all. The goddamn thing was aluminum, which seemed like cheating.

"Let's go, Valley! Let's go, Valley!" Bruce Delgado's fighters sounded like a high school football crowd whose team was driving. The rival shouts of "Topanga!" were fewer and more ragged. Sure as hell, this didn't look like one of the movies with a happy ending. By post-Change standards, Hollywood was a devil of a long way from here.

Jared cut at an enemy foot soldier. The guy jerked back, so the stroke missed. Bruce Delgado was smart to have his men cheer for the whole Valley (well, the whole west end of the Valley), not just for Chatsworth. The Lancers lived up in the north, but these guys might come from West Hills or Canoga Park or Reseda or Woodland Hills or Northridge. Those had all been district names before the Change. They might harden into towns or even tiny countries, or they might get subsumed into Chatsworth or the Valley. Time would tell, but it hadn't told yet.

Someone behind Jared blared something horrible on a bugle. A moment later, he blew the same call—Jared thought it was the same call—again. The high, shrill notes did pierce the battlefield din. The call rang out once more. This time, Jared actually recognized it. It was *Retreat*.

He didn't want to do that. But, when he looked around, he saw that the attackers had got over or through the wall at a couple of other spots, too. If the outnumbered Topangans didn't fall back and make a stand somewhere farther down Topanga Canyon, they'd get cut off and cut to pieces right here. Then the Lancers could advance at their leisure.

Of course, breaking away from a fight was harder than getting into one. The enemy's tails were up. They wanted to go right on killing people here. A baseball-sized stone clanged off Jared's helmet—luckily, just a glancing blow or it would have left him loopy even if it didn't cave in his skull.

As the Topangans fell back from the wall, they retreated south down the highway toward the village. Topanga Canyon Boulevard had been hacked out of the cliffside. The Valley men could fight on a narrow front.

Or they could go down deeper into the canyon and try to get behind the Topangans. Some did the one, some the other. The Valley had the manpower for both. The Topangans . . . didn't.

Horns also brayed from the north. Jared was afraid he knew what that meant: the Lancers were past the wall. If facing too many foot soldiers was bad, facing homemade knights in homemade armor was worse.

Somebody'd set up a breastwork of sorts at one of the many twists in the road. Rocks, boards, old trash cans full of dirt. None of it would hold up a determined foe very long. Here were the Fernwood men at last, though, doing what they could. One of them helped haul Jared over the breastwork. "You're Connor's dad, aren't you?" he said.

"That's right. Why?" Fear twisted Jared's gut as he came out with the last word.

"'Cause he saved Topanga village's bacon, that's why." The guy from Fernwood—Jared thought his name was Lou, but he wasn't sure—filled him in on what had been going on farther south. Jared had just enough time for a little pride. Then the fighting picked up again, and he got too busy trying to stay alive to worry about anything else.

Bruce Delgado's lance had blood on the iron head and on the shaft. He wasn't especially proud of the kill—he'd skewered a fleeing man from behind—but it was better than nothing. Every Topangan down was a Topangan he wouldn't have to worry about later on.

This was building up to be the biggest victory Chatsworth had won over the hippies in a hell of a long time. Maybe the biggest ever. Eddie Epstein grinned at him from behind another catcher's mask. "You ready to go surfing in the Pacific, boss?" he asked.

"That'd be something," Bruce said. "I haven't even seen the fucking Pacific since the Change."

"Bet it's still cold," Eddie said.

"Ya think?" Bruce said. They both chuckled. Los Angeles, of course, got hot. The Valley, and especially the north end, got blazing hot in the summertime. Bruce had heard the ocean off places like Florida was warm as bathwater. Strangers who'd come to L.A. before the Change often figured the Pacific worked the same way.

And they'd frozen their asses off finding out it didn't. A current from the north or something kept the water cold all the time. As long as Bruce could claim a stretch of beach as his own, he didn't care if polar bears sunbathed on it.

He gulped mixed wine and water from his canteen. He wished that were cold, but it wasn't. One of the things he missed most from the pre-Change days was ice cubes. You didn't see those in Chatsworth any more.

"Come on, man!" Garth Hoskins called to him. "Let's clean these fuckers out once and for all, y'know?"

"Sounds good to me." Bruce waved the Lancers forward. Infantry screened them. Longbows or crossbows gave even the heaviest cavalry grief. So did barricades. You wanted your horsemen out in the open and moving fast. Momentum was a big part of what made a charging knight so formidable. Yes, you had a nice, pointy lance. But you also had a ton or so of horse and man and ironmongery behind the point. Get all that moving at fifteen or twenty miles an hour . . .

And it's a medium-bad fender-bender in the old days. There were times when Bruce envied people like Garth. They didn't have memories from a dead world rising up all uneasy out of the grave.

Out in the open and moving fast was what the Chatsworth Lancers couldn't manage here. From Glenview down to the Pacific, Topanga Canyon Boulevard had always been only two lanes wide. The people who'd built it must have been proud they'd managed even that. The road wasn't quite so winding as Pacific Coast Highway or the route along the north shore of Maui, but it wasn't wide and it wasn't straight. Well, if this were ideal terrain for knights, Chatsworth would have reached the sea a long time ago.

A Topangan halfway up the hillside shot an arrow that splintered on the beat-up asphalt a few feet in front of Bruce. That it splintered meant it was post-Change work with a wooden shaft. Valley archers went to war with aluminum-shafted hunting arrows made for deer and bear. Aluminum was wonderful stuff. But they had to keep reusing what they already had. Without electricity, they'd never get more.

Some Valley men shot at the Topangan. Nobody hit him. Agile as a monkey, he scrambled out of range up the steep hillside.

A foot soldier came trotting back to the Lancers. "Little trouble up ahead," he reported, sketching a salute to Bruce. "They've got this chickenshit barricade across the road. It's only, like chest high, but the way through is real narrow."

"Well, let's have a look." Bruce urged Sherman up to a trot. The rest of the Lancers followed. They were content to let him take the lead— partly because he was the leader, partly because anything bad that happened would happen to him first.

He rounded one more kink in Topanga Canyon Boulevard. Sure as the devil, there it was: a chickenshit barricade. It was enough to have stalled his infantry. Knights weren't the ideal answer to barricades. They weren't bad on foot, either, though. The Lancers' protection wasn't too heavy to move in, but it was far better than anything the Topangans had. Force them back and clear the way . . . and then do it again half a mile deeper into the canyon?

Bruce was still mulling it over when he heard something and spied motion up the slope out of the corner of his eye. "Oh, shit," he muttered— uninspired last words, but what he came up with as the avalanche thundered down on him and the rest of the Lancers packed together on the narrow road.

Not all the rocks and rock piles up at the top of the canyon had got there by themselves, he realized now, when he couldn't do anything about it. And the Topangans hadn't set their half-assed barricade where they did by accident or happenstance, either. No, they'd known what they were up to, all right. Oh, hadn't they just? Plan A had been defending the works up at Glenview. This was Plan B.

Sherman snorted and reared. He knew those rocks rolling down on him—and, incidentally, on the man who rode him—were the worst news in the world. Knowing it didn't mean he could do thing one about it, either, though. A stone the size of a table slammed into his side. Another one, smaller but nothing like small, hit Bruce Delgado in the head. The Wehrmacht's finest manganese steel did zip against a blow like that. Bruce was mercifully unconscious as the rockslide swept him and his hopes off the road and down into the depths of the canyon.

Jared and Connor eyed the mess on Topanga Canyon Boulevard. The Topangans had cleared away their improvised breastwork. The avalanche still blocked the road, though. Under the watchful stares of Topangan guards with blowguns and bows, glum prisoners from the Valley's failed campaign swung picks and sledges and turned big ones into little ones.

When they got done with that, they'd repair the roadbed itself. The landslide had bitten a chunk out of it. Then the Valley men would go home. Turning them loose was cheaper and easier than feeding them. There'd been talk of putting them to work at the seaside salt pans, which wasn't a job many locals wanted. But Topanga had avoided slavery up to now, and the old farts like Jared, who felt especially hinky about it, still had enough clout to hold the beast at bay.

Kwame Curtis came up to study the prisoners at work. "Hey, it's the hippie Marine!" Jared said.

"Up yours, man," the fighting Brain answered without heat. "I managed to get something to work, that's all. We'd've been in deep kimchi if it didn't."

"Kimchi!" Connor grinned. He loved the stinky stuff. Jared didn't know what real Koreans would have thought of Topanga's pickled cabbage spiced with garlic and chilies, but he liked it, too. The strong flavors perked up food that was too often bland.

The breeze swung around to come from the north. Jared wrinkled his nose at a stink nothing like kimchi's. "I hate that smell," he said. Some men and horses still lay under the rockslide.

"Oh, me, too," Kwame Curtis said. "I smelled it in Kuwait and Iraq, and then in the Dieoff after the Change. Brings back bad memories, you know?"

"Yeah," Jared said. "This isn't as bad as the Dieoff. Then you couldn't get it out of your clothes or out of your hair or off your skin no matter how much you washed."

"I remember. I'm not likely to ever forget. Nobody who lived through it is," Curtis said.

Jared nodded. "You know that Lynyrd Skynyrd song?" he asked.

"'That Smell'?" Kwame Curtis asked. Jared nodded once more. Curtis went on, "The smell of death sure as hell surrounded us, didn't it?"

Connor looked from one of them to the other. There they went again, talking about shit from the dead world, the lost world, the world they still remembered and that still turned real for them in dreams. One of these years, the last person with memories and dreams like that would die. Then the post-Change folks, the ones who'd never known anything different from what they had now, would be able to go about their business without having to listen to *Back in my day, we could do this or that or the other impossible thing.*

It hadn't happened yet. Looking at his son, Jared guessed Connor wouldn't be altogether heartbroken when it did. He'd never lived in the United States, after all. His country was Topanga: a beach, a canyon, an uneasy border with the Chatsworth Lancers—who'd be having their own fun and games now that so many of them had suddenly vanished from the scene.

> My canyon, 'tis of thee,
> Sweet land of the hippie,
> Of thee I sing!

Jared snorted. Then he wondered why. *It might not make a bad anthem for Connor's grandchildren. And they wouldn't even know what they were missing. Poor, sorry buggers,* Jared thought. He turned back to watch the Valley men swinging sledgehammers under the warm sun.

THE HERMIT AND THE JACKALOPES

︽

BY JANE LINDSKOLD

JANE LINDSKOLD

Jane Lindskold is an award-winning, *New York Times* bestselling author of twenty-some novels, including the Firekeeper Saga and the Breaking the Wall novels, and more than sixty short stories.

About this story she says: In the southwest, availability of water and the many different cultures that have long shared the region mean the Change would take a very different shape. I'd like to thank Diana Northup, Kenneth Ingham, and Michael Wester for their tales and photographs of the malpais. Thanks also to Paul Dellinger who, many years ago, gave me a copy of Louis L'Amour's novel *Flint*, which inspired Brett's kipuka.

"Have you heard the news?" Nathan Tso asked almost before Brett Hawke had seated himself.

"News, Grandfather?"

Brett used the title out of habit. Nathan Tso wasn't his grandfather but, although there was no biological relationship, the old man was the closest thing to family Brett had left. The rest . . .

Memory shaded red tried to force its way up. Fiercely, Brett shoved it down, focusing hard on his surroundings. He wasn't in the Cloverleaf. He was sitting cross-legged on a handwoven rug spread over the floor of a small room in a cluster of buildings high atop Acoma mesa. Facing him was Nathan Tso: half Navajo, half Acoma Indian. Nathan's hair was iron fading into white, falling past his shoulders and bound by a faded blue bandanna.

His reddish brown skin was weathered and deeply lined. He possessed the stocky build that was the heritage of both his peoples, but not a trace of fat.

Grandfather Nathan hadn't been fat even before, when food had been more plentiful and many Indians had grown fleshy, victims of the white flour—and-lard diet that had bred the Navajo taco and related abominations: abominations that had led to disproportionate levels of diabetes, heart trouble, and related diseases among the Native peoples. Diseases that, in turn, had led to disproportionate levels of death when modern medicine was no longer available. There had been so many missing faces each time he'd visited . . .

Speaking rapidly, so that words might force memory away, Brett repeated, "News?"

"Yes. Riders came from the Double A Ranch. They wanted to know if some people had come here, if we were hiding them."

Acoma's spiritual center was the mesa that had been popularized as

Sky City by tourist promoters. It wasn't the biggest of villages, but it was arguably the most secure. Built up on a mesa that rose above the surrounding area, the village had successfully resisted attacks by the Spanish—even after some of those fiercely determined armored warriors had climbed all the way to the top.

After the End, the road that had been built to make possible a tourist shuttle had been left intact, but numerous walls and small forts built along its length assured that no one was riding up unseen and unchallenged. The only other "easy" access was a stair cut into the stone—and even though he'd been both up and down that narrow, twisting passage more times than he could remember, Brett wouldn't call the route "easy." A single man—heck, a child with a good-sized club—could defend the top long enough for help to be summoned.

When he wanted to, Nathan Tso could talk the hind leg off a donkey, as . . . Brett forced his mind away from who used to say things like that, concentrating on what Grandfather Nathan had said. More important, on what he hadn't said.

"Some people? Hiding? You mean criminals? Did someone steal something from La Padrona?"

"In a manner of speaking."

Grandfather Nathan nodded. Brett recognized the tiny quirk at the corner of his mouth that meant the old man was hiding a smile. A smile, Brett realized, because Brett was asking questions. Nathan Tso offered a little more information as a reward.

"She feels that they stole themselves from her."

"Huh? Stole themselves? Did they owe her labor for shelter or something?"

"No. They were longtime members of her ranchero: a blacksmith and farrier, a talented seamstress, a mechanic and metalworker, and a nurse who had studied both at college and with the *curanderas*. Oh, and their children, six in all, the eldest a girl of fourteen."

Brett shook his head as if a fly had landed in his ear, but it was jarring thoughts, not a bug, that were making his head buzz.

"That doesn't make sense. People with those skills would have earned their keep and more. They'd be welcome anywhere. Grants or San Rafael would take them in. Heck, even if they weren't Indian, any of the Native communities would find their way to giving them a place, maybe even adopt them into the tribe."

"Very true."

Silence again. Brett forced himself to puzzle through the problem as once, long ago, he might have puzzled his way back along a badger's scattered tracks for nothing other than the pleasure of finding the way to its den. This trail was hard. Brett didn't like thinking about how humans interacted, about the things they did to one another, even to those who offered only kindness. But Grandfather Nathan was looking at him, his dark eyes amid their deep lines watchful and sad. The little smile had vanished.

"Slavery!" Brett burst out at last. "No! That's not possible."

When the world had ended, the Acoma elders had claimed to have had visions that told them that the transformation of the world was long-term. They'd immediately put people to work clearing out the cisterns, hauling tanks for additional water storage, and otherwise preparing for siege. They succeeded not only in holding the mesa and the immediate watershed, but also the associated villages of McCartys and Acomita. Both Acoma's security and its strength as a community made it a likely destination for people on the run.

Brett didn't want to believe it. "They've got to have run for some other reason. No one around here would tolerate keeping slaves."

"Who will stop the practice once it begins?" came the reply—as once, when Brett had been nine, the old man had asked what diverted the flow of water or why a mountain lion had turned aside when tracking a deer.

"Begins? Oh . . ."

Brett understood. He didn't like understanding, but he did. In these years following what he had heard people call "the Change"—as if it were a natural thing, like a woman going through menopause, instead of a soul-ripping end of the world—the way in which people lived had, well, changed. He didn't know what had happened in other parts of the world, but here water ruled as it always had done.

Before the End, most of the local population had lived and worked in Grants, a city of some eight thousand or so, about an hour west, as I-40 flies, from Albuquerque. After the End, Grants had made a rebound of sorts—unlike much larger Albuquerque, which, except for a narrow strip along the Rio Grande, had depended on modern technology for its water. Even so, much of the region's surviving population had redistributed, so that Grants was just another village.

The Indians had formed communities in Acoma, Laguna, and Zuni. The Navajo—the largest nation, whose vast reservation lands were mostly desert—had divided into smaller groups, often seminomadic, following their sheep wherever they could find grazing.

San Rafael, a few miles southwest of Grants, which boasted a good water source from the Ojo del Gallo springs, had prospered. Indeed, where water was concerned, San Rafael was doing better than it had before, since, as the water table had recovered from excessive urban and industrial use, the springs had flowed more strongly. Farming was good and the mixed population fiercely protective of their rights.

The same pattern was true for various ranches farther south, including areas that had been the El Malpais National Conservation Area, the Cebolla Wilderness, and the plains.

La Padrona had staked her claim southeast of the malpais.

"La Padrona," Brett said, thinking aloud. "She's Anglo, isn't she, despite the title?"

"That's right," Nathan agreed. "Annabella Andersen. Along with her late husband, Andrew, she ran the Double A Ranch."

"Late?"

"Drew Andersen died a bit over two years ago. From what I've heard, Annabella is determined to hold on to the ranch for their children—especially for her son, Andy. Andy's eighteen now. When his father died, he was young for grown men to take orders from—especially when his mama was a very pretty woman and might be presumed to be looking for a husband to run the ranch for her. There are those who say Andy's too inexperienced, even now."

"I met Drew Andersen," Brett said thoughtfully. "Worked there a couple of times when they were looking for someone to train young horses."

"Then you might have met one of the men they're hunting," Nathan said. "Did you meet their farrier?"

"Emilio?" Brett dredged up the name as if from a lifetime ago, rather than only three years.

"Emilio Gallardo," Nathan replied, offering the little smile of approval. "That's right. He and his wife, Felicita, have decided they would like to leave La Padrona's employ. However, apparently, La Padrona feels this would be a mistake."

"But Emilio and his family didn't come here?"

"No. Neither to the high pueblo or the lower villages." Nathan leaned forward. "I dreamed you would be the one to find them and help them get away. Then you came to my door and I thought this would be so. You see, the Acoma elders have forbidden interference."

Brett understood. "The elders don't want to stir up something with Double A. One ranch alone wouldn't be a problem, but those ranchers are all allied."

"Yes. The elders of Acoma strongly disapprove of the Double A's actions. However, they also must think about the welfare of the rest of our community. You are an honored friend, but not a member of the tribe. Their commands do not bind you."

Brett remembered Emilio Gallardo, remembered their long talks about whether horseshoes were necessary, about weighting shoes to achieve certain gaits, and how best to trim a hoof for different sorts of terrain. He'd learned a lot during those talks, including things he still used, things necessary. He shifted uncomfortably.

Perhaps seeing Brett's unease, knowing that pushing him would make the young man bolt, Nathan deliberately turned the conversation to other things: the new bow he was making, the promising harvest, the strong late summer monsoons. He asked little about Brett's life, letting the younger man volunteer information about the health of his animals, his battles with squash bugs, the effectiveness of the new cistern he'd built last winter. They shared a meal of squash and speckled bean stew with pork, accompanied by yellow corn tortillas and thick honey.

As soon as it was polite, Brett excused himself. He collected his horses and supplies from the lower village, then rode south. Off to the west, the black flow of the malpais stretched, a land as rough and pockmarked as the moon and—even to the majority of those who lived right alongside it—just as alien.

As he rode, Brett tried to distract himself from Nathan's news. He thought about how well his business had gone. The general store in lower Acoma had given him good value for the boots he'd made. The rabbit pelts hadn't traded for as much as last time, but that was to be expected. Rabbits were plentiful this time of year, and the boys and girls set to guard the crops kept their rabbit sticks ready. He'd bought a jar of a strain of beans said to grow well in high heat and low water. It was always best to buy seed stock early, in case the winter was harsh, and hungry folk ate their future.

Thoughts of the foals he'd been approached about training over the winter kept Brett's thoughts occupied for a while longer, as did the question of whether he could cut enough hay to support an augmented herd. Nonetheless, inevitably Brett found his thoughts turning to what had happened to Emilio Gallardo and his family.

Why did La Padrona think she could start keeping slaves? Slavery was one foulness that hadn't arisen in this region since the End. Indentured servitude, sure, and people who sold their souls to the company store, as the old saying went, but outright slavery? Not yet. Too few people and too harsh a climate to support idlers—and, unless kept after with a lash, slaves were idlers. They had no incentive to be otherwise.

"What would Leo have thought?" Brett wondered aloud, causing his buckskin's ears to twitch back in startled response. "Would he have obeyed the elders?"

Leo had been Nathan's grandson. He and Brett had been closer than brothers. Brothers only share parents. Brett and Leo had shared a passion for the wilderness and all the skills needed to survive in it. They'd met when they were eight, in a Cub Scout troop associated with their grammar school. Leo's family was Acoma, but they had lived in Grants. Leo's mom, who always seemed to be pregnant or nursing, ran a sort of informal day care. Leo's dad did whatever came to hand, mostly construction, but he was a fair hand with stock as well. He wasn't exactly lazy; nonetheless, even as a boy, Brett could tell that Leo's parents had a different attitude about making money. They wanted enough to get by, but didn't necessarily care about getting ahead.

When Brett and Leo had been nine, Nathan Tso had come to live with his Acoma kin. The old man—for so he seemed even then, although his hair was still mostly black and the lines on his skin not so deep—had seemed to know everything about what the boys thought was important. He'd taught them how to track, to ride bareback, to shear a sheep. Later, he'd taught them how to hunt and—more important—how to dress their kills, use every part, and respect the lives they were taking.

Brett and Leo dropped out of Scouts in favor of becoming Nathan Tso's acolytes. Brett, who had black hair and dark brown eyes, courtesy of his Italian-American mother and Black Irish father, grew his hair long and didn't think there was any higher compliment than being mistaken for Leo's brother—as he often was, although Brett was taller and leaner, his skin tanning with a hint of olive, rather than to red-brown. When the boys were fourteen and fancied themselves men, they had sworn an oath as blood brothers, with Grandfather Nathan as witness.

After high school, they'd both gone off to Albuquerque to attend UNM. Brett couldn't figure out what he wanted to major in, but was leaning toward something to do with animals and maybe a minor in anthropology. Leo had immediately declared a double major in accounting and computers, but then he'd always been good at math.

A soft whicker from Little Warrior, his buckskin riding horse, brought Brett back to himself. Twilight was gathering and they were nearly to where they had to turn off. Brett patted the gelding on the side of his neck. He knew the horse could probably have taken him home, but he instilled in any horse he trained a respect for the rough lands in which they lived. Horses were good people, but they also had far too much imagination. On the plains or in the forest, a runaway horse was in danger of nothing worse that wearing itself out or straining a tendon. Here, the consequences for the same moment of panic were nothing short of mutilation and death.

"Malpais" means "bad lands" in Spanish.

In most situations, that was a pretty good name for the place. Contrary to popular belief, the rough volcanic terrain that began in the vicinity of Grants and flowed its erratic course over many acres to the south and west was not the result of the explosion of Mount Taylor. El Malpais resulted from the periodic eruption of numerous small vents. The most recent flows, from Bandera and McCarty's Crater, had happened only three thousand years earlier.

This relative youth meant much of the lava was sharp and jagged. The malpais ate boots, ripped into the soft parts of a horse's hooves, and sliced open skin. A horse who decided to panic at a fluttering leaf or bolt when a quail exploded up from underfoot was likely a dead horse. Brett had trained his horses to expect him to be alert and attentive, providing them with the confidence they themselves lacked.

Brett gave Little Warrior another "thank you" pat on the neck, then turned to check on Pintada, his brown-and-white paint pack mare. Both horses were of feral stock, acquired through the BLM's adoption program. If asked, Brett had always agreed that the horses were mustangs, although he knew the question merited a more complicated reply. However, he knew that, whatever their breed, his horses were tough and resilient, possessing strong legs and solid hooves. They were also a lot less picky about their diet than most horses. Sure, they were small and scrubby, classic round-bodied Indian ponies, but they were descended from generations of survivors.

Nathan had taken Brett and Leo hiking in the malpais and surrounding back country. They'd explored the caves, discovering areas where ice could be found in the middle of summer and where bats hung like gently rustling leaves. There had been moss gardens growing beneath tiny skylights and pools fed one drip at a time as rain seeped down from above. Nathan had explained that these caves were actually tubes formed when the lava had begun to cool. The hot lava had flowed through, leaving an open space. Some of the tubes ran for miles—sixteen was the largest measured. Others were huge—over fifty feet in diameter.

El Malpais embraced green islands called "kipukas" within its black flow. The largest of these kipukas was called Hole in the Wall. The boys had been a little disappointed to learn that it wasn't the Hole in the Wall made famous by Butch Cassidy, but this Hole in the Wall was marvelous in its own right. It embraced some six thousand acres. Tales were told of outlaws using it as a staging ground and deserters hiding during various wars. Antelope had somehow found their way in, as had any number of smaller animals and a host of birds. When they were in high school, Brett and Leo had hiked in any number of times to camp, feeling as if they were in a world all their own.

After the boys had graduated from high school, Grandfather Nathan made them a present of a secret that—as Brett learned later—not even the park service knew. Nathan had learned the secret from an old cowboy, long ago when he himself had been just a boy. He told them that, even with the old cowboy's description, it had taken him several weeks to find the place. Working as a team, the boys found it sooner.

They were carefully tracing their way along the fifty-foot-high lava wall as they had so many times before, painstakingly examining every crack and crevice, looking for one that penetrated more deeply than the rest. They stabbed themselves on prickly pear and thorny cholla. They wore thick gloves thin while moving chunks of rough, pockmarked basalt. Then they had realized that one narrow crevice was a whole lot wider than it looked, the result of an optical illusion caused by the junction of two sections of stone. Wild with excitement, they'd probed into the crevice. Their hopes had crashed when they saw what seemed to be a solid wall ahead of them but, when they followed the passage to its end, they realized the crevice actually curved, transforming into what they now recognized as the end of a lava tube.

After going back for their lights and packs, they carefully made their way along the tube's length. Open sky vanished as the crumbling edges of the tube's uppermost reaches became entire. Even with flashlights, they stumbled over chunks of basalt or bits of detritus that had drifted down from the upper world. Several times they splashed into puddles that had formed in a low section of the passage. Slimy drips trickled from above, running down their faces and hair onto the bare skin of their necks like the chill fingers of some ghostly denizen of the darkness.

Their efforts were rewarded first by a distant flicker of light, then when the tube opened out into an oasis of green, an acre-sized meadow surrounded on all sides by walls of cracked, black rock that bent in at the top, as if cradling the meadow. The stream that ran across the meadow was marked by thicker and greener growth. Whooping with enthusiasm, they drank and refilled their canteens. After they had washed off accumulated grime, they set about exploring their new domain.

Across from where they'd entered, an odd jumble of rocks caught their attention. Trotting over to investigate, they discovered that someone had built a wall from irregularly shaped chunks of basalt. Off to one side, hidden by the angle of the wall, was a thick plank door. Opening it, they discovered a tidy cabin, constructed by walling up a section of cave. The rock overhang served as a roof and light came from deep windows with thick glass set into wooden frames. The cabin was quite large. Bunk beds were built into one wall, and the area near the fireplace was furnished with a pair of handmade chairs and a table. A channel carved into the floor carried a trickle from the stream that vanished beneath a farther wall.

A door to one side showed the way into a second cave, reached down a short passage beneath the overhang and walled in after the same fashion as the front of the cabin. This second area's purpose was evident from a manger containing a few pieces of desiccated hay and a scattering of brittle straw on the stone floor. From this side, it was easy to find the hidden door that let out into the meadow.

"That manger's oddly placed," Brett said, after they'd poked around for a time, discovering an old bucket with the bottom out, a burlap sack that might have once held grain, some chewed bits of leather. "Why build it into the wall that way? Why not just make it freestanding? That took a lot of extra work."

Bringing his flashlight close to the manger, Brett examined the thick planks carefully. He'd split planks from logs and, even when you knew the trick, it wasn't exactly easy. Someone had gone to a lot of trouble to set these planks, then anchor the manger to them. Eventually, Brett found the hidden latch. It was quite heavy and took a moment to work loose, but when he did the section of planking holding the manger swung on hidden hinges, revealing a second tunnel.

This tunnel was shorter than the one that they'd followed in from the edge of the malpais and ended in a huge green space, with trees.

"How big is it?" he asked Leo. Leo had a good head for such things. He always won when Grandfather Nathan asked them to judge area or volume.

Leo frowned thoughtfully. "Hard to tell with the trees, but I'd say twenty-five or thirty acres. You could keep horses here, a couple cows, even. The grass is good and thick."

"The stream probably feeds under the walls to here," Brett said. "I think that the tube we followed in, the first meadow, and this were all part of one lava tube system. This section was probably never entirely covered."

"Suspect you're right," Leo agreed. "Shame that Grandpa didn't show us this a few years ago. We could have had a lot of fun during high school. Now we're off to college."

"But we'll come back," Brett said.

They had, many times. After college, Leo had gotten a job with a big accounting firm in Denver. He'd been flying back to New Mexico for a Saint Patrick's Day binge at Brett's parents' Cloverleaf Tavern when his plane went down. There had been no survivors.

*   *   *

Brett and his horses made their way through the crevice, down the tunnel, and into the first meadow a lot more quickly than Brett and Leo had that first time. Working by lantern light, Brett had carefully cleared away all the loose rock so the horses would have safe footing. The little pools came and went with the seasons, but never became deep enough to provide an obstruction. He'd hammered flat the worst of the protrusions. The one thing he hadn't made easier to use was the hidden entrance. Indeed, he'd done what he could to make it harder to find without blocking access for the horses.

It had taken a long time, but Brett hadn't been in a hurry. Far from it. He had nowhere to go and wanted to go anywhere even less.

He was tired when he got in—more tired than he remembered being for quite a while. Still, Little Warrior and Pintada had to be unpacked, untacked, rubbed down, then turned out to pasture. The dogs and cats pretty much took care of their own meals this time of year, but they still wanted attention. The chickens needed to be shut away and the goats milked. There had been rain earlier, so he didn't need to haul water to his garden. He decided he'd pick first thing in the morning.

One of the things he'd treated himself to in Acoma was a large side of bacon. Brett cut off thick slabs, fried them up, then cooked eggs in some of the grease. The rest he put aside for another time. He'd also bought bread, something he rarely made himself. After the heavy meal and the long day's ride, he should have slept like a log. Instead, he lay awake, a cat on his pillow, another on his chest, the Pomeranian snoring by his feet.

He thought about Emilio Gallardo. About how he'd taught Brett about taking care of horse's hooves. How Brett used that knowledge every day, owed a great deal to what he'd been taught. He dozed and in those dreams Leo was still alive. He was upset at the decision the Acoma elders had made, trying to show them how wrong they were with a cost/benefit analysis painted on a hide, but resembling a power point presentation. He waved a long stick as a pointer and lightning shot out from the tips and became a red-tailed hawk.

The hawk spiraled up, riding the thermals over the malpais, circling wider and wider to the south. Far below, the hawk spotted a cluster of jackrabbits. No. Jackalopes, for they had little horns. The jackalopes were huddled near an upthrust bit of sandstone. They were wearing horseshoes.

Brett drifted with the hawk, sleeping in perfect peace until cockcrow. He rose at first crow, made a large mug of hoarded instant coffee, and went out to gather eggs, milk the goats, and make a quick survey of the garden for produce that would spoil if he didn't pick it. He fried more bacon, ate some with more eggs and soft goat cheese, then wrapped up a couple of thick burritos. These went with some freshly picked cucumbers in a box that, in turn, went into his saddlebags.

Brett let the chickens out, but only as far as the wire mesh—covered enclosure he'd built to surround their coop. The goats protested being left in their run, but he didn't know if he'd be back before dark and, while the chickens would retire to their coop, the goats were much more confident of their ability to take care of themselves, something the coyotes sometimes took advantage of.

These chores taken care of, Brett went through the tunnel into the back pasture. Since he almost always brought a treat along, his small horse herd ambled over to greet him. While they were all busy with carrots, he slipped a halter over the head of Timpani, his choice for the day's work.

Timpani's owner had always said the mare was pure Arabian. Certainly, she had the Arab's high crest and delicate head. Her coloring was what the Old West had called steeldust, grey liberally sprinkled with darker hairs. Her mane and tail were a shadowy grey, darker than her coat, reminding Brett of gathering storm clouds. Although she played at being high-strung, Timpani liked work that demanded her attention and intelligence. Acting up was a sure sign that she was bored.

While he was tacking up Timpani, Brett had a serious chat with Rover and Fida, two dogs who had come to live with him that first winter. The pair looked as if they might have a lot of blue heeler—an Australian cat-

tle dog—in them. There'd been a fad for the breed about the time everything went to hell, so they could well be purebred. Rover and Fida weren't
pretty in the way border collies were pretty. Their coats were short,
colored a bluish grey, and overlaid with black blotches. Their muzzles
were somewhere between short and long, and held a good number of
very white teeth. Rover's perked ears were neat upright triangles, but one
of Fida's flopped, giving her a quizzical look. Their tails curved up over
their backs.

Like Timpani, Rover and Fida liked having work to do. They were also
completely convinced that they could handle the show without human
assistance. When Brett told them to guard the place, they looked at him
seriously, their alert ears and gently wagging tails saying:

"Don't we always, boss?"

Next, Brett whistled up Xenophon. The mutt hauled himself from
where he was sleeping in the shade of the cottonwood that grew near the
cabin door. Xenophon was a long-legged, long-nosed, floppy-eared
hound of no particular breed. His tail was long and straight; his coat an
unremarkable shade of tan. What was remarkable about him was his
sense of smell. Brett had picked him as a puppy from a litter sired by a
male who—so his owner claimed—could track a rolling rock through a
gully washer in the middle of the night. The bitch who mothered him
could perform the same miracles—but with a head cold. Xenophon's
biggest problem was that most of the time he was about as lazy as a dog
could be. Even when he'd been a puppy, he'd preferred sleeping with his
belly to the sun rather than romping about. Put him on a scent, though,
and he'd follow until forced to take a break.

After securing the Pom and several of the older cats inside the cabin,
Brett swung into the saddle. As Timpani walked purposefully in the direction of the exit tunnel, he checked his supplies: food, water, first aid
kit, bow and arrows, knives at his waist and in his boot tops. He didn't
figure he'd be fighting, but it was best to be prepared. He had a good
lasso in easy reach, as well as odds and ends of wire, string, and suchlike
tucked into his saddlebags. His best binoculars were in a case where he

could easily reach them. Given that he had no idea what he'd find, if anything, he was as prepared as he could be.

Once out in the open, Brett directed Timpani to a sheltered rise where he could scan the area without being seen himself. Grandfather Nathan hadn't said how long the Gallardos and their friends had been missing from the Double A, but if riders had come to Acoma to ask questions, it probably had been a few days. Riders wouldn't have come asking unless the area had already been searched and nothing conclusive found.

And they wouldn't make that choice lightly, Brett thought as he methodically scanned the terrain, because they'd be giving away that La Padrona was starting to think of some people as her property.

Brett's inspection of the area didn't show him anything as obvious as a posse neatly displayed out in the middle of the tall grass or threading their way through the scatterings of piñon, juniper, and other scrubby trees that were interspersed in copses through the plains. Last winter's rains had been good—by area standards—and the monsoons had established right on schedule, so there was as much green as brown in the undulating land.

Lowering his binoculars, Brett considered. *The people I'm looking for probably chose to leave the Double A at this time precisely because they could count on water and a certain amount of cover. The ranch is south of here; access used to be off 117. Acoma's certainly the closest community, but the runaways might have figured that's where La Padrona would look first. In that case . . .*

Brett reviewed a mental map. Options for people who didn't want to be returned to La Padrona weren't good. There were other ranching operations south of El Malpais, but the ranchers were loosely allied, respecting one another's brands and sharing resources. All Annabella Andersen would need to do was tell some tale about the Gallardos owing her and they'd be turned back. So not the ranches . . .

It would be a long trip, Brett thought, *but if I were them, I just might consider going west, then north, up toward some of the settlements in the Zuni Mountains or even to San Rafael. The Double A riders have got to have figured that, too. So why haven't*

Emilio and his band been found? Even with a head start, if they have children with them, a bunch of determined cowhands should be able to catch up.

He felt a tingle run up his spine, just like it had when Grandfather Nathan had posed one of those questions that had been meant to teach him and Leo to track with their minds, not just with their eyes and ears.

What if they're still close by? What if something happened to slow them up? A lamed horse, an injured person, a kid with a bellyache . . . I can think of a dozen possibilities. At this point, the riders would be looking farther afield, not behind. I wonder . . .

He tapped Timpani on one shoulder. In response to the command, the mare began to pick her surefooted way down the slope. Xenophon rose, shook himself, and followed.

Suddenly, Brett felt as eager as initially he had been reluctant.

Grandfather Nathan . . . Did he know? When he said he'd "dreamed" I'd be the one to stop the Double A, I just translated his words into Anglo—as "imagined" or "hoped"—but what if he meant it literally? What if he prayed for a solution and this was the answer?

In a twisted way, it made sense. Why else would Grandfather Nathan believe Brett had a chance to intercept people who should have been long gone from the area? Back when everything stopped working and the clear Western skies had shown all too clearly planes plummeting toward the earth as their engines failed, the elders had prayed—as tradition said Acoma had always prayed—for the well-being of the world. They had been certain that the catastrophic events were not caused by a short-term flicker in the electromagnetic field or any of the other bullshit explanations Brett had heard bandied around in Grants.

Brett guided Timpani south, skirting trees and larger rocks, rather than riding in the open: not hiding, but not making it easy for him to be seen either. After the third time he'd scanned the horizon, Brett realized that he wasn't looking for people so much as a landmark—a large rock, surrounded by trees. He could see the shape in his mind, clear as if he'd been there before, but he was certain that he hadn't. Problem was, he knew how the rock looked from a hawk's eye view, but not from the side.

As they had ridden their aimless course, Xenophon had decided that they must be searching for something. In his methodical hound's way, he had concluded that the something wasn't a deer or a cow or badger's den, since they'd passed up several interesting options in those categories already.

For the last few miles, the dog had been playing a sort of canine twenty questions with his human. He'd cast widely back and forth along either side of where Brett rode, snuffling enthusiastically. When he found something that he thought was interesting, he would woof softly to draw Brett's attention. Brett would dismount and inspect the find, rejecting a dead squirrel, an old quail's nest, a tree that a bear had recently clawed, and a neatly buried bit of porcupine scat. When Xenophon woofed and gently scraped his paw where something else had been covered with dirt and pine needles, Brett expected more of the same.

What confronted him was a neat deposit of human waste, almost certainly from several people.

"Good boy!" Brett said, rubbing Xenophon's ears and rewarding him with a piece of bacon. "I don't think the Double A riders would all share a hole, but if I were traveling with kids and didn't want to leave sign, this is just what I'd do. Can you find the people who left this?"

Xenophon wagged his tail and began casting around, making the whining, snuffling noises that Brett translated as "I'm working on it." Brett had barely settled back in the saddle before Xenophon gave a short bark and lined himself up along what, to Brett, was a still invisible trail.

"Go slowly," Brett commanded and Xenophon, his tail wagging like a metronome, put his nose to the ground and led.

It didn't take long for Brett to find visual indications that they were indeed tracking humans who had been through the area within the last day. They'd been careful. Whenever possible, they had ridden over pine needles or gravel that wouldn't hold a print. However, with this being monsoon season, hiding the trail wasn't always possible. After examining the prints, Brett decided they were tracking four to six horses going no more than two abreast, often single file.

The riders were careful to keep to cover. When he saw the greyish white sandstone upthrust ahead, he knew that must be their destination. Chewing thoughtfully on his lower lip, he considered his options. He couldn't just ride up. These people were on edge. If they thought they'd been found, but only by a single man, they'd probably shoot—and surely someone would be good enough with a bow to hit if not him, then Timpani. He wasn't going to put the horse at risk.

With this in mind, he dismounted in a sheltered clearing, loosening Timpani's girth so she'd be more comfortable. The mare was content to nibble on stray bits of grass. Xenophon, of course, promptly went to sleep. Leaving behind his bow and arrows as both too cumbersome and too provocative, Brett crept forward until he could see his quarry's camp.

The chunk of sandstone was larger than he'd realized at first—but then Leo had always been better at estimating size and distance. It also was two pieces, not one. The refugees had picketed their horses between the two sections, where there was a little grass, then dragged a deadfall to close off the far end. In front of this rough corral, they'd pitched several small tents. The space was sheltered and somewhat defensible, but those very qualities also made it a potential trap. Something in the bearing of the people gathered within told Brett they knew this.

There were four adults—two black, two Spanish—four small children, all black, and a baby on the Spanish woman's hip. The black man and several of the children were napping. The older girl Nathan had mentioned wasn't visible. Brett guessed she was keeping watch from atop one of the chunks of sandstone. She was probably doing her best, but after Xenophon had found the spoor the trail had led through cover. Then, too, the girl was probably alert for a group of riders. One man could easily be missed.

Brett belly-crawled as close as he could, then took shelter behind a boulder that had probably once belonged to the larger chunk.

Trying not to sound threatening, he called, "Emilio, it's Brett Hawke. I've come to help you."

Emilio Gallardo dropped the branch he'd been breaking into firewood, his expression shifting from surprise to suspicion so quickly that

Brett could almost read his thoughts. Emilio was a broad-shouldered man with the heavy torso of the classic blacksmith and sturdy legs. He was clean-shaven and wore his hair cut short. Suspicion still coloring his features, he rose, as if by doing so he could protect the entire group. Then, holding his branch firmly, he made a gesture that invited Brett to come forward.

Brett rose from behind his rock, stood so they could see he held no weapon, and stepped lightly forward. The black woman, broad-hipped, with heavy breasts, had her arms around her two older children. The littler ones—one hardly more than a toddler—clung to her voluminous ankle-length skirts. The Spanish woman—Felicita Gallardo, Brett guessed—hushed the baby. Only the last adult, a wiry man with skin the color of coffee with two splashes of cream, didn't move, but continued slumbering.

"Brett Hawke," Emilio said, a smile breaking through his suspicion, "by damn and all, it is you." He indicated the rest. "That's my wife, Felicita. Our friends, the Murchinsons: Winna, Jerome, and their kids."

Emilio might have said more, but Winna Murchinson interrupted. "You've come to help us? How do you know we need help? You sure you aren't coming from La Padrona?"

"I'm here because Nathan Tso of Acoma mentioned that La Padrona was hunting some folks," Brett replied. "He told me that one of them was Emilio here. I got to thinking about how I wouldn't have horses with sound hooves if it weren't for what Emilio taught me, and so I came. What's the problem? Why are you holed up, rather than moving along?"

"It's my husband," Winna said. "He was riding point. Jerome has a good eye for the land."

"He does," Brett agreed. "He did a fine job of hiding your trail. Not easy to do with so many horses."

Winna flashed him a smile. "Jerome was being so careful about making sure we rode where we wouldn't leave too much sign that he missed a big old rattlesnake sleeping in the sun across our trail. The snake missed us, too, I guess, because Jerome's horse was right on top of it before it set to rattling. Horse spooked. Jerome went off, busted a leg. I've got it set, but he's in a right large amount of hurt."

This must be the nurse and *curandera* Nathan had mentioned. Brett could see that all three adults had questions, but he held up a hand to forestall them.

"Ma'am, can your husband ride?"

A rusty voice, thick with sleep, cut in. "I can. It'll hurt, but if someone will lift me up, I'll hang on. The worst of the pain let up after Winna got it set, just that the setting hurt like . . ."

He stopped, obviously swallowing a profanity in deference to his wide-eyed children.

"Where were you heading?" Brett asked.

"San Rafael," Felicita Gallardo replied. Like Emilio, she spoke English perfectly, but with the accent of the New Mexico Hispanic who is bilingual from childhood on. "Can't hope Jerome can make it that far now."

"No," Brett agreed before Jerome could insist otherwise. "Am I right that you folks were going to lie low until the hunt died down, give Jerome a chance to rest, then move on?"

Nods.

"What if I offered you a safer place to do just that? There's a risk, because once we start moving, it's possible that La Padrona's posse will see us, but this is big country and it's possible they're visiting the other ranches, seeing if you're hiding out there."

The adults exchanged glances. Winna, perhaps because she had the most to risk, spoke first. "That would be kind of you, but where can we hide that they won't find us as easily as they would here?"

"In the malpais," Brett said. He glanced up. Thunderheads were gathering. "If we're lucky, it's going to rain this afternoon. That will give us cover and wash out our trail. Even if La Padrona is offering a bonus, her riders aren't going to figure they'll see much in the rain. They'll find cover. I suggest we pack you up and get moving. That way we can take advantage of the rain when we get to the point where we need to cross open ground."

Emilio forced a smile. "Ah, the summer monsoons. You can set your watch by them."

"It rained yesterday," said a little girl of about four. Something about her big dark eyes and soft wooly hair made her look like a lamb. "We got wet, even in the tents."

"And we'll get wetter today," Brett promised.

He tried to sound cheerful, but he knew it was going to be a miserable trip. The monsoon rains were usually what the Navajo called "male rain"—hard, driving wetness that soaked you to the skin in minutes. Its blessing and curse both was that the actual rainfall didn't usually last long but, by the time it stopped, drying out took hours.

"Rosamaria!" Emilio called softly. "Come down now. We're leaving."

Brett shook his head. "If that's your scout, have her stay up there until we're packed. I'd feel better knowing someone was keeping watch."

"Rosamaria didn't see you," said the oldest little boy. "Are you an Indian?"

"Not quite," Brett said, "but I try. Now, scamper and help your mama."

The refugees didn't have all that much. Felicita and Winna took charge of breaking camp while Emilio and Brett tacked up the horses and consulted on how best to distribute the weight.

"My Rosamaria can ride with Jerome," Emilio said. "She's not full-grown and he's not a bruiser like me. He can hold on to her, and she'll let us know if he's slipping. Yolanda"—this was the little lamb—"can ride with her mama. Carl and Oscar can ride together. I'll take Nancy."

Felicita nodded. "I'll carry Ignacio with me. That leaves Puff—the horse that threw Jerome—to carry the gear. He's still jumpy. I don't trust him with a rider."

Brett agreed. He left them to finish their arrangements while he collected Timpani and Xenophon, calculating their route back as he did so.

If Brett had still believed in any sort of beneficent deity, he might have thought the Creator was watching over them that day. The skies grew heavier and darker—reminding Brett that New Mexico had been notorious for deaths and injuries caused by lightning, back when people had the leisure to keep track of such things. Maybe the posse remembered this, too, because they saw neither hide nor hair of any other humans. When the rain came down, it fell in sheets. If it hadn't been for Xenophon's absolute certainty as to their trail, even Brett might have gotten lost. But the hound kept on point, his upright stick of a tail guiding them right up to the hidden entry into the kipuka.

The rain was letting up as Brett emerged from the tube that led to what had been his sanctuary from the world. He whistled to Fida and Rover, reassuring them that all was well.

"It's like a dollhouse!" exclaimed Rosamaria, looking with wonder around the still-dripping meadow. "I mean, not a dollhouse, but those little landscapes they make in boxes. It's so cute!"

Brett had not yet exchanged more than four words with this girl, since she had stayed on watch until they were ready to depart. Rosamaria Gallardo wasn't pretty, caught between coltish gawkiness and a young woman's figure she didn't know how to handle. Like her parents, she had brown hair and dark eyes, though her hair showed reddish highlights that time had dimmed in theirs.

However, he'd had ample opportunity to observe Rosamaria as she tenaciously kept her chestnut gelding in line. The chestnut—unimaginatively named Star, for the large white splash on his forehead—seemed offended by having to carry two riders. Maybe, as horses will, he realized that Jerome's seat was anything but sound and wanted him off. Rosamaria was having none of this. Star gave her trouble for the first mile, but by the second he was behaving, and by the third he had resigned himself to the fact that this featherweight was in charge. Better, Rosamaria had managed this feat without a crop or thudding of her heels into the horse's flanks. She'd simply met stubbornness with stubbornness.

Brett was irresistibly reminded of his and Leo's reaction to the hidden meadow what seemed like lifetimes ago. Swinging down from Timpani's saddle, he set about getting everyone—human and equine alike—settled. Despite ample and willing help, this wasn't a fast job. Twilight had turned to full dark by the time everyone had been fed, watered, and bedded down. The stable—not used this time of year except for its connection to the back thirty acres—was swept out and enlisted as a dormitory. Brett's bunk was given to Winna. A raised bed was constructed for Jerome by placing planks between chairs and padding the lot with the tents and one of Brett's rugs.

Overwhelmed by so much company—more than he'd had for over three years, for even on his visits to Acoma, Brett had tended to camp on the fringes of the lower village—Brett stepped outside. He was scratching the nanny goat between her horns when Felicita Gallardo came out, baby Ignacio gently fussing in her arms.

"Thank you, Brett," she said, "for everything you have done for us today. You haven't asked, but do you wish to know why we were running from La Padrona's ranch?"

"I did wonder," Brett admitted. "You'd lived there a long while, even, well . . . before."

Felicita nodded, rummaged in the pockets of her skirt, and came up with a bottle, which she gave to Ignacio. "Yes, we had—since Rosamaria was little. Emilio started as a rider, became a wrangler, then was assistant to the farrier. He was interested in smithing, and Drew encouraged him to learn, even set up a proper forge. When the first farrier got tired of living nowhere, Emilio was given the job."

"And you?"

Felicita flashed a warm smile. "I liked living there. Before we went to the Double A, I had a little business making alterations to garments and making custom dresses. After we moved, I continued doing the fancy work. With that, with Emilio, with our children, I was very happy.

"Even after the Change, we did very well. Emilio's skills were in great demand. He trained others to do much of the shoeing, because suddenly there were no stores where you could order hinges or latches or a hundred and one other things you never think about until they are gone. My skills as a seamstress were much in demand. Annabella Andersen was not going to stop looking good, even after—maybe especially after—Drew died."

Felicita's expression grew somber. "It was not all good. There was a sickness—maybe a flu—in the second year. Most of the adults who caught it lived, but Rosamaria's little brother and sister both died."

"I . . . I'm very sorry."

In the moonlight, Brett saw the fierce shake of her head. "We have all had losses. I am not asking for your pity. I tell you to explain why we left. Rosamaria is our only remaining child. I do not seem to be able to have any more. Ignacio is an orphan we took. Winna tried, but she could not save his mother. Valerie was too young and he was a large baby. Many things we took for granted—like mothers surviving childbirth—are gone now. Emilio and I took the child. But having Ignacio does not mean that we no longer cared for our Rosamaria. When . . ."

Her voice trailed off. Brett waited, uneasy but knowing he wanted to hear. Yet, when Felicita began to speak again, he wondered if she'd forgotten what she'd been talking about.

"Annabella took Drew's death hard. She had her children—the boy, Andrew, and two younger girls—but she has always been a woman who lives for the admiration and control of men. Now she had lost her man— and in losing her man, she had lost all men. Do you understand?"

"Not really."

"Annabella wanted to keep the Double A, for her, for her Andy when he was man enough to hold it. To do this, she must play the men off each other."

"Like Queen Elizabeth," Brett said, "the first one, I mean. Everyone wanted her to marry, but she wouldn't give control over to a man."

"Like that," Felicita agreed. "Maybe Elizabeth really was a virgin queen. Maybe she was sterile. Maybe she was just lucky. But Annabella knew she was not sterile. For a woman who had access to reliable birth control all her life, to suddenly be so vulnerable was agony. I know this, because she consulted Winna and Winna told me. So Annabella Andersen, who liked men very much, and who probably had lovers even when her husband was alive, was suddenly forced to celibacy. I think this is why, when Andy grew old enough to be, as they joke, 'randy' she did not discourage him."

"She was living through him?" Brett asked. "Like that. For sex?"

He was glad there was only moonlight, because he knew he was blushing.

"That is so," Felicita agreed coolly. "But for both of them, sex is bound up with power. Within the last year, Andy has developed a taste not so much for virgins, but for 'deflowering.'"

Brett saw where this was heading and cut in to spare Felicita the pain of explaining. "Rosamaria."

"Yes. He was waiting until she turned fifteen because, in Spanish culture, fifteen is when a girl is considered a woman."

"There's a celebration for that, isn't there?" Brett said. "I remember some of the girls in my school talking about it. Fancy dresses, like prom dresses, and a big party. But I thought that just meant they were allowed to start dating?"

"That's how many families interpreted the custom. A fifteen-year-old girl is often not strong enough to bear a child and live." She bounced the baby in her arms. "Ignacio's mother was fifteen when she became pregnant."

"Oh . . ."

"Emilio and I decided we must get Rosamaria away from there. Emilio worked closely with Jerome. Before the Change, Jerome was a mechanic. Although internal combustion engines have stopped working, there is still a demand for his skills."

"For mills," Brett thought aloud. "Clockwork of any sort. Even simple things like lifts would work better if someone who understood bracings and such was involved."

"More," Felicita said. "There has been talk about things like crossbows and catapults. I often worked in the big house, and overheard a great deal."

"And Jerome wanted nothing to do with that?"

"Nothing. What tipped the balance was when Winna overheard some jokes about 'darkies,' including a reference to her as an 'Aunt Jemima' and another very cruel routine that ended with 'But I don't know nothing about birthin' no babies.' Given that this was soon after she lost Ignacio's mother . . ."

Brett's fists tightened. "Grandfather Nathan hinted that La Padrona was beginning to think of people as her property. No easier place to start than with black folk. Move to darker Spanish and Indians, then . . . After a while, there wouldn't be a need to make excuses."

"Slavery has been reborn elsewhere," Felicita said, "or so we hear, without the excuse of race, only with power. Jerome realized that his scruples would mean nothing with Winna and the children as hostages. He asked Emilio for advice and Emilio—with my full enthusiasm—suggested they run away with us."

"Ah . . ."

There was a long silence, then Felicita said softly, "And you? How did you come to help us? You said something about Nathan Tso of Acoma. This is the same as the Grandfather Nathan you mentioned? Are you also of Acoma? Tso is a Navajo name, but you do not look Navajo, either."

"My best friend, Leo, was Nathan Tso's grandson. Nathan had a Navajo father, Acoma mother. His daughter married an Acoma man, and eventually Nathan settled with his Acoma family. That's how I met Nathan. He taught me—and Leo—a lot. Anyhow, by chance, I was in Acoma trading for supplies soon after riders from Double A had been through asking after you. Grandfather Nathan told me and he mentioned Emilio."

"Good chance for us," Felicita said. "Without you, we probably would have been found."

"Almost certainly," Brett said. "Once they learned you folks hadn't shown up anywhere, they'd have figured like I did and started looking closer in. Even if you got Jerome up on a horse, he wouldn't have been able to ride point and find you a good route like he'd been."

"Then God was looking out for us," Felicita said.

Long buried anger surged up, anger Brett hadn't admitted to for years. His hands wrapped around the top rail of the goat enclosure so tightly that he felt the wood creak.

"God looking out for you! How can you say that? You lost two children to an illness that would have kept them in bed a few days before. If they caught something really bad, they could have gone to the hospital, been put on fluids. You'd still have them . . ."

"Maybe," Felicita said, carefully, as if she were trying to convince herself. "Maybe not. We cannot read the future. Maybe humanity needed to learn a lesson."

Brett heard her pain, but his bottled-up anger had a life of its own. "What about all the nonhumans who died? I worked part-time in a pet shop, before. Do you know what happens to tropical fish when the power fails and the back-up generators don't come on? Even goldfish can't live once the pumps are off too long. March gets damn cold here, especially at night. Do you know what happens to little animals that don't have heat? Do you know what happens to animals that need a special diet? They start dying, slowly and painfully. Do you know what we had to do when we realized that the power wasn't coming back?"

Even in the moonlight, he could see Felicita's eyes widen and knew that she did. He didn't spare her—or maybe he wasn't sparing himself.

"We killed them. All those little creatures who trusted us, who looked up with big eyes when we came over because we were the ones who fed them and fussed over them. We killed them. And what did they ever do to deserve that?"

"You gave them mercy."

"I killed them. Me, because I knew how to do it cleanly. I sang the songs Grandfather Nathan had taught us, but still, I killed them. Birds, chinchillas, hedgehogs, guinea pigs, sugar gliders, exotic reptiles, all the creatures who couldn't hope to live because it was cold and the food they needed would never arrive. We waited a week, a week too long. They were already beginning to suffer."

"Oh, Brett . . ." The pity was real. So was the wisdom in her dark eyes. "But that wasn't all, was it?"

"I'd worked part-time at the pet store. My other job was at my family's business: the Cloverleaf, a restaurant and Irish tavern."

He laughed, a hard, barking sound. "It actually did pretty well. Lots of tourists get sick of everything with green chili and tortillas. My parents didn't believe that things wouldn't get 'right' again. I tried to tell them, tried to get them away, but they kept talking about this blackout or that storm. Never mind that planes didn't fall out of the sky during those. Never mind that every engine didn't stop working.

"My parents weren't dumb. They knew that any place with liquor would attract looters. So they brought people in to help hold the building. They used their supplies—they had extra because this all happened on Saint Patrick's Day—to set up a sort of soup kitchen, feeding people in return for wood or additional food. They fed a lot of people who didn't bring anything.

"The day after the pet store . . . closed, I left to go pick up some donations. Sacks of beans, I think. I got back after dark. The place was still—and it was never that way. Even at night, someone was up cooking or keeping watch. I went in the back way, lit a candle . . . They'd all been murdered: Mom and Dad, my younger brother and sister, my older sister and her kids, who had come back to be 'safe.' Her husband. Old man Seamus, who'd bartended for as long as anyone could remember, was behind the bar. Someone had slashed his throat. They'd walked on his body to break down the door to the liquor cellar.

"As I went through, looking for anyone who might still be alive, I realized that some of the neighbors who'd been given a refuge weren't there. I think they did it. At the very least, they ran, didn't do anything to stop the people who did.

"I found the Pomeranian puppy I'd given my mother for her birthday hiding under a table, too scared to even whimper. He was the only thing alive. I grabbed him and walked out of there. I had Little Warrior and Pintada with me. I went back to the house and started getting what I needed to make it on my own. I packed the family cats into carriers and strapped them onto Pintada. Left the damn beans. Whistled up Xenophon and another of the dogs—she's dead now. We got out of there while it was still dark. Headed for the malpais. Here. I didn't come out until September. Realized I'd need supplies for winter. Figured Acoma would have held out and I was right."

"How old were you?"

"Twenty-two. I'd graduated from college the year before and had been trying to figure out what to do with a B.S. in Biology and a minor in Anthropology."

"And now? Have you been alone all this time?"

"Mostly. I go to Acoma a few times a year to trade. Once I got the chickens and goats, I was pretty self-sufficient. I'd grabbed seed packets when I left Grants. My mom and I were going to start plants from seed that next weekend. I knew how to save seed, to tan leather, dry meat and vegetables. Lately, I've been making boots and sandals soled with old tires. The shopkeeper in Acoma saves me tire tread if I give him first shot at what I've made. Works."

"Aren't you lonely?"

"I've the horses, dogs, cats, goats, chickens. Some ducks flew over and decided to stay. Then there're the animals who come through with the seasons. That's enough."

"But you came out to save us."

"I owed Emilio."

"So you said . . . And now we have invaded your refuge."

"For now. We're going to have to get you out of here."

"Yes, even with the big pasture out in back, there's not enough to support us all."

"Not just that," Brett said. "You ran away so you could make a life for your children. This here isn't a life for them."

It's hardly even, he thought, *a life for me.*

When Brett returned from scouting early the next morning, he could tell that Felicita had shared his story. He was glad. He didn't want to tell it again and, from their expressions, he could tell no one was going to ask questions. His guests had taken care of the milking, egg gathering, and picking vegetables. Breakfast was waiting for him. As he ate, he called the adults in for a counsel.

"No sign of anyone near. That's good. Jerome needs a chance to mend a bit before we even think about having him ride."

There, Brett thought. *I've reassured them that I'm not interested in moving them along anytime soon. Now for the hard part.*

"I've been thinking over what Felicita told me last night, about why you folks decided to leave the Double A. I was wondering if you wanted to try and put a hobble on how Annabella and Andy think they can treat people."

From the way their eyes brightened, the Gallardos and Murchinsons were indeed interested. That was reassuring. He'd thought they might just care about getting away—and with six kids, that would be sensible.

"Here's how I see it," Brett went on. "La Padrona values two things: her control of the ranch and her son. Andy values himself pretty highly, too. So how about we arrange to acquire Andy? After all, if she can keep slaves, so can other people. Might help her see her behavior in another light."

Winna wrinkled her nose. "I don't want to keep any sort of slaves, especially not that tomcat."

"I didn't think you would, but it's funny how often people believe that everyone is like them. La Padrona will believe it and that's what matters."

"So," Emilio asked, "how do we catch him? He's not going to be alone."

"We set a trap." Brett dipped the tip of one finger in his mug and drew a few lines on the table. "This is a rough outline of the malpais. This space here is what's called a 'kipuka'—an island. In the day, it was called Hole in the Wall."

"Like Butch Cassidy?" asked Jerome, just as Brett and Leo had all those years before.

"Same name, different place. This Hole in the Wall is some six thousand acres of grassland and trees, surrounded on all sides by the lava flow. The easiest way to get into it is on the south side of the malpais. The lava is only three miles wide there and there's an old trail in. As hikes in the malpais go, it's an easy one. Thing is, you really shouldn't ride in. The lava's dangerous footing for horses. That's going to cut down on Andy's troops right there. Unless cowboys have changed a lot these past three years, they'll do just about anything unless they have to get off a horse to do it."

Emilio flashed a grin. "That hasn't changed. Gotten worse if anything. Man on a horse is somebody. Man walking's just a peon."

"So we make it look as if you folks decided to head into Hole in the Wall. Why not? It's close. There's water, game, even the means to build shelter. Probably the reason no one ever settled in there is the isolation. But for people who want to hide out, it would be a good choice."

"What about our horses?" Emilio asked. "They'll know we had horses."

"If you don't mind," Brett said, "I was going to ask if I could turn a couple loose in the right area—sort of place us. They'll figure you turned them loose when you couldn't take them into the malpais."

"Nice," Jerome said. "Take that son of a storm cloud that threw me. Puff's bad-tempered enough that anything short of a mountain lion won't be able to faze him."

"They're all pretty tough," Emilio agreed. "They might even head back for the ranch—or if they scent horses they know, they may join them. Either way, they'll help point the Double A riders where we want them."

"Good thought," Brett said. "Now, remember. Our plan is to grab Andy. We're not looking for a fight."

Winna frowned. "If we're not going to keep Andy as a slave, then what are we going to do with him?"

"Use him to make this whole thing public. When La Padrona complains that we kidnapped her kid, you folks can explain why."

"Who would listen?"

"I think plenty of people," Brett said. "Grandfather Nathan gave me the impression that Acoma wasn't happy about her hunting after you. Even the other ranchers might not be thrilled. Once humans start using other humans as property, it sets a dangerous precedent."

He was pushing back his chair and grabbing his hat, planning to leave the others to confer in decent privacy, when the door was flung open. Rosamaria strode in, shutting the door firmly behind her.

"I listened," she said defiantly. "The window was open. I want to help."

Felicita said, "You will, *mija.* Someone's got to watch over the children. I don't think Carl's up to keeping them in line, especially since they're his brother and sisters."

"Aunt Winna should," Rosamaria said. "Anyhow, she'd be best to take care of Uncle Jerome. He's being a hero but, even with his leg set, he's got to hurt a lot. I held the basin while Aunt Winna washed him and he's all over bruises."

Brett considered. Rosamaria had already shown herself tough and stubborn. And Andy was a whole lot more likely to be dumb if he caught a glimpse of his prey, but Brett kept his thoughts to himself. This had to be between the kid and her folks.

Rosamaria continued, her voice sinking to a fierce whisper. "You think I don't know why we left Double A, but I'm not dumb and I'm not just a kid. Valerie was my friend and I know what Andy did to her. She told me and she cried because he kept doing it. A couple times he's come up to me, right in public, and said things about the nice big present he has for me on my birthday."

"Oh!" Felicita's soft gasp was pure pain. Emilio's expression was grim. Winna and Jerome looked uneasy.

Brett continued his interrupted departure. "You folks'll talk better without me listening, but I'll say one thing. Think about what she said."

The refugees resolved matters faster than Brett had dared hope. The Gallardo family would be backing Brett in Hole in the Wall. The Murchinsons would remain behind. It hadn't been an easy choice for anyone, but Brett was coming to see that lately these folks had made enough hard choices that one more didn't come as hard as it might have.

Even so, by the time they finished their confab, the day was already getting hot and midday was no time to cross the black rock of the malpais.

In the distance, thunderheads were building up, promising a storm to match that of the day before. First, Brett briefed Jerome and Winna on the various security precautions he'd made. Next he taught them the commands to work with Fida and Rover. Then he went out to set the decoy horses loose.

The afternoon rains came a touch earlier than the day before. "We'll go now," he said, when the worst of the storm had rolled passed.

Winna accepted baby Ignacio from Felicita. Both women's eyes were bright with tears, but neither admitted how scared they were.

Brett found a grin. "Don't you worry, Ms. Winna. I've got a few tricks to make sure Andy and his posse come right where we want 'em. Help yourself to whatever's in the garden and stores. We might not be back for supper, but with any luck you'll see us by this time tomorrow."

On the western side of the back thirty, Brett pulled a pueblo-style ladder from where he'd stowed it in a cleft in the rock. As he checked the lashings that held the crosspieces in place, Brett talked to ease the sudden tense expectancy.

"Thirty acres is a good pasture, but it isn't enough to support my horses through the winter. I've been cutting hay in Hole in the Wall since my first year."

Emilio raised his bushy eyebrows. "Hard work, that."

Brett shrugged. "Grass there's belly high on a tall horse, just like when the European's first came to this part of the world. It hasn't been over-grazed like so many other places around here. When the weeds got out of control at my parents' house, we'd have to cut 'em by hand, so I know how to use a scythe. I didn't want to always go the long way around, though, so I scouted a shorter way over the malpais. That's what we're taking.

"I'll point out my trail markers as we go," Brett continued as he led the way up the first ladder. "If we get separated, look for them. Don't trust your compasses. There's enough iron ore in the malpais to screw them up. My trail weaves about a bit, but there's a reason. All lava isn't the same. *Aa* will chew your boots to shreds. *Pahoehoe* gives better footing, but still can be tricky. Some of the basalt offers pretty good walking, other times a block that looks stable might wobble so you turn an ankle. I've filled in a couple of crevices, to make the route a touch more direct. Miss my bridges and you're going to have to go a long way around."

Rosamaria followed him up the ladder. "Those words—pah-hoy-hoy and ah-ah and kipuka—are they Indian words?"

"Hawaiian," Brett said, getting out the second ladder and setting it in place. "Their words for things you find in lava flows became sort of common currency. Even Grandfather Nathan uses them."

Brett climbed the second ladder, then looked down to check the others' progress. "Emilio, gloves on. I know it's hot, but if you grab the wrong rock, or stumble and tear up your hands, you're going to be no good to your wife and daughter."

When Brett checked at the top of the third ladder, he saw that Emilio had complied. All of them wore clothing that would blend into the reddish browns and blacks of the surrounding terrain. All wore broad-brimmed hats. Long hair—his own included—was tightly braided, so as not to get in the way. Each wore a bulky pack, topped with a rolled tarp.

As always when he emerged from within the kipuka's surrounding walls, Brett felt like a bug on a tabletop. The sense of being exposed was an illusion. The lava field was far from smooth. Although barren compared to the surrounding forested plains, it was not without vegetation— including trees. Slender aspen grew alongside scrubby piñon and juniper. There were ponderosa pines, Douglas fir, and rough barked alligator juniper. Vegetation tended to be widely scattered, taking advantage of moisture invisible to human or animal. Combined with erratic upthrusts of broken stone, there was ample cover.

Though Brett set a stiff pace, the Gallardos kept up with him. The rain had finished by the time they came to Brett's personal entry into Hole in the Wall.

"There're remnants of an old road over west," Brett said, waving a hand in the general direction. "We'll set our trap closer to that. Once we're down, you can take off your gloves, but keep a watch out for cactus and the like."

He saw Rosamaria roll her eyes.

"I know you've lived in New Mexico all your lives, but I'm just doing my job."

She flashed him a smile, part-embarrassed, completely amused. "Sorry."

After hiking over the uncertain footing of the malpais, the relatively regular footing down in the kipuka's grasslands made the next part of their journey seem easy. Eventually, they came to where the old trail in from the malpais merged into thick grass interspersed with scattered trees.

A denser copse of trees grew slightly west of the trail, near where a narrow streamlet augmented by runoff provided encouragement to vegetation.

Brett pointed to the copse. "I was thinking we should set up 'camp' there. Do you think we need to go farther in?"

Emilio shook his head. "If we'd just hiked three miles through malpais anywhere near as rough as what we crossed just now, I don't think we'd have gone much farther—not with the Murchinson kids. Along with our packs, we'd have had to carry Yolanda, Nancy, and our own Ignacio. Carl would be beat."

"We'd all be beat," Rosamaria said, wiping a hand across her forehead. "If I wasn't so scared they'll get here before we're ready, I'd just flop down."

Brett shrugged out of his pack. "I'm going to get a fire started. You folks set up tents. Do it just like you would have if you were really using this as a hideout."

They did so, choosing an area that offered some concealment in a patch of cottonwood and scrub growth. From their packs they took props to give the impression that their entire group was present. Felicita strung a line between two saplings and pinned some diapers and pair of Oscar's trousers on to it. Rosamaria carried a bucket over to the rain-fed streamlet and arranged it artistically.

Brett called, "Rosamaria, get me some wet grass—not soggy, but a bit more than damp. I'm going to need a fair amount."

The girl complied, streaking her shirt with mud in the process. "Why wet grass?"

"I want them to see our smoke," Brett explained. "Wet grass will create a darker smoke. The Indians used it when they sent smoke signals."

"Won't the posse be suspicious?" Emilio asked.

"Not after all the rain," Brett said. "They'd figure someone threw a bundle of damp wood on the fire. We can hope they find the horses, but, even if they don't, this should help them draw the 'right' conclusion."

"I hope the smoke shows far enough," Felicita said with soft intensity.

"If they don't see it, they're too dumb for the job," Brett said. "Leo and I were into smoke signals in junior high. You can see smoke for quite a distance."

After the dummy camp was set up and a few other arrangements made, they took turns keeping watch from a big piece of basalt that had calved off the lava wall a long time back. Brett was beginning to wonder if they might need to try fresh smoke in the morning when Rosamaria slid down and came running over, Brett's binoculars bouncing around her neck.

"They're coming! Eight men."

"Eight men," Brett repeated amused, "to go after four adults and a passel of children. They certainly think you jackalopes have horns."

"Jackalopes?" Rosamaria asked, too startled to object at being lumped in with the children.

Brett strung his bow. "I had a dream. Now, get to your places, folks. Remember they've got to think there are a lot more of you."

Reclaiming his binoculars from Rosamaria, Brett moved to a place he'd already marked as giving him a good vantage from which to cover the area with his bow. He wished he could have brought along Fida and Rover. A couple of guard dogs would have evened the odds a lot, but walking over the malpais would have ruined their paws. Even the wild creatures crossed the lava flow with care.

Careful to ensure that the westering sun didn't reflect off the lenses, Brett periodically checked the trail, picking up details as the group came closer. Eight men trudged along—uniformed in worn blue jeans, Western shirts, and broad-brimmed hats. Several wore sunglasses. Of them, only three—a sandy-haired fellow wearing a big Stetson, who Brett recognized as Andy Andrews, and the two closest behind him—looked at all eager. The other five just looked beat. Two of these were limping, one badly enough that he was leaning on a stick. One had his right hand bound up in a bandanna.

Not dressed for the malpais, Brett thought scornfully. *A couple are wearing riding boots, I bet, and not all of them are wearing gloves. They all have truncheons, though. I see at least three whips. Lassos. No bows or spears, but then they didn't want to kill anybody, just haul them back. Probably planned to grab a kid or two, use them to make the adults cooperate. Good plan if you're chasing rabbits, but these are jackalopes.*

One of their preparations had been to tromp a path through the grass in the vicinity of the "camp." The widest path led in from the trail, as if a whole group had trooped along it. Various narrower paths radiated out of the grove, presumably created when collecting firewood. Brett found himself impressed by the impression of activity created by these vegetative hieroglyphs. Within the shelter of the trees, Felicita was just visible, singing in Spanish to shadowy shapes that looked convincingly—at least from a distance—like a group of children. Out in the open, Rosamaria was tending the fire.

Brett held his breath, counting down. In a few steps, the first members of the posse would have a clear line of sight on the camp, then . . .

Andy strode down the trail as confidently as if he were on his own ranch. Maybe he fancied he was. Men often laid claim to lands they'd never seen. In addition to sandy hair and the oversize hat, Andy possessed an abundance of freckles. His build was lanky and his ears stuck out a little. He had strong shoulders, though, and the slightly bowlegged gait of a man who spent a lot of time in the saddle. Heir apparent to the Double A he might be, but he was no idler.

The two men backing him both looked like trouble. One was big and broad all over, with white-blond hair and a close-cut beard. From his time working at the Double A, Brett recognized him as a bull wrestler called the Finn. The other was darker, a young tough probably Brett's own age. His nose had been broken and inexpertly set, giving him an unbalanced look. As they came forward, the Finn uncoiled a bullwhip with an easy grace that said he knew how to use it. The Tough only smiled, showing a broken front tooth in an unlovely grin.

Andy Andersen called out, "What's for dinner, *chiquita?* Where's your dad and Jerome Murchinson?"

Rosamaria froze. Brett didn't think the fear on her face was all play-acting, but her voice was only a little higher and tighter when she answered.

"They're setting snares. Aunt Winna's off with Carl, digging some sort of roots for tomorrow's dinner. We had to leave some of our supplies, so I can't offer you much for dinner."

She rose. If a piece of the sapling she'd been feeding the fire remained in her hand, it looked like an oversight. Felicita had stopped singing and could be heard hushing frightened children. She did the voices for them, too. Brett was impressed.

"So you and your mama are all alone except for the bambinos, eh?" Andy's use of Spanish was flawed, like something learned from a television Western. "And here we were all ready to escort you home. I guess while we wait, we should come in and get warm."

Given that the temperature had gone back up into the eighties following the rain, it was very clear that Andy didn't have the fire in mind for warming himself. When Rosamaria gave a nervous nod, Andy strode along the wide path that led into camp. The Tough fanned left, moving toward the tents under the trees, while the Finn fanned right, obviously moving to where he could strike with the whip. The other five men had slowed. One of the footsore ones sat on a rock and started working off a boot. The one with the hurt hand was eyeing the stream, clearly thinking about soaking his wound.

The two hale ones were scanning the area, looking for the absent members of the group. They didn't look too worried, though. After all, they had women and children as hostages.

They're overconfident. Maybe some aren't crazy about Master Andy's hunt. They've followed, but they're not going to make it easy for him. The Finn, though. He's dangerous. The other one . . . He's just mean.

Brett fit an arrow to his bowstring. He kept his gaze on Andy, silently counting off each stride: "One step, two, three . . . Now!"

As Andy passed between two trees, a sharp snap broke the uneasy hush.

"God damn!" The young rancher struggled to keep his balance.

Brett knew that his legs were looped in wire snares hidden in the grass. Without waiting to see how tightly Andy had been caught, Brett drew back his bowstring and shot at the Finn. He didn't want to kill the man, but that whip couldn't be allowed to get into play. His first arrow passed through the man's upper torso, his second caught him in the thigh.

The Tough, no idiot, rushed at Felicita, looking to secure hostages. Running at her, arms outstretched to grab a woman encumbered by a baby, he discovered just how much a length of wood, even when wrapped in a baby blanket, can hurt. He went down, his nose broken yet again. Felicita hit him a second blow, this time on the back of the head, and he stayed down.

Rosamaria, her length of firewood gripped firmly in both hands, darted over and walloped the struggling Andy. Brett had been worried the girl wouldn't be strong enough to do any real damage, but figured he'd cut over to help her. He didn't bother. Whether from fury at what Andy had planned to do to her or in memory of her dead friend, Rosa-maria proved that a solid length of greenwood, when wielded by a furious fourteen-year-old, could be a punishing weapon.

Brett ran to assist Emilio, who had been hidden to one side of the trail, in securing the remaining five. Only two proved much of a problem and when Brett—a completely unknown quantity—came out from cover, swinging a stone-headed war club, a rage-filled scream on his lips, they surrendered at once. Brett was almost disappointed. He'd wanted to strike out for so long, but reason, speaking with Leo's voice, said, "These men didn't do it. They didn't kill your family. They didn't crash my plane. Let them pay for the crimes they've committed, no more."

By the time he and Emilio had secured the five stragglers, Brett saw that Rosamaria and Felicita had gotten Andy tied. They'd left the young rancher where he was rather than risk letting him loose from the snares that fouled his ankles. With his hat knocked off and his shirt torn, bruises already purpling where Rosamaria had hit him, Andy Andersen looked young and frightened. Remembering rapes past and intended, dead girls and unacknowledged bastards, Brett felt no pity for him.

The Tough probably had a concussion, but they trussed him up anyhow. The Finn was the most seriously injured, but he'd had plenty of muscle and the arrows hadn't gone deep. Brett patched him up and thought that if infection didn't set in, he'd likely live. He looked like the type who was distilled from equal parts piss and vinegar.

"Now," Brett said slowly, "I think it's time we had a talk."

Two weeks later, the first ever regional conference and inquiry met at Acoma, this being not only the closest to a midpoint between Grants and the ranches south of El Malpais, but also near where many of the witnesses lived. Representatives came from Grants, San Rafael, Zuni, Laguna, local ranches, and from various Navajo bands. Even a few rugged Apache warriors, their faces streaked red and yellow, showed up.

The issue at hand was forming local policy regarding various forms of human servitude, up to and including slavery. Accusations of attempted enslavement were made against Annabella Andersen and her eldest son, Andrew: to wit, that they had restricted the freedom of unindebted members of the Double A community and that when, having decided to try their lot elsewhere, some of these had intended to leave, the Andersens had sent a posse to retrieve them by force.

Brett testified, as did members of the Gallardo and Murchinson families, and elders of Acoma pueblo. These last testified to having been asked about the whereabouts of the missing parties in a fashion that might have been interpreted as threatening, if the elders had been inclined to take it so. (Which, of course, they had not been, something they managed to make clear, while at the same time also making clear they hadn't much liked being threatened.)

In the course of the Gallardo and Murchinson testimony, Andy Andersen's forcing of his dubious charms on the women of the Double A was mentioned as the impetus for their flight. This did not support the Andersens' depiction of the Double A as a strong, vital, healthy community that no one would ever wish to leave.

The Andersens' assertion that the riders had been sent out when the Gallardos and Murchinsons had failed to return from a picnic fell apart when several of the cowhands testified. These men told not only how they had been ordered to bring back the Murchinson and Gallardo families, but how subtle threats had been made regarding the continuation of their own livelihoods and the safety of their dear ones. This testimony in particular brought home how easy it was—especially in the absence of a larger community upholding agreed upon standards of behavior—for a few powerful people to ignore the rights of the individual.

When the inquiry had adjourned, having made clear that slavery would not be tolerated and that other forms of servitude needed to be monitored, the Gallardos and Murchinsons invited Brett Hawke and Nathan Tso to share a meal at the house in Lower Acoma where they were currently staying.

"San Rafael made clear we are welcome," Winna said, passing around a platter of carne adovada burritos, "but Acoma has offered us a family compound in Acomita, along with a winter stipend, since it's late for us to put in crops. I'm going to start a clinic. We've been promised help starting a forge as well."

"It will be easier for us to visit the Double A from Acomita," Emilio added as he poured everyone strong mint tea with honey. "We still have friends there, and La Padrona will be more careful knowing we're looking in."

"I think," said Nathan Tso, "there will be much more 'looking in' between communities from here forward. Already there is discussion of seasonal festivals to make certain that we remember all we have in common. It has been too easy to believe that apart is safest. Recent events remind us that it is not."

Brett knew Nathan's words were intended for him. Leaning forward, elbows on knees, he forced himself to speak, although, since the immediate crisis had ended, the pull of silence and solitude was very strong.

"I've been thanked over and over for what I did," he said slowly. "But I need to do some thanking myself." He looked to where Felicita cradled Ignacio, finding speech easier if he focused on just one person. "When we talked that night, I began to realize that I wasn't so much angry at God as at me. I blamed myself for everything that had happened. I blamed myself for not saving the animals at the pet store. I felt that what had happened to my family was somehow punishment for that failure. I even blamed myself for Leo's death because, if he hadn't been flying back to celebrate Saint Patrick's Day with us at Cloverleaf, he would have been safely on the ground—and if anyone could have managed to make it back from Denver, it would have been Leo."

Several voices started to offer reassurance, but Brett waved them down.

"I know. You don't have to say it. So I hid myself away, trying to make amends by protecting what little I had left. If I hadn't had to lay in supplies to keep my critters alive, I might never have come out of that kipuka."

He managed a twisted smile. "But when I saw jackrabbits growing horns, fighting for the best lives for themselves and their children, willing to take risks to expose a danger they had escaped . . . When I saw Rosamaria stand out in the open as bait for a man who meant her harm—that's when I realized there could be more. I had chosen not to die.

"Now I see that I need to learn how to live."

THE NEW NORMAL

BY JODY LYNN NYE

Jody Lynn Nye

I write science fiction and fantasy, mostly of the humorous variety, although I explore many different settings and universes. Steve's world touches upon a sneaking paranoia many of us have: Could we survive if the machinery that makes current civilization what it is suddenly stopped functioning? It's not a new notion that those of us who are a part of back-to-Earth movements and the New Middle Ages would be better fit to cope than those who rely too heavily upon technology for survival, let alone entertainment. I also love the New Forest in Hampshire, U.K., both for its beauty and its history. I was inspired by a single mention in *The Protector's War* of a small coven who had managed to survive there, and the rest is where the thought took me.

"**B**rung y' another one, doc," Tim Brunton said, leaning in the kitchen door of the Alice Lisle pub. He was liberally smeared with blood, and there was a body draped over one huge shoulder. "Martin got bit by one of them Eaters."

Dr. Rebecca Saltford looked up, from the Bunsen burner she was nursing, at the big man, his rusty hair disheveled over his broad forehead. He grinned. His yellow teeth, splayed in a dozen directions, whether by Mother Nature or the many football brawls he had participated in over the years in which there had been football, gleamed in his filthy face. He edged sideways into the flagstone-floored room and dumped his unconscious colleague on the scrubbed metal table in the center.

In better days, it had been used for food preparation. Since the Change, it had become Dr. Saltford's surgery. Tim stripped the protective pads off his friend and removed the plastic and leather helmet to reveal a gash in his forehead and a deep bite mark in the patient's right arm. One of Rebecca's two teenage assistants, Nora Lytton, dipped a bucket of water from the barrel just inside the door and began to clean him up with a sponge. Water mixed with a few precious ounces of Dettol attacked the mucky mix. Blood and mud dribbled to the floor around their feet, which Stephen Dobbs mopped away. The dark-skinned man on the table moaned and stirred slightly.

From long experience, having delivered his burden, Tim retreated to the doorway, where he wouldn't be in the way. Rebecca shot him a look of reproof.

"Really, Tim, you cannot keep baiting those cannibals! One of these days they will trail you back to this place, and then where will the rest of us be?"

"Sorry, doc," Tim said sheepishly, his booted feet scuffing the floor.

He was twenty-five, but she could reduce him in a sentence to an eight-year-old.

"But we gotta clean them out, or it's us for the stew pot. We took out seven of 'em. Last one tried to take a bite out o' both of us."

He held out a wrist, but the only mark was on his filthy vambrace. Everyone who could fight to defend the settlement wore some kind of makeshift armor. Tim was too large to wear any that they had taken from Buckler's Hard Maritime Museum, but he had fashioned himself the nearest equivalent from motorcycle leathers and football gear.

Rebecca relented and smiled at him.

"Well, I'm grateful to you. The gods must be at your side, my lad. I give thanks for your safe return."

His big shoulders relaxed. She moved the burning candles to a safer distance from the bottom of the retort and its attached spiraled tubing. She had only six retorts left. Laboratory glass, however breakage-resistant, was irreplaceable, as were so many things these days. It was a wonder how much she had once owned, and how she had been reduced to the barest of bare necessities. Everything had to be treated with the greatest of care. A fruity whiff escaped from the clear liquid in the three gallon receiving bottle.

"Sure there's none of that to drink, missus?" Tim asked hopefully.

"No, you great oaf," Rebecca said, for perhaps the thousandth time. "It's wood alcohol. It will blind or kill you. It's for medicinal use only, to sanitize the utensils."

"You could make the real stuff," Tim said. "I miss a tipple, bad."

"I know." She sighed.

In her mind's eye, she could still see the neat bottles from Oddbins on the drinks trolley in her tidy sitting room. The house had burned with a thousand of its neighbors in the first month. The coven had long ago drunk up the contents of the cellar of this pub, what hadn't been stolen by other raiders in the first few days after the Change.

"I wish I could have a nice chardonnay or a good real ale in the evening myself. Hold on for a while yet, will you? We're doing our best."

Tim nodded toward Martin. "Will he be right?"

Donning a cotton cap over her graying chestnut curls and a pair of gloves with fancy cuffs better suited to plunging into a sink filled with Fairy Liquid foam, Rebecca mounted the box next to the table to look down at him. She wished that the steel legs could be reduced so her five foot two inch height did not put her at such a disadvantage while operating. She touched the pulse point in the right side of the man's neck and counted. "Ninety beats per minute. A little elevated, but fine. He'll do."

"Sorry about the mess, mum," Tim said. "He took the brunt of it."

"You're doing the work I can't. I'm grateful, lad. Go on and get yourself cleaned up. Have you reported to Ben yet? Stuart is cooking the meal tonight."

Tim wrinkled his nose.

"That'll mean stew," he said. "Stew Stu. That man can make a potato feed sixteen."

"And aren't you glad he can?" Rebecca said, with a wry smile. "Go along and let me concentrate."

The big man fled, and Rebecca warded the door after him with two fingers, closing the circle she habitually drew at the beginning of her workday. Everything she did in her surgery, she considered sacred to the gods. When she took the Hippocratic Oath at medical school, she swore by the Greek god Asclepius, but in her mind she pictured the goddesses Brigid and Eir, her patrons.

Three years, three terrible years, since the day everything stopped working. Rebecca had been called to help, along with every other medic, EMT, nurse, surgeon, and herbalist in the Southampton area, to save those who had been in collisions or trapped by machinery. It was no good arguing that she was an obstetrician/gynecologist with little surgical experience but for Caesarian sections and episiotomies. Everyone had pulled together in true English fashion, and done their best for their fellow man and woman. It was only when it slowly became evident that nothing was going to begin to work that the accusations, riots, then actual horrors began. She hated to relive those days, and dismissed them from her mind to concentrate on the poor man on the table.

She always began with a short prayer. The room was always warded, day in and out, as a matter of habit. She blessed herself and her two assistants standing by. Nora and Stephen pushed forward draped utensil trays, one with neatly folded boiled rags and pots of homemade salve, and the other with a tray of sterilized needles threaded with nylon fishing line. In happier times, those rolling carts had been dessert trolleys in the pub's dining room. With two fingers, she drew an invoking pentacle over the man's heart.

"Hail, guardians of the watchtowers, lord of death and rebirth and lady of life and love, be here now! Bless thy servant Martin here. Breathe with his breath, course with his blood, be strong in his bones. Let all darkness be cast forth from him and health return to him. So mote it be."

Her apprentices echoed behind her, "So mote it be."

She cleaned the wounds and prepared to stitch them. Surgical sutures were long gone. Dissolving stitches were a thing of the past. For internal injuries, when she stood a chance of saving the patient, she used biodegradable materials such as her dwindling supply of silk, counting on the patient's own healthy immune system to dispose of it once the trauma had resolved. For surface injuries, she used everything from fishing line to embroidery thread. She could no longer be fussy, nor could her patients. The knot of refugees living there in the New Forest couldn't spare anything. Not food. Not drink. And certainly not lives.

The Beech Grove Coven had met in the New Forest, probably since time immemorial, but certainly since Gerald Gardner had revived the Old Religion in the 1950s. Rebecca's parents had been among his devotees. Not so strange, if one thought about it. Carvings in churches had always featured images of the Green Man, with a face made of oak leaves.

The fact was, she reminded herself, that if one scratched even the most fervent British Christian, one touched a pagan core who leaped over bonfires under the full moon.

The coven in its heyday was large by any standard, up to forty souls who attended the solstices and equinoxes, if not the esbats in between. She had been Beech Grove's high priestess since old Mary Valentine had retired. Rebecca's husband had been its high priest far longer, after Mary's husband had died. Rebecca herself had been without a regular high priest for three years. Noel had traveled to London on the morning of the Change. After three years, she had admitted he wasn't ever coming home again. She had known the truth far longer. Ben Glass had substituted for him willingly, but it was time she acknowledged his place at her side and in her heart.

When the disaster had struck, Rebecca and all her fellow medical professionals had attended the scenes of accidents and fires, doing their best to save the victims, using whatever supplies they could find. No one had survived any of the hundreds of planes that had crashed on their way to or from British airports. Momentum had caused numerous train wrecks and boat catastrophes. Everyone, no matter of what origin, pulled together at that time and become splendidly, cooperatively English.

Within weeks, though, when the Change did not change back, Rebecca fled Southampton with her three children, trying not to look as desperate as she felt. She begged a ride across Hamble Water on a rowboat that had taken the place of the Hythe Ferry, paying with her gold wristwatch. Hidden in her holdall under magazines and a spare jumper were all the medical implements she could carry. A hysterical woman had ripped her Coach purse from her shoulder as soon as she came ashore and run off with it. Rebecca had let her go. Nothing in it was of any value any longer, not her mobile phone, not her electronic car key fob, or really her Lancôme cosmetics, and especially not the thirty pounds in notes or her credit cards. Only the skill in her hands and the knowledge in her head were of any value any longer. Her ordeal had not yet ended. Desperate men surrounded her, reaching for the holdall. The children cowered around her. The men were beaten back by the sudden appearance of a rearing horse and a riding crop in their faces. Rebecca had looked up to see a dark-haired man on a dappled horse. It was Ben Glass.

"I would never let anything happen to you, my lady," he had said. Rebecca felt her heart turn inside her with relief and dread. He had realized, as she had not, that her husband was gone, almost certainly for good. She could not, would not, believe it. Not then. But Ben was always at her side from then on.

He helped her up on pillion behind him on Dinnie the gelding, baggage and all. Together, they retreated to the New Forest, along with her three children and most of the coven, not a day before the real atrocities began. Rebecca knew very well that almost all the visitors to the forest never penetrated beyond a hundred yards or so from the car parks, leaving the rest of the wilderness to the rangers, wardens, and such enthusiasts as her family. Thank all gods, she had thought, that reluctance to brave the woods still held true. Occupation of the enclosure was in defiance of the rules and the regulations of the Royal Forestry Commission that employed Ben, but those who had made the rules never anticipated what would follow the death of civilization.

As well as she knew the ins and outs of the great forest founded by William the Conqueror in 1079, Ben knew it better. He had been a forester for eleven years. He kept the group moving from place to place, always hiding the traces of their passage from those who would follow and kill. What he did to prevent the enemy from pursuing them, she didn't ask and really didn't want to know.

Ben never pushed the reality in her face, and she did not want him to stop doing what he was doing. He was a natural leader, and she was grateful for his take-charge ways. She didn't mind sewing up the wounds or bandaging the bruises as long as she didn't have to watch them being inflicted.

Rebecca hated herself for being so squeamishly suburban. A few of the other adults felt the same way. On the other hand, the nine children, her three among them, all aged ten to eighteen, had become scouts in his small army, then fighters, helping to defend their small group from raiders and worse. Her youngest, James, had become a deadly archer who could make his own arrows with pheasant feathers. All she was called upon to do was heal, soothe, and organize—three skills she was glad to employ toward their survival.

Their numbers had dropped horribly and irrevocably during the starvation times that followed. The first winter was the worst. It nearly broke the coven into bits numerous times. Only hope and faith and a firm attitude on her part and a good deal of raiding from now tragically empty suburban homes on Ben's part kept them alive through the cold season and the hungry spring that followed. All of them had to dismiss their scruples on what constituted housebreaking or looting. Mary Valentine, the eldest and last of the OAPs who survived, preached the litany of "make do and mend." She also told them about the victory gardens of her youth. With the help of her son, Frank, a keen gardener who was not a Wiccan but indulged his mother in her faith, Beech Grove started miniature farms all over the New Forest that next spring. Wherever there was an open bit of ground, shielded by bracken, gorse, or bramble, the thirty-odd members of Beech Grove planted whatever seeds and tubers they could find. Though a number of the plants were uprooted by hungry animals and the desperate survivors outside the coven, enough food grew to keep them alive, if thin as wraiths. It surprised them all how many natural foodstuffs were to be found in the Forest. They supplemented the small crops with hazelnuts, beechnuts, herbs, tree fruit, and acorns, plus whatever fish, deer and, with immense regret, a few of the remaining New Forest ponies they could hunt for protein. They lived on swedes, turnips, potatoes, and other root vegetables, too boring during most times, but desperately welcomed now. If Rebecca could avoid ever being reminded of acorn bread, she would be grateful beyond words to the Goddess.

Frank and Ellie Valentine had come to her in April with an almost priceless treasure. Undiscovered in the back of the abandoned garden center just off the A326 was a bag of seed barley. Rebecca could have cried for joy. With a liberated scratch-plow pulled by Dinnie, they sowed a field and guarded it night and day until the seed sprouted. The group created a rota to hoe and weed. They used the old means of driving pests away, including scarecrows. Unfortunately, the hungry deer and ponies saw it as an open buffet lunch. Their scrawny carcasses added to the larder of the coven.

The first harvest was small, but the dusty-golden grain heads nodding heavily on their stalks raised everyone's spirits. At summer solstice, the Valentines proudly served barley bread, baked with sodium bitartrate gleaned from the skins of their wine grapes as a leavening. The loaves were broken up and shared with the gods, then devoured. The rest of the barley had gone to soups and morning porridge, with a precious tenth set aside for the next crop, but bread was a sign of normalcy returning.

At all the festivals and esbats, Rebecca, with Ben acting as her high priest, gave thanks for the gifts of food and survival. Come the fall, they made a thin, sour wine from the wild grapevines that twined everywhere up the sturdy, shaggy trunks of the oaks, and shared it at the rituals. Every other crumb or drop was hoarded against the winter, which they spent in a longhouse constructed from wooden fences ripped from the back gardens of every housing estate within half a day's trot and insulated with blocks of polystyrene. The longhouse was not a pretty sight, made as it was to blend with the undergrowth, but Ben warned them against using any of the surviving houses or inns until this third year, when they moved into the old red-brick pub, still with its FULLER'S ALE sign on the crumbling facade. They all slept in the great room, warmed by a log fire burning in the huge hearth they now used for cooking. Rebecca still missed her three-bar fire and her comfortable sitting room and the cryptic crossword in the newspaper of an evening and knew the others did, too, but she was impressed that everyone had adapted so well to living in primitive conditions. On the other hand, not one of them was more than three generations from an outdoor toilet in the back garden, nor five from cooking over a wood or peat fire.

Starvation, of course, was not their only enemy. As a doctor, she oversaw the construction of reasonably hygienic pit toilets to prevent the group from suffering cholera, but they passed influenza and colds around to one another like a favorite book. Everyone broke a bone or so, or gashed themselves doing chores. Or were injured by raiders or worse, like this poor lad here. Rebecca made sure the bleeding had stopped, then cleaned out the wound with saline from a squeeze bottle that had once held malt vinegar.

At the first thrust of the needle, Martin woke up. His dark brown eyes opened, staring at her in terror.

"Aaagh!" he cried. It was clear he didn't recognize her. The assistants leaped to hold him down. They had had a great deal of practice. Rebecca murmured to him, trying to keep from hurting him, or vice versa.

"It's Dr. Saltford, Martin. I'm sewing up the wound on your forehead. Now, hold still, there's a good lad. Brigid is with you."

The young man squeezed his eyes shut and held on to the edge of the steel prep table with both hands. Rebecca murmured to him soothingly throughout the rest of the operation. He'd have a scar worthy of Harry Potter, but if that was the worst that ever happened to him, he'd do fine.

She laid dressings over the wound and tied them in place with strips of sterilized cotton cloth. The bandages were printed with a cheerful pattern of flowers and butterflies. They had come from a hoard of quilting fabrics taken from a house on the edge of Dibden. The men scoffed when she insisted they bring it all back to the longhouse, but they'd ended up wearing a good deal of it over their many injuries since then.

And some of them had been sewn into shrouds made from that same wildly colorful cloth. Even with modern medical techniques, she couldn't have saved some of the wounded, not with what humans' inhumanity to others had become. She had had to learn to give mercy as well as healing. As one who took her Hippocratic oath seriously, it had been hard to learn to let patients die. She had no choice now.

Wearily, she washed herself and helped clean the operating room.

Ben was waiting for her in the garden at a rough table and bench hewed from whole logs. She studied him fondly. With the broad-brimmed hat to shield his eyes from the sun and the shaggy cloak he wore, he could have been a seventeenth century highwayman or Odin with both eyes intact. He wore a beard now, which he kept trimmed neatly to a point. It suited him. He studied her, too, then reached for the straw-lined basket in the center of the table and poured steaming liquid into a cup. She drank the tea gratefully.

"Will he live?" Ben asked. "Martin's my second-best man after Tim."

"I think so," Rebecca said. She finished the tea and held out a hand against a refill. Ben put the pot back into its protective basket. He stood up and helped her to her feet.

"Come and see the crops," he said. "I have a surprise for you."

Though she was tired from her surgery and the morning antenatal class with the two girls who had fallen pregnant over the last few months, curiosity stirred her enough to put on her Wellington boots and follow him. His hunting hounds, an assortment of sight hounds of all varieties, trotted obediently at their heels.

How strangely silent the Forest had become. In the old days, the susurrus of distant traffic had been a constant undertone. Now the song of larks and cuckoos rang out clear in the bright sky. They passed the longhouse, now used as storage for food. It was constantly patrolled by their young scouts and by a troupe of cats who traded their rat-assassin skills for fish and the remains from the evening meals. Close by was the grove of beeches that had given the coven its name, surrounding the stump of an ancient tree that acted as their altar. The woods were full of bluebells from April to mid-May. Their perfume was her favorite scent on Earth.

Ben held her hand firm in his, helping her over the uneven ground. Rockford Common stood almost chest-deep in grass and gorse after three years without cattle grazing. The sheer height of the greenery concealed their cultivation from easy observation. They waded across the small, brown forest stream with stickleback fry hovering in the clear water. Up the hill and over it, past an enormous blackberry bramble that was their landmark, Ben parted the grasses to let her see. She gasped with wonder. The barley was easily double or triple the previous year's crop.

"'England's green and pleasant land,' indeed," she said, with pleasure. "We won't run out this winter, not even with more mouths to feed."

"I have a mind to use it for more than bread and soup," Ben said. He swept up a punnet that sat on the ground at the corner of the field and presented it to her. "My wedding gift to you at the solstice next week, my lady dear."

A wave of heady perfume rose from the mass of tight little white blossoms nestled within it.

"Hops?" she asked, hardly daring to believe it.

"Aye," he said, thickening his natural lilt to a countryman's drawl, and matching her delighted grin with his own. "We'll have beer to drink to the longest day and our future together."

"So mote it be," Rebecca said.

Brewing was a messy and smelly job that was impossible to conceal. Ben and Rebecca had to resort to all the tools in their power to prevent anyone tapping the tanks in the microbrewery before the beer was ready. At the crack of dawn on the solstice, almost before the birds were up and singing, all twenty-three surviving souls put on the best clothes they had left. Julie wore a new dress she had made herself entirely out of scavenged T-shirts. The entire coven assembled in the Alice Lisle's microbrewery and waited avidly around the enormous copper tank. With solemn ceremony, Ben opened the cock and let the golden beer pour into a waiting keg. Rebecca thrust a huge tankard under the stream, poured a little on the stone floor for the gods and took a sip, and sighed with pleasure. The heady, yeasty scent tickled her nose, and the flavor made her tongue dance. It was good! Though she longed to drain the whole mug, she passed it to Ben. The first taste was only ceremonial. He held the beaker high.

"To a new day, my friends! Let the festivities begin."

The others cheered. He drank and handed the tankard to Mary Valentine with a bow and a flourish.

Beer, Rebecca thought in delight, watching him. *Beer, celebration, and love.* The latter thought made her heart twist with regret. She glanced at her children, each taking their sips from the big pewter mug and making faces at the strong flavor. *Ah, Noel, you'd be so proud of them.* But, as always, Ben was watching her, too. He reached out to touch her chin with his calloused fingertips.

"Now, now, my dear," he said. "This is the new normal. It'll be good. You'll see. We can live with this."

The day started out with a surprise for the adults. The children had been very secretive, whispering to one another in the shadowed corner of the sleeping room. Nora came around with wreaths of climbing roses and ivy for everyone's head. Rebecca shook down her hair under the fragrant circlet, feeling quite like a girl again. Ben wrapped his right arm around her, squeezing her tight. Then, to the strains of Tim's acoustic guitar, the children sang the ancient lay, "Sumer is A-Cumen In," with acrobatic dancing that would have done credit to Cirque du Soleil. The adults battered their palms with applause. The children bowed, gratified, but were even more delighted when Rebecca rewarded them with a rare treat of barley sugar candy.

Nearly everyone had a turn at the impromptu cabaret. Tim knew every word of every skit ever performed by Monty Python, and chanted Eric Idle's scurrilous "Philosopher's Song," to the cheers and whoops of his audience. Frank Valentine had been practicing in secret with a whip, and took a mug off his very trusting wife's head without hitting her.

A feast was laid out upon the pitted, elderly wooden tables. Sweet young peas still in the shell went down like candy as an appetizer. Roasted haunch of venison surrounded by tasty browned parsnips and carrots put everyone in a good mood. Rebecca had permitted a drain on the larder that she would never allow at other times, but this was a doubly joyous occasion. Ben went from person to person filling their mugs from a pitcher refreshed often from the first of the wooden kegs.

"Drink up, friends! There's five barrels to get through!" he announced. The others cheered.

"Two for today only," Rebecca corrected him. "Ethanol poisoning is no joke, and you have all lost your tolerance. Don't be silly. Today's an important festival."

"Enjoy yourself, love," Ben said, stooping to kiss the serious look off her face. "It's our wedding day. Remember the Goddess' charge. Reverence and mirth, both. Don't be a doctor for once. Be the priestess and my bride."

She put in the effort to let go of her most serious self, and found it was easier than she had thought. As Tim played tune after tune, she danced in a circle with her children and Ben.

"Are you happy to let him be your step-papa?" she had asked them again and again after Ben had proposed. "You know he will never replace your father, but Ben loves you."

"We're fine, Mum," David had assured her. Julie and James added their assent. "He's pretty great, you know."

"Yes," Rebecca remembered saying, and meaning it from the depths of her heart. "He is."

So it was no trouble, in the midst of the evening's rite after sunset, following the prayers for the midsummer, to stand before the candle- and flower-laden altar in the greenwood, hands bound together with a silk scarf, to repeat the words of the ancient vow. Fragrant resin gathered from fir trees that had come to substitute for the frankincense they could no longer obtain wafted its sacred scent upon the air. They took the aspects of God and Goddess into themselves, but also remained priest and priestess, man and woman.

"I, Rebecca, plight thee, Ben, my troth . . ." He repeated the vow, with their names reversed. No one needed to marry them to each other. They were priest and priestess, and the gods were eminently present, in tree, root and leaf, in bird and beast, in water and sky, and in the hearts of their loved ones around them. Her heart welling with joy, Rebecca kissed him. Ben wrapped her in his arms and picked her right up off the ground, squeezing her so tightly her ribs squeaked. She couldn't wait until the evening was over, so they could sneak away and consummate their marriage. By the light shining in his eyes, neither could he. Everyone cheered. Tim whistled and stamped.

A wind blew up suddenly, bringing with it a foul odor. The flames of the point candles danced, and two of them went out.

"Pretty, very pretty," said a man's voice. "What's this, a Renaissance fair?"

Rebecca spun. Everyone reached for their weapons, which were never far away. James slipped an arrow onto his bow.

Three men in canvas trousers and heavy leather jackets stumped toward them, hunting bows stretched in their hands with razor-pointed arrows nocked. Rebecca's heart pounded in her chest. They didn't look like the crazed cannibals that had stalked them before. They certainly weren't king's men. They were too filthy, and none of them had a badge on his sleeve. The weapons in their belts looked well used and well handled.

"Smelled your fires and thought we'd join you," said the leader, a stocky man of middle height. His brown hair was going gray at the temples, and he was missing two teeth in the front.

Rebecca glanced at Ben. Normally, two or more of the scouts would have been on watch outside the grove, probably up one of the enormous trees. It had been days since anyone had tried to attack their home, so he had taken a chance on allowing everyone to be in the circle for the festival.

More fool us, Rebecca thought. She trembled, but to her surprise, she stretched out her hand to the men.

"Welcome," she said. "We're celebrating the summer solstice."

"Witches?" the man at the leader's left shoulder asked.

"Nature worshippers," Rebecca said.

"We never put spells on people who don't deserve it," Mary Valentine said, her little dried walnut of a face set. All three arrows came around to point at her.

"Shh, Mum!" Frank Valentine hissed.

Ben glanced at Rebecca. She knew what he was thinking. Where had they come from, and how many of them were there? Their group was so small. While they might overmatch three men, they'd almost certainly lose one or more of their number, and what if there was an army of brutes in the shadows?

"I'm Ben and this is my wife, Rebecca," Ben said. "We're about to have our supper. Join us."

"We'll always take food," the first man said, trying not to look too eager. "Call me Boss Green. This is Jax and Tiger. Toss over all your weapons. Now! Not taking a knife in the ribs from someone who wants to be a hero."

Ben nodded carefully, and signaled to the others to comply. Rebecca tried to sum up the men. They were lean, as who wasn't these days, but fit as fighting dogs. Their gums and skin looked horrible, hinting that their diet was inadequate. They certainly hadn't been as well fed as Beech Grove. An idea began to form in her mind.

"We have food," she said. "And beer."

"Beer?" Even Boss Green's muddy eyes lit up at the word. He let the bowstring relax. "Hell's bells, where the fook did you find beer three years after the end of the world?"

"We made it," Ben said, giving his new wife a strange look. "Just tapped today. Come and try it."

Rebecca couldn't enjoy a mouthful of the succulent roast boar she ate. She was too worried about her children, who sat on their benches at the far end of the long table, pretending they weren't scared and wary. The strangers tore at their meat like the starving wolves that they were, and guzzled down beer as if to put out fires in their bellies. The pitch-soaked torches that lit the feast made the visitors look like demons.

In spite of their greed, the strangers were still cautious. They kept their feet on top of the pile of swords and bows they had taken. They had even collected the ritual athames.

"Why do you want to know where we live?" Boss Green demanded, angrily, as Ben asked for the seventh or eighth time. He pounded a fist on the tabletop, making the chewed bones around his platter jump.

"Well, there are only a few of us left practically in the world," Ben said, leaning back to show he was at ease. He toyed with his single glass of beer. "Stands to reason we might all join up. Against them cannibals out there and all."

"Don't want to join up with no witches," Tiger said, grouchily. The beer was beginning to affect him, but not quickly enough for Rebecca's taste. "T'others won't like it, neither."

"Sha!" Boss Green snapped. Tiger stopped talking and drained his glass. He waved to Nora to come and refill it. She did, although she had to keep dodging the hand he tried to put on her backside.

Others? Rebecca exchanged glances with Ben. Not close by, though, or he might have summoned them when he realized there were only twenty-three in Beech Grove.

"Well, perhaps you can take a vote on it," Ben said. "If there are a lot of you, we might move close to where you are instead of the other way around."

"What do you live in?" Boss Green asked. His voice was starting to slur, but he still sounded too alert.

"Huts," Rebecca said at once. "Lean-tos, mostly. We built them from garden fences. They're very cozy."

"Not a chance in hell. Got better digs." Boss Green realized that he was starting to speak too freely. He pulled himself to his feet. Curses! Rebecca thought. "Got to go. Men!" His bark brought Tiger and Jax upright. "Take the weapons. They ain't so good as ours, but better we have 'em then they."

"Thank you for joining us," Rebecca said. "Merry meet and merry part."

Boss Green spun to level a glare full of hate at her.

"You'll stop that pagan shite when we're done with you, madam," he said. "Maybe you'll be one of my wives instead of this mealy-mouthed bastard." He threw a scornful gesture in Ben's direction. Tim growled, and Boss Green pointed a dangerous finger in his direction. "Be back soon. Count on it."

Rebecca's belly roiled with seething anger and fear. If she had a knife, she might actually throw it into this monster's eye. She never wanted them to come back. If they made it out of the woods, a horde of barbarians would come and destroy the place that was just beginning to feel like home. They had nowhere else to go!

The idea that had been dancing in her mind came roaring to the fore, demanding to be heard. It was their only chance. The only thing she could think of. But she hesitated. What else could she do?

THE NEW NORMAL 551

"Wait," she said, standing up. She held out both hands to them. "It's the summer solstice and our wedding day. Let us give you a gift."

Boss Green echoed it uneasily.

"A gift?"

"You liked our beer," she said. She forced a trembling smile to her lips. "I have something special that I was saving for our full moon celebration later on, but I'd rather use it to seal our new friendship. Moonshine, the Americans call it. Grain alcohol."

"Moonshine?" Boss Green asked, his expression incredulous.

"It's absolutely delicious, but I couldn't let the children have it. It's too strong. Tim, won't you go and get it for me?"

Tim's small eyes widened, but he caught her meaning immediately.

"Do we have to give it to 'em, mum?" he asked, reluctantly. Thank all gods, the lad was a born Olivier.

"Yes, we do," Rebecca said. "Go."

The young man dashed off into the darkness, too swiftly for either Tiger or Jax to follow. He returned shortly with the enormous glass jug clasped in his arms.

Jax threw down the armloads of bows and swords. He seized the bottle from Tim.

"Try it," Boss Green said.

His henchman uncorked the container and splashed some of the contents into a cup. He took a small mouthful, and grinned widely.

"It's good, boss. Real good."

"Wanna get us drunk?" Boss Green snapped. Rebecca cringed, but she held herself erect. "Think we're stupid? Not stupid. Take it home, boys. We're going. Don't follow us unless you want an arrow in the guts. Be back again soon!"

He and Tiger drew their bows. Jax hurried out into the darkness. The other two backed out of the circle of firelight. Ben counted ten, then signaled to Julie and David. The scouts retrieved their own bows and glided silently after them.

The threshing footsteps receded. Rebecca found herself trembling with reaction. Ben sat down beside her and put his arm around her. She leaned against him, too frightened to cry.

"We've got to move!" Frank Valentine burst out. "Once they get over their drunk, they'll be on us in force! They'll take everything we've worked for. We're trapped. God help us!"

"They're not coming back," Rebecca said.

"What do you mean? We just fed them the best food we have all year, let them drown themselves in our beer, and now you make them a gift of white lightning? 'Course they'll be back."

"They won't, Granddad," Tim said. He knelt at Rebecca's feet. "You think we're brave, missus. You're the bravest of us all."

"Brave? She just let them take a year's worth of spirits!"

"She told them a little lie," Ben said, holding her close. "'Twasn't moonshine. It was the rubbing alcohol from the surgery. Smells just the same. How long do they have?"

"Not long once they drink it," Rebecca said. "Four ounces will kill a man. That container holds three gallons. As David might say, do the math. Goddess forgive me."

Ben smiled fiercely.

"Well done, my love. I'll recover our weapons and probably theirs as well in the morning. They won't need them any longer."

"How did you think to do that?" Ben said. "You've never wanted to be on the sharp end of the dagger."

She nestled close to him, staring up at the full moon almost exactly overhead, and listened to the owls calling to one another in the tree-tops.

"I never thought I could kill, until someone threatened the people I love," she said. He nodded understanding. "It's as you said before, Ben. We're trying to find our feet in a world that's different from anything we knew before. This is the new reality. I'm the only one who hadn't changed, and now I have."

"Ah, no, you haven't," Ben said gently. "The Goddess has many aspects. You just never wore this face before."

"How does it look on me?" Rebecca asked.

He studied her in the dying torchlight, then kissed her on the forehead.

"Surprisingly normal."

"Then it will be all right," Rebecca said. "I hope."

A MISSED CONNECTION

BY EMILY MAH

EMILY MAH

Emily Mah Tippetts writes science fiction and fantasy as Emily Mah and romance as E. M. Tippetts. A former attorney, she now runs a cover design and book formatting company for independent authors and publishers. She lives in New Mexico with her family. In the Change universe, she is the Premier of Western Canada, a place she's never really seen but would like to someday.

The doorbell rang at seven a.m. Marc stumbled out of bed, put on his bathrobe, and went to answer it, grateful that his roommate didn't seem to have awoken.

He assumed he'd see his ex, Chrissie, on his doorstep, but instead found himself face-to-face with Chrissie's older brother, Kevin; her younger sister, Rory; and Marc's own sister, Millie. Everyone from his tiny hometown of Bend, Idaho, who lived within forty minutes of the University of Utah campus.

"We need to talk," said his sister. The three of them pushed past him into the front room and Marc was powerless to stop them. They were all typically broad shouldered and muscular, good Bend farming stock. Marc had always been the scrawny, nerdy one.

"Mom says you've dumped Chrissie," said Millie.

"And Chrissie tells me you're interested in someone you talk to online," said Kevin.

"Did you guys have a dig-into-Marc's-business conference?" Marc demanded.

"No," said Rory. "Word gets around. You know how it is. I really think you've been awful to my sister. She waited for you your whole mission. Two years, she didn't date or even flirt with anyone else."

"Which you begged her to do when you left," added Kevin. "Now you won't even go out to dinner with her? Try to catch up?"

"Our families have been friends for how long?" said Millie.

"Chrissie's like a sister to us already. Everyone was so happy when you two started dating."

"Things have changed since then, all right?" said Marc.

"Specifically," said Kevin, "you aren't the runt of the litter anymore.

You're just back from your mission, which is when you are the most attractive you'll ever be to girls, by the way. Remember that Chrissie liked you even when you were the guy everyone picked on. And she'll still like you when the shine of your plastic name tag wears off."

Millie and Rory nodded in agreement.

"Guys . . ." said Marc.

"Name one reason why you shouldn't give her another chance," said Kevin.

"Because of where my life is going these days," said Marc. "Chrissie just wants to go back to Bend, and don't pretend that you guys aren't here because you know how hard it'd be for her to find someone else who'd ever want to live there. You think that because I know how to find it on a map, I'm better than some other random Utah guy. I'm not going back there. After I get my degree, I'm going to Silicon Valley, or maybe I'll start up a company here."

"Have you talked to her about any of this stuff?" asked Rory.

"And meeting someone online," said Millie, "sounds sketchy."

"I didn't meet her online," said Marc. "I met her on my mission."

"While my sister was writing to you?" said Kevin.

Marc rubbed his hands over his face in exasperation. "I didn't start dating this person back then. We got in touch after I got home, and after things ended with Chrissie."

"Marc, some advice, bro to bro?" said Kevin. "That plastic name tag with *Elder Branson* written on it that you wore for two years? Better than plastic surgery. A month from now, you'll be the same guy you were before, the computer science major with no friends."

Marc scowled at him.

"And this other girl is in Chile," said Rory. "It's not like you're going to see her ever again in your life."

"And have you considered that she may only be after a green card?" asked Millie.

"Give me a break," said Marc.

"There is that," agreed Rory.

Marc wished he hadn't gone to the door this morning. "You guys are living in the Stone Age. Just because you're not comfortable with the whole online thing doesn't mean that everyone who uses the Internet is a scammer of some kind."

"You do need to be careful," said Kevin. "You don't know what other people might do."

"What if she hacks into your bank account?" said Millie.

"She can't do that. Gimme a break. You guys don't understand anything about technology. You all plan to move back to Bend and take over the family farms—"

"And you look down on us for that," said Millie. "You think you're too good for Chrissie and for Bend."

"I just don't think I fit in there."

Aware they'd reached a stalemate, his guests exchanged looks of resignation.

Marc wanted to dance for joy when they finally let him usher them out.

Once back in his room, Marc took a deep breath, sat down on his bed, opened his laptop, and activated the dial-up connection.

Please, he thought as the modem hissed and boinged in its conversation across the ether. *Please, please, please!*

On the nightstand was the often folded and unfolded letter written in halting English, the words inscribed in purple ball point pen. In the other room, the doorbell rang again, but this time he ignored it.

As his e-mail inbox loaded, he crossed his fingers. Four new messages popped up, three from his mother and one from his ISP. He shut his eyes for a moment in frustration, then opened the last e-mail he'd sent.

From: MarcB@utah.edu
To: BellaFeliz@yahoo.com
Date: March 1, 1998

Dear Angela,

Thanks so much for your letter. Now you have my e-mail address. Hope to hear from you soon!

Marc (it's not Elder Branson anymore!)

He'd read and reread those lines, obsessing over every keystroke. Did he come on too strong? Did he e-mail too soon after he received her letter? Was she just not interested? Did it make her uncomfortable to use his first name? He smoothed open her letter and read it again.

February 5, 1998

Dear Elder Branson,

Thank you so much for your letter. I do remember who you are. You have green eyes and dark hair and a very nice smile. I hope you had a good trip back to Utah after your mission. Do you think you'll ever come back to Chile to visit?

To answer your question, yes, I have an e-mail. It is BellaFeliz@yahoo.com.

Sincerely,
Angela

He knew those words by heart now, and with each repetition became more aware of what they didn't say. She was being polite, not flirtatious. His interest in her wasn't reciprocated. All his talk about dating someone else was just that, talk. Angela was five and a half feet of slim elegant curves and a mocha complexion who seemed to like him in person, but

Kevin's words about girls digging missionaries stung. Perhaps he really had set his sights too high.

With resignation he folded her letter and put it in his pocket, then opened the first of his mother's e-mails. He skimmed it for news, to see if his other sister, Marie, had delivered her baby yet, or if his brother Max had his mission call. Finding no news of either in any of the three messages, he put them all in the trash.

In the other room, he heard the door open and shut, and then laughter of the exact pitch and tenor to make him cringe.

"Marc?" the feminine voice called out. "You ready for class?"

"I might be late," he yelled back.

Without even knocking, she opened his door.

"Whoa, hey!" he shouted, snatching his robe tight around himself. "Chrissie, seriously! First you send our families over for an intervention, and now you just barge in?"

The girl who stood in the doorway was plain with fine, blond hair. She tilted her head. "Intervention?"

"Yeah, play dumb."

Her bafflement seemed genuine, though. "You need to get ready. I don't want to be late."

"Then you go on ahead."

"No, it's okay. I'll wait for you. Just hurry okay?"

There was no point trying any harder to get her to leave. She had perfected her selective hearing of late.

Once she left the room, Marc picked up a dirty shirt and jeans from his floor and got dressed. His face had a three-day-old scruff on it that scratched the back of his hand as he pulled his shirt on. It was the latest of his attempts to put Chrissie off.

With one eye on the clock, Marc dragged his feet until five minutes past the start of class, only to emerge into the living room and find Chrissie on the couch, her backpack slung over one shoulder, one flip-flop clad foot tapping impatiently.

Good, he thought. *Get mad. Get furious. Storm out.*

She looked up at him, took in his rumpled clothing and blinked in dismay, but then a smile blossomed on her face.

"Okay, let's go."

"You don't have to walk with me to class."

"No, it's fine." She crossed to the front door and they were off.

Marc knew better than to drag his feet on the way. She'd only clamp on to his arm. The way to keep her from touching him was to walk fast.

"I seriously cannot learn HTML," she chattered as they dashed along. "I'm so bad at it. Maybe you can help me?"

"Or maybe you should switch to poetry or art," said Marc. "You don't have to take all the same classes as me."

"No, it's all right."

Marc pivoted on his heel and turned to face her. "You aren't interested in computers. It makes no sense for you to be a computer science major, okay? That's my thing, not yours."

For a moment she stared at him, aghast. Marc hoped against hope that this was it, that she'd snap, yell at him, and storm off.

But no, that glorious smile spread across her face again. "That's so you, caring like that. I'd rather spend time with you than paint pictures or write poems."

She looped her arm through his and tugged him on down the path. "Come on. I don't want to be too late. Oh, do you want to go to the movies on Friday?"

"Chrissie, we're not dating."

"Well, you aren't going to the movies with anyone else. It's been two years. Would it kill you to go on one date with me and see what I'm like these days?"

She was far too good at this. Rather than make puppy dog eyes or pretend she didn't hear him, she resorted to logic. Chrissie knew him better than anyone, as loathe as he was to admit it.

"You know I'm seeing someone," he said.

"That girl you're e-mailing? I'll believe it when it happens. I know you think the Internet is the way of the future, but I don't see the point of it at all. You can't really connect via e-mail."

Marc knew better than to mount an argument. He knew the Internet was the way of the future because he just felt it, in his bones. Five years from now, geography would be irrellevant. They'd be able to talk every day. They'd use video chat rather than phone calls.

If only that day were today.

It was past five when he finally made it home again and retreated to his room and his Internet connection. He found two e-mail messages in his inbox. One from his mother and one from BellaFeliz@yahoo.com.

He blinked and looked again. No, it was there all right, an e-mail from Angela. With shaking hands he clicked it open.

```
               From: BellaFeliz@yahoo.com
                 To: MarcB@utah.edu
               Date: March 5, 1998


Hi Marc,

It is very strange to call you by your first name (but
nice). I'm so glad you e-mailed me. I am still figuring
out how e-mail works. Perhaps with you I can practice.

Did you have a good trip home to Utah? Do you see any
of your other mission companions there? It is strange
to not have you in our ward anymore. Maybe someday I
can visit you in the USA.

Angela
```

His heart soared as he read the words again and again until they were seared into his retinas. He clicked to reply and wrote:

From: MarcB@utah.edu

To: BellaFeliz@yahoo.com

Date: March 5, 1998

Hi Angela,

It's great to hear from you! I did have a good trip
home to Utah, and yes, some of the missionaries I
served with go to school here with me.

It's strange to be up in the northern hemisphere
again, speaking English. Some days I feel like I
almost forget how.

Have you ever tried using a chat room? It's a way to
type to each other in real time. There's a chat room
called LDSChat with the password: Moroni, if you
click this link.

Marc

He pasted the link, hit SEND, and the agony kicked in before the
screen even refreshed. He should have reread that e-mail. He'd probably
sounded overeager, and she'd definitely be scared off by that.

After an hour of lurking in the chat room with no sign of Angela,
Marc emerged to forage in his freezer for a Hot Pocket. His roommate,
Jake, sat on the couch reading for his homework and waved without look-
ing up.

"No Chrissie tonight?"

"I hope not."

"Aw, just buy her a ring." He looked up, eyes twinkling with amusement.

"Right, because that'll fix things."

"She's the most stubborn girl I've ever seen."

"She and my mother believe that God's in favor of us getting married, so who cares about trivialities like my opinion?"

Jake chuckled. He was Mormon by upbringing, but hadn't been to church in as long as Marc had known him, and hadn't gone on a mission. He thought the whole prayer to God and getting detailed answers was a sign of lunacy, and in the current situation, Marc couldn't argue.

Right then, there was a knock at the front door. "Hey!" chirped Chrissie's voice. "I brought dinner."

Jake got to his feet, shook his head, and retreated into his bedroom.

"Come on, bro," Marc called after him.

"She is your problem."

"You don't even want to help me eat her food? She's a good cook."

"For a crazy person, sure." He shut his door behind him.

Marc answered the door, but kept his foot braced against it so that Chrissie couldn't open it all the way.

"I'm not feeling well," he lied.

"I made tuna casserole, and blondies for dessert."

"Thanks, but I'm good."

"No, you just take them. You can put them in the fridge or whatever."

"Chrissie, you don't need to cook for me."

"I know. I chose to. And I don't mind. You know how much I like to cook."

"Well I do mind, okay? I do."

"Just take the food. It's better than that microwave crap you always eat."

"I'll see you later." He shut the door in her face.

"I'm leaving it on the doorstep," she hollered through the door. "Let it spoil if you want, I guess."

Back in his room, he glanced at the chat room, then turned away, only to spin around and look again.

BellaFeliz: Is Marc in here?

Marc dove across the room and hit the keyboard, hard.

Marc: Yep! Hello!
BellaFeliz: Hello. Nice to see you.
Marc: Nice to see you, too.

The next line from Angela was in Spanish.

BellaFeliz: So how are you?

Marc switched languages too.

Marc: All right. Just working hard at school.
BellaFeliz: Are you in university?
Marc: Yes.
BellaFeliz: What's your degree in?
Marc: I'm not sure how to say "computer science" in Spanish.
BellaFeliz: No, I understand. That's very exciting. So that's why you
    know how to use e-mail and chat rooms.
Marc: This is the kind of stuff I'm interested in.
BellaFeliz: And now you know it works as far away as Chile.
Marc: Yep, but that's not why I wrote to you.

He winced. That was way too obvious. She'd shy away for sure.

BellaFeliz: So do you have a girlfriend?

Marc had to reread that one, to make sure that he'd seen it right.

Marc: No, I don't. Do you have a boyfriend?
BellaFeliz: No.
Marc: Oh good, no one to come kick my teeth in for talking to you.
BellaFeliz: You are funny.
Marc: I'm really glad you logged in.

BellaFeliz: Yes?
Marc: Yes.
BellaFeliz: Me too. This is fun.
Marc: You asked if I'd ever be back in Chile for a visit.
BellaFeliz: Yes?

He took a deep breath, as he knew his answer could put her off.

Marc: Not for a long time. I can't afford it.
BellaFeliz: Well, my cousin lives in Utah and I am going to visit her in
  a couple of weeks. Is Provo close to where you are?

He had to wipe his eyes and read that again. She was coming here?
To the United States? He'd be able to see her?

Marc: Not too far!
BellaFeliz: Maybe I can visit you?
Marc: Or I can come see you.

He ignored the pointed remarks of other people in the chat room who
didn't like the unending stream of Spanish. She filled him in on the details of
her trip. She'd be in Utah for a month to help her cousin with newborn twins.
  That was plenty of time to really get to know each other.

BellaFeliz: Okay, it's late. I will talk to you in here some other time?
Marc: Yes, see you later.
BellaFeliz: Good night.

A knock on his door five minutes later startled him. He'd been reading and rereading the chat room conversation until he'd put himself in a
trance.
  "Dude," said Jake's voice, "phone. It's your mother."

Marc groaned as he got up from his desk and accepted the phone from his roommate's hand. "Hi—"

"Marc, what's going on? Why don't you even talk to Chrissie when she does something nice like make you dinner?"

"Did she call you, Mom?"

"No, her mother did. She called home. That is a sweet girl, Marc, and she waited for you through your whole mission. Do you know how rare that is?"

"Listen, I'm sorry, but I'm dating someone else now."

"Not the girl on the Internet, from your mission?"

"I gotta go." He hung up fast.

Before he turned in for the night, he did remember to retrieve the food Chrissie had left him off the doorstep. She was an excellent cook, but she spent so much time at it and was the only person Marc knew who actually used the wheat-grinder attachment on her KitchenAid.

Angela was online when Marc got back to his apartment after class the next day and he talked to her for an hour, during which she sent him three pictures of herself, looking gorgeous, toned, and tanned. She really was out of his league, but while he might not have the looks of her usual suitors, he bet he had many times the income potential.

That night he shaved off his scruff and even tried to work out a little. Jake, passing through, gave him an indulgent smirk.

Two days later, as he took his time to get to class, he noted the mountains towering over the campus and the pioneer-built city of Salt Lake spread across the Wasatch Front below. How had he never noticed how beautiful it was? He could even make out the temple, jutting up from its spot on Temple Square.

Someone bumped shoulders with him, knocking his books out of his hand, and when he turned to see who it was, Rick Gardner, a guy on the football team, was glaring back over a well-muscled shoulder. He wasn't from Bend, but rather a little town outside of Bend. He'd gone to the next high school over, but now apparently he was inserting himself into the

Bend High School pecking order to help remind Marc of the fact that he was at the bottom.

Marc brushed it off. If a bunch of Idaho hicks had it in for him, he didn't care. They would matter less and less as his life went on.

BellaFeliz: Do you miss Chilean food?

Marc: Oh yeah. There's a guy from Chile in my class, and we complain about how much we miss it all the time.

BellaFeliz: I'll have to cook for you, then.

Marc: And I'll have to take you to some American restaurants.

BellaFeliz: To eat hamburgers?

Marc: Yeah, if you want. Or I need to take you someplace to get a good milkshake. Utah has some of the best milkshakes in the world.

BellaFeliz: Sounds like fun. So I arrive in ten days at 3 p.m.

Marc: Do you want me to pick you up?

BellaFeliz: No, I don't want to bother you.

Marc: No, let me pick you up. That way your cousin's husband doesn't need to take time off work. And it'd save your cousin from having to drive.

BellaFeliz: You're sure?

Marc: Positive.

BellaFeliz: Okay, I will e-mail my cousin.

BellaFeliz: I made a mistake today, I think.

Marc: What's that?

BellaFeliz: I showed your picture to my friend, Gertrudes, and when she asked who you were, I said you were a guy I'm seeing.

Marc sat back from his desk, a smile stretching from ear to ear.

Marc: Is it a mistake?

BellaFeliz: Do you think it is?

Marc: I don't mind if it's not.
BellaFeliz: Really?
Marc: Unless you don't want to go on a date when you're out here.
BellaFeliz: No, I do.

Marc pumped his fist in the air. "Yesss!"

He didn't get to bed that night until two a.m. Even after Angela signed off, he was aglow, unable to settle down, let alone go to sleep.

Computers and the Internet were the best inventions ever.

More than a week later, someone rang his doorbell at eleven at night, which didn't cause him to look up from his computer and his chat with Angela, until Jake knocked on his door. "It's your girl," he said.

Marc: Be right back.
BellaFeliz: Okay.

He found Chrissie seated on the couch, her eyes red and her cheeks raw from tears. "What is it?" he asked.

"Um . . . okay, so, I was praying and . . . something happened. Someone came."

"Who came?"

"An angel. With a sword."

"Who said what? You and I are meant to be together forever?"

She burst into fresh tears. "No, and I'm not joking. It's what I saw."

"Why are you telling me?"

"Because up until recently, you were my best friend. Now it's like you don't care about me at all."

"Chrissie, we aren't together anymore."

"Does this look like a romantic visit to you? Have I said one thing about us getting back together? You and I used to talk."

"Listen, I'm sorry. It's just that you and I have drifted apart."

"You've drifted. I'm still the same person I always was. And I can take a hint." She got to her feet, crossed over to the front door, and let herself out.

The next morning, Chrissie was back to walk with him to class. He scowled at her but she had her jaw set in such a way that he knew there was no point arguing. Best to let her do her pathetic, clingy thing.

Only, she didn't grasp his arm and beg him for a date. She walked beside him with her bag slung over her shoulder and said, "The world as we know it is about to change."

"That your revelation?" Marc sneered.

"Yeah." She gave him a sidelong look. "I don't normally go around telling people the answers to my prayers, but—"

"Excuse me?" snapped Marc. "You've been telling me for months that we're meant to be together."

"I think you're exaggerating there."

"Oh, right."

"I'm over you and I'm over us. Now will you listen to me? Did you even pray about what I told you last night?"

He shook his head and walked faster. She made no effort to catch up.

BellaFeliz: When I arrive in the USA, are you going to take me for a milkshake right away?
Marc: Yeah, if your cousin can spare you for a little while.
BellaFeliz: I'll have to dress nice on the plane, then.
Marc: Nah, it's casual.

A sudden kick to the head, pain like he'd never felt before—and then gone . . . The screen and all the lights went dark. *Dangit.* Marc fumbled along the wall for his emergency flashlight, pulled it from the plug, and switched it on.

It didn't work.

"Marc?" Jake yelled from the other room. "My CD player isn't working."

"It's a power outage," he yelled back.

"My CD player runs on batteries. It wasn't plugged in."

Marc's grip on the handle of his flashlight tightened. "Okay, that is completely weird."

Outside came the sound like boulders rolling downhill. "An airplane just crashed into campus!" a hysterical voice yelled.

"People's cars aren't working!" yelled another.

Then so many voices began to shout that it became impossible to tell one from another. Heavy footsteps sounded in the hallway, as the voices faded into the distance.

Marc fumbled in his desk for a box of matches and one of his safety candles. That worked. He hoisted the candle above his head, but the light was too weak to reveal much. He shouldered open his door and the light fell on Jake's face, shining with sweat.

"What's going on?"

"It's a really bad power outage?" guessed Marc.

"That stops cars? And their headlights. Look out the window. It's pitch-black."

Marc obeyed, going to open the blinds of the window in their living room. He thought he'd seen darkness before, but this was something else. It was as if the very air had gone opaque. A quick gaze upward reassured him that at least the stars still shone, but even they seemed more distant and tiny than usual.

"Come on," said Jake. "Let's try my car."

When he and Jake emerged in the hall, the scene was relatively sane. People stood with their doors open, chatting, candles held aloft as if at a rock concert during a slow song.

Marc nodded a greeting to anyone who called out to him as he and Jake made their way down the candlelit gauntlet to the stairs—though Marc did hit the button for the elevator on the way past, just to be sure.

The carpark had more groups of people standing in small clusters. Someone had built a campfire on the asphalt, which lit up the rows of cars in its bronze light.

"Hey, it's no good," someone called out when Jake and Marc stopped at the car. "They're all not working."

"I'm just gonna try," Jake hollered back.

He tried to unlock his car with his key fob, but it didn't even chirp, so he inserted the key in the lock and popped it open that way.

Marc climbed into shotgun, still holding the candle in one hand. It was fat enough that the wax didn't drip, but rather formed a pool in the center.

When Jake turned the key in the ignition, there was nothing, not even the sound of the starter.

He and Marc exchanged a look. A second attempt had the same result. They might as well have jabbed the key into the ground and turned it. The result would have been the same.

"We'll, I'm gonna start walking," said Jake. "Head down into the city. You coming?"

"Nah, I'm gonna wait it out here."

Jake shook his head. "Suit yourself."

Marc got a second candle out of his pocket and lit it for his roommate. The two said good-bye as Jake started off toward the exit and Marc headed back upstairs. One backward glance at Jake's retreating figure made Marc wonder if that would be the last time they ever saw each other, then he pushed that morbid thought to the side.

Whatever this was would get fixed soon.

Marc returned to his apartment, sat down in his chair, and positioned himself in front of his computer. As soon as electricity was restored, he was getting back online to make sure Angela was okay.

He woke with a start, a sharp cramp in his back from sleeping in a chair. At least he'd had the foresight to put out his candle.

The computer didn't work, the flashlight didn't work, the lights didn't work, and the building was deathly quiet. He ate a hasty breakfast of a granola bar and checked his roommate's room, only to find it empty.

It occurred to him that he should go find his home teachees. The

Church assigned every worthy priesthood holder a list of families to check on once a month, and in emergencies such as this. In Marc's case, he had three single girls he was responsible for, people from his church congregation who lived on their own, away from their families.

The charred fuselage of a commercial jet lay jammed up against the side of one of his home teachees' apartment building. Everything had gone up in flames and even still a fire burned far back in the plane's cabin.

The walls of the building had buckled and the scorching went clear through to the far side. The fire burned too hot for Marc to get any closer.

"I don't think anyone survived that," said a voice at his elbow.

He turned to see Dr. Holmes, the music professor, who stood with his backpack on one shoulder and his violin slung over the other.

"Has your ward been in touch with you? Have you got somewhere safe to go?" the professor asked. "Stay out of the city. It didn't fare well overnight."

"Excuse me?" said Marc.

"People are talking about seeing things. Shadows of figures that aren't there. Flames that dance in midair without burning anything. It might just be mass hysteria, or it might be something more."

"Over a blackout?"

"This is worse than a blackout," said the professor. "Better go see what your ward's emergency plan is. We don't know how long this'll last."

Marc looked over the man's heavy luggage. "Where are you going?"

"Out. I just feel like I need to get away from whatever's going on in the city. I figure I'll walk south and see if this phenomenon extends to the suburbs. I'd hope people would drive up here if they could, but who knows? You take care."

For the second time, as he watched the professor walk on and disappear around the corner, Marc had the uneasy feeling that he'd seen someone for the last time in his life.

Stop it, he told himself.

It was Chrissie's dire predictions that had him on edge, and he needed to not let that happen.

His other home teachees' dorm was blocked off by a barricade of broken furniture. He didn't have much time to take this in because as soon as he was spotted, shouts broke out and something whizzed past his head. He hit the ground and took a moment to process this. They were throwing stuff at him? Had they gone insane? Had whatever force that took out the electricity addled their brains as well? When he turned to see what it was they'd thrown, he found an aluminum shaft arrow lying in the gutter. That convinced him to get out of there.

By now he was closer to the city and was getting a sense of what Dr. Holmes had said. There were multiple fires eating their way through buildings and a steady stream of people, carrying heavy backpacks, hiking up from the wreckage.

"Don't go down there," a woman herding two small children warned. "Whatever happened, there's something sinister behind it."

Marc angled his steps toward her, threading his way past other refugees who looked disturbingly dead eyed. "Are you okay?" he asked.

"I'm going to try to get to my sister's farm. The cities won't hold together without electricity or transportation. Food will start to spoil and the grocery stores won't be restocking."

"But it's only been like this for a day," said Marc.

"Yeah, but that's too many people all in one place. There are already reports of looting." Her two children looked up at him with wide, frightened eyes. "Best to get to the country," she admonished.

Marc watched as she took her children's hands and pushed on.

It was definitely time to see what his ward was doing about all this.

Once back at his apartment, he found a note on the door telling him to meet at the next apartment building over with any food and supplies he had and could carry. He went in and retrieved his seventy-two-hour kit—enough nonperishable food to last three days. Chrissie had made it for him as a coming home present.

She was the first person he saw when he arrived at the next apartment building over. Everyone was in the lobby, sitting in little groups talking. She glanced at him, but looked away.

Bishop Atwood, wearing shorts and a T-shirt, walked among them with a notepad in hand.

"Marc," he said, checking something off on his paper. "Good to see you. Your home teachees?"

"I think one of them might have been killed by a plane," said Marc. "And the other two might be hostages to some nutsos with bows and arrows. I'm not kidding."

The bishop nodded. "There's been a lot of strangeness. People are all reacting to this in different ways."

"It won't last forever."

"We certainly hope not. We're not marching to retake Missouri just yet." He winked. "Still, we're moving the ward into this building and your building. So let me know if you've got space for someone to crash with you?"

Marc nodded. "We have our couch." He wasn't going to give up Jake's room yet. Odds were high his roommate would return. Eventually a truck or a cavalcade of tanks or a helicopter would arrive with a message from whatever parts of the world were unaffected, and this would be sorted out.

Ten days later, he sat in front of his still dead computer and looked out the window to see yet another cluster of people leaving. While everyone had started out in high spirits, now people were starting to despair. More rumors of riots and looting came from the city, and there was even a report of cannibalism, which Marc didn't believe. The university had posted handwritten flyers stating that classes were suspended indefinitely.

A knock on his door made him look up.

Chrissie stood in his doorway. "Hi," she said. "Your front door was unlocked."

"Hey."

"So . . . you need to see something." She bit her lip, a habit she had when she was nervous.

"I do?"

"Yeah."

He didn't want to be bossed around, but he was curious. She led him downstairs to the car park where Rick was holding a rifle, squinting down the length of the barrel at someone's car.

"What?" said Marc. "Is he nuts?"

Chrissie shook her head. "Wait. Watch."

Marc's pulse thundered in his ears as he watched Rick pull the trigger. Nothing happened. There was no bang, no puff of smoke, nothing.

"I'm telling you," Rick said, "the powder's not wet. It's like the laws of combustion have been rewritten. Electricity doesn't work, and neither does gunpowder."

Marc exchanged a worried look with Chrissie. "What," she asked, "could shut off power and gunpowder?"

Marc shrugged. "I don't know."

"Well whatever it is, we're screwed. Cars can't drive. Radios don't work. Even if it's possible to make new radios that would work, I bet the factories don't work right now. Neither does the kind of equipment we need to make factories, or the equipment to mine the metal we'd need to use in the first place. This is major."

That much was obvious. In the ten days since the blackout began, Marc had bathed only campground style, with a wet washcloth dipped into a basin of soapy water. His scruff was growing out again because he didn't want to take the time to shave it.

"So . . ." Chrissie squared her shoulders and turned toward him. "We're going to start to walk north. Toward home. See if we can get somewhere that has working electricity."

Marc nodded. "Okay."

"Are you coming with?"

"Nah. I'll wait it out here."

"Okay, well, if you change your mind, we leave tomorrow morning."

"Who's we?" Marc asked.

"Me, Rick, and a couple other guys from Idaho, and a girl who's brother is at Ricks." That was the Church-owned junior college in Idaho.

"Good luck," said Marc.

In the late afternoon, the bikers arrived in a swarm. Not guys on motorcycles, but rather bicycles, wielding baseball bats and machetes. Everyone retreated inside the buildings at the sight of them, so they cycled on past without incident. Marc watched this spectacle from his window, and while the bikers pedaled on past, the rust-colored blotches of liquid on their weapons caused Marc to decide then and there, he was leaving with the Idaho crowd.

Dear Angela,

I hope by the time you get this letter, we'll be together and can laugh about this strange turn of events. I hope you are safe, wherever you are, and that you know I didn't just sign off for no reason. I imagine the news down there has to be talking about what's happened here in Utah.

My guess is that it was a solar flare or some other kind of electromagnetic pulse that fried all our electronics, so it will take a while to replace all the damaged equipment, but in time things will be restored. Meanwhile, I'm just hoping things here don't get too violent.

I want you to know my home address as well as my address in Utah. It's 4 Main Street, Bend ID 88777, USA. That's where I think we're going—I'm with a group of people from Idaho. I hope that if we can walk far enough, we'll get to where the cars and phones and all that work again and can contact our families.

Marc laid his pen aside and finished packing up his backpack. While everyone in the building had pooled their resources, the food would last only another week at most, and the water pressure in the sinks continued to drop by the hour, despite all their efforts to conserve what was left in the tower. Marc packed dry pasta, salt, and olive oil along with his laptop, and a change of clothing. More than that, he didn't dare try to carry.

The group bound for Idaho was in his lobby when he arrived. Rick and Kevin took one look at him and turned to Chrissie, who glanced at Marc and nodded. It stung that he had to rely on her in order to be included, but he had little choice. He wasn't of any particular use to this group while the power was still out.

"All right," Kevin called out. "We've got three large packs of supplies here."

He gestured to some oversize duffels propped against the wall.

"We take turns carrying them. No exceptions. We'll try to find a wagon or a shopping cart or something on the way."

"The area's pretty picked over for that kind of stuff," said a girl, whom Marc didn't know.

"Then we make do with what we've got," said Kevin. He hefted one bag, Rick another, and a guy Marc had seen in the halls (but had never learned the name of) grabbed the third one.

Marc fell in step as the group moved out. Bishop Atwood stood outside the front door, and at the sight of them packed and ready to go, he gave a small, sad smile.

"Good luck," he said.

"You, too," said Chrissie.

This time, Marc didn't look back as they walked away. He'd see Bishop Atwood again, he decided. This disaster couldn't last forever.

We've walked for six days and think that we are perhaps nearing Logan, though it is hard to say for sure because we've kept off the roads. There's still no radio, but there are more rumors of gangs riding bicycles, with chains and baseball bats. I'd rather not run into one of those.

We've been able to spend nights in small towns and in the odd barn. Two more people have been added to our group and we've actually managed to gain supplies on the way. The only other big group that is taking our same path is being led by Emily

Mah—leader of the Student Democrats at the U and a really obnoxious person we want to avoid at all costs. She'll probably want to go to Canada or something, liberal that she is.

I miss talking to you and I wonder how long this outage will continue. I can't wait until we can speak to each other again.

I'm so mad at myself for not printing out the pictures I have of you. Often I wonder what's happened to my apartment. Has someone else gotten in and are they tearing up my mission albums and journals? Are they sleeping in my bed and eating what's left of my food?

This whole experience is a nightmare, and I can't wait to wake up.

A holler made him look up and snap his journal shut. They'd reached another barbed wire fence to cross and while he could walk and write, he couldn't climb through a fence and write.

As they made their way through a gap where the fence had collapsed, Chrissie fell into step next to Marc and looked sidelong at him.

"Hi," she said, with hesitation.

"Hi, Chrissie."

"So, how're you holding up?"

Marc shrugged, which ignited more pain in that cramp in his back. That had returned with a vengeance the first night they'd slept rough. He did his best to put one foot in front of the other, though, and keep up with the herd.

He waited for Chrissie to keep prattling, but she was silent.

Upon thinking it over, he wasn't sure what he really expected. Her infatuation with him seemed to have waned. She hadn't cast him a single longing look this entire time.

"Can I just say something?" she said.

"Sure."

"You've got to let her go. Not because I'm saying you should be with me. I'm not sure that makes sense anymore, but you can't be with her. She's gone. The plane that would have brought her here will never fly again and your laptop is taking up space and weight we can't afford."

"I'll need it after the blackout."

Chrissie looked sidelong at him again. "That won't ever happen. And I think deep down, you know that."

Her tone was odd enough to make him look over at her.

"I know you think I'm crazy," she went on, "but I did have a visitation before this started, and correct me if I'm wrong, but you haven't even offered one prayer for answers. This change is for good. This is our life now."

Marc shook his head. He couldn't accept that.

"Okay, fine," she said. "How about you let me carry your laptop? Your knees are about to buckle and that's seven pounds I can take off you."

"No," he said.

While she wasn't scrawny, she was slim. She didn't have a whole lot of muscle mass, and the rationed food they were eating made everyone's faces more gaunt and eyes more prominent. He shook his head.

"I couldn't."

A root caught his foot and he went down, spraying alkaline soil in an arc, his hands smarting as the skin peeled from his palms. The rest of the group paused, but no one stopped to help him up.

No one but Chrissie.

Marc made sure to get up on his own.

The next morning, when the load was divvied up, the largest bag plopped in front of Marc. He stared at it despairingly, knowing he couldn't ask anyone for help. Chrissie stood by, her hand out, offering to take the laptop.

With tears pricking at his eyes, he pulled it out of his bag and laid it on the ground. "Let's go," he said.

Chrissie didn't argue, but she did stare.

"I just need a minute," he told the group.

They all stood politely as he knelt and bowed his head. *Lord,* he thought, *I guess I should be thankful I've lasted this long. Thou must have a million prayers from people asking Thee to fix all this. Add my voice to that crowd and . . . otherwise just help me along here.*

He opened his eyes and saw that no one tapped their foot or glared at him.

Marc drew himself up as straight as his aching spine would allow. He tucked his journal, with his letter in progress for Angela, into his pack. No one smiled or snickered, but the pity was as tangible as the ground beneath his feet. He ignored it, shouldered his bag, and the group moved on out.

The laptop grew smaller and smaller until it was nothing but a dark dot in the distance. Chrissie walked next to Rick, who hung on her every word. Marc brought up the rear with an aching back and a limp. He wanted to look back one last time, but he knew that if he didn't keep up, he was a goner.

DEOR

BY DIANA PAXSON

DIANA PAXSON

I have written a lot of short stories and novels on legendary themes, from Siegfried and Brunahild (the Wodan's Children trilogy) to the Avalon series that I took over from Marion Zimmer Bradley, and some nonfiction books, including *The Way of the Oracle*. I hosted the first tournament of what became the Society for Creative Anachronism in my backyard. My first publications were the chronicles of Westria, set in a world several centuries after a somewhat different Change. When I read *Dies the Fire* I was fascinated to find that Steve had come to many of the same conclusions I had regarding who would survive, which made more sense when I found out that he liked Westria! I've been following the series eagerly ever since and I'm delighted to have this opportunity to play in the world of the Change.

For more about what I'm doing, see diana-paxson.com.

The ocean was a tumult of white and gray, misting into bars of cloud through which the setting sun sent a glimmer of gold. Deor squinted as another roller crashed against the point, glimpsing for a moment an iridescent form shaped from sea wrack and spray, mutating as he watched into a hint of bright eyes and laughter. Was that what he was waiting for?

"Sae-aelfen baill!" he whispered. He hunkered back into the dubious shelter of the pine, automatically shifting the sheathed seax to one side, and shook back his hair. Dry, it was curly enough to stay off his face, but wet it lengthened, and the wind was whipping the dark strands into his eyes.

"That passed, so shall this."

For most of his life he had hated that quote, but at moments like this he could appreciate its grim philosophy. He had been born twelve years after the cataclysm that rendered the old world more distant than Old England, and his parents had named him Deor for the long-ago poet who wrote that line. It was the Saxons, or so his father said, whose ways had saved them when nothing from the old world worked anymore. Their arms, their crafts, and their poetry were equally appropriate to a grim life in what had become a grim land. Deor dreamed sometimes of building a ship that could venture beyond the cove and see what else had survived the cataclysm, but even a Saxon ship would have trouble in such a storm.

Why, he wondered, had he wanted to come to Albion Cove? It was the season for harvesting crabs, and he wanted to escape the confines of Hraefnbeorg one last time before winter closed in, but the season was changing early this year.

From the bluff on the northern side he could see across the cove. Waves were rolling all the way in to froth around the tangled iron stubs of the bridge where the Albion River joined the sea. The leather scales of his jack were slick with moisture, his cloak was growing heavy, and the damp would not be doing his bow any good either. On this trip, flotsam was the only harvest they were likely to gather from the sea.

Branches thrashed above him as the wind rose. There were fell voices on that blast. Not evil, but heedless of humankind. His father and older brother were always telling him to pay attention to the dangers he could see. They honored the spirits of the land, but sometimes he wondered if they understood that they were real.

"Deor! Are you froze, man, or just crazed!"

A hard hand closed on his arm. He started to swing, recognized the touch, and pulled the punch as Alfwin leaned away, brown hair tossing. His friend laughed.

"Guess you're not frozen, then—but stay here an' ye will be. Th' others are already headin' back t' the village—" He motioned toward the flat beyond the bridge, where a few houses and a boat-barn still stood, despite the river's habit of flooding every year or two.

The bit of sky that showed between the bands of cloud was deepening to flame. Deor pulled himself upright, scanning the horizon through slitted eyes. And stilled, blinking, as beyond the rocks at the northern headland something moved. He took a step down the path.

"Man, what're ye doing? I'm not gonna freeze my butt—"

"Alf, can't you see?" Deor found his voice. "Look there, at the point—by Thunor's beard, 'tis a sail!"

"Crazed—" Alfwin draped an arm across Deor's shoulders and stood

beside him, leaning into the wind. They had sometimes seen ships slipping along at the edge of sight offshore, long, low vessels like the ones
the Pomo tribesmen up at Kah-la-deh-mun said had burned half the town
the year before. But this one was closer. Too close, for one who did not
know the channel, and in such a sea.

"Not to worry—" said Alfwin grimly. "Rocks'll get 'em if they go on
that way . . ."

Deor squinted into the sunset. "No . . ." he breathed. "This one's different. Like the picture in *Treasure Island!*" Alfwin was not much of a reader,
but Deor had taken to it, and when they could escape the endless chores
he read to his friends from the lore books at Hraefnbeorg.

Alfwin peered at the angled black wedge that leaped against the sky.
"Maybe . . ."

A host of wordless intuitions coalesced into certainty. "She's in trouble!" Deor pulled off his cloak and began to sweep twigs and fallen
branches into it. "I'll light a beacon. Run back t' the village! Get boats
out—pick up survivors if she goes down!"

The wind had torn a long branch from the pine. He tossed it down to
the spit of land at the foot of the bluff, then pulled the hatchet from his
belt and began to hack at the brush. By the time he had bundled it all into
his cloak and scrambled down the slope the ship had passed the point.
He stopped short as the sun, sinking below the clouds, painted the vessel
a sudden vivid gold.

Need propelled him into action once more, piling the wood, using his
belt knife to shave tinder down to the dry pith and fumbling with the flint
and steel. He had been doing this since he was old enough to hold the
striker, but never when lives might depend on that flame.

"*Neid, Ken!*" Deor sketched the rune above the wood. "*Loge* damn you,
burn!" He struck again, saw the spark catch, and spread his cloak to shield
the infant flame. In moments, the resinous wood was flaring, fanned by the
wind. Smoke billowed upward. Surely they would see. He flapped at the
flames with his cloak until they roared.

When he dared look again, the ship was turning! Now he could see battered timbers and a white, desperate face at the rail. Even if mortal, the ship was amazing, maybe fifty feet in length with two masts, though one had snapped and the other bore only a tattered trysail. She leaped like a horse with a burr beneath the saddle, but she still swam.

He snatched a brand and loosed it in an arc to land in the slack water just beyond the guano-covered rock. "Here!" he shouted. "Anchor here!" The cove had seen no ship of any size since the Cataclysm, but the fisherfolk said that long ago, big ships had anchored there to load the great logs men cut in the hills.

Someone shouted from the deck. Deor snatched up another brand and waved it around to the left, willing them to turn. The boat heeled over, foam frothing at her prow. With a crack the sail split, but the wind at her stern was pushing her now. He gazed hungrily as she neared. Everything—her size, her elegant lines, even the bright paint on her battered sides, proclaimed, "Not from here . . ."

Until this moment he had not believed, not really, that beyond this small corner of what had once been California there were other communities of men in the world who still deserved to be called human.

The ship shot into the lee of the white rock and slowed. Men heaved at the anchor and with a splash it shot downward. The ship jerked as it caught, then came to a halt a short stone's throw away.

Deor let out his pent breath in a long sigh. Alfwin waved from the shore below the bridge, Willa and Manfred behind him, as two rowboats from the fishing village nosed between the pillars and headed into the cove.

"Ahoy!" came a call from the deck.

The man's graying dark hair was cropped shorter than he'd ever seen a free man wear, but it was clear that this was no thrall. Beside him a youth leaned over the rail. He looked to be a little less than Deor's age, but what wonders must he have already seen?

The captain's dark eyes met his own. "What place is this?"

Deor's pulse quickened. "Albion Cove!" he called in reply. "Barony of Mist Hills! I hight Deor Godulfson. *Wes hail!* Be welcome here!"

"Captain-owner Daniel Feldman," the man replied. "Of the *Ark;* what's left of her," he added ruefully.

Four machines crouched on either side—catapults, he realized, but they hadn't been enough. The sides and deck were peppered with holes as if someone had been using the boat for a target, even through the thin metal that covered much of the hull. In fact, in several places below the waterline something that looked very much like the sort of arrow an etin might shoot was still wedged in the planking, broken off and caulked with pitch to plug the hole. The rowboats had reached the vessel now and were taking off the first load of crew. To Deor's surprise there were women among them. At home both lads and lasses trained in the basic skills, but only the men of Albion Cove went to sea.

It's me—Deor hugged himself, controlling the impulse to laugh from sheer joy. *Not my father, who dreamed of this day, or my brother, who never believed it would come. I'm the one who will welcome these folk and get first news of the weird of the world.*

Still grinning, he kicked the remains of the fire into the sea and scrambled back up the hill.

By the time Deor had made his way back along the bluffs and down to the village, most of the ship's crew had been ferried ashore. A cauldron of chowder was already steaming over the fire. In their sodden shirts and breeches the strangers looked human enough. Alfwin's leather bota of brandy was being passed around, but they were clearly waiting for him, as the baron's son, to make the first move. As he came forward, the captain nodded and gestured toward the sea.

"Thanks for the signal fire."

"I could see your trouble. From the look of your ship, ye've had a hard time."

"Without ending in a whale's belly like Jonah, it would be hard to have worse," the captain agreed. "There are tiger teeth on this coast of yours. We were on our way back from a run to Hawaii when we got jumped by pirates out of Mindanao; Suluk corsairs, I think. Chased us all the way across the sea and cut us off before we could reach home."

Deor took a deep breath, still not certain in his soul that questioning these strangers would not cause them to vanish away. "And where might that be?"

"Newport," said the captain. "The Faculty of Economics, Entrepreneurial Studies."

"No—" Deor spoke more sharply than he had intended. "What land?"

The man's fine-boned face brightened suddenly. "Ah—" He looked around him at the broken bridge and the ruined buildings on the cliff above. "Of course, you wouldn't know . . . We're from the High Kingdom of Montival. The heart of it is the Willamette Valley, north of here, though come to think of it, in theory California is a part of the High King's realm."

A king . . . breathed Deor.

Alfwin grinned. "Wonder what Duke Morgruen will think o' that?" For the children of men who had played at knights in the Society for Creative Anachronism before the old world fell, the word "king" had power.

"You're ruled by a duke here?" asked a sturdy young woman who was trying to dry a short coat made of closely woven brown wool at the fire. One of the others had called her Thora. She had a snub nose and a rather determined expression, and a mop of red hair stiff with salt spray. For a moment Deor stared. The thought came to him. *She's going to be important to me.*

"He thinks so—" murmured Willa. Her father had lost a leg in one of Morgruen's cattle raids.

Deor turned back to the captain. "My father's the Baron of Mist Hills. Our burg lies a day's walk or so inland." He gestured toward the slopes that rose behind them. Clad thickly in pine and fir, their tops stood out in stark silhouette against the dimming sky. "Morgruen has a fortress down on the Rushing River near where Healdsburg used to be. He farms the valley with cannibals he's captured and masterless men."

"We like t' say he guards our southern borders from the cannibal band." Alfwin grinned. "We can't take him, an' he says these hills aren't worth his while, but I think he don't dare try us on our own ground."

That balance might change, thought Deor, *if the barony can establish contact with Montival.* The crew of the *Ark* were good-looking men, agile and strong. As their clothing dried he could see that the fabric was near as finely woven as the stuff from the old times, but strong and new. And the rest of their gear—the metal fittings on belts and boots, and the steel cuirass that one man wore—was better than anything they could make at Hraefnbeorg. Any man could claim a grand title. But the newcomers' gear and that ship could only have come from a prosperous community.

"You'll be safe with us," he said quickly. "You can shelter here tonight. Tomorrow we'll take ye to the burg."

"We'll need to repair our ship—" said Captain Feldman, clearly uncertain what resources the Hraefnbeorg folk might have.

Deor nodded.

"You have a smith?"

"And supplies—whatever you need. We've seasoned wood, and it's been a good year—we can replace your stores. My father will want to talk to you about trade," he finished in a burst, flushing a little at the captain's understanding smile.

He must know we'd do almost anything to get them to come back again.

"Then I think we can do business," Captain Feldman replied. "I'd like to leave half my crew to start the work and bring the rest to the burg."

"How many might that be?"

The captain sighed. "We've twenty-eight remaining—no, twenty-seven, and of them, six are too hurt to be much use. So it would be about a dozen."

"Here in the cove your ship should be secure." Deor paused, thinking. "Willa"—he turned to the girl—"you ride lightest. Can you leave at dawn? Bag up the fish we traded for and take the pack pony. Get back to Hraefnbeorg fast as you can and tell 'em we're coming. If my mother fails in hospitality because I brought strangers with no warning she'll have my hide."

"I'd hate to cause her any trouble—" the captain began, but his eyes were smiling.

"Oh no, sir," Alfwin said earnestly. "Lady Avisa'll be delighted. Better'n a wedding, this. Only, y'see, she likes to be prepared."

My mother wasn't prepared for the Cataclysm, thought Deor. It seemed to him that she had been trying to make up for it ever since. He was her last child, after two who died, and one of the things she tried to control most often was him.

The headman of the village came toward them with wooden mugs of steaming tea. His folk had been here since before the Change. One of the two houses belonged to his family, the second to his brother.

"Th' woman says dinner's ready soon. We'll lay straw on old sails in th' boat-barn t' make beds for ye, get sleeping gear from th' ship next trip. Come see—"

"That would be . . . welcome," the captain replied.

Thora Garwood set down her pack and scanned the clearing. It had been noon before they left Albion Cove and at this season darkness drew in early. She had expected they would have to spend at least one night on the trail.

"What's the best wood here to burn?" she called.

Once they left the coast the terrain had changed. The higher slopes were thickly forested with mixed oak and fir where remnants of cloud still clung like the shreds of wool sheep left behind them. Mist Hills indeed! The trail wound inland through groves of the tall evergreens they called redwoods, following a creek swollen now from the recent rain. She grimaced as a drop from one of the overhanging branches rolled down her neck. The sailors were stretching a sail between the trees with their usual efficiency, but they needed a fire.

The dark-haired young man who had appointed himself their guide had drifted to the edge of the stream bank. He looked a little younger than her own twenty years. He would probably have been a military apprentice at home. She rubbed the space between her brows where the

A-list mark would go, if the Bear-Lord found her worthy once she got home. A day ago she had been wondering if she would live that long, but hope had returned now that she was on solid ground.

"Lord Deor?" she called again. The last visitors had left a pile of small logs and kindling under a rude shelter, but they would need more, and the light was fading fast.

He turned, blinking. "Th' wights say to take wood from the river. All that debris from the storm is blocking the flow. The bits that stick out won't be any wetter'n what you find in the forest," he added as she frowned.

At least the sailors didn't mind getting their feet wet, she thought as Captain Feldman gave the orders. Neither did Deor. She watched as he led them down the bank, leaping over rock and snag as if he had eyes in his feet. In a moment he reappeared dragging a long branch tangled with weed, and began to chop the wood with swift, efficient blows.

The captain's son was darting about with the others, collecting kindling, but his father had eased down with his back against a redwood tree as two of his men hung a pot over the fire. Thora grinned. It was probably just as well it had been a short march. The sailors were tough, but their expertise was in running up and down rigging and hauling on lines. Bear-killers were trained to long marches, but it had been a while since she had scampered in full field kit up the trail they called Satan's Staircase at home.

She noted Deor's lithe grace with appreciation as he bent to spoon up more stew. Barely more than her own height and wiry, still, he moved well. *He'd do better as a scout,* she thought, *than in the line.* He straightened, looking around the circle of firelight with his slightly abstracted gaze, then stepped to the edge and dropped a spoonful of stew into a hollow at the base of one of the trees. He said something to his friend Alfwin, who grinned and punched his arm, then started toward her.

As Deor settled himself she moved politely to make room. His gaze was intense, but as she met those gray eyes she realized that if it was not the avid appreciation she might have expected from a young man her own age, neither was it the evaluation of a warrior.

"They say you are not from Cor-vallis—" His glance flicked from the basket-hilted sword that lay at her side to her brigandine, its leather worn through in places to show the layer of mail beneath, but still a more serious form of armor than the jacks of cuir-bouilli over heavy knit sweaters and loose pants that most of the sailors wore.

"I'm a Bearkiller." She touched the snarling bear-mask over her breast. "Most of our territory is inland, and we don't have a port or ships bigger than fishing boats. Since the war with the Cutters ended, things have been pretty quiet in Montival. I wanted to see the world, so I signed on with the captain. Never expected to see California, though. We thought there'd be nothing but a few Eaters skulking through the ruins down here."

Deor's face darkened. "There's some bad ones . . . in San Francisco and 'cross the Bay, but we cleaned out the nest in Santa Rosa. There's folk still hiding in the mountains, but they live on game. And there's Duke Morgruen's thralls." He spat. "He keeps plowing more land and needs all the hands he can get, so I don't suppose he lets them eat each other anymore."

He looked down at the bowl on his lap and took a deep breath. It was only reheated fish and barley from last night's meal, but it smelled wonderful.

"Thanks to the food that fills us, thanks for the hands that feed us, thanks to all wights with whom we share this land!"

He sketched a Jera rune in the steam.

"Hail holy earth that givest to all!" Thora echoed.

She looked at him for a moment, then fished out the Thor's hammer pendant from beneath her tunic. Her family was one of those that had followed Lady Signe in adopting the faith of Ásatrú some dozen years before.

He stared. "You honor the old gods in Montival?"

"You have no idea—" Thora grinned. "I think that every god anyone ever thought of must be worshipped by somebody in the High Kingdom. But if you mean Thor and Odin and all that lot, yeah, my folks do, and a fair chunk of the Outfit as well."

She'd never thought about it much, beyond that it was a good faith for a warrior.

"Mine too, though we call Them Thunor and Woden. But in some of my father's books They're called by those names." His gaze turned thoughtful. "In the old days, in the Society, he had what they called an Anglo-Saxon persona, but he took it seriously. There's some in the barony who still follow the White Christ, and there's the monks at the City of Ten Thousand Buddhas, but most folk are Heathen here. Myself, I'm training to be a scop—a singer—so I offer to Woden."

Thora shrugged. "I think it's pretty much that way all over. In Hawaii they offer to Pele and Kane. That was worth leaving home to see! The old, old ways go better with the life we live now."

A smile lit Deor's gray eyes and she felt a flicker of attraction. To let the crew even think of her as a woman could have caused stresses in the little world of the vessel. She had been wary even of making a friend, though the sailor-girls seemed to get along okay. But they were not on shipboard now. *I could take Deor in a fight,* she thought, *but if he invited me to share his blankets, I wouldn't say no . . .*

"My father leads the rites, and my sister Gytha uses healing spells, but my brother puts his faith in the spear and the plow," he replied. "I've tried to learn the runes. Do you have anyone who knows more?" Any thought of dalliance was clearly miles away.

Thora sighed. Admittedly she did not look her best, though she had bathed at the village and washed the salt out of her hair. But she didn't know the customs here, and anyway, there was no privacy.

"Not on the ship, certainly. In Montival, for magic I guess you'd go to the Mackenzies. Or the High King."

"Tell me—" Deor's eyes shone. "Tell me about your king . . ."

What will King Artos think of this land?

As the road wound upward Deor took a deep breath and looked back the way they had come.

If it is his, will he belong to it in turn? Will he see how beautiful it can be? Surely Mist Hills was a part of Montival.

The previous night the heroic figure of the High King had filled his dreams. And the Sword of the Lady—and Woden speaking through the godwoman to say it was forged for the hand of a King!

The rain had ceased. The rich scent of damp earth and mulching leaves lay heavy on the air, spiced by an occasional breath of wood smoke from the farmhouses in the valley below. He thought the valley had impressed the visitors with its well-kept farmsteads, each surrounded by a stout palisade, and the stock grazing in the pastures and the orchards where a few apples still clung to the trees. They had stopped at Gowan's farm for cider and meat pies, but that seemed a long time ago.

The setting sun shafted between bands of cloud, illuminating ochre slopes half covered by oak forest, the wet leaves shining richly orange and bronze and gold. Farther down he could see the thick band of trees that edged the river, and mist smoking off the fir-clad ridges beyond. He had dreamed of seeing the world beyond this valley, but for a moment a sudden awareness of the land overwhelmed him, as if all the myriad lives around him had fused into a single Spirit that welcomed him home.

Thora trudged beside him. She looked weary, but her hazel eyes missed nothing. He was surprised to realize how much he liked her. Lately his mother had started matchmaking, and it made him feel as if walls were closing in. Perhaps it was because all the girls at the burg felt like his sisters. His older brother had three children already and Gytha had two. The Godulfsons were not going to go extinct if he did not breed.

He grinned as the long blare of a horn rose and fell beyond the trees.

"It's a fair land, your Mist Hills, and reminds me a bit of home. I take it we're almost there?"

After hearing about the wonders of Montival Deor did not expect to impress her, but he could not resist a spurt of pride as the rock wall and the palisade came into view. Beyond them rose the peaked roof of the mead-hall and a tower where two banners snapped in the wind, the one per fess azure and vert a fess wavy argent, and the other per chevron or and sable, a raven volant bendwise sable.

His father's huscarles were marching out to form two lines before the

gatehouse. The last sunlight sparkled on the serried links of their hau-
berks of riveted mail and gleamed from the curve of the spangenhelms
and the points of their spears and the bosses of their round gold and black
painted shields.

Beneath the arch of the gate waited the baron and his lady. For a moment Deor saw his parents through the strangers' eyes—a man of sixty-
two with scarred face and hands, still big in the shoulders though his
body had thickened with age; a woman whose crisp linen wimple hid
fading hair and a double chin, but whose erect posture and sharp gray
eyes conceded nothing to the years.

"Food and baths and beds for all!" he grinned. "And if I know my
mother, a feast tomorrow. Welcome to Hraefnbeorg!"

I've made it to Meduseld . . . thought Thora as the summoning horn ceased to
blow. *The Rangers will love it here!*

She had never seriously considered joining them, but she had read the
books the Dunedain called the Histories. The rest of Hraefnbeorg's
buildings were a maze connected by covered passages, the older sections
weathered and much repaired, the new with a rough vitality. The kitchen
was separate, and there was a small house for the images of the gods.

The feasting hall was also new. It stood at the highest point of the hill,
where the summit had been built out with stone. Timbers braced the
sides, and the lower part of the shingled roof was angled outward over a
porch. Above, crossed timbers ended in raven heads, stark against the
sky. For a moment she stared, then followed Captain Feldman up the
steps and into the hall.

Her legs felt naked beneath the long skirts of the russet gown they
had given her. Bearkiller women rarely wore them, but all her other
clothes had been carried off to be cleaned. The meat must have gone into
the pit and onto the spit as soon as they were sighted coming up the hill.
Her stomach had been growling all morning as the scent of roasting pig
wafted through the air.

At the door a boy stood with a basin and towel so that the guests could wash their hands. Deor's friend had said Lady Avisa liked to be prepared. *To be in control was more like it,* she thought wryly. *Some people had reacted that way, after the Change.*

Light shafted down from windows at each end and from the dormers over the doors at the sides, but at first all she could make out were the two rows of pillars that ran lengthwise to support the upper part of the roof. As her eyes adjusted she could see that the uprights were carved and painted with bands and chevrons, as were the crossbeams that braced them. The long tables were filling with solid-looking folk, most of them in some kind of T-tunic or gown, though a few wore carefully preserved dresses or jackets and trousers. They must be the eorl's guard and the more prominent farmers from the valley below.

"This way, mistress—" Deor's friend Willa appeared at her elbow and pointed her toward the trestle tables set up along the left side of the hall.

Captain Feldman was already waiting by a carved chair in the middle, where the long hearth had been divided so that people could pass between the two sides of the hall. The crew sat on the benches beyond him. He seemed a little self-conscious in a tunic of purple cloth that looked as if it had been packed away somewhere since the Change.

On the other side of the hall Deor's father stood by a dais that held two even more ornate chairs with a small table between them. The lord's seat was carved with a sinuous interlace within which she glimpsed the horns and muzzles, curving tails, beaks and bright eyes of every bird and beast one might find in these hills. The lady's chair bore all the fruits of orchard and forest and field. A tapestry had been stretched between the pillars behind the high seats, cross-stitched with the arms of the barony. There were discolored spots on the green, as if new stitching had replaced a wreath that had once been there.

Eorl Godulf's tunic was made of very finely woven saffron wool, heavily embroidered across the breast and shoulders with twining beasts. The cloth was a little faded with age, and strips of a cruder weave and slightly different color had been set into the sides to expand it. He wore a white belt like an Association knight and a pendant Thor's Hammer on a complex linked chain. The jutting nose above the strong, bearded jaw was that of a man accustomed to being obeyed, but he did not seem unkind. Close to the lord's high seat she noted a strongly built man in his thirties who was the image of what Godulf must have been when he was young, with a pregnant woman beside him.

"The countess will come—" Willa followed her glance. "We sit here. Usually I help serve, but Deor said stay t' tell you what's goin' on."

"I thought Godulf was a baron—" said Thora as she took her place behind the bench next to the first mate from the *Ark*. And where was Deor? He was surprisingly easy to be with, and she had hoped he could sit with her to explain.

"For Mist Hills, aye, but in th' old days he won the rank of eorl by arms. He was noble afore the cataclysm"—Willa pointed proudly to the embattled silver band that held the eorl's silver hair—"an' he saved us all!"

Loaves of brown bread and a variety of sliced cheeses were already on the table, but no one else was eating, so she controlled the impulse to tear off a piece and wolf it down. There was a stir at the end of the hall as Countess Avisa appeared in the doorway, bearing a large silver-mounted drinking horn. Several young women with pitchers followed. All fell silent as Godulf lifted his hand.

"Laid are the boards and the guests assembled. *Wilcuma!* Be welcome!" He stepped onto the dais and took his seat. Thora felt the prickle of awareness that came sometimes at home when they sat at sumble, as if the visible guests were not the only ones in the hall.

Lady Avisa passed between the tables and the hearth to stand before the dais. "Hail the hall!" She turned to face her husband. "Hail Godulf Eorl! This drink I bear to bless the land-father, wine and wynn for the boar of battle!" She held out the horn.

The eorl made the sign of the Hammer over the top and lifted the horn. "Hail to the gods, hail to the goddesses, hail to the fathers and mothers of our folk! Hail to the sele-aelf, to mund-aelfen and aecere-aelfen, hail the wights that ward us all!" He took a long swallow. "*Wuton wesan wel!* Let us be well!" He handed the horn back to his lady.

Once more the countess faced the hall. "To all our guests a host of welcomes!" Her face shone. "Far have they fared, bringing hope unlooked for!"

Traditional words, but rarely so sincerely spoken, thought Thora as Lady Avisa paced across the gap between the hearths and offered the horn to Captain Feldman.

Clearly the captain had been warned. He took the horn a little awkwardly, but this was no real challenge to one who had feasted Association-style.

"Greetings to you, my lord and lady, and to all here. On behalf of myself and my crew I thank you for this welcome. And your son Deor, lord Baron, I thank for his quick wit and quick action! Not so long ago I thought our next meal would be at the bottom of the sea! He saved our ship and cargo at the very least, and likely our lives as well."

Feldman laid his hand on the shoulder of the youth beside him. "Including my son Moishe here, who is on his first voyage to learn the trade. If you or yours ever come to my home, my lord, my house is your house and any help I can give is yours for the asking. But I'm grateful also to find yet another community that has survived the wreck of the old world. I drink to a long and profitable relationship between your barony and the Kingdom of Montival!"

He drank, then looked at the horn with an appreciative smile.

Has he told our hosts that from Montival's point of view, Mist Hills is already a part of the kingdom? Thora wondered as she sat down. Until now the Province of Westria had existed only in theory, but she guessed that once the *Ark* got home plans to reclaim it might start moving faster.

As the countess went to her seat the girls spread out to fill everyone's cup or glass. The wine went down like silk, leaving a complexity of flavors, rich and earthy beneath the hints of fruit and flower that preserved the essence of the land from which they came. A pinot noir, she thought, as good as anything she had tasted at home, perhaps from one of the vineyards they had passed on their way.

But the friendly fire in her belly only whetted her appetite for the dishes that the children of the burg, faces scrubbed and shining, were bearing in. Leading the procession came a platter with the head of the boar wreathed in bay laurel, an apple in its tusked mouth, followed by trays with steaming slabs of pork dripping with fat and some spicy marinade and accompanied by bowls of barley with little bits of dried fruit mixed in.

At the sound of a plucked chord everyone looked up, though they did not cease to chew. Deor was standing before his father's high seat with a rectangular lyre cradled in one arm. She noted with approval that he cleaned up nice. His wild hair had been combed and he was wearing cross-gartered gray breeches and a T-tunic of muted blue wool that had been lavishly embroidered around the neck and hem and along the seams by a loving hand. There were silver plates on his belt and the sheath of his seax, and around his neck a valknut on a silver chain. His gear, like most she had seen here, lacked the polish she would have expected for folks of their rank in Montival, but really, for what must be a relatively small community, they were doing pretty well.

He cleared his throat. "Here we have no scop, but my father grants me leave to offer some entertainment." He half bowed to Captain Feldman. "This is a poem from long before the Cataclysm, that I've put into our tongue. 'Tis by another man who was a wanderer. I think things long ago were a lot like today . . ." Once more he struck the strings. His voice was unexpectedly precise and commanding as he began to declaim.

> *Oft the lone-dweller must wait for honor*
> *For the Measurer's mercy, though he be anxious,*
> *Over the seaways wide he shall wander*
> *With his hands stroking through the frost-cold sea,*
> *Far from home faring. Weird does what it will.*

Thora lost track as the servers returned with thin-sliced venison garnished with mint and baked apples and drizzled with a sauce made with a cider reduction and local bearberries. With it came bowls of red cabbage cooked with raisins and purple onion and bits of grated carrot. The drink they served with this course was a cider just at the edge of dry.

She looked up again at a sudden bitter quality in the chanting—

> . . . *many the places in middle-earth now,*
> *where walls stand wind-blown,*
> *forced down by frost, storm-beaten the shelters.*
> *The wine-halls totter, the lords laid low.*

Thora shivered, remembering a scavenging expedition when the wall of an old building had shuddered in the wind and then with a groan collapsed into the road. This had all happened before! Maybe not the same Change, but something that destroyed a world. The ruins of Portland would not have surprised the man who wrote those words.

They were bringing in a third course of wild geese stuffed with garlic and onion, with roasted root vegetables on the side. She wondered when Deor would get a chance to eat, but now at last he seemed to be drawing to a close.

> *Well for the one who keeps his troth,*
> *Unwise for a warrior to speak of his worry*
> *Unless for the care he has the cure.*
> *The eorl goes bravely. Well for him who seeks blessing*
> *From All-father in heaven, in whom our help stands.*

As he ended, there was some scattered applause, but really, it had been a depressing poem. People were getting up and moving around, taking a break before the dessert that Thora felt sure would be coming along soon. Eorl Godulf invited Captain Feldman to take one of the empty seats nearby.

Deor reappeared, carrying a full plate, and slid onto the bench beside her. "My father wants t' set up a regular trading schedule. What d'ye think the captain'll say?"

"What can your people offer?" she said as Deor sketched a rune above his plate and began to devour the food. "He can't afford to sail without some profit. We already have enough cattle and timber and wine at home."

"D'ye have any cider good as this?" Deor held out his cup as one of the girls came around. "Gowan has all kinds of apples. Might be some your folk have never seen."

"That's a thought." She stopped, as above the conversation she heard the long call of a horn that sounded as if it came from the tower. Deor jerked upright, hand on his seax, and the huscarles reached for the weapons they had leaned against the wall. Thora grabbed fruitlessly at her side, cursing the convention that forbade her to wear her sword with this gown.

The horn blew again. "Someone coming," Deor relaxed. "Not expected, but not wild men, or Eadric would still be blowing."

A young man with flyaway fair hair burst through the door and sketched a bow. "Milord! It's Morgruen and Orsa, decked out in their best an' trottin' up the road with their merry men behind."

"How many?" Godulf rose.

"A dozen—"

The baron nodded. "He can bring four with him into the hall. We'll talk in the rede-room." He gestured toward the door that led to a smaller chamber at the end of the hall. "Bring food, but not too much. Those who come to a feast without invitation can't complain if leftovers is all they are served."

"Hail to the hall!" Duke Morgruen's voice seemed to vibrate in the painted timbers. "Hail to Godulf Eorl and Countess Avisa. Hail to all here, and especially to your guests from the northern realm." Duke Morgruen and his lady bowed to the high seat and then to Captain Feldman.

Just as if they had been invited! Deor thought indignantly. He was not the only one whose hand had gone to his blade. Morgruen had not quite apologized for being late to the feast, but somehow it was implied. Someone in the duke's pay must have scurried off to Guildengard as soon as Willa brought word of the ship's arrival.

The duke moved forward to shake hands with Captain Feldman. He and his lady were wearing crimson silk and a king's ransom in gems set in gold. He was a big man, but looked now as if some of his height had slid down to his middle.

"We're delighted to meet you, sir! I'd heard things were happening up north. Been meaning to send an expedition to see. And now here you are!" Morgruen said genially.

Deor bristled. Surely that kind of rumor should have been shared!

"I'm sure Eorl Godulf here has been making you offers," Morgruen went on, "but you'll want to make the best deals you can. I've had good hunting in the dead cities—" He patted the massive gold of the necklet beneath his pointed beard. "Don't make any promises till you've heard what I have to say—"

Duchess Orsa handed her cloak to one of the girls, looking around her as if she were setting a price on the tapestries. The collar was of fox fur, a shade lighter than her dyed hair. A faceted red stone winked from her cleavage. In a predatory way, thought Deor, she was still beautiful. He stilled as he realized that the duchess was looking at him. He could smell her perfume from here. Seeing him flush, she smiled without showing her teeth, then followed her husband and Godulf into the rede-room.

"Thinks a lot of himself, doesn't he?" Thora said softly. "Don't fear we'll be too impressed. You've never seen an Association noble in full court drag . . ."

The odd chill that had followed Deor's blush eased. "Looks as if they're not getting leftovers—" she added as two boys headed toward the rede-room with plates heaped high.

"My mother won't let you guests see her fail in hospitality, even to an enemy." Deor's breath caught as he realized how easily he had used that word.

"An enemy, or a rival?"

"I don't . . . know. I think the stakes just got higher."

"Because of us."

He nodded. "There's things worth fighting over now. My father says the folk from the old kingdom—the Society—used t' joke about gathering at the Beltane tourney site near Cloverdale if there was a zombie apocalypse, whatever that was. So when the Cataclysm happened, my parents armed up, piled everything they could carry on the tourney wagon, put my brother atop it and started walking. They lived in Santa Rosa then." He shivered. He'd been to the old city once, scavenging. It wasn't as bad as the great cities by the Bay, but he remembered his mother's silent tears as they picked through the wreckage that had been her home.

"Morgruen said he should lead because he was a duke. My father said the kingdom was dead, but if we fortified Hraefnbeorg, the barony could survive. But he'd have to command, 'cause it was our family's land—my great-grandfather's buried here, and his spirit guards us. Godulf was baron in the first place 'cause the people had wanted him—in the old days that rank wasn't won by arms—so when he headed up Highway 128 most of them followed him."

"And the local farmers?" she asked.

"Well, they knew him too. There was a bit of an argument when he ordered them at sword's point to pack up every bit of food they had stored and bring it to the burg, but most were just glad t' see someone who sounded like he knew what t' do. By the time refugees got this far, the valley was stripped and we had a palisade up round the burg." He looked at the shut door of the rede-room, wondering what they were saying in there. Captain Feldman's son, still sitting on the other side of his father's fancy chair, looked as if he wondered too.

"Do you wish you had been invited?" asked the Bearkiller girl, following his gaze.

"Yes . . . I'm the one brought you here, after all. But while he has Godric, my father has no need for me."

"Trade is not all that could come of this, you know," Thora said then. "If you're not required here, you could come back with us to Montival."

But that would mean leaving Mist Hills . . .

Suddenly uncomfortable, Deor swung his legs over the bench and stood.

"There'll be no dessert till they're done," he said brightly, "but if I ask nicely Auntie Hilda will give us a pie. Come along and I'll show you round the burg."

The morning had dawned crisp and clear. Men and horses filled the space before the Gatehouse as Duke Morgruen prepared to escort the Montivallans and a party from the burg to his hold. Godulf's raven fluttered in the wind. The duke's banner, gules five bezants in annulo, had been stiffened with a rod to hold it steady in the still air.

As the baron had put it, Captain Feldman already knew what Hraefnbeorg had to offer, but if Morgruen tried to underbid him he wanted to be there to get his counteroffer in. Deor suspected he also wanted a new look at Morgruen's defenses. They might have something to fight over now.

Captain Feldman was giving his son some last directions for the work on the *Ark*. As Godulf kissed his lady and swung up on his big bay, Deor stepped forward.

"Father, will you give me leave to accompany you?"

"You ran off to Albion Cove without telling anyone," his mother's gray eyes narrowed. "And you expect to be rewarded?"

"To see Morgruen's rock pile? Hardly a reward," murmured Godric. Deor sent his brother a grateful glance. Godric had teased him unmercifully when he was a child, but fatherhood had mellowed him.

"Not as a reward," he said loudly, "as a responsibility. If 'twere not for me the Montivallans wouldn't be here!"

"I don't like the way Orsa looked at you . . ." his mother muttered.

Deor glanced across the courtyard, where Duke Morgruen and his consort were already mounted. Had they heard? He suppressed a shudder. If he wasn't tempted by the girls his mother sent his way surely he wouldn't succumb to a painted hag like Orsa!

"They won't do anything dishonorable. They want to impress the captain with how civilized they are. If 'tis safe enough for Father, surely I'll come to no harm!"

Thora took a step forward. "I owe your son my life. Will it content you if I pledge to ward him?"

Alfwin and some of the other lads snickered and she glared them to silence. Girls in the barony trained in archery, pole-arms, and fortress defense, not swordplay, but Deor felt an odd relief. Thora didn't boast of her deeds, but she had let fall enough in passing to convince him that she could hold her own against any man here. Captain Feldman's own escort included several stout sailors, but only Thora had been trained in land warfare. He would need her expertise to interpret what he saw.

Eorl Godulf sighed and nodded, and Deor swung into the saddle, smirking at Alfwin.

Avisa lifted her hands in blessing. "Thunor give you good weather and Woden show you the way! May all the Powers watch over you and bring you safe home once more."

The gates swung open, and Deor followed the fluttering raven banner through.

Thora straightened in the saddle and looked behind her. The night before they had camped at the old tourney site near the point where Highway 128 joined 101. Now they were leaving the first range of coastal mountains behind them and coming into a long valley where the Rushing River flowed close to the highway.

"Forth, Eorlingas!" she grinned.

The dozen Hraefnbeorg huscarles had clearly taken their inspiration from the Warrior Series Number Five: *Anglo-Saxon Thegn*. There was a copy in the library at Larsdalen too.

"What?" asked Deor, bringing his mare alongside.

She gestured at the knee-length mail-shirts and the gilded boars on the ridges of the conical helms. Deor himself had exchanged his leather jack for a shirt of gleaming scales. "The Rangers are going to love you people. You look just like the Rohirrim."

"Do you think so!" Deor sounded pleased. "I found those stories in my father's bookcase when I was small. They made a lot more sense than most of the books that were there."

Thora snickered. "Just remember to refer to them as the *Histories* and you'll do fine. Though Mithrilwood is well worth a visit, I must say."

The valley began to open out. To the east, a tangle of willow mixed with oak and poplar and western maple marked the course of the river. On the other side mounds of underbrush showed where the ruined town had been. The occasional rusted vehicle, covered now with wild blackberry, had been pulled to the side of the road. Farther along, native shrubs were competing with tangled vines to which a few withered grapes still clung. From time to time they glimpsed deer and once some kind of horned beast that bounded off as if on springs, pursued by a tawny streak with a spotted hide whose scent made the horses snort and plunge.

"Cheetah—" said Godulf when the captain asked. "There was a Safari Park a little south of here. The rhinos couldn't take the cold and the giraffes and the zebras got eaten, but the antelopes and the cheetahs survived. They do well where there's open ground."

"Up north, it's tigers," Captain Feldman grimaced. "They like heavily forested mountains just fine, and after the Change they developed a taste for men. When there's a man-eater in a district, the local lord has to go after him. Sometimes the High King himself leads the hunt. He says it's duty, but I suspect that he feels the need for an occasional challenge, now that the Cutters are gone."

"Those were the foes you were speaking of last night—" said Duke Morgruen. "That was a great victory."

"Thanks to the Lord of Hosts, it was indeed," said the captain, "and a great evil banished from the world. I was in the Corvallan contingent there at the Horse Heaven Hills where we broke the Prophet's army, with the field-catapults. A sailor learns that trade."

Eyes distant for an instant, he added softly, "It was . . . a long day. Very long."

"And now your king rules all their territories as well?"

"He keeps the peace." Captain Feldman shrugged. "I've heard him say it's more a matter of *reigns over lightly* than *rules*. We have pretty good communications via courier and the trains, but you can't maintain the kind of Federal government we had before the Change. Each land is governed in its own fashion, whether that be the ways of the Seven Council Fires of the Lakota tunwan or the Faculty Senate and Popular Assembly in Corvallis, or the neo-feudalism the Armingers set up in the Portland Protective Association."

"*Norman* Arminger?" asked Godulf.

"Blackthorn of Malmsey?" echoed Morgruen.

For a moment their eyes met with a shared speculation that held no hint of rivalry.

"I fought him at the eighth West/An-Tir War," Morgruen said then. "He was an arrogant son of a bitch and a period-Nazi, but very, very good with the blade."

"Yeah," agreed Godulf, "I suppose he would survive."

"He's dead now. He was killed by King Artos' father in Change Year Ten," Captain Feldman said dryly. "Though Sandra Arminger . . . the Queen Mother—her daughter is High Queen Mathilda—is very much alive, up in Castle Todenangst. She ruled the Association territories, the Protectorate, for a long time after the Lord Protector died, and she's still . . . very influential."

Duchess Orsa laughed, a sound that seemed bitter and amused at the same time. "I'm even less surprised to hear that. That woman was always so twisty that she could have met herself coming down the stairs."

"They call her the Spider of the Silver Tower," Thora blurted; she'd heard her elders say the like more than once. Captain Feldman gave her an odd unreadable look and nodded.

"Her Majesty is known for her . . . ah . . . very keen intelligence. It's said she was the one who proposed that California be called the Province of Westria when it's reclaimed . . ."

For some reason the three older local nobles all laughed at that.

"The same King Artos who now claims California . . ." said Eorl Godulf thoughtfully.

"In theory—" Captain Feldman smiled. "But you needn't fear he'll come marching in any time soon. Even if the High King wanted to impose one system on everybody, helping the places that were hit worst by the war to get back on their feet is enough to keep any ruler busy just now. His rule is to confirm anyone who'll swear allegiance to him and the Great Charter in their own lands and local law and customs; he says that is Montival's strength. But one of these days he will send colonists to the empty spaces down here, and they'll be glad to have allies already on the ground."

Thora nudged her horse closer to Deor and grinned. "All the better for you. King Artos' sept totem is the Raven, and they say that She who the Mackenzies call the Crow Goddess claimed him when he was a boy. I expect he'll call you folks at Hraefnbeorg his kin!"

Presently the course of the river veered away from the highway. To the east, forest rose above what had been a sizeable town. On the bank of the river she could see what looked like a tannery and a mill. To the west, tilled fields reminded her of the heavy cultivation around Corvallis, with plots that lay fallow alternating with those that were being plowed and those in which the winter wheat had already been sown.

Gray figures moved in the fields. As they got closer Thora realized that it was not the people but their garments that were all the same— rough gray woolen smocks on both men and, she thought, women too. Since all of them had their hair cropped close it was hard to tell. She glanced ahead, where Duke Morgruen was talking to Captain Feldman about wine, and edged her horse closer to Deor's.

"Are those the duke's workers?" After a quick glance, most kept their eyes on the ground, but a big fellow with Hispanic coloring straightened, glaring, and Thora recoiled from the rage she saw in his eyes.

"You joked about Morgruen's thralls at the cove, but this . . ." She shook her head. "Are those neck rings made of iron?"

He nodded. "Sometimes a man escapes to us, and our smith has to cut it off. We hide him at an outlying hold till his hair grows."

"Deor—this is wrong!"

He turned to her, eyes wide. "Do you feel the evil too? For the past few miles I've been wanting to turn my horse and head for home. I . . . sense things sometimes. Even before I saw your ship my heart was pounding though I didn't know what I was waiting for."

Thora's indignation had been at the injustice. Clearly Deor meant something different.

"Does that happen often?"

"All the time when I was little—one reason, I guess, my mama tries t' protect me. Then I learned to get it under control by chanting the runes. But here"—he signed himself with the protection rune—"it's all around us. I never felt anything quite this bad before."

He was staring at a stand of trees, no, at the rising ground on the other side of the river where a fortress of yellow stone squatted toadlike atop the hill. "Guildengard . . ." he whispered.

Thora was familiar with castles. This one had a curtain wall with four towers and a gatehouse, surrounding a keep. A good siege-train with artillery could take it down, but clearly they had never had a modern war here. Compared to Gervais or Molalla it was a minor fortress, but crude as it was, it menaced the valley.

"Before the War of the Eye, in the PPA the peasants used to be tied to the land," she said softly. "They wore thrall-rings too. If they escaped to our territory we protected them, but we weren't strong enough to take on Portland alone."

"I think my father would like to free them," Deor replied soberly. "But if Guildengard and Hraefnbeorg fought in earnest we'd destroy each other, and only cannibals and the wild men would remain in this land."

She nodded. Deor might feel dread, but outrage was burning in her belly, kindled by the glance of the man she had seen in the field.

*　　*　　*

"At least once a year I send a party down to the dead cities." Morgruen gestured with the hand that was not holding his wine. "There's still a lot of good stuff to be had . . ." He pointed a ringed finger toward a corner where bolts of bright fabric leaned against the wall. The previous room had been full of brown boxes inscribed with the faded printing of the olden times. Deor wondered why one would make towels out of paper, and what Huggies were for.

"Even Lady Orsa can't wear all that," hissed Thora, "and he's certainly not using it to clothe his household—why is he saving all those things?"

"For some future that's only in his head? Or maybe for replacement wall hangings? I think mice have got at some of the ones in the hall." He gave her a doubtful glance.

Dinner had been served in a chamber hung with lengths of multicolored silk, even the ceiling, with paintings jostling for space on every wall. The beefsteaks were tough and the vegetables overdone. Deor could tell when food had been prepared with care, and there was none here. When he tried to pay his respects to the house wight he got only a resentful turmoil in return.

"These are your trade goods?" asked the captain.

The huscarles had been given a feast of their own in the barracks with the duke's men, and were probably having a better time. The food might be uninspired, but there was nothing wrong with Morgruen's wine.

"Some of them, certainly," Duke Morgruen smiled, "but some must be saved for our own needs. When I have enough land under cultivation to support my city we'll need supplies."

"A city? And who will live there?" Godulf said sharply.

"Are you afraid your farmers will run away to join me?" Orsa tipped her head to one side and gave a tinkling laugh. "No, we shall breed up our own folk. And then the High King will say who is worthy to rule this land."

"A populace bred from your slaves?" The eorl's tone sharpened, and he turned to Captain Feldman, who had gone very still. "And what will this High King you have been praising think of that?"

Deor's skin prickled suddenly.

"Before we fought the Cutters, before the High Kingdom, we fought the War of the Eye against the PPA, and the serfs were set free," Thora burst out when Captain Feldman did not reply. "There is no slavery in Montival. It's one of the few laws the High King enforces in all his lands, it's in the Great Charter that any who wish may leave their own land for one that will take them in, even if they must leave with nothing but the clothes on their backs."

The sense of danger deepened. Duke Morgruen blinked, then took another sip of wine. For a moment he rolled it on his tongue, then he swallowed and smiled.

"Oh, we will not have slaves either, by the time Montival is able to concern itself with what we are doing here . . . You must understand—these were wild folk when I took them in, cannibals or the next thing to it, not worthy to be classed as men. First they must learn discipline. Orsa, my dear—" he beckoned to his wife. "I fear our guests are growing weary. I believe you had a dessert in mind? Some of those butter cakes you do so well? Why don't you see to it now? In the meantime"—he turned back to the others—"in the next room, we have machine parts and tools . . ."

By the time the tour brought them back to the silk-lined room it was growing late. Thora's neck was stiff with tension despite the wine. Why hadn't Captain Feldman said anything about Montival's position on slavery? Was it because he saw a chance for profit here? She would not have thought he could be tempted, but she was a Bearkiller. How would she know what a Corvallis merchant might choose? Eorl Godulf didn't look happy either. Her military instinct told her to leave, but Captain Feldman continued to chat with their host with every appearance of bland unconcern.

As they settled back around the table, Orsa returned, followed by several children and a young woman with black curls. They carried trays of dark brown cupcakes still warm from the oven, drizzled with honey, and topped with crumbled walnuts. They were all in the same shapeless shifts, but they looked considerably better than the thralls she had seen in the fields. Thora's mouth watered as a spicy, buttery scent filled the room.

"Do I smell molasses?" exclaimed the captain. "We've begun to import it from the islands, but I never expected to find any here!"

"And chocolate—" Duchess Orsa's eyes gleamed. "From a warehouse in Oakland. We've been saving it for a special occasion."

As the servant held out the tray, Thora realized that what she had taken for a smudge of dirt on the young woman's cheek was a bruise. A good figure gave some shape to the rough shift she wore. It was none too clean, but at least she was not collared like the thralls. As Thora reached for a cupcake, it seemed to her that the woman started to shake her head.

"Just set the tray on the table, Mousey—our guests can help themselves."

As the Duchess spoke whatever had been in the woman's eyes was replaced by fear. The tray clattered as she set it down, bowed and hurried from the room.

The others were already eating, and the last tray was beginning to look rather empty. Thora bit into a cupcake, savoring the rich mix of flavors. They must have scavenged a gourmet supply store, she thought as beneath the robust flavor of the molasses she recognized spices and a hint of herbs. Deor was chewing blissfully. She had noticed that he had a sweet tooth, and desserts were not part of most meals.

By the time they had finished, the children had brought in straw pallets covered with a motley collection of cloth. Guesting at Hraefnbeorg had felt like visiting another part of Montival. Guildengard was like something the Questers might have encountered during one of the less pleasant parts of their epic journey. However the coals were glowing gently in the fireplace, and it had been a long day. The others were already rolling themselves up in their draperies. Eorl Godulf looked more relaxed than she had ever seen him, and Deor, the pig, had collapsed almost immediately and was beginning to snore.

"I'll take the first watch," Thora announced, placing her arms handy and settling herself with her back against the wall. Through the silk hangings she could feel the stones. Perhaps they would keep her awake. She felt oddly twitchy, though she knew that she was tired.

Captain Feldman raised an eyebrow. "Do you think that's necessary? They clearly want to impress us, even though I wish you hadn't said—" For a moment he frowned, then shrugged. "Probably doesn't matter. We'll talk about it on the way back."

"Sir, the only reason I'm here instead of in the barracks with the rest of our escort is because I'm a woman. They probably thought my sword was just for show, but you hired me as a marine. Let me feel useful, okay?"

"Knowing when to let an expert do his—or her—job is one reason I've lived so long." The captain smiled. "But I'm sure everything will be fine . . ."

Thora roused from evil dreams with the sense of movement in the room. Shadows moved between her and the dimming coals. Her head was pounding, but beneath the pain she realized that her heartbeat had accelerated. *The cupcakes*, she thought. They were laced with something— might have been weed. The stuff had made her paranoid the one time she had had it before.

"Sleepin' like babies! Get the boy first—Her ladyship wants 'im safe 'n sound . . ." came a whisper, and someone else cut short a laugh.

Her heart was racing; she fought to move leaden limbs. The men carrying Deor passed her as others bent over the captain and the eorl. Thora settled her bowl helm on her head and sucked in breath.

"Awake! Ware foes! Captain, danger! Wake up now!"

Someone turned with an oath. Thora staggered to her feet, unhooking the buckler and bringing the sword up to guard. A shape blurred toward her and her buckler clanged as it deflected a blow.

"Ho La Thor!" she yelled, and lightning drove the last of the drug from her limbs. A grunt told her that Captain Feldman was up and fighting, and an oath in what sounded like Anglo-Saxon came from the spot where Deor's father had lain. She lunged, felt the point of the blade catch in someone's mail. He yelled and reeled aside as it drove in. She twisted, jerking her blade free as a shape loomed over her, ducked, thrusting up the buckler, and rolled aside.

"Thora, run! Get help!"

"Get the bitch!" The gruff voice clashed with Captain Feldman's cry. "That's an or—" the captain's last word ended in a groan.

For a moment she wavered, every hero tale she had ever heard battling every lecture on military necessity. They had taken Deor. She was outnumbered, Eorl Godulf and the captain were about to be captured if they were not already slain. She could do nothing here. Weeping with rage, she put all her strength into a slash that half severed a man's arm and ran for the door.

As she reached the bottom of the stairs to the yard she wavered, trying to remember where they had lodged the Hraefnbeorg men. A waxing moon gave just enough light to see. From the barracks built against the northern wall she heard shouting and then the kettle-mending clash of arms. Light flowed through an open door; a man reeled through, blood spurted crimson as two others cut him down, then went back to rejoin the fray. No help there. Their escort must have been drugged too.

Where else could she look for allies? Bearkillers were expected to use their heads for more than something to hang a helmet on. The woman the Duchess had called "Mousey" had tried to warn her, and the thralls had an even better reason to hate their master.

She eased around the building, keeping close to the wall. Smoke from a chimney identified the kitchen, and through the bars on the window of the next building a light showed. She dashed across the yard. The door was barred from the outside—carefully she slid back the heavy board. Sword at the ready, she opened the door.

Terrified faces greeted her, but the dice had come up sixes at last, and she recognized the woman, who seemed to be in charge of the children here.

"You, Mousey! Do you want freedom? Show me where they keep the thralls! Now, while the duke's men are distracted, we can surprise them."

"The pens, guarded—" the woman began.

"But not by many," Thora said grimly, "not tonight!" She flourished her sword. "Mousey, help me now—you'll never have a better chance."

Hope sparked in the woman's eyes. "My name Maria," she replied. "Manuelito, *mi hermano*, there. He fight for sure."

At the side gate, there was only one man on guard. As they approached, Maria ran forward.

"There's trouble—the señora, she need you!"

As the man came into the moonlight Thora saw handsome features and guessed why he might believe the duchess wanted him.

"But I, on the other hand, find you entirely superfluous!" She came in with a rushing lunge that drove the point of her sword into his throat while he was just beginning to draw. Maria was already opening the gate.

The slave pens had been built on an outthrust halfway between the castle and the fields. Thora thought she could have found them by the smell of night-soil that drifted up the hill. A log palisade surrounded an area the size of an old city block. Inside were metal sheathed pre-Change buildings where Maria had said the slaves were locked when night fell. Thora began to work her way closer.

The night was chilly, and the guards, two of them, were sitting in a lean-to close to a small fire. That was good. The firelight would negate their night vision. They had sleeveless leather jacks with metallic strips riveted on and swords. Spears and bows leaned ready against the shed's wall, so they were not totally incompetent.

Thora told herself that would make killing them more satisfying. She'd survived boarding battles with pirates, but it was different with your comrades beside you and no time to think about what you'd just done. The catch and crunch as her sword went into the gate guard's throat was still with her, and the little jerk when she pulled back that meant the point had lodged in a vertebra. She realized she was shaking, stopped and pulled in a deep breath, then one more, wishing she had her bow, wishing she was not alone.

She had just resumed her stalk when one of the men by the fire sat up suddenly, staring. She froze, but the man was not looking at her.

Maria was walking toward the fire. She had torn open the neck of her shift and let it gape so that her breasts were bare. Silently Thora grinned.

Guess I'm not alone after all. She just uses different weapons than me.

Now both men were on their feet, slavering. Thora worked her way from shadow to shadow until she was behind them. Just out of reach Maria paused. As one man stepped toward her, Thora darted in and hamstrung the other. Maria sped past her and Thora danced forward, point and buckler moving in confusing swirls.

"Gawd damn, 'tis a bitch!" the first guard exclaimed. "One for each of—" He glanced at his groaning comrade and laughed. "That's two fer me!"

He outmatched her both in weight and reach. But nobody made it through Bearkiller training unless they were both fast and strong. He came in swinging and she swayed aside. Steel screeched as she deflected his blow and her blade sliced along the inside of his arm. She dodged back to give him time to feel the sting. Blood loss would slow him soon, but she was in a hurry. She came back to the attack, feinting up and to the left, and when his sword followed the move, knocked it the rest of the way up with the buckler and drove past to sink her own point past the edge of the jack, into his armpit and up into the shoulder joint from below.

His sword went flying from suddenly nerveless fingers. She freed her blade, brought it up and across in a smooth stroke that cut short his cry. Blood spurted in a glittering stream as he fell.

Maria was back with a length of board. She bashed the man Thora had hamstrung in the head and flipped him over, wrenched his dagger from its sheath and sank it into his eye as he tried to rise, then fumbled with his belt-pouch and came up with a key.

"Come! Manuelito's ready—has them all!"

As they ran toward the old warehouse Thora could hear a feral murmur from within. Maria jammed the key into the massive padlock and turned. As it came off, the doors burst open and the thralls surged through.

"The guards in the barracks are fighting the Hraefnbeorg men! You lot, grab tools and go help them—" Thora gestured up the hill. "I need a dozen more for the castle. Maria, where would the captives be?"

"The pig's torture chamber!" growled the man who must be Maria's brother, reflexively massaging his shoulder joints. Thora thought she recognized those eyes. "Where he go for fun. You and you." He pointed to three women and several men. "You hate him most. You come."

"I know where," said Maria. "Follow me!"

Thora was sweating beneath her brigandine but adrenaline surged through her veins. What was happening in there? They had had Deor and the captain for nigh on half an hour. Remembering the way the duchess had looked at him made her belly churn. She swung her dripping sword toward the castle.

"Go! Go! Go!"

"I would rather have whiskey, but they give me blood . . ."

Deor blinked, wondering what had happened to his beautiful dream. The shape of the house wight wavered in and out of visibility, a hunched, misshapen being who glowered at him before receding back into the wall.

A rainbow flicker of candlelight danced across stones. He tried to reach for it, winced at the rasp of rope around his arms and began to struggle, caught in the old nightmare in which he was stuck in a place he did not belong and could never get away. The candle approached once more, cupped in Duchess Orsa's hands. Her face was a demon-mask, lit from below.

"Wake up, little hero!" She slapped him with the back of her hand, gashing his cheek with her rings.

"Why?" Pain shocked him to awareness.

"Because I fancy a toy that doesn't stink?"

She came closer, her scent sweet as corruption. He flinched as she set her lips to his cheek and licked the blood away. She laughed, ran her fingers down his chest to his loins, and kissed him. He tasted his own blood and wrenched his head away.

"Oh come now," her voice grew hard. "You're too pretty to be a virgin."

He spat. Colors still tended to waver, but he could see. Duke Morgruen sat at a rough table, pouring wine from a crystal carafe into a massive silver chalice. For a moment this vision was overlaid by an image of fire and blood. The warriors wore the badly cured leathers of wild men. One of them drank from the chalice and in the next moment was struck down. The chalice rolled across the floor . . . and then he was looking at the stone wall of the chamber, where chains and manacles hung. Coals glowed in the brazier, with some unpleasant looking devices resting on a rack nearby.

"Doesn't make sense," Deor said aloud. "You want the Montivallans to like you . . ."

"We did—" the duke said regretfully. He brightened as the door swung open.

Two of the bravos Morgruen called knights pushed their way in, dragging a third man. Horror shocked through Deor as he recognized his father. A bandage had been wound around Godulf's torso, but at the rough handling the stain reddened once more.

"Gently, lads, gently," Morgruen said as they lowered the baron into a rough chair. "Wouldn't want our guest to leave us too soon!"

From outside came an unfamiliar oath, then two more guards manhandled Captain Feldman into the room. His hands were bound and a purple bruise was swelling on his brow.

"What's the meaning of this, damn you? What have you done with my men?" roared the captain as the guards shoved him down on a bench and took up position around the room.

And what about Thora? thought Deor. Had they tossed her to the duke's guards, or had she fought her way free?

From the state of Deor's head, they had all been stupefied by something in the cupcakes. Before the Cataclysm weed had been a cash crop here. This must have been a really big dose. He blinked as spectral figures moved between him and the others, mouths opening in silent agony.

Morgruen shrugged. "Oh, they're being taken care of. You'll all be taken care of. The only question is how. Really, I was looking forward to working with you. I'm afraid your little redheaded whore's outburst about my thralls put an end to that possibility. But she'll not get far."

Thora was not a prisoner! Deor sagged, beginning to fade out once more.

"I had no idea you would be so old-fashioned about such things," Morgruen went on. "Hard times require hard ways. Don't tell me the peasants who built those castles you were talking about were all volunteers."

"We put an end to that."

"You could afford to."

The captain's face flushed. "You can't hope to get away with this! By God, when King Artos hears—"

"Who will tell him? Even in the old days ships were sometimes lost. The *Ark* will be one more that never returned. They'll drink to your health on the holy days and get on with their lives. So sad. But there it is."

"I will . . ."

At the sound of his father's voice, Deor focused once more. Godulf sounded a little weak, but perfectly clear. He was sitting up now, his pale face showing every groove and scar. He had always been the great oak that sheltered them all. Deor had never thought of him as looking old.

Morgruen smiled. "Ah—my lord baron, you are with us once more. I apologize for the rough invitation, but you should not have resisted."

Deor's bonds were too stout to break. He giggled, wondering if he could bore them to insensibility with Anglo-Saxon poetry, then started to recite the futhorc, hoping it would give him some control. But he could not keep the order. Each one opened into a vision—the rich fields of Feo, a forest of birch trees, a standing stone . . .

"Kill us, and there are still the men at Albion Cove," said Godulf.

"True, but the wild men have been very active this year . . . not to mention the pirates. Once the sailors are dead and the boat burned, who's to say who killed them? Of course, if we make alliance all this will be much easier to arrange."

"And help you murder my guests?" Godulf shook his head. "No."

"Not even to preserve your son?"

"Such a pretty boy," purred Orsa. She pricked Deor over the breast-bone. "Your concern for him when we left the burg was touching. He didn't react to me, but some of our men would find him delightful. Whether from self-interest or sentiment, I suggest you rethink your stand."

Reidh, thought Deor, legs twitching. *Get me out of here!*

"You can't imagine you will get away with this—" Captain Feldman exclaimed.

"Why not?" The duke grinned, and the rainbow ripples surrounding the candle flames began to grow dark. "If all the men from Montival are dead, they cannot accuse us to your king, and if everyone who knows who really killed them also dies, when colonists from the north finally arrive there will be no one to complain."

"There are your slaves," said Godulf.

"My workforce? But by then I will have bred up an obedient peas-antry. I take the children and raise them separately, you see. The only law they know is mine."

"Reminds me of the Cutters' breeding pits," muttered the captain.

"I don't need your approval," the duke told Godulf. "Become my vassal and your own guilt will keep you silent."

Deor felt himself fading out again. *Ear . . . the grave . . .* The house wight was back, and the ghosts. Death didn't require a legendary conflict. Men died for senseless reasons all the time—from the scratch of a rusty nail, or a fall. Compared to the Cutter High Seekers who the captain had described Morgruen had been little better than a wild man with preten-sions. Until now. Was it the drug that made Deor feel as if something lurked in the shadows, waiting to be invited in?

"When the old world died"—Godulf's voice was low, and he had become even paler—"it was kill or be killed. We did what our weird required to win a chance to start over . . . to live the Dream . . ." he said bitterly.

Morgruen gave a short laugh. "My dream rules now. Do you think your heir will rescue you? I had no real reason to attack Hraefnbeorg before, but if you refuse me, I will destroy the burg. In the meantime, this boy will be an entertaining hostage."

"Ask for mercy, boy. Persuade your father," came a whisper in Deor's ear.

He jerked back to focus as the point of Orsa's blade hovered before his left eye.

"No!" He wrenched his gaze from the dagger to his father's face. "I'm only the spare. Don't sacrifice your honor for me!"

For the first time since he had been dragged in, Godulf met his son's eyes, and Deor saw an agony there that was more than physical.

"Is that what you thought? You were our hope, Deor, our promise that the bad times were finally passing away!"

Oethal . . . A vision of Hraefnbeorg bloomed in memory, but he could feel it fading.

Deor swallowed. "'Each of us must accept the end of life here in this world, so before death we must seek honor while we can . . .' Beowulf said that, and you taught us to live by it, even"—his voice faltered despite his resolve—"if no one ever knows how we died." For the first time in Deor's life, he met his father's gaze as an equal.

He looked at the duke in appeal. "Free the thralls and we'll help you train them—kill us and you will be all alone!" For a moment he could feel the balance wavering. Something darker than shadow hovered in the room. *Choose life* . . . Deor thought, *choose!*

The duke giggled suddenly. "There can only be One . . ." He heaved himself to his feet and grasped the leather-wrapped handle of one of the instruments that had been heating on the coals. Its tip glowed like an evil red eye. "A pity, really. You were a beautiful boy—"

As he swung it toward Deor, Godulf surged upright. "Not while I have breath, you troll!"

Haegl . . . Nydh . . . Hailstone strike them all, for our need is near! The nearest guard drew, but Godulf was already falling.

"Os! Ing!" Deor cried aloud, and the words resonated as if through the mouth of a god. "Aelfen aid!"

Deor's vision prismed. He saw blood blooming crimson on the bandage across his father's breast, and the shape of his spirit rising to confront his foe. Death confronted Life, and it was Godulf's spirit that blazed while Morgruen was swathed in darkness. The duke dropped the glowing poker as other spirits flickered into visibility around him.

Then the door crashed open and the shapes grew flesh. Suddenly the room was full of struggling figures led by a red-haired valkyrie, faces contorted with rage. Flailing shovels, rakes, clubs, they overwhelmed the guards. Orsa's scream turned to a gurgle as a gaunt woman grabbed her by the throat and bore her down. Deor glimpsed Captain Feldman wielding one of the guards' swords with his bound hands.

Duke Morgruen swept out his own blade. He had been a warrior once, and the superior steel of his sword scythed through the farm tools and the arms that bore them. The bitter tang of blood filled the room. The thralls fell back and Morgruen started toward Captain Feldman.

"Isa! Ice! Limbs grow stiff and blood grow cold!" Deor put all his will into the spell, and then, "Whiskey for the wight that helps us now!"

A chill passed through the room and Morgruen's sword slowed. A shadow by his feet grew solid, and as he tripped, Captain Feldman swung. Then the duke's body thumped to the floor, spraying blood, and his head went spinning across the room.

Thora was coming toward him.

"Are you all right?" The outer layer of her brigandine had been slashed across and blood splattered her face, but at Deor's smile, her hazel eyes glowed. Then a rainbow shimmer veiled his vision and he knew no more.

On the third day after the fight, Godric and the full fyrd of Hraefnbeorg came trotting up the road, spears in hand, shields on their backs and crossbows thumping at their sides. His brother had made good time.

By dawn the last of the drug had left Deor's system, and he found himself in charge. As soon as it was light, he had given the fastest horse to the least wounded of the huscarles and sent him off with the news.

The wait gave them time to establish some kind of order. Three of the huscarles and one of the sailors were whole enough to be helpful. Maria and the children were nursing the two who were not, along with the wounded thralls, while her brother tried to forge the others into some kind of community. Many had been killed and some had run for the hills, but the rest stayed to hunt down their tormentors. Deor wondered how long it would take for the scent of blood to leave the ground.

He had found a bottle of whiskey labeled OBAN, and left it in a dark corner for the house wight. Deor hoped the being was pleased—his inner senses had been numb since Duke Morgruen died. Perhaps, he thought, what he had done had burned them out.

Godric had not said much, but Deor knew now how his brother would look when he was old. They stood together to watch the burning of the dead, and then, just in case any of the escaped thralls were too crazed to be grateful, Godric assigned a dozen of his men to escort them and told Deor to take their surviving guests back to the burg.

That night they camped once more at the old tourney grounds.

No one seemed very eager to go to bed when the meal was done. Deor understood. They all feared bad dreams.

"It was my fault—" Thora said suddenly as the captain added another stick of wood to the fire. "I was so angry about the thralls, and you didn't seem to care. I never thought—"

"Nor did I. I should have told you we would not be making any deals with Guildengard," Captain Feldman replied, "but I did not think the man capable of such treachery."

The past few days had aged him, too. "After dealing with the Armingers, how could anyone take small fry like Morgruen and Orsa seriously? And I think the Cutters were so far off the scale it desensitized us for anything less profound. But this—we should have learned from

Norman Arminger that men don't need alien devils to turn them to evil. A little tin-pot dictator in isolation can be corrupted all on his own."

Deor frowned, trying to see if the glitter in Thora's eyes came from tears. When the captain turned to one of his men with a comment about the ship, she got to her feet.

"I'm going to take a walk."

"I'll come with you." He was painfully aware that once the *Ark* was repaired she would be gone.

As the moon rose, the trees stretched a tracery of interlace against the midnight blue of the sky. From time to time something scuttled through the undergrowth. Farther off he heard the cry of a hunting owl.

"Don't torment yourself," he said after a while. "You freed the thralls. I couldn't even strike a blow."

"You may have been tied up, but you were doing *something*! I felt the chill when you galdored the runes!" she answered indignantly.

Deor sighed. "I don't know what I did or how. But my father died trying to protect me, and that's all anyone will remember once I get home."

Thora turned suddenly. "Then come to Montival! We'll find someone to teach you even if we have to go all the way to that seeress King Artos met in Norrheim." She stopped, then suddenly grasped his shoulders and kissed him.

Her lips were cool and friendly. He hugged her back, hoping he would feel something more, but after a moment she stepped away and sighed.

"Deor—have you ever kissed a girl before?"

"Not really. Unless you count Orsa—" He shuddered.

"Have you kissed a boy?"

"Yes . . ." He had always known the direction of his desires. "I thought it might be different, with you."

"I suppose I should take that as a compliment." Thora shook her head. "Just my luck. I've spent a year avoiding advances and the first time I find someone I like, he likes boys!"

"Thora . . ." His spirit strained to reach her as his body had fought his bonds. "I can't be your lover, but . . . I would give my life for you."

She stroked the tumbled hair back from his brow.

"Then come with me! Be my brother, my comrade. Valkyrie and vitki—we'll be invincible! There's a *world* out there, my friend—waiting to be seen!"

Suddenly it all came flooding back—his connection with the wights of stream and rock and tree, the blessing of the guardian who watched over this land—and Thora's spirit, burning like a tiny sun. He had feared to leave Mist Hills, but a world waited.

"Soul-sister!" he breathed, and some last barrier disappeared and set him free.